The red eyes blinked but the pack did not mo

Rix took another step. Only eight more to the door. He could hear Glynnie's heavy breathing behind him.

"It's all right, Benn," she whispered. "Rix'll save us."

The tone of her voice wasn't convincing. He lowered the torch, holding it out in front of him at the chest level of the shifters. Another step.

"To get to me, you've got to pass the fire," said Rix, swinging it back and forth.

The pack leader's eyes followed the flame. It double-blinked.

Now! Rix leapt forwards, thrusting out the burning torch with his right hand and Maloch with his left. Up one step, two, three and still the shifter had not budged. If he had misjudged, the children would die. Four, five, six. He let out a furious battle cry and swung Maloch at the beast's snout.

REBELLION

THE TAINTED REALM TRILOGY
BOOK TWO

IAN IRVINE

orbit

www.orbitbooks.net

Orbit
Hachette Book Group
237 Park Avenue, New York, NY 10017
HachetteBookGroup.com

First U.S. Edition: March 2013
First published in Australia and New Zealand in 2012 by Orbit (An Imprint of Hachette Australia Pty Limited), Level 17, 207 Kent Street, Sydney NSW 2000

Orbit is an imprint of Hachette Book Group, Inc. The Orbit name and logo are trademarks of Little, Brown Book Group Limited.

The Hachette Speakers Bureau provides a wide range of authors for speaking events. To find out more, go to www.hachettespeakersbureau.com or call (866) 376-6591.

The publisher is not responsible for websites (or their content) that are not owned by the publisher.

The characters and events in this book are fictitious. Any similarity to real persons, living or dead, is coincidental and not intended by the author.

Library of Congress Control Number: 2012955593
ISBN: 978-0-316-07285-4

10 9 8 7 6 5 4 3 2 1

RRD-C

Printed in the United States of America

CONTENTS

TO BLEDDIMIRE

GARRAMIDE

TIRNAN TWIL

SWIRE

TOGL

LAKE
FUMEROUS

CAULDERON

THE VOMITS

RUTHERIN

THE CAPE

ESTERLYZ

N

MILES
0   5   10

GREATER
HIGHTSPALL

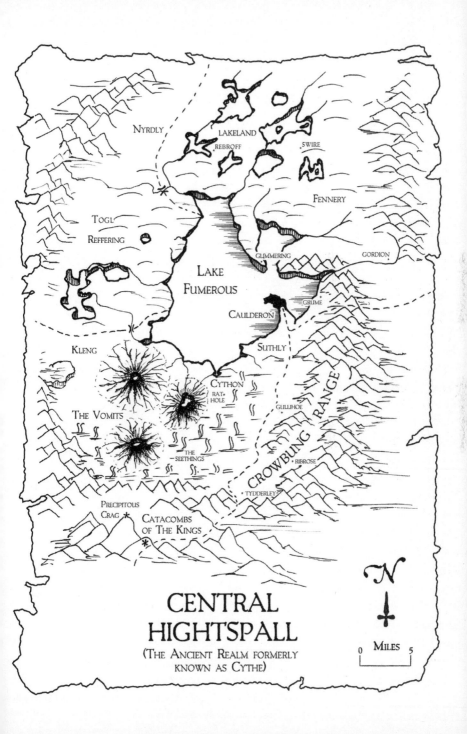

NYRDLY

LAKELAND

REBROFF

SWIRE

FENNERY

TOGL

REFFERING

GLIMMERING

GORDION

LAKE
FUMEROUS

GRUME

CAULDERON

SUTHLY

KLENG

CYTHON

RAT·
HOLE

GULLIHOE

THE VOMITS

CROWBUNG RANGE

THE
SEETHINGS

RIBROSE

TYDDERLEY

PRECIPITOUS
CRAG

CATACOMBS
OF THE KINGS

CENTRAL
HIGHTSPALL
(THE ANCIENT REALM FORMERLY
KNOWN AS CYTHE)

N

0   MILES   5

CHARACTERS

Arkyz Leatherhead: A gigantic, murderous bandit.

Astatin: A witch-woman and healer in Garramide.

Benn: Glynnie's little brother, aged ten.

Blathy: Leatherhead's mistress – a bold, vengeful gambler.

Chancellor, the: The leader of Hightspall, a small, twisted, cunning man.

Crebb: A black-bearded thug.

Dibly, Madam: An aged healer.

Errek First-King: The legendary inventor of king-magery, recreated in spirit form by Lyf.

Gauntling, the: A humanoid, winged shifter.

Glynnie: A young maidservant from Palace Ricinus, Benn's big sister.

Grandys, Axil: A brutal, treacherous man, the first of the Five Heroes and the legendary founder of Hightspall.

Holm: An old, mysterious man, very clever with his hands. Also known as Kroni.

Lirriam: One of the Five Heroes, a cold, buxom temptress.

Lizue: A beautiful prisoner in Fortress Rutherin.

Lyf, King Lyf: The last king of Cythe, recently reincarnated from his ghostly wrythen, and now the king of the Cythonians.

Maloch: Rix's enchanted sword, which originally belonged to Axil Grandys.

Nuddell: One of Leatherhead's gang, later Rix's loyal sergeant.

Porfry: The Keeper of the Records at Garramide; a fanatical Herovian.

Radl: A tall, beautiful Pale slave in Cython. Tali's enemy since childhood.

Rannilt: A slave girl, aged ten, who has an enigmatic gift for magery. She escaped from Cython with Tali.

Rezire: The curator at Tirnan Twil.

Rixium (Rix): Formerly heir to the vast estates of House Ricinus. Also known as Deadhand.

Rochlis: Lyf's greatest general. A man with a conscience.

Rufuss: One of the Five Heroes, a tall, gaunt man whose only pleasure is denial.

Sullen Man, the: A cold-eyed prisoner in Fortress Rutherin.

Swelt: The castellan of Garramide, a greedy, corpulent man.

Syrten: One of the Five Heroes, a massive, golem-like man.

Tali: A Pale slave, the first to ever escape from Cython.

Tobry: Rix's closest friend, who became a caitsthe to save his friends.

Wil: A blind Cythonian, addicted to sniffing alkoyl. Also known as Mad Wil, Wil the Sump.

Yestin: A local lord who helps Rix in the raid on Jadgery.

Yulia: One of the Five Heroes, a slender, sad-eyed, moral woman.

PRÉCIS OF VENGEANCE

In the underground city of Cython, a simple youth called WIL reads the forbidden but incomplete iron book, *The Consolation of Vengeance*. It burns his eyes out, but he also has a foreseeing about *the one*, a slave girl of the Pale who will grow up to challenge the Cythonians' legendary leader, King LYF. Wil should have told the matriarchs where to find *the one*, so they could have her killed, but he lies, and other girls are killed in her place.

Lyf, the creator of the iron book, was murdered two thousand years ago but still exists as a bodiless wrythen bent on two things: restoring his dispossessed people to the land above, and taking revenge on the Hightspallers who killed him and drove his people out.

TALI, an eight-year-old slave girl in Cython, is led, along with her mother IUSIA, on a secret escape route by TINYHEAD, a Cythonian. But Tinyhead betrays them, and in a gloomy cellar Iusia is caught by a masked man and woman. Though Tali has a gift for magery, she is unable to summon it in her mother's defence – using magery in Cython means instant death and she has been taught to suppress it.

While the terrified child watches from hiding, Iusia's captors hack something out of her head, killing her, then take her blood. After they have gone, Tali sees a richly dressed boy hiding on the other side of the cellar. He flees and she returns to her slave's existence, swearing to bring the killers to justice when she grows up.

In a cavern deep in the mountains, Lyf's wrythen is trying to bring his two-thousand-year-old plan to completion. To do so he has to recover his king-magery, the mighty healing force that was lost when he was murdered by the legendary Five Heroes at the behest of their leader, AXIL GRANDYS. But first, Lyf needs all five ebony pearls, powerful magical artefacts that only form in the heads of rare, female Pale slaves.

Lacking a body, Lyf cannot take the pearls himself, and long ago he forced the sorcerer DEROE to get each new pearl for him, possessing Deroe to make sure he complied. To escape the agony of possession, Deroe employed LORD and LADY RICINUS to take the second, third and fourth pearls for him, hoping thereby to drive Lyf out and kill him. For this service, Deroe made House Ricinus fabulously wealthy.

Now Lyf forms a long-term plan to get the fifth pearl – the master pearl – by compelling the Ricinus's son and heir, RIXIUM (RIX), via the great heatstone in Rix's room, to take the master pearl once the host slave girl comes of age.

Tali turns eighteen, discovers that three more of her direct female ancestors were also murdered at a young age, and knows that the killers will soon be hunting her. She has to escape Cython but does not know how – the Pale have been enslaved for a thousand years and in that time none have ever escaped. At the same time she begins to have terrible headaches, as though something is grinding against the inside of her skull. The master pearl is waking (though she does not know they exist).

The pain accentuates Tali's rebellious streak, but her attack on a vicious guard results in the execution of her only friend, MIA, by their overseer, BANJ. Stricken with guilt, Tali swears that one day she will save her enslaved people. Then she realises that Tinyhead is hunting her.

Tali also discovers that the Cythonians, who are masters of alchymie and have invented many alchymical weapons, are preparing to go to war on Hightspall, the land above, where Tali's ancestors came from. Tali feels sure that Hightspall is unprepared; she has to warn her country.

With the aid of a ten-year-old slave girl, RANNILT, who has an unfathomable gift for magery, and MIMOY, a foul-mouthed old woman who turns out to be Tali's ancestor, she escapes, beating Tinyhead and killing Banj with an uncontrollable burst of magery. For that crime, if the Cythonians catch her, she will suffer the most terrible death they can devise. Mimoy dies, but Tali and Rannilt get away and Tali sets off across Hightspall to try and find clues to the killers' identities.

In Palace Ricinus, Rix is about to come of age. Soon he will inherit one of the greatest fortunes in Hightspall. He's a trained warrior as well as a gifted artist, though some of his paintings are disturbingly divinatory. But Rix is troubled by nightmares about doom and destruction, the fall of his house, and his role in a future, terrible murder. He is supposed to be completing his father's portrait for Lord Ricinus's Honouring, which Rix's social-climbing mother, Lady Ricinus, plans to use to raise House Ricinus to the First Circle, the highest families of all.

Rix can't bear the hypocrisy, for his father is a disgusting drunk and his mother a cold, merciless woman without a good word for anyone. The Honouring will be a travesty and he has to get away. With his reckless and impoverished friend TOBRY, Rix goes off to the mountains, hunting, in the middle of the night. He takes MALOCH, a battered old sword that bears a protective enchantment, though on the way Maloch seems to be leading him.

Rix and Tobry are attacked by a caitsthe, a huge shifter cat, and only a brilliant attack by Rix drives the injured beast off. They pursue it into a deep cavern, but are forced to flee from Lyf's malevolent wrythen. Tobry is knocked out by a rock fall; Rix, after an almighty battle, kills the caitsthe but is immediately attacked by the wrythen, which is trying to possess Tobry. On driving it off, Rix discovers that the wrythen is afraid of Maloch, which it recognises as the sword Axil Grandys used to hack Lyf's feet off before he was murdered two thousand years ago.

Rix carries Tobry to safety. On the way home they realise that preparations they saw in the wrythen's caverns presage war, and head across the thermal wasteland of the Seethings to check on the Rat Hole, a shaft up to the surface used by the Cythonians.

Rix and Tobry encounter Tali and Rannilt in the Seethings. Tobry is immediately smitten by Tali, but Rix and Tali clash and, when he recognises her as a Pale, he rides off in a fury – in Hightspall the Pale are regarded as traitors for serving the enemy. Tobry apologises and goes after him. Once they're gone, Tali has a blinding revelation – Rix is the boy she saw in the murder cellar! He's her best clue to the killers' identities, and she has to go after him, though how can she ever trust him?

Tali's escape causes the Cythonians to bring forward their plans for war. They attack Hightspall, using devastating chymical weaponry and causing great destruction. Hordes of shifters go on the rampage; the great volcanoes known as the Vomits erupt violently; and from across the sea the ice sheets are closing in. It feels as though the land is rising up to cast the Hightspallers out.

After a series of captures, escapes and recaptures, Rix and Tobry rescue Tali from her Cythonian hunters, though even now Tali isn't sure she can trust Rix. She tells him about her mother's murder but he doesn't react – it's as if he doesn't remember, though she knows he was there.

Rix returns to the palace, in the capital city of Caulderon, to complete his father's portrait, a painting he loathes. Lady Ricinus is furious that he has neglected his responsibilities. The portrait must be completed by the Honouring – the future of House Ricinus depends on it – and she confines Rix to his rooms until it's completed.

Rix's nightmares and premonitions of doom return, stronger than ever. He works on the portrait as long as he can bear it, and also begins another painting that comes from his subconscious – a haunting cellar, a woman laid on a bench, two people standing by her and a wide-eyed child in the background. He can't paint their faces, nor work out why the scene fills him with such horror, for in a childhood illness he lost all memory of the murder he witnessed.

Tobry brings Tali and Rannilt to Caulderon and hides them, knowing that Lady Ricinus would never allow a despised Pale in the palace. Tali is also being hunted by the CHANCELLOR, the supreme ruler of Hightspall, since her knowledge of Cython will be invaluable to the war. Tali sneaks into the palace anyway; she has to pursue the clues to her mother's murder.

The Cythonians besiege Caulderon. Rix, more and more disturbed at what he's painting, goes to see his old nurse, LUZIA, to ask her about his childhood, but finds her murdered, presumably to stop her talking to him. Rix is shattered. And Rannilt, whom Tobry had left with Luzia, is missing.

Tali gets into Rix's rooms and sees the painting, which she recognises instantly as the murder scene. How can Rix not know? He goes on with it, working unconsciously, and to his horror Tali's face appears on the prone woman. It's his nightmare made real; is Tali the woman he's doomed to kill? He fights the compulsion with all he has.

The wrythen is pleased. His plans are finally back on track; soon he will tighten the compulsion on Rix and force him to cut the master pearl from Tali. Then he will dispose of Deroe and, with all five pearls, recover king-magery and exact his vengeance.

The war is going badly for Hightspall; the Cythonians are winning everywhere. The chancellor orders Palace Ricinus searched for Tali, and gives Lady Ricinus an ultimatum – find Tali, or House Ricinus will be crushed. She knows he'll do it, too, because the chancellor has always despised House Ricinus. Lady Ricinus plots the worst treason of all – to have him killed.

Rix and Tali discover the plot, separately, and Rix is torn by an impossible conflict. If he does not betray his mother, he too will be guilty of treason. But if he does betray her, how could he live with himself?

Rix redoes the cellar painting and to his horror, this time he sees what the two unidentified people by the bench are doing – gouging an ebony pearl from the dying woman's head. Then Tali confronts Rix, screaming at him, "That's my mother. You were there! How can you not know? And now Lyf wants you to do it to me."

The chancellor is an unpleasant, vengeful man but Tali can't stand by and see him killed. She tells him about the treason, though he does not say what he plans to do about it. He also holds Rannilt and has been interrogating her for her knowledge of Cython.

The following day Rix, tormented by his own conflict, also visits the chancellor, who forces the truth out of him. He throws Rix out, saying that he could never trust a man who would betray his own mother.

Rix, now utterly dishonoured, feels that he has only one way out. He completes his father's portrait then, in a drunken frenzy, repaints the cellar picture from scratch. But this time he paints the faces of the killers – Lord and Lady Ricinus. House Ricinus, and everything Rix has, comes from the depraved, murderous trade in ebony pearls.

He staggers up to the roof to cast himself off to his death, but slips, knocks himself out and only recovers as the Honouring is beginning. He'd promised to be there, and he plans to do this last duty before he dies.

Tali, in disguise, goes to the Honouring Ball with Tobry, and begins to feel that she loves him, though she tries to deny it. At the Honouring, Lady Ricinus's triumph is complete – the forged documents she presents are verified and House Ricinus is accepted into the First Circle. Then Rix unveils his portrait of Lord Ricinus, but to his horror someone has switched paintings, and he actually reveals the painting of the murder cellar, clearly showing both the killers' faces and the ebony pearl. The chancellor smiles; he's about to have his revenge.

Lady Ricinus is defiant, blaming everyone else, even her own son, but Lord Ricinus can't take any more. He confesses everything, revealing that Rix was taken down to witness the murder as a boy, to make him complicit in the family business. And they took Iusia's blood because it has healing powers.

House Ricinus is condemned, its assets confiscated, the servants cast out and the disembowelled lord and lady hung from the front gates. Rix survives because he's not yet of age, but is universally condemned for betraying his parents.

GLYNNIE, a young maidservant, begs refuge for herself and her little brother, BENN, and Rix takes them in. That night the three Vomits erupt at once, a sign of the fall of nations. Rix is plagued by murderous nightmares, sent by Lyf, and plans to take his own life in the morning. A colossal eruption causes a tidal wave in Lake Fumerous which washes the city walls away. Caulderon is defenceless and now the enemy attack.

Rix prepares to ride out and die. Tali begs Tobry to stop him, saying that she loves Rix, though this is a lie – she actually loves Tobry. Tobry, in despair, stops Rix.

Tali knows Lyf is coming, and Deroe too; he has been lured to the cellar by Lyf in pursuit of the master pearl. Tali plans to seize the three pearls from Deroe, but he turns the tables on her and prepares to cut out her master pearl for himself.

Lyf wakes the compulsion, using the heatstone, and forces Rix to go to the cellar to kill Tali. Rix fights the compulsion but cannot defeat it. Tobry realises what is happening and smashes the heat-stone, which lets off a tremendous blast of force that knocks everyone down and frees Rix from the compulsion.

A horde of shifters attack, led by a caitsthe. The only way the allies can be saved is for Tobry to face his worst nightmare – to become a caitsthe himself. In despair at losing Tali, he does so and manages to hold the attack off.

During a battle in the cellar, Lyf's faithful servant, Tinyhead, goes for Rix, but Wil, now hopelessly addled from sniffing the alchymical solvent *alkoyl* to assuage his guilt, strangles Tinyhead and flees with Lyf's iron book.

Tali recovers and seizes the three pearls from Deroe, but Lyf breaks through and holds the lives of Rix, Tobry, Glynnie and Benn in his hands. Tali can still execute Lyf and gain justice for her mother, but only at the cost of her friends' lives. She can't do it. Lyf kills Deroe, seizes the three pearls to add to his own and calls his armies to attack the city.

They storm Caulderon and soon the city is doomed; Tali, Rix, Tobry, Rannilt, Glynnie and Benn are trapped in the palace. They are at the top of Rix's tower when the chancellor appears and orders Tobry killed, because he's a shifter. Tali realises that her own heal-ing blood might be able to turn him back, and it seems to work. But the vengeful chancellor, who has always hated Tobry, has him cast off the tower to his death. He orders Rix's right hand severed with Maloch, then takes Tali and Rannilt prisoner for their healing blood, and flees Caulderon.

PART ONE

HEALING BLOOD

CHAPTER 1

"Lord Rixium?" Her voice was desperate. "You gotta get up now. The enemy are coming. Coming fast."

Rix's right wrist throbbed abominably, and so did the back of his head. He groaned, rolled over and cracked his ear on a stone edge. His cheek and chest were numb, as if he'd been lying on ice.

"What . . . ?" he mumbled. "Where . . . ?" His eyes were gummed shut and he didn't want to open them. Didn't want to see.

"Chancellor's stolen Tali and Rannilt away, to milk their healing blood."

He recognised her voice now. A maidservant, Glynnie.

"And Lord Tobry's been chucked off the tower, head-first. Splat!" said a boy's voice from behind Rix.

"Benn!" Glynnie said sharply.

Rix winced. Did he have to be so matter-of-fact about it? "Tobe was my oldest friend."

"I'm sorry, Lord," said Glynnie.

"How long was I out?"

"Only five minutes, but you're first on their death list, Lord. If we don't go now, we're gonna die."

"Don't call me Lord, Glynnie."

"Lord?"

"My parents were executed for high treason," he said softly. "House Ricinus has fallen, the palace lies in ruins and I betrayed my own mother. I am utterly dishonoured. *Don't call me Lord!*"

"R-Rixium?" She tugged at his arm, the good one.

"That's what my murdering mother called me. Call me Rix."

Glynnie rubbed his eyelids with her fingertips. The sticky secretions parted to reveal a slender servant girl, about seventeen years old. Tangled masses of flame-coloured hair, dark green eyes and a scatter of freckles on her nose. Rix had not yet turned twenty yet he felt a lifetime older. Foul and corrupt.

"Get up," she said.

"Give me a minute."

They were on the top of his tower, at the rear of what remained of Palace Ricinus. From where Rix lay he could not see over the surrounding wall – and did not want to. Did not want to see the ruin a hundred-foot fall had done his dearest friend.

A freezing wind carried the stink of burned deer meat, the forgotten skewers Glynnie had been cooking over the embers of Rix's artist's easel. He would never paint again. Beside the fire stood a wide-eyed boy of ten, her little brother. A metal drinking cup sat on the stone floor. Some distance away lay a bloody sword. And a small puddle of blood, already frozen over.

And a right hand, severed at the wrist.

Rix's right hand.

Something collapsed with a thundering crash not far away, and the tower shook.

"What was that?" said Rix.

Glynnie ran to the wall, went up on tiptoes and looked over. "Enemy's blasting down the palace towers."

"What about Caulderon?"

Her small head turned this way and that, surveying the great city. What was left of it.

"There's smoke and flame everywhere. Rix, they're coming. Tell me what to do."

"Take your brother and run for your life. Don't look back."

"We've nowhere to go, Lord."

"Go anywhere. It's all the same now."

"Not for us. We served House Ricinus; we're condemned with our house."

"As am I," said Rix.

"We swore to serve you. We're not running away."

"Lyf hates Herovians, especially me. He plans to put me to death. But he doesn't know you exist."

"I'm not leaving you, Lord – Rix."

Rix did not have the strength to argue. "What about Benn? If the Cythonians find him with me, they'll kill him too."

"Not runnin' either," said Benn. "We can't break our sworn word, Lord."

Unlike me, Rix thought bitterly. The servants outreach the master. "Ah, my head aches."

"That mongrel captain knocked you out," said Glynnie. "And the chancellor – he –" Her small jaw tightened. "He's a useless, evil old windbag. He's lost Caulderon and he's going to lose the war. No one can save us now."

"*You* can, Lord," said Benn, his eyes shining. "You can lead Hightspall to victory, I know it."

"Hush, Benn," said Glynnie. "Poor Rix has enough troubles as it is."

But he could see the light in her eyes as well, her absolute belief in him. It was an impossible burden for a condemned man and he had to strike it down. Hightspall was lost; nothing could be done about it.

"Benn," he said softly, speaking to them both. "I can't lead *anyone*. The chancellor has destroyed my name and all Hightspall despises me—"

"Not all, Rix," said Glynnie. "Not us. We know you can—"

"No!" he roared, trying to get up but crashing painfully onto his knees. "I don't even believe in myself. No army would follow me."

Benn's face crumpled. "But, Lord—"

"Shh, Benn," said Glynnie hastily. "Let me help you up, Lord."

She was stronger than she looked, but Rix was a huge man and it was a struggle for her to raise him to his feet. The moment he stood upright it felt as though his head was going to crack open. Through a haze of pain and dizziness he heard someone shouting orders.

"Search the rear towers next." The man had a heavy Cythonian accent.

"Where are we going, Rix?" said Glynnie.

He swayed, his wrist throbbing. She steadied him.

"Don't know." He looked around. "I need Maloch. It's enchanted to protect me."

That was ironic. A command spell cast on Rix when he was a boy of ten had left him with a deep-seated fear of magery, and recent events had proven his fear to be justified.

"Didn't do a very good job," she sniffed. "Benn, get Rix's sword. And ... and bring his hand."

"His hand?" Benn said in a squeaky voice. "But − it's all bloody ... and dead ..."

"I'm not leaving it for the crows to peck. Fetch the cup, too."

Benn handed the ancient, wire-handled sword to Rix, who sheathed it left-handed. The roof door stood open. Glynnie helped him through it and onto the steep stair that wound down his tower. Rix swayed, threw out his right arm to steady himself and his bloody stump cracked against the wall.

"Aaarrgh!" he bellowed.

"Sorry, Lord," whispered Glynnie. "I'll be more careful."

"Stop apologising. It's not your damn fault." Rix pulled away from her. "I've got to stand on my own feet. It's only a hand. Plenty of people have survived worse."

"Yes, Lord."

But few men had lost more than Rix. He'd been heir to the biggest fortune in the land, and now he had nothing. His family had been one of the noblest − on the surface, anyway. For a few moments, House Ricinus had even been a member of the First Circle, the founding families of Hightspall. Then the chancellor had torn it all down.

Rix's parents had been hung from the front gates of the palace, then ritually disembowelled for high treason and murder, and everything they owned had been confiscated. Now, not even the most debased beggar or street girl was lower than the sole surviving member of House Ricinus.

He had also been physically perfect − tall, handsome, immensely strong, yet dexterous and fleet − and accomplished. Not just a brilliant swordsman, but a masterful artist − the best of the new generation, the chancellor had said in happier times. Now Rix was maimed, tainted, useless. And soon to die, which was only right for a man so dishonourable that he had betrayed his own mother. As soon as Glynnie and Benn got away, he planned to take the only way out left to him – hurl himself at the enemy, sword in hand, and end it all.

He reached the bottom of the tower stair, ignored Glynnie's silent offer of help and lurched into his ruined studio. When Tobry had smashed the great heatstone in Rix's chambers the other day, and it burst asunder, it had brought down several of the palace walls. There were cracks in the walls, part of the ceiling had fallen and the scattered paints, brushes and canvases were coated in grey dust. He crunched across chunks of plaster, stolidly looking ahead.

"Where we going, Lord?" Glynnie repeated.

"How the hell would I know?"

Not far away, sledgehammers thudded against stone and axes rang on timber. The Cythonians were breaking in and they would come straight here.

"We're trapped," said Glynnie, her jaw trembling. She stretched an arm around Benn and hugged him to her. "They're going to kill us, Lord."

"Go out the window—"

Rix looked down. From here the drop was nearly thirty feet. If they weren't killed outright, they'd break their legs, and in a city at war that meant the same thing. He cursed, for it left him with no choice. Glynnie and Benn were his people, all he had left, and as their former lord he had a duty to protect them. A duty that out-weighed his longing for oblivion. He would devote his strength to getting them out of Caulderon, and to safety. And then . . .

He headed down the steps into his once-magnificent, six-sided salon, now filled with rubble, dust and smashed, charred furniture. The crashing was louder here. The enemy would soon break through. The only hope of escape, and that a feeble one, was to go underground.

"Get warm clothing for yourself and Benn," he said to Glynnie. "And your money. Hurry!"

"Got no money," said Glynnie, trembling with every hammer and axe blow. "We got nothing, Lord."

"Tobry—" Rix choked. How was he going to do without him? "Tobry brought in spare clothes for Tali. She's nearly your size. Take them."

Glynnie stood there, trembling. "Where, Lord?"

"In the closet in my bedchamber. Run."

He still had coin, at least. Rix filled a canvas money belt with gold and other small, precious items, and buckled it on one-handed. He packed spare clothing into an oilskin bag to keep it dry, and put it, plus various other useful items, into a pack.

The crashing grew louder, closer. Glynnie filled another two oil-skin bags, packed two small packs and dressed herself and Benn in such warm clothes as would fit. She strapped on a knife the length of her forearm and collected the dusty food in the salon.

"They're nearly through," she said, white-faced. "Where are we going, Lord?"

Benn still held Rix's severed hand in his own small, freckled hand. His wide grey eyes were fixed on Rix's crusted stump, which was still ebbing blood. Benn caught Rix's gaze, flushed and looked away.

Rix gestured to a broad crack, low down in the wall at the back of the salon. The edges resembled bubbly melted cheese, the plaster and stonework etched away and stained in mottled greens and yellows.

He hacked away the foamy muck to reveal fresh stone, though when he flicked the clinging stuff off the knife the blade was so corroded that it snapped. He tossed it into the rubble. Benn ran back and fetched him another knife, which Rix sheathed.

"Go through," said Rix. "Don't touch the edges."

"What is that stuff?" said Benn.

"Alkoyl. Mad Wil squirted it around the crack to stop us following him."

"What's alkoyl?"

"An alchymical fluid, the most dangerous in the world. Dissolves anything. Even stone, even metal — even the flesh of a ten-year-old boy." Rix took Benn's free hand and helped him through.

"We'll need a lantern," said Glynnie.

"No, they'd track us by its smell," said Rix.

He handed the boy a glowstone disc, though its light was so feeble it barely illuminated his arm. Tobry, an accomplished magian, could have coaxed more light from it, but ... Rix avoided the rest of the thought.

"We'll need more light than that," said Glynnie.

She bundled some pieces of wood together from a broken chair, tied them together with strips of fabric, tied on more fabric at one end and shoved it in her pack.

They went through, holding their breath. The crack snaked ever down, shortly intersecting a network of other cracks that appeared to have freshly opened — and might close again just as suddenly.

"If they shut, they'll squeeze the juice out of us like a turnip," whispered Glynnie.

Rix stopped, frowning. "Can you smell alkoyl?"

"No," she said softly, "but I *can* smell stink-damp."

"That's bad."

Stink-damp smelled like rotten eggs. The deadly vapour seeped up from deep underground and collected in caverns, from where it was piped to the street lamps of Caulderon and the great houses such as Palace Ricinus. Stink-damp was heavier than air, however. It settled in sumps, basements and other low places, and sometimes exploded.

"*I* can smell alkoyl," said Benn.

"Good man," said Rix. "Can you follow it?"

"I think so."

Benn sniffed the air and moved down the crack.

"Why are we following alkoyl?" said Glynnie.

"Wil was carrying a tube of it," said Rix. "He also stole Lyf's iron book, and if anyone can find a safe way out of here, Wil the Sump can, the little weasel."

"Isn't he dangerous?"

"Not as dangerous as I am."

The boast was hollow. Down here, Rix's size put him at a disadvantage, whereas Wil could hide in any crevice and reach out to a naked throat with those powerful strangler's hands.

They squeezed down cracks so narrow that Rix could not take a full breath, under a tilted slab of stone that quivered at the touch, then through an oval stonework pipe coated with feathery mould. Dust tickled the back of his throat; he suppressed a sneeze.

After half an hour, Benn could no longer smell alkoyl.

"Have we gone the wrong way?" said Rix. "Or is Wil in hiding, waiting to strike?"

Neither Glynnie nor Benn answered. They were at the intersection of two low passages that burrowed like rat holes through native rock. Many tunnels were known to run under the palace and the ancient city of Cauldron, some dating back thousands of years to when it had been the enemy's royal city, Lucidand; others had been forgotten long ago. Rix's wrist, which had struck many obstacles in the dark, was oozing blood and throbbing mercilessly.

"Lord?" said Glynnie.

"Yes?"

"I don't think anyone's following. Let me bandage your wrist."

"It hardly matters," he said carelessly. "Someone is bound to kill me before an infection could."

"Sit down!" she snapped. "Hold out your arm."

An angry retort sprang to his lips, but he did not utter it. He had been about to scathe Glynnie the way his late mother, Lady Ricinus, would have done. But Glynnie had never done other than to serve as best she could. She was the worthy one; he should be serving her.

"Not here. They can come at us four ways. We need a hiding place with an escape route."

It took another half hour of creeping and crawling before they found somewhere safe, a vault excavated from the bedrock. It must have dated back to ancient times, judging by the stonework and the crumbling wall carvings. A second stone door stood half open on the other side, its hinges frozen with rust. To the left, water seeped from a crack into a basin carved into the wall, its overflow leaving orange streaks down the stone.

"I don't like this place," said Benn, huddling on a dusty stone bench, one of two.

"Shh," said Glynnie.

In the far right corner a pile of ash was scattered with wood charcoal and pieces of burnt bone, as if someone had cooked meat there and tossed the bones on the fire afterwards.

Rix perched on the other bench and extended his wrist to Glynnie. "Do you know how to treat wounds?"

"I can do *everything*." It was a statement, not a boast.

"But you're just – you're a maidservant. How do you know healing?"

She pursed her lips. "I watch. I listen. I learn. Benn, bring the glowstone. Rix, hold this."

Gingerly, as though she would have preferred not to touch it, she pressed Maloch's hilt into Rix's left hand.

"Why?" he said.

"It's supposed to protect you."

"Only against magery."

She knelt in the dust before him, then took a bottle of priceless brandy from her pack, Rix's last surviving bottle, and rinsed her hands with it. She laid a little bundle containing rags, needle and thread and scissors on her pack, poured a slug of brandy onto a piece of linen and began to clean his stump.

Rix tried not to groan. Blood began to drip. By the time she finished, Glynnie was red to the elbows.

He leaned back against the wall and closed his eyes, for once content to do as he was told.

"Hold his wrist steady, Benn," said Glynnie.

A pair of smaller, colder hands took hold of Rix's lower arm. He heard Glynnie moving about but did not open his eyes. She began to tear linen into strips. Liquid gurgled and he caught a whiff of the brandy, then a *chink* as she set down a metal cup.

"I could do with a drop of that," he murmured.

Glynnie gave a disapproving sniff. She was washing her hands again.

"Steady now," she said. "Hold the sword. This could hurt."

She began to spread something over his stump, an unguent that stung worse than the brandy. Rix's fingers clenched around Maloch's hilt.

"Ready, Benn?" said Glynnie.

"Yes," he whispered.

Her hand steadied his wrist. There came a gentle, painful pressure on the stump. Where his fingers touched the hilt, they tingled like a nettle sting. Then Rix felt a burning pain as though she had poured brandy over his stump and set it alight. His eyes sprang open.

Glynnie had pressed his severed hand against the stump, and now the pain was running up his arm and down into his fingers. Cold blue flames flickered around the amputation site then, with the most shocking pain Rix had ever experienced, the bones of his severed hand ground against his wrist bones – *and seemed to fuse.*

He had the good sense not to move, though he could not hold back the agony. It burst out in a bellow that sifted dust down from the roof onto them, like a million tiny drops falling through a sunbeam.

"What are you doing to me?"

CHAPTER 2

B enn let go and scrambled backwards into the dark, out of harm's way.

Glynnie went so pale that the freckles stood out down her nose. She swayed backwards as though afraid Rix was going to strike her, but her bloody hands were rock-steady, one on his wrist, the other on his partly rejoined hand.

"Don't move!" she said.

Hope and fear went to war in Rix. The foolish, foolish hope that Glynnie knew what she was doing and could give him his right hand back. And the gut-crawling fear that it would go desperately wrong and would be worse than having a stump on the end of his arm. He clutched the hilt of Maloch so hard that it hurt – and prayed.

It was impossible to keep still. The pain was a dog mauling his wrist, splintering the bones. Then, out of nowhere, he *felt* his amputated hand as an ice-cold, dangling extremity. He felt the blood oozing sluggishly through each of the collapsed veins, dilating them one by one.

His hand was no longer cold, no longer grey-blue. A warm pinkness was spreading through it. Red scabs formed in three places across his wrist and slowly extended along the amputation line until they ran most of the way around, though a spot near his wrist bone, and another underneath, still ebbed blood.

His little finger twitched; pins and needles pricked all over his hand. And then – Rix flexed his index finger, and it *moved*. Tears sprang to his eyes.

"How did you do that?" he said hoarsely. "Who are you?"

Glynnie shook her head, slumped onto the other bench and wiped her brow with her forearm, leaving a streak of blood there. "I'm not a healer, nor a magian – just a maidservant."

"I don't understand . . ."

Glynnie tilted the metal cup towards him. The bottom was covered with a smear of blood.

"What's that for?" said Rix.

"It's the cup Tali used to try and heal Tobry. With her healing blood."

"But she didn't heal him. He's dead."

"Maybe shifters can't be healed," said Glynnie. "But Tali's blood can heal ordinary wounds. That's all I did."

"Go on."

"I covered both edges of your wrist with the blood left in the cup. It was frozen; I had to warm it in my hands. I pushed your hand and wrist together and held them. That's all."

Rix's other hand was still clenched tightly around Maloch's hilt. He let go. "You also used the protective magery of my sword."

"*I* didn't use it," said Glynnie. "I only put it where it could do you some good."

"You gave me back my hand. I can never thank you—"

"It could get infected," said Glynnie. "I'll have to look after it."

She stood up, swaying with exhaustion, and Rix realised how much he had taken her for granted. Why should the great Lord Rixium notice a little, freckled maidservant? Palace Ricinus had employed a hundred maids, each as replaceable as every other.

"Sit down," he said, reaching up to her. "Rest. Let me wait on you."

Her eyes widened; a blotchy flush spread across her cheeks. "You can't wait on *me*."

Glynnie washed the blood off her hands and forearms in the basin niche, then took a rag from her pack and scrubbed Benn's grubby face and hands. He was half asleep and made no protest. She cleaned her blood-spotted garments as best she could, took stale bread and hard cheese from her pack, cut a portion for Rix and another for her brother, then a little for herself. She resumed her seat, nibbled at a crust, leaned back and closed her eyes. The flush slowly faded.

Her eyes sprang open. "Lord, we got to fly. They could be creeping after us right now."

"Maloch will warn me. Rest. You've been up all night."

"So have you."

"I couldn't sleep even if I wanted to. Hush now. I need to think."

It was a lie. So much was whirling through his mind that he was incapable of coherent thought. Rix clenched his right fist, for the pleasure of being able to do so. It did not feel as natural as his left hand, and the scabbed seam around his wrist would leave a raised scar, but he had his hand back, and it worked. He could ask for nothing more.

"How did you know it would rejoin, Glynnie?"

"Didn't. But the captain cut your hand off with that sword . . ."

"Yes?" he said when she did not go on.

"It's supposed to protect you. So I thought . . . I thought it might not have severed your hand on all the levels . . ."

"What do you mean, *all the levels?*"

"I don't know. Heard it mentioned by the chancellor's chief magian one time . . . when . . ."

"When you were watching and listening?" said Rix.

"Servants spend half their time waiting," said Glynnie. "I like to make sense of things. I thought, if your hand hadn't been severed on all the levels, it might join up."

He rested his back against the wall. Though it was deep winter in Cauldron, this far below the palace it was pleasantly warm. He raised his hand. Two places were still ebbing blood, though they were smaller than before. The healing was almost complete.

He closed his eyes for a minute, but felt himself sinking into a dreamy haze and forced them open. The enemy were too many and too clever. It would not take them long to discover which way he had gone, and if he were asleep he might miss Maloch's warning.

He rose, paced across the square vault and back. Then again and again. His eyes were accustomed to the dimness now and the glow-stone shed light into the corners of the vault. The stonework was unlike anything he had seen before. The wall stone was as smooth as plaster, yet the door frame, and each corner of the wall, was shaped from undressed stone, crudely shaped with pick and chisel. Though odd, it seemed right.

These walls are crying out for a mural, he thought, and his hand rose involuntarily to the wall, as though he held a brush. He cursed, remembered that there was a child present and bit the oaths off. Again his hand rose. Painting had been his solace in many of the worst times of his childhood, and Rix longed for that solace now.

"Lord?" said Glynnie, softly.

"It's all right. I'll wake you if anything happens. Sleep now."

She trudged across, holding out a long object, like a stick or baton, though it took a while for him to recognise it as one of his paintbrushes.

"Thought you might need it," she said.

"After I finished the picture of the murder cellar, I swore I'd never paint again."

"Painting is your life, Lord."

"That life is over."

"It might help to heal you."

He took the brush. His restored hand felt like a miracle, but it would take a far greater one to heal the inner man who had betrayed his mother and helped to bring down his house.

Yet if he could lose himself in his art, even for a few minutes, it would do more for him than a night's sleep. Rix set down the brush, since he had no paint, and looked for something he could use to sketch on the wall. There was charcoal in the ashes of the ancient campfire, though when he picked it up the pieces crumbled in his hand.

Behind the ashes he spied several lengths of bone charcoal. He reached for a piece the length of his hand and the thickness of his middle finger. His fingers and thumb took a second to close around it, then locked and he began to sketch on the wall. His hand lacked its previous dexterity so he drew with sweeps of his arm.

He had no idea what he was drawing. This was often the case when he began – it worked better if he did not think about the subject. On one notable occasion he had done the first sketch blindfolded, and the resulting painting had been one of his best. The chancellor had called it a masterpiece.

It had also been a divination of the future, and Hightspall's future was bleak enough already. If there was worse to come, he did not want to know about it in advance.

As he worked, Rix tried to work on an escape plan. It would not be easy, for the enemy occupied the city and guarded all exits. They knew what he looked like and, being one of the biggest men in Caulderon, he had no hope of disguising himself. There were many tunnels and passages, of course, and some led out of the city, but the enemy were masters of the subterranean world and he had little hope of escaping them there. The tunnels would be patrolled by jackal shifters and other shifters. They could sniff him out a hundred yards away.

That only left the lake. Having dwelt underground for well over a thousand years, the Cythonians could have little knowledge of boats, while Rix had been sailing since he could walk. And many forgotten drains led to the lake. Some had been exposed by the great tidal wave several days ago, burst open by the pressure of water. If he could get Glynnie and Benn onto a boat, they would have a hope.

The worn length of bone charcoal snapped. He selected another from the ashes and sketched on.

If he succeeded in escaping, where could he go? Not over the sea; Hightspall was almost ice-locked. For centuries the ice sheets had been spreading up from the southern pole to surround the land, as they had already enveloped the long, mountainous island called Suden.

Southern Hightspall was mostly open farmland that offered few hiding places; his way must be to the rugged west or the mountainous north-east.

He had lost everything, but the chancellor had also given him something – the Herovian heritage Rix had not known he had. He ran his fingers along the weathered words down Maloch's blade – *Heroes must fight to preserve the race.* Who were the Herovians, anyway? They had come here two thousand years ago on the First Fleet, a persecuted minority following a path set down in their sacred book, the *Immortal Text*, searching for their Promised Realm.

They had been led by Axil Grandys, the founder of Hightspall, and his allies who together made up the Five Herovians, or Five Heroes as they were to become known.

"It's beautiful," sighed Glynnie. "Where is it?"

Rix focused on his sketch, almost afraid to look. It showed a pretty glade by a winding stream, the water so clear that cobbles in the stream bed could clearly be seen. Wildflowers dotted the grass. Hoary old trees framed the glade and in the distance was a vista of snowy mountains.

He let out his breath with a rush. "I don't know. I've never seen the place before."

Glynnie returned to the bench, put her arm around Benn and her eyes closed. For the first time since he had known her, she looked at peace. Rix laid down the charcoal, sat on a block of stone and compared his hands. His wrist still throbbed and his fingers tingled. When he opened and closed his hand it moved stiffly, though less stiffly than before.

One of the ebbing wounds had closed; the other still oozed blood. Idly, Rix wiped it away with the paintbrush, then studied his blood in the bluish light of the glowstone. It looked richer than before, almost purple. He admired the colour for a moment, as artists are wont to do then, without thinking, stepped across to the sketch and began to paint.

When the brush was empty he touched up his sketch with the charcoal, using his left hand. Taking more blood on the paintbrush he continued, eyes unfocused so he could not influence the work; painting on blind inspiration.

After a while he began to feel weary and drained. He often did at the end of a painting session. He dabbed at his wrist but it was no longer bleeding. The last section of the wound had sealed over and he had nothing left to paint with.

He glanced at the stick of charcoal and realised that it wasn't some animal bone, cast onto the fire after dinner. It was part of a human arm bone, the smaller bone of the forearm.

Rix tossed it away with a shudder and let the brush fall. He slumped onto his seat, head hanging, arms dangling, longing to lie down and sleep. He fought it; the longer they delayed, the more difficult it would be to get out of Cauldero. He shivered. Why was it so cold? His fingers were freezing.

The fingers of his right hand were hooked and he could not straighten them. They no longer moved when he willed them to. And they were cold; dead cold. The tips of his fingers weren't pink any more, but blue-grey, and grey was spreading towards his hand.

"Lord, what have you done?" cried Glynnie.

He started and looked around wildly. She was on her feet, staring at the painting on the wall. Red as blood it was, black as charred bone. Rix blinked at it, rubbed his eyes and recoiled.

It still showed the glade by the stream, but it was no longer enchanting. The sky was blood-dark and its reflection turned the water the same colour. There were two figures in the clearing now, a man with a sword and a woman with a knife. No, three. The third was up against the trunk of the largest tree, chained to it, helpless.

It was Tobry, and his shirt had been torn open, baring his chest.

The man was Rix, the woman, Tali, and they were advancing on Tobry, preparing to murder their best friend. But he was already dead, so what could it mean? Was it meant to symbolise the way Tali and Rix had, without meaning to, destroyed Tobry's last hope, leaving him with no choice but to sacrifice himself to the fate he most feared? Or could the mural be an expression of Rix's own sickening guilt? Or did he bear Tobry a secret resentment because the chancellor had forced Rix to choose between Tobry's life and betraying his own, evil mother?

Am I even more dishonourable than I've been made out to be? Rix thought.

Cold rushed along the fingers of his right hand, then across his hand to the wrist. Blue followed it, slowly turning grey. All feeling vanished up to the wrist and Rix felt sure it would never come back.

Henceforth he would go by another name.
Deadhand.

CHAPTER 3

L *ike the first trickle down a drought-baked river bed it came. But it*
wasn't a river bed, it was a paved corridor, the stone walls of which
were carved into scenes of forest glades – it was the main tunnel in the
underground city, Cython. It wasn't water either, for it was thick and red
and sluggish, and had a smell like iron.

"Bare your throat," said the chancellor's principal healer, Madam
Dibly, a scrawny old woman with a dowager's hump.

Tali was jerked out of her daze and the vision of that red flood
vanished. "My – *throat?*"

"To best preserve its potency, your healing blood has to be taken
fast. And the carotid artery is the fastest."

"Why not take it directly from my heart?" Tali snapped. "That'd
be even quicker."

The old healer's pouched eyes double-blinked at her. "I don't like
the treacherous Pale, Thalalie vi Torgrist, and I don't like you. It's
a great honour to serve your country this way. Why can't you see
that?"

"I don't see you giving up your life's blood."

"If my blood had healing powers, I would do so gladly, but I can
only heal with my hands." Dibly studied her fingers. The knuckles were swollen and her fingers moved stiffly.

"You're not a healer, Madam *Dribbly*, you're a butcher. Are you
making blood pudding from my left-overs? If it heals so well, you
could live forever on it."

"Bare. Your. Throat!"

It wasn't wise to make an enemy out of one so exalted, who was,
in any case, following the orders of the chancellor. But Tali had to
fight. Robbed of her friends, her quest, and the man she had only

realised she loved when he had been condemned in front of her, resistance was all she had left. She didn't even have the use of her magery. Afraid that Lyf would lock onto it and track her down, she had buried her gift so deeply that she could not find it again.

It wasn't right that Lyf, the man ultimately responsible for her mother's death and the deaths of her other ancestors, was not only free, but stronger than ever. Yet Tali, even as a slave, had not been as powerless as she was now. One thing had not changed, however – her determination to escape and bring him to justice.

Resistance was useless here. If she did not obey, Dibly would call her attendants and they would not be gentle. Tali took off her jacket and unfastened her high-collared blouse, her cold fingers fumbling with the buttons. She pulled it down over her shoulders, then lay back on the camp stretcher, shivering.

The chancellor's cavalcade had fled the ruins of Caulderon three days ago, using powerful magery to cover their tracks. Now they were high in the Crowbung Range, heading west, travelling at night by secret paths and hiding by day. It had been cold enough in Caulderon, but at this altitude winter was so bitter that everyone slept fully clothed. Tali had not bathed since they left, and itched all over. As a slave in Cython, she had bathed every day. Going without all this time was torment.

Madam Dibly passed a broad strap across Tali's forehead and pulled it tight.

"What's that for?" Tali cried.

Straps were passed around both her arms, above the elbows, then Dibly waved a cannula, large enough to take blood from a whale, in Tali's face. The slanted steel tip winked at her in the lantern light.

"Were you to move or twitch with this deep in your throat," the healer said with the ghoulish relish peculiar to her profession, "it might go ill for you."

"Not if you know your job," Tali said coldly.

"I do. That's why I'm strapping you down. And if you curb your insolence I might even unstrap you afterwards."

The healer set a pyramid-shaped bottle, made from green glass, on the floor. It looked as though it would hold a quart. So much?

Tali thought. Can I live if they take all that? Does the chancellor care if I don't?

Dibly crushed a head of garlic and rubbed the reeking pulp all over her palms and fingers to disinfect them. Tali's stomach heaved. The smell reminded her of her years of slavery in the toadstool grottoes. One of the most common toadstools grown there had smelled powerfully of garlic.

The collapsed vessel of a boar's artery ran from the cannula to the bottle. Madam Dibly inspected the point of the cannula and wiped Tali's throat with a paste of crushed garlic and rosemary. She could feel her pulse ticking there.

Why did her blood heal? Was it because she was Pale and had spent her whole life in Cython? If so, her healing blood was not rare at all – all eighty-five thousand Pale could share it. Or was there more to it? Did it have anything to do with the master pearl in her head? The missing fifth ebony pearl that everyone wanted so desperately?

"Steady now," said Dibly.

The cannula looked like a harpoon. The old healer's snaggly teeth were bared, yet there was a twinkle in her colourless eyes that Tali did not like at all. She was taking far too much pleasure in what she was about to do.

"W-will it hurt?" said Tali.

"My patients never stop whining and squealing, but it isn't *real* pain."

"Why don't we swap places?" said Tali. "You bare your grimy, wattled old neck and I'll stab the cannula into it up to the hilt, and we'll see how pig-like your squeals are."

Madam Dibly ground her yellow teeth, then in a single, precise movement thrust the cannula through Tali's carotid artery and down it for a good three inches.

Tali screamed. It felt as though her throat had been penetrated by a spike of glacial ice. For some seconds her blood seemed to stop flowing, as if it had frozen solid. Then it resumed, though it all appeared to be flowing down the boar's artery, dilating it and colouring it scarlet, then pouring into the green glass bottle.

It was already an inch deep. The watching healer separated into two fuzzy images and Tali's head seemed to be revolving independently of her body, a sickening feeling that made her worry about throwing up. What would happen if she did while that great hollow spike ran down her artery? Would it tear out the other side? Not even Dibly could save her then.

Tali's vision blurred until all she could see was a uniform brown. Her senses disconnected save for the freezing feeling in her neck and a *tick, tick, tick* as her lifeblood drained away—

The brownness was blown into banners like smog before the wind and she saw him. Her enemy, Lyf! She shivered. He was feeling in a crevice in the wall. She cried out, involuntarily, for he was in a chamber that looked eerily like the cellar where her eight-year-old self had seen her mother murdered for her ebony pearl. It had the same half-domed shape, not unlike a skull ...

It was *the murder cellar, though everything had been removed and every surface scrubbed back to expose the bare stone of the ceiling and walls. Before being profaned by treachery and murder, this chamber had been one of the oldest and most sacred places in ancient Cythe – the private temple of the kings.*

What was Lyf doing? He was alone save for a group of greybeard ghosts – Tali recognised some of them from the ancestor's gallery he had created long ago in the wrythen's caverns. Lyf had a furtive air, lifting stones up and putting them down, then checking over his shoulder as though afraid he was being watched.

"Hurry!" said a spectre so ancient that he had faded to a transparent wisp, though his voice was strong and urgent. "The key must be found. Without it, all you've done is for nothing."

What key? What could be so vital that without it everything Lyf had done – saving his people and capturing the great city at the heart of Hightspall – was as nothing? And who was this ancient spectre who was telling the king what to do?

The blood-loss vision faded and she saw nothing more.

"You shouldn't bait her, Tali. Madam Dibly is just doing what I ordered her to do."

Tali was so weak that she could not open her eyes, but she recognised the voice coming from the folding chair beside the camp bed. The chancellor.

"Ugh!" she said.

She tried to form words but they would not come, and that frightened her. She had been robbed of far more than two pints of blood. Part of her life and health had been taken from her. She was enslaved again, but this was far worse than the enslavement she had endured in Cython. There she'd had a degree of freedom, and vigorous health. There, those who worked hard and never caused trouble were relatively safe.

But the chancellor was using her like a prized cow – she was fed and looked after to ensure she could be milked of the maximum amount of blood. And once her body gave out, would she be discarded like a milkless cow?

There was also Rannilt to consider. If the blood-taking could weaken Tali so drastically, what must it be doing to the skinny little child who had been near death only days ago?

"You can stop all this," said the chancellor. For such a small, ugly, hunchbacked man, his voice was surprisingly deep and authoritative.

"How?" she managed to whisper.

Her eyes fluttered open. She was in his tent, the largest of all, and she saw the shadow of a guard outside the flap. The man was not needed; Tali lacked the strength to raise her head.

The side of her neck throbbed. She felt bruised from shoulder bone to ear.

"I know you're holding out on me," said the chancellor. "Tell me what I need to know and I'll order Madam Dibly to stop."

Had Tali not been so weak, she would have started and given her secret away. If he guessed that she hosted the fifth pearl inside her, the master pearl that could magnify his chief magian's wizardry tenfold, how could the chancellor resist cutting it out?

Hightspall was losing the war because its magery had dwindled drastically over the centuries. With the master pearl the chancellor could have it back. With the master pearl, his adepts might even command the four pearls that Lyf held. He might win the war, and even undo some of the harm Lyf's corrupt sorcery had done to Hightspall. Such as the shifters that Lyf had created for one purpose only – to spread terror and ruin throughout the land, and turn good people into ravening monsters like themselves.

Like Tobry, her first and only love turned into the kind of beast he had dreaded becoming all his life. But Tobry's suffering was over.

Should she give up the master pearl? It wasn't that simple. According to Deroe, ebony pearls could not be used properly within – or by – the women who hosted them, though he might have been lying. She could not tell. To gain their full strength, the pearls had to be cut out and healed in the host's blood, which was invariably fatal. Tali could only give up the pearl by sacrificing her own life.

Someone nobler than her might have made that sacrifice for her country, but Tali could not. Before escaping from Cython she had sworn a binding blood oath, and until she had fulfilled it she did not have the freedom to consider any other course.

"Don't know . . . what you're talking about," she said at last.

"You're lying," said the chancellor. "But I can wait."

"You're a failure, Chancellor. You've lost the centre of Hightspall and you're losing the war."

He winced. "I admit it, though only to you. According to my spies, Lyf is already tearing down Caulderon, the greatest city in the known world, and rounding up a long list of enemies."

She hadn't thought of that. "What's he going to do to them?"

"Put them to death, of course."

"But that's . . . evil!"

The chancellor sighed. "No, just practical. It's what you do when you capture a city – you hunt down the troublemakers and make sure they can't cause any trouble."

"Does that include Rix?" said Tali.

"I'm told he's number one on Lyf's list." The chancellor smiled wryly. "I feel a little hurt – why aren't *I* on top?"

"I wish you were!" she snapped, then added, "I couldn't bear it if Rix was killed as well."

Though the chancellor despised Rix, he had the decency not to show it this time. "He's a resourceful man. He could have escaped."

"You chopped his hand off!" she said furiously. "How's he supposed to fight without a right hand?"

"To escape a besieged city you need to avoid attention, not attract it."

After a lengthy pause, he continued as though her problems, her tragedies, were irrelevant. Which, to him, they were.

"The enemy hold all of central Hightspall – the wealthy, fertile part. Now I'm limping like a three-legged hound to the fringes. But where am I to go, Tali, when the ice sheets are closing around the land from three sides? What am I to do?"

This was the strangest aspect of their relationship. One minute he was the ruthless master and she the helpless victim; the next he was confiding in her and seeking her advice as though she were his one true friend.

The chancellor was not, and could never be, her friend. He was a ruthless man who surrounded himself in surreal, twisted artworks, and with beautiful young women he never laid a finger on. He was not a kind man, or even a good one, but he had two virtues: he held to his word and he loved his country. He would do almost anything, sacrifice almost anyone, to save it, and if she wasn't strong enough, if she didn't fight him all the way, he would sacrifice her too.

"Why ask me? Where are you running to, Chancellor, with your tail between your crooked little legs?"

His smile was crooked, too. "I've been insulted by the best in the land. Do you think your second-rate jibes can scratch my corrugated hide?"

Tali slumped. She was so weak that five minutes of verbal jousting was all she could manage.

"Is all lost, then?" she said faintly.

He took her hand, which was even more surprising. The chancellor was not given to touching.

"Not yet, but it could soon be. I fear the worst, Tali, I'm not afraid to tell you. If you know anything that can help us, anything at all . . ."

She had to distract him from that line of thought. "Do you have a plan? For the war, I mean?"

"Rebuild my army and forge alliances, so when the time comes . . ."

"For a bold stroke?"

"Or a last desperate gamble. Possibly using you."

Tali froze. Did he know about the ebony pearl? She turned to the brazier, afraid that her eyes would give her away.

"You gave me your word," he went on.

Not her pearl. *Worse.* He was referring to the promise he had forced out of her in his red palace in Caulderon. That one day he might ask her to do the impossible and sneak into Cython to rouse the Pale to rebellion.

She did not consider the promise binding since it had been given under duress. But the blood oath she had sworn before escaping from Cython *was* binding, and it amounted to the same thing. With Cython depopulated because most of its troops had marched out to war, the vast numbers of Pale slaves there were a threat at the heart of Lyf's empire.

Sooner or later he would decide to deal with the threat, and that was where Tali's blood oath came in. She had sworn to do whatever it took to save her people. But before she could hope to, she would have to overcome her darkest fear – a return to slavery.

CHAPTER 4

The winter journey over the Crowbung Mountains, and the lower ranges beyond, took eight days of cold, exhaustion and pain. Tali saw nothing of the lands they were passing through, for the chancellor had taken pains to ensure that no spy could discover where she was.

She was confined to a covered wagon all the hours of daylight, disguised by a glamour the chief magian had cast over her. All she knew, from glimpses of the setting sun, was that they were heading west, then south-west.

Twice more she was taken to the healer's tent at night so Madam Dibly could draw more blood. It was needed to heal valued people who had been bitten by shifters and thus turned to shifters themselves.

Tali had been waiting for it, hoping to have another of those blood-loss visions. What key was Lyf looking for, that mattered more than anything he had done so far? Finding out was the one way she could help the war effort. But, frustratingly, the vision had not been repeated.

"Does it work?" said Tali on the second occasion, "or are you putting me through all this out of spite?"

"I'm a healer!" cried Dibly, deeply affronted. "I look after my patients no matter what I think of them." Her scowl indicated exactly what she thought of Tali.

"Does my blood work?" Tali repeated. "Or aren't I *allowed* to know."

"It heals most shifters—"

"But not all?"

"Few panaceas work on every patient," said Madam Dibly. "The blood you give so grudgingly heals most shifters, as long as it's administered within a few days after they've been turned."

"But not after that?"

"The longer they've been a shifter, the harder it is to turn them back. And once the shifter madness comes on them it's no use at all . . ." Dibly looked away, her jaw tight, her eyelids screwed shut. "My brother was one of the bitten ones. Your blood came too late for him."

"What happened?" said Tali, moved despite her dislike of the old healer.

"For everyone's safety, the bitten ones have to be put down – like rabid dogs." Madam Dibly wiped her eyes, then said harshly, "Lie down. Bare your throat."

She only took a pint of blood this time. Tali tried to force another blood-loss vision by envisaging Lyf in his temple, but saw nothing. She was so exhausted she could only doze on the camp bed afterwards. If they took any more it was bound to be the end of her.

She was given the best of food, including more meat than she had eaten in her life, though after the third blood-taking Tali lacked the energy to chew it. Dibly had it made into rich stews which she dribbled down Tali's throat from a spoon.

But today, the eighth day since leaving Caulderon, she felt better. The cold wasn't so bitter, her throat felt less bruised, and she had enough strength to pull herself up to a sitting position, wedged in place by pillows. The cavalcade was heading down a steep, pot-holed track, the brakes squealing and the wagon lurching each time they grabbed the rims of the six-foot-high wheels.

"Where are we?" she asked.

"Approaching Rutherin," said the healer, who was trying to write in a small, red-bound herbal.

Ruth-erin. The name had an unpleasant sound. "Is that a town?"

"It is, but we're going to Fortress Rutherin, which is on the cliff-top above the town."

"Can I see?"

Madam Dibly had mellowed after seeing how badly Tali had been affected by blood loss. She peered out between the curtains. "It can't hurt, I suppose, since we're high up and no one can see in."

She drew the curtains wide and white light flooded in, momen-tarily dazzling Tali. Her throat constricted. For a few seconds the wagon rocked, as the dome of the sky had rocked the first time she had left the dim underworld of Cython for Hightspall. She had suf-fered her first attack of agoraphobia then, and now thought she was about to have another, but everything settled.

They had crossed the mountains and were winding down a steep hill towards the south-west coast. The sun was out and in the dis-tance, as far as she could see, a dazzling field of white extended across the ocean. "Is that the *ice*?"

Madam Dibly seemed amused, in a grim sort of way. "Indeed it is, and creeping closer to Hightspall every year. When I was a girl it could only be seen from here in winter, at the furthest horizon."

"Why is it coming closer?"

"The land we took from the enemy long ago is rising up against us."

So people said, but Tali found it hard to believe. "But ... so much ice. Where does it come from?"

"No one knows, but it cut Hightspall off long ago. Now we're alone in the world – perhaps the only nation left ..."

"Alone in the world," said Tali, "and at the mercy of the ice." She shivered.

"It's closing off our southern ports, one by one, and creeping up the east and west coasts. Soon Hightspall will be ice-locked. Some say that our great volcanoes will stop it from covering the land the way it's buried Suden, but surely ice will win over fire." The grim smile faded.

"Is Rutherin a port town?" Tali said, trying to sound casual.

"It was, but don't think there's any escape that way. It's a stranded port."

"How do you mean?"

"As the ice sheets grow, the sea falls. It's now a mile offshore and the old port – see it there, beside the town – is dry land. The fishing fleets no longer dock at Rutherin."

Madam Dibly busied herself with her herbal. Tali stared hungrily out the gap in the curtains. But escape was impossible when she barely had the strength to stand up.

The wagon turned a corner, rattling and thumping down a track surfaced with chunks of broken rock. Over the heads of the horses she saw an ominous bastion of black stone. The native rock had been cut into knife-edged ridges around it to enclose it on both sides and the rear, while at the front there was a high wall and a pair of massive wooden gates which now stood open. On her left, the ridge fell away in a glassy black cliff that plunged down towards the town.

"What's that place?" said Tali.

Madam Dibly whipped the curtains closed and sat down, breathing raggedly. "I told you, Fortress Rutherin." She bent over her herbal.

"Aren't I supposed to see it?"

"You can see it. No one is allowed to see you."

"Why not?" said Tali, though she could guess the answer.

"You know Cython's secrets, and the enemy wants you dead."

No, Lyf wants me very much alive, so he can crack my head open and gouge out the master pearl. It had to be taken while she were alive; if she died, the pearl died with her.

Tali realised that Madam Dibly was looking at her curiously. Had she given something away? "Fortress Rutherin doesn't look a very nice place," she said hastily.

"It wasn't . . . even before the blood-bath lady became its mistress."

Tali had to ask. "Who was the blood-bath lady?"

"It takes a lot of victims to fill a bathtub with blood. And she bathed daily. Or so the tales say."

Was this another of Dibly's macabre jokes? Tali tried not to think about it, but the image of all those people being bled to death each day was not easily banished.

"Puts your little problem into perspective, doesn't it?" Dibly said with a sidelong glance at Tali. "But Fortress Rutherin is strong; it's what the chancellor needs. It's easy to defend, hard to attack and has underground water enough to withstand a year-long siege."

One wheel crashed into a deep pothole, jerked out of it and fell into another. There came the sharp crack of breaking wood. The wagon tilted sharply to the left, slamming Tali's camp bed into the left-hand wall.

"Are we being attacked?" she cried.

Dibly tore open the front curtains and was leaning out when there came another crack, from the rear. The left-hand side of the wagon slammed down onto the rocky road, hurling her out, and the wagon bed came to rest at a steep angle. Tali was toppled from the camp bed, which overturned onto her.

Struggling out from under the bed was like climbing a mountain. Her heart was pounding by the time she freed herself. Outside, people were shouting and a rider was galloping towards them. If it was an attack, was she better off inside the wagon or out? Out, she thought. She could not bear to be trapped.

Tali crawled along the sloping bed of the wagon to the curtains, and peered out. "Madam Dibly?"

The old woman lay on the rocky ground, unmoving. There was blood all over her face. Tali slid down, half falling. Both of the left-side wheels lay on the ground. It wasn't an attack. The first jolt must have broken the front axle of the wagon and then the strain had snapped the rear one.

Tali felt so faint that she had to hang on. She crawled to the healer.

"Madam Dibly?" she said, turning her head upright.

It moved too easily, and when Tali released it, flopped back at an odd angle. Dibly was dead. Her neck was broken.

Tali closed the healer's eyes, then pushed herself to her feet. The faintness returned. She took a lurching step forwards, clambered over the wagon tongue and out into the middle of the track. A line of wagons had stopped behind hers and several drivers had gathered around it, studying the broken axles.

Ahead, most of the riders were still heading for the closed gates of Fortress Rutherin, but three horses had turned out of the line and were coming back. Two were ridden by big men who had the look of the chancellor's elite guard, while the fellow between them was small, hunchbacked and rode slumped in the saddle like a bag of wheat. The chancellor.

Tali had to know where they were taking her and what the surroundings were like. The moment she was strong enough, she was going to escape. She moved out on to the road, clear of the wagon, and looked around.

The black cliff to the left of the fortress dropped several hundred feet to a narrow coastal plain, below which she could see the tangled streets and smoke-stained buildings of the former port town of Rutherin. It had a forlorn and neglected air. In the distance, the ice sheet covered the ocean in all directions, unimaginably vast. Its advancing front was formed from ice cliffs nearly as high as the track on which she stood.

Behind her, up the winding road, were the snow-covered mountains they had recently crossed. No escape that way; not on foot, anyhow.

Kaark! Kaark!

The hoarse cries caused her to look up. Squinting against the bright sky, she saw a large bird wheeling, thousands of feet up. An unusual bird; or was it a huge bat? Shivers ran down her back.

As it came lower, circling above the fortress and the road with the stalled wagons, Tali saw that it was neither bird nor bat, but some flying creature bigger than either, with man-like shoulders and head, and wings at least twelve feet across, but spindly legs that could not have supported its weight. She had never heard of such a creature. Tali was studying it, shading her eyes from the bright, when the chancellor let out a furious bellow.

The guards came hurtling up. The leading rider scooped Tali off her feet, dropped her face-down across his saddle and threw a cloak over her.

"What are you doing?" she cried, struggling to free her face.

The guard's big hand pressed her down. He wheeled his horse and raced for the gates of Rutherin. The chancellor and the other guard turned and matched his pace, and within a minute they had passed through and were under a covered ride-way inside. Further on, the ground sloped so steeply that the rear of the fortress was thirty feet lower than the front.

"You bloody fool!" cried the chancellor, dragging Tali off the saddle. "You bloody, bloody fool."

She had to sit down; her head was whirling. "Dibly was thrown out of the wagon," said Tali. "I went to help her . . . but she broke her neck."

A triumphant cry echoed across the yard. *Kaark! Kaark!*

The chancellor jerked his head at the first guard. "Shoot the damn thing, Regg."

Regg grabbed his bow, darted to the edge of the ride-way and looked up, but shook his head. "It's too high, well out of range."

"What's it doing?"

"Flying away, waggling its wings – looks like it's giving us the finger."

The chancellor slumped onto a bench, breathing hard. His eyes met Tali's.

"It's a gauntling, a kind of flying shifter. *A spy*, Tali. A key purpose of this trip was to get you here without the enemy knowing. Why did you think I kept you disguised and indoors the whole time?"

"I assumed it was to torment and punish me."

"Aaarrgh!" he roared, tearing at his scanty hair. "And now it's all been for nothing. It won't take the gauntling long to fly back to Caulderon. By midnight, Lyf will know you're here."

CHAPTER 5

Rix shuddered. Why had he painted that dreadful mural? Was it symbolic – the despised Pale and the disgraced former nobleman collectively destroying their country? Or did it mean nothing at all?

He could feel Glynnie's gaze on him. No, on his dead hand. Her mouth was open, her eyes huge. He scowled and she lowered her head. A creeping flush passed up her cheeks.

"Why didn't you leave it up on the roof?" Rix said quietly. "Why did you have to interfere?"

Her reply was barely audible. "You done so much for us. I wanted to help you . . ."

"But you didn't know what you were doing!" he cried.

Benn whimpered and scrunched himself in the corner. For once, Glynnie ignored him. "You . . . you could have told me to stop."

"I didn't know you were planning to reattach it. I had my eyes closed. I couldn't bear to look at the damn, dead thing."

He raised his lifeless right hand, wanting to be rid of it. Should he hack it off? Rix did not have the courage for such a bloody, final act. And, if he admitted it, he could not abandon hope that whatever had withdrawn the life from it might restore it again.

"Sorry, Lord," whispered Glynnie, falling to her knees before him. "I'm just a stupid maidservant. Beat me black and blue; I deserve it . . . but please don't take it out on Benn. Please don't abandon us now."

He wanted to, but he could not abandon a young woman and a child, for any reason. Without him they had no hope. With him, maimed and useless though he was, they had a tiny chance.

"I'm not going to beat anyone—"

Somewhere behind and above them a beast howled, an eerie sound that echoed down the tunnels. It was followed by a frantic scratching, panting and yelping. Rix imagined a shifter's blood-stained claws tearing at the lid of a coffin, trying to get at the dead meat inside.

"They've sniffed us out," whispered Glynnie. "We'll never get away now. Lord, please don't leave us."

"I'm not going to leave you. Get Benn up."

Instinctively, Rix reached for Maloch, but his dead hand could not grip the hilt. He drew it left-handed and held it up. The blade, which had a bluish tint, was made from the immensely strong metal titane, the secret of whose forging had long been lost. The very tip of the sword had no point, for it had been melted by magery in the battle with Lyf. Rix would have to grind a new tip – assuming his sharpening stone could grind titane.

He checked the passage outside the vault. There was no sign of a light, but neither the Cythonians nor their shifters needed light to travel underground. The enemy could feel their way, and their shifters could smell it out.

He sniffed and caught a faint, rank odour, like a jackal shifter, yet more dog-like. Whatever kind of shifter it was, a pack of them would have the advantage down here. Rix had defended Glynnie and Benn from jackal shifters a few days back and never wanted to do so again. Had Tobry not eaten that piece of caitsthe's liver and become one himself to fight them off, they would all be dead—

He forced the memories away. Concentrate on survival; nothing else is relevant. Glynnie and Benn were staring at him, holding their knives. They knew what was coming, and how little chance they had. Even with his right hand, Rix would have struggled to beat a pack of shifters. Without it, what hope did he have?

"Shut that door," he said, indicating the one through which they had entered. "We'll go out the other way."

Glynnie pushed the door closed. "There's no lock."

"Damn!" Rix looked around. "Give us a hand with the bench."

They heaved at it but it was fixed to the floor, and so was the other one.

"Maybe they'll go straight past," said Benn.

"They'll sniff us out, lad."

They went through the far door and tried to close it but the rusted hinges would not budge. Beyond, a well-made tunnel curved around to the right, then down in a series of long, shallow steps in a sweeping left-hand curve.

"Go ahead, Glynnie," said Rix. "Hold the light high so I can guard our backs."

They went down. Rix backed after them, straining to see into the darkness, for the bluish light of the glowstone only extended up a few yards past him. Not nearly enough. The sly creatures would creep down in the dark, attack in a mass, and he'd have less than a second to defend.

"What's down below, Glynnie?" he said. "Can you see?"

"No, but it's getting steeper," she whispered. "Wait, there's a door going off to the right."

"Can we lock it behind us?"

"No."

"Keep going down."

A minute later, Rix caught a characteristic rank whiff on an air current. Hyena shifters. They were through the vault door, high above. And he couldn't fight them without light.

"Smelling stink-damp again," said Benn.

"Me too," said Glynnie, a moment later. "It's getting stronger with every step. Lord, if we keep going down . . ."

Now Rix could smell it. "It'll poison us. We'll go back up to that door."

They turned and went up, but now the reek of hyena shifters was overpowering.

"They're close," quavered Glynnie. "Lord, Lord—?"

"Light the torch, quick."

"But there's stink-damp! I can't make a flame here."

"I don't think there's enough of it to explode up here."

She gave him a dubious glance and handed the glowstone to her brother. Taking out the fabric-wrapped bundle of wood, then a small wrapped lump, which she unwrapped and began to rub into the cloth with her hands. Butter. Rix could smell it. She wiped her hands on her pants then, gingerly, struck sparks with her flint striker. The buttered cloth caught and burned with a sizzling yellow flame.

He clamped his dead fingers around the bundle and held it high. And recoiled. Glynnie gasped. Benn let out a strangled squeal.

The light reflected back from a dozen pairs of eyes, less than ten yards up. Red eyes, though the hyena shifters had black fur that made them almost invisible.

Rix drew Maloch and held it out. "Got your knives?"

"Yes, Lord," whispered Benn and Glynnie together.

"If one attacks you, go for the throat."

It might not be enough to stop a hyena shifter, but it was the best they could do. Rix swallowed. His heart was thundering, but inside he was calm, focused. He'd faced death many times in the past weeks. He'd even wanted death at his darkest moments. But not now. It was up to him to protect the innocents.

Taking a step up the slope, he met the eyes of the pack leader.

"I'm going to spill your guts on the steps," said Rix. "You're going to die and the other hyenas will eat you. You haven't got a hope against me."

Another step. The words were nonsense, but the steely self-confidence he projected was not. To beat the pack, he had to assert dominance over its leader. "I'm the top dog. Come onto me and I'll kill you, first stroke. Turn away."

The red eyes blinked but the pack did not move. Rix took another step. Only eight more to the door. He could hear Glynnie's heavy breathing behind him.

"It's all right, Benn," she whispered. "Rix'll save us."

The tone of her voice wasn't convincing. He lowered the torch, holding it out in front of him at the chest level of the shifters. Another step.

"To get to me, you've got to pass the fire," said Rix, swinging it back and forth.

The pack leader's eyes followed the flame. It double-blinked.

Now! Rix leapt forwards, thrusting out the burning torch with his right hand and Maloch with his left. Up one step, two, three and still the shifter had not budged. If he had misjudged, the children would die. Four, five, six. He let out a furious battle cry and swung Maloch at the beast's snout.

It ran, and the others did too. But not far. Only ten yards up the steps. Hyena shifters knew how to play this game. Even if it took a day to wear their prey down, they could wait.

He took another step. The door was on his left. He pushed it open. "Glynnie, Benn?"

They came up.

"Go through."

"But, Lord . . ." said Glynnie. "What about you?"

"Now!"

They went through. The pack leader was up on its toes, its tongue out. Rix swung the torch back and forth, but this time the beast's eyes didn't follow. It was a bad sign. It had his measure and was getting ready to attack.

Now! And if he was wrong, it was all over. He swung the blazing torch around, turned on the balls of his feet and tossed it out and down towards the bottom of the steps. The pack charged. He hurled himself through the door.

"Hold it shut!" he panted, taking hold of the door and forcing it closed.

The pack was clawing at the door when an enormous thudding boom was followed by a blow on the door that burst it wide open and hurled Rix, Glynnie and Benn six feet backwards. Tongues of fire licked in, then a rolling blast of sulphurous heat. The pack leader tumbled past them, its fur blazing, snapping uselessly at the flames and howling in agony. It raced down the tunnel, lighting the way for a few seconds, then disappeared.

Rix heaved the door shut and slumped against it, panting.

Glynnie was staring at him, wide-eyed. "Lord, I didn't know you could use *magery*."

"I can't. Stink-damp is heavy and it pools in low places. I tossed the torch down to the bottom, praying it would be thick enough there for it to explode."

"And you saved us, Lord." The light was back in her eyes. The belief that he could do anything.

"Not yet. The enemy will send people to investigate. We'd better get going."

The hero-worship made him acutely uncomfortable, nonetheless there was a kind of solace in doing his duty by Glynnie and Benn.

Without them, he would have hurled himself at the shifters in a suicidal attack.

They crawled through another fissure that appeared to have opened recently, then continued along one passage after another. The air reeked of burnt fur for a while, though they did not see the shifter again.

"Do you think it's dead?" said Benn.

"Yes, lad." Rix put a hand on the boy's shoulder. "I'm sure it is."

But there would be others, and soldiers, too. The enemy did not give up.

"I knew you could do it, Lord," said Benn. "And . . . and you can save Hightspall, too."

"Don't start that again," Rix growled.

"But it's true," said Benn, bewildered. "You're strong and clever and brave, and Hightspall needs you, Lord. Why can't you see?"

"Benn!" said Glynnie.

They continued in an uncomfortable silence. Benn was plodding now.

"Anyone smell water?" Rix said after several minutes. "Benn?"

"Sorry, Lord," said Benn after a long pause.

"I think . . . the lake is this way," said Glynnie, pointing to a passage that went left, sloping gently down.

"How can you tell?" Rix did not like being underground and had no idea which way to go.

"It feels colder and danker . . . and there's a rotting smell."

After the tidal wave and the brutal enemy onslaught, the main things rotting in the lake would be bodies. "We're still under the palace, so it can't be more than a few hundred yards to the water. Let's try it."

Shortly they came to a broad crack running across the passage; the floor on the other side had also dropped a foot. The crack was only three feet across but the bottom could not be seen.

"Jump," said Rix.

Benn leapt across but Glynnie, so brave in every other way, baulked at the gap.

"It's only a yard," said Rix.

"I can't do it."

"Come on, Sis," said Benn.

She tried to jump, froze on the edge and teetered there, her arms windmilling.

"Sis!" screamed Benn.

Rix dived for her, caught her with his good arm, swung her around and, before she could resist, heaved her across.

He sprang over. "Come on."

Glynnie did not move. She was looking up at him, tears filling her dark green eyes. Rix pretended he hadn't noticed.

Further down, they entered an ancient drainage line built from neat stone blocks. Puddles of water lay here and there, and scatters of rotting fish.

"This must date to Cythian times," said Rix, noting the quality of the stonework. "That means it's more than two thousand years old," he explained to Benn.

"What are the fish doing here?" said Benn.

"The great tidal wave forced lake water right up these drains, lad. In places, it squirted up through the lawn in fountains twenty feet high. We could find anything down here."

Benn shivered and took his sister's hand. Rix wished he hadn't said anything when, several minutes later, they turned a gentle bend and found a tangle of broken bodies lodged in a collapsed section of the wall.

As they edged by, Glynnie put her hand over Benn's eyes. He tore it away.

"Got to see everything," he said. "Got to know what happened."

Rix did not look, for fear he would recognise people from the palace. Too many good memories had been destroyed in the past few days; he wanted to preserve the few he had left.

"I can hear waves breaking," said Glynnie. "Lord, we must be near the lake."

"Carefully," said Rix. "They'll have guards along the shoreline, and they may have located all the tunnel exits by now."

But before they had gone another fifty yards Rix realised that the enemy could not have discovered this exit. The rest of the tunnel was full of water; the outlet must lie beneath the lake. And surely the pursuit could not be far away. The stink-damp explosion would have shaken the whole palace.

"Can either of you swim? You, Glynnie?" Rix could not resist adding, "You said you could do everything."

"I can swim a bit," she said, gnawing her knuckles. "Old Rennible taught me when I was little."

The former Master of the Palace, a gentle and kindly old man. The chancellor had hanged him from the front gates along with the lord and lady, plus all the other heads of Palace Ricinus. Guilty, innocent, it mattered not, as long as the lesson was taken. When a great house fell, everyone who had belonged to that house, or served in it, fell with it.

"How far can you swim?" said Rix.

"Twenty yards." She faltered. "But I never swum underwater."

"What about you, Benn?"

"I can learn," said Benn, uneasily.

"There's no time to teach you." Rix looked up the tunnel, then down at the dark water. "I can't see any light, though it can't yet be dark outside."

"Does that mean it's a long way to the end?" said Glynnie.

"Could be. Or it could be deep underwater. The lake's full of churned-up mud; you can't see far at all. I need to know how far it is to the outlet – if it's more than forty yards, we'll run out of air getting there."

She also scanned the conduit behind them, swallowing. "Can you swim through to check?"

"It'd take too long." Rix was infected by her unease. How long before the pursuit found them? He frowned, rubbed his jaw. "I can't take you both at once. If we lose contact I'll never find you again."

"Take Glynnie," said Benn. "I'll be all right."

Memories of the time Rix had lost contact with Tali in a lake out in the Seethings still burned him. She had been within seconds of drowning and it had been his fault. "You're smaller. It'll be easier if I take you first."

"Where would you leave him when you get out?" said Glynnie. "You can't take him to shore; there'll be guards everywhere."

"I don't like either option," said Rix. "What do you think, Benn?

If I take Glynnie first, will you be all right by yourself? It'd only be for five minutes."

"Of course," said Benn, thrusting his knife out menacingly, though his arm shook. "Don't worry about me, Sis."

Glynnie's face told a different story, but she said, "All right." She hugged him impulsively.

They took off their coats and boots and packed them in the oil-skin bags. "No, lad," said Rix. "Keep yours on until I come back. You'll need all the warmth you've got."

He stepped in and Glynnie went with him. The water, though chilly, wasn't as cold as might have been expected given the bitter winter outside. Lake Fumerous, which had filled the void created when the fourth of the volcanoes called the Vomits had blown itself to bits in ancient times, was warmed from beneath by subterranean furnaces.

"Take three slow, deep breaths," said Rix, "then hang on tight. Don't try to swim – you need to save your air. If it looks to be more than forty yards, I'll bring us back. Ready?"

She nodded stiffly, trying not to worry Benn, whose knife was drooping. Standing there all alone, he made a small, forlorn figure. Rix swallowed his own misgivings. Had it been Glynnie he would have felt just as bad.

"Now!" he said.

He pulled Glynnie under, holding her against his side, and swam down the drainpipe, following the gentle slope of its top and counting his strokes. The buoyancy of the oilskin bag helped to counteract the weight of the gold in his money belt, though it tended to pull him sideways. The light faded. Was she all right? She held herself so rigidly that he could not tell. Twenty strokes; twenty-five. He must have gone twenty yards by now, surely.

Rix could swim fifty yards underwater, at a desperate pinch, but Glynnie could hardly hold her breath that long. Thirty strokes. Should he turn back? If he went any further he wouldn't be able to – he'd run out of air on the way.

It wasn't easy, swimming one-handed. Was that light up ahead? It was hard to tell in the turbid water; his eyes felt gritty. Go on, or turn back? He must be beyond the point of no return now.

Yes, it was light, the faintest glimmer. Rix kept going, fighting the urge to breathe in. Glynnie was making small, panicky motions of her hands but there was nothing he could do for her. The light grew; they passed through a waving fringe of algae and he swam up to the surface. He held her with one arm while she gasped down air, raised himself head and shoulders out of the water, then hastily sank to chin level.

"What's the matter?" panted Glynnie.

"Guards, all along the shore." He could hear their boots crunching on the ice along the waterline.

"What are we going to do?" Her green eyes went wide. "Benn——"

"I haven't forgotten him."

He turned, turned again. At various points into the bay, huge timber mooring piles had been driven deep into the mud, though all were empty. The ships that had been moored there had either been sailed away, or wrecked in the tidal wave.

The nearest pile was thirty yards away. Rix fixed the location of the end of the drainpipe in mind as best he could in the featureless water, then swam with Glynnie to the pile, which extended six feet out of the water and had a copper cap on top.

"Hang onto the mooring ropes," he said, and made sure she had a tight hold. "I'll be as quick as I can."

He scanned the water for boats and other dangers. Several hundred yards further offshore, wind and currents had collected a mass of timber and floating debris into a loose, bobbing raft at least a hundred yards across. Dinghies were drawn up on the shore but he could not reach any without being spotted.

"Benn's in trouble, I know it," she wept. "I should have let you bring him first. I'm so stupid. I can't do anything right."

"He'll be all right. I'm going back now."

"What if you can't find the end of the drainpipe?"

"I'll find it."

"If something's happened——"

Now Rix was worried too, but he couldn't bear to listen. "I'll be quick. Stay low. Don't do anything to attract attention."

He swam back thirty yards, dived and went down with powerful strokes of his left hand, his right flopping uselessly. The bottom was some fifteen feet down, but there were no waving streamers of algae and no sign of the drainpipe. Rix cursed and swam in a widening spiral until lack of air forced him to the surface. He trod water, gasping, eyeing the patrolling guards until he got his breath back, then dived again.

The drainpipe was not below him here, either. How could he be so far out? He swam another spiral, another. Ah, there it was, but he lacked the air to swim all the way back to Benn. Another breath and down he went, into the drainpipe and up. Despite his words to Glynnie, Rix was starting to panic. He'd told Benn that they'd be five minutes but fifteen must have passed by now, and in fifteen minutes anything could have happened.

He swam furiously until he approached the upper end of the drainpipe, then slowed and approached it carefully, just in case. Now he could make out a faint bluish light, coming from the glow-stone. It was all right.

He eased his head through the surface and looked around. The air reeked of rotting fish and decaying bodies. He hadn't noticed how bad it was before. The glowstone sat on a rock by the water's edge, and Benn's little pack was beside it. But Benn was not there.

CHAPTER 6

Rix threw himself out of the water, grabbed the glowstone and held it high. "Benn?"

No answer. What had happened to the boy? Could a hyena shifter have survived the explosion and taken him? It seemed unlikely; there was no blood, no shredded clothing, no shifter stink. If one of the rank beasts had been here, the smell would linger . . .

Had Benn been captured by the enemy? The floor of the drain was bare stone here and showed no tracks, but surely they would have taken his pack, or tipped everything out to search it.

Had he gone back up the tunnel? Why would he? More likely,

after a wait that must have seemed interminable to a small boy, Benn had tried to go down the drainpipe in a vain attempt to find his sister. He could not swim, and must have drowned if he had tried ... though he might have held his breath and pulled himself along the rough stone on the bottom of the drainpipe. Could Rix have passed him, coming back? It was possible, because he had swum along the top. They would not have seen each other in the murky water.

Check the water, quick. If Benn had only gone in a minute or two ago, he could still be alive. Rix dived in and swam furiously along the bottom, sweeping his arms out to either side, feeling for anything lying there. Nothing. He reached the outlet without encountering anything other than broken rock and leathery weed, then felt around the exit for snags and projections. Nothing. Nor could he see the boy on the muddy lake bed immediately outside.

Though he was desperately low on air, he swam back along the roof of the drainpipe in case Benn had passed out and floated up. Nothing there either. Rix burst out of the water, gasping, lay on the stone for a minute while he got his breath back, then picked up the glowstone and checked up the drain again. There was no sign that anyone had ever been here.

Could Benn have reached the outlet? It was barely conceivable that he could hold his breath that long, but if he had, Rix would never find his body in the murky lake waters. Benn was a skinny lad, and if he had drowned, his body wouldn't float.

Only one hope remained – that he had wandered up the drain, back the way they had come. What could have made him do such a thing, though? He was a sensible boy and would not have headed back into danger. Besides, he would never have left his sister.

Rix stared up the dark drain, then down at the murky water. Benn might have been captured by the enemy, though if so, why hadn't they touched his bag? Holding the glowstone high, he ran up the tunnel to the first bend. There was no trace of the boy. He stumbled on, to the point where the broken bodies were jammed into the wall. There was mud on the floor here but it showed only their three sets of tracks, heading down.

He rubbed his numb fingers, clawed at his scalp. What else

could he do? If Benn *had* been taken by the enemy, they would be on watch for a rescue attempt. If Rix tried, he would be killed or taken and Glynnie would drown, all alone, never knowing what had happened to either of them.

How long could she last in the water? Slender little thing that she was, half an hour might finish her. An hour certainly would. If she climbed out onto the mooring pile, the icy wind on her wet skin would kill her more quickly.

And if he did not come back? Glynnie *might* manage to swim to shore, though it was a hundred yards away from the pile and she had never swum more than twenty. She would be captured and probably killed for having been a servant of Palace Ricinus.

Rix groaned, turned, turned again. He could do no more for the boy. His duty was to the living now, and if he spent any more time looking for Benn, Glynnie would die. He headed back to the water. How was he going to tell her that her brother was lost, almost certainly dead?

This swim down the drainpipe was interminable, yet not long enough. A thousand miles would not have sufficed to find the words to confess his failure. If he could not protect these two innocents, what was he good for? Nothing.

He struggled on, exhausted in body and mind, and every injury he'd suffered in the past few days, every bruise he'd taken after throwing himself down five levels of the corkscrew stair to the murder cellar two days ago, throbbed to remind him of the pain he was about to cause Glynnie.

Rix reached the end of the drainpipe so breathless that he had no energy to swim further. All he could do was float to the surface and bob there, gasping so hard that surely the troops patrolling the shore must hear him.

It was after four in the afternoon. The short winter day was fading, mist rising to drift in wisps above the water. The breeze had picked up and was icy on his cheek and shoulder. It drove more debris ahead of it, the final fruits of the tidal wave that had engulfed the lower areas of Hightspall a few days ago.

A large, solid front door, intricately carved and inlaid with freshwater pearl shell, but splintered along one side where the water had torn it from its hinges. An empty pottery flagon, green and white, slowly turning as it drifted. The body of a stocky, balding man, his fish-white skull gleaming like glowstone through strands of sparse black hair. His belly was swollen and his eye sockets empty, picked clean.

The cold was seeping into Rix now, making his bones ache. And none worse than his regrown wrist bones, where the pain was a clawing beast trying to take the dead hand off forever.

He had to ignore it. He had a duty to Glynnie. Rix swam around the body, keeping well clear, picked up the flagon and set it on the door to use as a float, then swam towards the pile where he had left Glynnie, pushing the door before him.

There was no sign of her. Had he lost her too? Was fate determined to strip every good thing from him, grinding him down with failure after failure until he had nothing left?

He checked the shore, keeping low in the water. The mist was thickening, the guards appearing and disappearing behind it, but they were ever-watchful and if he made a mistake they would have him.

He steered the door around the mooring pile, scanned its sides and could not see Glynnie. She was not on top, either. Then a small head bobbed out of the water and she was staring at him with those huge green eyes. Her teeth were chattering.

Her gaze narrowed, raked the lake all around Rix. Her eyes went dark and she sagged in the water. "Where's Benn?"

"I'm sorry," said Rix, wishing he was a thousand miles away; wishing he had died with his family; anything to escape the desperate ache in her eyes. "I looked everywhere. That's why I've been so long. I – I had to make sure."

Her voice rose. "What do you mean, *make sure?*"

"I'm sorry," Rix repeated. "Benn's gone. I don't—"

"No!" she whispered, let go of the rope, and sank.

Rix lunged, caught her by the tangled hair streaming up above her head and drew her to the surface. The moment her chin was above water, she opened her mouth wide, as if to scream. He thrust the heel of his dead hand across her lips, indicating the guards on the shore with a jerk of his head.

"If you scream, we're dead!"

Again Glynnie closed her eyes and sank. Again he lifted her up. Again she went to scream. This time he pulled her to him until her face was pressed against his chest, then put both arms around her, holding her tightly. She heaved against him, thrashing her legs, kicking with her feet. He squeezed the air out of her, and kept doing so each time she took a breath, until she gave in and sagged against him.

The pain in his wrist eased, then came shrieking back. It was getting worse. Something was badly wrong with his right hand. Of course there was – it was dead, and still attached. Rix frog-kicked to the door, which had drifted a few yards away, fought the pain and put her hands on the edge.

"All – all right now?" he said.

It was a stupid thing to say. For a few seconds he thought she was going to punch his teeth down his throat, but she restrained herself. She dashed the water off her face, then looked up at him.

"What happened? Is Benn ... he wasn't ...?"

He had to conceal his pain from her. They couldn't both crack up. "The glowstone was there, and so was his pack, but he was gone."

"If you mean *killed* – if you mean ... *eaten*—"

"There was no evidence he was attacked at all ..."

"He didn't come down the drainpipe after us?"

"I think he must have. I'm sorry, Glynnie ..." The useless words failed on his lips.

She pulled herself up on the door, crouched there.

"What are you doing?" hissed Rix. "Get down! The guards will see you."

Glynnie slowly stood up, rocking the door and knocking the flagon off. She swayed, threw her arms out, then turned in a circle, surveying the grey water. As she turned another circle, the light in her eyes slowly went out. The wind fluttered her wet hair. Her teeth chattered and she slipped back into the water.

"Maybe ..." She blanched. "What if a shifter ...?"

"There was no sign of a struggle. No—"

"*Blood!* If there was no blood, why don't you say it?"

"All right – there was no blood. No shifter stink, either."

"He wouldn't have gone into the water. He must have been captured. We've got to rescue him."

"I don't think he's been captured. His pack hadn't been touched. I went back up the tunnel to those bodies and the only tracks I saw were ours."

"But it's *possible* he's been captured," she said desperately.

The pain in his wrist came back, worse than before, jagged spears along the bones. After a long pause, Rix said, "Yes. It's possible."

"Then we have to rescue him."

"How, Glynnie?"

"I don't know!" she wailed.

"Shh! Sound carries across water." He checked on the guards. They were still patrolling, watchful as ever.

"*It's my fault.* I should have let you take him first."

"If I had, you'd have been captured and he'd now be begging me to rescue you."

"That's different."

"Why?"

"I swore I'd look after Benn. He's just a little boy."

"And you're a girl."

She bridled. "I'm a grown woman. I'm *seventeen*. Nearly as old as you."

She said it with such earnestness that Rix had to smile. "Not quite." He counted the days. "Tomorrow's my twentieth birthday."

"Besides," she said with quiet dignity, "Benn's the one who matters."

"Why does he matter more than you?"

Tears welled in her eyes. "I promised Mama, before she died, that I'd look after him. I've been looking after myself since I was twelve—"

Someone bellowed, from the shore. Rix twisted around and squeezed her left shoulder, hard. "Don't move."

She broke off. "What's that?"

"Someone shouting orders. At the guards."

They lowered themselves until their eyes were just above the water and edged around the door to face the shore. Mist danced and drifted in the wind, revealing then concealing the guards patrolling the edge of the lake. A burly officer was running towards a group of guards, waving a signal flag and shouting.

"What's he saying?" said Glynnie. "Is it about us?"

"I couldn't hear. But I'm prepared to bet it is. Back."

Rix turned the door and began to push it out into the lake, using great scissor kicks. The effort sent jags of pain through his wrist; it felt as though the join was on fire again.

"We can't leave Benn," said Glynnie.

It was a struggle to break through the pain now. Just speaking took an effort. "He's lost to us, Glynnie, and he wouldn't want you—"

"How would you know what Benn would want?" she hissed. "You don't know him. You don't know any of us."

"I know he loved his big sister," said Rix. "And he'd do anything to protect you."

She did not respond.

Rix started panting. It was the only way to control the pain.

"What's the matter?" said Glynnie sharply. "You sound like you're having a baby."

"I'm all right." He lifted his arm off the door, into the water. The cold did not ease the pain this time.

Glynnie lifted his arm. His wrist was crimson and swollen all around the join with his dead hand.

"Oh!" she said, like a healer realising the worst.

Onshore, the officer skidded to a stop, let out an indecipherable bellow, then pointed out into the lake towards the submerged outlet of the drainpipe. Several of the guards ran to him. Others raced back along the shore and were lost behind a banner of mist.

"They know how we got out, and they'll have a boat in the water in minutes." He looked around for inspiration but found none in the grey water or the leaden sky. Hope evaporated. "I can't fight any more. We're lost."

"We're *never* giving up, Lord," Glynnie said fiercely. "We got to survive – then come back and find Benn."

"Yes," he said dully.

They were making slow progress, less than ten yards in a minute, and it was not enough. The cold was seeping into Rix's bones now and it was a struggle to think. He vaguely remembered seeing something earlier that might help them, but could not dredge up the memory.

"Nowhere to go – can't swim ashore – find us right away—"

"What about a boat?" said Glynnie. "There are dinghies on the shore."

"We can't get to them."

"We'll have to leave the door in a minute. It's too big; too easily spotted."

Glynnie's teeth chattered again. She was trembling from the cold and her lips were blue. "Where can we go?"

"We can't stay in the water much longer," said Rix, kicking as hard as he could. "But we've no way of getting out."

"There's a lot of rubbish floating further out."

The memory resurfaced – that gyre where all the timber had collected, forming a great wheel of debris on the water. If the wind hadn't drifted it away.

A rattling sound echoed across the water, followed by a thump, then a rhythmical splashing.

"What's that?" said Glynnie.

"Someone pulling up an anchor chain and rowing to the outlet. Then they'll check the mooring piles . . ."

Another anchor chain was pulled up, and a third. The enemy must know that the escapee was Rix, and they were determined to find him. He had fought Lyf twice with Maloch, and hurt him, too. Lyf would want him dead.

"And then?" said Glynnie.

The light was fading now, though it could not save them.

"With three boats, and lanterns, they can search the whole area in half an hour, and turn over every bit of floating debris."

Nothing would escape them. No one.

CHAPTER 7

"How fares the destruction, General?"

Lyf was perched on the wall at the top of Rix's leaning

tower, half a day after the fall of Caulderon. He was often drawn to the place, perhaps for the contrast with his reeking temple and his ever-more frantic search for the key.

"My king, a third of Palace Ricinus had been blasted down already," said General Hillish, a squat, muscle-bound man with slash-tattoos across his forehead. A round head joined his torso without any visible neck. He stood on a box so he could see over the wall and pointed out the details.

"I have a thousand Hightspaller slaves hauling the rubble away," Hillish continued. "Another thousand are digging out the cleared area to expose the foundations of the kings' palace of old."

"Very good," said Lyf. "Before the invaders came, our palace stood there since the beginning of recorded history. Are you searching out its original stones?"

"We are, my king. Many were re-used in later buildings. I have a hundred masons checking every stone and marking all those from the kings' palace."

"Excellent. I'm going to rebuild it exactly the way it was before, to show that Cythe will always prevail. Where's Rochlis?"

"Here, my king," said General Rochlis, from the doorway.

"What progress can you report?"

"We've rounded up more than half the people on your list, including a goodly number of Herovians, and taken them away . . . to be dealt with."

"Why did you hesitate, Rochlis?"

"My king, I'm a professional soldier. In battle I ask no quarter, and give none . . ."

"But?" said Lyf, irritably. One after another, his people were questioning or reinterpreting his orders.

"But putting people to death simply because they *might* cause trouble . . . my king, it . . ." Rochlis, an honourable man who always did his best, was struggling to find the words.

"It's not that many," said Lyf. "Barely two hundred."

"Nonetheless, it turns my stomach. I'm sorry, my king."

Lyf had once been an honourable man too. He was no longer honourable, but a good leader was careful not to drive his people too far.

"I won't force you," said Lyf, making his displeasure evident. "I'll see to the executions myself."

"My king," said Rochlis, sweating, "I believe it to be unwise. It can only make the ones who escaped—"

"Who escaped?" cried Lyf. "The city was sealed."

"The chancellor and his retinue, for starters."

"I suppose I should have expected him to get away. He's a wily foe."

"But he's taken Tali with him."

Lyf's face froze. "How did this happen?"

"He must have had a hidden escape tunnel, further concealed by magery."

"Find her! If the chancellor discovers that she bears the master pearl, and cuts it out, his magians might be able to command my four pearls."

"We're hunting her now, with every means at our disposal."

"What about my other enemies?"

"We can't find Rixium Ricinus," said Rochlis.

Lyf let out a bellow of fury. "You told me the shifters had him trapped way down under the palace."

"He killed them and disappeared."

"One man killed a whole pack of shifters? How?"

"With that underground explosion we felt earlier. We believe he set off a sump full of stink-damp and burned them alive."

"But not himself?"

"It's thought that he crawled through a freshly opened fissure and found a way down into the ancient tunnels. We haven't mapped them all yet."

"He's too quick, too clever," said Lyf. "He must not escape."

Not just because Rix was descended from that treacherous swine, Axil Grandys, who had betrayed, mutilated and murdered Lyf so long ago. And not just because Rix bore the cursed sword, Maloch, that had caused Lyf an aeon of pain and torment. Rix had fought Lyf twice, and twice had wounded him. He had a genius for escaping; he was an intuitive fighter and a leader who inspired loyalty. That made him a most dangerous man.

"Find him. And if he looks like getting away, kill him."

CHAPTER 8

Regg carried Tali down three flights of an age-blackened stairway to a once grand, ornately decorated chamber with a carved ceiling and elaborate cornices. One half was now a fifteen-foot-wide corridor with an iron door at the far end. The other half had been divided into a dozen large, cold cells. The guard opened the fifth cell, dropped her on the bunk and locked her in.

The bunk was a mouldy palliasse, the toilet a filthy wooden bucket; the floor was puddled with water oozing from every crack in the ceiling and walls. The side and rear walls were stone, but the front wall was made of wrought-iron bars that writhed and twisted like a lunatic's nightmare. Large portholes had been carved through the side walls and she could see into the adjoining cells, though the portholes were also meshed with tormented iron bars.

It was a struggle to stand up, but she had to know where she was. Tali tottered across to the right porthole and clung to the bars. Five or six cells away, a bent old man was shuffling back and forth. She called out several times but he did not look up. None of the other cells were occupied.

She wrapped her coat around her and lay on the palliasse. How long before the chancellor sent another healer to take her blood? He was a vengeful man, and how better to punish Tali than by rendering her so weak that she could not cause any more trouble?

She closed her eyes, longing for the oblivion of sleep, but it would not come. Enslaved again, and it was all her fault. Everything was her fault.

"Tali?" said a shrill little voice she had not heard in more than a week.

She looked up. "Rannilt?"

Two of the chancellor's personal guards were at the door, one working the massive lock while the other held the child by the arm.

She was a skinny, knock-kneed little thing, though not as skinny as the last time Tali had seen her.

Rannilt turned to her, frowned, looked up at the guards questioningly, then back.

"Where's Tali?" she said, taking a dragging step through the door. The guards locked it and turned away.

"I'm right here," said Tali. What was the matter?

Rannilt stretched out a skinny finger. A little golden bubble formed at her fingertip, some product of her unfathomable gift for magery. It separated, drifted towards Tali and burst on the tip of her nose with a small, cold pop, and Tali felt something stir inside her, her own buried magery. But it subsided again.

"Ah!" sighed Rannilt. "Chief magian put a glamour on, to hide you."

She bolted across the cell and threw herself at Tali so hard that she was knocked back against the wall. Rannilt hauled Tali to her feet and danced her around the cell until her head whirled.

"Enough, child," she said, groping back for the bed. "If I don't sit down, I'm going to throw up."

Rannilt sat beside Tali, holding her right arm with both hands and staring hungrily at her.

"I didn't know there was a glamour," Tali said hoarsely. She hadn't seen her face since leaving Caulderon. "Can you see the real me?"

"Of course not, silly," said Rannilt.

Tali's shoulders slumped. "Then how do you know it's me?"

"Checked your aura, of course."

"Didn't know I had one."

"Don't worry." Rannilt patted Tali's shoulder condescendingly. "You're still Tali on the inside."

"You can't call me by name," said Tali. "Lyf's after me."

"I know. Old Chancellor said to call you Grizel."

An ugly name, thought Tali. He's doing it to punish me.

"Someone's comin', Grizel," said Rannilt.

They squatted in the corner while orderlies bustled in and out, sweeping the puddles down a drain hole, exchanging Tali's mouldy mattress for a fresh one and bringing in another bunk for Rannilt, providing a table and two chairs and, finally, a steaming bowl of stew, two plates, cutlery and a third of a loaf of grainy bread. All was done under the watchful eyes of the chancellor's guards, then the cell was relocked and they were alone.

"You're shakin'," said Rannilt, helping Tali across to her bunk. "Are you sick?"

Tali leaned back against the cold wall. Rannilt snuggled up against her. The child, starved of human contact most of her life, had always been clingy, but Tali needed the contact now. She put an arm around her.

"They've taken pints and pints of my blood," she said dully. "I'm so weak I can barely walk. Aren't they taking yours?"

"Healer Dibly took some on the first day out of Caulderon. But only half a cup, and she was really cross about it. She called the old chancellor some wicked names, I can tell you."

"Really?" said Tali, revising her opinion of Madam Dibly.

"I'm sorry she's dead," said Rannilt. "I liked her."

"Did they only take your blood the once?"

"Yes, Dibly said it didn't heal. But she kept feedin' me just as much. Said I needed feedin' up."

"And so you do," said Tali, feeling ravenous herself. "Could you get me something to eat?"

Rannilt went to the table, spooned stew onto the plates and brought them back. When Tali had first met her, Rannilt had been as skinny as a stick and covered in bruises, for the other slave girls had picked on her constantly.

Tali lowered her voice. "We're in trouble, child. Did you hear—"

"About the gauntlin'? Yes."

Tali ate some stew. "We've got to escape, like we did from Cython. Can you wake my gift again?"

Without Rannilt's last-minute intervention that had, in some inexplicable way, roused Tali's gift, she would have died in the sunstone shaft within sight of her destination, beheaded by Overseer Banj's Living Blade, and Rannilt, too.

"No," said Rannilt. "Chancellor told me to make sure you don't escape."

Tali pulled away. "I thought you were on my side."

Rannilt put her plate down, snuggled up and curled Tali's arm around her. "I am, Grizel. The only place you're safe is here, under guard."

If only you knew, thought Tali.

"I'm no good to you anyway," said Rannilt. "As soon as it's dark . . ." She shuddered. "Things get bad when it's dark."

"What kind of things?"

"It was really bad after we went to Precipitous Crag and fought Lyf's wicked old wrythen."

"I was sure you were going to die," said Tali, realising that she needed to know what had happened. "What did he do to you?"

Lyf had made some kind of connection to Rannilt's gift and had started drawing it out of her. He had fed on it to strengthen himself so he could escape his intangible wrythen form and get back a real, physical body that would make him so much more powerful – and free him from the caverns the wrythen was bound to.

Rannilt's eyes turned inward. "I don't know. He was suckin' the gift out of me. The golden threads were streamin' out and up and away, but I couldn't do nothin' about it. I was gettin' weaker and weaker. I knew I was goin' to die."

"We were really worried about you," said Tali. "Me and Rix and Tobry."

"I really miss them," said Rannilt wistfully. "Especially Tobry. He was so kind to me."

"Me too," said Tali, turning away. Her eyes blurred.

"When my eyes were closed I saw all kinds of things I didn't want to see."

"Were they coming from the wrythen?" said Tali.

Rannilt shrugged her thin shoulders. "Maybe. Stories were gushin' into my head, a hundred at once. Wars and traitors and people bein' killed just for nothin'. Had to hide in my own head to get away."

Tali sat up. She'd thought that Rannilt had collapsed because Lyf had stolen too much of her gift, but if she had retreated to escape the unbearable stories flooding into her mind, it put a very different complexion on matters.

"Then there was the healin'," Rannilt added, reflecting.

"What about it?"

"The old kings of Cython were the only ones who were allowed to use magery, and they used it only for healin'. Healin' the land, and healin' their people."

Tali knew that, but did not say so. It was so good to hear Rannilt talking again.

"It's why that rotter Axil Grandys betrayed King Lyf, then chopped his feet off and walled him up in the Cat – Catacombs, to die," the girl added. "He wanted the king-magery for himself, but he could only steal it when Lyf died and the magery was released—"

Tali finished the sentence. "To pass to the new king. But it didn't pass on, did it?"

"It couldn't."

"Why not?"

"Because no one in Cython knew what had happened to Lyf." Rannilt thought for a moment. "And without his body they couldn't do all the fancy stuff to make sure his gift went to the new king. The king-magery left him when he died, but Axil Grandys didn't get it. No one knows where it went."

"That's why Lyf became a wrythen," said Tali. "Without the proper rituals, his spirit couldn't pass on, either."

"Serves him right, after all the horrid things he did."

"He hadn't done them, then. Until he was betrayed and left to die, Lyf was a good king."

Rannilt shivered. "I'd love to be a proper healer. Reckon I'd be a good one." She studied her small hands. Several of her fingers were crooked, as if they'd been broken more than once.

"I'm sure you would," Tali said absently. "Though it's curious your blood doesn't heal."

"What if that's what old Lyf was really after?" said Rannilt. "My healin' gift. Maybe that's what he was tryin' to steal from me."

"Why would he want your healing gift when he has his own?" said Tali.

"He's healed all sorts of things, but he's never been able to heal his legs, has he? I'll bet he wants that more than anythin'."

And if he had stolen Rannilt's healing gift, rendering her blood

useless for healing, maybe he could do it, too. All the more reason
for Tali to uncover his secret, as soon as possible.

"Rannilt, can you help me with something? But you can't tell
anyone."

CHAPTER 9

"Told you, I'm not helpin' you escape," said Rannilt.

"I didn't mean that," said Tali. She lowered her voice. "After
Dibly took blood the first time, I had a vision of Lyf, in his temple,
and—"

Rannilt started. "No!" she cried.

"He's looking for something really important. I need to find out
what it is."

"You can't ask me to look," Rannilt said shrilly, and covered her
face with her hands. "You can't! You can't!"

"What's the matter?"

"He'll get into my head again. He'll rob my gift. It's horrible,
horrible . . ."

Tali cursed herself. Why hadn't she thought before she opened
her mouth? She hugged the trembling child. "I wasn't going to ask
you to look. I just thought you might be able to make it easier for
me."

"No," Rannilt said faintly. "Nooo . . ."

Tali held her tightly, thinking hard. The only other way to spy
on Lyf was with magery, if she could recover hers, but it would be
taking a terrible risk.

Rannilt's mood went steadily downhill after that, and became
ever worse as the afternoon waned. She was dreading the night.

"Can I push my bunk against yours?" she asked around 4 p.m.,
when the distant light from a slit window above the stair was
fading. Most of the lanterns had been extinguished to save lamp oil
and it was almost dark in the cell.

"Of course," said Tali.

In the night something roused Tali, a rustling in the straw. Just a mouse, she thought until Rannilt began to kick and bang her head on her pillow. She had crept closer in the night and was now lying against Tali.

She put an arm around the child and she lay still. But as Tali was dozing off again, Rannilt moaned, went rigid, then began to thrash so violently that Tali couldn't hold her.

"Rannilt, wake up. It's just a nightmare. You're all right."

Rannilt shot upright and stared around wildly, the faint light from the corridor reflecting eerily off her wet eyes. She shuddered, groaned, then seized Tali's wrist and sank her teeth into it, at the little scar where Tali had drawn her own blood in that ill-fated attempt to heal Tobry on top of Rix's tower.

Before she could pull away, Rannilt's sharp little teeth broke the skin and the tip of her tongue began lapping at the wound, taking Tali's healing blood for herself.

She tried to pull free. "Rannilt, what are you doing? Stop it, this instant."

Rannilt's bony fingers were locked around Tali's wrist so tightly that, in her weakened state, she could not tear them off. Rannilt pressed her mouth over Tali's wrist and bit down hard, hungry for her blood. No, *desperate* for it.

Tali swung her free hand at the child, smacking her across the face. Rannilt let go, swallowed then lay back and slipped into a peaceful sleep – if, indeed, she had ever woken.

Tali stumbled across to the table and collapsed into a chair, shaking so violently that she had to cling to the table. It could almost have been *her* nightmare, save for the pain in her torn wrist and the tang of blood in the cold air.

Had Rannilt reverted to the time when Lyf had been stealing her gift to strengthen himself, and unwittingly – or wittingly? – revealing the nightmares of his own distant past? Could Lyf use his connection with Rannilt to get at Tali? Was that what he was up to now? If he could, spying on him with magery would be the height of folly.

Or did Tali's blood have some other value? Of course it did –

while the master pearl remained inside her, it was bathed in her blood, and perhaps that was the connection Lyf really wanted.

Or was she over-analysing it? Was Rannilt subconsciously attempting to undo the damage Lyf had done to her the only way she could, by stealing Tali's healing blood?

Whatever the reason, Tali thought guiltily, I precipitated it.

"I've spread a cover story about you being a traitor and spy," the chancellor said the next morning, "to ensure neither the guards nor the prisoners will have anything to do with you. I'm sure you won't mind." He bared his crooked teeth.

His guards had come for her at first light. Rannilt had not stirred, which put off one problem, at least – what to say to the child when she woke. Tali looked down at the wounds on her wrist. Was she being used more ill by her enemies, like the chancellor, or her friends?

"I'm sure you don't give a damn either way," she snapped.

"No, I don't."

A burly guard stood on watch near the door. "When I first met you," said Tali, "you surrounded yourself with women. How come you have male guards now?"

"After you deceived me and let me down, I came to realise that men are more reliable – at least in wartime. Enough talking. Eat!" A large table was set in a corner, by a window covered in a translucent membrane, perhaps the stretched stomach of a cow or buffalo. "You're weak, and that's no good to me."

"You want to fatten me up so you can milk more of my blood."

"So I do," he said jovially. "The blood of a weakling is unlikely to have strong healing powers."

The words stung, which doubtless was his intention.

"I'm just a living tool to you, something to be used then thrown away once I'm broken."

When he did not react, she added, nastily, "Are you winning the war yet?"

"I'm not your enemy. Why do you keep fighting me?"

To distract you from thinking about the pearls, and reaching the conclusion that I bear the master pearl.

"How does it go, then? What's your latest disaster?"

His lips tightened. He went to the table, which was set with an array of covered dishes at one end, and a small plate containing two slices of black bread and a thin wedge of green cheese at the other. After gesturing her to a chair, he sat, nibbled at a corner of black bread, then tossed it aside and picked up a yellow oval object.

Tali took a helping of white fish cooked in a spicy sauce. It tasted wonderful. Since her escape from slavery, almost everything did.

"The only news I've had in the past week has come via this speaking egg," said the chancellor, fondling the yellow ovoid, "though I'm not sure it's reliable any more. Now that Lyf has four ebony pearls, he might be able to corrupt the messages my spies send me. Or send lying messages of his own."

His eyes rested on Tali as he said "ebony pearls', and her heart skipped a beat. Did he know she bore the master pearl? Was he toying with her for his own amusement? It would be just like him.

The chancellor grimaced and set the ovoid down. He did not speak for some time, but the lines on his face deepened and the flesh seemed to sag.

"I don't know where to turn, Tali. He's intercepting my couriers and killing my spies. How can I fight a war when I can't find out what's going on?"

She didn't answer.

"My only experienced generals died in the storming of Caulderon," he went on. "Who can I turn to? And if I had good leaders, where could I strike that would make any difference?"

"You had a good man, one of the best. You cut his right hand off and left him to die."

"Rix betrayed his own mother," he snapped, nettled for the first time. "How could I trust a man like that?"

"You already knew Lady Ricinus was plotting high treason. I told you myself."

"That's not the point. He informed on her."

"You're a swine, Chancellor! You drove Rix to it, coldly and deliberately, because you were determined to crush House Ricinus. You gave him an impossible choice – between his mother and his dearest friend. She was a monster who abused him cruelly. Is it Rix's fault that he cared more for Tobry than he did her?"

"It's entirely understandable," said the chancellor. "But how could I trust him?"

"For a man with his back to the wall, you're overly discriminating. A good leader crafts his plans to take advantage of his officers' strengths and compensate for their failings."

He leaned back, folded his hands over his scrawny chest, and she saw his first genuine smile since their flight from Caulderon. "You speak boldly for a helpless prisoner. Perhaps next time *I* should insert the cannula into your carotid."

The long bruise on her neck pulsed. "If I get hold of it, I'm liable to insert it through your larynx and out the back of your spine."

His eyes widened. He rubbed his throat.

"How are you going to save the country you profess to love so dearly, Chancellor?"

"Again you put your finger on the nub of the matter. I used to be feared for my grasp of political strategy and my bold tactics, but now I've got no idea what to do, and the people of the west have sensed it. I've dispatched envoys to provincial leaders far and wide, trying to raise an army to replace the ones lost in the ruin of Caulderon. And what do my envoys tell me when they return?"

"Nothing good," said Tali.

"Some were turned away at the gates, their pleas unheard. Others were invited in to hear lies and excuses. Only unity can save us but the west is falling into chaos, and every mayor and petty lordling is trying to set up his own kingdom. Soon there will be anarchy, and then where will we be?"

"There must be some loyal men in the west," said Tali.

"I have pledges for four hundred mounted troops and four thousand foot soldiers, and there will be more. A goodly force, you might think, but—"

"I would have done, until I saw twice that many cut down in an hour at the storming of Caulderon. But you haven't answered my question."

"How the war is going? Badly. Lyf now holds all of central

Hightspall and he has small forces advancing on the south and the north. I'm told that they're meeting no organised resistance."

"Does that mean Hightspall's troops there are *surrendering?*"

"Pretty much. News spreads fast. Everyone knows how quickly our armies were defeated in the first days of the war." He lowered his voice. "Too quickly, in my opinion."

"Meaning?"

"I suspect that Lyf used pearl magery in the storming of Caulderon. His soldiers aren't superhuman, but that's how they seemed."

"Is there any good news?" said Tali.

"Good and bad. The people of the north-west peninsula still hold loyal to Hightspall. Bleddimire is almost as wealthy as Caulderon and they're doubling their army. Unfortunately, they won't be coming a hundred and fifty miles south to help me."

"Why not?"

"Lyf is marching an army of twenty thousand north-west at this moment, and Bleddimire is his next target."

"It could defeat him."

"I pray that it does, but all the evidence tells me I should prepare for bad news."

"Why don't you send your own army north, catch his force between yours and Bleddimire's, and destroy him?"

"His army is five times as big as mine," said the chancellor. "Nonetheless, if I could march an army north in secret, I would. But he can spy on us from the air, with gauntlings, and we can do nothing about them."

CHAPTER 10

"What do the planets say?" Tali said, panting. Walking fifty yards had exhausted her, but it was twice as far as she could have gone yesterday.

They were up in the chancellor's observatory, at the highest point of Fortress Rutherin. It was a cold, still night with a red moon and a scattering of the brightest stars.

The chancellor, swathed in a fur-lined cloak, was studying the motions of the planets through a telescope. He had provided a padded chair for Tali, and a charcoal brazier, but she was pacing around the triangular roof. If a chance came to escape, she must be ready to take it.

"That if I don't do something brilliant now," he replied, "it will be too late."

He warmed his hands over the coals and hunched in his chair. He looked defeated.

She continued her circuits, counting the steps. One hundred, two hundred, two hundred and fifty—

"You're up to something," he said. "Come here."

Tali returned to the chairs and put on her cloak, but did not sit down. She did not speak; it was the safest way with the chancellor. He was a cunning interrogator and the most innocent questions had a way of leading into quicksand.

"We could be friends," he said mildly. "You don't have any friends, only the child."

"I had two friends," she blurted. "You killed one and condemned the other."

"The necessities of war."

"That's your excuse for everything. You always hated Tobry."

"It wasn't hate I felt for the man – it was *contempt*. How could I respect a fellow who made a joke of all I held dear, yet himself believed in nothing?"

"He'd lost his house, his family and all *he held dear*, through no fault of his own."

"I know his story," the chancellor said indifferently.

"Not all of it. The Tobry I knew, *and came to love*, was fighting for his country as bravely as any man I've ever met."

"You haven't met many men, have you? In Cython, the Pale men are kept apart from the women."

Tali wasn't going to be distracted that easily. "Tobry made the ultimate sacrifice to save his friends – he became a shifter because it was the only way to save us from a horde of them. That's not the action of a man who believes in nothing!"

The chancellor waved a twisted hand. "Perhaps I was wrong about him. I'm fallible, like everyone else."

"Unlike everyone else, your mistakes kill people!" she said furiously.

He jerked the cloak more tightly around his meagre frame. "Do you think I don't lie awake at night reliving my failures? I had eighteen thousand troops in Caulderon. How many do you think I got out with me?"

Tali had no idea. "Two thousand?"

His laugh was like metal tearing. "I couldn't even save two *hundred*. Most of those eighteen thousand died in the storming of Caulderon, along with thousands of civilians, because I underestimated the enemy."

The pain in his voice was evident; the agony of command, but after all he had done to her friends she could not feel any sympathy for him. "When are you going to stand up and fight?"

"When my army is ready."

"It'll never be ready," Tali guessed.

"You are at my mercy," he reminded her coldly.

"But unlike you, I haven't given up."

"What are you talking about?"

"You're just going through the motions. You don't have what it takes to lead Hightspall in war."

His face flushed. She had stung him. Good!

"Will you be as diligent in fulfilling your blood oath as you are in criticising my failings?" said the chancellor.

She looked down at her hands. How *could* she rescue the Pale? In a thousand years, no other slave had ever escaped from Cython, and there was a good reason why. Every entrance was heavily guarded and the entry passages were mined with all kinds of ingenious traps.

And even if she could overcome her terror of slavery enough to go back, and even if she could get inside, how would she ever rouse the cowed, unarmed, untrusting Pale to rebellion and get them out again? In Cython, betrayal was the way to favour and most of them would inform on her in an instant.

The chancellor rose and warmed his hands over the brazier again. A momentary breeze stirred the coals, sending a single spark drifting up and wafting warmth towards her.

"Sit down, Tali."

She sat by the brazier.

"You've suddenly regained a sense of purpose," he said.

A chill crept over her. This was why he had called her up here. How could she hold him out?

"After a week and a half abed you've suddenly started exercising. Why?"

"You're spying on me."

"I spy on everyone. Answer the question!"

"Why do I need a reason to eat, or to rise from my sickbed and regain my health?"

"I wouldn't advise you to play games with me, Thalalie vi Torgrist."

What could she say? Nothing that would heighten his suspicions.

"It's Rannilt," said Tali.

The chancellor's eyes met hers. "What about her?" he said mildly. "She's no use to me. Her blood doesn't heal. Now why would that be?"

"I think Lyf stole her healing gift in the caverns under Precipitous Crag."

"Is that so? My spies tell me Rannilt has nightmares and comes to you for comfort."

"Not the kind of comfort you're imagining," said Tali, and showed him her scabbed wrist.

The chancellor stared. "She's taking your *blood*?"

"I love the child, and I owe her my life, but . . ."

"But she's like a little parasite, sucking your blood."

"Yes, she is!" Tali cried, rising abruptly and lurching, stiff-legged, around the chairs. "You can't imagine how much I resent it." She used her passion to try and conceal the coming lie. "I'm not taking it any more – *letting* her take it," she amended hastily.

His enigmatic smile troubled her. He knew she was concealing something. She had to give him more.

"There's something else," said Tali. "About Lyf."

"Go on."

"I've *seen* him."

He raised an eyebrow.

"I – I connected to Lyf after Dibly took my blood the first time. He's searching for something, lost long ago."

"What?" the chancellor said sharply.

"Some kind of a key. The ghost king with Lyf said, *The key must be found. Without it, all you've done is for nothing.*"

"A key lost long ago?" The chancellor leapt up and paced around the brazier. "Do you mean from the time he was abducted by the Five Heroes?"

That hadn't occurred to Tali. "I suppose it must be."

"What kind of a key? To a lock? Or a puzzle?"

"I don't know."

"And you've known this for how long?"

"A week or so."

Purple flooded his face. He was angrier than she had ever seen him. "Yet you kept it from me."

"You've treated me and my friends like enemies."

"I'm trying to win the war."

"Not hard enough!"

"If I'd known this a week ago I might have been able to do something. Find out!"

"What?" she said, shivering.

"Do whatever it takes. I've got to know what the key is."

"I – I'll do my best, but—"

"I don't want your best," he said savagely. "I want the answer, *now*!"

"It's dangerous. Lyf—"

"Not as dangerous as I am when people fail me. We'll start with another blood-letting. Right now!"

CHAPTER 11

Glynnie's knuckles were white where she gripped the edge of the floating door. She was staring back towards the lake shore as if expecting to hear someone cry out that they had found a body. Benn's.

In the other direction the edge of the wheel of flotsam, thirty or forty yards away, stretched further than Rix could see. Mist was rising everywhere now, banners streaming up into the icy air to be drifted into fog banks by the breeze. It would soon be dark.

He had lost sight of the dinghies, though he could hear the searchers talking and the gunwales knocking together. They must have anchored above the outlet to the drainpipe, sending divers down to see if any of the escapees had drowned there. The search would not take long.

"We'd better abandon the door," said Rix. "It's too easily spotted."

"Don't think I can last much longer." Glynnie's teeth chattered. She clenched her jaw.

Rix didn't have much left either. Between the cold, the pain in his wrist, the lack of sleep and the battering his body had taken in recent days, his strength was fading.

But he wasn't beaten yet. "Come here. Put your arms around me."

"Lord?"

"It'll keep the cold away."

She bit her lip. Was she afraid of him? No, Glynnie was still in awe of House Ricinus, and the mighty lord that Rix was in her eyes, rather than the dishonoured man he was in his own. He pulled her against his chest with his free arm and held her tightly, and after a while she put her arms around him and clasped her hands behind his back. The pain in his wrist faded a little.

"You're warm!" she said in amazement.

"I was swimming hard."

As warmth spread between them, Rix found himself clinging to her for comfort. All his life he had known where he belonged – the heir to a noble house – and where everyone around him fitted into the vast entity that had been House Ricinus. Now he had no house, no family, no place, and in this savage land a man who belonged nowhere was prey to all.

They pulled apart at the same moment. Pain lanced into Rix's wrist bones.

"Can you swim out to the flotsam, Glynnie? You've got to be able to do it by yourself . . ."

If I'm killed, lay unspoken between them.

She looked that way and her small shoulders hunched. "I – I'll try."

It was little more than a dog paddle at first, but as she swam Glynnie's stroke changed to imitate his. She was painfully slow; he could have towed her there in half the time, but she was a good learner. Her courage and determination were an inspiration.

They limped thirty yards before they reached the edge of the slowly wheeling gyre of debris. Glynnie was tiring, starting to thrash.

"Can't go – any—" She was gasping, making no progress.

Rix pushed a floating plank to her. She clung to it the way she had clung to him earlier.

He surveyed the gyre. There were scores of uprooted trees, a timber yard's worth of lumber, hundreds of pieces of furniture – some broken, others unmarked – empty bottles of many sizes, shapes and colours, an inflated wine skin that might have been used as an emergency float, a white china teapot with a red rose painted on the side, bobbing its handle and spout. The water seemed thicker here and had an unpleasant red-brown tinge. And a smell Rix did not want to dwell on.

Dead seabirds, white wings spread upon the water, eyes pecked out. A drowned goat with bloated belly and four legs standing vertical. And bodies, some broken by the force of the tidal wave, some apparently unharmed, but all dead and eyeless, as if they could not bear to look upon the horror that had befallen them.

The gyre might have been a hundred yards across, or thrice that far. He could not see the further edge through the mist. It was the best hiding place they had, though only a miracle could save them from a determined search by three boats.

Rix looked over his shoulder but the mist had closed in along the shore as well; he could not see anything there. He could hear the faintest rasping though, the rhythm unmistakeable to one who had spent his youth in boats.

Glynnie caught the direction of his gaze. "What's that funny noise?"

"Rowing. They've packed sacking into the rowlocks to muffle the oars."

"They're coming after us?"

"Yes."

Rix caught the drifting wine skin. "Put this under your shirt. It'll hold you up . . ."

She held onto it to support herself. "If the cold gets me, a float isn't going to help."

They headed towards the centre of the gyre, passing more broken timber, more dead animals, more bodies. One was a boy, floating face down with his arms and legs rigidly outstretched. And he had red hair—

"Benn?" said Glynnie in a cracked voice.

She sagged on the wine skin, her weight pressing it beneath the surface, then let go and it shot out of the water. She began to thrash towards the boy, making little progress and far too much noise. Rix caught her by the shoulder. She swung around and punched him in the nose, then flailed off. He caught her by the hair, holding her until she exhausted herself.

"It's not him, Glynnie."

"How would you know?" she sobbed. "I got to be sure."

He didn't want to look at any more bodies, and definitely didn't want to see what time and predators had done to an innocent child, but there was no help for it. He swam with her to the body and turned it over.

She gave a muffled shriek, then turned away and clung to him, desperately. "That poor little boy."

Rix turned the lad face down again. It seemed more respectful. He swam away, carrying her with him, to a pine table floating on its side.

"How did you know it wasn't Benn?" said Glynnie, hanging onto the edge of the table.

"This gyre must have been here since the tidal wave, and the wind isn't strong enough to mix it up. Any body in the middle of the gyre must have been here for days."

She seemed to take comfort from that. It allowed her to keep hoping. Rix rubbed his nose, which was throbbing from the blow, and found a smear of blood on his hand.

"Lord, I'm sorry," said Glynnie, hanging her head. "You must think—"

"I dare say I deserved it." He stiffened. The muffled sound of rowing was louder than before and coming from several places at once.

"Have I given us away?" she whispered.

"They know we escaped, and since they haven't found us in their drag nets, or ashore, there's only one place we can be."

"What are we going to do?"

Die, he thought, and that will put an end to all pain.

"Keep going. There could be a storm . . . or we might find a boat in the rubbish. You never know."

They were in an impossible situation and she knew it. He was about to swim on when a dinghy emerged from a mist bank, barely thirty yards away. A man at the bow held a lantern up on the end of a pole; a yellow halo surrounded it.

Rix pulled her down until only their eyes were above the water. "Don't look at the light," he whispered. "They'll see it reflected in your eyes. Look down."

He did the same, one arm around her chest. He could feel the thumping of her heart, her chest rising and falling with each breath. The lantern man swung his light from one side to the other, scanning the debris-littered water. The boat passed through a banner of low-hanging mist. The light made a brighter halo, then disappeared.

"Another boat behind us," breathed Glynnie. "They're searching in a pattern."

Rix rotated. The second boat was mere shadow and rainbow-ringed light, moving steadily through the mist, then gone.

"The next pass will come right through here. And that close, nothing can hide us. Come on."

He set off towards the line the first boat had followed. Glynnie followed for a while, then stopped, and when he turned to check she was going under. He raced back, hauled her up. Her face and hands were mottled blue and purple from the cold and she was shuddering fitfully.

"Leave me," she said dully. "Can't go – any further."

"I'm not leaving you. Shh! You're breathing like a walrus."

He towed her across, taking advantage of the cover of a drifting sideboard here, a dead donkey there. Rix was very cold now and an icy lethargy was creeping through him too. If they stayed in the water much longer Glynnie would collapse from exposure. He pulled her against his chest but this time no warmth grew between them, not a trace. He was numb from cold, save for his right wrist, which burned with fire.

"We're going to die, Lord," she whispered. "Right here."

Better we do than the enemy take us, he thought. "Not yet, Glynnie. You've got to hang on. We'll beat them yet."

He played hide-and-seek with the three boats for another few minutes as they crisscrossed the gyre. It was almost dark now but the fog was lifting and Rix was losing hope; he could feel Glynnie slipping away. The water was taking her body heat faster than she could generate it.

They were in the meagre shelter of an almost submerged log when the three dinghies came together in an open space forty yards away. The leader of the searchers stood up in the dinghy and swept his arm out in a circle that seemed to indicate the circumference of the gyre.

"I don't like this," Rix muttered in Glynnie's ear. "What Cythonian devilry have they got in mind now?"

Glynnie's head lolled onto his shoulder. She was fading fast, and if he couldn't warm her she would die. He pulled his shirt up, and hers, pressed his bare chest against her and crushed them together. A faint warmth grew there.

After a minute or two, Glynnie roused. Her head wobbled, steadied. Her eyes drifted open, unfocused, then suddenly widened.

"Lord!" she croaked, trying to pull away. "What are you doing?"

He held her. "Saving our lives. Shh!"

Clots of mist drifted by, momentarily obscuring the three dinghies, then cleared. They separated and were rowed out in widening spirals, each lantern man now supporting a barrel on the transom. From the bung holes, an oily liquid gurgled into the water.

The enemy were masters of the alchymical arts and had developed all manner of terrifying new weapons. Rix had seen more than enough of their effects in the first days of the war and did not want to experience them here. He went backwards, using just his feet.

"Is it poison?" said Glynnie.

Every possibility Rix could think of was horrifying. "I don't know."

"They're trying to kill you."

Glynnie would have been safer if he'd left her behind. Being with him was a death warrant. "We've got to get out of the gyre. Hold tight!"

The dinghies were rowing quickly now, as if they did not want to be anywhere near the gyre when their mission was completed. They would reach the outside before he and Glynnie were a quarter of the way, and he could not swim any faster without alerting the enemy. His wrist was so painful that he could scarcely think. It felt as though acid was eating through the bones.

The stuff from the barrels gave off fumes that burned his nose, and Glynnie's eyes were watering. The dinghies reached the outside of the gyre, equally spaced around it. The last of the fluid was emptied out. The oarsmen rowed another ten yards, then stopped and the lantern men returned to the bow and stood there, watching the gyre.

Glynnie threw her hands up, clutching the sides of her head.

"Head feels like it's bursting."

"Try not to breathe the fumes."

They had gone another thirty yards when the captain swung a brawny arm, hurling a glowing object hard and high. It wheeled over three times before smacking into the water. Nothing happened for one, two, three seconds.

Then flames exploded up and raced across the gyre from one side to the other.

CHAPTER 12

Glynnie screamed.

The captain bellowed, "There they are. They're mine!"

Fire was racing towards Rix and Glynnie. It wasn't orange like normal fire, but an ominous, chymical crimson. He could not see the other boats through the flames, but he had no choice. He had to take the fastest way out of the gyre even though it led directly to the captain's dinghy. If it was the last thing Rix ever did, he was going to save her.

He hissed, "Deepest breath you can, *now*!"

Glynnie was used to obeying without question. He pulled her under, fixed the position of the dinghy in his mind and dived deep. Flames rushed across the water above them. The light turned an unpleasant red, tinged with black.

Rix kept going down; it would make it easier to stay under. He had to do the swim of his life this time. He pushed on past the first pain barrier, then the second. Past the moment when his lungs began to heave and the only urge he had left was the desperate need to breathe in. Another five seconds, he told himself, and when that was up, just another five seconds.

He was out of the zone of flames now, and praying that the enemy didn't guess what he was up to. They would hardly think he could swim so far with such desperate purpose. At least, he hoped they wouldn't.

Glynnie couldn't last much longer and neither could he. Where was the dinghy? Ah, he saw its shadow not far ahead. He swam beneath. Just five more seconds. Just four. Just three.

He curved up to the surface. The men in the dinghy were standing up with their backs to him, staring into the gyre, which was a roaring vision of Hades. There was no time to tell Glynnie his plan. He pushed her away, swam to the dinghy, put his hands on the gunwale and heaved with all his strength, as if to haul himself aboard.

As he had hoped, his great weight was too much for the craft. It rocked wildly, throwing the standing men into the water, then slowly overturned on top of him. But he had snatched a breath and was already diving away as everything inside the boat fell into the lake.

The lantern landed on the water, bobbed there and remained alight. The men were not so fortunate. Few Cythonians knew how to swim and these three had not learned. One of the rowers drifted past, his mouth wide open, his arms thrashing uselessly. Rix slammed his left fist into the man's belly, driving all the air out of him. He doubled up and sank.

The second rower was clinging to the keel of the upturned boat. Rix tore his hands free and, when the man began to thrash, used both feet to send him head-first against the transom. His forehead cracked into it and he went under.

"Rix!" Glynnie cried.

Rix whirled. The captain was clinging to her, and he was so stocky and heavy-boned that he was pulling them both under. He glanced over his shoulder, saw Rix approaching, then shifted his big hands from Glynnie's shoulders to her throat. He was going to take her down with him.

No time to think. Rix picked up a floating oar, balanced it on his right forearm, then drove the end of the blade against the back of the captain's neck. His head snapped backwards and he sank, his hands still locked around Glynnie's throat.

Rix was diving after them when Glynnie doubled up, slid her hands up inside the captain's hands to break his grip, then straightened her legs and forced him away. He went down, she was propelled up and reached the surface at the same time as Rix got to her.

"Well done," he said. "Now, if we can just—"

"Hoy?" someone called across the gyre to the other boats. "You fellows all right?"

The chymical flames on the water were dying out, though objects still burned in a hundred places – floating furniture, pieces of timber, bodies ... Through the smoke and mist, it was impossible to tell where the other two dinghies were.

"It's worrying – we can't see – their lights," panted Glynnie.

Rix was thinking the same thing. "They can't know I overturned the boat. I don't think they're too concerned."

"Of course they are."

"Why?"

She rolled her eyes. "Because you're the great Lord Rixium, who attacked Lyf in his own lair and hurt him badly – *with Maloch*. The same Rixium who rescued Tali from a band of Cythonians, then helped her defeat the magian, Deroe – and almost Lyf himself."

"We almost died a dozen times."

"Maybe that's what the enemy are afraid of – that you have the good luck, and they have the bad."

Rix was about to remind her of the downfall of his house when a signal rocket soared high above the mist and burst in a yellow star.

"They know something's wrong," he whispered. "They're calling for reinforcements. To the boat, quick!"

They swam to the dinghy, which was floating face down.

"Don't see how it can be turned over," said Glynnie.

"I do, but it won't be easy one-handed. Go up near the bow, lie across the keel and take hold of the gunwale on the other side. I'll do the same amidships, where it's heaviest."

"What's the gunwale?"

"The raised side, where the oars are attached."

She did so. He stretched his frame across the middle and took hold of the gunwale with his left hand.

"I can hear them," said Glynnie. "They're coming fast."

"Then we'd better be faster. When I give the word, throw your weight backwards and we'll try to heave it over. One, two, three ... *heave*."

The dinghy heaved a few inches out of the water but Rix lost his grip and the boat smacked down, cracking his jaw so hard on the planking that tears formed in his eyes.

"I can't do it one-handed." He frowned at the underside of the dinghy. "If I jam my bad hand through the rowlock—"

"You might do more damage," said Glynnie.

"Not as much as the enemy will do if they catch us."

Rix put his right hand through the rowlock, locked his fingers around the iron, then took hold of the gunwale with his left. "Ready? One, two, three, heave!"

He threw himself backwards, swinging his legs for extra leverage, and Glynnie did the same. Excruciating pain speared through his right wrist. He felt something tear and for an awful second thought his rejoined hand was going to rip off at the wrist. The side of the dinghy rose – rose until it was almost vertical – then teetered.

He gave another swing of his legs, felt an equally appalling pain in his wrist, then the dinghy passed the vertical and slapped down on the water with a noise that would have been audible a quarter of a mile away. It also smashed the bobbing lantern, leaving them in a smoky gloom.

"If they're any kind of boatmen they'll know what that sound means," said Rix. Glynnie groaned. "Are you all right?"

"Bow cracked me on the shoulder," she said. "It's not broken."

"Bail the water out. There's a wooden pail tied to a rope." He boosted her in.

"What are you doing?" said Glynnie, bailing furiously.

"Looking for the oars."

He swam around the dinghy, found one and slid it over the side. "How's it going?"

She tossed half a bucket of water in his face. "Oops, sorry! Nearly done."

"Any sign of the enemy?"

"No."

He swam around the dinghy again, and again, but could not find the second oar. He had to have it. One oar was useless.

"Another boat's coming, Rix!"

He saw a light off to the left, higher than the flickering flames. Rix remembered that he'd attacked the captain with the other oar;

it must be further out. He swam five or six yards and ran into it. He stroked back, slid the oar in, dragged himself over the transom and flopped into the bottom of the boat, landing on his injured wrist. He was hard pressed not to scream.

"Is there some trick to rowing?" muttered Glynnie. She had fitted the oars into the rowlocks but, being small, was having trouble catching the water with the oar blades.

"Long practice. I'll have to do it."

"But your hand, Lord . . ."

"I *know*," he said savagely, for the pain was so intense that he was scarcely capable of thought. "Out of the way. Check on the other dinghies."

She vacated the bench. "One's racing at us. I can't see the other."

He thumped onto the middle bench, took hold of an oar with his left hand and slapped his dead right hand down on the other oar. "Tie it on."

"What?"

He wasn't capable of politeness. "Rope, *there*!" A loop of thin rope hung from under the gunwale. "Tie my hand to the oar."

She cut a length of rope and did so. It took more time than he would have liked but her knot work was first class, secure yet allowing a degree of movement.

"Lord, you got to hurry," whispered Glynnie.

Rix quickly fell into the rhythm he'd had as a youth, when he had rowed nearly every day, and soon the warmth was flowing back into his limbs. It was tiring work, though, and he could exert far less force with his bound hand, so he had to match the other to it. The rope was already chafing the skin off his inflamed wrist. Off the back of his dead hand too, though he did not give a damn about that.

"Stay low," he said, fighting the pain, which was almost unbearable. "They could have bows."

Glynnie's glance told him that he made a bigger target than she did, and a far more likely one.

"They're turning towards us," she said. "Can you go any faster?"

"I'm saving my strength."

"If you save it much longer—"

"Hold on," said Rix.

"What for?"

"We'll never outrun them. I'm going to try something else. Come right back. I need your weight at the stern."

As Glynnie did so, the stern sank and the bow rose a little. The other dinghy was running a parallel course, only ten yards away and a couple of boat lengths behind. The lantern man held his lantern high as if to show their location to the third boat, or to the reinforcements. Rix might, just possibly, deal with one boat, but two was out of the question. It had to be now.

He turned sharply as if to veer across the bows of the second dinghy and escape into a patch of smoky fog.

"Faster!" cried the lantern man. "Don't let them get away."

The second dinghy accelerated. Then, when only a few yards separated them, Rix sharpened his turn until his craft was perpendicular to the other. His bow slammed into the enemy dinghy amidships and he dug deep with his oars, using all the strength he had to drive the high bow up over the side of the other dinghy which, with three burly Cythonians aboard, sat low in the water.

The crash threw the rower and the other man off their benches and the lantern man over the side, then the weight of the bow drove the enemy's gunwale under. Water poured in. Rix kept rowing desperately until, with the front half of his dinghy lying over the other one, it sank.

The rower went with it, leaving his discarded set of oilskins floating on the water. The other man made a desperate leap, caught hold of the bow of Rix's dinghy and swung himself in. He was going for his sword when Glynnie swung the wooden bucket around her head on its rope. Rix ducked as it passed perilously close to his forehead, then cracked the rower in the face. He fell backwards, dazed. Glynnie took hold of his feet and tipped him over, and Rix ran him down.

"Great bucket work," he said, admiring her presence of mind.

Glynnie reached over and hauled in the oilskin coat. The trousers had sunk.

The lantern man, still holding his lantern on its pole, slid beneath the water. The lantern fizzed and went out, leaving them in darkness apart from a handful of the brightest stars. The lantern of the third dinghy was just visible through the smoke, a couple of hundred yards off. Rix took up the oars and rowed quietly into the darkness.

Glynnie looked back at the lights of Caulderon, barely visible through fog and smoke. She sniffled. "Do you think he suffered?" she said softly.

"No," said Rix. "I don't think Benn suffered at all."

"I – I know we can't go back. We don't even know where to look . . ."

"But it feels wrong to be leaving him," said Rix. "As though we're letting him down."

"We'll come back, won't we?" Her voice was barely audible. "We'll find out what happened to Benn."

She had to think that, though Rix knew how faint the hope was. "Yes, we will."

Glynnie rubbed her eyes, then leaned forwards. "Your wrist needs tending."

"I'll put up with it. Let's put as much distance between the enemy and us as we can. Get your coat on."

Glynnie took her heavy coat from its waterproof bag and pulled it around herself. "Where's your pack?"

"Lost it in the fighting." He donned the oilskin coat, which was wet on the inside and tight across the shoulders, but better than nothing. "Rowing will keep me warm. Get some sleep."

Glynnie hunched down out of the wind but did not sleep. She was weeping silently; weeping for Benn.

Rix rowed on, shaken by the chymical attack. It meant that Lyf wanted him dead at any cost, and wherever he went, he would be hunted ruthlessly. If they caught him they would kill Glynnie too.

She was all he had left now. At all costs he had to protect her, and there was only one way to do that. He had to find a place for her, as far away from himself as possible.

CHAPTER 13

The chancellor carried out his threat at once. His guards hauled Tali down to his chambers and he called a junior healer, who took blood while he stood beside her. Tali watched it pumping into the bottle and thought that it did not look as red as previously. Had they taken too much? Was the new blood she was making no good?

"Anything?" said the chancellor.

"No. But when it happened before—"

"You kept it from me. Try harder."

"I must protest," said the healer.

"Get out!" said the chancellor.

She went, tight-lipped.

He bent over Tali until his crooked nose touched hers. "If you'd told me when it happened, I might have been able to find this key. But all my spies in Caulderon are dead now. All I have is you, and if I have to break you to get this secret, I will."

Tali fought down her panic, and her terror of another reliving of her ancestor's murder, and focused on her memory of the temple – the skull-shaped chamber, the freshly scrubbed stone walls. Suddenly the master pearl began to beat in her head like a pumping heart. Her vision blurred and she was in another time, another place. But it wasn't the temple, not as it was now.

It was a horribly familiar place, despite it being in darkness, for it reeked of mould and damp, rotting wood and the stench of poisoned, decaying rats. She was looking back in the murder cellar underneath Palace Ricinus, the chamber that had once, in the distant days of old Cythe, been the Cythian kings' private temple. The place where they had worked their king-magery to heal the land and its people.

But Axil Grandys had violated the temple and, beginning nineteen hundred years later, the lords and ladies of Palace Ricinus had debauched it by committing foul murders there. Four murders. Tali's closest female ancestors.

A pinpoint of light on the far side of the cellar grew to a candle flame, flickering as it was lit and raised high. But this was not the cellar as Tali knew it, piled high with rotten crates, empty barrels and other discarded things. This cellar was almost empty, the only furnishings being a line of stone bins along the walls and a simple wooden bench in the centre—

Sulien's heart was beating furiously; the floor was damp under her bare feet. She looked left, looked right. Why had she been led here, so far from home? And why, oh, why hadn't she listened to Mimoy? Her mother had warned her to trust no one, but the young man had been so handsome and charming and kind, and all her life she had yearned for a little kindness. There was precious little among the Pale slaves, who treated each other more ruthlessly than their slave masters did.

The young man had disappeared the moment she had entered the room. Sulien had called out to him but her voice had echoed so alarmingly in the vast, empty room that she dared not call again. Yet the silence was worse.

Crack!

The sound raised the little hairs on the back of Sulien's neck, for it was like the sound their masters' chymical chuck-lashes made when they went off across a slave girl's bare back. Sulien had not felt one herself, for Mimoy had taught her the rule of survival harshly – obey or suffer.

Her mother was a hard woman but a good teacher, and until today Sulien had not disobeyed any of her lessons. Even now, as a grown woman with a little daughter at home in the Empound, she was afraid of her mother. What had made Mimoy so hard and suspicious? Did it have to do with the terrible scar across the top of her head, which she would never talk about?

Another candle appeared to Sulien's left, a third to her right. A stocky, well-dressed woman carried one candle, a beanpole of a man another. She could not see who carried the third candle but she could smell him: the pungent odour of a man dehydrated to stringy meat, twanging lengths of taut sinew, and brittle bone. He was the one she was really afraid of.

Sulien revolved on her small feet. What could they want of her? It had to be a mistake – she was just a little slave, of no value to anyone, and surely if she told them so they would let her go.

She smoothed down her sweat-drenched loincloth, raked her fingers through her blonde hair to tidy it, then put on a feeble smile and stepped into the light.

"Hello," she said. "I'm Sulien and I'm lost. Can you tell me the way back to the Pales' Empound?"

The desiccated man stopped, staring at her, then rubbed his forearms. Flakes of dry skin whirled up through the light of his candle. He swallowed; he seemed nervous. And so was the beanpole on her right. He did not want to be there. The stocky woman was the one driving them. Sulien turned to her and stretched out a hand. Surely, as one woman to another—

"How dare you approach me!" raged the stocky woman, "Filthy Pale swine. Take her and hold her down."

Only now did Sulien understand how naïve she had been, how foolish to trust the handsome young man, but it was too late. She tried to run but the tall man darted and caught her with arms almost the length of her own body. He held her tightly, then stood there as if he didn't know what to do with her.

The woman was another matter. She struck Sulien in the belly so hard that it drove all the wind out of her. She slumped in the man's arms while he carried her to the bench and laid her on it.

"You paid a fortune for the little bitch, Deroe," the woman said to the desiccated man. "Come and take it."

Deroe's mouth worked and his shoulders heaved, as though he was going to be sick, but he got out his bone gouging tools and moved slowly towards Sulien—

With a convulsion of horror, Tali separated from her great-great-grandmother and tried to block out the vision, the nightmare. But she could not; it only made things worse. At the same time that Tali was herself observing the sickening violence being done to her great-great-grandmother, she was also Sulien—

Trapped.

Helpless.

Watching the hideous tools approach the top of her head.

The victim having no idea what her captors' intentions were until the toothed tube ground into the top of her skull. Her great-great-granddaughter knowing all too well what was going to happen and being utterly powerless to stop it, for it had happened almost a hundred years ago.

Sulien screaming and writhing until, suddenly, the cord between the pres-
ent and the past snapped, taking her with it.

Tali was sitting upright, gasping. Her fists were clenched so
tightly that she could not open them, and the pain in the top of her
head went on and on, as if that ebony pearl – the very first – had
been gouged out of her.

The nightmare was so much worse because she had seen the same
thing happen to her mother. And because two weeks ago it had
almost been repeated on herself.

"Well?" said the chancellor.

She couldn't tell him what she'd seen. If he knew that another
of her ancestors had been killed for a pearl, he would realise she bore
the master pearl. But she had to tell him something. "I just relived
my mother's murder." Her heart was still racing. "I can't look
again!"

"Not today, at any rate," said the chancellor, ominously.

The guards took her back to her cell. Half of them had occupants
now. On Tali's right was a black-clad, sour-faced fellow who wore
a perpetual scowl when he looked at her; she called him the Sullen
Man. Evidently he knew her reputation as a traitor.

On the other side was an astonishingly pretty young woman
whose mass of shining black curls hung halfway down her back. She
had been imprisoned for some unspecified theft or fraud. Her name
was Lizue and she seemed remarkably cheerful about her plight,
evidently thinking that she would soon be released. Given her
charm and physical assets, Tali did not doubt it.

Lizue and Rannilt were already chattering through the wall
though, presumably because of Tali's reputation, Lizue did not
speak to her.

Tali lay on her bed, still shaken by the reliving. She tried to
ignore the smouldering gaze of the Sullen Man, then realised that
his eyes were fixed on Lizue who, as far as Tali could tell, had never
once glanced his way.

Built into a niche in the far wall of the corridor outside Tali's cell
was a ten-foot-high water clock, a beautiful device made of brass,
with three pink and gold dials, one for the hours, one for the days

and one for the months. It was incredibly ancient, and must have been of great value, for an attendant appeared each morning to rub it down and polish its rock crystal dial covers.

Tali wondered what it was doing down here. It seemed out of place next to the cells, until she remembered that this level had once been a grand, ornate chamber. It had been divided up into cells at a later date. The water clock kept stopping, however, and, not long after she was returned to the cell, a man called Kroni was sent to fix it.

He was an oldish fellow, lean and middling tall, with sparse grey hair and a short grey beard. His face and hands were weathered the colour of cedar wood, and his fingers were crisscrossed with pale scars. He spent hours taking parts out of the clock and putting them back, to no avail. He's not a clock mechanic, Tali thought. And I'll bet his name isn't *Kroni*, either – that's too obvious a reference to time. The chancellor must have sent him down to spy on me.

Well, he wasn't going to see anything, and she could not put off talking to Rannilt any longer. She was drawing on the wall with a piece of white stone.

"Child?" Tali said, "I need to talk to you."

Rannilt was so absorbed in her drawing that she did not look up for some time. "Yes, Grizel?"

Mutely, Tali held out her bitten and scabbed wrist.

"What happened?" said Rannilt. "Does it hurt? Let me heal it."

"No!" Tali said sharply.

Rannilt's lower lip trembled.

"Your healing gift is gone, child."

"No, it's not!" Rannilt wailed.

"Yes, it is. Madam Dibly told me. Lyf must have stolen it."

"He didn't! He didn't! He didn't!" Rannilt wept.

"Anyway," said Tali, discontinuing the fruitless argument, "You did this to me and it can't ever—"

"Don't say that!" Rannilt howled. "It's not true. You saved my life. I'd never hurt you. Never, ever, *ever*!"

Tali tried again. "Look, I do understand, but—"

"No, no, no! Why are you bein' so horrible?"

Rannilt collapsed on her bunk, weeping so piteously that Tali said no more.

The child had another nightmare that night, though the first Tali knew of it was when Rannilt's teeth sank into her wrist. She tried to push Rannilt away but she scrambled onto Tali's chest, pressing her down with two bony knees and holding her wrist with both hands while she lapped at her blood with quiet, clinging desperation. Tali whacked at her feebly, then Rannilt toppled off onto her own bunk and was instantly asleep.

Tali did not think she would ever dare sleep again. Her wrist was aching, the top of her head throbbing and the pearl was again beating like a frantic heart. For a few horrified seconds she thought the loss of blood was going to drive her into reliving Sulien's murder again.

The feeling passed but the terror did not. What if Lyf was trying to get at her through Rannilt?

Tali sat up all the following night, determined to repulse Rannilt when next she came to her veins, but the girl had no nightmares and slept soundly all night. Tali snatched what sleep she could during the day after that. She felt sure she was safe in daytime. Safe from her, at least, but not from the chancellor. What would he do next time? She could not face that nightmare again.

"You're looking mighty well today, Rannilt," said Kroni, the clock attendant, who had his hands in the bowels of the clock mechanism again. "It must be good to be back with your old friend, *Grizel*."

"No, it's the diet," Tali said sourly.

The old man glanced at her. "Doesn't seem to be doing *you* any good."

"Every bloodsucker in the fortress is using me. Most of all, the chancellor."

"I'm sure he's doing his best for Hightspall," said Kroni.

"There is no Hightspall!" she snapped. "The enemy is tearing down the best of it and a hundred vultures are making civil war over the rest."

"How would you know that," he said in a steely voice, "when you're confined to your cell with no visitors?"

"Just a guess." Tali turned away, her heart beating erratically. She knew because the chancellor had confided in her. Why, why had she blurted it out to his spy?

She lay on her bunk and closed her eyes. Kroni was right about Rannilt, though. Every day she looked stronger; less scrawny and waif-like. The scars on her arms and legs, where the other slave girls had tormented her, were fading and her formerly sallow skin had developed a golden bloom. Healing blood indeed.

And of all the people who had taken her blood, Rannilt was the one Tali did not begrudge. She would have given it to her willingly.

She could not but resent the way it was taken, however.

CHAPTER 14

"Why do you hate me, Grizel?" Rannilt said late that afternoon.

Tali sighed. "I don't hate you."

"You seemed to like me, *after I saved your life*, but you don't care for me any more. You're always tryin' to get away. You want to get rid of me, don't you?"

The emotional blackmail had been going on for hours, and Tali was fed up with it. "All right! It's because you've turned into a little bloodsucker."

Rannilt froze. "What are you talkin' about?"

The Sullen Man's face appeared at the bars, though he was looking through Tali's cell, to Lizue's. Out in the corridor, old Kroni was bowed over part of the water clock mechanism but he was quite still. Spying for the chancellor.

"I tried to tell you the other day." Tali thrust her wrist in the child's face. "This! You're like a vampire bat – no, like a leech."

Rannilt blanched. "I take your *blood*?"

"I was too weak to stop you. And ... and I thought, why

shouldn't you have it, if it would make you better? But you're feeding on me like a horrible little leech, *and I can't bear it*."

"I thought we were friends," whispered Rannilt. "But I'm a horrible little leech."

"I shouldn't have said that," Tali said hastily. "But Rannilt—"

"Don't worry!" the child said stiffly. "I'll never come near you again." She dragged her bunk across to the far side of the cell. "Never, ever!"

"Please, come back," said Tali. "I didn't mean it like that."

"If you didn't mean it, why did you say it?"

Rannilt stalked across to the porthole into Lizue's cell and began an animated conversation with her. Tali raked her fingers through her hair, knowing there was nothing to be done. She had never met a child with more unwavering determination than Rannilt. Only time could heal the injury – if anything could.

She was pacing away when she realised that Rannilt was telling Lizue a story about their escape, and how determined Tali was to avenge her mother, *and her other murdered ancestors*. Did Rannilt know that each of them bore an ebony pearl, and that Tali did as well?

"Rannilt?" she said sharply. "Could you come here, please?"

Rannilt gave Tali a look of childish malice, then turned back to Lizue and said in a shrill, raised voice. "It's my story too and I'll tell it how I like."

She began to tell Lizue about Overseer Banj's attack on Tali in the sunstone shaft leading up from Cython. Tali's heart nearly stopped – if Kroni told the chancellor that story in all its bloody detail, he would know how powerful Tali's magery was and must guess where it came from.

She glanced across to the water clock but Kroni had gone. Shaking with relief, Tali slumped on her bunk, then noticed the Sullen Man's shocked expression. He must be a spy as well.

But then it got worse.

"Then Tali killed Banj with a white blizzard," Rannilt was saying in her bloodthirsty way. "Burst out of her fingertips, it did, and took his big round head right off and sent it bouncin' down the steps."

Tali's mouth went dry. Rannilt had used her real name.

In an instant, Lizue's face changed, as if a glamour cast on her had broken. Though she was still remarkably pretty, she no longer looked like a Hightspaller. She had the grey skin and black eyes of a Cythonian.

Lyf must have put the glamour on her before he sent her into Rutherin to try and locate Tali.

Lizue pointed a crystalline rod at Tali. A red beam touched her forehead, stinging it, and she felt the chief magian's glamour disappear.

"Guards!" cried the Sullen Man, who now looked alert, focused. "Gua—"

Lizue hurled a glass phial, which smashed on his bars, spattering his face with brown droplets that fizzed and released thin white fumes. He fell out of sight, choking and clawing at his nose and eyes.

Lizue ran the pointed tip of another phial across the tops and bottoms of the twisted bars between her cell and Tali's. Whatever chymical potion the phial held, it dissolved the metal within seconds. From inside her coat, she withdrew a clear bag and a long, heavy blade, rather like a machete.

Only then did Tali realise her peril. She ran to the front of the cell and clung to the bars. Where were the guards? Where was Kroni?

"Help! I'm being attacked. Help, help!"

Lizue pulled out the eaten-away bars and tossed them on the floor, *clang*. She went back several steps, ran and dived through the hole, into Tali's cell.

"What are you doing, Lizue," cried Rannilt, trying to stop her. "Tali's my friend. I didn't mean it. Please, no—"

Lizue elbowed Rannilt in the nose, driving her backwards onto her bunk. Blood flooded from her nose onto the mattress. Lizue turned to Tali, put down the knife and shook out the clear bag until it could have enveloped a melon. Or a head. It resembled the head bag that a healer in Cython had once used to save the guard Orlyk's life. This bag wasn't intended to save a life, though, but to take it.

Tali's knees were trembling. She did not have the strength for a fight, even a brief one. She struck at Lizue's eyes, and then her throat. The assassin avoided the blows lazily, almost contemptuously.

Tali drove a blow at Lizue's midriff; again she avoided it. She knew what Tali intended as soon as she moved, and that could mean only one thing. Lizue must have interrogated Nurse Bet back in Cython, and knew exactly how she had trained Tali in the bare-handed art.

"Stop it, stop it!" wailed Rannilt.

From the corner of an eye Tali saw the child racing at Lizue, her fingers hooked, blood still dripping off her chin. Without looking, Lizue backhanded her halfway across the cell.

A blow to the belly dropped Tali to her knees. In another second, Lizue had whipped the bag over Tali's head and twisted it around her throat to seal it. Lizue picked up the heavy knife and swung it back. She wasn't planning to cut the pearl out of Tali here – that would take far too long. She was going to cut Tali's head off and seal it in the bag with her blood, which would preserve the pearl long enough for it to be extracted elsewhere.

Tali couldn't get out of the way in time. She was watching the swinging blade when the Sullen Man broke open the door of the cell and slammed it into Lizue's back. She dropped the knife, but dived for it and swung it at her attacker, wounding him in the shoulder. He drove a punch at her throat. She swayed away and the blow did little damage.

Tali clawed at the head bag. It had been made from the intestines of the Cythonian elephant eel and the membrane was so strong that her short nails made no impression on it. It was tight around her nose and mouth and there was no air inside. If she could not get it off in the next minute she would suffocate.

She forced her fingers in under the tight opening of the bag and tried to stretch it enough to get it over her head. It gave a little, then snapped back – it was immensely strong. Stronger than she was in her weakened state. She tried again, failed again.

Gasping like a stranded fish, she tried to force the membrane into her mouth so she could bite through it. It would not stretch far enough. Her head was spinning. She had only moments of consciousness left.

The Sullen Man leapt at Lizue, feinted, then kicked her legs from under her. She landed hard and groped for the knife. He drew a knife of his own and stabbed her in the left thigh, the blade going in all the way to the bone. She cried out and slumped, the wound gushing blood.

He ran to Tali, who was starting to choke, and tore the clear bag apart.

"Out!" he gasped. "Run upstairs."

Lizue staggered to her feet, the heavy knife in her hand, and plunged it through the Sullen Man's chest into his heart. He fell dead without a sound.

Rannilt leapt up, picked up a fallen chair and whacked Lizue across the back with it. She reached out to Tali, her face twisted in anguish. "I'm sorry, I'm sorry."

Another of those golden bubbles formed at her fingertip, shot across the cell, struck Tali on the forehead and burst there with a hot flare of light. Rannilt bolted out the door and up the steps, screaming for help.

Tali was rubbing her throbbing forehead when she felt her gift rising – rising all the way this time. Lizue staggered towards her, swinging the knife. Tali thrust out her right arm, her fingers pointing towards Lizue's throat. Lizue froze.

The power was there but it would not come. They stared at one another for a long time, then Lizue smiled and lurched forwards. Tali threw herself through the open cell door and slammed it in Lizue's face.

Rannilt had disappeared up the steps; Lizue was struggling to get the door open with her bloody hands. Tali looked around. If she remained here, she would die, for she was too weak to fight.

The stairs and the main part of the fortress were to the left, but Rannilt would have alerted the guards up there by now. Tali turned right and was heading down the dimly lit corridor when a rear door opened and Kroni came through, carrying a bucket of water for the water clock. Tali froze for a second, then continued, her face turned away, but he merely nodded and continued past. With the glamour gone, he had not recognised her, but he would soon discover what had happened. She lurched through the door, closed it behind her and ran.

But without food, winter clothing or any knowledge of where she might get help, where was she to run to? The Sullen Man might be dead, but Lizue would come after her. And the chancellor would soon read the signs. The head bag would give her secret away.

Within the hour, he would know she bore the master pearl.

And he would kill her before he allowed the enemy to get it.

CHAPTER 15

"What's that smell?" said Lyf. He was at the door of his underground temple, formerly the murder cellar beneath Palace Ricinus. After many days of labour all traces of the cellar had been removed and the temple stripped back to its original stonework. "You told me it had been thoroughly scrubbed."

"Three times it's been cleaned, Lord King," said his personal attendant, Moley Gryle, "and the final time I did it myself. When we're finished, it's as perfect as we can make it, yet within hours the smell comes back."

"Where's it coming from?"

Lyf hobbled inside on his crutches. He could have floated in, or flown, but it would have felt sacrilegious to use the magery of the pearls in such a place. In olden times, the temple had one purpose only – healing. Besides, the pearl magery had been weakening rapidly of late. Had he drawn too much to ensure his fabulous victories? All the more reason to get the master pearl as soon as possible.

Before the Hightspallers had arrived on the First Fleet, this temple had been one of the most sacred places in Cythe, the private temple of the king. Here a succession of kings had worked their king-magery to heal the turbulent and disaster-prone land, as well as those unfortunate people whom ordinary healers could not help. At least, most of them. Some people suffered ailments beyond even the kings' healing.

But the temple had been debauched by Axil Grandys, who had betrayed the young, naïve King Lyf there, hacked off his feet and dragged him away to his death. Curiously, though, Grandys had protected the temple when every other building in the capital city of Lucidand had been torn down, and he had spent the following years in a fruitless attempt to find the secret of king-magery.

"There, Lord King," said Gryle, pointing.

She ushered him in and across to the centre. Everything had been removed from the former cellar, even the plaster on the walls and the staircase that had spiralled down through the ceiling when it had been the murder cellar. Now it was an empty, ovoid space some forty yards long and twenty-five wide, with a curving ceiling like the top of a skull. A skull with a hole in it, for the staircase opening had not yet been plugged. Lyf wondered if that was the problem.

"This is the spot." Gryle indicated the large flagstone in front of her.

Lyf measured the cellar with his eyes. "The altar stood here. The table and benches were over there – that's where the Five Herovians used their foul magery to compel my signature onto the lying charter they used to justify the theft of our country. And here—" He choked, but collected himself. "Here – see the gash in the stone – this is the place where they held me down while Grandys hacked my feet off with his accursed blade."

"The sacred stones cannot forget the crime that was committed here," Gryle said sententiously. "They reek to remind us that we must never forget."

"I wonder," said Lyf. "After I've completed my morning's devotions, take up the stones, remove the earth beneath and re-lay them."

"It will be done." Gryle went to speak, hesitated for almost a minute, then said, "Lord King, may I raise a matter with you?"

"If you must."

"Lord King, this is not something that concerns me personally . . .

not deeply, at any rate – but so many of your people are talking about it that I feel I must speak."

Lyf made an impatient gesture, and she hurried on.

"Many people are troubled by the way the war is, um ... going, Lord King."

"You may speak candidly, Gryle."

"Our people want Cythe back, and the enemy punished. But they feel the destruction of every house, every palace, every library and every temple built by the enemy over the past two thousand years is ... excessive."

"It's what they did to us," said Lyf, nettled.

"And they're sickened by all the unnecessary killing."

"Do you know how many Cythians they put down?" bellowed Lyf, brandishing a fist at her. "Fifty thousand, at least."

Gryle held her ground, though only with an effort. "Lord King, I do. But that was long ago and we – they – we feel—"

"You asked to speak, Gryle, and I have heard you."

"Yes, Lord King. And may I say—"

"You may not!"

"Lord King?"

"Get out."

As she was leaving, a courier came running. "Lord King, an urgent message from Lizue, at Rutherin."

"Yes?"

"The disguised prisoner *was* the escaped Pale, Tali vi Torgrist. Lizue almost took her head, but one of the chancellor's spies interfered and the Pale got away. Lizue is injured, though not badly enough to stop her from trying again."

His severed shinbones began to throb. Could victory be slipping from his grasp already? No, he would not allow it.

"Send gauntlings," said Lyf. "All we have. Find Tali."

The courier withdrew. Lyf called for his daily report on the war. An officer he did not recognise came to present it, a slender young man with prematurely white hair. General Hillish was leading the army against Bleddimire, and Lyf had banished General Rochlis, that great hero of the war, to a fortress in the north, for insubordination.

"Who are you?" said Lyf.

"Captain Durling, Lord King."

"Make it quick, Durling. I've much on my mind today."

Durling bowed. "Caulderon is quiet, Lord King. The people are thoroughly cowed."

"No signs of insurrection anywhere?"

"There are, from time to time, but we put them down swiftly and execute the ringleaders, which serves as a lesson to the rest of the city."

"Good. Continue."

"There was some trouble in the north, around Lakeland, but Rochlis has sorted it out. He's a good man, Lord King."

"He has an overly sensitive conscience for a military man," Lyf said coldly. All was not forgiven. "What's the state of the south?"

"Steady. It's too miserably cold there for trouble, Lord King. I doubt you'll have to worry about it until the spring."

"How about the west? What's the chancellor up to?"

"Growing his army and making alliances."

"How many troops does he have now?"

"About seven thousand, according to our spies. But most are inexperienced, and they're poorly led."

"I had all his officers killed after we took Caulderon," said Lyf. "You can train a soldier in a couple of weeks, but it takes months to produce a good officer – or years. And Bleddimire?"

"Your army is in position for battle and morale is good."

"Have my spies mentioned Bleddimire's morale?"

"Weakening by the hour."

"Then I can safely leave the business to Hillish. He'll soon have another famous victory. That only leaves the Nandeloch Mountains."

"The north-east is as rebellious as ever," said Durling, "but we can't do anything about it until spring."

"Why not?"

"The mountains are too high, too rugged, too cold. We'd need an army of twenty-five thousand to subdue the area and we don't even have five thousand to spare. Besides, if we tried to fight there in winter we could lose half an army."

"Why?" Lyf said coldly. He did not appreciate such advice.

"The roads are bad and the snow heavy. We run the risk of having our forces cut off by avalanches and freezing to death."

"Their petty little earldoms can wait until spring," said Lyf. "Is there any news of Rixium Ricinus?"

"I'm afraid not, Lord King ... though we have hundreds of troops looking."

"I am displeased. Find him!"

Durling withdrew.

Lyf closed the doors, barred them and walked around the temple. He knew it was empty, but caution was ingrained in him and in this matter he could not take any risks. Once sure that no spying device had been hidden inside, he continued his painstaking search. He would remove every stone in the walls and ceiling if he had to.

The key had to be found. The need was becoming desperate.

CHAPTER 16

"Where did I go wrong?" wailed Wil the Sump, rubbing his cavernous, eaten-away nostril until it bled.

The little man was deep underground in the Hellish Conduit, a down-plunging passageway so sweltering and humid that each breath clagged in his throat and had to be consciously swallowed. A place where green, corrosive fluids seeped from the walls and welled sluggishly up through cracks in the floor; where sickening emanations howled out of the depths; where luminous, tentacled growths sprouted from every crack and cranny, and tiny multi-legged creatures cowered in cracks while the plants were the predators.

Wil clawed at the encrusted wall until his fingernails tore to splinters, but it did not ease the agony he felt inside. The only thing that could take away the pain of his failure was the perilous alchymical solvent called alkoyl. But he had sniffed the last of his alkoyl eight days ago, he had no way of getting more, and with-drawal was like fishhooks dragging through his brain.

That wasn't the worst, though. Wil's beloved land was in danger and no one else could save it. The ice sheets were creeping up from the southern pole, closing in around the coast, and if they were not stopped they would grind all life off the face of the land, as they had already extinguished everything on the great southern island of Suden.

To save his country, Wil had to erase the iron book, *The Consolation of Vengeance*, that he had stolen from under Lyf's nose, then reforge the pages and rewrite them to tell the true story. Wil loved books and stories more than he loved his own miserable life, and the true story of Cython had to be told. He had to know how the story ended, but how could he find the right ending now?

He felt sure it involved the subterranean Engine, way down the Hellish Conduit at the heart of the world. Cythonians believed that the Engine powered the workings of the land itself, and Wil had planned to open the stopcocks to make the Engine race and melt the ice away. But the Engine had proven to be so vast, hot and terrifying that his courage had failed him, and he had run and kept on running. The Engine's story was beyond his power to write.

Nor could he rewrite the iron book. He had not yet succeeded in erasing the words Lyf had written, the words that had seemed so right until *the one* had appeared and made Lyf's story go wrong. That was Wil's fault too. Long ago he had lied to the matriarchs about *the one*, and though they had put all those little slave girls to death to get rid of her, Tali had survived and changed the story. She had changed everything.

To erase the iron book, Wil had to have more alkoyl, but the stores held in Cython were closed to him now. The only other place to get more was the source, the Engine itself, for as it worked the Engine wept small quantities of the universal solvent. However he dared not approach the source.

Until something changed, he would have to wait. But his pain could be endured no longer and he had a remedy for that. In the dark of night he would creep up the Hellish Conduit into Cython, and there he would strangle the life out of the first Pale he encountered. He should have killed Tali the first time he had seen her.

That was only right and just.

Tali was *the one*.

It was all her fault.

CHAPTER 17

"Are you going to rescue the Lady Tali?" said Glynnie. Rix had been rowing across the lake for an hour, guided through the black night by a single bright star.

"How could I?" he said curtly, for the rope binding his dead hand to the oar had chafed most of the skin off his wrist and the pain was unrelenting.

"You killed a whole pack of shifters," she said, and the awe in her voice was evident. "And with only your bare hands, you beat all those guards to save us. You can do *anything*."

Mentioning Benn would have been needlessly cruel. "I can't rescue Tali," said Rix. "I don't know where the chancellor's taken her. Besides, he'll have her hidden by the best magery there is – magery that even Lyf would struggle to break." He rowed on, wincing with every stroke. "Anyway, I couldn't have done anything without you."

"Of course you could. I was in the way—"

"Without you and Benn I'd be dead," he said bleakly.

"Rix!" she cried.

"I'm a dishonoured man, and I was going to—"

"You're a wonderful man," she said passionately. "You're brave and noble and true to your word. And kind. In all my life I've never known anyone as kind as you."

A tight feeling in his chest prevented him from speaking for a while. "Thank you for saying so," he said gruffly. "If it wasn't for you . . ."

"What?" said Glynnie. "What were you going to do?"

"Give my life away, fighting the enemy."

"No!" Her cry rang out across the water.

"Hush!" He stopped rowing and cupped a hand to his ear, but heard no sound save ripples lapping against the dinghy.

"Why would you do that?" said Glynnie.

"I've lost everything. Destroyed my family and my house. Betrayed my mother—"

"You didn't do any of those things," Glynnie said stoutly. "The stinking chancellor destroyed House Ricinus out of spite. And he *forced* you to name your mother; if you didn't, he was going to kill Tobry. Then he did anyway. He's a wicked, stupid man and he's going to lose the war." She looked up at him, her eyes reflecting the starlight. "Rix?"

He could see where this was going. "I can't do anything about the chancellor, Glynnie. He's made me an outlaw; no one would listen to me."

She put a hand on his good hand. "But we're never giving in. We're not running off and hiding. We're going to fight Lyf all the way – *aren't we*?"

Again the servant gives lessons to the master, he thought wryly. She saw things far more clearly than he did. "Yes, Glynnie. I'm going to fight for our country – to the very end."

Glynnie leaned forwards, impulsively, and threw her arms around him. "Thank you!" She sat back at once. "Where are we going?"

How could he tell her his plan? It would crush her, but he had to see her safe. "I don't know. It'll take time to build a rebel army, so I need a hideout that's easy to defend and hard to attack."

He stood up, the dinghy rocking under his weight, then drew Maloch, rested it on the bench seat and spun it. It stopped, pointing to the right. Rix checked the angle of the bright star. "Maloch is telling me to go north-east."

"What's there?"

He sheathed the sword. Ahead, there was nothing to see but darkness. "Beyond the lake, there's Grume, then Gordion. After that, the Nandeloch Mountains run north-east for a hundred and fifty miles."

"What are they like?" said Glynnie.

"Rugged. High peaks, deep valleys, snow and ice, rebellious people and bad roads. The last place Lyf would want to fight in mid-winter – and therefore the best place for me to go."

And, Rix belatedly recalled, he had a manor there. Fortress Garramide.

It had been left to him by a great-aunt last year. At the time, he had been due to inherit a hundred manors and three million acres of land upon his father's death, and Rix had taken no interest in another manor in the distant, uncouth uplands. But the world had changed. His main inheritance had been lost with House Ricinus's disgrace and fall, yet Garramide was untainted, still legally his.

Rix let out a sigh. He had a purpose in life and a place to go. It was all he needed. He took up the oars, braced himself against the agony in his wrist, and rowed on.

"I'm not overly keen on that sword," said Glynnie.

"Me either, but without it, we wouldn't be here."

"That's what worries me. Where is it sending us? And how does it know the way?"

Rix shrugged. "It's enchanted to protect me."

"Who enchanted it?"

"Who knows? It's a very old sword."

"Then the enchantment can't have been made for you."

"I suppose not. Maloch belonged to Axil Grandys, originally."

"The chancellor called it a *foul blade*," said Glynnie.

"When?" said Rix.

"Before he ordered his captain to chop off your right hand with it. Maloch didn't protect you then."

Something scuttled across Rix's grave. "Then why did you ask me to hold it while you were reattaching my hand?"

"I thought it might help."

Rix swallowed a bitter retort. They'd been through that before. "We'd better keep moving."

Hours after their escape from the gyre he pulled the dinghy into a wooded cove and the keel rasped on sand. A yard-wide stream ran into the cove at its upper end. There were no buildings, no lights or smell of wood smoke, no sign that anyone lived nearby. They climbed out into ankle-deep water with nothing save the clothes they were wearing, Glynnie's small pack and the money belt around Rix's waist. He reached into the dinghy and retrieved the rope.

"Where are we?" Glynnie asked listlessly.

She had not spoken in the past hour, just sat there, staring into the darkness, shivering and wracked by bouts of quiet weeping for her lost brother. It might have been better if she had seen the lad's body. At least she would know.

Rix was no longer troubled by doubt. Everything in his life was certain, including its brevity. Henceforth, he had nothing save the sword in his left hand ... and lost, loyal Glynnie. For a few days, at least, until he found a place for her. He shied away from the thought.

"A mile north of Grume," he said, belatedly answering her question. "We can't leave any traces here, so stay in the water. I'll get rid of the dinghy."

"How?"

Rix took off his coat and handed it to her, then waded out, pushing the boat, until the water was up to his shoulders. Taking Maloch in his left hand, he thrust it through the planks, well below the waterline, then drove the blade down to the keel, across and back up. The enchanted sword cut through the tough wood as though it was card and the dinghy sank.

He went back to Glynnie. "We'll go up the stream until we come to a path, or rocks, and leave the water there."

"We could still leave tracks," she said.

"If they don't come out of the lake, there's no reason to suspect the tracks are ours. They could belong to anyone."

They walked up the stream for several hundred yards before the land rose in a ramp, the stream chuckling down over a series of rock shelves like broad, shallow steps. Rix turned left across the shelf into a low woodland. Dry bark rustled beneath their feet. They climbed a hill and at its crest he stopped to survey the land around.

Away to their left he saw a scatter of lights, the town of Grume. In every other direction the land lay in darkness. It was getting colder and their clothes were still damp, but he dared not light a fire here.

"What now?" said Glynnie.

"Get away from the lake as quickly as possible. Then buy two horses, or steal them, head for the mountains and hope there's enough snowfall to hide our tracks."

"How long will it take to get there?" she said as they headed down the other side of the hill.

"Depends how long it takes to find a place for you," he said without thinking.

She stopped dead. *"You're sending me away?"*

Rix cursed himself for putting it so baldly. "No, I'm going to find a safe household for you—"

"I thought we were allies, working together," she cried. "What have I done wrong?"

He caught her by the shoulders. "Shh! There could be hunters out, or shepherds."

"Answer. The. Question." Her voice was ground ice.

"You saw what they did back at the gyre. They plan to kill me."

"And you need a fr— an *ally* to watch your back," she said, her voice quavering.

"I vowed to look after you and Benn," said Rix. "I failed Benn; I'm not losing you as well."

"And my feelings don't come into it?"

He scanned the darkness, uneasily. "We can't talk about this now. We've got to get clear."

She turned and walked away.

Rix ran after her. "You're going the wrong way."

"You go your way, I'm going mine."

He groaned. "If we split up, it doubles the chance of discovery. And when they find one of us they'll know where to look for the other. Anyway, you've got no money or anything."

"What do you care? You're planning to dump me the minute you can."

"I'm not planning to *dump* you. Glynnie, be realistic. I'm going to do Lyf as much damage as I can, but in the end . . . I'm just one man, and I'm bound to be killed."

"So it's all right for you to fight for our country, but not for me?"

"I have a duty to look after you."

"House Ricinus has fallen! You're not my master. I'm nothing to you."

"You mean a lot to me! But I vowed to look after you and I'm going to."

Her voice went even colder. "So after all we've gone through together, you're *getting rid of* me?"

"No, I'll be providing for you as best I can. You're a clever, capable girl. I'm sure you'll do well."

"I'm not a girl," she said, stamping her foot. "I'm a woman."

"And you have a life to live."

"So do you."

He groaned. "I'm Lyf's number one enemy – and high on the chancellor's list as well. Whoever wins, they'll come after my head and they'll probably get it."

"But you're all I have left," said Glynnie. "I can't bear to lose you too."

CHAPTER 18

Three days had passed. Today was the day. Glynnie sank ever lower in the saddle of her stolen horse and refused to meet Rix's eye.

"It's for the best," he said. "What else can I do?"

She did not reply.

"It wouldn't be right to take you with me."

"Which is why you're casting me off like a worn-out pair of trews."

"I'm not casting you off. I'm setting you up for your future."

"Whether I like it or not."

"I'm responsible for you. You're not—"

"Will you shut up! I've been looking after myself since I was twelve and I don't want to be set up for my future. Damn you. You can go to hell."

Glynnie stared at him for thirty seconds, her fists clenched, then the ferocity drained out of her. Her face took on the resigned look he had seen all too often on the faces of the house servants – that this was her lot and she had no option but to accept it. A look he could not bear to see on her.

"All right, Lord," she said. "I can't fight you any more."

"I'm not a lord. I'm just Rix."

"You're disposing of me. That makes you my lord."

"What else can I do? I've lost everything and I'm probably going to die."

"You still have allies, and a belt full of gold. And now you've rejected me, no one in the world cares if I exist – or if I die."

"I'm not rejecting you. I do care!"

"Then take me with you." She said it dully, knowing the answer before he spoke.

"I – can't!"

She bent her head to him, servant to master. "All I had was you. You were my family. Now I'm alone in the world."

Rix's mouth tasted of ashes.

"Where are you dumping me?" said Glynnie as they approached the situation Rix had picked out for her.

"Canticleer Manor. A friend of mine, Jondo Canty, stands to inherit it when his father dies. He may already have done; the old man was ailing ten years ago. Jondo was the youngest," Rix reflected. "He's got five older sisters, but they're an old, traditional family. Daughters only inherit when there are no sons, can you believe it?"

"I can believe it," she muttered.

It occurred to Rix, for the first time, that the Cantys might be Herovian. Inheritance through the male line was a Herovian custom, he recalled. And since Rix was descended from the great Axil Grandys, they would certainly want to keep his favour.

The track was winding, potholed and the wagon ruts almost axle deep. Had Canticleer fallen on hard times? It might not be a bad thing – it made the place less of a target.

It was drizzling as they turned the corner and rode up to the gate, which was sagging on its hinges. Weeds sprouted along the wall to either side. The manor was small, square and very plain. Rix's heart sank as he studied the tiny windows, the mean, nail-studded front door and the dozen squat chimneys. It was a miserably cold day yet only one chimney was smoking. Canticleer did not look welcoming.

He pounded on the gate, and shortly a thin, slatternly young woman appeared on the other side. Her clothes were grimy and so was her hair. She looked him over. "What do you want?"

"Good day to you," said Rix. "I've come to see Jondo."

"What name?"

"Rixium Ricinus."

She stiffened and went back inside. Several minutes passed. Rix studied Glynnie from the corner of an eye. The reins were twisted around her hands so tightly that they scored purple marks across the backs. He could imagine what she was thinking. He would not want to be left here either.

The young woman returned with a matron of perhaps fifty years. She was short and stout, with a purple, jowled face and plump fingers, and her grey hair was draggled and stringy. Rix had been looking at her for some moments before he recognised Jondo's mother, whom he had not seen in ten years. She had not aged well.

"Good day to you, Madam Canty," he said politely. "You may not remember—"

"I remember your bitch of a mother," said Madam Canty. "And how she mocked my son for his old-fashioned manners and rustic dress."

Rix had not expected such naked hostility. "But—"

"Our living may have been meagre, but at least it was earned honestly."

"My mother is dead, and so is my father," said Rix. "And I—"

"Executed for high treason and murder! And now your house has collapsed like a rotten melon, you dare come begging at my door?"

"I am no beggar, Madam. I am riding to war to defend my country. I have a maidservant, a clever, hardworking girl who would be an asset to any household. As I have none, I'm seeking a place for her."

Madam Canty's hard little eyes surveyed Glynnie, then flicked

back to Rix. "Knowing Ricinus's way with maids, I cannot believe
she is one."

Glynnie flushed the colour of her hair.

Rix dared not speak his rage. "She is an excellent maidservant,
Madam. Will you have her?"

"I have five daughters, no husband and no son. I have no need of
servants."

"Ah, I'm sorry. Was Jondo killed in the war?"

Her mouth turned down, became a savage gash. "He was put to
death in Caulderon, five days ago. Would that they had done the
same to you." She looked him up and down, her contempt deep-
ening. "Though being your mother's son, Lord Ricinus, I dare say
you bought your freedom with the blood of those more scrupulous
and less fortunate."

Fury was rising in Rix but he clamped down on it. Madam
Canty had much to be bitter about and he could not blame her for
speaking her mind. He nodded stiffly and was turning away when
Glynnie let out a cry of fury.

"How dare you speak about Lord Rixium like that, you ugly old
cow! He's a good and noble man—"

"Who betrayed his treacherous mother to her death," Madam
Canty said icily. "He's just as foul as she was." She met Rix's eyes.
"Begone, Lord Ricinus, and take your leman with you, before I set
the dogs on you both."

They rode away with as much dignity as they could manage.
Glynnie was shaking and almost incoherent with fury. "How. Dare.
She?" she finally ground out.

"She's lost her only son," he said mildly, "and she's wondering
how they'll survive the war – or *if* they will."

"You didn't *buy* your freedom. And ... and ..."

She was flushing again, and he felt an urge to tease her, gently.
"What are you trying to say?"

"You're a gentleman. You would never take advantage of ...
of ..."

"Of a maidservant who had no one to protect her? Ah, Glynnie,
if you only knew what gentlemen are really like. Taking advantage
of innocent maids is one of their principal sports."

"I know exactly what *those* gentlemen are like," she said hotly. "And I also know you. I trust you with my life, Lord. My life and . . . and everything."

She jabbed the horse with her heels and it trotted ahead. Her head was held high and she wore a faint, enigmatic smile. Glynnie was not altogether displeased with the way things had turned out.

Rix felt a slight heat in his cheeks. Someone should remind her that it was possible to trust too much.

"I'm sure we'll have better luck at Corkyle Manor," Rix said that afternoon. "Tyne is an old friend."

Glynnie went pale. "Better luck at what?"

"Finding you a place."

"But . . . I thought you'd given up on that."

"They're going to hunt me down like a dog, Glynnie. And even if I could escape them, I can't take you to war."

"I thought you were going to find a place to build an army."

"I am." Why hadn't he told her about Garramide? If he mentioned it now it would only infuriate her more.

"That'll take weeks, even months. Why do you want to get rid of me now?"

"You're deliberately misunderstanding me. I don't want to get rid of you. But I don't want you in danger, either."

"Hightspall is at war. Wherever you *banish* me to, I'll be in danger."

He ground his teeth. "Not as much as if you were with me."

"Your refuge in the mountains — it'll be a castle or fortress, I assume."

"Yes, a place with strong defences."

"And you'll have soldiers to help you defend it?"

"As many as I can round up. Hundreds, hopefully."

"And dozens of servants to manage daily life in the fortress?"

"I'll need servants, and you're not going to be one of them."

"What's wrong with me? If you can fight for our country, why can't I?"

"You're going, and that's that."

"Arrogant pig!" she muttered.

"I beg your pardon?"

"Madam Canty was right about you," she snapped. "There's nothing noble about you; you're not even a gentleman's . . . *backside*." She galloped ahead.

He gave her fifteen minutes, then rode up beside her. "It's still no."

Her shoulders sagged. "What about Tyne's lady? What's she like?"

"Tall, bony, sharp tongued, but underneath it all, Felmae is a kindly woman."

"I suppose she'll have to do, then. How long have I got?"

"Before we get there? About five minutes."

"You . . . you *bastard*!" she shrieked, so self-consciously that he was sure she'd never used the word before. "Why didn't you tell me we were so close?"

"Must have slipped my mind," he lied.

"You're a stinking liar, Deadhand." She wrenched her horse's head around and faced him, a compact ball of fury dwarfed by the enormous horse. Glynnie swallowed the fury with an effort and said calmly, "At least your treachery has solved one problem."

"What's that?" Rix said uneasily.

"I hate you! I'm glad to be getting rid of you, you great arrogant lump. And . . . and, if you should ever come by to visit me, not that you would, *I won't be in*."

She turned away, evidently thinking she had won a great victory.

It was snowing gently as they rode up a winding track between small, leafless trees. Granite boulders dotted the slopes to either side and the air was very still, with a hint of wood smoke.

"It'll be nice to relax by the fire with old friends," said Rix. "And sleep in a proper bed."

"Are you staying the night, then? I thought you'd dump me and run away to play at your wars."

Rix felt his jaw muscles tighten. "You never let up, do you?"

"Surely you didn't think I was going to make it easy for you, Deadhand?"

Rix couldn't take any more. He spurred his horse and galloped ahead, up the hill, around a tight corner where the trees grew so closely together that they made a black wall to either side, then down a straight drive. Ahead were the simple, elegant lines of the old keep, built in pink granite a thousand years ago. The smell of wood smoke was stronger here, and he soon saw why. The manor behind the keep was a smoking ruin.

He careered down the track. It need not mean what he feared. The keep was strong; a hundred people could hold up there for weeks. But as he came closer Rix saw that its doors had been smashed in. A trail of smoke still issued from inside, as though the last combustible items had almost been consumed.

He was staring numbly at the hacked bodies of the lord and lady of Corkyle when Glynnie reached him. Many other bodies were scattered around them, but not all looked as though they had been killed in battle. Several, including the lady, appeared to have been cut down after they had surrendered.

They searched the keep and the ruins but found not a living soul. Not even children had been spared. Yet the manor had not been looted. Most of its artworks and other treasures had been burned or hacked to pieces, as if the intention of the raid had not been conquest, but simple, bloody destruction of all that had been built here.

"Why would the enemy do this?" said Rix.

"They hate us."

If he'd left Glynnie here a day ago, she would have been one of the butchered. His eyes moistened; he had not appreciated how dear she had become to him. He turned away and she went with him.

"I'm sorry, Lord," she said quietly. "To see your friends like that must be the worst thing in the world."

"They were good people. They never hurt anyone."

"Do you want to bury them?"

Rix put a hand on the hilt of Maloch and felt a shock that jolted his hand into the air.

"What was that?" whispered Glynnie.

"A warning. Maloch keeps doing that. We're in danger and it's getting closer."

"We have to go, don't we?"

"The least I could do would be to honour my friends with a respectable burial, and I can't even do that. It'd take a day to dig graves in this rocky ground. Come on."

"Where are you going?" said Glynnie.

Previously she would have said, *Where are we going?* Had she given up?

He balanced his sword on a rock, and spun it.

Glynnie checked the angle of the sun. "Maloch always points in the same direction, north-east. What's it pointing to?"

"There's a fortress called Garramide. A very old place, high up."

She stared at him. "Lady Ricinus talked about Garramide." Her green eyes narrowed. "Wasn't it—?"

"It's mine," Rix admitted.

"But you lost it when House Ricinus fell."

"No, it's still legally mine. I inherited it last year from a great-aunt who had nothing to do with House Ricinus, so not even the chancellor could confiscate it."

"And you've known this all along," she said, sparks flashing in her eyes. "When did you propose to tell me? Or were you going to dispose of me first, so I'd never know?"

"Not all along. I'd forgotten I owned it."

It was the wrong thing to say. "How could you forget you owned a *manor*?" she shrieked.

"When I was heir to House Ricinus, I stood to inherit a hundred manors," he said lamely. "What difference does it make? You know now."

"I thought we were the same," she said bitterly. "Two people who'd lost everything, working together like friends, just trying to survive. But we were never the same; you've been acting under false pretences."

"I don't understand what's bothering you," said Rix.

"That makes it even worse," she screamed. "If I had one lousy brass *chalt* in my purse, I couldn't forget I had it – yet the great Lord Rixium is so stinkingly rich he forgets he owns a *manor*! No wonder you want to get rid of me. There's no place for me in your world."

And she broke down and wept.

Rix stood there awkwardly, trying to work out why she was so upset. *I thought we were the same.* Did she think he was rejecting her, or repudiating what had grown between them during the escape and the journey?

Or did it go deeper? She was no fool; she knew that wealthy lords often dallied with maids, but they never took them as equal partners. Yes, that had to be it.

What was he going to do about it? There *was* a vast gulf between them, but not the way she imagined it. Glynnie was strong and brave, but she was also an innocent, while Rix felt old and tainted. In no way was he worthy of her. Besides, any friend, any partner of his would be in as much danger as he was, and he wasn't going to inflict that on her.

He let out an almighty groan. "I'm sorry, Glynnie."

She wiped her eyes, squared her shoulders and looked up, the good servant again. "Forget I said anything, Lord. I was just being silly. Emotional. It ... losing Benn, and everything ... it's all been a bit much. And here's you with your friends murdered ... I'm sorry."

She mounted her horse. It wasn't over, nothing like it, but Rix seized the diversion gratefully. "I can't do anything for them. We'd better go."

"What's your manor like?"

He shrugged. "I don't know. I haven't been within twenty miles of the place. But I may have to fight for it."

"Why?"

"In times of war, the moment a great house falls, the hyenas move in to take everything left undefended." He climbed onto his horse. "Coming?"

"Where?"

"To Garramide."

She did not move. "You're not sending me away? You're taking me with you?"

"I'm not letting you out of my sight," said Rix.

CHAPTER 19

Tali bolted down the black stone corridor past the last of the cells to the great iron rear door she had seen the day she arrived. An icy draught whistled underneath it, suggesting that it led outside. She was not dressed for winter, she had neither money nor food, but she did not hesitate. If she could not escape she was going to die, one way or another. She raised the latch, slipped through into the dark and the wind-driven rain, and closed the door behind her.

Where to go? She had no idea. All she knew about the fortress, and the town of Rutherin below the cliff, was the glimpse she'd had after the wagon's axles broke.

She was in a large, paved yard surrounded by the knife-edged ridges she had seen as she arrived, which were too steep to climb even had she been fit. The main building loomed behind her against a dark sky. There was no moon to guide her, not even a star. Everything was obscured by a heavy overcast. The only light came from several small windows on the topmost level of the fortress, barely enough to see by.

First she must get out of the fortress. If she did, she would worry about where to run, where to hide, how to survive. She turned around and around, willing her underground-sensitive eyes to reveal what normal people would never see. There, up the steeply sloping yard, two shadowy rises in the wall must be the gate towers.

She had to hurry – Kroni would have seen the blood-drenched, empty cell by now. Within minutes the gates would be sealed and everyone would be on the hunt. Nothing mattered but speed.

Tali darted across the yard and scuttled along beside the wall. She wasn't used to running and already her knees felt weak. There was a light in the guard box and she saw a shadow there, and heard a rhythmic thudding. It was miserably cold; the guard must be stamping his feet to keep warm.

She felt her way along to the main gates, but they were locked and barred at night. A small gate beside the guard post, only wide enough to admit one person at a time, was also closed and she could not open it without being seen.

The gate was her only chance, so she had to distract the guard. If she'd had command of her gift it would have been easy, but even after Rannilt's intervention Tali could raise no more than a trickle of magery.

She crept closer until she could see the guard in his little wooden guard box. An elderly, sad-eyed fellow with sagging jowls and pouched eyes, he looked as though he had seen more than enough of the misery of the world. Did he have a soft heart, though? If his troubles had hardened him, her plan would fail.

The great fortress gates were made from six-inch-thick slabs of timber reinforced with vertical lengths of the same timber, though here and there she could feel cracks between the slabs. She slid along the gate until she was behind the reinforcing slab nearest the guard box, praying that it was enough to conceal her. It might do, as long as he didn't shine his lantern along the gate.

In Cython, Tali had been the best of all the slave-kids at hiding, and Nurse Bet had taught her to throw her voice so as to send pursuers the wrong way. Could she still do it?

She put her lips to a crack between two slabs, cupped her hands around her mouth, then threw her voice so it would seem to come from outside. She had to use a trickle of her precious magery to make sure, and it still did not sound very convincing, so she picked up a small piece of rock from the road and tossed it over the gate. It clattered away, outside.

"Help," she moaned in her highest, most child-like voice. "Help, help!"

"Who's there?" said the guard, coming to the door of his box.

"Lost my mummy. Help me."

The guard opened the viewing flap and shone the lantern around outside. "Come to the gate."

"Broke my ankle," Tali whimpered. "Please help me."

"Not allowed to open the gate without seeing who's outside."

Tali let out a groan.

"You've got to come to the gate, girlie," said the guard. "If I break the rules, I'll get a flogging."

Tali let out another moan, then said no more. The guard swore, checked back towards the fortress, then opened the side gate and looked out.

"Where the blazes are you, girl?"

Tali crept towards the guard box. The old guard, muttering to himself, went through and she heard his boots crunching on the gravel outside. Now!

"Where are you, girlie?"

She slipped through the gate behind him. He walked a few paces, swinging the lantern back and forth, trying to penetrate the shadows down the slope to the right side of the road. He stopped. It did not look as if he was going to go any further, and the moment he turned back he would see her and shout the alarm.

Tali picked up a chunk of rock, stepped up behind him and, as the lantern swung back in his hand, slammed the rock into the glass. The lantern went out and darkness descended. She ducked aside and crouched down.

"What the bloody hell happened?" said the old man. "Girlie, I've got to go back."

A klaxon sounded from the fortress and someone bellowed, "Seal the gates. Let no one in or out. Guards, be on alert for a small, blonde woman."

"Oh, gawd!" cried the old man. "Oh gawd, oh gawd, I'm for it now."

Almost sobbing, he groped his way back to his box. Tali felt a spasm of pity for the kindly old man. She had used him ill, and now he would get a flogging. She began to run off, hesitated, then turned back. Could she make it appear that it wasn't his fault? And could she still get away if she took the time to help him?

She followed the old man back. In his distress he had neglected to bolt the side gate, and she slipped through. He had a burning taper and was trying to light his lantern, wheezing, "Oh gawd, oh gawd," but his hand was shaking so badly that the wick would not catch.

She took the lantern from his hand and shook the oil out all over the walls of the guard box. "Run," said Tali. "Yell for help. Tell them I set your box on fire."

He stared at her as though she were an apparition. Tali took the taper from his hand and touched it to the furthest wall. Flames licked up.

"Go!" she hissed.

He stumbled away, croaking, "Help! Fire!"

Tali tossed the taper at the other wall, went through the side gate, pushed it shut and looked around her. The road from the gate ran up into the mountains, she knew, though without clothing and proper gear she had no hope of surviving there. To her right, a steep track wound down the cliff towards the town of Rutherin. After they searched the immediate surrounds of the fortress, Rutherin was the first place they would look, but she had no alternative.

Tali headed down the road at a trot, though before she had gone a hundred yards she knew she would be lucky to reach the bottom. She was already exhausted. Could she do this? Would her strength last?

She stumbled on. Behind her, the fortress was lit with a hundred lights and flames from the blazing guard box could be seen above the gates. The side gate was blocked by fire but it would only take a minute to swing the main gates open, and then they would come after her.

Where could she hide? The steep ground beside the track was bare rock save for a few miserable bushes that would not conceal her for a minute. She had no choice but to follow the track, though every breath was burning in her throat and a pain in her side was getting worse with every step. She had never run down such a steep slope before. Her knees were already wobbly.

Tali looked over her shoulder, stumbled and crashed to the rocky ground on her knees and outstretched hands. Pain pierced her right palm; she staggered to her feet and lurched on. Both palms were bleeding and so was her left knee. She could feel the blood trickling down her leg.

"She must have gone down!" a man roared. "Get horses and go after her!"

The searchers were at the top, waving lanterns. They would have to ride carefully down the steep track but they would be faster than her.

She reached the base of the cliff, caught her breath for a second, then plodded on. Houses sprouted on both sides of the track, mostly shanties and lean-tos, though in this miserable weather the doors were all closed and the streets empty. Alleys meandered between the shanties. In the distance she could see taller buildings. She headed in that direction.

The streets of Rutherin were poorly lit, only a lamp every fifty yards or so, and the alleys were dark, stinking tunnels through a maze of filth. Tali followed a random path through them, stumbling on broken cobbles, slipping on greasy clay and, more than once, on human waste dumped in the street. She moved into the middle of the alley and sank to mid-shin in a pot-hole filled with muck that oozed into her boots, squelching with every step.

She struggled out again, her heart racing; each step was like climbing a mountain now. Several streets away she heard horses galloping, men and women shouting, and someone roaring at the townsfolk.

"Light the lanterns. An escaped prisoner. A small, blonde girl. Big reward. *Huge* reward!"

Lights blossomed behind Tali. She headed away down another series of mean alleys, each fouler and darker than the one before. As she turned a corner, someone caught her arm and a blast of grog breath made her reel.

"Bin waitin' all night for you, dearie. Right here'll do."

She reacted without thinking, using Nurse Bet's favourite defence, and this time it worked. A knee to the groin doubled the man over onto her fist, which she drove hard into his throat. He fell backwards against a shanty wall, the impact rattling the flimsy boards, and swayed there, gasping for breath. From inside, a high voice cursed him. Tali ran.

She zigged and zagged through the alleys, following an instinct that told her to go towards the sea, but could not shake her pursuers. There must have been dozens of them, all mounted. It felt as though they were driving her into a corner, trapping her – but against what?

The old docks, where for centuries uncounted the fishing fleet and the merchant vessels had moored to unload their cargoes. The timbers loomed above her and along the old shoreline in either direction as far as she could see, but the docks were derelict now, and rotting. It took a while to remember why. As the ice had spread, the level of the sea had dropped, and now it was a mile offshore.

Tali assumed that the odd tingling in her nose, a combination of salt and rotting weed, was the smell of the sea. She could also smell the tarred wharves and decaying wood.

Not that way, not that way! It was Rannilt, screaming into Tali's mind.

Tali stopped. "Rannilt?" she whispered. She had no idea how to speak back to her, one mind to another. She could not comprehend how the child had done it in the first place.

I'm sorry, Rannilt wept. *I'm sorry, Tali. I didn't mean it.*

Tali tried to reach her but the connection was gone.

She crouched in the shadows and looked back for her pursuers. They were making no effort to conceal themselves; she could see riders to the left, riders to the right, and more ahead, coming out of the alleys with their bright lanterns held high.

They seemed to know which way she had gone and they weren't hurrying any more. They were methodically searching every street, every alley, making sure she could not slip through their line. In five minutes, ten at the most, they would know she wasn't in that quarter of Rutherin, and equally well that she had not escaped them. Only one place would remain to be searched.

The docks.

There was nowhere else to go. Tali clambered up onto the empty docks, praying for a miracle. The effort took the last of her strength; she had to lie on the icy boards with her pulse pounding in her ears and little bright flashes going off in her eyes for several minutes before she could raise her head.

A broad boardwalk ran off the seaward side of the docks, out across mudflats and marshland in the direction of the distant sea, but on it she would be visible for a hundred yards. She might take to the marshlands, she supposed, though they looked treacherous. No, she was bound to be trapped there.

The first of the riders were approaching. It was hopeless but she could not give in. She was never giving in. Unable to stand up, she crawled in among the myriad crumbling storerooms and little warehouses. Wherever she hid, they would find her and drag her back to the fortress and the bloodstained cell, and the cannula that would take her blood until there was nothing left of her but a dried-up husk that would blow away in the wind.

Someone was walking along the docks, a slow, careful tread. She crouched down, heart crashing and breath burning in her throat. She could not run any further; she had nothing left.

He approached, looking left then right. She tried to shrink into a tighter ball but it was no use. She could smell her sweat, her terror. He must be able to smell her too.

He turned, walked past, then back. She prepared to defend her-self, though she could barely lift her arms. Past he went, came back, then lunged, caught her by the shoulder and dragged her out into the light. He looked like an old man of sixty, with that grey hair and beard, though he had such strong fingers that he might not be as old as he appeared. Fingers crisscrossed with little white scars.

"Kroni," she whispered. "All along I knew you were a spy."

He blinked at her for a few seconds, frowning. He had not seen her true face clearly on her way out. He knew her as the older woman the chief magian's glamour had made her into.

"Then all along you knew wrong."

CHAPTER 20

"What are you doing?" said Tali. "Where are you taking me?" Kroni did not answer. She tried to dredge up her magery, anything at all, but exhaustion would not allow her to focus.

He dragged her into the shadows between two storerooms, then out onto the seaward side of the docks, down twenty steps and onto the boardwalk that led to the distant boats and the sea. Before they had gone a hundred yards the riders clattered onto the docks, shining their lanterns about and roaring at one another.

"Don't move." Kroni pulled her down onto the boards and cast a grey cloak over them both. "Don't look towards the lanterns."

From the corner of an eye she saw a tall fellow come to the top of the steps and shine his lantern along the boardwalk. It cast a bright light and she was sure it would pick them out. He waved it back and forth, evidently watching for moving shadows, then turned away.

Tali was about to stand up when Kroni crushed her shoulder. His fingers were hard as brass. "I said, don't move!"

The tall man turned suddenly and shone his lantern down the boardwalk again. Tali's heart slammed into her ribs. He would have seen her. He studied the boardwalk, the mudflats on the left and the marshlands to the right, then turned back to the search of the docks.

"Now," said Kroni.

He heaved her to her feet and led her down towards the sea. She stumbled; his arm went around her shoulders and held her up.

"What's the matter with you?"

"Lost too much blood," she said limply. "Hardly stand up."

His arm curled around her waist, taking most of her weight, and he hurried on.

"Where you taking me?" she panted.

"Depends on the answers you give me."

"What answers?"

"Good ones."

"You – a spy for Lyf?" gasped Tali. "You – working for Lyf?"

He gave a derisory snort.

"Who then?"

When he did not reply, a cold fist clenched around her heart. Kroni must be a privateer, and she was worth a fortune. He had been watching her for ages, and now he was planning to carry her away and sell her to the highest bidder. How much would Lyf pay to be delivered the host of the master pearl? What would the chancellor give? Enough to corrupt almost any man.

She tried to pull free. Even if she fell off into the marsh and drowned it would be better than having her head hacked open while she was still alive. If she drowned, she would thwart them all. The pearl had to be harvested from a live host.

"Don't!" said Kroni, holding her easily.

In another five minutes she heard water lapping and the boardwalk ended in a T shape, running to left and right beside ragged lines of piles driven into the mud. Several boats were moored there and the reek of fishy water in the bilges took her breath away.

He hauled her to the left, then along a series of slimy, algae-covered planks to three pairs of piles where a number of smaller boats were tied up. He thrust her down in the shadows between two boats. It was exposed here, and an icy wind was blowing across the water, stirring her short hair.

He glanced back towards the main boardwalk. "They're coming, and I need answers, fast. What's your name? Your real name?"

Could she trust him? Could she trust anyone? She didn't know anything about Kroni – he might be a privateer, or he might, possibly, be genuine. On the other hand, she knew what the chancellor would do if he got her back.

"There's no time left," said Kroni, and she could hear the urgency in his voice.

If she went with him, it would buy her time, at least. "It's Tali," she burst out. "Thalalie vi Torgrist."

He whistled. "You're the escaped Pale?"

"Yes."

"But what are you – patriot or traitor?"

"I love my country," said Tali.

"Which one?" he said roughly. "Hightspall or Cython?"

"Hightspall, of course. What do you take me for?"

"I haven't decided, though the chancellor did imprison you, and the word in Fortress Rutherin names you a traitor."

"He spread that lie to conceal me from my enemies. You saw how Lizue tried to kill me."

"Kill *you?*" said Kroni. "The way I read the evidence, she tried to save you from the sour fellow in the other cell."

"No; Lizue's Cythonian. She burned through the bars and tried to kill me. The Sullen Man is – was – the chancellor's spy. He tried to save my life, and died for it."

"She didn't look Cythonian," said Kroni.

"She does now. The glamour on her broke at the same time as the one the chief magian put on me."

"The Cythonians don't use magery."

"But Lyf does."

"How would you know that?"

"Because I've met him. Fought him."

"Now I know you're lying. You're just a slip of a girl—"

Tali's fury gave her strength. "I'm the first Pale to escape Cython in a thousand years," she snapped. "I've been to the wrythen's caverns under Precipitous Crag, I've jousted verbally with the chancellor himself and given as good as I got. And he rewarded me, too—"

She was getting into dangerous waters. Old Kroni had a remarkably keen mind for a clock mechanic, and there were certain questions she didn't want raised at any price.

"Really?" said Kroni. "What for?"

"Mind your own business."

He glanced along the boardwalk. "You've got one minute to satisfy me that you're on our side. If you can't, I'll give you up to the chancellor."

"And pocket a fat reward," she said bitterly.

"Should I not be rewarded for capturing such a valuable and elusive spy and traitor?" he said mildly. "Why did the chancellor reward you, incidentally?"

She did not think Kroni was much better than her pursuers, but he was the only hope she had. And the searchers were getting closer; she could see their lights clearly now.

"I told him that Lady and Lord Ricinus were planning his assassination."

He let out a low whistle. She'd surprised him.

"I understood that Rix Ricinus informed on his mother for high treason," said Kroni, "and that's why the chancellor refused to have him."

"He forced it out of Rix; but the chancellor already knew, because I'd told him the day before. But he's a vengeful man; that's why he hacked Rix's hand off with his own sword. And because Rix is Herovian."

"Is that so?" said Kroni.

"Yes. He carries Axil Grandys' enchanted sword."

"He carries Maloch?"

"You know the name of his sword?"

"I like to read. It's in the history books. What was your reward?"

"The chancellor's spectible."

"He gave you his *spectible*?"

"I did him a mighty favour. Besides, his chief magian couldn't use it."

"And you can, I assume? What did you want it for?"

"To try and get control of my magery—"

"All right, I've heard enough. Come on." He jerked her to her feet.

"Where are we going?"

He pointed to the cabin boat they had been sheltering behind. It was about thirty feet long, with a small deck in front of the little cabin and a larger deck behind it with a tall mast in the middle.

"Get in."

"You're . . . going out to sea?"

"Why else would I have come this way? What's the matter?"

"I'm afraid . . . of the water," she said quietly.

"More afraid than you are of them? *Get in!*"

"Hoy! You! Stop right there." The leading group on the board-walk, five or six of them, broke into a run.

Kroni threw Tali over the rail, cast off the mooring ropes fore and aft, and leapt nimbly in. The boat began to drift seawards with the wind, which was blowing down from the mountains. He unfurled a scrap of sail then ran into the cabin to the wheel. He spun it and the boat heeled over.

But it was still moving slowly and the guards were hurtling down the boardwalk. The gap between the boat and the pier was only three feet, four, five. Still an easy leap. Six feet ... seven ... eight – a difficult jump now, but possible.

The guards hurtled up. Ten feet ... twelve. They skidded to a stop at the end of the pier, screaming abuse, for the gap was now beyond any man to jump. Fifteen feet ... twenty. Kroni left the wheel and hauled on ropes, trimming the sail. It caught the wind and shot down the channel into the bay, and she was safe. From immediate pursuit, at least. Though not from the water, and perhaps not from Kroni either.

"Come in out of the wind," said Kroni.

She followed him into the cabin. It was about six feet by eight, beautifully built from honey-coloured timber that had been polished until it shone and coated with layers of varnish. There was a large round window forward, small portholes to either side and a sliding door onto the rear deck.

Bench seats ran along the left side and the rear, to the door, and there was a small fixed table in the corner in front of the seats. A low door, latched open, led to a square hatch and a ladder that ran down into a lower cabin, or perhaps the hold. She couldn't tell; it was dark down there.

"Anything else you want to tell me?" said Kroni, gesturing to the seats.

"Don't think so." Tali sat, wanting to lie down and close her eyes and not move for a week. "What about you, Kroni?"

"Kroni," he said, smiling. "That takes me back. I really am a clockmaker, you know. A good one, though you may think me boastful for saying it. You would have realised that Kroni was a pseudonym. My name is Holm."

"Holm what?"

"It'll do for the time being."

"Whose boat is this?"

"Mine. I built it twenty years ago."

"So you're also a master boat builder?"

"I dabble."

"What do you want me for?"

"Youth of today!" he sighed theatrically. "So suspicious. I don't want you for anything."

"Everyone I've ever met wanted something from me . . . except Tobry." Tears welled and she turned away hastily.

He adjusted the pocket handkerchief sail and returned to the wheel. "The only Tobry I've heard of came from the fallen House of Lagger."

She nodded. She could not trust herself to speak.

"And?" he prompted.

She told the bitter story in as few words as possible.

"And you had feelings for him?" said Holm.

"I didn't plan to."

"Does anyone ever *plan* to have feelings for another person?" he asked mildly.

Tali felt a fool. "I swore to gain justice for my murdered mother. I didn't have time for anything else . . ."

"But those treacherous feelings crept up on you anyway?" Holm was smirking now.

"I was too busy. I was on a quest."

"So you denied your own feelings."

"All right! Yes, I loved Tobry," she said, sniffling. "But I didn't realise it until it was too late."

"I'm sorry."

She did not want his sorrow or his pity. She wiped her eyes. "Where are you taking me?"

"Won't know until we get out through the heads."

"Why not?"

"Depends what we see. It's been weeks since I was out on the open sea. Things change rapidly at this time of year."

"Which way do you want to go?"

"North towards Bleddimire, of course."

"Why there?" said Tali.

"It's warmer, safer and further from the enemy."

"What if you can't go north?"

"Not west. There's solid ice for a thousand miles."

"South?"

"I hope not. Too much pack ice. Get some rest."

She shivered. "Have you got a spare coat?"

He took a heavy, fur-lined coat from a long, narrow compartment and handed it to her. Tali wrapped it around herself. He closed the cabin door. She hunched in the corner of the two bench seats, behind the table, braced herself against the rolling and closed her eyes, hoping for sleep.

It did not come, and she knew why. She was in a tiny, flimsy piece of wood, on the vast and endless sea, and if anything went wrong she was going to drown. She had nearly drowned once, crossing a lake in the Seethings with Rix and Tobry, and it had left her with a terror of water.

Time drifted; she could not have told whether ten minutes had passed, or an hour. Then suddenly the movement of the vessel changed. Instead of rolling gently it was pitching up and down, as well as rocking back and forth in plank-creaking jerks that kept hurling her off her seat.

She became aware of the wind whistling through the lines and shaking the boat violently. Occasionally a gust would heel it over until the rail almost broke the sea and all she could see were enormous, foaming waves rolling towards them in every direction. They were passing through the heads, out into the open sea.

"Coming up for a bit of weather," Holm said laconically.

The boat righted itself. They passed out through the heads. The wind howled and hurled rain at them like solid pellets. The waves out here seemed twice as high as before. Holm turned north. They crested a wave bigger than any they had encountered before. The wind flung them over, the boat righted itself like a cork, and ahead, covering the sea from east to west, Tali saw it.

A wall of ice, hundreds of feet high.

"Guess we're not going north after all," said Holm.

CHAPTER 21

The night dragged on, one of the most gut-gnawing of Tali's life. Every minute she expected the little craft to founder and plunge to the bottom, or to strike one of the many floes and icebergs that

littered the sea like white confetti. They were larger, more jagged
and more numerous the further south they went.

But whatever else Holm was, he was a master seaman. He handled
the little craft with the delicacy of a surgeon, picking his way between
the bergs and floes without so much as a scrape in the varnish.

As the hours crept by, her need for sleep became a desperate, all-
consuming ache, but the more she tried to sleep the more it eluded
her. Whenever she closed her eyes her head spun until she thought
she was going to throw up. She hunched in the corner with a blanket wrapped around her sea coat and endured the dizziness and
nausea as best she could.

"Drink this," he said, shaking her by the shoulder.

He was holding a steaming metal cup. "What is it?"

"Ginger tea. It'll settle your stomach."

"Stomach isn't the problem. It's my spinning head."

"It'll do your head some good, too."

She took the cup and warmed her cold fingers around it. "How
do you boil water on a wooden boat?"

"There's a stove. We have all the comforts here. It's just like
home."

The boat climbed a monster swell, up and up, revealing terrifying, white-capped waves through the round front window. She
shuddered.

"When I was a slave in Cython, home was a tiny cell carved out
of rock, with a stone bunk, and my only possession was a loincloth."

"But it felt like home?"

"When I was little. When my mother was alive. It was all I
knew."

"Well, there you are. And this boat is my home."

Tali sipped her tea. The sickening motion inside her head eased,
though it did not disappear.

"Would you like breakfast? Bacon? Eggs?"

She salivated. "I . . . don't think I'll risk it."

"You've got to eat something."

He checked all around, lashed the wheel so the boat would run
straight, then went down the ladder, returning with a steaming
saucepan.

"That was quick," said Tali.

"I put it on when I made the tea."

He dropped a knob of butter into the saucepan, spooned in a quarter of a cup of honey and handed her the saucepan and a spoon.

"What is it?" she said, eyeing the grey, buttery mess uneasily.

"Just porridge. It'll put a healthy lining on your stomach – what there is of it."

She sampled it. "It's good!" she exclaimed. "It's – it's wonderful."

He smiled with his eyes. "Compliments, eh? I'll cook for you any day."

The porridge settled her stomach and the honey sent a surge of energy through her. The weakness in her knees retreated a little.

They sailed on. Holm went in and out many times, adjusting the little sail. The hot tea delivered a tingling heat and the wonderful coat kept it in. It was the first time she had been truly warm since Caulderon. She dozed.

"Where *are* we going?" she said, as a watery, haloed sun clawed its way over the horizon. She rubbed her sore eyes.

"South to The Cape, then east along the strait between Hightspall and Suden – if we can manage it."

"Why wouldn't we?"

"Pack ice. We can't go far offshore, but close to shore is equally dangerous."

"Why?" She didn't know much about the sea. "Are there reefs?"

"Yes, and shoals, and dangerous currents, but they're not the main dangers. People are."

"Pirates?" She wasn't entirely sure that Holm wasn't one.

"The chancellor controls the land south of Rutherin to The Cape, and he'll be watching for us. But after we round The Cape, southern Hightspall is now Cythonian territory all the way to Esterlyz."

"What's Esterlyz?"

"The south-eastern corner of Hightspall. Why does the enemy want to kill you, anyway?"

"I told you," Tali muttered, not meeting his eye. These waters were as dangerous to navigate as the ones he was sailing through.

"I don't believe you did."

"Well, I would have thought it was obvious."

"I'm set in my ways and I like things spelled out. Indulge me."

"Because I was the first slave to escape from Cython. They have to punish me and set an example to the other slaves."

"That all?"

"I also know Cython's secrets."

"What, all of them?" he said, grinning.

Was he mocking her? "Enough to be invaluable if the chancellor ever attacks Cython."

"I still don't see why *he* wants you so badly. Didn't he question you about Cython?"

"At length."

"And all the enemy prisoners would have been interrogated. The chancellor's cartographers would have made maps of Cython."

"A map's not as good as a guide!" she blurted, then flushed.

"A guide for what? Leading an army into Cython?" For the first time, Holm seemed off-balance.

"How would I know?" she said lamely.

The muscles along his jaw had gone tight. "What the hell is he thinking?"

"He's preparing the ground; gathering his forces; evaluating all kinds of options." Why was she defending him?

"While the enemy is seizing the ground and destroying our forces."

"Well, he's making alliances . . ." Tali noticed Holm's grim smile. "What's the matter?"

"Why are you apologising for your enemy's failures?"

"I – I don't know. We often talked. The chancellor told me things he can't say to anyone else."

"If he doesn't stop talking and start fighting it'll be too late. Then all the strategies and alliances won't make a jot of difference—"

Holm broke off, adjusted the sail then took the wheel again, rubbing his jaw.

Tali looked out but saw nothing save ice and heavy seas. "Is something wrong?"

"Thought I saw something in the water, way across to port."

"What do you mean, 'to port'?"

He jerked a gnarled thumb to the left. "That way."

In the morning light, the crisscrossing scars on his fingers stood out against the tanned skin. "Have you been tortured?"

He looked down. "They're work scars. From clock springs, mostly."

"I've no idea what a clock spring is."

"It's a long strip of metal – steel or brass – wound into a tight coil. The tension drives the clock. Some clocks, anyway. But when you have to take a coil out, sometimes it snaps open. Bloody business."

"How did you come to be a clockmaker?"

"I failed at something important—" His mouth tightened; he looked away. "The opportunity came up. Always been good with my hands."

He went out and climbed twenty feet up the mast, hanging on with one hand and staring off to port. With every sickening roll of the boat the mast swayed halfway across the sky and she felt sure he was going to be hurled off, to break every bone in his body. Or go over the side and never be seen again.

What would she do if he went into the water? How would she get him out? In her present state she would not have a hope.

Tali imagined being trapped on a boat she had no idea how to sail, frantically trying to work the sail and the rudder without having any idea what she was doing, fighting the wind and the waves at the same time ... Then the slow, sickening roll, the monstrous seas coming over the side and the little vessel foundering and carrying her down with it, the icy water flooding into her lungs—

Holm hit the deck with a thump, burst in and spun the wheel.

"What's the matter?" cried Tali.

"Shell racers."

"What are shell racers?"

"Long, low racing craft, rowed by four oarsmen. With a scrap of sail they're faster than anything in the water, downwind. And infinitely manoeuvrable. They can go anywhere, even upwind."

"I wouldn't want to be out in these seas on a little rowing boat."

"Nor I," said Holm. "I've rowed them. They break up too easily."

"What happens if they break up?"

"Go in water this cold and there's only one minute to get you out. Beyond a minute, you die." He closed his eyes for a moment, then opened them again, studying her face. "But the massive reward the chancellor will be offering for you is worth any risk."

And Tali still had no idea what Holm wanted from her.

He paused, then went on, slowly, "Time was when I would have thought the same. I was a great risk taker when I was young ... though not all of them came off."

Tali wasn't sure how to interpret that. "What do we do when they catch us?"

"Can you shoot a bow and arrow?"

"No."

"But you do know how to fight?"

"Only with my hands."

"How good are you?"

"Not good enough to beat armed men."

CHAPTER 22

"Not long now," said Rix, frowning at the immense range that ran across their path. "Garramide is up there."

It was raining again. Ten days had passed since they fled Caulderon, and it had snowed or rained every day. Ten days of travelling by night through the wildest country he could find, constantly looking behind, expecting his enemies to be there. Ten days of covering their tracks; ten days of practising with Maloch left-handed until he burst the blisters on his palm over and again. He would never be as good as he had been with his right hand, but he had to be good enough to beat most swordsmen.

The escarpment was covered in thick forest woven with vines and from this vantage point it blocked out half the sky. Inside the forest, the ground, the rocks and fallen trees were carpeted in moss, vivid green in the dull light. Water ran out of the slope in a dozen places, forming little, trickling rivulets only a foot across.

"It looks awfully steep. And wet," said Glynnie.

"It's rainforest."

"Rainforest?"

"*Temperate* rainforest. It rains here two hundred days a year, I've heard. And snows for fifty."

"How do we get up?"

"There's a road of sorts up the eastern end. They can haul carts up in dry weather, but when it's wet, or deep in snow as it is now, the only way up is on foot. But we can't go that way. Their sentinels would see us hours before we got there."

"But if Garramide is yours—"

"It's *legally* mine – but since the war began, anything could have happened."

"So how do *we* get up?"

"According to the letter my great-aunt wrote me before she died, there's a secret way up the western end. But we'll have to set the horses free. It's too steep for them."

"What's up there?"

"A volcanic plateau, four thousand feet high."

"Sounds miserably cold," said Glynnie.

"It has hard winters, to be sure," said Rix, "but fertile soil and plenty of rain. There's a good living to be had. More importantly, with mountains on three sides and this escarpment on the fourth, it's easily defended."

They dismounted, set the horses free and turned to the slope. "It's as high as a mountain," muttered Glynnie. "This is going to take a week."

"At least half a day, I'm told, so we'd better get going."

"It's desolate," said Glynnie, when they reached the top in the early afternoon and scaled a rocky hilltop to get a better view.

The plateau was about four miles long by two wide, undulating farmland covered in snow. She made out several manors and half a dozen villages. Black, ice-sheathed mountains defended the far sides.

"Pretty country though," said Rix. "And the most beautiful fortress I've ever seen. One of the strongest, too," he added approvingly.

Fortress Garramide was only a few hundred yards away. It had been built on a rocky hill at the edge of the plateau, an outcrop cliffed on two sides and surrounded by a thirty-foot-high wall that must have enclosed forty acres. Every fifty yards along the wall was a watchtower.

"The wall is eight feet thick at the top, and solid stone all the way through," he recalled.

"It's enormous," said Glynnie.

The inner fortress arose from the highest point of the hill and contained a great, stepped castle built from golden stone and topped with five towers, four at the corners and a larger one in the centre, surmounted by copper-clad domes tarnished to a rusty green. A tall, narrow tower behind the others had no dome, and neither did a separate tower immediately behind the gates. It ended in a flat war platform a hundred feet up, surrounded by walls with arrow slits through them.

He studied the defences, assessing the fortress's strengths and weaknesses. "Water should never be a problem with all the rain here. If they've got enough cisterns, they could store enough for a thousand people, for a year."

"Food might be."

"There's a lot of land inside the walls, and as long as they keep the barns well stacked with hay, they could feed their stock through a month's long siege. There's only one problem I see—"

"The walls are too long," said Glynnie. "It'd take an army to defend them."

She constantly surprised him. "Precisely." He studied the sky, which was a billowing black in the south. "Looks like snow, and lots of it. We'd better move."

It was heavily overcast by the time they reached the gates of Garramide, and snow was falling, though not thickly enough to disguise the stench, nor the mess of blood and rotting entrails protruding through the crust of last night's snow.

"What the blazes is going on?" said Rix, covering his nose. "Has the enemy beaten us here as well?"

"Hooves," said Glynnie, who had ventured closer. "And horns. Looks like they do their butchering here."

"Outside the main gates of *my* fortress?" cried Rix.

Striding to the gates, he hammered on them with the hilt of his sword. "Garramide, open to your lord."

A filthy, bewhiskered fellow opened a viewing flap. "Who the hell are you?"

"I'm Rixium Ricinus and I've come to claim my estate. Open the gates."

"The boy lordling," sneered the guard. He turned away, saying, "Get Arkyz." He turned back, grinning, to reveal a mouth full of rotten teeth. "Garramide ain't yours any more, kid. Clear out."

Rix did not look prepossessing. In his dirty, ragged coat and mud-caked pants, he could have been any miserable vagabond on the road, though he was bigger than most. "Who's in charge here?" he said evenly.

When the guard's gaze fell upon Rix's grey hand, he snorted mucus from his nose and grey slime from his mouth. "Arkyz Leatherhead, and he chops trespassers up into little bits and dumps them in the ditch."

"Not any more," said Rix.

He reached in, caught the guard by the throat and dragged him through the flap, tearing the shirt off his back. Hauling him one-handed to the rotting remains, Rix dumped him in a half-frozen heap of entrails.

"Run for your life. If you're still on the plateau in an hour, I'll cut you into little pieces and feed you to the crows."

"Who's Arkyz Leatherhead?" Glynnie said quietly.

"A murdering, raping bandit. He's been terrorising these mountains for years with a gang of cutthroats, preying on the weak and the helpless."

"What's he doing here?"

"He must've broken in and seized Garramide after the war began. Before House Ricinus fell, he wouldn't have dared."

Rix was walking back to the gate when Glynnie shrieked, "Look out!"

The guard was racing towards him, swinging a double-edged knife. Rix swayed out of its way, allowing the man to lumber past. He skidded to a stop outside the gates and came racing back. Rix lazily avoided another couple of killing blows then, without seeming to move, punched the guard's teeth down his throat. He was driven three yards through the air, landed hard, rolled over and vomited up his shattered teeth onto the boots of the man who had thrust the gates wide.

A man so huge that beside him Rix looked like a pup.

"Rix, no," whispered Glynnie.

I can't do this, Rix thought. I've met my match and I'm going to die.

Arkyz Leatherhead was a vast slab of beef, near to seven feet tall and a yard across the shoulders, with long, swinging arms that came down past his knees. He might have been forty, and looked as though he had spent every minute of that time outdoors, for his hairless skin was as coarse and leathery as cowhide. The top of his bald head, so flat that it might have been sawn off, was covered in freckles and black moles.

Leatherhead was clad in horsehide – a thick leather jerkin with the hair on, laced together across his boulder chest with leather thongs as thick as Rix's little finger, and baggy leather knee britches. Behind him, grinning and rubbing their grimy hands together, were twenty of the filthiest and foulest ruffians Rix had ever seen.

"Lord Deadhand!" Leatherhead said in a rumble so deep that loose planks in the gate rattled. "Come forward and die." His meaty hands dropped onto the hilts of twin swords. "Or run like a dog. I'll give you five minutes to get to your kennel, hur, hur!"

He grinned at his feeble wit and looked back to his men for approval. They roared, clapped their thighs and stamped their feet.

Rix drew Maloch, but as he raised the sword his dead right hand throbbed. Despite all the practice, he wasn't sure he could beat this giant left-handed, unless Leatherhead's great size made him slow.

Leatherhead's matched swords were the longest Rix had ever seen, a handspan longer than his own. With his enormous height and unusually long arms, Leatherhead's reach was a good two feet more than Rix's – with either hand.

Then, as Leatherhead slashed with his twin swords and Rix back-pedalled desperately, he knew he was in diabolical danger. The brute was just as good with his left hand as with the right, capable of using both at once, and fast as well.

Rix wasn't even sure he could have beaten him with his right hand.

He ducked and the blades howled over his head, intersecting like a pair of scissors and clipping off a lock of his black hair. Glynnie gasped. Rix lunged and hacked at Leatherhead's left kneecap but it wasn't there – he'd anticipated the stroke and moved too quickly. Despite his age, he was fast and experienced. By the way he fought, he must have been in hundreds of fights. And won them all.

Leatherhead drew back, held a sword out to either side, then paused. But he wasn't watching Rix. He was staring at Glynnie and a slow smile cracked his beefy face.

"Spoils o' war, girlie."

Rix's skin crawled. Why had he brought her here? She would have been better off as a prisoner in Caulderon than in the hands of these scum. And that's where she was going to end up, for he was losing hope of beating Leatherhead.

"Run, Glynnie."

Glynnie let out a little, muffled cry, but did not back away. The lesson in courage stiffened Rix's own. He had to beat Leatherhead so convincingly that none of the followers would dare take him on. And he had to do it soon.

He feinted to the left, then struck at Leatherhead's left hand. Leatherhead slipped it aside, hacked at Rix's throat, and he felt his coat collar give as the tip of the blade cut through it.

The men behind Leatherhead clapped and jeered. Rix raised his sword and swung it with all his strength, down at his opponent's mole-covered skull. Again Leatherhead anticipated the blow and danced away, and Maloch struck a rock in a shower of sparks. Rix needed to be closer, but when his opponent had a longer reach and a sword in each hand, going in close was a sure way to die.

He backpedalled, checking the blade. Maloch was not a heavy weapon, but the titane blade must have been supremely well forged, for it had not been damaged striking the rock – nor previously, when the chancellor's captain had hacked through Rix's wrist and deep into a flagstone.

They matched strokes for several minutes, by which time his legs were tiring. Fighting was the hardest work anyone could do and the exhausting climb up the escarpment had taken its toll. The longer they fought, the more the balance would tip.

Yet he could not rely on Maloch to save him. Its protection was against magery, not might . . .

Wait – if he could not beat the man, could he beat his weapons?

It was a desperate gamble. If he was wrong, if he damaged Maloch, he would die. But it was the only hope he had. He backpedalled again, luring Leatherhead forwards. The man was enormously strong but had no subtlety; he used the same few strokes over and again.

Rix waited until Leatherhead struck another of those scissoring double blows, then swung Maloch into the path of the swords. It missed his opponent's left-hand blade by a whisker and struck the right blade side-on, near the hilt.

Maloch rang like a tower bell. A hot shock passed up Rix's arm and for an awful second he thought his own blade was going to shatter. There was a screech of metal and a red-hot spray that spattered Leatherhead's jerkin and pants, then Maloch sheared through the other blade, which was hurled sideways to embed itself in the muddy snow.

Leatherhead looked down uncomprehendingly at the semi-molten hilt, then dropped it and began to claw at his chest, trying to tear off the smoking jerkin. But the thick leather thongs did not give, and now smoke was issuing from within. The spray of molten metal had burned through the leather, only to be trapped against Leatherhead's skin.

His guard was down, and Rix was not one to miss an opportunity. He sprang forwards and, with a stroke of surgical accuracy, lifted Leatherhead's pumpkin-sized head off his stump of a neck and sent it rolling down the slope to the piled offal. His hands were still clawing at his smouldering chest when his blood-drenched body hit the ground.

Rix fixed his gaze on the goggling brutes in the gateway, then put his right boot on Leatherhead's chest and raised Maloch high.

"I am Rixium Deadhand, heir to Garramide," he said in a voice that could have been heard at the top of the highest dome of the fortress. He deliberately did not mention the tainted name, Ricinus. "This sword, Maloch, came to me in direct line from my ancestor – the First Hero, Axil Grandys, who built this fortress."

He paused to allow that to sink in. Grandys was a legend, the Founding Hero, and the connection meant that any challenge to Rix was a challenge to the legitimacy of Grandys himself. At least, Rix hoped so, though with brainless thugs like these, you couldn't always tell.

"Garramide is mine and I claim my inheritance. If any here challenge my claim, speak now – *and die*."

CHAPTER 23

The outlaws shuffled their filthy feet, staring at Maloch, and Rix's grey right hand, and the body of their fallen leader, as if they could not comprehend it. No one spoke. No one met his eyes.

There were more than forty of them now, and despite that some were clearly drunk, and others barefoot and only armed with knives, they were a formidable force.

Behind them, through the gate, the fortress servants were gathering, at least a hundred of them. Quite a few were armed, and Rix saw a dawning hope in their eyes. Though the fall of House Ricinus had damaged his reputation, the old dame they'd loved had named him her heir and given him the sword, and he could hardly be as bad as these outlaws. Rix saw no uniformed guards, though, and that was a worry. Presumably Leatherhead had killed them when he'd attacked the fortress. Rix had to have guards, and plenty of them. The fortress could not be defended without them.

What would the outlaws do? If they rushed him, he might kill three or four before they overwhelmed and killed him, but kill him they would. But would they attack? They seemed like common thugs to Rix; no one had the look of a leader. It wasn't surprising –

men like Leatherhead kept order with brutish violence and did not encourage rivals.

"What are you going to do?" said Rix quietly, so they had to strain forwards to hear. He raised Maloch. "No one bearing this sword – *Axil Grandys' enchanted sword* – has ever been beaten in battle."

"Deadhand's just one man," said a toothless, brawny thug at the front. "We can take him." He reached for the sword sheathed at his hip.

Rix leapt forwards and pressed Maloch's tip against the man's throat. Blood threaded a path down his dirty neck. "Touch your weapon and you die."

The thug choked. He couldn't speak; the tip was pressing into his voicebox. His hand froze in mid-air, inches above the hilt. Rix lowered Maloch, cut the thongs of the man's sheath and it fell to the ground. He forced him backwards to the gate, then kicked the sheath back to Glynnie, who drew the sword.

"When we escaped from Caulderon," said Rix, "I killed six men with my bare hands – plus a whole pack of hyena shifters."

He paused to let that sink in. Every eye was on his dead hand.

"And even if you could beat me, where can you go in midwinter? The fortress is armed against you now; try to retake it and you will die."

The thugs turned, saw the great line of armed servants, turned back to Rix. "But we're at war," said Rix, "and I need men who can fight, so I'll make you an offer. Swear to serve and obey me, and I'll take you on – and any raids we make against the enemy, you get a share of the plunder."

The servants stared at one another, then there was a furious muttering among them. They weren't happy. Perhaps they were wondering if Rix would be any better than Leatherhead.

"But be warned!" Rix said in a booming voice. "I intend to run Garramide as my great-aunt ran it. You will live like men, not pigs, and any violence against the people of this household will be punished by exile – or death. There will be no more warnings. Well? Do you swear to serve me and follow the laws of the fortress, on pain of death?"

There was some sullen nodding among Leatherhead's men, a few quiet affirmations, some whispered oaths.

"Aloud!" cried Rix, brandishing Maloch. "On your knees."

They went to their knees in the freezing mud and swore.

Rix gestured to them to rise. As he studied the faces, trying to take their measure, it occurred to Rix that Glynnie was still at risk.

He gestured behind him and she came to his side. "Glynnie will be in charge of my household. You will obey her as you do me."

One of the outlaws, a big lout of a man, round-faced, with a beard as coarse as the bristles of a boar, sniggered and made a vulgar gesture.

Rix leapt forwards and struck the man down with the flat of his sword. "Get off my land."

"But Deadhand, this is my home," whined the lout, struggling to his knees. "I've lived here all my life."

"Liar!" yelled a stocky maid whose yellow hair hung in a single braid to her waist. "You slaughtered your way in last week."

"No warnings, I said," said Rix. "You've got ten minutes to be gone. After an hour, I'm giving the hunting dogs your scent and setting them loose."

The man looked vainly for help among his fellows, then trudged in through the gates. Rix studied the faces before him, one by one. None of the outlaws met his gaze.

"Anyone else disagree with my orders?"

No one spoke.

"I asked a question," Rix said, lowering his voice so they would have to strain to hear. "As the master of Garramide, I expect instant and total obedience. Does anyone disagree with my orders?"

"No, Lord Deadhand," they said in a ragged chorus.

"Get this muck cleared away." The sweep of his hand included both the offal and Leatherhead. "Then go to the bathing house and scrub yourselves clean. I'll have no filth in this house."

The man Rix had struck down reappeared with a thin, shrew-faced woman who was whacking him with a knobbly walking stick.

"Stupid, useless lump," she shrilled. "Why I put up with you I'll never know." She came up to Rix, put on a sickly smile that did not approach her eyes, curtsied clumsily and said, "He's a fool, Lord.

Never opens his mouth but to vomit out his stupidity, but he don't mean it. He's a good man, deep down. And we don't got nowhere to go, Lord. Please—"

Momentarily, Rix's heart softened at the appeal, and against his better judgement he was considering relenting when Glynnie spoke.

"He's rotten all the way through, and you're no better. Get going."

"You little bitch," cried the shrew-faced woman. "I'm not taking orders from a half-grown scrag I could break over my knee." She launched herself at Glynnie, hissing and spitting.

Glynnie sprang forwards but Rix thrust his sword between them. "Go, or your man joins Leatherhead – in two pieces."

"Couldn't care less if he does," muttered the shrew-faced woman.

She gave Rix a hard glare, and Glynnie a look of fire and brimstone, then resumed belabouring her man about the shoulders, driving him down the road. But before they turned the corner she looked back, and Rix could have sworn he saw a grin of triumph. It troubled him, momentarily. Then they were gone and he put her out of mind.

Rix gestured with his sword towards the offal. Men ran to clean it up with shovels and buckets.

"You shouldn't have stopped me," said Glynnie quietly. "It's bound to cause trouble now."

"They won't be back," said Rix.

"Maybe not, but everyone in the fortress saw you interfere to protect me. Now they'll think I'm a helpless girl put in a place I don't belong. That the only authority I have comes from you—"

"If they challenge my authority I'll put them out the door."

"They won't challenge *your* authority, Rix. But they'll undermine me at every turn, and—"

"Let's worry about that when it happens. I've got a million things to do and I haven't even gone through the gates."

Before they could pass inside a woman came hurtling out, howling like a mad thing. She wore an embroidered white blouse, a brightly patterned skirt, and despite the cold her arms and feet were bare.

Tall, she was, very tall, with a mass of chestnut hair, thick and wavy and wild, a full mouth, white teeth bared in a rictus of pain, and a proud, arching nose. She shot past Rix and Glynnie and threw herself onto the headless body of Arkyz Leatherhead, embracing it and smearing his blood all over herself.

She let out a howl of anguish, sprang up, looking around wildly, then plunged down the slope to the remains of the offal heap, where his head lay. The woman picked it up, kissed his bloody mouth then, cradling the dripping head against her bosom, lurched back to the body and fitted the head in place. Letting out another savage moan, she lay full length on the body, embracing it again, then rose and rent her garments, baring herself to the waist.

She stalked up to Rix, her full skirts swishing. She must have been thirty-five, and was by no means a beautiful woman, but even in her bloodstained fury, she was a majestic one.

"Who are you?" he said.

"I am Blathy."

Rix knew her by reputation. "Leatherhead's long-time mistress," he said quietly to Glynnie, "and said to be just as bad." Rix met Blathy's eye. "What do you want?"

"You killed my man. I demand the blood-price."

"Blood-price isn't payable for self-defence."

"My man was defending his hearth. His death is murder."

"He took Garramide by force. I'm the legitimate heir—"

"Garramide belonged to Arkyz by right of might."

"He's dead," said Rix, "and the fortress is mine, by right *and* by might. Begone." He raised the bloody sword.

She ignored the blade. Blathy was no coward. "I won't go, and you can't compel me."

"I'll carry you to the edge of the escarpment and dump you over if I have to," said Rix.

"According to the founding charter of Garramide, the widow of the old lord must be given an apartment here for as long as she cares to stay. If the new lord does not make such provision, his lordship is void."

"What a load of rubbish," said Glynnie. "You made that up."

Blathy looked down at Glynnie, who was a head shorter, then up again, dismissing her. "Ask Porfry."

"And Porfry is?" said Rix.

"Keeper of the Records."

Without taking another look at her dead man, nor pulling her blouse together over her naked chest, Blathy stormed in through the gate.

He looked down to see Glynnie scowling at him. "What have I done now?"

"You're going to regret not casting her out," said Glynnie.

"She's just lost her man."

"It doesn't make her any less of a viper, and now you've given her the freedom of your house."

"She'll take another man within a fortnight, and once she does I'll see her gone."

"What if she doesn't?"

"I don't follow."

"There are women who will only have one man, and if they lose him they never take another. I think Blathy is such a woman. You've got to get rid of her."

"I took a vow to protect vulnerable women. I can't cast her out in the middle of a war, in mid-winter."

"She's no more vulnerable than you are," Glynnie said furiously. "And . . . and you'd better watch out. She'll be after you next."

"You just said she'd never take another man. You're rambling, Glynnie."

"And you're stupid. You can't see what's in front of your own face."

Rix's wrist gave an agonising throb. He looked up at the brooding sky, and the fortress he must make his own against all opposition, then prepare it for an enemy attack that was bound to come before he was ready. Suddenly he felt exhausted, and unaccountably irritable.

"What makes you, a girl of seventeen who's lived all her life in one great house, so wise about the ways of the world?"

It was a stupid thing to say, for all kinds of reasons. The great houses were miniatures of the world, with all its lessons in close-up.

She sprang away as though he'd slapped her, rubbing her cheeks with her hands. "I'll never be anything but a maidservant to you. Someone to be dumped on the first doorstep, and never to be taken seriously. Never to be treated like a woman."

"Can we talk about this later?" said Rix. "I'm—"

"Don't bother, Lord Deadhand."

CHAPTER 24

Swelt, the castellan of Garramide for the past thirty years, was five feet high and four feet wide, and had the appearance of as greedy a man as ever lived. From the middle of his triple chins bulged a goitre the size of a melon, his fingers were so fat that he could not bend them around his spoon, and his eyes were little black dots swimming in seas of lard.

But appearances were deceptive. Rix's great-aunt, a clever and perceptive woman, had trusted Swelt implicitly and by letter had recommended him to Rix before her death.

Swelt was also the most well organised man Rix had yet encountered. Swelt had every detail of the fortress, its staff and its resources at his fingertips.

"You want a healer for *that*?" said Swelt, frowning at Rix's dead hand and shaking his head.

"Surely Garramide has a healer," said Rix.

"We have three – Oosta and her two assistants. And some of the men can poultice an infected wound, or saw off a smashed limb at need. But there's no one here who can help you with a mage-grown member."

"Does no one in Garramide know magery? No one at all?"

"I dabble. And Blathy can work a fine curse when she needs to – only against her enemies, though, and those who have injured her ..." Swelt gave Rix an assessing glance. "But as for healing magery ... well, there's only the witch-woman, Astatin, though I wouldn't trust a healthy member with her, much less an ailing one."

Swelt's gaze skidded off Rix's grey hand. "You'd need to go to Rebroff or Swire for that."

"How far are they from here?" said Rix, whose knowledge of the geography of the area was patchy.

"In dry weather, on a fast horse, you can reach Swire, in Lakeland, in three hard days' riding, and Rebroff a few hours longer. But in winter, with rain and snow—" Swelt inflated his quivering cheeks, "— you might not do it in a week."

"Then I'll have to put up with it," said Rix. "I can't waste a day on a hope that's probably forlorn, much less a fortnight there and back. Now, to business."

"Indeed. Was it wise to take on Leatherhead's men, after all they've done here? It hasn't endeared you to the servants."

"To defend Garramide I've got to have experienced fighters. There was no other way to get them in a hurry."

"After all they've done here you'll have to work damn hard to get the people on side. And make sure your thugs keep to their barracks."

"I meant what I said," said Rix. "I plan to run Garramide the way my great-aunt did. I expect you to advise me on that."

"I will," said Swelt. "What are you going to do about Blathy?"

"She said she was entitled to remain in Garramide. Is that correct? Or should I ask Porfry?"

"I wouldn't bother."

"Why not?"

"He's a fanatical Herovian. He sees you as an upstart who has just discovered his true heritage and plans on using it to his advantage."

"You don't like him?"

"His first loyalty isn't to Garramide," Swelt said simply.

Rix put that aside for later. "You tell me, then."

"Blathy quoted the founding charter correctly – the widow of the previous lord is entitled to remain here ..."

"But?"

"Two points." Swelt studied his sausage-like fingers. "The intent of the provision was to provide for the widow of a *legitimate* lord – not a passing bandit who seized Garramide by killing everyone who opposed him."

"And the second point?"

"In law, before becoming a widow, it's necessary to be a wife. Mistresses don't count."

"So I can get rid of her . . ."

"Why do you hesitate?"

"It feels like a dishonourable thing to do . . . even knowing that she's hardly better than Leatherhead."

"Honour can be taken too far, Rixium."

"The fall of House Ricinus has given me a new appreciation of its value," Rix said drily.

"If you want to take the place of your great-aunt, you'll have to take the hard decisions."

"I'll think on it. What's the state of the fortress?"

"You tell me. You've just spent all afternoon inspecting it."

"The defences are in good condition, apart from the gate itself. I've ordered the carpenters and masons to begin strengthening it in the morning. But I wasn't talking about the walls."

"Depends what you plan to use Garramide for," said Swelt.

"I didn't come here to hide."

"I'm pleased to hear it. Why did you come?"

"To fight for my country. I'm going to raise a small army and harry the enemy every way I can." Rix studied Swelt's round face, expecting him to demur. He did not have the look of a fighter.

Again Swelt surprised him. "Your great-aunt would have been proud."

"It'll put Garramide in danger," said Rix.

"As one of the oldest Herovian houses in the land, built by Grandys himself, Garramide is already threatened. We can either fight, and probably lose, or hide like craven cowards and gain another few months. Either way, Lyf is coming." The tiny eyes drifted around the room, then settled on Rix again. "But you've just shortened the time by weeks."

"I don't follow."

"You sent Tordy and his wife away with nothing."

Rix frowned. Glynnie had said the same thing, but he was so tired he could not think straight. "Yes?"

"Tordy's a moron, but his wife is stiletto-sharp, and she'll sell the news for a high price."

A throbbing pain in Rix's belly matched the agony in his wrist.

"In two or three days," said Swelt, "Lyf will know where you've gone to ground, and he'll come after you."

"How long have I got?"

"Perhaps a fortnight." Swelt's gaze drifted back and forth across Rix before settling on his face.

"Where's the best place to cut them off?" said Rix, cursing his poor judgement.

"Tordy's been hunting in the rainforest all his life. You'll *never* find them."

"Damn! Well, give me your report."

Swelt produced a set of hand-written inventories which he passed to Rix, then proceeded to recite them word for word and number for number – the entire contents of the pantries, larders and cellar, the number and state of the arms in the armoury, the kinds and numbers of the beasts grazing in the outer yard and on the many farms.

"Enough!" cried Rix, his eyes glazing at the thought of so much book learning. "Just give me the gist."

"Which particular gist would that be, Rixium?"

"What we have plenty of for a siege, what we lack, where our strengths and weaknesses lie, the state of the treasury—"

"Ah," said Swelt. "The treasury."

"What about it?"

"It was most handsomely endowed when your great-aunt died, but since then . . ." Swelt spread his pudgy hands.

"You're the damned castellan," Rix said savagely. "You're the man in charge."

"I was when your great-aunt was alive. But after you inherited . . ." Swelt peeled off a piece of torn thumbnail.

"Get on with it!" cried Rix, the pain in his wrist growing by the second.

"You weren't of age, and Lady Ricinus did not entrust the job to me." There was a hint of bitterness in his voice. "She sent in a factor of her own, a fellow called Scunlees . . ."

The name meant nothing to Rix. His mother had employed dozens of factors. "And?"

"Scunlees' instructions weren't to manage your estate, but to strip it."

Rix studied Swelt, wondering if he were lying and had stolen the treasury for himself. But he did not think so. It fitted too well.

"Go on," he said.

"It appears that the stories about House Ricinus's vast wealth were exaggerated, Rixium ... but I don't think that comes as news to you."

"It doesn't," Rix said slowly. "Mother spent staggering sums on bribes to get us into the First Circle of families. And Father squandered an even greater amount training and equipping the Third Army."

"An army that was wiped out in the first hours of the invasion of Caulderon."

Rix shook his head, trying to clear his memories of that horror. "By the time of the Honouring we were on the brink of bankruptcy. Tell me the worst," he said grimly.

"The treasury is almost bare," said Swelt. "Had I not hidden part of it, Scunlees would have taken every last *chalt*. And he sold half the flocks and stores a month ago; more than we could afford to lose."

"Where is the bastard?" Rix said furiously. "I'll wring his miserable neck."

"When the news came of House Ricinus's fall he was gone within the hour – with everything he could cram into his saddlebags. The great dame would weep."

"I don't remember her being the weeping sort," said Rix.

"Just an expression," said Swelt. "She would have nailed his head to the barn door."

"Go on with your gist. What about men to man the walls?"

"With the fortress servants, the labourers from our farms and stables, the bakers and brewers, masons and smiths and so forth, we can muster three hundred men at need. Though only a handful are experienced fighters."

"Plus Leatherhead's fifty. I'll knock them into line and start training your folk in the morning. How many other people are there?"

"Another few hundred. Plus children, nursing mothers and pensioners."

"That's a lot of mouths."

"We've stores in the fortress to withstand a siege, though they won't last for months. And if winter gets any harder we'll have to feed half the serfs on the plateau, or see them starve."

"We won't see them starve," said Rix. "We'll all tighten our belts." His eyes slipped to Swelt's astounding middle.

"Some more than others," Swelt said drily, though Rix sensed approval. "Your great-aunt would have said the same."

"And after Scunlees was gone?"

"Leatherhead turned up the next day. He knows these mountains – he's been terrorising them for a decade. He stormed the gates, hacked the guards to death and burst in. Within a day he had turned this lovely old fortress into a slaughterhouse, a tavern and a brothel."

"What's your view of his men? They're experienced fighters and I need all I can get."

"A third of them are worthless scum who'd cut your throat for a pair of boots—"

"But I dare say they'll follow if I beat them into line."

"I dare say they will – if you prove you're as tough as Leatherhead. And if Garramide is attacked, they'll fight for it, since they've nowhere else to go." Swelt shook his head. "The rest are recent recruits, men who lost everything when the war began and had no choice. I expect you can make something of them – with the right leadership."

That word again. "I'm not sure leadership is my strong point." Rix hadn't even succeeded with Glynnie. He lowered his head into his hands.

"Then you'd better learn fast. No one else can do it."

"If I lead, will you follow?"

Swelt snorted. "I loved the old dame I served for thirty years, and she thought highly of you. I'll do my best for you, Rixium, and so will most of the household, but be warned. You have enemies here, and they'll do everything they can to bring you down."

"I grew up in an adder's nest; I think I can handle—"

"It's one thing to know your enemies. It's entirely another when you can't tell who's holding a dagger behind their back."

"Perhaps even you?" Rix asked with a quirk of an eyebrow.

"You don't know me either."

"I wasn't allowed to manage my inheritance a year ago, but I made proper enquiries about my castellan."

"Might I ask what they reported?" said Swelt, not entirely hiding his anxiety.

"A gross and greedy man at the dinner table." Rix met Swelt's eye. "But honest, and fiercely loyal to Garramide and the old dame."

"So I am. But I don't give my loyalty to fools or knaves."

"And I am?" said Rix.

"More fool than knave, since you ask. We'll obey your orders, Rixium, because you're the lord of Garramide and we believe in fighting for our house and our country. But you'll have to *earn* our loyalty – and you come with a handicap."

"The evil reputation of House Ricinus," said Rix.

"Just so."

The pain was back, worse than ever. How could any man over-come such a disadvantage?

"On the other hand," said Swelt, "at a blow you've freed us from a vicious tyrant, and the old household thanks you for that. You've made a good start – apart from one decision . . ."

"What's that?"

"The maidservant you put in charge of the household servants. It was a mistake to raise her above her station. Only anger and resentment can come of it."

"Glynnie has many fine qualities."

"I don't doubt it, and her green eyes and charming smile not the least of them. But the servants will never accept her orders. It's quite impossible."

"They accept mine."

"You're the heir, and from birth you were trained to command. Glynnie has no right, and it shows. Persist in this decision, Rixium, and you'll lose far more than you hope to gain from her . . . what-ever that may be."

CHAPTER 25

"I can see them now," called Tali. "Five shell racers. Closing in fast." She jabbed her finger behind the boat and around to port, indicating their positions.

She was on deck, hanging onto a rope, enveloped in her oilskin sea coat and trousers, and wearing rubber-coated boots that came up to her knees. The wind blew icy spray in her face, but the porridge had given her a satisfying feeling of fullness and she felt alive for the first time since leaving Caulderon.

Tali looked forwards, to the scattered floes and the great ice cliffs in the distance, and shuddered. How could one old man, no matter how wily, outwit five shell racers and their combined crew of twenty men?

Holm put up a bigger sail and with the wind behind them his boat was hurtling through the water, rising up each swell then crashing down in fusillades of spray. But the shell racers were faster. In ten or fifteen minutes they would come alongside, and it would be over.

"They'll try to shoot me," said Holm, as if he had heard her thoughts. He had lashed the wheel and was standing in the cabin doorway.

"Wouldn't that send the boat out of control?"

He shook his head. "Wind's steady behind us. We could sail on for a good while."

"Have you got a plan?"

"Get among the icebergs before they catch us."

"How will that help?"

"It's tricky sailing in there. The winds are constantly shifting and there'll be broken ice in the water, barely visible. If a shell racer hits a chunk of ice at speed, it goes straight to the bottom."

"So will we," said Tali.

"I built this boat. It can take a hell of a lot more than their cockle-shell racers can. And we're a lot higher in the water. We can see what's ahead."

But they're far more manoeuvrable, she thought. And they can go upwind.

The shell racers were only a few hundred yards behind now, the icebergs about the same distance ahead.

"What are you going to do once we get among them?" said Tali.

"Take advantage of what comes up."

Frustrating man! "What do you think will come up?"

"How would I know? I didn't expect this."

"What did you expect?"

"That we'd sail merrily north, out to sea where the pursuit would never find us, sipping our afternoon tea and reciting odes to the creeping ice."

"There's no need to be sarcastic."

"Me?" He grinned.

He went inside. Tali watched the shell racers, her heart beating erratically, now racing, now creeping. Two of the racers were heading out to the left, another two to the right, while the fifth continued directly behind them.

"Looks like they're planning to close around us and attack together," she said over her shoulder.

"That's how I'd do it," said Holm, adjusting the sail and putting up another, smaller one.

It gained them a little more speed, but not enough. Something went *whirr-click*. She looked around and he was holding a small crossbow.

"Don't suppose you've fired one of these?"

"Oddly enough, the enemy don't hand them out to their slaves," said Tali.

"Making jokes now," said Holm. "You have improved." He handed her the weapon. "Unlike an ordinary bow, any fool can shoot straight with a crossbow."

"Any fool?"

"No insult intended, but it takes hundreds of hours of practice to be any good with a true bow."

He showed her how to work the crank, load the quarrels and use the sights, and made her practise until she could load and crank back the bow in thirty seconds.

"Don't try anything fancy. Just aim for the middle of the man's chest."

"Just like that?"

"It's him or you, Tali, so yes, just like that. But no further than thirty yards away – if you shoot, you have to hit."

Clearly, Holm wasn't planning to sell her to the chancellor, but who he was and what he really wanted was no clearer. Tali sighted on the leading man in the racer behind them, felt an inner squirm, and lowered the crossbow. Could she shoot a man dead, just like that?

Remembering her mother's murder, and that sickening reliving of her great-great-grandmother's death, she knew there was no choice. If they caught her, the chancellor would do the same to her. He might do it reluctantly, and perhaps with regret, but nothing would stop him from taking the master pearl that could win the war. Or lose Hightspall forever, if Lyf got it.

The racers were only a hundred yards away when she felt a chilly blast of wind. They were flashing past a white mountain, a cracked and cratered iceberg towering as high as the twisted spire on top of Rix's tower in Palace Ricinus.

The boat heeled so violently that Tali was thrown off her feet and went sliding towards the side, the cocked crossbow spinning ahead of her. If it went off . . .

Snap, thud, crash!

"What the hell are you doing?" roared Holm, who was fighting the wheel.

Tali struck the side, whacking her head on a timber rib. Holm raced out but did not look her way; he was heaving on the lines, adjusting the sails. He ran in, spun the wheel, then called over his shoulder, "You all right?"

She got up, rubbing her head, picked up the crossbow and lurched across the deck. Ahead was a maze of icebergs, hundreds of them, ranging from monsters the size of a small town down to berglets no bigger than a house, and pancake floes that only stood a few inches out of the water. How was Holm going to manoeuvre through all that?

Tali went into the cabin. "What happened?"

He indicated a gouge in the brass wheel. "Your bolt glanced off the wheel and struck the porridge pot amidships. I'm afraid it's gone down with all hands."

The saucepan, which Tali had left on the bench, was crumpled on the side facing her and had a neat hole through it.

"Sorry. Was thrown off my feet. Why did the boat heel over that way?"

"Sudden wind shift," said Holm. "Among the bergs, the wind can come from any direction, and there's no predicting it. Reload your bow. You're going to need it."

She did so, hastily.

"This time, *hang on*," said Holm.

They shot through a narrow gap between two icebergs. The sides matched so well that Tali wondered if they had been one iceberg that had split in half.

"Only three racers are following us," said Tali. "Do you think we've lost the others?"

"Not a chance. They'll have gone out wide, hoping to find a quicker way through the ice to cut us off."

"I suppose they'll be a lot quicker in here."

"You suppose right. Manoeuvrability is everything when you're in the ice. And with their shallow keels they can cut through places I don't dare. Brace yourself – and don't point that thing anywhere near me."

Tali clamped onto the rail and lowered the crossbow. They headed out into open water.

"Or yourself!" yelled Holm.

Tali realised it was aimed at her left foot. She directed it away and clung on as the boat heeled again.

"Look out!" roared Holm, and spun the wheel hard. Something struck the starboard side of the boat a glancing blow, driving it sideways, then they shot past. A little ice floe, awash and almost invisible in the water.

She looked up and there, directly ahead, were the other two shell racers.

"They're planning to board us from either side," said Holm. "Shoot!"

She aimed at the middle of the leading rower, a barrel-chested fellow wearing a red, tasselled hat, but as she fired, Holm spun the wheel the other way. The bolt went wide as the boat veered off to starboard.

The two racers turned in their own length and raced ahead to cut them off. The three behind were only forty yards away. The enemy's plan had gone perfectly. In a minute or two they would be surrounded.

"Shoot!" yelled Holm.

Which target? The racer following in their wake was the closest. Tali inserted another bolt, aimed at the leading man, but as she was about to fire the bow dropped. She could not shoot him in cold blood, just like that.

She fired. He let out a yelp as the bolt passed between his shins and slammed into the floor of the boat.

"If you can't kill him, at least disable the bastard," said Holm.

Tali took aim at the side of the man's chest but, before she could fire, the shell racer slowed sharply. It was noticeably bow-down now, and the leading rower was groping in water that must have been flooding in through a hole in the bottom.

"Your bolt smashed through a plank," said Holm. "Hull must be thin as an egg."

The leading man dropped his oar and bent over, pushing down as though trying to block the hole with his fist, but it wasn't working. The racer was filling fast, the waves already lapping at its low sides.

"One wave and they're gone," whispered Tali.

As she spoke, a little wave curled over the side and the long, low craft sank beneath the rowers, leaving them struggling in the water.

"Help!" they cried, waving frantically to their fellows.

Their pleas were ignored and, one by one, the cold got to them and they sank.

"The others are greedy for the prize," said Holm, shaking his head.

Tali did not reply. She was too shocked. She stared at the grey water, imagining that she was thrashing uselessly in the cold sea, about to drown.

"Hang on!" Holm yelled.

He heeled the boat over so sharply that she was flung against the side once more. This time she took the blow on shoulder and hip, managing to keep her grip on the crossbow. She looked up and gasped. Holm was hurtling towards a tiny gap, only twenty feet wide, between two icebergs. It was a clever strategy, if it worked, for the shell racers could not attack from the sides and would have to follow. But if the boat struck hard enough, it would go straight to the bottom.

They hurtled down the gap, driven by a strong wind funnelled between the two icebergs. Tali could not bear to look ahead. Not far behind, the leading two shell racers were flying after them into the gap.

"We've got you now," a yellow-haired giant in the first craft roared.

Then suddenly they were hauling on their oars, churning the water to foam as they frantically tried to row backwards out of the gap. But, outside, the wind was gusting one way, then the other, and their sail was driving them forwards. The third rower yanked down the sail, the oars dug deep and the craft shot backwards, colliding with the second craft, whose sail had jammed on the mast, and snapping its two front oars.

"Why are they going backwards?" said Tali. "I don't understand."

"I've raced those craft, and the oars span twenty-four feet," Holm said smugly. "Unless they ship them, they won't fit through the gap."

The leading craft kept going, driving past the second shell racer and back out to safety. The other craft wasn't so lucky. In the confusion after its front oars were broken the wind drove it into the gap between the icebergs, snapping the remaining oars. Now it was driven sideways. The bow struck one iceberg, the stern another, and the wind blowing into the sail turned the shell racer upside-down.

None of its crew came to the surface.

"They should have shipped their oars and gone through on the wind," said Holm. "It's wild outside, but good and steady in here. But it's not easy to do the right thing in an emergency."

"Like the emergency of our gap closing?" said Tali, who was looking ahead.

Holm cursed, wiggled the wheel to glide them past a projection of the right-hand berg, then back the other way to escape an out-jutting ledge of the iceberg on the left. Deep down, wood groaned as it scraped past a submerged obstacle.

Holm looked grave. "That didn't sound good. I hope it hasn't sprung the planking."

Tali didn't ask what that meant. "Three racers left. Can the one behind catch us?"

"Depends. It's the other two I'm worried about. I've no idea where they went."

"But these icebergs must be shifting all the time. They can't know where we'll end up."

"They can't," Holm agreed. "Passages that are open one hour are gone the next. But if they're sound judges of wind and current they might guess where we'll appear."

Ahead, the gap opened out to fifty feet, then closed again to less than twenty, and the boat was hurtling. There was no room for error and no leeway to manoeuvre.

"At least the wind is steady in here," said Holm.

"More like a gale," Tali muttered.

"The ice sheet creates its own wind, and the gaps between the bergs funnel it. Ah, I see the end."

They shot out of the gap, the boat heeled under a crosswind, and Holm checked all around. Ahead were more icebergs, as far as she could see.

"I believe we've lost them," said Holm.

"No, we haven't."

CHAPTER 26

The missing two shell racers had been hiding behind a house-sized iceberg. As Holm's boat went past they burst out and closed in from either side.

Tali fired at the biggest man in the leading racer and struck him in the shoulder. He lost his stroke and clutched at the wound, baring his teeth.

The ferret-faced man behind him yelled, "Row, dammit!"

The injured man took hold of the oar with a bloody hand and resumed his beat. She snatched another bolt, laid it in the groove of the crossbow and gave the crank a furious turn. Too furious – the bolt slipped sideways, jammed, and before she could free it the racer was alongside. The injured man and the fellow at the bow held it steady while the other two began to scramble up onto Holm's boat.

She dropped the crossbow, picked up a length of anchor chain and swung it like a flail, striking the ferret-faced boarder around the head. He fell back into the racer, which rocked wildly. The rower at the bow lost his grip but the injured man did not, and now the second man was aboard and coming right for her.

She swung the chain again. He caught it, tore it out of her hands and tossed it aside. He wore a sword but did not draw it – clearly, he wanted her alive and unharmed. Tali backpedalled around the deck, looking for something she could use to hold him off. There, under the rail, was a boathook used for hauling in lines. She grabbed it and moved it back and forth in front of her. It was a poor weapon because the hook was U-shaped, the point facing her.

The man she had shot in the shoulder was holding the shell racer against the side of the boat. His sleeve was drenched in blood and he was white-faced, swaying in his seat. She did not think she had to worry about him. The fellow she had knocked back into his own position in the racer had recovered. He began to haul himself aboard, blood dribbling from his ear, a gash on his right cheek and a deadly expression on his ferret face.

Now the second craft was only yards away. With eight against two there was no hope. Where was Holm? The boat was drifting. She could not see him anywhere.

"Holm?" she yelled. "Holm, where are you?"

It came out as a screech. Her opponent grinned — he didn't think much of her. She struck at him with the boathook, missed. Struck again, and this time the curving brass hook slammed into his knuckles. He tried to snatch it out of her hands but she managed to tear it free, gashing his arm.

Tali swung the boathook wildly. It caught in one of the sail lines. She freed it and backed away, but she was up against the side with nowhere to go.

"Holm, they're aboard! Get out here."

He burst up from a hatch at the bow, carrying a metal canister the size of the porridge pot, with a lid on. Tali's opponent drew his sword and went for Holm. Holm bent, did something with the canister then, almost casually, tossed it at the approaching shell racer. It smacked into the water near the bow, sank, and went off like a small Cythonian bombast.

The bow of the racer was lifted fifteen feet into the air. The stern remained where it was. The bow kept going up, up, up until it was vertical, tumbling the rowers back onto the lowest man, then the craft sliced down through the water, carrying the four rowers with it, and disappeared.

The boat heeled violently under the water-blast but Tali, who had her back to the rail, kept her feet. The ferret-faced man had fallen to one knee. She sprang across the deck and dealt him a monumental blow to the head with the boathook, right where she had hit him with the chain. It felled him but did not knock him out. He struggled to his hands and knees, collapsed and struggled up again, fumbling out a knife.

If it's you or me, thought Tali, it's not going to be me. She whacked him again and this time he did not get up.

Where were the others? She looked around. The man who had gone for Holm lay unconscious — no, surely dead with that great wound in his neck. Holm was pursuing another man around the deck with the weapon that had done the damage – a harpoon. The fellow turned and struck at Holm with a curved sword like a scimitar.

He ran backwards, raising the harpoon. "Surrender or die."

The man lunged at him and Holm put the harpoon through his breastbone.

Holm wrenched it out, went to the side and said to the injured man holding the boat, "I'll give you the same choice."

The man looked at the bloody harpoon, and then at Holm, and said, "I'm going."

"Take him with you."

Holm dragged the semi-conscious ferret-faced man to the side, heaved him onto it, then dropped him into the shell racer, head-first. The injured man rowed awkwardly away.

"Give us a hand with these, will you?" said Holm.

He took the man with the neck wound under the arms. Tali lifted his feet and they heaved him over. The harpooned man was much bigger. It took three goes before they could get him up onto the side and by then Tali was seeing double. She held the man there; Holm rolled him into the sea.

They watched the little shell racer limp out of sight. "Do you think they'll get back to tell the story?" she said, swaying on her feet.

"With that injury, I'll be surprised if he gets a mile. Better sit down before you fall down."

Tali slumped down with her back to the mast. "What about the other racer? The fifth one?"

"I'd say we've lost it. But keep an eye out, just in case."

Holm sighed, collected water in a bucket on a rope and scrubbed the blood off the deck. Tali crawled across to the crossbow, cleared the jammed bolt and put it away, trying not to think about the violence and her part in all those men's deaths.

"How did you make that canister go off like that?"

"Got the idea from some of the enemy's weapons," said Holm. "I used to dabble in alchymie when I was young—"

"Is there anything you haven't done?"

"Not much, but now isn't the time for it. You're shaking. Come inside, I'll make you a cup of tea?"

"Thank you. And maybe I'll have the bacon and eggs after all. I think I could hold it down now."

"It's hungry work, fighting for your life."

"And taking other people's lives."

"It was them or us."

"We still killed them."

"I know, I know."

Holm set a course south and east, heading inshore until they were within sight of land, where the icebergs were fewer and further apart. They ate bacon and eggs, soaked up the fat with chunks of bread, and sailed on. In an hour or two they were passing The Cape, an outjutting finger of mountainous land that marked the south-westerly end of Hightspall.

"Beyond here we'll be sailing east, through the straits between Hightspall and ice-bound Suden. We'll have to keep a sharp lookout there. The straits are shallow, treacherous waters, full of rocky reefs and sandbanks, and the tidal currents are fast and treacherous."

"Anything else we have to worry about?"

"As I said earlier, it's Cythonian territory."

"But they're not sailors, are they?"

"You know them better than anyone. You tell me."

"I never heard of any of them being sailors ... though they could have practised sailing on the lake at night."

"I'd better keep a sharp lookout."

"I'll take a watch," said Tali.

"Not now you won't. Go below, have a sleep and don't come back 'til dark."

Despite her exhaustion, sleep was a long time coming. She kept seeing the faces of the dead, and the way each man had died ... Tali woke abruptly and she could still see daylight through the porthole. What had roused her?

"*Tali!*"

It was Holm, yelling. "What's the matter?" she said sleepily, pulling on the oversized sea boots he had given her.

"Up here, quick!"

She clumped up the ladder into the cabin. He was out on deck, staring up at the sky. She went out. The sea was dotted with low-hanging patches of mist or fog and a scattering of icebergs, large and small.

"What do you make of that?" said Holm, pointing.

She squinted up at the sky, which was half covered in grey, wind-shredded cloud. She rubbed her eyes and looked again, but she was so tired her eyes would not focus. All she could see was a faint dark shape. "A bird, I assume."

He gave her a sardonic glance. "A bird?"

"Until a month ago I'd never seen the sky, much less a live bird. If you know, why don't you tell me?"

"I don't know what it is. That's the problem."

"What do you think it is?"

"It's not a bird, and it's not a bat. That rules out anything natural."

"A blown-away kite?" said Tali. She had seen children playing with kites in Caulderon.

"It's flying, not drifting."

"Haven't you got a telescope or anything?"

"I fell on hard times a while ago and had to sell it. Haven't replaced it yet."

"But you're afraid of something."

"Yes."

"Are you going to tell me what it is?"

"I don't want to alarm you."

"You're alarming me."

"I think it's a shifter."

A line of shivers ran up the back of her neck and over the top of her head. "A flying shifter?"

"Yes."

Memory stirred, sank, stirred again. "Is it a gauntling?"

"It looks like one – and that's bad. Of all the shifters Lyf has created, gauntlings are the most troubling."

"I would have thought that caitsthes were the worst."

"They're powerful, and vicious, but they're also predictable. Gauntlings aren't – but they are intelligent."

"How do you know?"

"Shifters are one of my hobbies."

Tali liked nothing about that statement, and it aroused her dormant worries about Holm. Though he had rescued her, and though he had saved her life, she felt sure that he wanted something from her. Did he also want her healing blood, so he could test it on his *hobby*?

"How long has it been there?" said Tali.

"I first noticed it half an hour ago."

"What's it been doing all that time?"

He stared up at the creature, clenching and unclenching his jaw.

"I'm very much afraid," said Holm, "that it's watching us."

CHAPTER 27

The gauntling turned and began to describe slow, descending circles, high above the boat.

"It's coming down." Tali retrieved the crossbow and loaded it.

"Not sure it'll be much use against a shifter that size," said Holm.

"How can you tell how big it is?"

"You get used to judging sizes and distances, at sea. Reckon its wingspan is a good fifteen feet."

Three times Tali's own height.

"And it'd need to be ..."

"Why?" said Tali.

"I reckon it's carrying a rider."

Tali rubbed her eyes, which were sore from all the sea spray. As the gauntling descended, she made out legs hanging below the middle, but not the spindly little legs of the gauntling she had seen above Fortress Rutherin.

"It's spying for Lyf. When it reports back, they'll send a boat after us."

"And not cockleshell craft like we dealt with last time," said Holm. "They'll send a proper boat, and they'll be prepared for anything."

"Can you hide from it?"

"Pray for a storm, or for the fog to thicken," he said, "though I wouldn't want to navigate these waters in either. Likely as not we'd come to grief on a reef or a berg. Keep watch."

The gauntling was still descending in slow, sweeping circles. Was it coming down to make sure of her identity? She paced the deck, checked the crossbow, and checked it again.

She put it down and bent over, rubbing her sore eyes. When she straightened up, the gauntling was gone.

It could not have disappeared; it must be behind a cloud. Though the clouds were too high, and the scattered fog banks, hanging above the water, seemed too low.

"Holm?"

"Yes?"

"The gauntling's disappeared."

He ran out. "Where did you see it last?"

"Up there. I just rubbed my eyes for a few seconds, and when I looked for it, it wasn't there."

"I suppose it's gone back to report," said Holm. "Keep watch in case it's hiding behind an iceberg. I'm just popping below."

The nearest iceberg was a good mile away. He returned to the wheel and the boat turned towards a fog bank half a mile off. It wasn't much of a hiding place. The gauntling could circle above it, waiting for the fog to thin, or direct searchers in boats back to the area.

She was staring up at the sky when there came a shrieking whistle behind her, like wind howling across tortured wings. Tali whirled to see the gauntling hurtling low over the water, its clawed feet extended, straight for her.

"Holm! It's here!"

Where had she put the crossbow? She turned around, around, around. There it was, right where she had left it. She grabbed it, aimed for the creature's chest and fired, but her hands were shaking and the bolt missed.

Still Holm did not reply. The rider stood upright in the stirrups, pulled off a helmet and a cascade of black, wavy hair streamed out behind her. Lizue! She had tried to kill Tali before and she was here to finish the job.

"Holm," she shrilled. "It's Lizue."

Tali scrabbled another bolt out of the bag, slammed it into the groove and desperately wound the crank. She would not hesitate this time. If she got a chance to draw bead on Lizue's chest, she would put a bolt right into her heart.

Where was Holm? She shot a glance over her shoulder and he was not at the wheel. That's right; he'd gone down the ladder and might not have heard her.

The gauntling shot across the deck, directly above. Tali fired and seemed to get it in the tail, which lashed about like a dying snake. Lizue sprang off. As she soared through the air, arms outstretched, Tali was struck by two contrasting thoughts: how extraordinarily beautiful Lizue was, and how determined she was to cut Tali's head off.

There wasn't time to reload the crossbow. Lizue slammed into Tali, knocking her to the deck. She tried to whack Lizue in the face with the crossbow. Lizue elbowed Tali so hard in the nose that her eyes flooded with tears, momentarily blinding her, then struck her on the elbow. Tali's forearm went numb and the crossbow skidded away across the deck.

She blinked away the tears and jammed a finger into one of Lizue's eyes. Lizue reared back, dropped her head and attempted to butt Tali in the face. Tali elbowed her in the mouth, splitting her lip.

Lizue heaved Tali onto her back and jammed her left knee into Tali's belly, pinning her to the deck. Her thigh was bandaged where the Sullen Man had stabbed her. It looked swollen and fresh blood was seeping through the bandage.

The injury must be exceedingly painful – how had Lizue kept going all this time? After Tali had taken that Cythonian arrow in the thigh, out in the Seethings, only intensive healing magery had allowed her to walk on it. Tali clubbed her fist, swung it around and drove it against the stab wound with all her might.

Lizue threw her head back, let out a shriek and fell backwards, her teeth bared. Tali rolled over and scrabbled across the deck, desperate to get out of reach. Lizue was her master in every respect and fighting her hand-to-hand could only end one way. But as she regained her feet, Lizue overcame the pain and attacked with a flurry of punches, trying to finish Tali as quickly as possible.

A blow to the jaw rocked her backwards; a second blow to her nose sent blood gushing from it.

"Holm!" she gasped. "Help."

Was he absenting himself deliberately? Could he be working with Lizue? He had tracked Tali down immediately after Lizue's first, failed attack, after all. Had he brought Tali this way so as to sell her to Lyf?

She stumbled backwards, looking around for a spar, the boathook, or anything else she could use as a weapon. Her lack of fitness was telling on her, and the weakness in her knees told her she could not resist much longer.

From a small pack on her back, Lizue withdrew a head bag like the one she had used in the cells. She slid a heavy knife from a sheath on her left thigh, and advanced. Tali went backwards until her back was against the side of the boat. If she moved left she would be trapped at the stern; on her right, a winch blocked her way.

How could she beat a fanatical opponent who carried a knife as big as a machete? Tali's one advantage was that Lizue could not do her serious harm before she had the head bag securely over Tali's head. She could not risk destroying the pearl. And Lizue had a weakness. Her thigh.

Tali groped behind her in the open compartments that ran along the sides of the boat, but felt only coils of rope and other items that were useless for self-defence. How could she attack Lizue's thigh wound? She could not use any of the tricks Nurse Bet had taught her, for Lizue knew them all. Something new, then? No, a combination of old and new.

Tali attacked with a flurry of right-handed blows intended to divert her attacker from her real attack, a roundhouse left to the throat. Then, as soon as Lizue moved to defend against the blow,

Tali raised her right foot and slammed her boot heel into the thigh wound.

Lizue screamed, dropped the head bag and fell back against the side of the boat, blood flooding from the wound. Her beautiful face was twisted in agony. Tali had to finish this now; she could not fight for one more minute. She crouched, seized her attacker's ankles and, with a swift heave, dumped her overboard.

"Did I hear you call?" said Holm from the top of the cabin ladder.

"About an hour ago," she snapped. "Where the hell have you been?"

She picked up the boathook she had used earlier and stood ready for when Lizue tried to reboard.

"I was at the crapper," said Holm, coming to the cabin door. "Wasn't aware that I was supposed to ask your permission." He looked down at the bloody deck, up at Tali's heaving bosom and scarlet, bloody face, and his weathered face paled. "What's going on?"

"Lizue happened. She tried to take my head. Again!"

Lizue's head and shoulders shot from the water. Her eyes were staring and the sea was red with her blood. Her arms caught the side of the boat, heaved and she was on the side.

"Not this time," Tali said savagely.

She jammed the curve of the boathook against Lizue's chest and shoved hard. Lizue slid off into the water and floated there on her back, her blood staining the sea around her.

A grey fin cut the water. The sea churned and a huge, grey head burst out. Jaws opened, revealing dozens of backwards-angled teeth. A single snap took Lizue's bleeding leg off at mid-thigh. She screamed until foam gushed from her mouth. Her hands caught the gunwale and she tried to pull herself up, but the jaws opened again, closed around her middle and pulled her under.

Even when she was screaming, even when she was about to die, Lizue was still the most beautiful woman Tali had ever seen.

CHAPTER 28

"I bear dreadful news, Rixium," said Swelt, three days later, "and I'd prefer the whole household did not hear of it. At least, not yet."

"News of the war?"

"Yes."

"How did you hear?"

"Your great-aunt insisted on knowing the affairs of Hightspall, and I've maintained her network of informers."

"It's a long walk from any of the battlefronts to here."

"We use carrier hawks. One flew in an hour ago."

"You'd better come in." Rix opened the door to its fullest extent and Swelt squeezed through.

Out of respect for his great-aunt, and the feelings of the household about her, Rix had not taken her chambers for himself. He had occupied the rooms of her late husband, Rorke, an ineffectual man who had died thirty years before and not been missed by his spouse or anyone else.

Rix gestured Swelt to the chair by the fire and resumed his seat at an ornate desk by a narrow window. The only light in the chamber came from the fire but he did not light a candle. If they would soon be besieged, every candle was precious.

"What news?"

"You knew that Lyf had sent an army of twenty thousand across the mountains to attack Bleddimire?" said Swelt.

Rix's stomach knotted. "I'd heard he'd sent an army. I didn't know it was that big." The army of wealthy Bleddimire was Hightspall's main hope of relief. "What's happened?"

"There was a battle by Lilluly Water yesterday."

"Where's that?"

"Two hours' march south of Bledd. Lyf's forces wiped Bleddimire's army out, leaving the capital undefended. They'll be attacking the walls of Bledd by now."

Rix rose abruptly, stalked to the fire and stirred it with a poker. Sparks shot out onto the floor. He crushed them under his boot. "What about the chancellor?"

"He's holed up in Fortress Rutherin, a hundred and fifty miles to the south."

"But . . . he must have known Lyf was marching on Bleddimire."

"He must have," said Swelt. "Not even Lyf can move so great an army in secret."

"Why didn't the chancellor go after him? He could have attacked from the rear."

"At a guess, because he's a schemer, not a fighter."

"But he's got half a dozen generals . . ." said Rix. Swelt was shaking his round head, his jowls quivering like dewlaps. "Hasn't he?"

"It seems Lyf targeted our commanders in the initial attack on Caulderon. All the chancellor's generals and senior officers were killed or captured on the first day."

"Even so—"

"The chancellor's army is small, and his only officers are raw lieutenants. They don't know anything about military strategy and they've got no battle experience."

Rix drew another chair up to the fire and sat down abruptly. "So we've lost the centre, the south and now the north-west. Half of Hightspall will soon be occupied – the strongest and wealthiest half. And the chancellor, who's useless, is stuck in Rutherin, a hundred miles across the mountains from anywhere. What do we do, Swelt?"

"Why ask me? You're the lord of Garramide."

Rix had already come to rely on the old man, and valued his advice. In some respects, Swelt was the kind of father figure Rix had yearned for, but never had. "I haven't been in charge of a fortress before. I don't know these mountains and I don't know the servants. What are they like? Will they support me?"

"Depends what you want to do?"

"I told you, fight for my country."

"Then most will support you – as long as you don't just talk about it."

"But some won't."

"The ones who served your great-aunt – a couple of hundred, all up, including myself – are loyal. Most of them have lived and worked at Garramide for generations and they loved the old lady. Since she named you her heir, they'll follow you."

"Even to war?"

"Of course – they know what the alternative is if Lyf wins."

"What about the others?"

"The war has brought over a hundred new people in, counting Leatherhead's fighters and their hangers-on. In the absence of anyone stronger, most of them will follow you ..."

"And the rest?"

"Troublemakers. They'll obey you if you're strong enough, but you'll never gain their loyalty."

Rix sat back. "What about the enemy?"

"Lyf has a few garrisons lower down in the mountains. There's one at Jadgery, one at Fladzey, further east, and another way up north at Twounce. Only forty or fifty men at each; he's just showing the flag."

"I know Jadgery," said Rix. "I spent some time there when I was a kid." He rubbed his jaw. "So ... if we could take one of their garrisons ..."

"Jadgery is closest," said Swelt.

"It would inspire everyone else. It would be the first start to an uprising."

"Which would bring Lyf down on us, quick-smart."

"But with all the battles he's fighting, and all the provinces and cities he's occupying, he can't have many troops to spare right now."

"It'll be different in spring."

"Once he controls his captured lands, he'll be able to spare an army. If we wait until spring to take him on, it'll be too late."

"What's your plan?"

"A raid on his garrison at Jadgery."

"If you succeed it'll be a great boost to morale," said Swelt.

"I'll take Leatherhead's fifty. They're the only experienced fighters I have."

"How can you be sure they'll fight?"

"If we win, they get a share of the plunder."

Swelt shrugged, his shoulders wobbling. "If you win, it'll also bind them to you."

"What if I lose?"

"Try to lose the thugs we don't want back."

As Swelt was waddling out, panting with each breath, Rix said, "Swelt?"

He turned. "Yes?"

"How's Glynnie getting on?"

"Surely you know better than I do?"

"She's been avoiding me," said Rix.

Swelt inflated his cheeks. "I'm not one to carry tales, Rixium!"

"I need to know."

"Well, I have to admire the girl."

"For taking charge of the household?"

"No," said Swelt, "for taking on the lowest, dirtiest and most menial tasks of all, and doing them perfectly."

He went out, leaving Rix staring after him.

"You called for me, Lord Deadhand?" said Glynnie, from behind Rix.

He had not realised she was there. He started and knocked the ink bottle across his map.

"Sorry, Lord Deadhand. Let me clean it up."

"I'll do it!" he said, more brusquely than he had intended. "And call me Rix, dammit."

She stepped back smartly, until he could barely see her in the dim light, then stood stiffly to attention as though awaiting Lady Ricinus's pleasure.

"Don't be like that, Glynnie," he said, sighing.

"How may I serve you, Lord?" she said in a voice stripped of all emotion, though it quavered on *Lord*.

"Please, not after all we've been through together."

"That was then," she said quietly. "This is now."

"We were friends. I miss you. I need you."

Her face was tilted away from him. "You're back where you

belong, the lord of a manor with thousands of rich acres and hundreds of servants. And I'm back where I belong – the least of them all. I'm not making that mistake again."

"You're not least," said Rix. "I gave you charge of the household servants."

"I begged you not to. I'm just a maid – the least of all."

"You're strong and clever, and you know how House Ricinus was run."

"*But I didn't run it*. I don't give orders, I obey them."

"You can run this household; I know you can."

"They won't have me, and I don't want it."

"Is that why you're doing the dirty jobs? To spite me?"

"When I see a job that needs doing, I do it. There's nothing more to say. Will that be all, Lord?"

She was turning to go when he said sharply, "What's happened? What did they do?"

"Nothing, Deadhand," she muttered. "Just the everyday life of a servant in a great house."

He sprang up, caught her by the shoulder and turned her around. She resisted, then obeyed. Her left eyebrow was badly cut and swollen, the area around her eye turning blue-black.

"Who hit you?" he raged.

"I'll never say and you can't make me."

"I'll have the lot of them up here. I'll make the bastards talk."

"And they'll get me for it. Rix – Lord," she clutched at his hands. "I told you this would happen. Why wouldn't you listen?"

"I was trying to do the right thing. You're so clever and capable, and you've done so much for me."

Glynnie exploded. "You're so stupid!"

"What are you talking about?" he said, genuinely bewildered.

"Ten days ago you were looking for a housemaid's position for me, without asking me, because I'm an inexperienced girl who knows nothing of the ways of the world. Now, suddenly I'm old and experienced enough to be put in charge of a vast household?"

After a long pause, he said quietly, "I – wanted to make up for the way I'd treated you."

"You've got to take it back."

"If I do, they'll assume I'm weak. They'll know they've won."

"They have won. You know the rumours Blathy is spreading about me?"

"No," said Rix, frowning. "How could I?"

She made an exasperated noise. "She's calling me your mistress – though that's not the word she uses." She flushed.

"What word does she use?"

"Slut! Your *slut*, Rix."

"But I'm trying to do the right thing," he bellowed.

"It's not working." She went out.

Rix threw himself on the huge old bed, which emitted clouds of mouldy dust.

Damn Blathy. He had to get rid of her, right now. He could not put off the evil moment any longer. He sprang up and headed downstairs to the servants' quarters, feeling that familiar pain in his belly again. What if she wouldn't go and he had to throw her out?

"Where's Blathy?" he said to the widow Lobb, a toothless crone who was sitting by a narrow window, using a darning needle to gouge an ugly splinter from a boy's hand, and making a bloody mess of it. She must have been half blind. The boy's eyes were damp and he was trying not to cry out.

"I'll take you to her, Lord," said the boy – a sturdy, grey-eyed lad of about eight years, with wild sandy hair and a gap where he'd lost two front teeth.

Rix looked down at the boy's raw hand. "Yes, right away."

The boy wriggled free of the widow Lobb. "This way, Lord Deadhand."

"Mind you come straight back," Lobb said sharply.

"What's your name, lad?" said Rix, following.

"Thom, Lord. I'm one of the wood boys."

"An important job. I'll see you get leather gloves in future."

"Thank you, Lord."

Thom led Rix through a maze of passages and up a damp, south-facing tower to a weathered plank door. "Here's Blathy's room, Lord."

"Thanks." The boy was waiting, watching him, and Rix didn't want any witnesses. "Better run back and get that splinter out."

Thom studied his butchered palm, trembling. Rix took pity on him. "Go down and find Glynnie – you know her, don't you?"

"Yes, Lord. She's pretty." Thom reddened. "And kind."

"Tell her I sent you. She'll have that splinter out so quick you won't even feel it."

"Thank you, Lord." Thom ran.

Rix took a deep breath and rapped on the door. "Blathy, come out." What if she wouldn't go? He should have brought some guards.

After a minute or two she wrenched the door open and stood there in her shift, staring at him. She must have come from her bed, for her heavy-lidded eyes were half closed, her long hair was a tangled mess and her feet were bare.

"What do you want, Deadhand?" she said imperiously.

"According to the official charter, you have no right here. I'm putting you out. Gather your things."

She stared at him for a long time, then strode across to the rumpled bed and in one swift movement drew her shift over her head and dropped it on the floor. She stood before him, proud, majestic and completely naked.

"Throw me out."

She was bluffing. She had to be.

"Get dressed."

"Make me."

He wasn't going along that road. "I'll send the guards up, and some women to dress you."

She picked up a heavy knife. "They'd better come armed."

"They will," said Rix, cursing her.

"If you expel me I'll tear my clothes off and walk naked into the snow, to freeze to death."

"That's your choice, not mine."

"But you'll be blamed. You'll bear it for the rest of your life."

She threw her head back, proudly meeting his eyes, staring him down. She wasn't bluffing. Blathy was a terrible, vindictive woman, but a magnificent one too – she was prepared to risk everything on her estimate of his character, and face the consequences if she was wrong.

"What do I care if you live or die?" he muttered.

"You're chivalrous, Deadhand. With my death on your conscience, you'll burn with guilt."

"You're assuming I have a conscience."

"When it comes to dealing with women, you're weak. It's your curse."

There was nothing to say. He walked out, cursing his folly. I am weak, he thought, and she's beaten me. How will I ever get rid of her now?

His wrist was aching worse than ever. He manually flexed the fingers of his dead hand, then rubbed the inflamed scar where it joined the healthy flesh of his wrist. It did not ease the pain. If there had been more of Tali's healing blood, might it have saved his hand?

He had not thought about her in ages. In truth, he'd avoided thinking about Tali because her small betrayals – notably, not telling him about Lord and Lady Ricinus's treasonous plan to assassinate the chancellor – had been too painful. Now he realised that her failings paled beside his own.

He flexed his fingers again. Why had his rejoined hand worked so well, then gone dead? He should never have used his own blood to paint with. Had the prophetic mural ended the life of his hand?

In the past, Rix had often painted things he did not want to see, yet painting had also been his main solace in childhood. It had been the one thing that had not been bought by the wealth of House Ricinus. He wanted to paint now. No – to get the insoluble problems of Glynnie and Blathy out of his head he *needed* to paint. Even something crude, which was all he could manage left-handed, would be better than nothing.

He turned and went up to see the castellan.

"Paintbrushes?" said Swelt, as though he'd never heard of such arcane objects. He peeled a dried fig off a string, popped it in his mouth and contemplated another. "Why would you want paintbrushes?"

"Painting helps me to think," said Rix. "Do you have any artist's brushes in the stores?"

"Certainly not. But . . ." Swelt masticated another fig, like a cow chewing its cud. "In the days when the great dame had ladies to stay, some of them used to paint. I'll see what I can find."

He lumbered out, and shortly returned, red in the face and gasping for breath, bearing a handful of brushes in one balloon-like hand and a rack of six little paint pots in the other.

Rix took them and thanked him. "Where did the ladies paint?"

"Out on the lawns, when the weather was clement. In the solar when it was cold or wet. Splendid light in the solar, they used to say."

"Not at this time of night," said Rix. "Is there a high room somewhere, quiet and away from everything else?"

"The great dame was fond of looking at the stars from her observatory," said Swelt. "It's a hundred and eighty steps up the rear tower – the one without a dome. You won't mind if I give you directions?"

Rix preferred it. He took the rusty old key Swelt was holding out, a bracket of candles, the paint pots and brushes and some oil, and headed up the tower.

The observatory was open, windy and miserably cold, though in his present mood that suited Rix. Cold not only numbed his wrist, it also occupied his mind and turned off his endlessly cycling worries. About Glynnie, and the enemy, and all the other problems he had created for himself and could do nothing about.

He had no paper, no canvas, no board, but that didn't matter. Rix was happy to paint on the pale stone. It would fade in months, and weather away in years, though that didn't bother him either – it was the sheer act of creation that mattered, not what was done with the work afterwards.

He unfastened the lids of the paint pots, resurrected the desiccated contents by stirring with a little oil, took a handful of brushes, not sure which one to use, then out of habit thrust the largest brush through the hooked fingers of his dead hand.

And the fingers moved.

CHAPTER 29

Rix dropped the brush and stared at his dead hand in the yellow candlelight. His heart was thundering. Were his fingers less grey than before? It was hard to tell in this light, though he thought they were.

What was going on?

He flexed his fingers, one by one. This time they moved more easily and he felt a tingling pain in the middle finger. They were definitely pink now, though he could not imagine it would last. It had to be some cruel trick of the magery that had rejoined hand to wrist. But oh, the joy of holding a brush again.

He stirred in more oil until the paint was the right consistency, fretting at the time it was taking and afraid his hand would go dead. He mixed paint on the flat mount of a sundial, took some black on the largest brush and swept it across the wall. Rix eyed it for a minute or two, decided it was a meaningless swirl and rubbed it off with the heel of his hand.

He began again. And again rubbed it off.

Rix clamped his left hand around Maloch's hilt, in case its protective magery had something to do with his previous painting, and blanked his mind.

Blathy appeared in his inner eye, imperiously naked, daring him to throw her out. Rix groaned and blanked his mind again.

He scrawled on the wall a third time, went to rub out the black marks then stopped with his right hand outstretched. Was that a figure in full flight? Or someone leaping into a pool, arms and legs spread? Or a man roaring in fury? Yes, definitely a man.

But the more he thought about it, the more inspiration was draining out of him. His artistic gift was intuitive and analysis always defeated it. Don't ask what the man is doing. Don't try to paint what you're thinking. Concentrate on something else and let your painter's hand, your magical, sometimes-live-and-sometimes-dead hand, paint what *it* sees. Concentrate on striking a blow against Lyf that will shake his confidence and boost Hightspall's shattered morale.

He was painting unconsciously now, his eyes unfocused, indifferent to what he was doing, totally absorbed by a developing plan.

Rix was a gifted warrior of the rarest sort – not just enormously strong, but fast and dexterous too. And his tutors had been the best in the land. He had never been beaten in a fight and, with the enchanted sword in his hand, even his left hand, he was almost invincible.

Almost, he reminded himself. Pride leads to bad outcomes.

His first action on entering the fortress had been to review its defences, and Rix knew there was no immediate threat. No roving band of villains would dare attack such a well-fortified place while he was in charge.

At some stage the enemy would come after him, though moving troops in winter was difficult and it could take a fortnight to march a sizeable force here. In that time he had to unite the fortress behind him, and the best way to do that was by proving himself against the enemy.

He would lead Leatherhead's fifty men down the mountain road in darkness and attack the enemy garrison at Jadgery, ten miles away. House Ricinus once held a manor near Jadgery, and Rix had spent several weeks in the area when he was fifteen. He had roamed all over the place and knew the land and the town well.

As he painted, he planned the route of the march and how he would attack the garrison. Were fifty men enough? Ideally, he needed a lot more attackers than there were defenders, but he dared take no more from here; he could not leave Garramide undefended. How could he get more?

The clatter of the falling brush roused him from his reverie. A minute ago his hand had been pink and warm, but it had suddenly gone cold, as if all the blood had withdrawn from it. His fingers were stiff and blue. Was the painting finished? It was hard to tell in this light.

He carried the bracket of candles to the wall. And started. The painting was crude, but it was definitely a man. A dark-skinned man, darker than any Cythonian he had ever seen, almost black. Their skin was pale grey, or occasionally a steely blue-grey, but seldom dark. Though it might darken in the sun, he supposed.

This man was heavily built but not fat – he was massively muscular, yet his arms and legs were thrown out in unnatural angles as though he was doing a dervish dance. No, not a dance. Rix looked closer. The man was in pain – an agony so intense that it had twisted him in ways no normal human could be twisted. He was screaming in agony.

As Rix moved the light, a fleck of paint reflected it back at him in brilliant, shimmering red. Odd, Rix thought. He moved the light the other way. This time the reflection was emerald, and then it was black.

Hair stirred on the top of Rix's head. What did that remind him of? How could the light be reflected in completely different colours?

Opal could. Where had he seen opal that looked like this? He could not recall; he had emptied his mind too thoroughly. Without thinking, he rubbed the worn wire-bound hilt of his sword, and the image he had drawn blasted into his mind so clearly that he cried out.

He had seen that tormented figure several times before – a man carved from a single enormous mass of black opal – and each time it had been after touching Maloch's hilt. Tali had seen it too; it had been floating in the white shaft of the Abysm, next to Lyf's caverns under Precipitous Crag. The Abysm: the most sacred of all the enemy's holy places, the very conduit between death and life.

Rix also knew *who* it was, for Lyf had told him and Tali in the cellar before stealing Deroe's three ebony pearls. The figure wasn't *carved* from opal – it was a man *turned* to opal.

It was the petrified body of the greatest of the Five Heroes, the man who had begun the war with Cythe and founded Hightspall. Rix had been drawn to him from the very first time he had heard the story, and was drawn to him still. Powerful, ruthless, creative and endlessly fascinating, he was a man Rix would have followed anywhere.

The black opal figure was the remains of his ancestor, the first Herovian to step ashore in the land he would take for his own. The man who had brought Maloch to Cythe.

Axil Grandys.

"You should not have painted that."

Rix whirled. A woman stood in the doorway, one pale arm out-flung, pointing to the mural. In the dim light he could not make out her features, only the hook of a mouth, a plough nose and one dark-shadowed, staring eye. And layer upon layer of garments, all odd sizes and unmatched colours. It was the witch-woman, Astatin.

"You should not have painted that."

"Why not?" said Rix.

"Garramide will fall and all its ancient, secret treasures will be lost."

Then she was gone, silent on slippered feet.

He rubbed his dead hand and shivered. It was colder than it had ever been; icy. What had changed since he'd painted Grandys? Was the enchantment of the sword involved, and if so, what did it want? Why had it brought him here, anyway?

Why had Maloch involved itself in the rejoining of Rix's hand? He knew it had; the magery of the sword had made his fingers tingle at the time. Why had the sword given him this gift?

He lowered the sword and walked around the outer wall of the observatory, the tip of the blade scraping along the flagstones behind him. What was the sword's price? He knew there had to be one – it must have been enchanted for a purpose.

Was it the remnant of an ancient enchantment that had nothing to do with Rix, as the chancellor had said? Maloch was an ancient family heirloom. But who had put the protection on it; and why?

Or had it been placed on the sword by one of Lady Ricinus's magians, before she gave the sword to Rix? He had no way of find-ing out. The high magian of the palace had been hung from the front gates of the palace beside his master and mistress.

He had to know more about Maloch, and about the man who had owned it, perhaps even forged and enchanted it. Rix had to find out everything he could about Axil Grandys. If his restored hand was the gift of the sword, he had better find out its price as well.

And if he could not pay the price, he should cut his hand off right now and feed it to the dogs.

Assuming they would have it.

CHAPTER 30

"What happened to the gauntling?" said Holm.

"I don't know. Lizue leapt off onto the deck and it flew away."

Holm picked up the head bag and stretched it between his fingers. Tali tensed. Had he been at the crapper? Or had he absented himself while Lizue did the gruesome business? He might well have betrayed Tali, for a fortune. It did not mean that he would want to see her head cut off.

"What's this for?" said Holm.

"No idea," Tali lied.

He tossed it overboard. Tali tested Lizue's blade on her forearm; it shaved the tiny hairs off like a razor. She swung it through the air. It was heavy enough to take her head off with a single blow, but well balanced. And she needed a weapon.

"The gauntling can't have gone far," she said. "It would have come back to pick Lizue up once she killed me."

"Then I dare say it's up there somewhere, watching for her signal."

He looked up and Tali did too, but during the battle they had sailed into a fog bank and only small patches of sky could be seen through it. "It could be anywhere. Or gone."

"Either way, we can expect to be harried all the way across the straits until we get to Esterlyz, the furthest that the enemy's writ currently extends. Or so I'm told."

"You seem remarkably well informed for a humble clock attendant."

"It does seem odd, now you mention it," he said cheerfully.

"Are you planning to tell me how you know so much?" And who you really are, and what you want of me.

"I don't believe so."

"Why not?"

"I don't want to."

She had no answer to that. "Where are you taking me?" she said waspishly. "I'm entitled to ask that, aren't I?"

"You can ask whatever you like."

"Well?"

"I'm taking you somewhere safe – assuming I can find such a place."

"Where?"

"I haven't decided yet, but probably the Nandeloch Mountains."

"I don't know anything about them," said Tali. "My tutors in Cython were a little hazy on geography."

"Come inside."

In the cabin, he withdrew a map from a chart drawer, spread it on the little table, and circled his forefinger around the north-eastern corner of Hightspall.

"These are the Nandelochs," said Holm. "Hundreds of little valleys separated by high ranges. Brutal frosts and heavy snow in winter; torrential rain in summer. The people there are fiercely independent, and the Nandelochs are the best place in Hightspall to hide."

"How do we get there?" she said warily.

"I haven't worked that out yet—"

The distinctive shrieking whistle raised Tali's hackles. As Holm ran to the cabin door, a round, glass object the size of a large melon smashed on the front deck, spilling a thick yellow fluid everywhere.

"What the hell was that?" said Holm.

"The gauntling," said Tali, darting back for the crossbow.

It came around again. She aimed for its round yellow eye, but missed. Before she could reload, it dropped a blazing, pitch-covered brand onto the front deck and kept going. The yellow fluid exploded in flame.

Tali snatched another bolt. "It – it's trying to kill us . . ."

"Like I said, gauntlings aren't predictable. And there's a powerful psychic bond between gauntling and rider . . ."

Tali slammed the bolt into its groove and wound the crank. "What are you saying?"

"That when it saw its rider killed, and the psychic bond between rider and gauntling snapped, it went renegade," said Holm. "It's disobeying its orders; it's bent on revenge."

"I'll give it something to think about first." Tali aimed and fired.

"Well shot!" said Holm, running for a bucket. "Straight up the tail vent."

The gauntling's wings faltered and it curved down towards the sea, streaming blood from its rear. Had she killed it? The flow of blood stopped. It skimmed the water and laboured up again, then she lost sight of it in the fog, heading towards the distant shore.

"Not well enough," she said darkly.

"It's mighty hard to kill a shifter, but you've certainly hurt it. Give us a hand."

He tied a rope around the handle of a bucket, tossed it overboard then hauled it up and hurled the water at the flames. Tali did the same, but after a minute Holm put a hand on her shoulder.

"It's no use. The water's just spreading the oil."

"There must be a way to put it out," said Tali, imagining their fate when they ended up in the water. Either the sea beast that had taken Lizue, or the icy cold. At least it would be quick.

"There isn't," said Holm.

"Can we reach the shore?"

"No, it's miles away."

He heaved up his largest sail, turned to port and lashed the wheel so the boat would run true. "Come on!"

She followed him down into the cabin. "What are we doing?"

"Gathering everything we'll need to survive on an iceberg. Assuming we can reach one."

They heaped warm clothes and blankets into sacks. Holm tossed in a case of balms and bandages, a pot and a pan from the little galley, and the food in the cupboards. There wasn't much. His boat was not stocked for a long voyage.

"Carry it up." He began to pack tools and other gear into a haversack.

Tali lugged the sacks to the deck and put them down near the stern. The boat was moving swiftly under the larger sail, but the wind was fanning the flames on the front deck and driving them against the cabin. The smoke was thick and black, and the varnish was bubbling.

"Holm, *hurry*."

He came up, swaying on the ladder, carrying a square, heavy-looking box under one arm and a rucksack over the other shoulder.

"What's that box?" said Tali, feeling a familiar prickling and throbbing in her head.

"A heatstone stove."

"I don't like heatstone." Her father had died a terrible death slaving in the Cythonian heatstone mines.

"On an ice floe, it could mean the difference between life and . . . the thing we've been trying to avoid all day."

He ducked through the door into the cabin and went down the ladder.

"Come back!" Tali yelled.

The roof of the cabin was aflame now, and the inside could catch at any moment. If he were trapped below, if it fell in on him . . .

He came staggering up, coughing, his eyes watering, carrying a brown leather case.

"What's that?" said Tali.

"Memories."

"Are they really worth risking your life for?"

"Are yours?" said Holm, putting the bag down between his feet and turning a key in the lock.

Clockmaker, master mariner, expert in everything, and man of many secrets. What else was he?

The roof collapsed and in seconds the cabin was ablaze. Holm was peering out to the starboard side, sighting on the iceberg he had aimed for. It was a couple of hundred yards away and Tali didn't see how they were going to make it.

"We have a small problem," he said, in the conversational tone he used to make light of the gravest problems.

"And that is?"

"As soon as my wheel lashings burn through, the course we take is anyone's guess."

Tali squirmed. If they had to jump into the sea, she would die even if the iceberg was only ten feet away. She could not swim a stroke and knew she would panic in the frigid water – assuming the shock did not stop her heart.

"Actually, there are *two* problems," Holm went on, watching the flames roar ever higher. "As soon as the sail catches . . ."

The prospect seemed to amuse him. He went to the stern and began lashing spars to an oar. Tali wondered if he had lost his wits. She could not focus on anything but the blaze and how soon it would consume everything.

The iceberg was a hundred yards away when something broke in the cabin and the boat began to turn to port. Holm thrust his oar over the other side. He'd lashed some cross-pieces to it and a large square of canvas to the cross-pieces. He shoved it under and heaved.

"Makeshift rudder," he said. "Not near as efficient as the boat's rudder, but it's a darn sight bigger."

He heaved again. The boat turned back on course, then too far. He heaved the oar the other way. The iceberg was only sixty yards away now. Now only fifty . . . forty . . . thirty.

Whoomph! Flame leapt to the sail, and in seconds it was ablaze from bottom to top.

"We're goners," said Tali, thinking that the boat would stop dead in the water.

"It takes a little while for a heavy boat to lose way."

But it was slowing rapidly, and the bow was lower than it had been. "Water's coming in. We're sinking!"

It must have burned through the planking at the waterline and water was pouring in, though not quickly enough to douse the flames.

Fifteen yards. "We're not going to make it."

"I'll try to swing her alongside," yelled Holm. "Get ready to chuck everything onto the ice."

He wrenched out the makeshift rudder. The boat began to turn, very sluggishly. He ran to the other side and paddled. Ten yards. The boat slowed, but kept turning. Five yards . . . four. It was almost parallel to the rough side of the iceberg now. Three . . . two.

The bow dropped sharply. "Get the gear over. She's going down."

Tali heaved the bags across, then Holm's rucksack. He came hurtling back, tossed the leather case onto the ice, then picked up the heavy heatstone stove.

The gap started to widen again. "Jump, jump!" he roared.

Tali hesitated, sure she was going to end up in the water. No, better the water than the flames. With the boat tilting down steeply, the flames were licking around her. She dived for the ice, landed hard on her breasts and belly, then began to slide backwards towards the water.

Holm sprang, landed badly and dropped the stove, which broke apart, scattering slabs of heatstone across the ice. He scrabbled around, caught Tali's outstretched hand and yanked her up onto flat ice.

"Move the gear up."

He began to gather the pieces of heatstone, which were melting square and rectangular depressions in the ice, and wrapped a tattered blanket around them. They carried the gear up another ten yards, well out of the way of the breaking waves. When they turned around, the beautiful little boat was gone.

"Twenty years ago I built her, with my own hands," he said, holding them out before him. "I cut every plank, shaped every nail and peg by hand, and sailed the seas for many a year with her my only companion. And I didn't even see her go."

Tali put a hand on his shoulder. "I'm sorry."

"Ah well," he said. "It doesn't do to grow attached to things that can't last. Nor people, either."

CHAPTER 31

"It's going to rain, then freeze," said Holm, studying the sky. "If we're to survive the night, we'll need a cave, though I don't think we're going to find one."

Shock had finally set in and Tali was shivering in spasms. "We'd better look right away. It'll be dark in half an hour."

Fog closed around them, cold and dank, as they trudged along. The iceberg was a hundred yards long and shaped like a ragged, stretched-out pentangle. At the end where they had landed, a jagged peak rose steeply to sixty feet, then sloped away to only a few feet above the sea at the other end.

"No cave," said Tali, when they returned to the gear. "There's not even a crevasse or a hollow to break the wind. What are we going to do?"

Holm sat on a blanket and stared into the fog.

Had he gone into a decline because of the loss of his boat? Was it all up to her? Well, the lesson that had been reinforced many times in her eighteen years was that those who never gave up, those who kept searching for a way out to the very end, sometimes did survive against all odds.

Her head throbbed. Heatstone always had that effect on her. She moved a couple of yards further away from the wrapped slabs and sat down again. Then scrambled to her feet.

"Heatstone!" said Tali.

"What about it?"

"It's the answer."

Tali put on a pair of heavy gloves and picked up one of the slabs, which was the size of a brick sliced in two along its length. Even through the leather her skin tingled and prickled, she had put up with the effects before and could do so again.

She walked up the slope, wondering where to begin. Which way was the wind blowing? No, which way was it likely to blow hardest and longest and coldest? She spent several minutes wrestling with the question before realising that it was irrelevant. If the iceberg turned as it drifted, it would expose all sides to the prevailing wind.

Above her, the ice rose almost sheer in the lower part of the peak. If she started there, she would have less to remove. She picked a spot, held the edge of the heatstone to the ice, and pushed. *Sssss.* It began to melt its way in. Her head gave a sickening throb. She closed her eyes and continued.

"That'll never work," said Holm sourly. "You'll use all the heat in an hour or two, and what will it have gained you?"

"Shows how much you know about heatstone," she muttered.

"Beg pardon?"

"In Cython we often talked about heatstone — where it came from, and what the source could be that gave it such peculiar properties."

"What peculiar properties?"

"For one, you can't cool it. It gives off the same amount of heat no matter what."

"Is that so?"

"You mean there's something the great Holm doesn't know?" she said sarcastically.

"There's no need to be like that."

"Sorry. Heatstone makes my head ache."

Tali pushed harder and the heatstone melted its way in, faster. She withdrew it.

"Feel the edge. It's as hot as it ever was. Melting all that ice hasn't cooled it one bit. It keeps on heating whatever is around it for years, until one day it goes dead in a few seconds."

"I wonder why?" said Holm.

"No one knows whether the heat comes from within the heatstone itself, or whether it draws heat from somewhere else."

"You've convinced me."

Holm fetched another stove slab and pressed it into the ice a yard away from Tali. After ten minutes they had made a series of crisscrossing channels. With hammer and chisel, Holm cut away the ice in between and they began again.

Night closed in. The fog thickened until visibility was only a few yards, and their hair and eyebrows were dripping. They continued working by the subtle scintillations from the heatstone. It was slow and tiring, and Tali's head was throbbing mercilessly, but at least it was warm work.

At eight o'clock it started to rain, though by then they were sheltered by the cavity, kneeling side by side working at the ice face four feet inside the iceberg. By ten o'clock they had excavated a cave eight feet long, three wide and high enough to sit up in.

"That'll do for now," said Holm. "Let's get dinner."

They carried their gear in and stacked it at the front to break the wind. Holm reassembled the stove and began to cook a stew from smoked fish, dried vegetables, and copious amounts of spices. Tali sat at the back with her head in her hands, enduring the pain.

"Something the matter?" he asked, half an hour later.

"Ever since I dropped the sunstone down the shaft at Cython, and it imploded, heatstone makes my head feel strange and gives me terrible headaches. And each time I go near it, it's worse."

"I wonder why?" said Holm.

Tali had a fair idea why – because the sunstone implosion had woken the master pearl inside her and briefly liberated her recalcitrant gift for magery – but she dared not say anything that would make him think about ebony pearls and where they came from. Or who had been killed for them and how they were related to her.

She shrugged. "I should have known better than to use it for so long."

"Have some stew. Life always looks better after fish-head stew."

"You're really weird, Holm."

He chuckled.

She did not see how it could do anything for her ailment, but ate a bowlful then bedded down on the oilskin. After wrapping all her winter clothing around her, Tali closed her eyes.

When she finally clawed her way up from the deepest sleep she could remember, Holm was working at the back of the cave.

"What are you doing?" she said, yawning under her covers.

"Making a right-angle bend to give us more protection from the wind." He glanced up at the ice hanging above him, uneasily.

She looked out the entrance. Wind-driven snow, fine and hard, sandblasted her cheeks. All the gear was covered in powdery snow and drifts lay alongside her.

"What time is it?"

"Three in the afternoon."

"What, tomorrow?"

He laughed, and so did she.

"You didn't stir all night, or all day. How's your head?"

"Almost normal. Normally the headache goes, but I suppose I'm too close to heatstone."

He reinserted his slab into the stove and made a pot of tea. Holm drank at least six pots a day. She wondered how he fitted it all in.

"What's going to become of us?" she asked.

"Depends where the iceberg goes," he said, slurping his tea.

"Where's it likely to go?"

"Depends on the winds and currents."

"You've been sailing these waters for twenty years. You must have a fair idea."

"Everything's different now."

"How so?"

"When the sea level dropped, it exposed the sea bed out for miles. Tens of miles in some places. That changed the currents. And the ice sheet creates its own wind."

Tali sighed. Getting anything out of Holm was like prising open a barnacle. "If you had to guess, just to humour me, where would you guess this berg would drift?"

"More or less east."

"And that will take us where?"

"If it goes a bit north of east, it'll run aground in the shallows of Hightspall and stay there until enough ice melts that it can float away again in spring. If it drifts south of east, it'll jam into the ice packs around the edge of the Suden ice sheet and freeze there until the spring. And we'll starve when we run out of food."

"What if it drifts due east?"

"Out of the straits into the ocean?" he said grimly.

"Yes."

"We die."

"Just like that? No chance?"

"Nope."

He went back to his work, carrying his mug of tea. He kept checking the ice behind and above him, uneasily.

"Something the matter?" said Tali.

"Just wouldn't want to be trapped in here, is all."

"Looks pretty solid to me," she smirked. "Old Holm doesn't have a phobia, does he?"

"Mind your own business."

Tali had some more fish-head stew, walked around the iceberg several times in the clinging fog and returned to the cave. Holm came out of the entrance, carrying a bucket of ice chippings which he put on the stove to melt for water.

Tali inspected his work. It ran for another six feet around the corner.

"That's probably enough, don't you think?"

"Depends how long we're stuck here." He thrust the heatstone slab in as far as it would go, *sssss*.

"If we are stuck here, we can worry about it then."

"I like to keep busy."

"Have a break. Why don't you tell me about your life?"

"I've told you all that's worth hearing about."

Her eye fell on the locked black bag. "What's in the bag?"

"Two deaths on my conscience," he said curtly, then picked up the bag, checked the lock and carried it around the corner to where he was working.

It did not help her state of mind.

Tali did not use heatstone again, and kept as far away from it as possible, and gradually the headache went away.

The day passed, then the next, and the one after. Holm was increasingly taciturn. He spent his time either fishing, sleeping, or enlarging the cave with heatstone. After creating two rooms around the corner, he had chipped a number of shards off one of the heatstones to make carving tools, and was carving intricate patterns into the ice around the doorways. The work seemed pointless to Tali, but if it kept him happy, what did it matter?

The fog did not lift, so there was no way of knowing where the iceberg was taking them. They took it in turns climbing to the top of the peak, which they were using as a lookout, but the only thing they could see was the fuzzy disc of the sun, rising and setting. There was little wind now, and no sense of movement. They might have been trapped in an endless sea and the rest of the world vanished.

It rained heavily that night, and after it stopped, everything froze. In the morning Tali climbed up to the lookout and, in a few steps, broke out of thick fog into clear air. It was a bright sunny day and she could see over the roiling fog banks to the horizon – north to the green landscape and snowy mountains of Hightspall, south to ice-capped Suden, east—

The dome of the sky tilted, her throat closed over in panic and terror overwhelmed her. Her world had been closed in for so long that she had forgotten her own phobia. And she had no hat; she had nothing to cut off the terrifying, rocking sky.

Tali choked and stumbled backwards, desperately trying to reach the shelter of the fog, only a few feet down. She stepped onto a frozen rainwater puddle, moving too quickly, for the surface was as slippery as oiled glass.

Her feet went from under her, she fell forwards and struck a jagged edge of ice where part of the berg had broken away. The edge sliced deep into her left shoulder and she felt the blood flooding out.

"Holm?" she called weakly. "Holm?"

If he was working in the back of the cave, tapping away with hammer and chisel, he would never hear her. She yelled a couple more times, then began to make her way down backwards, terrified of falling again and rolling all the way down, into the sea.

But then she lost sight completely, and a blackness was growing inside her, a horribly familiar dark. She tried to fight it but did not have the strength.

CHAPTER 32

Someone had picked her up and was carrying her down a steep slope, then into a room out of the wind. It was warmer here, but she did not like it. A disgusting reek was growing with every step.

"Tali?" a man's voice said. He sounded worried. "Tali, wake up."
She could not wake up, and she had never heard of Tali.

"I'm Zenda!" she wailed. "I told you already; I'm not the one you're looking for."

"Sweet Zenda," a man said silkily. "Gentle, stupid Zenda, trapped like a mouse. You've got no idea what to do, have you? Come here, Zenda."

"Don't want to," she moaned. "Please don't make me."

"You don't want to," said the woman, "but you're going to. You're not a fighter like Mimula, nor a thinker like Sulien. You're apathetic, Zenda; the perfect slave. Come here!*"*

Zenda knew what they were going to do, because they had told her what they had done to her mother twenty years ago. They had exulted in the savage tale, feasted on her terror, fed on the blood.

But they were right about her. Sweet little Zenda *was* the perfect slave. *She had no idea what to do and did not even think about fighting for her life.*

She stumbled forwards, whimpering, "No, no, no," and put herself in their hands.

They cut the pearl out savagely, as though they blamed her for her fate. As only her agony could assuage their guilt.

Tali woke screaming, and it took ages to come down from the nightmare. No, the *reliving*.

The best part of an hour passed before she came back to who she was and where she was. Before the pain where the top of Zenda's head had been gouged away shifted and blurred into the pain in Tali's shoulder.

"It's all right," someone was saying, over and again. "You're safe now. No one can hurt you."

She forced her eyes open. Outside, the wind was howling again, but in the back of the cave, with Holm's carved ice door closed and the heatstone stove open, it was almost warm.

Holm's own eyes were closed. He was holding her in his arms, rocking her back and forth. Tali lay still, and gradually the nightmare of her *reliving* was replaced by a new fear – that she could have revealed her deepest secret to Holm, whom, after all this time, she knew little about.

"Stupid nightmares," she said with a false laugh. "I've been having them for ages."

"Right now, I'm more concerned about what happened up on the peak," said Holm, setting her down on the floor. The ice was carpeted with their oilskins.

As she sat upright, pain speared through her left shoulder. He made her a cup of spiced tea. She clamped her cold hands around it.

"On the peak?" she said, struggling to dredge up the memory.

"You fell and gashed your shoulder badly. I had to sew the wound back together."

Tali felt her shoulder, winced. Scraps of the moment came back.

"I reached the top and the fog lifted." She frowned. "No, I broke through it. The top was a few yards below me. There wasn't a cloud in the sky. It was glorious; I could see in all directions for a hundred miles . . ."

"And then?"

She did not want to tell him. Why should she reveal her secrets when Holm kept his from her? Besides, it would make her seem weak.

"How come you fell?" he persisted. "You're usually so sure-footed."

She was being silly. He needed to know. And if she opened up, perhaps he would too.

"I had a panic attack. I've been having them ever since I got out of Cython. The world is too big, and sometimes, on bright clear days, it feels as though the sky is overturning on me. I need a hat," she said plaintively. "Have you got a hat?"

"You can have my hat any time you want. And because of the panic attack, you fell."

"The ice was like greasy glass. I just slipped, that's all."

"No harm done, then. It's a nice clean wound. It'll heal quickly."

"I do heal quickly," said Tali. On the outside, anyway.

"Lunch?" said Holm.

"As long as it's not fish-head stew."

"I caught some fresh fish last night, while you were asleep. You can have them grilled if you like."

"I would like." Anything to distract him from asking about the reliving, though she thought she had got away with it by passing it off as a recurring nightmare.

He grilled the fish in a pan on top of the heatstone stove, which only took a few minutes, and served it with pepper and salt. It was the best meal she had ever eaten.

She started to get up to clean the plates.

"I'll do it," said Holm. "I don't want you moving that shoulder for a while."

He returned, made more tea then lay back on his covers.

Tali closed her eyes and was drifting to sleep when he said suddenly, "What was all that about Zenda?"

She jumped, fighting to calm herself. She hadn't got away with it at all. "Just a nightmare."

"Like the other one you had a while back, about a woman called Sulien?"

"How did you hear about that?"

"The healer in Rutherin told me. She was worried."

"Why did she tell you?" Tali said hotly. "She had no right. What's it got to do with you?"

"I've picked up a bit about healing in my travels," he said airily. "Unusual things. She thought I might be able to advise her. Who's Sulien?"

"No one you'd know."

"You mentioned a great-grandmother. Was that Sulien?"

His questions were like arrows, striking all around the target, perhaps deliberately. He was a clever man. Would he put the next one in the bull's eye?

"Or was Zenda your great-grandmother? And Sulien the one before that?"

Her only refuge was silence. She felt too weak to spar with him, or evade his probing questions.

After a couple of minutes of silence, he said, "Hold your tongue all you like. I think I can answer for you."

She started but did not speak.

"You keep having nightmares about murders," said Holm, sipping his tea. "Hardly surprising since you saw your mother murdered for an ebony pearl ten years ago, when you were the tender age of eight."

She opened her mouth to speak but he held up a callused, square hand. "There's no point denying it."

"I wasn't going to."

"Just as well. Since the scandalous revelations at the late Lord Ricinus's Honouring, any denial on your part would only heighten my suspicions."

Her attempt at an indifferent shrug sent pain spearing through her shoulder.

He continued. "Everyone with an interest in ebony pearls knows that four have been harvested, from four young Pale women. But no one knows who the other hosts were. They could have been any four out of a hundred thousand young women born in Cython over the past hundred years."

"Or more," said Tali desperately. "There are eighty-five thousand Pale, and if there were five generations, say, and half of them women—"

The number reminded her of her unbreakable blood oath, and her impossible duty to save her people. Every new victory by Lyf brought the fatal day closer – the day when he would have to move against the Pale, the threat at the heart of his empire.

"Something the matter?" said Holm.

"No," she lied.

"Good. The number of Pale isn't relevant," said Holm, "because there's another possibility – equally plausible. That those women belonged to a single, extraordinary family."

Her blood ran as cold as the ice the room was carved from. He knew! He knew everything.

"Your great-great-grandmother, Sulien; then your great-grandmother, Zenda. And your grandmother ..." Holm looked at her expectantly.

Tali could not fight him any longer. There was no point. "Nusee," she whispered.

"And finally your own mother, whose death you witnessed."

"Iusia."

"One thing puzzles me, though," said Holm. "Who was Mimula?"

"Mimoy. She was my thrice-grandmother, Sulien's mother. She had a gift of magery and she was a tough, cranky old cow."

"*You knew her?* Your thrice-grandmother?"

"She lived to be a hundred and nineteen. Though not *naturally*, Mimoy said."

"I wonder if she could have been the first intended victim, but she got away?"

"It never occurred to me . . . though she did have an old scar on the top of her head."

She looked across from him, sick with dread. "Well, you know my secret, and what I'm worth. What are you going to do with it?"

"Why would I want to do anything with it?" Holm said mildly.

"Everyone wants something from me."

"You should learn to trust more."

"That's not easy to do when you're *the one*, and bear a pearl in your head that's worth a province."

"Makes no difference to me. I have all the possessions I want."

"You just lost your beautiful boat because of me. With the pearl you could buy another one tomorrow."

"My boat was precious because I built it with my own hands, and because of the memories – of the places we voyaged together over twenty years. Neither can be replaced with any amount of money."

"All right. If you're a patriot, the master pearl could win the war for whoever you give it to."

"I am a patriot. Doesn't mean I'll do *anything* to save my country."

"Why did you hunt me down to the docks, if not for the pearl?"

"I didn't know you had it. Didn't even suspect it."

"Why did you risk your life helping me, then?"

"When I took you aboard, I didn't expect to be risking my life. If not for the ice, we would have escaped north and no one would have known where we were."

"You're a liar!" she yelled. "You were stealing the chancellor's most valuable prisoner, and in wartime that's treason. You didn't do that on a whim. What patriot would? *What do you want?*"

He buried his head in his hands.

"Well?" said Tali. "I've told you my deepest secrets. You could at least tell me something."

After a long interval, he said, "You can call it atonement, if it helps."

"It doesn't. Why atonement? Whose?"

"Let's just say that I did a terrible wrong once. Not deliberately, nor by accident, but through my own negligent arrogance. Others paid dearly for my wrong, and I took a vow, long ago, to try and make up for what I'd done."

"Oh!" she said, and knew by the way he spoke that he was telling the truth. At least, a small part of the truth. *Two deaths on my conscience*, he had said the other day. "What wrong did you do?"

"I don't see that it's any of your business." He rose, looking old and haggard, and went to the entrance. "The best thing you can do for your shoulder is to get a good night's sleep."

"I might say the same thing about your own ailment."

"I dare say you're right. But there'll be no sleep tonight for me, so I might as well go fishing."

He wrapped himself in his oilskins, put on fur-lined sea boots and stomped down to the water.

CHAPTER 33

"Do I have your blessing for this raid?" said Rix after outlining his plan to Swelt.

"If we don't fight for our country, we'll lose it."

"It's just the first stroke." Rix rose and began to pace. "If it succeeds, people will flock here to join my army and I'll plan a bigger strike."

"You have bold plans," said Swelt.

"We can't save Hightspall by hiding and hoping Lyf will go away."

"I agree. But when it does come to war, how are you going to pay the troops? Our treasury is almost empty."

"Every able-bodied man has to do thirty days customary service. After that, I'll pay them. I brought a small treasury of my own," said Rix, and was pleased to note Swelt's eyes widen. "Did you think I came empty-handed, like a beggar on the road?"

"Of course not," Swelt said hastily. "And when it's exhausted? Need I remind you how ruinously expensive war is?"

"I checked Father's accounts for the Third Army. I know the cost of a soldier, and a war, to the penny. And since we're on the topic, Astatin mentioned the ancient, secret treasures of Garramide."

Swelt rolled his eyes. "Many have sought them, but nothing has been found."

"Do you think there are treasures to be found?"

"Old manors are characterised by three things, Rixium. Ghosts, secrets and rumours of lost treasure. I put my faith in things I can count and measure." He looked down at the ledgers and lists on the table.

"Then why was Garramide built so strong?" said Rix. "It's the strongest fortress I've seen outside Caulderon."

"They say it was to protect Grandys' daughter – his only child, only relative. She was the only Herovian rescued from the wreck of the Third Fleet. Blood was everything to him."

Swelt turned the pages of a ledger, then added, "What if the raid isn't the success you expect?"

"It'll still worry Lyf."

"How so?"

With a flourish, Rix drew Maloch and held it high. "Grandys maimed Lyf with this sword, and I've fought Lyf with it, twice. And hurt him, too. More than anything in the world, he's afraid of Maloch."

Swelt smiled. "I'm pleased to hear it. What do you ask of me?"

"I need more men."

"Why?" said Swelt, frowning until his forehead bulged out over his deep-set eyes.

"The enemy garrison is forty or fifty strong. To be sure of success I need a hundred men—"

"You can't take a hundred from here."

"I wasn't planning to. Look, Swelt, you know everyone in these parts. Give me introductions to one or two young lords, of a like mind to me. Men who chafe under the yoke of this war and want to strike a blow against the enemy."

Swelt said nothing for a very long time.

"Is there a problem?" said Rix.

"I advise against it."

"Why?" cried Rix.

"I can introduce you to several young hotbloods who, according to reputation, would be only too happy to join with you on such a raid. But reputation isn't reality, and the men with the loudest mouths don't necessarily make the best allies."

"As long as they support me with a small number of fighting men—"

"They might say one thing and do another. They might agree to support you, then go running to the enemy. Or their wives or mistresses might talk them out of it—"

"Do you think I haven't thought about that?"

"If you plan to go to war relying on men you don't know, you haven't thought about it enough."

"Just do the introductions. I'll worry about the quality of the men I'm dealing with."

Though Rix was forcing their pace to the limit, he dared no light. They had to cover the twenty miles from Garramide to Jadgery and back in darkness, unseen, otherwise the enemy would follow them home. The Cythonians might suspect that the attack came from Garramide, but they must not know.

The track down the escarpment was by turns greasy, a knee-deep bog, and crisscrossed by sharp-edged outcrops. Rix, who had been riding since he was three and was an accomplished horseman, fell twice, and he was the best of them. By the time they reached the bottom two horses had broken their legs and one rider his neck. Rix left the man without a mount to bury the dead man, then walk back up to the mountaintop sentry post.

It was snowing gently as they gathered at the foot of the escarpment. At least one thing was going right.

"We're down to forty-eight," said Rix. It was barely enough for the main attack on Jadgery, and only if everything went perfectly, though he wasn't going to say that.

"Where are the others meeting us, Deadhand?" said Riddum, a lanky, sarcastic man who had been one of Leatherhead's strongest supporters. Rix *thought* he could trust him, though he wasn't absolutely sure he could trust any of them.

"The lord of Bedderlees has sent twenty men. They'll signal once they're in place at the rear of the garrison, then set fire to the barracks—"

"How?" said a voice from the darkness. Rix had no idea who it was.

"They'll hurl blazing oil bottles onto the roof, each holding enough oil to burn through wet thatch to the dry straw underneath. Yestin's thirty-five are attacking the right-hand wall. They're going to send a wagon filled with black powder down the hill into the palisade, aiming to blow a hole through it into the armoury on the other side and destroy their chymical weaponry."

"What's our plan?" said Riddum. "I assume you do have one?"

The disrespect was palpable, but the middle of a raid was no time for a lesson. Rix made a note to take the man down once they returned.

"We creep up to the garrison gates and wait for the signals. When the other attacks begin, we storm the gates and take the officers' quarters. It's the stone building around to the right. We want to capture their commanding officer, and any other officers we can find."

"Better to kill them so we can loot the place in peace," said Riddum.

"Are you leading this raid?" Rix said in a dangerous voice.

"We're taking our pay in plunder, Deadhand. We've got to make sure of it."

They went at a steady pace through the night, seeing no one on the way. Rix rode absently, trying to imagine all the ways the raid could go wrong and working out what to do about each problem. If the alert was raised before his allies were in position, for instance. Should he attack by himself, or abort the raid? His allies were to signal that they were in place, but in the dark he had no way to modify their orders. The question should have been decided in advance.

He scratched an itch under his chest-plate. He was wearing chest and back armour. It was heavy, ill-fitting and cold as an icicle.

At three in the morning they bypassed the town of Jadgery and walked their horses across a snow-covered field towards the garrison, which lay half a mile beyond the town. From his saddlebags Rix drew the steel gauntlet he'd taken from an old suit of armour. He straightened his dead fingers to slip the gauntlet on and closed its fingers into a fist. It wasn't as good as a sword in his right hand, but after a blow from his steel fist his opponent would not get up.

"Keep the horses calm," said Rix. "If one of them whinnies—"

"We know our business," growled Riddum. "Most of us were a'raiding when your mummy was still wipin'—"

Someone shushed him, which was just as well. Rix was considering knocking him cold and dumping him in the snow.

"Bedderlees and Yestin will signal when they're in place," said Rix. "That'll be in a quarter of an hour, if all goes to plan."

"You know them?" said Nuddell, a middle-aged raider with no hair and few teeth, a steady fellow who Rix felt he could rely on.

"I met them three days ago. Swelt introduced them as sound men. They seemed solid enough."

"Folk usually are in the security of their own manors." Nuddell spat sideways into the snow. "But when the night's cold and the wife is warm, staying a'bed can seem a better option than going a'raiding. Not that I know these young fellers, Lord."

Suddenly the night seemed a lot colder. Rix pulled his coat around him. "They gave their word. They'll be here."

"I'm just saying, is all."

The rendezvous time passed, then another quarter of an hour. Neither Bedderlees nor Yestin signalled.

"What's keeping them?" muttered Rix. His feet were freezing.

"They're not coming," said Riddum. "They've pulled a swift one on you, *Lord*."

"Shut up!" Rix ground out. "There's still time. We can still do it."

He swept the area with a pair of night glasses that had been his great-aunt's. She had used them for studying the planets and they had the finest lenses Rix had seen, but on such a dark night he could see no more than shades of shadow.

"Wait," he said, focusing on the steep slope up from the right-hand palisade wall, where Yestin's attack was to take place. "I think I can see movement up there."

The tiniest light flickered near the top of the slope, just below a crown of trees.

"What the hell are they doing?" said Rix. "The guards are bound to see that."

"Lighting the fuse to the black powder wagon, I'd say," said Nuddell.

Rix cursed fervently. Surely they knew enough to light it under cover? Evidently not.

"Tell the men to get ready," he said to Riddum. "We attack the moment the wagon blows up."

"What about Bedderlees? If he doesn't attack the barracks, they'll all swarm out to the gates."

"I'm sure he's in place," said Rix. He checked through the night glasses again. No signal could be seen from the rear. "All right. They've set it moving."

The clouds parted and a sliver of moonlight revealed the wagon trundling down the slope. But instead of rolling straight towards the wall it was curving around, across the decline. It teetered onto two wheels, then settled back and stopped, halfway down the slope. Dark-clad figures swarmed after it and tried to heave it back in line, though it did not budge.

"What the hell are they doing?" said Rix. "Never seen such incompetence."

"Looks like it's bogged." Riddum chuckled. "This is comical."

Rix resisted the urge to slug the man with his mailed fist.

"The fuse is sizzling," said Nuddell. "They'd better get a move on."

About twenty men had gathered around the sides and rear of the wagon. They swung it around and heaved it down the boggy slope towards the palisade.

"If it were me," said Riddum, "I'd be slipping quietly away. This ain't going to work."

Rix was of the same mind but he had given his word. He could not abandon his allies, no matter what a mess they were making of things. "It'll work – and whoever goes first gets a double share of plunder."

A cry rang out from the wall. Rix saw a signal lantern being waved there, and heard the clang of a bell.

"They've been seen. Attack. Attack now!"

As he raced for the front gates, a flare burst over the hill slope. Yestin's men were struggling with the wagon, which was bogged again, twenty feet from the wall. Yestin, a bear of a man, was heaving with the rest. I hope they're counting the seconds on the fuse, Rix thought—

With a colossal boom, the wagon exploded, scattering men everywhere and lighting up the area so brightly that Rix could see the outlines of the enemy guards running along the top of the wall.

He reached the gate with a dozen others. "Up and over," Rix said quietly. "First men in, slip the bar and open the gates. The rest of you, prepare the way."

He boosted a man up to grab hold of the top of the gate, which was twelve feet high, then another. Riddum and three of the other tallest men were doing the same. In a minute and a half, fifteen men had gone over.

As the last one dropped, a skyrocket soared up from the direction of the munitions store, then another. Could the blast from the wagon have set the store off? No, the rockets burst into half a dozen brilliant flares that lit up the buildings and yard of the garrison, and the area outside the walls, almost as brightly as day.

Rix drew his sword and waited for the gates to open. He did not hear the bar sliding. He heard nothing at all.

"What the hell's going on?" he muttered. "Riddum, get up on the gate and have a look."

Riddum might have been the focus of discontent but he was no coward. One of the men heaved him up. He leaned over, then threw his arms out, toppled backwards and crashed to the ground with an arrow through his chest.

"Dead," he said. "Throats cut. They were waiting for us . . ."

"Retreat!" roared Rix. "We've been betrayed. Retreat, retreat!"

He bent to pick Riddum up but he was dead. As Rix straightened, the gates were wrenched open and a squad of the enemy stormed out. Rix froze – he had only thirty-two men left, and if they ran the enemy archers would shoot them in the back.

But he also had Maloch. And here, the best defence was to attack.

"Stand firm!" he bellowed. "Attack!"

Without waiting to see if anyone was following, Rix hurled himself at the enemy, swinging the sword with his left hand and driving his steel-encased right fist into every vulnerable body part that presented itself. In one furious minute he drove three lines deep into the enemy, leaving a trail of fallen enemy behind him. He was surrounded on all sides. A sword he did not see clanged off his chest-plate. He struck the man down then whirled, slashing and striking, and around him several of his men were doing the same. Suddenly the enemy broke under the onslaught and began to retreat back through the gates.

For a mad moment Rix considered driving through them and on to the officers' quarters, to make something from this fiasco, but the officers were already streaming through the doors. Besides, only a handful of his men had followed him. The rest were either dead or had fled.

The light of the flares was fading as they dropped lower, and now they went out, leaving the scene lit only by slanting lantern rays from inside. He yelled, "Retreat! Retreat, while the dark lasts."

Suddenly Rix was alone. He was backing away, watching for archers, when he stepped on a body that moved under him.

"Ahh," yelped Nuddell.

"Sorry," said Rix, hefting him up.

"I'm done, Deadhand. Save yourself," groaned Nuddell.

"I don't leave my men behind."

"Then you're a bloody fool, if you don't mind me saying."

Three of the enemy attacked. Rix dropped Nuddell and cut down the first with a sword blow to the neck and the second with a steel-fisted punch that broke his jaw. The third was a huge man who, like Leatherhead, fought with a sword in each hand.

Rix matched him blow for blow, standing over Nuddell so the enemy could not strike him dead, then snapped the enemy's right-hand sword with a sideways blow of his mailed fist and slid Maloch through the gap into the fellow's lung. Air hissed out; the man slumped sideways and Rix ran him through.

He hefted Nuddell and ran with him towards the hidden horses, though before he was halfway the enemy had another flare up and the archers were firing. Ahead of him, several men fell. Arrows whizzed past on all sides, one sticking in the heel of Nuddell's left boot, two more shattering on the hardened steel of Rix's back-plate.

He heaved Nuddell over an empty saddle – there were plenty to choose from – bound him on, and checked on his men. Half the survivors had fled, not looking back to see if their fellows were all right, but there were twenty riderless horses. Horses Garramide could not do without.

"Get going, Deadhand," said Nuddell. "They're after us."

Rix slashed the tie ropes, roared at the horses and they bolted. He dragged himself into the saddle, only now realising that he was wounded in half a dozen places, and followed them.

From the top of the hill he looked back. The remains of the black powder wagon were blazing fiercely, and part of the palisade wall nearby. At least a dozen bodies were scattered around, the men who had been pushing the wagon when it went off. The closer ones must have been blown to bits. Another dozen had been taken prisoner and, knowing how the enemy treated prisoners, were bound for a cruel death.

Rix spurred his horse and raced after Nuddell, reckoning up the toll as he rode. Twenty of his men dead, plus at least fifteen of Yestin's, almost certainly including the lord himself. Another dozen taken prisoner and soon to be executed. An unknown number injured.

Bedderlees had not shown up, and clearly the knife men waiting at the gate had known the details of the attack. He must be a traitor.

And what had been gained? Neither the walls nor the gate had been breached, and the barracks and armoury were unharmed. They had killed at least ten of the enemy but the attack he had invested his credibility in had been a failure.

No, Yestin's incompetence had turned it into a fiasco.

To make matters worse, the snow had stopped and now the

moon came out. Rix rode wearily home, knowing they were leaving tracks that a child could have followed. They led directly to the escarpment track, and Garramide.

He should have listened to Swelt.

PART TWO

OPAL ARMOUR

CHAPTER 34

When Holm finally reappeared in the middle of the night, carrying a string of cleaned fish, Tali reached out to him.

"You said I should trust more, and I'm going to. Will you help me?"

"Depends what you're asking," he said gruffly. "I'm good with my hands, and I can add two facts together and get a third, but I'm no warrior."

She sat up on her covers. "I'm not asking you to fight."

"Yet I've been fighting ever since you landed in my lap."

"You came after me."

"Are you complaining?"

It silenced her for a while. "Of course not . . . Holm, I need to get control of my magery and I don't know how."

"You're asking the wrong man. Magery isn't one of my gifts, thankfully."

"Why thankfully?"

"If I'd had it when I was young, I would have done even more damage."

"I'm not asking you to use magery."

"What are you asking?"

"You understand how things work . . ."

"Some things." He pursed his weathered lips, puffed his cheeks in and out. "All right – a lot of things. So?"

"Can you tell me where I'm going wrong?"

"I doubt it."

"Will you try?"

"All I can do is listen and see if I notice something you've missed."

Holm made yet another pot of tea and offered her the first cup. She shook her head.

"Begin," he said.

She wasn't sure how to start. Or where. "Magery is forbidden in Cython."

"It always has been," said Holm. "Even in old Cythe, before the First Fleet came, magery was forbidden to the people. Using it was an insult to the king."

"But in Cython, any Pale with the gift are killed out of hand."

"What, even if they don't use it?" he said in a deceptively mild voice.

"Yes. Even little children."

His eye glinted. "Go on."

She told him about her own developing gift, and how her mother had warned her never to use it. Yet several times, when she was a little girl, it had exploded out of her, wreaking havoc, then it disappeared for years.

"It only happened when I was furiously angry, but I never had any control of it. Then, the night I turned eighteen and came of age—"

"When was that?"

"Um, I suppose it was five or six weeks ago."

"So young," Holm said to himself. "I can hardly remember that far back."

"That night I started getting dreadful, grinding headaches. I think they've got to do with the master pearl maturing."

She told him how the imploding sunstone in the shaft had seemed to release a block on her magery, temporarily at least. Next, when Banj had attacked, that a golden radiance had streamed out from Rannilt and touched her. Something seemed to burst inside Tali, then the white blizzard had burst from her fingertips to shear Banj's head off.

"He wasn't a bad man. Of all the Cythonians I knew, I liked Banj best." Tali hugged her arms around herself, staring into nothingness. "It was horrible. The sight will live with me all my days." She rubbed her fingertips. "But I still couldn't control my gift, or even call it at will."

She looked hopefully at Holm, hoping he could make sense of it. He said, "Continue."

"Later on, I had a theory that breaking a heatstone could release my gift."

"Did it work?"

"The chancellor gave me a little heatstone to break, when he sent me to the wrythen's caverns."

"And?"

"It released a lot of power, but Lyf stole most of it. Then he robbed Rannilt of her gift and after that he was ten times as strong. We were lucky to escape."

Holm indicated that she should continue.

"In the Abysm I saw power swirling around in vast, complex patterns, too strong for anyone to use."

"Really? Where did it come from?"

"It was spiralling up from deep in the earth. I also saw little coloured loops and whorls of power in the pattern. I thought they were the key to using my gift – if only I knew how to see them in the real world.

"In the three-way battle in the cellar, Lyf held a loop of power up in front of me," she concluded, "and I took power from it to defeat Deroe. I thought it was what Mimoy had meant – my enemy teaching me to use magery—"

"Maybe it was," said Holm.

"But I haven't seen those patterns again. I could only see them with the chancellor's spectible, and it was lost when the palace was attacked."

"That all?" said Holm.

"Yes."

She expected him to say something, or question her further, but he merely leaned back and closed his eyes. Occasionally he opened them to take another sip of tea, or replenish his mug. Tali lay down and closed her eyes. Time passed, at least half an hour, and her faint hope began to fade. When it came to her magery, every hope had turned to ashes.

"Heatstone," he said at last.

Assuming he was referring to the stove, she said nothing. Why had she imagined that Holm could help her?

"What about it?" said Tali.

"Where does it come from?"

"The heatstone mine."

"How did heatstone get there?"

"I assume it was always there."

"I don't think it was there when Cython was established."

"How would you know?"

"I've talked to a lot of people about heatstone," said Holm. "Such as the Vicini traders who buy and sell it. It was unknown to either side during the first war, so how did it suddenly appear?"

Tali did not reply. It was a good question.

"I think something *turned* the rock there to heatstone," Holm continued, "some time after Cython was founded. And later on, the first ebony pearls began to form in the women of your family."

"Why are you so focused on heatstone, anyway?"

"I think it's the key to your magery."

"How can it be? It hurts every time I go near a piece."

"And so does your magery, and the pearl you host. Doesn't that tell you that they're linked in some way?"

"I hadn't thought of it like that."

"So! If heatstone is the key, to unlock the lock we have to know how it formed." He looked up at Tali. "But right now, the important thing is your master pearl – *and how heatstone created it.*"

Tali jerked upright. "The pearls were *created* by heatstone?"

"By emanations from heatstone, I'd guess."

"Then why do pearls only form in my family?"

"Why does a gift for music, or dance, or magery run in some families and not in others?"

"All right, I'll clutch at the straw. Supposing you're right, how does it help me?"

"If your magery is blocked in some way, heatstone might liberate it."

"Are you planning to break one over my head?"

"Not unless you're more irritating than usual," he said, smiling.

"If heatstone can liberate my magery, what's that going to do to me?"

"That would depend on how you use it."

"Deroe said that ebony pearls were too strong for any host to use safely."

"He might have been lying; he might have been wrong. It's a risk *you* have to take. I can't advise you."

"I think I'll have a cup after all," said Tali.

He made a fresh pot. She pulled her coat around her and warmed her hands around the mug. It didn't feel as though they were getting anywhere.

"You might also ask yourself why this matters so much," said Holm.

"I swore a blood oath to save my people."

"You mean the Pale?" said Holm.

"Yes."

"How?"

She might as well tell him. "I'm afraid Lyf wants to get rid of them."

"Cast them out of Cython, you mean?"

"No – they know too much to be set free."

"About what?"

"How the enemy think, how Cython's defences work, where their water and air supplies come from and how they operate, how they grow food underground – the lot!"

"If the chancellor knew all that," mused Holm, "he'd identify Cython's weaknesses and find a way to attack it – poison the water supply, for instance. You're right, Lyf can't cast them out."

"And with the place nearly emptied of Cythonians, the Pale are a much greater threat than before. I'm worried, Holm."

"Why?"

"I think he'll order them to be put down."

"He's got the best of Hightspall already. Why would he care about protecting Cython?"

"The enemy were almost wiped out in the first war. They were driven out of their homelands and herded into filthy *degrado* camps, and they swore they'd never allow that to happen again."

"You mean—?"

"They'll *never* give up Cython. And I've often heard them threatening to get rid of the Pale. 'Come the day when we don't need your kind any more,' Orlyk used to say, and I think that day's nearly here. I think it's the ending Lyf plans to write in *The Consolation of Vengeance*."

"You may be right," said Holm, "but I don't see—"

"If the Pale are facing genocide, I have to fulfil my blood oath. I have to rescue them."

CHAPTER 35

Holm whistled. "Has it occurred to you that you're taking on the impossible?"

"Every day," said Tali. "Every hour! But what option do I have?"

"Was your blood oath that specific? Did you actually swear to go back to Cython and rescue them?"

"I'm not going to weasel out of it." How she wanted to; Tali knew she wasn't up to the job.

"Answer the question."

"No, it wasn't that specific, but it's what I have to do. So I'm going to need my magery."

"Ah, yes," said Holm. "And all the evidence suggests that emanations from heatstone created the ebony pearls – in you and your ancestors."

"By itself?" said Tali. "Or did Lyf have something to do with it?"

He must have. She could not bear the thought that her family's agony had a natural cause. Someone had to be at fault. Someone had to pay.

"But once created," Holm continued as if she had not spoken, "there's a tension between these emanations and the pearls. That must be why being near heatstone causes you such pain."

"I don't see—"

"I wonder if that tension might be used to unlock the power of your pearl?"

"How?"

"In a nutshell – ha! – by surrounding your head with it."

"Wouldn't that be painful?"

"Agonising," he said cheerfully. "I'm not sure I could bear to watch."

"Yet you're suggesting I do it."

"I suggest nothing. I advise nothing. You asked for my help. I'm telling you what I think. No more."

"If our positions were reversed, what would you do?"

"Our positions can't be reversed."

"Just answer the damn question," Tali snapped. "What would you do?"

"You're a prickly little thing, aren't you?"

"Especially when ugly old coots call me a *little thing*."

He sipped, refilled his cup and drained it. "A few things in life are worth the price one pays for them. Magery isn't one of them."

She stared at him, mouth open.

"No more questions," he said.

"Are you going to help me?"

"Are you asking me to, knowing the likely consequences?"

She licked her lips, which were unaccountably dry. "Yes."

"Then I'll do it – for my own reasons. Go to bed. You've got a long and painful day ahead ... *assuming you survive*."

"But I might not?" she said hoarsely.

"I'll do my best. I'd miss your company."

"But?"

"Death is a possible consequence."

She woke during the night. Holm had not moved in hours. He was sitting cross-legged on his oilskins, cutting the heatstones to pieces, shaping each piece and testing how it fitted together with its neighbours.

When she roused to see daylight streaming in, he was still leaning back against the ice wall, snoring gently. On the floor before him sat a heatstone helmet made of hundreds of perfectly shaped pieces, each slotted so they locked together like a three-dimensional jigsaw. What a marvellous craftsman he was.

The helmet was ten feet away, yet her head throbbed. How bad would it be with it on her head, surrounding her pearl to force the gift out of it into herself? It would be agonising; it might be unbearable.

There was no point dwelling on it; her oath must be kept. Just get on with it!

She put on the helmet and the pain was so bad that she wanted to scream. But she could not. She couldn't see, couldn't hear, couldn't speak, couldn't move – then her senses overloaded and the pain vanished—

"*I can't find it anywhere, Errek,*" *said Lyf.* "*What if it's been destroyed?*"

He was searching frantically, tearing the stones out of the wall of his temple with his bare hands and breaking his nails as he did.

"*Pray it has not,*" *said the faded wisp that was Errek First-King.* "*The balance is tilting rapidly now – far more rapidly than it should – and all forms of magery are failing with it. You've been profligate, Lyf.*"

Lyf hurled the stone aside, checked the space where it had been, then heaved at another. "*The enemy are devils. I had to make sure we won the first battles within hours. I had to make them believe we were invincible.*"

"*Was it worth it? We would have won within days anyway.*"

"*I hadn't realised that pearl magery was limited; that the well could be emptied so easily.*"

"*And now you know,*" *said Errek.* "*Don't waste any more magery on the war. You've got to save it for your greatest task – if it's not done soon, the balance will tilt so far that it'll be irreversible.*"

"*Without the key, I can't even begin.*"

Too late for what? thought Tali. What balance? Why irreversible?

"*Then get the master pearl,*" *said Errek.* "*It'll lead you to the key.*"

The pain flooded back and overwhelmed her again.

Tali wrenched off the helmet. Her head felt as though an axe was buried in it. She rolled over, crawled out to the entrance and vomited down the icy slope.

Holm handed her a cup. She rinsed her mouth with it and allowed the rest to run down her throat, which felt hot and inflamed, as if she had been screaming.

"Better?"

"No!" she croaked. "Why did you let me do such a stupid thing?"

"You only had it on for ten minutes."

"Ten very bad minutes."

"Not as bad as they might have been. Did it work?"

"I don't know; all I remember is pain. But I don't feel any different."

"Why don't you test your magery?"

"Don't have the strength."

"Or are you afraid to try in case you fail?"

She didn't answer.

"Success is built on the failures you learn from. If you're afraid to fail, you'll never succeed."

Tali pointed a trembling finger at him. "I'm getting an urge to blast every grey hair off your leathery old head."

"I could use a haircut."

She sat down, abruptly, as the memories flooded back. "I saw something."

"What?"

She told him. "And it's not the first time. I also saw Lyf and the same ancient ghost after my first blood-loss reliving. His name was Errek and he was telling Lyf what to do. Who was he?"

"Errek First-King. The very first of the line of Cythonian kings, ten millennia ago. He's a legend, credited with saving the land and inventing king-magery."

"Is it true?"

"After all this time, who could tell?"

"Well, Lyf was asking Errek's advice and taking his orders."

"It raises many questions," said Holm. "What *balance* was Lyf talking about, and why is it *tilting* so rapidly? What's changed?"

"And what's the key he needs so badly? Is it a key to a safe? Or a secret door?"

"When was it lost? Did he say?"

"No; but I first envisaged him searching his temple not long after the chancellor fled Caulderon," said Tali, thinking it through. "And that's the first time Lyf had been alone in his temple since the Five Heroes abducted him—"

"Two thousand years ago. So he's looking for something hidden – or put away – before then."

"Which he needs for his *greatest task*. But what could be more important than winning the war?"

"I don't know ..." Holm got up, went to the entrance and looked out, then came back. "But we have learned a piece of vital intelligence."

"What's that?"

"Lyf's speedy victories weren't due to his superior armies after all. They came because he used colossal amounts of magery."

"Why is that important?"

"If magery is failing everywhere, he won't be able to use it in battles to come. It evens things out."

"It explains why mine has been so hard to use," said Tali.

"Which brings me back to the link between your pearl, your magery and heatstone. Why would its emanations create pearls and be linked to their magery?" Holm paced to the entrance again, strode back. "Got it!"

"Got what?"

"Heatstone was unknown in the ancient world. So what brought it into being?"

"No idea," said Tali.

"Yes, you do," said Holm. "It was created by a great and powerful event, to do with magery, long ago ..."

"I don't know enough about history—"

"Yes, you do."

She stared at Holm. "Are you talking about Lyf's lost king-magery?"

"It seems the most likely answer."

"Are you saying that, after Lyf's death, his king-magery sank into the earth and turned a great area of rock to heatstone?"

"It explains the link between heatstone and the pearls, and their magery. It explains everything – and raises a worrying question."

"But king-magery was a vast force," said Tali. "Far greater than any other kind of magery. So why is it failing?"

"Maybe it isn't. But lesser kinds of magery we know *are* dwindling. It's time to test yours. Let's see if the helmet has worked."

Tali looked into her inner eye, and for the first time in the real world she saw the coloured loops and whorls that held power. They were dull, though, far weaker than they had appeared in the Abysm. She reached to the nearest loop and drew power. Her skull throbbed.

She pointed her right hand at the wall.

"Not there," Holm said hastily. "You might bring a hundred tons of iceberg down on our heads."

She went to the entrance and pointed at the edge, down near the waterline.

Ice, break!

Three feet of iceberg shattered and cascaded into the water.

"Power *and* control," said Holm. "I'm impressed. How are you feeling?"

"My head hurts, though not as badly as I would have expected." She shivered.

Tali went inside and pulled her coat around her.

"Well, you can't expect miracles."

"What was the worrying question?"

"What?"

"You said the link between heatstone, the pearls and magery raised a worrying question."

He frowned. "King-magery was only ever used by the kings – and ruling queens – of Cythe. And only for healing the wounded land and people."

"Why is that worrying?"

"On becoming king, every Cythian king of old made the choice to use the great power of king-magery only for healing, not for destruction – because to do otherwise would be disastrous."

"How do you know this?"

"I told you, I've always been fascinated by both history and magery. Each king had to affirm his choice, for healing, in a great public ceremony."

"What's the worrying bit?"

"Your magery comes from heatstone, which formed from king-magery. If you use magery for purposes *inimical* to healing, it's likely to damage your ability to heal."

"I wasn't planning on doing much healing," said Tali.

"That's all right then," said Holm.

"Why?"

"I believe that, with pearl magery, you can be a destroyer or a healer, but not both. You have to choose — then keep to that choice — forever."

CHAPTER 36

The whole of Palace Ricinus had been torn down, save for Rix's leaning tower. The rubble had been cleared away and the land dug deep to expose the foundations of the kings' palace that had stood here in ancient Cythe, when the royal city had been called Lucidand. Lyf had sketched the great buildings of the city as he remembered them before the First Fleet came, and given the sketches to his architects. Soon he would make a start on the restoration.

"This is an unhealthy obsession, Lyf," the shades of his ancestors kept telling him. "Our past means nothing to your people any more."

There were a hundred and six of these shades, and each, in life, had been one of the greater kings or ruling queens of old Cythe. Lyf had created them, his ancestor gallery as he liked to think of them, during his long exile as a wrythen. For centuries he had relied on them for advice and support, though latterly their advice had mostly been contrary, and he was fed up with it.

"It does, it does," said Lyf.

"No, it doesn't," said Bloody Herrie, the angriest and most contrary shade of them all. He rubbed his red, hacked throat. "The remnants of old Cythe were extinguished when our *degrado* camps were burned by the enemy and you allowed the last of our people to die."

"Not the last — just the last of the adult *degradoes*. They were fatally corrupted. We had to start again, with the children. The untainted ones."

"Your aim may have been noble, but in doing so you wiped our past clean. You took those children and remade our people from them, but they have no history save the one you fabricated for them, in your blasphemous *Solaces*. Why should any of this matter to them? Let Cythe go, Lyf."

"I can't!" he cried.

The kings' temple had been restored to its simple, ancient beauty. Yet, though every flagstone had been torn up, cleaned, and the soil for a yard beneath it had been removed and replaced, still the foul odour lingered.

But all would be well, in time. After the war had been won Lyf would use king-magery to heal his land and his troubled people.

"I'll have the daily war report," he said to his waiting generals.

"The chancellor is playing at war in the south-west," said General Hramm, "but he's plagued by self-doubt and struggling to make alliances. We can discount him."

"I never discount an enemy until his head is impaled on a pole," said Lyf. "The chancellor may be down, but he's a wily, formidable foe. He may be making his case look worse than it is to gull us. Redouble the watch. Urge our saboteurs and insurrectionists to greater efforts. Undermine him every way we can."

"It will be done, Lord King. In the north-west, there have been a number of skirmishes north of Bledd. Though none to trouble us."

"What about the hunt for the slave, Tali, and my master pearl? Surely you have some good news there?"

General Hramm looked all around the room.

"Well?" said Lyf.

It burst out. "Tali escaped from Fortress Rutherin with a man called Holm. They were pursued out to sea but escaped again, sinking most of the pursuing boats. Lizue found them in the Southern Strait and attempted to take Tali's head in a bag—"

"Well?" said Lyf.

"Tali beat Lizue in combat, threw her overboard, and she was eaten by a shark."

Lyf reeled. "Not Lizue! She was my best. How do you know this?"

"Her gauntling came back, eventually . . ."

"Yes? Go on."

"The bond between gauntling and rider is strong, Lord King, and when she died in so bloody a way, the balance of its mind was broken. It turned renegade and dropped an oil bombast onto Holm's boat. It burned and sank."

"It *sank*?" Lyf stared into empty space. Could two thousand years of planning be defeated by the malice of a deranged shifter? He had created shifters specifically to terrorise the enemy and the irony was too painful to contemplate. "What about Tali?"

"Her fate isn't known. The gauntling was badly injured by a crossbow bolt, and fled. I'm sorry, Lord King. The treacherous beast will be put down once it's found, of course."

Lyf clacked back and forth on his crutches, struggling to breathe, then whirled and stalked to the pearls. Taking them in his hand, he sent out the *call*. It was not answered, but neither did he feel the painful emptiness that would signify the master pearl had been destroyed.

"Don't put the beast down. I don't believe the pearl has been lost. Identify the location, then redouble the search where the boat sank, and for a hundred miles around."

"Yes, Lord King. We'll have to be more careful with gauntlings in future."

"They're a flawed creation," said Lyf. "The intelligence that makes them such useful spies also gives them less desirable attributes. They're headstrong, vengeful, malicious . . ."

"And always looking to break our control. I recommend that you put them all down, Lord King."

"Once the master pearl has been found and the war won, I will. Until that time, they're the only aerial spies I have, and I can't do without them."

Lyf floated up into the air, as if the extra height could enable his inner eye to see further, but it did not. He descended to the floor. "What else?"

"Lord King," said General Hramm, with a show of reluctance, "the ice grows ever closer, and the weather colder. With so many prisoners to feed, it will be a struggle to survive the winter."

"There is a solution," Lyf said softly.

"Not one that is palatable to your people, Lord King. As you know, for some time there has been muttering about the senseless bloodshed and wanton destruction."

"Very well," snapped Lyf. "A wise king listens to the voice of his people. What are they saying?"

"That we've done enough. That we should negotiate for peace. And coincidentally, the chancellor has sent a second lot of envoys."

"I know," said Lyf. "They've been waiting for three days, trying to see me, and I've been refusing them."

"It never hurts to talk, Lord King. They're bound to reveal more than you will."

"I suppose so. Send them in. But I'll never trust the chancellor. And I'm making no concessions, nor giving back any territory."

After seeing the envoys, he called Hramm back to complete the war report.

"What's the situation in the north-east?"

"Mostly quiet, but underneath, rebellion seethes," said Hramm. "As you know, there are many Herovian manors in that area."

"That irks me," said Lyf. "Have we the strength to subdue the region?"

"It would take another two armies. The mountains are difficult to fight in, the manors isolated and well fortified, the people of a rebellious disposition – and the weather very bad."

"Are they preparing for war?"

"Not that we know, save for the place where your most bitter enemy, Deadhand, has taken refuge."

"Does this place have a name?"

"Garramide. And he has the sword, Maloch, with him."

Lyf let out a hiss. "How did you find him?"

"A lord in our pay brought news of a planned raid on our garrison at Jadgery. Our troops were waiting. They crushed the attack and followed the tracks of the survivors. Deadhand – Lord Rixium – was their leader."

"Garramide," said Lyf. "Do I know it?"

"The manor of Wendand Nil stood there in your time—"

"My time? *Now* is my time."

"When you were king of all Cythe, my king," Hramm said hastily. "It was torn down, and Garramide built in its place by Axil Grandys for his bastard daughter. It's been a Herovian outpost ever since."

"Hand-pick a force, the best we have. Crush Garramide and raze it."

"Yes, Lord King," said Hramm.

"Then bring me the sword, and Deadhand's hands – and his head, impaled on a spike."

CHAPTER 37

The whole of Garramide was waiting in the main courtyard when Rix rode in with Nuddell and the twenty riderless horses, though they weren't waiting for news. The survivors of the raid had told the bitter tale an hour ago.

"What went wrong?" said Swelt, gnawing at a blood sausage.

"Bedderlees betrayed us. The enemy knew when we were coming and how we planned to attack. They were waiting inside the gate."

"And they'll follow you back," said Porfry, colourless and dry as dust. "For nineteen hundred years Garramide has been unassailed. Now, in one reckless night, you've destroyed it, Deadhand."

"Doom, doom on us all," howled the witch-woman, Astatin.

Blathy stared at Rix, arms folded over her bosom. No doubt comparing him to Leatherhead, who had never been known to fail in a raid.

"When the enemy attacks, hundreds of us are going to die," said Porfry.

No one felt his failure more keenly than Rix, but he was the lord and had to protect morale. "The doom of this fortress was set in ancient times, when Axil Grandys tore down the Cythian manor that once stood here and built Garramide in its place."

"How dare you blame our noblest ancestor for your failings!"

"The past has created the present, every bit of it—" Rix broke off, reflecting wryly that Tobry had not long ago made the same point to him. "As soon as the centre is secure, Lyf will attack the provinces. Garramide would have been high on his list whether I came here or not."

"It's higher now," Porfry said mulishly.

"Our country is being torn apart by a brutal enemy, Porfry, and if we don't fight for it we're going to lose it. Would you have me hide like a coward?"

"Enough, Porfry," snapped Swelt. "A garrison that size can't attack a mighty fortress like Garramide. Lyf will have to send a force from Caulderon – if it isn't already on its way."

"The result is the same," said Porfry, shooting Swelt a hostile glance.

"And you're a whining coward who wouldn't fight to save your own mother!"

"I think that'll do," said Rix. "Let's go in."

"Besides," Swelt went on, "Garramide is the greatest surviving Herovian manor, built by Axil Grandys. And Maloch – the weapon Lyf fears more than any other – lay hidden here for the next nineteen centuries. Lyf's attention would have turned to us sooner, not later."

Most of the servants had gone inside, but a small group lingered, shooting Rix dark looks, and Blathy was among them. He could see the fierce joy in her dark eyes.

Swelt turned to Rix and said quietly, "Don't take any notice of that rabble. The servants that count aren't *too* upset."

"Why not?"

"Surely that's obvious?"

"Enlighten me."

"The dead men were the worst of Leatherhead's thugs and they treated the servants badly. They won't shed any tears."

"It doesn't lessen my failure."

"But it will reduce the consequences. I'll send messengers to every hut and steading on the plateau, telling them to be ready to bring their people and livestock to Garramide. We've got to get ready for a siege."

"Thank you, Swelt," said Rix. He had one ally in Garramide, at least.

Glynnie was also watching him but her eyes were hooded and he could not tell what she was thinking. She had a livid mark on her right cheek, and her arms and legs were covered in bruises.

She had always been his stoutest defender, and look how he had repaid her.

What have I done? Rix thought. And how am I ever going to fix it?

The fire in his suite was blazing and the room was full of welcoming steam. Rix had never been more glad to see it. He stripped off his filthy, bloodstained garments and collapsed into the bath that had been drawn for him. He was pouring a dipper of water over his head when the latch on the outside door clicked.

He started up, water going everywhere, and was reaching for Maloch when Glynnie came through the inner door with an armload of clean clothes. She yelped and looked away. He sat down in the tub, hastily.

"You're hurt, Lord Deadhand." It sounded like an accusation.

"Just scratches."

She approached the tub, inspected his chest, arms and back. Glynnie was trying to look like an impassive servant, but she was trembling. She put down his clothes.

"They look bad. Let me tend—"

It wasn't right that she should be looking after him when he had done her such wrong. "No!" he said, more harshly than he had intended. "It's nothing. I can do it."

"You rob me of every little thing we had together," she said. "You must really hate me."

"I don't! I care—"

She went out as quietly as she had entered.

Rix flopped back in the tub. What could he do for her? He couldn't give her a new role – that would only make her position worse, and heighten the rumours that she was his lover.

As he sat there, brooding, an image of the raid came to mind, a moment he had not seen but had thought about constantly on the long ride home. Fifteen men climbing over the gate in the dark, only to have their throats slit as they reached the ground on the other side. Many had been thugs, even brutes, but Rix had trained and fought with them, and none of them had been wholly bad. They had all cared about someone, or something.

Fifteen fathers, sons or brothers who would never come home to their weeping womenfolk, their grieving fathers, their families who might now starve in this most bitter of all winters. And he had given the order that had sent them to their deaths.

It was an inevitable consequence of being a leader in wartime. The chancellor's orders had led to tens of thousands of deaths – soldiers and civilians – and perhaps, after a while, the body count grew so high that one became numb to it. Rix had not reached that stage. He could see all their faces.

Hours later he was still sitting in the icy tub when Glynnie reappeared, wringing her small hands.

"What are you doing?" she said softly.

"Counting my failures and reckoning up the toll. Trying to make peace with all those men I sent to their deaths."

"Well, stop!"

"The faces won't go away."

"They went willingly – for plunder." She thumped him on the shoulder, hard. "Get out."

"What?" he said dazedly.

"Get out of the tub."

"Why?"

"I've got to tend to your wounds."

"They don't matter. Nothing matters."

She slapped him across the face, a stinging blow with all her strength behind it. "Get. Out!"

He looked up at her, rubbing his cheek. "What was that for?"

"I liked you better as a good man who had failed than I do you wallowing in self-pity, Lord."

"I'm not wallowing . . ." But he was.

"Get up and do something about your problems."

She fetched the red towel and stood by, waiting.

He crouched in the icy bath. "I'll get out when you leave."

"I'm not a *real* person, just a maidservant here to attend your needs."

Rix did not have the energy to fight her. He rose from the tub and allowed her to dry him, which she did with a servant's thoroughness. Her cheeks were pink when she finished. He slipped into the fur-lined robe she held out for him.

"On the bed," she said.

He blinked. "I beg your pardon?"

Her flush deepened. "The enemy are going to attack us, aren't they?"

"Yes."

"How soon?"

"Too soon."

"Then you've got to be in a fit state to take charge of the defences."

She wrenched the robe down over his shoulders, slapped a handful of some foul-smelling paste into the long gash down his upper arm, and rubbed it in with furious strokes.

Glynnie climbed onto the high bed and loomed over him, using her weight to force the paste deep into a puncture wound in his upper chest, then a slash between his ribs, jamming it into the inflamed area with her thumbs. He bit back a groan.

"Something the matter?" said Glynnie.

"No."

"It'd serve you right if you got infected and had to rely on other people for a change. I almost hope—" She broke off, her cheeks crimson. "Lord, forgive me. Sometimes my mouth runs away with me."

It was time for a truce. "Sorry. Didn't hear what you said."

"Garramide needs you sound and healthy, Lord. You're its leader, its inspiration. Its hope, and Garramide can't do without you."

"All except you." Rix took her hand. "I'm really sorry. I've treated you badly."

"Yes, you have," she said softly, staring into his eyes. Her green eyes were huge.

"But not because I don't care about you . . ."

"I don't understand what you're saying."

"It's because I care too much."

Tears quivered on her lashes. "You've got to look after yourself, Rix. You're all I have now." She turned away, turned back. "Don't worry about my little problem with the servants. I can fix it."

CHAPTER 38

"That mural is bad luck, Rix," said Glynnie, several days later. "I wish you'd paint over it."

He did not like it either, but Rix was constantly drawn back to the work, as if his crude dabs of paint could reveal the man within. Swelt had given him a book on Grandys and Rix now knew all the man's astonishing achievements, though little about Grandys himself.

He had been everything Rix was not – a brilliant, charismatic leader who had pulled off one impossible victory after another. His troops would have followed him anywhere, but what had he really been like?

"Have you been listening to Astatin again?" he said, belatedly responding to Glynnie's remark.

"It's impossible not to. She stalks the halls by day and the battlements in the starlight, forecasting doom and disaster. And Blathy is worse. Is everything ready?"

Everyone in the fortress had been working night and day to ready the defences, and Rix and Glynnie were snatching a few minutes' break up in the old dame's observatory.

He went to the wall and looked down on the yard. The carpenters had almost finished strengthening the gates. Behind them the masons were raising a second line of defence, a wall of basalt blocks, but cutting and laying such hard stone was slow work and after a week and a half it was only shoulder-high. Better than nothing, if the enemy broke through the gates, though not much better.

"You can never be truly ready for war – there's always more that can be done. But the walls are strong, the stores are in, the weapons ready and the new wall guards trained . . . At least, as best I could in the time."

"And we've all had some training with a knife or a sword," said Glynnie. "We're ready to fight for our house and our country."

If only servants could be trained to fight battle-hardened warriors that easily. If he survived the coming struggle, which seemed unlikely, how many more dead faces would he have to endure? And would Glynnie's be among them? If only things could go back to the way they were . . . but that offered no comfort, either. House Ricinus's wealthy, privileged life had been built on the murder of innocents and the near slavery of its servants and serfs.

"Is Oosta back yet?" said Rix.

The chief healer was a law unto herself and, without telling Swelt or Rix, she had taken both her assistants to a village on the far side of the plateau two days ago, to attend a serious outbreak of buboes. They had not yet returned.

"No," said Glynnie, "but I've had the healery scrubbed down and a dozen beds moved into the recovery room next door, and I've used her recipes to make extra balms and healing draughts. The amputation saws have been sharpened and . . ."

What would I do without you? Rix thought. While I agonise, you just get on with all the jobs that need doing.

His belly was aching. He'd fought in various skirmishes before, but never a proper battle. War was a terrible business and, as Jadgery had shown, the most carefully laid plans could end in disaster. What if this great fortress fell, and all its people were put to the sword, solely because of his failures?

He turned his great-aunt's field glasses towards the track that wound up the escarpment. Only glimpses could be seen from here, but anyone reaching the top of the track was immediately visible.

"How long until they come?" said Glynnie, beside him.

"No idea. Why did I make that foolish raid on Jadgery?"

Nowadays, she was his staunchest defender. "We came here to fight, Rix. If the raid had succeeded, people would be praising your name all across Hightspall. How long until the wall behind the gate is finished?"

"Another three or four days, if the masons can keep up the pace."

"There's one more thing."

Something flashed in a gap between the trees. Someone was riding up the track. No, racing up it, which was liable to kill the horse or break his own neck. "Mmm?" he said absently.

"I'm really worried about Blathy. She hates you. You've got to get rid of her."

"You're right. I should have taken your advice. But it's too late now."

"Give me three guards and I'll have her off the plateau within the hour."

He felt the tendons in his neck go rigid.

She stood up on tiptoe and looked over the wall. "What is it? I can't see anything."

"See that speck at the top?" said Rix, handing her the glasses. "It's a horseman, and he's just come hurtling up the mountain track."

She lowered the glasses, staring at him. "No one would gallop up the escarpment unless it was an emergency."

"He's waving a red warning flag."

"Does that mean—?"

"Yes, the enemy are coming."

He ran to the bell that stood beside every watch post in the fortress and swung the clapper against the side, three times, then three more. The signal that an enemy attack was imminent.

"How did they get an army here so quickly?" said Glynnie. "Rix?"

"What?"

"Get going."

"Where?" he said dazedly. He sagged against the wall. This was it. The fortress was ready, but he was not. Normally, he was good in a crisis but he could not think where to begin.

"Signal the other manors and villages," said Glynnie. "If they're not inside our walls by nightfall, they're lost."

"The emergency signal, yes!"

"And Oosta. Signal the healers to come back immediately."

Rix's thoughts unfroze and he set off at a run, down the observatory tower steps and across the yard towards the battle tower behind the gates. "Why didn't I consider that the enemy might make a forced march and get here in half the time? Because I'm a fool."

"If they've been on a forced march for a week," said Glynnie, "won't they be exhausted?"

"Utterly."

"So they won't be able to fight very well."

"Neither well, nor for long," said Rix. "That's the first positive thing I've heard all day."

He crashed his way up the steps to the top of the battle tower. Glynnie came after him, red-faced and gasping. A watchman stood by the great cast-iron fire box. He had taken the rain cover off, and the fire box was piled high with kindling and tar-soaked wood.

"What are you waiting for?" panted Rix.

"Orders, Lord Deadhand," said the watchman.

A brazier stood in an angle of the wall, occasional raindrops spitting and hissing as they struck the coals. Rix wrenched a tar-coated stick out of the fire box and jammed it into the coals. It caught at once. He thrust it into the centre of the fire box. The tarred wood exploded into fire that leapt ten feet high.

"What's the signal, man?" Rix yelled.

"For what?" said the watchman. "Heard the bell but don't know why it was rung."

"Can't you see the enemy?"

"He doesn't have field glasses, Rix," said Glynnie quietly. "And, by the way he's squinting, I'd guess he's short-sighted."

"A short-sighted watchman," Rix said in disgust.

Glynnie opened her mouth to speak, but closed it again.

Rix knew what she had been going to say. He was thinking it too. *You're the leader. You should have checked.*

"You can't think of everything," said Glynnie. "You've never done this before."

"There are no excuses in war – you win, or you lose." He turned to the watchman. "What's the signal for an enemy attack?"

"Green flame."

"Make it."

The watchman ducked into his booth and came out holding a heavy bag.

"All of it?" said Rix.

"Just half."

Rix slashed the top of the bag open. The watchman heaved half the white mixture in the bag into the fire box. The dancing, whirling flames turned green.

"Go down to the wall," said Rix. He sprang up on top of the watch post and roared, "The enemy are coming! Where's Captain Noys?"

"Here, Lord Deadhand," said a stocky man wearing a jerkin of crimson leather.

"They'll be here in under an hour. Rouse out the men. Get them fed. Unlock the armoury and arm everyone."

Noys began to shout orders.

"Even Blathy?" said Glynnie.

"She can kill me as easily with a kitchen knife as a sword."

"Then you'd better watch your back. What do you want me to do?"

"If Oosta and her healers are cut off, we're in dire trouble."

"I know a bit about healing."

"Good! Take charge. Swelt will know who can help you. Round them up, and make sure they scrub their hands. Oh – and Astatin knows some healing magery."

"Anything else?"

"If there's any trouble among the servants, report it directly to me. I'm going to see Swelt and after that I'll be on the outside wall, by the gates."

Glynnie gathered her skirts and ran. Rix headed the other way, down to the castellan's little empire. Swelt wore a battered old sword that was too long for him; its tip dragged on the floor as the round little man paced. Rix smiled at the sight, but he appreciated the effort.

"A little earlier than you were expecting," said Swelt.

"But not you?"

"A good castellan hopes for the best and prepares for the worst."

"How well prepared are we?"

"We went through all this the other day."

"Tell me again."

"If it'll soothe your nerves," said Swelt. "We're as well prepared as we can be. The cellars are stocked, the cisterns full and the barns stacked with hay and silage. We have carcasses enough in the cold rooms—"

"Not a complete inventory, Swelt, or the enemy will be at the gates before you complete it. Just the overview."

"I am giving you the overview. Oh, very well! We have food and drink for ourselves and our beasts, and weapons enough. And the walls are in sound shape, all things considered. What we lack, and you already know this, is men to defend them."

"We have three hundred and twenty armed and ready," said Rix, "and another forty or fifty still to come in from outlying manors and steadings. But . . ."

"To defend the walls from a serious attack we'd need twice that number."

"Before we panic, let's see how big the enemy force is."

Rix nodded his thanks, turned away, then swung back. "I've told Glynnie to take charge of the healery. I'd appreciate if you could back her up."

"The girl has spirit," said Swelt. "And many talents. And she never complains, no matter the . . . er, setback. She just tries harder. I find, to my surprise, that I admire her . . ."

"But?" said Rix.

"We're at war. I'll support her all the way."

"Thank you."

He headed down through the halls to the front gate, but at the front door he decided to climb back to the battle tower instead, where he could gain an overview of the situation. Nuddell was there on watch, along with three other men whose names Rix had not yet learned.

Nuddell saluted him smartly. After Rix had saved his life at Jadgery, Nuddell had become his man, one of only a few of Leatherhead's crew that Rix was sure of.

"Rather a lot of the buggers, Deadhand," he said laconically.

The Cythonian force was visible with the naked eye now, a brown stain spreading across the snow at the top of the escarpment track. Rix checked with his great-aunt's field glasses, trying to estimate their numbers.

"Four hundred, so far."

"At least," said a tall, bald, badly scarred fellow with two front teeth missing. He looked like a brawler, though not a successful one. "And still comin'. They can be here within the hour if they want to."

"But I'm guessing they don't," said Nuddell. "If I were leading them—"

The brawler fell about laughing. "You couldn't lead a pig into a pie shop, and that's a fact."

"I'll tell you what's a fact," Nuddell said heatedly.

"Save it for the enemy," snapped Rix. "You," he said to the brawler, "what's your name?"

"Droag, Lord."

"Why is your sword rusty, Droag?"

Droag shrugged. "Once I stick it through a couple of the enemy, no one will notice."

"A man who's too lazy to look after his weapons is a man I put in the front line. When he's killed, I haven't lost anyone who matters. Clean it. *Now*!"

Droag borrowed a sharpening stone and began to rasp the rust off the blade.

"I hope they're not all like him," Rix muttered.

"Garramide hasn't been besieged in a thousand years, Deadhand," Nuddell said quietly. "They're just farm lads. They don't know what war is."

"But you do."

"I've seen some raiding over the years. And a pitched battle or two; only short ones though."

"Splendid. You're promoted. Take charge here, Sergeant."

CHAPTER 39

"Tali?" said Holm, shaking her. "It's time to go."

It took her a long time to rouse. Since he'd woken her pearl with the heatstone helmet she had spent twelve hours a day sleeping, and even when wide awake she found it difficult to rise from her bed.

"Go?" she said blankly. "Where?"

Holm was packing their gear as he spoke. "The wind turned southerly in the night and it's drifted the iceberg ashore."

She struggled to her feet and dressed in her outside gear. "To Hightspall?"

"Yes, but if it changes it could take us back out to sea. We've got to go now, and find a place to hide while it's still dark. The land hereabouts is enemy-controlled territory and there're bound to be guard posts everywhere."

"But I've got magery now. Why do I have to hide?"

"That you ask the question shows how much you have to learn. The greater the art, the less you should use it. And never if there's any other way of getting what you need."

"Why not?" said Tali, struggling to come to terms with this. She'd spent so long trying to find her magery, and now she had, she wasn't supposed to use it?

"It leaves traces, and the print of every magian's gift is different. Yours is not subtle. If you use a lot of power, Lyf will know. Beware!"

They went out, taking their packs and the remaining food but leaving the heavy gear behind, since they would be travelling on foot once they reached shore. The overcast had lifted and there was a little light from the stars and a paring of moon.

Waves were lapping at the iceberg. Tali looked around and there was water as far as she could see. "Thought you said we'd run aground?"

"We have. But most of an iceberg lies beneath the water."

Tali did a quick calculation. "So the water here could be a hundred feet deep. Or more. How do we get to shore?"

"One of my more remarkable creations," Holm said smugly, and led her down to the lower end of the iceberg. "Made it while you were snoring the night away. It's a bit rough, but it should do."

He had used heatstones to carve a little oval dinghy out of a bulge in the side of the iceberg. He had done a remarkable job as he'd said, and Tali knew he was a master boat builder, but she eyed the craft uneasily.

"How far have we got to go to shore?"

"Quarter of a mile."

"Are you sure an ice dinghy will last that long?"

"In water this cold, it should last a week," he said cheerily, though she detected a faint tone of unease in his voice.

"What's holding it in place?"

"This beam of ice." He pointed below the water. "Once I carve it off, we're away. Jump in."

Not knowing how thick the bottom was, she climbed in carefully and crouched down, shivering. Holm took a blanket-wrapped heatstone from his pack and unwrapped it. After passing her the packs, he lowered the heatstone into the water, towards the beam.

"Ahh! That's cold."

He held it below the water for a minute or two then, with a little twitch, the ice dinghy came free and was bobbing on the water. He wrapped the heatstone and handed it to Tali.

"Put that somewhere safe. We're bound to need it later on."

As Tali took it, pain sheared through her head from the top of her skull to her jawbone. She set the heatstone down and held her head with both hands. Holm took up a paddle carved from ice and began to paddle the dinghy on one side, then the other.

It was miserably cold. The little ice boat rocked with every movement and, once they were out of the shelter of the iceberg, every wave slopped water over the bow. Tali had to bail constantly with Holm's pot. In a minute, her hands were numb.

"Can you bail a bit faster?" said Holm. "It's rising up my boots."

Tali bailed more furiously. "It doesn't seem to be making any difference. How far do we have to go now?"

"Not far." He rowed faster.

"Some master craftsman you are. The boat must have sprung a leak."

"The bottom is six inches think, and I checked everything carefully."

"You must have missed a crack."

"I don't miss things like that; not when our lives depend on them. Just as a matter of interest," he said in an overly casual voice, "where did you put the heatstone?"

"On the floor—" She felt around for it and found the blanket it had been wrapped in, but the heatstone was gone and water was bubbling up from a slot in the bottom. She put her boot on it. "Ulp! Sorry. It gave me a dreadful headache and I wasn't thinking straight. Must've knocked it out of the blanket with my foot."

He shook his head. "For someone with a phobia about drowning, you're awfully blasé about ice-boat safety."

He paddled furiously and drove the ice boat onto a mud bank, just in time.

"We'll have to travel light, and fast," said Holm. "The price on your head will be big enough to corrupt even the most decent of people."

Tali jumped out and sank calf-deep in black, stinking ooze, almost as cold as the ice.

"Should have warned you," chuckled Holm, passing Tali her pack. "Keep to the sandbanks." He indicated the paler, wavy lines, just visible in the moonlight, stretching into the distance.

"How long 'til dawn?"

"Three hours. And it'll take half that time to cross the former sea bed to reach dry land. Can you go any faster?"

Tali did her best, but the fitness she'd had as a slave had gone with the blood stolen from her.

"Take off your boots," said Holm when they reached the sandbank. "Dry them inside, as best you can. Put on dry socks, otherwise you could get frostbite."

She did so. Two cold and exhausting hours passed before they reached the edge of the old sea bed and began to climb a sandy incline dotted with tussocks of coarse grass.

There were dunes after that, a series rising progressively to a hundred feet. Spiky bushes with narrow grey leaves formed scattered clumps along the low points between the dunes, but the ridges and crests were sandy. Tali and Holm left perfect tracks there. The sky was beginning to lighten in the east, though it had no colour yet.

"Got to get off the sand," said Holm. "We're making it easy for your enemies to find us."

Tali tried to reassure herself. "They're just tracks in the dunes. They could belong to anyone."

"An old man and a small, exhausted woman," said Holm, looking down at their tracks. His were broad but slow, hers small and dragging. "Coming from the sea. Any fool could read that."

"Where are we going?"

"Right now? Somewhere wild and empty."

"Is it far away?"

"A couple of days' walk, according to my map."

"I'm not sure how far I can walk in a day."

"Then push yourself. We don't only have to worry about your enemies. Anyone who sees our tracks will read us as prey."

"You're a treat," Tali said acidly. "When I'm down, you never fail to point out how much worse things are going to get."

"Would you rather I put icing on it?"

They passed off the dunes into silent marshland with scattered, stunted trees between the mires, a cold and desolate land where every bog and pool had brown ice on it, and no birds sang. There was no sign of life, not even a beetle or a gnat.

"Why is the ice brown?" said Tali.

"I don't know."

"Volcanic ash?"

"Could be."

Narrow paths wove through the marshlands, arched over by reeds. But at least the ground was beaten there, and if they trod carefully in the centre of the path they left only occasional smudged tracks.

"Any chance of breakfast?" said Tali. "My belly's about to dry up and blow away."

"Not until we find safe shelter."

They reached the edge of the marshes, Holm five or six paces ahead. Beyond was a scrubby, barren land with no signs of habitation. It was fully light now, a watery, wintry sun striking through the rushes from the north-east and catching them in the eyes. Perhaps that was why, as they climbed a gentle rise, Holm did not see the horsemen until it was too late.

He was rubbing his eyes, looking right and left, when three

riders burst out from between a clump of bushes and spurred towards him. Tali turned and skidded back down the slope, expecting Holm to follow, but he was slow to react, and when he did, he ran up the rise, not down.

"Not that way," she whispered.

Knowing how capable he was, she wasn't too worried at first. He'd outwitted every foe they'd met so far, and she felt sure he was capable of dealing with three ruffians. That was what she took them to be.

Only when Holm turned and ran sideways along the edge of the marshland did she realise what he was up to. He was leading them away in the hope that Tali, who had been well behind, had not been seen. He must have decided that they could not both escape, and was sacrificing himself for her.

The leading man, a big, red-whiskered fellow on a bony grey, leapt off his horse and ran down into the marshes to cut Holm off. The horse seemed glad to see its master go, for it whinnied, kicked up its heels and began to crop the coarse grass. Its mouth was torn from cruel use of the bit and there were bloody spur marks on its flanks.

Holm was darting and dodging, taking advantage of every bit of cover and the marshy ground where they dared not ride, though never going far into it. He could not, for the red-whiskered ruffian was always further out, blocking his escape, herding him back.

Tali lost sight of Holm behind a clump of rushes. She ran a few steps until she saw him again. He was plodding up a steeper slope, exhausted now. She lost him again and had to scurry back up to the point where they had first seen the riders.

When she finally located him, the other two riders were converging on him. One raised a cudgel and struck Holm down, then they dismounted and she saw clubs rising and falling. It looked like they were trying to beat him to death.

No time for thought. Tali ran up to the grey, gasping, and tried to haul herself into the saddle. It was a huge beast, at least seventeen hands, and the stirrups were so high that she could not get a foot into them.

Holm let out a terrible cry. She took hold of the harness. The horse turned its head and gave her a quizzical look. She stroked its flank.

"It's all right. I'll never hurt you like that whiskery bastard. Please, let me on."

It stared at her. Tali reached higher, caught the strap below the saddle, dragged herself up and managed to get a boot into the stirrup. The horse did not move; it hardly seemed to notice her weight. She got a leg over and tried to slide into the saddle, but had to pull out of the stirrup first – her legs weren't long enough.

The saddle was vast, barely holding her at all. Red-whiskers must have a backside the size of a warthog's. She took hold of the reins, gave them a gentle shake and said, "Go."

The horse gave her another quizzical look, but did not move.

"That way," said Tali, pointing to where the three ruffians had taken Holm. Were they still beating him? Did they plan to kill him because she had escaped, or just for the fun of it? "Go, please."

Nothing. She gave the horse a gentle nudge with her heels. Nothing.

Feeling exceedingly foolish, she reached out with her magery, gently and respectfully. *Please, run for me.*

The horse took off. Tali slid backwards in the saddle, then sideways. She grabbed desperately for the saddle horn, sure she was going to fall. She had been on a horse before, though for most of that time it had been with Tobry. No one would have called her an accomplished rider.

Even if she stayed on long enough to reach Holm, what was she to do? *Think, think!* Then something Tobry had once said about Rix popped into her mind. He had been talking about their plan to rescue her from Orlyk's Cythonians, out in the Seethings.

With respect, Lord Rixium, Tobry had quoted, smiling as he retold the story, *full gallop is the only plan you ever have. Subtle you are not.*

Why not? The plan, if she could get the horse to cooperate, had the merit of speed and simplicity. Yes, she would go straight at them and pray that it would work. Though three ruffians against one small woman . . . No, don't think of the problems or Holm will be dead. Do it!

She tugged gently on the reins, remembering the horse's bloody mouth, and eased the animal around towards Holm's attackers. *Sorry. I don't mean to hurt you.* The men were only sixty yards away now and did not seem to have noticed her, for the horse's hooves made little sound on the soft earth.

Go, my friend. Right at them. But look out for Holm, on the ground.

It accelerated so fast that she nearly slid off the back of the saddle. The horse leapt a bush, five feet in the air and fifteen at a stride.

One of the ruffians shouted, "Look out!" and scrambled to his feet.

But the great horse was travelling far faster than he could move. It crossed the last twenty yards in less than a second, hurtling towards the three ruffians, who were desperately trying to get out of its way.

They could not move fast enough. The horse's right shoulder struck the red-whiskered ruffian on chest and chin, snapping his head backwards and hurling him ten feet into a thorn bush. Its chest knocked the second man off his feet and Tali heard something crack as he went under the hooves. She did not see what happened to the third fellow.

The horse slowed, turned, and its great eye was on her again, as if asking, *is that enough?*

"Can you go back, please? I can't see Holm."

Had he been trampled? Was that what that hideous crack had been? She rode back warily, watching the ruffians. Were they dead, injured or only shamming?

The fellow who had gone under the horse was dead. There was a hoof print in the middle of his chest and blood around his mouth and nose. The horse's weight must have broken his ribs and stopped his heart.

The red-whiskered fellow was trying to free himself from the thorn bush, crying out with every jerk and twitch.

"You little bitch!" he said in a thick, pained voice. "Going to carve you into pieces."

Tali let out a gasp. He grinned, slack-jawed, as if it had been dislocated.

She turned the horse away. Red-whiskers was trapped by a network of needle-length thorns and he could hardly get free without making a lot of noise. But if he did – she shivered. At least she was armed.

The third man had disappeared, and he was the bigger worry. He was a burly fellow with a chest three times the size of her own and a dense stubble of coal-black beard. If he caught her he could snap her in half and, once the initial shock wore off, he was bound to come after her. If she dismounted she would have no chance against him. But she had to see how Holm was.

She loosened Lizue's big knife, which she wore in a canvas sheath across her back. "Thank you," she said, stroking her horse's neck. "You're a wonderful creature. Please don't go away. I'll just be a minute."

Talking to the horse helped to maintain the illusion that she was not alone. She had got into the habit back in Cython, with her beloved pet mouse.

The dead man had fallen across Holm, obscuring his face and chest. Without moving the body, Tali could not tell if he were alive or dead. There was a lot of blood on the ground, though. Her heart clenched like a fist.

She could not bear it if Holm were dead.

CHAPTER 40

Tali took hold of the dead man's ankles, trying not to look at the ruin the horse's hoof had made of him, and heaved. He barely budged; he was several times her weight. She went around to the side, pushed her hands under him and heaved.

He rolled over and flopped to the bare, gritty ground. Ants were already swarming there, going at the blood, and Holm's head was covered in it. Was he alive or dead? She wiped the worst of the blood off and felt his face. His nose was broken, his left eye black and swollen, there was a triangular cut across his left eyebrow and a long gash from that side of his forehead around into his thin hair.

And oddly, his muscles were knotted. In someone unconscious, she would have expected them to be relaxed.

"Holm?" she said softly.

He did not respond and, when she lifted his eyelids, his pupils hardly reacted to the light. Concussion. She leaned back on her heels. What was she supposed to do?

The thorn bush rustled and the red-whiskered villain let out a sharp groan, as if another of the thorns had pierced him. Good, I hope it hurts.

"Crebb?" he called. "Give us a hand, would you?"

There was no answer. Tali assumed Crebb was the burly black-beard. She crouched lower, turning in a circle, but saw nothing, heard nothing. Had he run off? She did not recall anyone crashing away, though in the drama of the attack she might not have noticed.

She slipped Lizue's knife from its sheath and laid it on the ground while she finished checking Holm. There was blood all over his face but none in his mouth, and no ribs or limbs had been broken. They'd mainly attacked his head and shoulders, thumping him with cudgels then punching him. They hadn't intended to kill him, then.

The horse was tearing at the coarse grass, watching her from one eye. She rose and stroked its flank. The beast snorted. It seemed to like her. She weighed nothing on its back and had treated it respect-fully, unlike its red-whiskered rider. She would try to get Holm onto the saddle.

She took him under the arms and heaved. Holm was not a big man but Tali's heart was pounding by the time she got him to a sit-ting position. She held him upright, worrying about the concussion. Head injuries were dangerous and unpredictable. If his skull was cracked, and a piece of bone was pressing on the brain, a tiny bump could kill him.

"Where are you, Crebb, you bastard?" yelled the man in the thorn bush. There was no answer and the rustling resumed, then he said to Tali, "Coming for you, bitch."

She had to hurry. Crebb might come back any second, with more villains. Or Red-whiskers might free himself from the thorns.

Tali shortened the stirrups so she could reach them from the saddle. She would need them if she were riding holding Holm, otherwise she was liable to drop him. Taking hold of the dangling reins, she led the horse back. It shied at the body and the smell of blood, whinnied and stamped around in a circle, wild-eyed, tossing its head and almost stepping on Holm's face.

"No!" She cried. Tali laid her hands on its long neck. "It's all right, it's all right." She rubbed the horse's nose, spoke quietly to it for a minute, and it steadied.

She led it away a few yards, upwind of the blood, and tethered it to the far side of a bush, putting it between the horse and the body. She would have to lug Holm yards further, but it could not be helped.

The horse began to tear at another clump of grass. She took Holm under the shoulders again, and heaved. The top of her head gave a painful throb, like a warning. She turned around and around. Was it Crebb? The hairs on her arms were standing up. Was he stalking her? She scanned past the thorn bush, froze. The red-whiskered fellow wasn't there.

How had he got free without her hearing him? He must have slipped out when the horse had panicked; he could be anywhere by now. She dragged Holm up beside the horse. The saddle looked a mile high. How could she get his dead weight up there? She would have to lift him well above her head.

She might have managed it when she had been a strong, healthy slave, but Tali could not do it now. It left only three choices: try to make a litter, capture Crebb or Red-whiskers and force them to put Holm on the horse for her, or heal him here and now.

She had no axe to cut saplings for a litter and no rope. The second alternative was even more hopeless. How was she to capture a big, brutish villain, then force him to do her bidding? She checked around her. There was no sign of either man, no sound. But Red-whiskers would not have gone far. He wanted revenge.

She considered her last option, healing.

Tali had always been able to heal without magery, for that gift was common among the Pale, though hers had never been strong. She could heal a cut, bruise or minor infection, though not broken bones, and serious wounds had been utterly beyond her. But with healing magery she might do all that, and more. Though—

You can be a destroyer or a healer, but not both. You have to choose – then keep to that choice.

If she chose to use her magery for destructive purposes – to defend herself, or attack an enemy – she might lose her ability to heal. Yet if she used her gift to heal, would she lose the ability to defend herself with magery? She looked down at Holm's battered, familiar face. He needed her help, now. It had to be healing.

Where was Red-whiskers? Tali walked around, peering behind the bushes. The uncertainty was more worrying than knowing where he was. She retrieved her knife and put it beside Holm. Quick, while you can.

She laid her hands across his broken nose and drew power, hard. The top of her head burned; she eased off. Fool! The master pearl gave her access to more power than human tissue could withstand. If she used it recklessly, it could cook her brain.

She tried again, gently, gently. Drawing a tiny wisp of power, she channelled it into her healing gift, visualised the nature of the injury, then felt the bone and cartilage of Holm's nose shift under her hand as it pulled back into shape and the broken bone began to grow together.

The bone would take hours, perhaps days, to regain its former solidity, but she could leave that to his natural healing processes. Tali touched the cuts and gashes, one by one, and the skin began to knit under her fingers. There would be scarring and bruising – she was a novice after all – but he would be whole again.

"Holm?" she whispered, when she had finished. The tension she had seen in his muscles previously had eased away but he lay as still as before.

Had she missed something? Or did he have internal injuries? If he did, she could do nothing about them – she could only heal those injuries she could see and understand. She opened Holm's eyes. His pupils still did not react to the light. There had to be a head injury.

Tali was so absorbed that she forgot to check around her. She probed his skull all over, pressing gently with a fingertip. Nothing,

nothing, nothing. Then, on the right side of his head, above the ear, it gave in a small depression no bigger than a coin. One of the blows he'd taken had cracked the skull in a small, ragged circle.

Tali had her hand over the depression and was preparing to move the bone back into place when the horse whinnied. She went for the knife, which was on the other side of Holm, but Red-whiskers charged from the bushes and kicked it out of her hand. The blackbeard, Crebb, hauled Tali up by the hair, put his arms around her middle from behind and held her in an unbreakable grip.

"Got you!" said Red-whiskers, and punched her in the mouth.

She sagged, staring at him in terror. The lower half of her face was a mass of pain, running all the way up along her jawline to the sides of her skull.

Tali had suffered a number of beatings in Cython, before she had mastered Nurse Bet's bare-handed art, but she had never experienced anything like the savage glee with which Red-whiskers had attacked her.

He drew back his fist for another blow, then clutched at his side, groaning. His own jaw hung oddly, dislocated when the horse's shoulder had struck him. His face was a swollen mess and each tortured breath made a bubbling sound in his chest. Had a broken rib punctured a lung? He also had dozens of bloody punctures from the thorn bush, and some were red and shiny.

Red-whiskers twitched, grimaced, shuddered. He was in agony and wanted to inflict as much pain on her. He thumped her again, then clutched at his chest. Strands of pink saliva hung from his gaping mouth. Tali swallowed a mouthful of her own blood, wondering if it would have any healing powers on her.

Red-whiskers spat blood onto the ground and raised his fist for a third blow.

"Enough!" said Crebb. "You'll kill her."

"Want to kill the little bitch," slurred Red-whiskers.

"No! Where do you think I've been while you were lazing in the thorn bush?"

"Running for your gutless life. You're never around when the dirty work needs doing."

Crebb dropped Tali beside Holm and put a hobnailed boot in the middle of her back. "I can safely leave that to you. Someone has to do the thinking."

"All right, I'll bite," Red-whiskers said sullenly. "Where did you get to?"

For the moment they weren't looking at Tali. She slid a hand across Holm's skull and located the depressed fracture. It was a far more difficult healing than fixing his broken nose, and more dangerous, too. If she moved a splinter of bone the wrong way, he could die.

She wasn't sure she could do it. What if she had judged wrong? No, hesitation would be just as fatal; just do it. Forcing the pain in her mouth and the throb in her jaw into the background, she drew power to ease the cracked skull bone into place.

"Followed their tracks back across the dunes," said Crebb. "They came from the sea, you moron. Across the mudflats from the iceberg that stranded last night."

He whistled up the other two horses. They came running, their manes streaming out behind them.

"Who cares where they came from?" Red-whiskers drew back a massive boot, as if to kick Tali in the head. She could see the hobnails in the sole.

Heal, heal! she thought frantically.

Crebb thrust him aside. "Enough! There's a reward, a big one."

"Never heard about no reward," Red-whiskers said sullenly.

"Because you can't read. There are notices along the road. A big reward for an old man and a young blonde woman who've come from the sea."

"How big?" Red-whiskers' manner implied a hope that it be not too big, so he could forgo it and get on with his battery.

"Big enough to satisfy both of us – *for life.*"

Heal, heal! The skull bone was hardly moving at all. Was she doing something wrong? Tali was starting to panic. If she did not succeed in the next minute, it would be too late. Once the villains tied her up there would be nothing she could do. *Heal, heal!*

Red-whiskers said hopefully, "Don't suppose the reward is for dead or alive?"

"If they're dead, our own lives are forfeit," said Crebb. "They're wanted alive *and unharmed.*"

"What for?"

"How would I know?"

"What are you gunna do with your share?"

"Haven't got it yet."

"When you do?"

"Head north where there's no stinking rock rats."

"They'll come," Red-whiskers said gloomily. "Reckon they'll hold the whole of Hightspall in another month."

"Reckon they won't," said Crebb. "Resistance is building up in the mountains."

"I didn't hear that. What's going on?"

"A bloke called Deadhand. A great warrior – he killed Arkyz Leatherhead in five minutes flat."

"Arkyz is dead?" said Red-whiskers.

"Deadhand took his head clean off in a single blow and sent it flying thirty feet into a dung heap."

"Where was this?"

"Some upland fortress in the Nandelochs. Place called Garramide."

"Is that where you're heading?"

"My fighting days are over, and my spending days are just beginning. I'll be heading well past Garramide. Enough talk. Help me get them on the nags."

CHAPTER 41

Crebb hauled Holm to his feet and held him there, head lolling. Red-whiskers kicked Tali in the kidneys, just for fun. He lifted her up, groaning at the pain in his side, and tossed her over his shoulder. After spitting blood onto the ground, he headed past the horse she thought of as her own, towards the other two horses.

Holm's right eye opened. His fist shot out and struck Tali's horse on the inflamed gouges on its left flank. It whinnied shrilly and kicked backwards at Red-whiskers with both hooves.

One hoof struck him on the right hip, which went *crack* and collapsed under him, spinning him around. The other hoof caught him in the left side, caved his chest in and blasted bloody foam six feet out of his mouth. He was driven backwards, dropping Tali and impaling himself on the thorn bush.

Crebb let Holm go and swung at his face, but the effort had been too much for the old man. His legs crumpled and the blow passed over his head.

Tali's hand closed around a stone the size of a grapefruit. She hurled it at Crebb's groin and, from five feet away, she could hardly miss. He doubled over, retching with the pain. She picked up another rock with both hands and knocked him out, then checked on Red-whiskers. He was twitching and shuddering, his malevolent eyes fixed on her, but he could not move. He gave a last shudder, and died.

Tali looked away from the ruined body. "That could have been me," she said, trembling all over.

"Sorry," he said in a frail voice. "It was then or never."

"Well, the horse did hate its master. It did seem to aim for him."

He did not reply. Holm was swaying back and forth.

"You okay?" It hurt to talk. The lower half of Tali's face felt like one enormous bruise and her swollen lips were very painful.

"No." He steadied himself with his arms. "But I'm alive. Thank you."

"Reckon you can get on a horse?"

"Suppose I'll have to."

"We'd better hurry," she said, glancing at Crebb. "He could come to any time."

"Tie him up."

"No rope."

She retrieved her knife, sheathed it and picked the smallest horse of the three. Holm took hold of the saddle, Tali boosted him from below and, with a lot of effort, got him into the saddle. Crebb groaned and clutched at his groin.

She took hold of the reins of the third horse, tied them to her saddle horn and clambered up like a crab trying to climb a wall.

"Where are we going?" she said.

"East then north."

She had lost all sense of direction. "Which way would that be?"

He pointed to the right. "Keep going that way 'til you reach a rugged range, then follow it north – which will be on your left. Keep to the wildest country you can find."

She directed her horse east, up and over a small hill, where she caught a last glimpse of the hostile sea, only a mile or two behind. The stranded iceberg was clearly visible and was bound to attract searchers.

A squall swept up from the south, dumping five minutes of heavy rain on them. Lightning flashed once, high up within a cloud; a rumble of thunder shook the ground. The rain died to a steady drizzle. Tali's stomach rumbled. She pulled her belt in another notch.

"Do you know anything about this fellow they mentioned – Deadhand?"

"Never heard of him," Holm said faintly. He did not look well.

"What was the name of the place?"

"Garramide."

"Do you know where it is?"

He did not reply.

"Should we go there? What do you think, Holm?"

"I'm going to have a little rest. Wake me when we get there."

Tali followed the range north, walking their horses along stream beds and across expanses of flat rock in an effort to disguise their tracks, and at sunset she holed up in a cave in the southern range. After tethering the horses where there was grass and water, and screening the cave entrance with a dense stack of bushes, she lit a small fire, checking twice to make sure no glow could be seen from outside. Holm was still poorly and she had to repeat her healing twice before, finally, he slept soundly.

Having slept so much in the past few days, she was wide awake. It was smoky in the little cave, but pleasantly warm, and for the first time since her escape from Cython she felt safe. No one knew she was here and their trail would be difficult to follow; though, sooner or later, a determined search must locate them. She had to be ready, and it would help if she knew what Lyf was up to.

Her previous seeings had been involuntary – either due to blood loss or to the effects of the heatstone helmet. But once before, when she had been in the Abysm trying to steal his pearl, Tali had seen Lyf at a distance, via magery. Could she use her newly recovered magery to see him again?

It proved easier than she had expected – she saw him the moment she looked. Tali drew back, afraid to go on. Had her unconscious visions of him in his temple created a mental pathway that allowed her to slip straight across? That could be dangerous. Such a pathway might reveal her to him. But she had to take the risk.

"Go through it all again," said Errek. "In case we've missed something."

Lyf related the tale of how the Five Heroes had betrayed him and Axil Grandys had hacked his feet off with the accursed blade.

"They bundled me up in a rug, disguised me with magery, then rode like fury to the Catacombs of the Kings and walled me in to die," Lyf concluded.

Why didn't you fight back, she wondered. You might have been an inexperienced king, but you were also an adept with the greatest magery of all at your disposal. Why didn't you use it to save yourself?

"And you have no memory of what happened to the key?" said Errek. "None at all?"

"It was in its hiding place," snapped Lyf. "No one knew it but me, and it's not there now. It's not in the temple."

"Then someone took it – probably Grandys."

"But he never used king-magery; he never even found where it had gone."

"Perhaps he took the key when he searched the temple, but did not know what it was."

"After all this time, we'll never know."

"There may be those in Hightspall who would know," said Errek. "There's a man outside you need to talk to."

"Who?"

"The historian mage, Wiven."

Lyf went to the temple door, unbolted it and said, "Bring him in."

A little old man was brought in. His dark face was as wrinkled as a prune.

"You are Wiven?" said Lyf, after the guards had gone and closed the door behind them.

"Yes," he said in a reedy little voice.

"Yes, Lord King!" corrected Errek.

Lyf waved a hand at him, irritably.

"I'm told that few people know more about the history of magery, and the time of Lyf's death, than you," said Errek.

"No one knows half as much as I do," said Wiven. "What do you want?"

"What happened to the contents of the temple after Lyf's disappearance?"

"It was raided in the night. Everything was taken."

"Who raided it?" said Lyf.

"Axil Grandys."

"Why? What was he looking for?"

"No one knows," said Wiven. "But—"

"Yes?"

"It was rumoured that he was looking for a talisman."

"A talisman?" said Lyf. "Why?"

"Grandys' own magery relied on them. Maloch, for instance, is a great talisman."

"Did he find one?"

"Since he never found the lost king-magery, it's assumed he did not."

"What happened to the contents of my temple?"

"No one knows."

Lyf recalled the guards. "Take him out. Far enough that you don't defile the temple."

The little old man was hauled out. There was a brief scuffle, a reedy cry, then the thump of a blade cleaving a head from a neck. Tali winced.

Lyf closed the door, bolted it and moved well away. "Another dead end."

"A poor choice of words, in the circumstances," Errek said drily. He looked around. "What's that?"

Had she been discovered? Tali broke the link and opened her eyes. So this vital key was definitely gone, probably taken by Grandys, but how could anyone find it after all this time?

Suddenly ravenous, she went through Holm's pack, discovered

a map which she put aside for later, then took out their remaining food – a chunk of fatty bacon, an onion, a couple of cups of oatmeal and some unidentifiable pieces of dried fruit. Tali had never cooked a meal but how difficult could it be? She chopped everything into small pieces, put it in the pan with some water and set it on the fire.

"I hope you've got an appetite," she said, on waking Holm an hour later. "This is the last of the food."

Holm eyed the grey, oily mess without enthusiasm. "What is it?"

"I'm calling it stew."

"What's in it?"

"All we had of everything."

"Boiled?" he cried. "Even the bacon?"

"Um," said Tali. "Isn't that how you do it?"

He sighed and took a cautious spoonful. "Oh, well, I dare say it'll be nourishing."

"Isn't that what people say when the food is horrible?"

"Did I say that?" he said with an innocent twinkle. He tasted, tasted again. "It's not too bad ... considering. Didn't your mother teach you to cook?"

"In Cython, the kitchen slaves do all the cooking."

They finished their stew in a companionable silence. The fire died low. She put more wood on.

"What now?" said Holm.

She debated whether or not to tell him about her seeing of Lyf and Errek, but decided to put it off a bit longer. "Er ... about my magery?"

"Yes?"

"Have I made my choice? Between healing and destruction, I mean?"

"By healing me?"

"Yes."

"I don't think so. The choice can't be any little old thing."

"I wouldn't call healing you a little old thing," she exclaimed.

"Neither would I, but I'm biased. Here's how the king's choice used to work, according to what I've read in the history books. You have to choose either to do a *great healing*, such as saving a life that could not be saved any other way. Or a *great destruction* – taking someone's life with magery, for instance, or destroying something vast, valuable or vital."

"I did save your life."

"From the thugs, not the head injury." He felt it carefully, wincing.

"So if you're right, I still have the option," she said quietly. It came as a great relief, though she could not have said why.

"Perhaps it's just as well," said Holm, "since you're *the one*. Lyf's your great enemy, and you're his. If he's to restore the ancient realm of Cythe, or if you're to rescue the Pale, sooner or later the battle has to be fought."

"The later the better, as far as I'm concerned," said Tali.

"And the sooner the better for him. He'll be planning to take you on the moment he finds you, so you've got to be ready."

"Um," said Tali, "he may already have found me. Or at least, seen me."

"What have you done now?"

She told him about her spying mission, and what she had seen and heard.

"He had the mage put to death at once, you say?"

"Yes," said Tali.

"So the secret of the lost key is so vital that he couldn't allow anyone to discover what questions he'd asked." Holm picked up his stew bowl and scraped the sides. "I wish you'd waited until I was awake."

"Sorry."

"But it has told us one thing," said Holm.

"What's that?"

"The key he's looking for is the key to king-magery. But what is it? Is it a physical key? A talisman? A document? A spell?"

"Judging by Lyf's reaction to the word it wasn't a talisman. And whatever it was, Grandys probably took it."

"Though if he did, presumably he couldn't get it to work – or didn't recognise it as the key."

"Since we don't know where it is now, or even if it still exists, it doesn't help us."

"I have an idea about that," said Holm.

"Really?"

"I was fascinated by Grandys at one stage, when I was young and proud and arrogant. I spent a couple of months reading his papers and studying his artefacts, and after that I didn't want to be like him at all. Not long afterwards I discovered . . . that I didn't want to be like me, either."

What could he mean? His eyes gave nothing away. "Do you want to tell—?"

"No, thanks."

After another pause she said, "Where is all Grandys' stuff?"

"Lost, mostly, or scattered. Some of it's at Tirnan Twil."

"Where's that?"

"In the Nandeloch Mountains."

"Everything seems to be in the Nandelochs."

"They've always been a Herovian stronghold. I think the rugged land and the wild weather was much akin to their racial dream of the Promised Realm."

She sighed. "About Tirnan Twil?"

"It's a homage to eternity."

"That may be poetic, but it doesn't give me the clearest picture."

"It's a library and museum, and, for some, a place of worship."

"What for?"

"The Five Heroes began it to glorify their achievements and maintain their heritage. The expense was staggering. It almost bankrupted the young nation – and Hightspall almost lost the war because of it. But that's ancient history."

"I take it, then, that we're going to Tirnan Twil?"

"If this key still exists, it's the first place I'd look."

CHAPTER 42

"What's the matter with them?" said Rix, punching the steel gauntlet on his dead hand into the palm of his other hand. He wore it all the time now, because it made his dead hand into a formidable weapon. "Why don't they attack?"

"Perhaps they're waiting for reinforcements," said Droag, idly polishing his sword.

"Any sign of the healers?" said Rix.

"No," said Nuddell gloomily. "Must've gone into hiding. No way they can reach us now."

Or else the enemy had caught or killed them.

They were up on the tower behind the gates again. The Cythonians had been outside for two days now, camped in the snow in a semicircle, several hundred yards out of arrow range. They had not fired at the fortress, nor used any of the chymical terror weapons they had employed to such devastating effect in the early days of the war.

From time to time they sent raiding parties across the plateau. The sentries on the walls would see smoke rising and know that another manor or village had been burned, along with anyone who had missed the call to take refuge in the fortress. The raiding party would return, driving cattle, sheep or goats before them, which they butchered and roasted over spits. Then the waiting resumed.

"They're doing it to wear us down," said Swelt, rubbing his depleted belly.

Now that the fortress was at war, everyone had to make do on reduced rations, even the castellan.

"They did the same thing at Caulderon," said Glynnie. "After they blasted the gates, they didn't attack for several days, and our armies couldn't touch them. By the time they stormed the walls, morale was in tatters."

"If they don't attack today, it'll be their last chance for a week," said Nuddell, who was studying the sky. "There's a blizzard coming, a big one."

Away in the south-west, a black cloud-bank had been developing for ages, thickening and spreading until it covered the southern sky.

"Those clouds haven't moved in days," scoffed Droag. "If it gets any warmer the daffodils will come out."

"Nor'westerlies are holding the blizzard back," said Nuddell, "but they can't last much longer. And once they break," he said with dire relish, "the coming blizzard will tear the hairs right out of your nose."

Droag plucked a clump of his luxuriant nose hairs, studied them incuriously, then let them fall. "Ain't a breath of wind, Nuddell."

"Mark my words, boy. It'll be howling by dinner time."

"Our biggest weakness is the length of the wall," said Rix to his officers. "Ignoring the escarpment side, which is too steep for anyone to attack, we've got over half a mile of wall to defend. And only three hundred and ninety men, counting the reserves."

"Surely they'll attack the gates," said Noys. "They're always the weakest point."

"But ours are strongly defended. And if they attack somewhere else under cover of darkness, they might get up onto the wall before we realise what they're doing."

"If you reinforce all the places they're likely to attack—"

"We don't have enough men," said Rix. "We'd need another two hundred, at least."

By noon the black cloud-bank was perceptibly closer and the towering storms at its front were illuminated by continuous flashes of lightning. By three in the afternoon, odd little puffs of warm air kept breaking the eerie calm. The high clouds ahead of the front had spread to cover all but a lens of sky in the north-west, through which were focused the slanting, blood-red rays of the descending sun.

At twenty to four, the storm struck with a flurry of heavy rain-drops, followed by a fusillade of hail. Rix clapped on his helmet. At the same moment, the lens of bright sky vanished and it became almost as dark as night.

Nuddell, grinning, said something Rix could not make out over the hammering of hailstones on his helmet.

"What did you say?" said Rix.

"You can stand down the extra men," Nuddell yelled. "There won't be an attack today."

"Why not?" said Droag.

"If they try to fight in a blizzard," said Rix, "half their troops are liable to die of exposure."

A red flash from the enemy's position was followed by a smashing thud below.

"What the hell was that?" said Nuddell, the whites of his eyes shining in the gloom.

"Bombast," said Rix.

He looked down. The exploding projectile must have been enormous, for it had blasted a ragged, cart-sized hole through the top of the great gates. Half a dozen guards on the right-hand wall lay dead or wounded, cut down by jagged, flying timber.

"Hope that's the only one they've got," said Nuddell.

"I doubt it," Rix said curtly.

One bombast blast would not let the enemy in. Rix, who knew the power of the enemy's weaponry first-hand, had ordered a stone wall built behind the gates. But the damage was worrying.

"Why now?" said Nuddell. "What's the point? They can't attack today."

The answer came like a flash of lightning. "Maybe they *are* going to attack – despite the weather. Come on!"

He bolted along the wall towards the gates, hailstones the size of plums bouncing off his helmet and cracking painfully into his shoulders, chest and knees. A minute ago he had been sweltering in tunic and leather armour. Now his breath steamed in front of him and the hail and rain was so thick that he could barely see the gate tower.

Lightning struck the largest copper dome behind him, sending sparks in all directions. Another bolt hit something on the wall ten yards to his left – a guard – blowing him to pieces.

The shockwave drove Rix down to hands and knees and he remained there for a couple of seconds, wiping blood off his face, before getting back to his feet. The lightning could as easily have struck him. Was there malice behind the storm, some purpose directing it to harry them before the attack began? Could Lyf's power have grown that strong? Perhaps, now that he had four ebony pearls, it could.

As Rix ran on, a Cythonian shriek-arrow shot past his nose, the eerie sound raising his hackles as it was intended to do. How could the enemy see to fire? Or were they firing blind in the hope of creating as much terror as possible before the storm, in all its fury, drove them into shelter?

He stopped to scan the area outside the wall. It was too dark to pick out individual details, but when the lightning flashed again he saw a brown, spreading mass. The army was moving! Unbelievably, they were attacking in the full ferocity of the storm; ignoring the lightning, the hailstones slamming into their helmets and shoulders, the icy rain in their eyes.

Fear shuddered through him. How could they be so driven? His men were huddled under whatever shelter they could find. They would not see the enemy raise their scaling ladders to the walls, or attach hand-carried bombasts to vulnerable points in the defences. Their plan was madness yet, if Rix could not get his men into position in time, it could succeed.

"They're attacking!" he bellowed, so loudly that it hurt.

He barely heard his own voice over the crashing hailstones, the shrieking wind and the continuous boom and thump of thunder. No one could hear anything; his men would be deafened.

He had to know where the attack was focused. Logic said that they would attack the damaged gates, but logic wasn't a reliable ally where the Cythonians were concerned. Rix leaned over the wall, trying not to think about the shriek-arrows flying all around.

A small company was attacking the gates, but the rest of the enemy force was heading hundreds of yards to the left, where Garramide's outer walls curved in around a black outcrop called Basalt Crag. It was a weak point in the wall and, because the enemy had been camped outside the gates, he had only left a handful of men up at the crag. Not nearly enough to defend it against a full attack.

"Nuddell, follow me!"

He raced along the wall to the gate tower; nothing mattered but speed. Rix burst onto the open top of the tower, skidding on an inch-deep layer of hailstones and nearly falling. It was empty. Where were his men? There! The bastards were huddling in a little wooden cabin and no one was keeping watch.

He kept running, leapt at the door, feet-first, burst it off its hinges and crashed in among them. Wild-eyed and covered in the dead man's blood, he must have looked like a lunatic.

"They're attacking up at the crag!" he bellowed.

"In *this*?" said a grizzled, toothless old fellow.

"Yes! Nuddell, take these men up to Basalt Crag. Keep low so they don't see you. Out!"

He drove the stragglers out with bruising blows of his steel-encased fist, then continued to the next watchtower, leaving the men stationed along the wall in place but ordering all those on the watchtowers, plus the reinforcements waiting below, up to Basalt Crag.

"We're the *reinforcements*," said a surly fellow that Rix remembered from the raid on Jadgery. He was one of those who had run at the first opportunity.

Rix clamped his steel fingers around the man's throat. "Get up there now or I'll choke the life out of you right here. And if you ever desert your post again, you're dead!"

The hailstones were only the size of grapes now, but the rain grew heavier. Rix had never seen such a storm. He was soaked to the pores of his skin, his feet were squelching in his boots and, despite the exertion, he was freezing.

He did the same at the next tower, but as he approached the one after that he saw no one there. What was the matter with the fools? He leapt a puddle six feet across and so deep that lemon-sized hailstones were bobbing in it, and raced on, his breath tearing in his throat and his fear growing. So far he'd only sent back twenty men. Not nearly enough. Without a hundred there was little hope of defending Basalt Crag.

Rix cursed his lack of foresight. He'd known it was vulnerable. Why hadn't he prepared a plan to deal with it? Because in good visibility he would know where the enemy were attacking and could reinforce Basalt Crag with a hundred men in minutes.

He leapt another pool and raced on to the tower. A triple lightning flash showed five or six men down, some lying in pools of water. And he had no proper healers. This was going to be a disaster.

There was no blast damage to the tower, so he assumed the troops had been struck by lightning. One or two people were bending over bodies. The rest of the guards were huddled under a lean-to roof on the far side, their white eyes picked out in every flash.

Rix bellowed his orders, saw the men away and was about to run on when another flash revealed Glynnie, kneeling in the water beside a man bleeding from the nose and mouth. She was only wearing her housemaid's gown, which was wet through and plastered to her slim figure by the wind.

His heart turned over. He ran across. "What are you doing up here, dressed like that? If the lightning strikes again, or a flight of arrows falls—"

"You do your job, I'll do mine," she said without looking around. Then something made her look up and she cried, "Rix, your face."

His right cheek was swollen and torn open. It was so numb from cold that he had not noticed.

"Must have been a hailstone. I'm all right."

She turned back to the bleeding man, wiped his face and yelled, "Stretcher bearers!"

Two wide-eyed lads came splashing through the water and took the man down the steps.

"At least put some leather armour on," said Rix.

Glynnie stood up, shivering and rubbing the small of her back. "There's none my size."

"Please take care of yourself."

He ran on to the next tower and sent its men back, then plodded to the one after that. The cold was getting to him now. His heavy armour and gear was a greater burden with every step and he wasn't halfway around the damned wall.

Fear gnawed at his belly. The enemy were ferocious fighters and gave no quarter. How many had headed across towards Basalt Crag? It had looked like hundreds. They would be raising their scaling ladders already, and no more than fifty of his men could have reached that part of the wall.

Too few! And most of his men were local yeomen and peasantry who had never fought before. Would any of them know how to repel men scaling the wall – which was the best way, which the worst? This savage storm was not the place to learn on the job.

Worst of all, they were leaderless and he was a third of a mile away on the other side of the fortress. He could not see the enemy from here, had no idea what was going on and, whether he turned back or kept going, it would take him precious minutes to reach the danger zone.

What had he been thinking? Why hadn't he sent runners to do the job for him, and run straight back?

Had he made the biggest mistake of his recent, disastrous life?

CHAPTER 43

Rix pounded around the battlements, praying that he would reach Basalt Crag in time. And that when he arrived, he still had strength to fight.

The hail had stopped and the rain had eased a little, but the lightning was as ferocious as ever. And he made a fine target, being the tallest man on the wall. The great dome had been struck repeatedly, and several of the smaller domes as well, while a strike on one of the lower roofs had blasted roof slates everywhere and set alight the framing timbers beneath, though the deluge had put the fire out in seconds.

The wind was gusting wildly, shifting from one quarter to another as the storm passed overhead. Now it was blasting hard rain into his face, stinging his battered cheek and getting into his eyes, half blinding him. A savage gust that almost lifted him off his feet drove him sideways into a battlement. Had he been passing a low point in the wall it might have carried him over the edge.

Where was everyone? There had been no guards at the last tower, and there were none on this section of wall either. He stopped, momentarily confused. No lightning had flashed for a minute now and the dark was impenetrable.

Rix forced the plan of the defences into his mind. Ah, yes! He was halfway along the escarpment side, where the wall rose up from solid rock to twice the height of the entrance wall, at least sixty feet. Not even the Cythonians would try to attack here, for there was no solid ground on which to place their ladders.

Focus! He was only a couple of hundred yards from Basalt Crag. Lightning flashed, illuminating the way ahead, and he put his head down and ran. If he got there in time, and by some miracle they beat off this attack, it would not only gain Garramide some breathing space, but it would improve morale in the fortress immeasurably.

Rix was only a hundred yards away when, in a momentary lull in the storm, he heard a curious clacking sound from below. He froze, ducked behind the battlement, and carefully peered over the wall.

A distant flash of lightning froze an instant of the scene below. Not enough to resolve the individual dark-clad figures huddled against the base of the wall, but enough to produce paired reflections from at least a dozen eyes, looking straight up.

Had they seen him? Since he had been looking down, there could be no reflection from his eyes, though they might have noticed the outline of his head against the lightning-lit sky. If they had, their archers would be waiting, and the next time he looked over they would put their arrows through his face.

Did they have scaling ladders, or were they attacking the wall itself? It was very thick here and quite a few bombasts would be needed to breach it. But for all he knew, they might have a dozen.

What to do? The bigger danger, he felt sure, was at Basalt Crag . . . though the men he'd sent would be there by now, and one more, even himself, would make little difference.

However if they climbed onto the wall here, or breached it and got into the fortress without anyone knowing, they could take the women and children hostage and force a surrender.

He dared not look down from here. Rix scurried along the wall for thirty feet, to a point where he would be in shadow when the lightning flashed, and gingerly peered over. Half a dozen troops were raising a scaling ladder. Further along, another group was working at the base of the wall. A faint light flickered there, though not enough to reveal what they were up to. It wasn't an orange light though, as though they had been igniting a fuse. It was a pale, steady blue, like the light of a partly shuttered glowstone lantern.

Could they be assembling some mechanical contrivance? There

was no way to tell. He crept back until he was directly above them, then rose to his full height and took hold of the heavy capstone on top of the riser of the battlement.

Loose capstones were a defensive innovation Swelt had mentioned in one of his inventories. At least, it had been an innovation a thousand years ago, though since Garramide had never been besieged it could not have been used. Would it still work?

The capstones were not mortared on, but mounted on brass pins set in the stone beneath. The capstones could not slide or fall, but two strong men could lift one off its pins and drop it on any attackers below. Could one very strong but weary man do it by himself? Or had time and the elements cemented the capstone immoveably onto the wall?

He rose beneath it, took hold of the overhang of the capstone on the left with his good hand, and the overhang on his right with the steel gauntlet, then strained until his back clicked. The capstone did not budge. He tried again, with the same result.

It could not be done. No man save the late, unlamented Arkyz Leatherhead could have lifted one of these. Nonetheless, Rix took another grip, crouched, raised his arms until they were straight, locked them and slowly, slowly began to straighten his legs.

The strain was immense. He could feel his back spasming, and began to fear that he would dislocate his shoulder, or that the steel gauntlet would shatter his right wrist bones. He strained harder, taking it slowly, and the capstone inched up on the right-hand side, then the left. Higher, higher. Not far to go now. Then it stopped and he could raise it no further.

He was about to let it down when a familiar voice spoke, in a hoarse whisper. "You bloody fool, Rix. Why can you never ask for help? I've got it. Heave, now!"

Rix heaved, the other man did too, and with a faint rasp of stone on stone the capstone went over the edge and fell away.

A muffled thud, a scream of agony, then a bombast went off with unimaginable ferocity, shaking the wall and grinding the other capstones back and forth on their pins.

Rix looked over the side, carefully. The wall was not badly damaged, for the bombast had not been fixed in place and most of the blast had gone outwards. But of the enemy soldiers who had been huddled there, there was no trace.

The other dozen, who had been halfway up the scaling ladder, were scattered across the rocky ground and the ladder was broken.

Rix rubbed his ringing ears and turned around, half expecting that the voice had been a hallucination brought on by the strain. If so, it was a fleshly one. His eyes stung with tears as successive flashes lit the dirty, bewhiskered, grinning face of the friend he had given up for dead weeks ago.

"Tobry? What the hell are you doing here?"

"I might ask the same of you, *Deadhand*."

"I thought you were done for."

"I should be, but this isn't the time for a beer and a yarn about it."

They embraced, and he clung to his friend for a long moment, before pulling away.

"They're attacking further along with scaling ladders. Have you been there?"

"Nope," said Tobry. "Heard the fighting and climbed the wall up from the escarpment. Seemed the safest way in, all things considered."

Rix froze. He'd ruled out an attack on the escarpment side because it was almost sheer. "Do you reckon the enemy could do the same?"

"One or two might get up, if they can climb wet rock as well as I can. Which seems doubtful, since they've lived all their lives in dry, horizontal tunnels."

Rix relaxed. "I've never met anyone who can climb as well as you. The night old Luzia was murdered, you carried me up the outside wall of my tower, single-handed."

"What a lousy night that was."

The storm was passing, but the icy southerly wind behind it was picking up, the rain turning to driven snow.

"It's damn cold up here," said Tobry.

"They say there's a blizzard coming. A bad one."

They headed around the wall. Tobry was limping badly, favouring his right thigh. Rix's back ached as if he had strained it. But the pain was nothing. It was irrelevant now. Tobry was back! The world had resumed its proper orbit. Everything was going to be all right.

"I'd sooner fight my way in through the front gate, personally. But then, you always did have a way with walls."

"Driving you up them, you mean?" Tobry chuckled.

"It's not far now," Rix said quietly.

They were approaching Basalt Crag, and when the lightning flashed he could see men fighting on the wall.

"The enemy are up," he whispered. "Keep low and we might take them by surprise."

He drew Maloch, and Tobry his own sword, then they crouched and ran. The fighting was furious; dozens of Cythonians had reached the top and Rix could not see many defenders. Three scaling ladders stood against the wall and more enemy troops were streaming up them.

"If we can make a bit of a breathing space," Rix said quietly, "we might be better off attacking the ladders."

"Good idea. I'll follow your lead. But first, let's hit the bastards hard."

They hurtled into the attack, side by side, carving through several lines of the enemy before they realised they were being attacked from behind. With Maloch in his left hand and Tobry by his side, Rix felt no harm could come to him. He dropped several of the enemy with blows from his steel fist.

A ragged cheer broke out from further along the wall. "Deadhand, Deadhand!" The defenders did not know Tobry but Rix's height, bulk and steel-gauntleted right hand were unmistakeable. They attacked with renewed vigour and soon the enemy on the wall, besieged on both sides, were fighting for their lives.

"I'll hold the line here," said Tobry. "Go after the ladders."

Rix hesitated, but only for a moment. Tobry was a fine swordsman.

Rix ran along the battlements, looking over. The soldiers on the furthest ladder were closest to the top of the wall. They would be attacking within a minute. He raced down, took hold of the top of the ladder and shook it.

The men were well trained; none of them fell. He shook it again.

They clung on, then resumed the climb. Rix wrenched the ladder from side to side, trying to make it slip at the base, but it was securely mounted and two men held it steady.

The wind howled and a flurry plastered them with snow. The blizzard was almost on them. Rix wiped snow out of his eyes.

This wasn't going to work. Unsheathing Maloch, he reached down as far as he could and, taking advantage of a momentary darkness, dealt the top three rungs a ferocious blow, cutting them in half. Had the men on the ladder seen? He did not think so. He took hold of the two sides of the ladder, locked his steel gauntlet against one side, then wrenched with all the strength in his arms.

Too late the soldiers realised what he was up to, but they were holding onto the rungs, not the side rails, and Rix's mighty heave tore the rungs out of the rails, all the way down. He thrust one rail left, the other right, and watched the men fall. It might not kill them, but after falling that far onto rock they were bound to break bones.

An arrow glanced off the battlements, driving chips of stone into his swollen cheek. He ignored the flare of pain and ran for the second ladder, though he did not plan to use the same trick twice. Not with their archers watching for him. He picked up a dead Cythonian lying on the wall and pushed his head and shoulders over. Three arrows went through the man's throat. The enemy archers were dangerously good.

Sheltering behind the body, Rix heaved the dead man down the ladder. As the body fell, it knocked the climbers off one by one and the tumbling figures cannoned into the men steadying the ladder, which toppled.

One ladder left. He was planning on dealing with it the same way when a cornet sounded from the darkness below. The surviving enemy scrambled down the ladder and retreated into the blizzard, leaving their dead behind.

The fighting on the wall was over. Rix leaned back against the wet stone and closed his eyes for a moment, but could still see the dead and the dying. Not far away, a signal horn sounded the three-note call — *send up the healers*.

If only he had proper healers. Damn Oosta. What kind of a

healer took both of her assistants away on the eve of battle? People were going to die because of her stupidity.

He wiped his face, then headed along to his troops. They were checking the fallen men, heaving the enemy over the side and laying Garramide's dead along the inside wall. The injured still lay where they had fallen on the bloody stone. A man and a woman, both wearing red healers' armbands, ran up. The man began checking the fallen, sorting them into those who needed immediate attention, those who could wait, and those who could not be saved. The other healer was Astatin, the witch-woman.

Glynnie wasn't there. What if she had been killed? "Where's Glynnie?" he called.

Astatin was holding a man's partly severed arm and muttering incantations. She did not reply.

"Don't know," said the man.

Rix told himself to calm down. It was impossible to keep track of everyone in the chaos of battle. Glynnie could be anywhere. But the fear would not go away. He looked around for Tobry but could not see him either.

"It's over," grinned a bloodstained Nuddell. "We must've killed a hundred of the buggers here."

"Plus another twenty or more round the corner. They were trying to blow a hole in the wall," said Rix, jerking his thumb over his shoulder. He shook hands with Nuddell and the other men at the front. "That was well fought, lads."

"We've done for a third of them, then, and plenty more injured. But without you coming up the back way and surprising them, it could have been tricky."

"Very tricky," said Rix. Running the long way around the wall hadn't been a stupid blunder – it had been the best thing he could do. He wasn't a fool and a failure after all. "How many have we lost?"

Nuddell's grin faded. "Fourteen men dead, here, and nineteen injured, some badly. Bad enough, but it could have been a lot worse."

"Any man lost is one too many," said Rix. And there had been more casualties along the wall, and at the gate. But thankfully

Tobry wasn't among them. He was limping up now. His clothes were in tatters and a bloody bandage was tied around his left thigh.

"Sergeant Nuddell, meet my old friend Tobry Lagger."

They shook hands. "Never seen a blade worked so well as yours," said Nuddell.

"I used to practise," said Tobry. "Have they gone?"

"Yes, but it's not over yet," said Rix. "Not by a long way."

"Still, something to celebrate," said Nuddell.

"Oh yes," said Rix, putting an arm around Tobry's shoulders. "I'm not planning to stop for a week."

He pulled free. There were a dozen things to do first, and not least of them, making sure Glynnie was all right. "Nuddell, take Tobry downstairs. Ask Swelt to fix him up with a bath and a room. I'm going to walk around the wall, just to make sure of everything."

"Keep your head down, Deadhand," said Nuddell. "They could have longbow snipers out."

Nuddell and Tobry went down. Rix continued along the wall to each of the towers, thanking his men individually and sending all but the night guards below.

"Do you think they'll attack again?" said his captain, Noys, who was on the left-hand tower beside the gates.

The wind shrieked. Rix took shelter behind one of the battlements, but the frigid wind had already leached the battle warmth out of him, and every bruise, wound and muscle strain was throbbing. For the enemy, exposed on the windswept plateau with no shelter save their tents, things would be getting desperate by midnight.

"Blizzard's going to get a lot worse, and it can kill them quicker than we can. They can't climb ladders in this wind; certainly can't fight in it. They'll have to take shelter until the blizzard passes."

"I'm going to keep watch for a while," said Noys. "I don't trust the bastards."

"Me either," said Rix. "Take special care of the sentries. Make sure they've got gloves and furs. No more than half an hour on the wall without going in to warm themselves at the braziers. And plenty of hot drinks."

Noys saluted. "I'll see to it." He turned away, then turned back. "Heard what you did further up, Lord Deadhand. You saved us, and we won't forget it."

"We all did our bit."

"Aye, but you made the difference. I'll follow you anywhere, Lord."

"Thank you, Noys." Rix swallowed. "That means everything to me."

He shivered convulsively. The cold was creeping right through him now, and as he went down the icy steps, his rubbery knees could barely support him. He'd been out in the cold far too long.

But there was so much to do. He clapped his hands together and headed across the yard, then into the healery. And froze, for it looked more like an abattoir.

Three lines of four trestle tables had been set out and a seriously injured man lay on each. Most were bleeding, the blood seeping from temporary bandages, puddling on the tables then dripping on the floor. Two servant girls, no more than ten years old, were cleaning the floor with bloody mops, though the blood accumulated as fast as they could clean it away. Two even smaller girls came staggering in carrying buckets of steaming water.

A severed right leg lay on a table inside the door, along with a mashed, freshly amputated pair of hands, and at the back a tall, bald soldier, dead from a horrific head wound. Droag. Rix hadn't liked the man, but he didn't want to see him like this, either – taken from life by a single smashing blow.

Two blood-covered men – amateur healers – were holding down an injured soldier while a woman with a bone saw cut off his shattered right arm. The man was eerily silent. And there was Glynnie, down the far end of the room, leaning over a screaming man who had been bound to the table, stitching a foot-long gash across his chest.

He went down to her as she completed the last stitch and began to bandage the wound. Glynnie was as pale as the snow on the windowsill and swaying with exhaustion. Her clothes were still wet and she was shivering fitfully.

"Have you had anything to eat or drink?" said Rix.

"There's no time. No one else knows as much about healing as I do. If I stop now, men will die."

Rix cursed Oosta yet again. "What can I do to help?"

"This is my job, not yours. You've been fighting for our lives."

"If there's no one else better to do it, it's my job. I've attended plenty of injuries in my time. Give the orders and I'll see them done."

CHAPTER 44

"If I try to climb up there, I'll die," said Tali.

"You're being hysterical," said Holm.

"I hate you."

"So you've been saying for the last three hours and twenty-seven minutes."

"Tirnan Twil had better be worth it."

"It is."

"I can't do it. I'll fall."

"Unless I throw you over the side first."

"I'm sure that's why you brought me here," she muttered.

"Don't tempt me. Take your right foot and put it in front of your left. Then move your left foot up in front of your right. Keep doing that and you'll reach the top in no time."

Tali would have thumped him, had she been game to take her eyes off the track.

An uneventful four days had passed as they rode north for Tirnan Twil, travelling through the wildest country they could find, fishing or scrounging for their dinner and some nights, when they could not find anything edible, going to their blankets hungry and rising hungrier.

Finally, last night, they had reached the tiny village of Tirnan Plat, where all the houses were made from red rammed earth roofed with yellow thatch. They had exchanged the horses for as much food as they could carry, Tali had said a teary goodbye to her mount, and they had set out on foot at first light.

The mountain track had grown progressively steeper all morning. She kept feeling that there was someone behind her, or watching her, but the track above and below them was empty. At midday she turned a corner and all the blood drained from her head. The track ran diagonally up a cliff, a good thousand feet high, where an ancient fault line had carved half the mountain away.

"I'm going to die without ever seeing the place," she said hoarsely.

Tali knew she sounded whiny, but even with her hat pulled down over her ears the sky was rocking. Her panic was rising, along with the sick fear that she was going to fall and be smashed to bits on the rocks far below.

"Steady," said Holm, not teasing her now.

His strong hand closed around her upper arm and the panic eased a little.

"Sorry," she croaked. "And to think I had a panic attack the first time I saw the open sky, yet it was all in my head."

Here, death lay on every side, only a misstep away. A momentary weakness of the knees, a pebble rolling underfoot, a piece of rotten rock crumbling, an attack of agoraphobia — any of those things could send her over. And that wasn't her only trouble. Something was wrong, she knew it. They should not have come here.

"You'll be all right," said Holm. "We've passed the worst. Tirnan Twil is just around the corner."

He did not seem fazed by the climb. But then, a man who could hang on with one hand, twenty feet up a mast in a gale, could not be afraid of many things.

"You've been saying that for three hours," said Tali.

"This time I mean it."

"You've been saying *that* for two hours."

"And this time it's true."

"And you've been saying — oh, what's the use?"

"Exactly," he beamed. "And since it's impossible to turn back, you might as well keep going as cheerfully as possible."

"It'd better be worth it," she muttered.

"The view's worth it, I promise you."

"I don't give a damn about the view. I meant Grandys' stuff."

"You should give a damn. Life is short and uncertain; you can't spend the whole of it chasing an obsession."

"Do we have to talk about this here?" said Tali.

He took her hand. "Come."

She allowed him to draw her around the corner of the cliff. Tali shuffled along, watching her feet and making sure she didn't stand on anything unstable that would tip her over. Then, a few yards around the corner, the foot-wide track broadened to a ledge ten times that width. She let go, looked up and out, and every hair on her body stood up.

"Oh!" she whispered. "That's . . . that's . . ."

"There aren't enough words," said Holm. He seemed as overcome as she was.

The other side of the chasm, two hundred yards away, was as sheer as the cliff she was standing on. The slanting afternoon light touched veins in the yellow stone as though there was a fire behind them. It was beautiful, but that was not it.

Tirnan Twil was it.

Five slender arches of golden stone, spanning the chasm. Each buttressed against the cliff on either side. All intersecting over the centre of the chasm, and that was marvel enough. It was incomprehensible that anyone could have built such vast unsupported spans, far greater than the greatest dome in Caulderon.

At the centre, rising up from the point of intersection, stood a building unlike anything Tali had ever seen, or imagined. A spire. No, a spike, for it did not aspire to the sky – it transfixed and impaled it.

It was extravagant, astonishing, impossible. It made no concessions to structure, function or practicality. Tirnan Twil was pure form.

No more than thirty feet in width, the golden stone smooth and unornamented save that the outside was shaped like a five-sided cloverleaf, it soared a thousand feet into the heavens. It was simplicity itself, and astoundingly beautiful.

Tali swallowed. "Five arches."

"For the Five Heroes who founded Hightspall. Though back then they were still known by their real name – the Five Herovians."

"Why the change?"

"The Herovians fell out of favour, but a nation has to have its heroes."

"And a five-sided spike."

"Like a nail through the celestial dome," said Holm. "An insight into the way they viewed the world, if you like."

She did not care to dwell on that. "I don't understand what holds it up."

"Arches are strong. And the weight of the spike on it only makes it stronger."

"Even the strongest stone will break if you put a big enough load on it. So the Cythonians say, and they're masters of stone."

Holm shrugged. "It's stood for a very long time."

"How do we get in?"

"We walk across the central arch. The shortest one."

"Aren't there guards, or gates?"

"There used to be. During the Two Hundred and Fifty Years War, and for a while afterwards, there were five Guardians, but then Tirnan Twil fell on hard times. Anyway, once the Cythians were defeated, Tirnan Twil faced no threats."

"Why not?"

"How would anyone attack it? Every approach runs along a cliff like this one, and from their cliff-top guard posts intruders can be seen coming for miles."

The broad ledge ran in a gentle curve out of sight. They reached the first arch which, though it appeared slender from a distance, was twenty feet deep and fifty feet broad. And the way across it was blocked.

"Every piece of stone in the arches is shaped to interlock like a three-dimensional jigsaw," said Holm.

"Like the pieces of the heatstone helmet you made for me," said Tali.

"Where do you think I got the idea?"

They passed the second arch, which had the same cross-section as the first but was shorter, and reached the third, the central arch. It crossed the chasm at right angles and was shorter yet, and unblocked. Holm headed across the arch, which had neither rail, kerb nor gutter.

"I wouldn't fancy walking across this in a high wind," said Tali, plodding after him and trying to look neither down nor up.

"Nor snow or ice. But I dare say one gets used to it."

At the other end, a large wooden door stood open. It was so old that the surface of the wood had weathered into corrugations along the grain, leaving little fibres standing out from the surface.

"After you," said Holm.

She didn't move. "Surely we can't just walk in unannounced?"

"If they didn't want us to come in, they wouldn't have opened the door."

A shadow passed across the sun. Tali shivered and looked over her shoulder. Again she felt as though someone was watching her, but there was nothing to see. Nonetheless, she felt as though she was an intruder, open door or not.

She went through and was immediately struck by how thick the walls were, and how small the rooms. Or room, for there was only one on this level. It was also shaped like a five-leaved cloverleaf on the inside, and each embayment contained an ancient tapestry depicting the life and glories of one of the Five Heroes. In the centre, a fixed steel ladder ran up vertically through a hole with the same shape.

As Tali studied the tapestries, the feeling of being watched grew until all the skin on her back crawled. She turned, looked across into the embayment on the other side, let out a yelp and instinctively sprang backwards.

Its tapestry depicted a man with the heavy-jawed, florid face she remembered from the Abysm – the face she had seen contorted in agony on the opalised figure of the First Hero.

Axil Grandys.

CHAPTER 45

A cool hand on Tali's elbow steadied her, and a soft, amused voice said, "He affects many visitors that way. A formidable man, our Axil Grandys."

She turned to see a neat, compact fellow dressed in an embroidered shirt and yellow pantaloons, and soft white shoes with the tips curled up.

Her face must have indicated surprise because he said at once, "You thought we would dress like monks? This is a place of scholarship, my lady, and preservation. Some people do worship at the altar of the Five Heroes, but I do not. My name is Rezire, and I am the curator. Your companion I remember from several visits, long ago. Greetings, Holm."

Holm bowed. "This is the Lady Thalalie vi Torgrist. But she answers to Tali."

Tali shot him a furious glance.

"We deal in truth here," said Rezire, who had intercepted Tali's glare. "Visitors must give their real names."

He returned Holm's bow, and bowed to Tali. "You are welcome, Lady Tali. But you have come a long way, with some urgency. If you would follow me." He turned to the ladder.

"How does he know that?" Tali said under her breath.

"Every visitor has come a long way. And considering how badly the war is going, our visit is bound to be urgent."

"I trust you have no fear of heights," said Rezire. "The design of Tirnan Twil, while breathtaking, makes no concession to practicality. The walls must be thick to support the weight, which leaves no room for a staircase."

He went up the ladder, which ran vertically for thirty feet before passing through a six-foot-high hole in the ceiling, with no more effort than walking from one room to another. Tali followed wearily, then Holm.

"Is it too much to hope that Grandys' stuff is on this level?" she said quietly.

"If memory serves me," said Holm, "his journals and papers are on the fifth level, and various devices, artefacts and memorabilia are on the floors above that."

"You remember," said Rezire, beaming down at them.

"I should have warned you, my Lady," he added politely. "The shape of the rooms focuses sounds to the centre, and upwards. There are few secrets in Tirnan Twil, but if you care to keep yours, make sure you're above anyone who may overhear you, rather than below."

The embayments on the second level had widely spaced, curving shelves made from thick glass that had developed a yellow tinge with age, though most of the shelves were empty. Tali looked into the embayment on her left. It contained only a pair of red shoes, the leather cracked, the toes scuffed. They were oddly shaped, almost square, with black laces.

"This room contains the oldest relics we have. Personal objects brought by the Five Heroes from our ancestral homeland," said Rezire.

"Why so few?" said Tali.

"Space on the First Fleet was limited: one chest per person."

"Even to the Five Heroes?"

"They were just ordinary citizens then."

"Whose are these?" She indicated the shoes.

"They're Syrten's baby shoes."

"Baby shoes!" Tali echoed. "They're almost as long as my shoes. And three times as wide."

"Syrten was an unusual man. Unique." Rezire turned away. "Over here we have the wooden flute carved for Lirriam by her grandfather, and—"

"Alas, we must take the tour on our next visit," said Holm. "Our time is short, and our enemies many."

The third level contained items of personal adornment owned by the Five Heroes – amulets, rings, torcs, armbands, anklets, and other items, mostly in heavy gold, though to Tali's eye they looked crude and unfinished.

"They're very . . . um . . ." said Tali.

"You find them a trifle rustic?" said Rezire, frowning. "You may say so. We believe in plain speaking here."

"They not what I'm used to, after Caulderon—"

"And Cython?" he said coolly. "The Herovians of old were crafts-men, but all their craft went into weaponry. Arts and crafts that were over-ornate, or *sophisticated*, offended them."

"They would have found much to be offended by in Palace Ricinus," said Tali. Everything in the palace had been elaborate, yet beautiful. And now it was all gone.

Every floor had one or two librarians or curators, silently dust-ing, polishing or writing in ledgers. On the fourth floor, which was empty as far as Tali could tell, three yellow-robed pilgrims knelt in the embayment on the right, facing each other, eyes closed.

"How many levels are there?" said Tali.

"Thirty-three," said Rezire, who was heading up into the fifth level.

"It seems an odd way to protect their treasures," said Tali.

"Ah," said Rezire, "but Tirnan Twil wasn't built to protect the Heroes' treasures."

"Why was it built?"

"To exhibit and glorify their lives."

"So all this stuff—?"

"Items that would be seen as treasures by those who worshipped the Five Heroes."

"Oh!"

"This level is entirely devoted to the papers of Axil Grandys," said Rezire.   •

The layout was the same as for the rooms below. Five embay-ments, each with widely set shelves of thick glass, though here the glass had a purple tinge rather than yellow. There was a small blackwood desk to the left, and three wooden benches.

"The embayment to your immediate left contains Axil Grandys' papers relating to the Two Hundred and Fifty Years War," said Rezire. "At least, the first decade of it, when he led our armies."

"Before he disappeared and was never seen again," Holm said quietly.

These shelves held hundreds of bound volumes, some books,

some journals, some ledgers of accounts, though most were collections of papers that had been bound together.

"The next embayment," Rezire continued, "has documents dealing with the establishment, laws and government of Hightspall. The third embayment, his household accounts and personal papers. The fourth, correspondence with the other Heroes and important figures of the day, and the fifth, miscellaneous papers. I hope you find what you're looking for."

He bowed and went up the ladder.

"What *are* we looking for?" said Tali quietly, so her voice would not carry.

"The key," said Holm, drawing her away into the corner of the room and lowered his voice even further.

"I know *that*. But what could it be?"

"Just about anything."

"Then how are we—?"

"You're not thinking, Tali. Lyf wants the master pearl because it'll help him to locate the key. And you've got the pearl . . ."

"So I need to look at everything that Grandys had, and see if anything resonates."

The room contained thousands of volumes. It would take hours just to take them down and look at them. Tali took down a volume at random, *Lessons from the Esterlyz Campaign*, and flipped the pages.

Holm sat on a bench, staring at the shelves.

"I hadn't realised it would be this hard to read," she said. Grandys' handwriting was spare, as befitted the simplicity of Herovian life and philosophy, but the language had changed in two thousand years and many of the words and expressions were meaningless.

Holm said something she could not make out. She was turning back to the book when again she had that feeling that someone was watching her – no, *looking down* at her.

She went to the ladder hole and looked up. There was no one in sight save a white-haired woman labouring up a ladder three levels above. She walked around the room, trailing her fingers across the spines of the books, but they told her nothing. She did the same with the two lower shelves, then the one higher than that, which was as high as she could reach.

"Nothing," said Tali. "Holm, I don't think it's here. Do you think—?"

"You're the one with the pearl."

"I think I'll try the next level."

It contained an array of weapons and armour – swords, daggers, war axes, bows and crossbows, and other weapons she did not know the names of, dozens of different kinds of each.

"They don't look like Cythonian weapons," she said to Holm, who had come up behind her.

"They're not, so they definitely didn't come from Lyf's temple. You don't have to worry about them."

It made her task a little easier. She wandered across to the opposite embayment, and recoiled. The shelves contained dozens of severed, embalmed heads, some worm-eaten and others, judging by the odour and appearance, beginning to decay despite the embalming fluid.

"Did Grandys collect these?" said Tali.

"Afraid so. Tells you what kind of man he was."

She went up to the level above that, which was a portrait gallery. There were nine portraits of Axil Grandys, plus several of each of the other heroes, but she gave them only a cursory glance. They hadn't come from Lyf's temple either.

The far embayment contained five portraits of Lyf, the young king of old. This is more like it, she thought.

"Would he have had portraits of himself in his temple?" she said to Holm.

"It hardly seems likely. It was his private temple; no one else ever entered there save at his invitation."

Four of the portraits were formal ones, masterly but stiff and over-formal. She continued to the fifth, a grimy, battered little miniature entitled *Self-Portrait of the Newly Crowned King, Age 18*. It showed Lyf in his temple, looking boyish, anxious and vulnerable.

"So he was eighteen when he became king," said Tali, drawn to the lonely figure despite all he had done since. "The same age as me."

"And not much older when they betrayed him and walled him up to die," said Holm. "Any resonance from it?"

"No." She went closer. "But it's so dirty, it's hard to see what he was like."

Tali continued around the portraits, but felt that feeling of foreboding again. She shuddered.

"What's the matter?"

"I keep feeling that we're being watched."

She drew a tiny amount of power and probed with her magery, above her, where the forebodings seemed to be coming from. They were diffuse and spread out over a wide area. What could it mean?

Tali looked up; looked down. Her foreboding was growing with every thickening breath, every racketing heartbeat.

"It feels like the danger's above us ... But not directly above. Not in the spike."

Tali paced around the five-lobed level. She had never felt claustrophobic in Cython, yet she felt trapped in this tower suspended over one of the most glorious views in Hightspall but lacking a single window. She had to see out; she was practically choking. She ran up the ladder to the next level. A young archivist, clad in green robes, was huddled over an object in an unlighted lobe of the room.

"Excuse me?" she cried.

He seemed surprised that she had addressed him, but bowed and said, "Yes, my lady?"

"Is there a window nearby? I've got to see out!"

"Tirnan Twil was designed without windows in the library and archive rooms, my lady."

"Anywhere?" she said thickly.

"In the early days, when the world was less benign, our designer had an eye to defence. Between a number of the levels there are places for sentries to hide and watch. And even defend if necessary, though I hardly think—"

"Where?" she screamed, barely restraining herself from shaking him. "Where's the nearest?"

"Just above, my lady. Would you like me to—?"

"Yes!" she shrieked. "Now!"

He bolted up the ladder, as if to escape her. As it passed through the hole to the floor above, he reached out to his left and opened a small, concealed door. He stepped through into a low-ceilinged service level, dark and musty.

"This way, my lady."

He had to crouch, and even Tali had to bend her head under the low ceiling. She followed him. Fifteen feet across, a pair of shutters had the same five-lobed shape as the tower.

He threw them, revealing a window set in the yard-thick wall. "There you are, my lady," he said with a trace of condescension. "You'll be all right now. You're not the first—"

He was turning away when something outside caught his eye. He thrust himself against the window, staring up, then heaved on a lever and the thick glass groaned out and down. He leaned out, his mouth hanging open.

"What is it?" said Tali.

He tried to speak but no words came out. Though he was much bigger than her, Tali thrust him aside and looked up.

Gauntlings! Dozens of them, circling around the tip of the spike that topped Tirnan Twil. Her heart stopped for a moment, then restarted with a lurch. But what could gauntlings do, up there?

"They can't get in, can they?"

His mouth worked; a globule of red saliva oozed onto his lower lip. He'd bitten his tongue in terror. Useless man! She ran past him to the ladder hole and yelled down.

"Holm! Gauntlings, dozens of them, high above!" She shouted the same message up to Rezire.

Holm came clattering up, the curator silently down. He thrust past her into the service level and across to the window. When he turned to them, his face was the colour of white marble. "It's an attack!"

"Surely gauntlings can't hurt this place?" said Tali.

"There is a way," said Rezire. "A flaw in the design. Though it was not a flaw when Tirnan Twil was built—"

"What flaw?" snapped Holm.

"The early curators discussed the issue for many decades."

Tali wanted to shake him. "What issue?"

"Whether an intelligent flying creature could ever be created. The best advice in Hightspall said no."

"So you did nothing."

"Are you without personal failings," said Rezire coldly, "that you judge others so readily, on so little evidence?"

"The question, however badly put," said Holm, "is an urgent one, Rezire."

"I'm sorry," said Tali. "But if the gauntlings have ill intentions—"

"This is a place of guardianship and contemplation," said Rezire. "We're used to thinking before we speak. Not a virtue held in high esteem in the outside world, I fear." His cold stare included Tali in that category.

"What was done?" she said.

"At crippling expense, Guardians were stationed at the ends of the arches, and up top, but no threat ever eventuated. The Two Hundred and Fifty Years War ended in our victory, and the danger passed. The Herovians who were our chief supporters fell on mean times. Support for Tirnan Twil dwindled, and we could no longer afford the Guardians. We kept watch ourselves, though Tirnan Twil has never been threatened ..."

"And now it is," said Tali. "What's the flaw in the defences?"

"Water."

"I don't understand."

"We need water to drink, and cook with, and bathe in," said Rezire, "but we can't carry it up a thousand feet from the river."

"How do you get it?

"Fans inside the top of the tower draw the misty gorge air in through slits in the stone. An array of condensers extract water from the air, and it's piped down to tanks on each level of the spike."

"Why is that a flaw?"

"An attack on the slits at the top of the tower could make its way all the way down the tower."

"What kind of an attack?" said Tali.

"Remember how the gauntling attacked my boat after Lizue was killed?" said Holm.

Tali stared at him. "Fire?"

"Fire."

CHAPTER 46

"Can't you block the slits?" said Tali.

"We could, if we had people stationed up there," said Rezire. "But it takes an hour to do so ..."

"And the gauntlings can attack in minutes," said Holm, "if that's their intention."

"If you turn off the taps," said Tali, "it'll stop fire coming down the pipes."

"However if the top level of Tirnan Twil should be set alight," said Rezire, "burning books and embers will cascade down through the ladder holes. There's no way to seal them."

"Then you've got to stop the gauntlings."

"I don't know how."

Tali tore at her hair. Could Rezire be that obtuse? But then, he was a man of learning. Battle and bloodshed wasn't real life to him, as they had become to her. War was something he read about in dusty old books. She looked to Holm to take the lead but he waved a hand as if to say, *continue.*

"You have defensive magery, don't you?" said Tali.

"We used to, devices of great power brought from ancestral Thanneron, but they failed long ago."

"They failed?"

"The land fights back. Most of the old magery has failed. Everything fails in the end, even steel and stone ..."

Rezire sounded resigned, accepting, and she could not comprehend it.

"Not Tirnan Twil!" said Tali. "Send men up to the tower top, armed with bows and spears."

"What would they do?"

"Attack the gauntlings. Drive them away from the air slits. *Hurry!*"

Rezire went to the ladder hole and shouted orders. Tali looked out the window at the circling gauntlings.

"Are they carrying riders?" said Holm.

"No."

"So what are they doing here?"

"They could be just spying for Lyf."

"Then why so many of them? One would be enough to shadow us here."

"I've ordered my most reliable people up to the defences," Rezire said dolefully, "but I fear it will do little good. Those attributes that make a good fighter are of little value in our work."

"Then you'd better tell your people that they don't have much time to escape – just in case it is an attack."

"Tirnan Twil is our home, our hope, our life, our future."

"If the gauntlings attack the air slits, some of your people may die."

"Everyone dies, Lady Tali."

"Not before their time."

"If Tirnan Twil's time has come, so has ours."

He trudged off, bent-shouldered and flat-footed.

"You've been very quiet," she said to Holm, who was looking up through the window.

"I'm wondering why the gauntlings are circling the tower. If they knew you were coming here – and presumably they've been spying on us from on high – why didn't they try to capture you on the way?"

"And carry me to Lyf?" said Tali. "I don't know."

"Wait a minute," said Holm, staring at her. "I don't think they're under Lyf's command at all."

"Why not?"

"He wouldn't order them to attack this place with you inside. That would risk losing the master pearl."

"Then who is commanding them?"

"No one," he said grimly.

"I don't understand."

"We talked about gauntlings after Lizue was killed, if you recall. They're troublesome, rebellious creatures, and Lyf would never send them out on attack without a rider to command them."

"Well, what do *you* think is going on?"

Holm took another look. "I think they've turned renegade. I think they're out for revenge because you killed Lizue and gravely injured her gauntling. They're not attacking Tirnan Twil for itself – they're trying to kill you."

"Sounds a bit far fetched."

"Gauntlings are vengeful, malicious and not entirely sane – madness is the bane of many kinds of shifters."

Tali checked on the gauntlings. "They're circling in towards the top of the spike. If they are planning to attack, it won't be long. Should we go up and help?"

"By the time we haul ourselves up another eight hundred and fifty feet of ladders, any attack will be long over."

"Then I've got to choose, right now – healing or destruction."

Holm said nothing.

"If I use it for destruction, what will happen if I need to heal someone to save their life?"

"I suspect you won't be able to heal anyone with magery, ever again."

"I don't know how to decide."

"If you freeze because you're afraid of the future, you'll never make *any* choice. You've got to choose now."

Tali had been through this before, before healing Holm's skull. Her frantic gaze fell on the scars on his brow and nose. "If I do choose destructive magery, could it undo the healing magery I did on you?"

"Possibly."

The gauntlings were using their little arms to heave barrels out of their panniers.

"They're going to attack," she said without turning around.

No answer. He had gone.

If she did not act, some of the people of Tirnan Twil were bound to die. She had to bring down the gauntlings, and if she could it would be a *great destruction* that would set the course of her gift forever.

Tali began to prepare for a magery greater than anything she had ever used before. She had to stop two dozen gauntlings and she only had minutes to do so — assuming that she could draw enough power, and focus it at such a distance. The way magery was failing everywhere, that was debatable.

But she was *the one*. This was what her gift was for and it was part of the great battle of the age. She reached deep, found power, then, in her mind's eye, located each of the twenty-four gauntlings.

They were arcing out and around and back in towards the spike, the single vulnerable point of Tirnan Twil. Their paths resembled a flower with twenty-four perfect petals.

She was about to direct her power at the gauntling coming in from due south, intending to burn its wing mounts away and send it plunging two thousand feet to the base of the gorge, when the image in her inner eye blurred. Then, ever so slowly, it changed.

Tali was staring at a man's face. A face that was familiar even though it was out of focus. A large, florid face. Shudders ran up her back and sweat dripped from the palms of her hands. She had seen that face in the Abysm, and the impossibly contorted body. Lyf had turned his greatest enemy to black opal and hurled his body into the Abysm. But the expression on the man's face was different here. He wasn't screaming in agony. He was roaring with rage.

The sweat froze on her palms. Her tongue filled her mouth and a weight on her shoulders was crushing her to the floor. Grandys was dead, turned to stone nearly two thousand years ago, so why did she keep seeing his image? Was it some kind of omen, like Rix's painting that had divined the future?

Was she some ignorant peasant, fearfully reading the sky for omens? No, she was the Lady Thalalie and the fate of many rested on her making the right decision.

Grandys' furious face vanished. Tali drew on her magery, focused it to a killing spell and checked out the window. But the sky was empty. She was looking up at the spike when flames burst out of dozens of slits near its tip, forming another beautiful red flower there, a deadly crimson one. She was too late. The gauntlings had attacked the tower's weak point and fire was roaring out of the condenser slits.

And if Rezire's people could not stop it from setting the top level alight, the embers would cascade down the ladders, level by level. Tirnan Twil had nothing to stop it coming all the way down.

CHAPTER 47

"How the blazes did you survive, Tobe?" said Rix late that night, after all the injured in the healery had been attended to and Glynnie had finally been relieved. "You fell a hundred feet, head-first, from my tower. It beggars belief."

The blizzard had struck in earnest and was blowing a near hurricane, with snow so thick and blinding that a man outside could not see his extended hand. Rix had no fear of the enemy attacking again while it raged, for they would die of exposure before they reached the top of the wall. Until it passed they would lie huddled in their miserable tents, wishing they were back in the warmth and safety of Cython. But once the blizzard passed, it would be on again.

Tobry did not reply. He was leaning towards the fire, staring fixedly into the flames.

Rix studied his old friend covertly, looking for signs of shifter in him, but saw none. Even after Tali had used her healing blood on Tobry, his cheeks had been downy, his eyes rounder, and his ears slightly furry and pointed. Tobry's eyes, Rix remembered, had still had a tinge of caitsthe yellow. There was no trace of it now; though bloodshot, they were the grey they'd always been. Her healing blood had worked, then.

The chancellor would be so pleased.

Tobry raised his glass, studied the play of light through the wine, and sipped appreciatively. "A fine cellar the old dame had. I wonder your mother's bandits didn't ship it away as well."

"They might have done had Swelt not realised what they were up to, and hidden the best of the drink in one of the abandoned cisterns."

"Is he a drinking man?"

"I don't think so."

"Then I praise him all the more." Tobry raised his glass. "It's a wonder none of the household gave the game away." He was a renowned cynic.

"Things are different in the provinces," said Rix. "Country folk cleave to their own and nurse their loyalties, and the old dame was greatly loved. But even had she not been, they would not have willingly given up Garramide's wealth to interlopers from Caulderon."

"From wicked House Ricinus, as was," said Tobry.

"We're the same now, you and I," Rix said without thinking. "Both ruined men whose houses have fallen."

"Not quite the same," said Tobry curtly.

Rix, assuming he was referring to Rix's inheritance of Garramide, bit his tongue.

"You've fallen on your feet, at any rate," Tobry added.

Rix snorted. "There are people here who would gladly cut my throat."

"You don't seem too worried."

"Once the enemy turned up, the servants realised that I'm the only one who can save them. My enemies had to pull their heads in – for a while, anyway."

Rix leaned back in his chair. They were in the grand dame's salon, a long rectangle of walnut-panelled walls with a painted ceiling twenty feet above them. The salon was a cold room, though with their chairs drawn up on either side of the fire it was almost cosy. It was the first time he had been able to relax since the war began.

"You were going to tell me your tale," said Rix.

"Later, if you don't mind." The wind howled outside the shuttered windows and Tobry shuddered, as if at some unpleasant memory. "The places I've been over the past weeks, the sights I've seen, have almost robbed me of the power of speech. I need to take it slowly."

Rix leaned back in his chair, studying his friend through the side of his glass. Tobry could be moody, and after all he'd suffered as a child, no wonder.

"No hurry. More wine?"

Tobry looked at him absently, then waved the bottle away. Rix wasn't sure what disturbed him more – that Tobry had been through a nightmare, or that he could refuse a second glass of the finest wine Rix had ever tasted.

"Am I talking too much?" said Rix. "Would you prefer I left you alone?"

"No!" Tobry said sharply. "My own company is the last thing I want. I've had far too much of it, and presently my mind isn't a fit state to visit, much less live. Tell me about yourself, and Glynnie and Benn. And . . . and Tali," he said in a rush, "if you've got any news of her."

"I wish I had. I haven't heard a whisper since the chancellor took her away."

Tobry hunched down in his chair, reached for his glass, found it empty and said, "Think I will have another drop."

Rix filled it to the brim. Tobry gulped it, spilling red wine down his chin without realising it. Rix pointed it out.

"Sorry." Tobry wiped his chin. "Been living like a pig for weeks. Hiding in drains, eating rats and other vermin. When you're bedding down in a sewer, manners don't seem so important." He looked up. "I spent most of that time searching for news of Tali and Rannilt, and the chancellor."

"That bastard!"

"Indeed," said Tobry. "But there was none, and I'm sure if the enemy had caught them I'd have heard about it. No, he ran away with his tail between his legs, somewhere west I'm guessing. But he's got Tali so well hidden by magery that no one knows where she is. After I exhausted my last lead, I came looking for you."

"Any news of the war?"

"Probably less than you have, given Swelt's network of informers. I can tell you that the centre of Caulderon lies in ruins – torn down so Lyf can rebuild old Lucidand."

"Any chance of a rebellion?"

"If there's one thing the enemy know, it's how to subdue a conquered people. They practised on the Pale for a thousand years."

"You mean there's no chance," said Rix.

"Lyf has fifty thousand troops in Caulderon, and the first thing they did was make a death list – all our leaders, military officers, thinkers, plus known troublemakers like you and me. The scaffolds have been working overtime. At the first hint of opposition, they round up all the ringleaders and put them to death."

"And now Bleddimire is going the same way. Is there any resistance in the provinces? Anywhere at all?"

"Not that I've heard. Lyf's victories have been too quick, too overpowering, too terrible ... and, for want of a better word, too *magical*. Rebels die swiftly and unpleasantly, and most local lordlings prefer to grab what they can get to fighting for their country – the gutless scum."

"But still ..."

"I've been among the common folk these past weeks, and they're terrified. People have lost hope for Hightspall. They're starting to think it's better to live as slaves than die as heroes."

Rix shivered. "I'm not thinking that!"

"Nor I. But to answer your question, as far as I know, organised resistance is confined to this fortress."

Tobry studied Rix thoughtfully, as though weighing him for the task, but said no more.

"What should I do, Tobe?"

"Unless a great leader steps forward, very soon, Hightspall is lost."

"In the past, you never stopped short of telling me what to do."

"I've been to hell and back, Rix. I'm not sending anyone else there."

Rix studied Tobry's worn face for a minute or two. "I'm no great leader. Doubt I ever will be. But even if I have to fight alone, I'm fighting for Hightspall – all the way."

"You're a good man, Rix. Did I ever tell you that?"

"Not as often as I'd like to hear it," said Rix, and they both laughed.

Tobry's smile faded. He leaned back in his chair and closed his eyes, as though the brief exchange had worn him out. "You ... talk."

"What about?" said Rix, feeling more than a little anxious.

"Anything. I just want to hear the sound of a friendly voice. It's ... it's a cruel world out there, Rix, when you're alone and friendless, and have no house to protect you. It's savage." His gaze fell on Rix's grey hand. "Tell me about it."

Rix didn't particularly want to. He still felt self-conscious about his dead hand, but Tobry was his oldest friend, and there were one or two curious things he might be able to cast some light on.

"It was Glynnie's idea. Didn't occur to me for an instant. She's a remarkable woman."

"I always thought so."

"She used the rest of Tali's healing blood. There wasn't much. Maybe that's why ..." He looked down at it. "She made me hold Maloch while she did it. Because Maloch was supposed to protect me, she said, and it might not have severed my hand on *all the levels*. Whatever the hell that means."

Tobry whistled. "How did she know that?"

"Something she picked up, listening to the magians talk."

"I gather your hand was alive for a while ... and then not?"

Rix froze. He had been trying not to think about the mural he'd painted on the wall of the little vault after Glynnie had rejoined his hand – the mural depicting himself and Tali about to kill Tobry, drawn with bone charcoal then painted with his own blood.

What could the mural mean? Do I secretly resent Tobry for gaining Tali's love? She's a beautiful and desirable woman. Do I, subconsciously, want to take her from him? No, that's absurd.

Should I tell him about the mural?

Rix wanted to tell Tobry and see him laugh it off, but couldn't bear to bring it up. It was too painful, too confronting. What would Tobry say? What would he think? He was a tolerant man, but could anyone be *that* tolerant? Revealing it could undermine Tobry's trust in him, even destroy their friendship. What if he walked out, never to return?

Rix could not take the chance. He needed Tobry's friendship, his wise counsel, his strength and not least his magery. Besides, Rix's paintings often portrayed strange, mysterious or alarming scenes. Occasionally – very occasionally – they divined some aspect of the future, though most of the time the paintings were mere figments of his artist's imagination. He wasn't going to risk Tobry's friendship and support over a mural that was so patently absurd.

"I used it for an hour or so," he said, looking into the fire, "while we hid in a forgotten vault deep beneath the palace. Then it went grey and dead in a few minutes. There can't have been enough of Tali's blood to heal it."

"I was talking to Glynnie earlier, down in the healery . . ." began Tobry.

Rix's heart thumped three times, close together, then missed the next three beats entirely. He looked away, afraid to meet Tobry's eyes; afraid he would read the sickening truth there. Rix's throat tightened until he could barely draw a breath. "What about?" he said with studied casualness.

Tobry favoured him with a sour smile, as if he knew Rix had left out something vital. In days gone by they had shared everything. Well, almost everything.

Could Tobry know what Rix was hiding? Surely not; Glynnie had the discretion of the perfect servant. She would never tell Tobry about a painting that concerned him so directly.

"The mural you painted up in the observatory. And how your hand came back to life when you took up your brushes."

"It's true," said Rix, wondering what Tobry was going to say next. Knowing him, it would not be positive.

Tobry didn't disappoint him. "Didn't you wonder how your hand could be dead all that time, then suddenly come to life when you began to paint?"

"Of course I did, but I decided to treat it as a gift."

"A miraculous gift, come to you because you're so deserving." Tobry heaped the sarcasm on with a shovel.

"Why not?" Rix said defensively.

"Glynnie as good as told you that there was magery involved—"

"What would she know about it?" Rix muttered, contradicting his earlier remark.

"And where can the magery have come from, but Maloch? In case you've forgotten, let me remind you. Nothing good has yet come from that sword."

"You've changed your tune. You're the one who urged me to wear it."

"I wish I hadn't."

"It saved both our lives in the wrythen's caverns," Rix pointed out.

"Only after it led us there for its own fell purposes."

"What rot!"

"Do you deny it led us there? You spun Maloch three times, remember, and each time it pointed to Precipitous Crag. I tried to stop it spinning, using the best magery I had, but it resisted me. No, it *beat* me."

"I don't deny it," said Rix, thinking about the sword and the strange pull it had on him. When he held it, all his doubts fell away. He felt strong, powerful, invincible. He wasn't planning to tell Tobry that either.

"Were you holding Maloch when you began the painting up in the observatory?"

Tobry had an unerring ability to make Rix feel like an idiot. "Er, yes."

"What did it tell you to paint?"

"It didn't *tell* me to paint anything," he snapped. "That's not how I work, as you know very well."

Tobry leaned back in his chair. The firelight played on his face and Rix saw that he looked much older – closer to forty than his true age, twenty-five. He wore scars Rix had not seen before and his eyes were brooding.

"Remind me how you do work."

"I disconnect my mind—"

"Never a hard thing, in your case."

Rix smiled, for the retort reminded him of the old, acerbic Tobry. He was far preferable to the new, harder man. The lost one.

"I deliberately didn't think about the painting. I didn't set out to paint Grandys—"

Tobry shot out of his chair, scattering wine across the floor. "*You painted Axil Grandys?*"

"I assumed Glynnie would have told you that."

"I tried to get it out of her, but she's like a clam where it concerns you. Go on."

"I needed to paint. You know how I get, sometimes – it's the only escape I have. I didn't care what I painted, so I deliberately disconnected. I spent the time planning the raid on Jadgery, as it happens."

"I heard about that on the way here. Not your most brilliant success."

"I came here to fight, and Swelt supported me. And," Rix realised, "I suppose I was obsessed with proving that I wasn't a true son of House Ricinus."

"Ah, well. You're not the only fool in this room."

"It wasn't until I'd finished working out the plan for the raid, and my right hand had gone icy cold, that I saw what I'd painted. Even then, it took a good while to realise I'd painted the image of Grandys I'd seen before."

"What image?" said Tobry.

"The one I saw when I put my hand on Maloch's hilt, on the way to Precipitous Crag."

"Like I say," said Tobry, "beware the sword. Whatever it's up to, it's not acting on your behalf."

"Then on whose behalf is it acting?"

"That," said Tobry, "is the question you should have asked yourself a long time ago."

CHAPTER 48

"Do you want to see the mural?" said Rix.

Tobry was slumped in his chair. "Not right now." He opened his eyes. "What happened to Benn?"

Rix told him. "He was just *gone*. No evidence, no trace."

"It happens in war. Happens all the time. Gods," cried Tobry, "I hate this world, this life." He held out his glass. Rix filled it. Tobry stared into the wine as though he might find the answers to the miseries of the world there. "He was a nice kid."

"Yes, he was," said Rix, a trifle shocked. Not because of the outburst – anyone was entitled to react that way on hearing of the disappearance of a child they knew – but because it was so uncharacteristic of his close-mouthed friend.

They finished the bottle and began another, not talking. Rix ran through his search for Benn yet again, in case he'd missed something, but his thoughts kept turning back to Maloch. The sword had belonged to Grandys, and Rix had spent all his spare time reading about the man, so it was hardly surprising that he had painted the petrified image while he was holding Maloch.

"I didn't land on the paving stones," said Tobry.

"What?" said Rix, dragged abruptly out of his own thoughts and not sure what Tobry was talking about.

"When the chancellor's guards threw me from the tower. The tidal wave must have collapsed the land beside the tower. I landed in a sinkhole full of water and slimy mud. And bodies; lots of drowned people."

"It's still a wonder you survived," said Rix. "A hundred feet!"

"I didn't survive by myself."

"Oh?"

"The impact knocked me out and hurt me badly. I was throwing up blood for a week."

He took a gulp of wine, which, as if to emphasise the point, stained his lips the colour of blood, then went on. "First thing I knew, Salyk was dragging me out over a pile of bodies." He shuddered.

"Who's Salyk?"

"A Cythonian soldier. Not much older than Glynnie, and quite unfit for soldiering . . ."

"Why so?"

"She was compassionate, gentle and caring, even to an ugly old enemy like me. She had nightmares from the atrocities she'd witnessed in the first days of the war. She should have been an artist . . ."

"Really?" said Rix, rolling his eyes.

"I mean it. We've talked before about Cythonians and their art. It seems to fill some great void in them, and even a humble soldier girl like her could tell the difference between good art and bad." He studied Rix's dead hand for a minute or two then said, with elaborate casualness, "I suppose that's why she saved your father's portrait."

Rix's heart stopped. "What portrait?" he said hoarsely. But he knew, he knew.

"The one you did for the Honouring."

"Where did she get it? I thought the chancellor took it."

"Evidently not. She found it in the ruins somewhere, and was so moved by it that she begged an audience with Lyf himself, to ask what to do with it."

Rix did not move or speak. He could not. Just when he thought House Ricinus's dreadful past had been erased, it rose up to haunt him.

"Lyf thought it a masterpiece, too. The finest work of Hightspall he'd ever seen." Tobry looked sideways at Rix.

"Is that supposed to console me?"

"I know how you artists crave the adoration of the masses." Tobry chuckled. "Ah, it's good to be back, Rix."

Rix scowled and did not reply.

Tobry went on. "In the early days of the war, Hightspall, at the instigation of Grandys and the other Heroes, wantonly destroyed almost all the treasures of old Cythe. Lyf ordered the portrait burned in retaliation."

"Good riddance!" said Rix.

"But Salyk couldn't burn it. It had moved her too deeply. She defied the express order of her lord king and hid the portrait where it would not be found. Though I've a feeling it will be found one day, and then it'll reveal its *true* divination."

"What do you mean, *true* divination?"

"I don't know – like I said, it's a feeling I have."

"How do you know all this?"

"Salyk hid me, and doctored my wounds, for quite a few days. I spent all my waking hours staring at the damn thing."

"Do you happen to know where the portrait is?"

"I dare say I could find it again, though I'm not planning to go back to Caulderon any time soon. They don't like me any more." Tobry chuckled. "Why do you ask?"

"It's the best painting I've ever done, yet I've never hated anything more. I've an urge to burn the damn thing myself."

"I wouldn't advise it. I heard Lyf's built a special scaffold, just for you."

Rix's lungs gave a convulsive heave. "Go on with your story."

"Not much to tell," Tobry said, a trifle hastily. "Salyk helped me to escape from Caulderon and I went looking for Tali. And a miserable time I had of it, too, until I gave up and ended up here."

Rix knew that Tobry had left out a large part of the story, but if he did not want to tell it there was no point asking him.

"How about you?" said Tobry. "What brought you to Garramide?"

"There's not a lot to tell that you don't know. Benn was lost, Glynnie and I fought a bunch of Cythonians in the lake. We escaped and made our way here."

"How come?"

"What?"

"Why here, as opposed to any other place?"

"My great-aunt left Garramide to me last year, in my own right. It didn't come through House Ricinus, so not even the chancellor could rob me of it."

"Were you consciously heading here? Or following the sword?"

"The sword pointed the way, and then I thought of Garramide."

Tobry frowned. "All right, let's assemble the evidence. You went to Precipitous Crag because Maloch pointed the way. You fought Lyf's wrythen there with Maloch, the sword that Lyf hates and fears. Lyf's ancient enemy was the great Herovian Axil Grandys, who started the war and owned the enchanted sword, Maloch. He hacked Lyf's feet off with it." Tobry's sardonic eye met Rix's bewildered one. "With me so far?"

Rix didn't bother to reply.

Tobry went on. "In the fight in the murder cellar, Tali hurled Maloch at the trophy case containing Lyf's severed foot bones, which Grandys had kept for some arcane purpose. Maloch destroyed the foot bones with a colossal burst of magery, hurting Lyf badly.

"Not long afterwards, you followed Maloch's directions to
Garramide, the fortress that Grandys' only child lived in until 1950
years ago. The Herovian fortress where Maloch lay hidden all this
time, until your great-aunt sent it to you a couple of years back."
Tobry raised an eyebrow. "Have I missed anything vital?"

Rix jerked his head from side to side.

"And what's the first thing you do when you get here?"

"You tell me. You know so much more than I do."

The sarcasm settled like a wet blanket.

"You call for paints and brushes," said Tobry, "even though your
hand has gone dead and you've vowed to never paint again. You
take Maloch in your good hand and, Lo! Tra la! Like magic, your
dead hand comes back to life just long enough to paint a mural
depicting the opalised body of Axil Grandys. And what do you do
then?"

Rix did not reply.

"Nothing!" said Tobry. "Nothing about the mural strikes you as
the least odd or worrying. You draw no parallels, see no omens. You
continue on your merry way as though nothing had happened."

"I've been sweating about it for ages," cried Rix, nettled beyond
forbearance.

"Yet you still wear the sword," Tobry said inexorably. "You
still go up to the observatory and moon over the mural every
night."

"How the hell would you know what I do?"

"I asked Glynnie and she told me that much, because she was so
worried about you. Rix, can't you see that this obsession with
Grandys – or perhaps a better word is *infatuation* – is perilous?"

"He's been dead almost two thousand years, Tobe."

"But his sword is up to something and it's out of your control.
And there's another thing—"

"Make it the last," snapped Rix.

"All right. I know it came as a shock when the chancellor told
you that you were Herovian, and directly descended from Grandys
himself. And I know your life had been shattered by the fall of your
house, and you felt you had nothing left—"

"Get to the point, if you've got one," Rix grated.

"You needed to fill the void in your life, but I wouldn't advise you to adopt Herovian ideals uncritically."

"I'm not like you, Tobe. I'm not a deep thinker."

"You've got that right. You're not even a *shallow* thinker."

Rix gritted his teeth but let it pass. "I don't know much about Herovian ideals – no one will tell me! But I know they believe in honour, nobility—"

"And *blood*, Rix. Bloodlines were everything to them. That's why Grandys made Garramide one of the strongest fortresses in Hightspall – to protect his only child. They also believe in racial purity, drunkenness, brawling and contempt for the arts, to name but a few. Grandys made a point of destroying every thing of beauty the Cythonians had created in thousands of years. How do you reconcile that, Rix?"

"I can't. But . . . he was just one man."

"A man who epitomised his people. He also believed that the mentally disabled, infirm and crippled should be done away with, to preserve the purity of the race."

Rix was in dangerous waters and had no way out. "That was all long ago—"

"Herovian beliefs haven't changed," said Tobry. "And before you get too involved with them, hasn't it occurred to you that you count as a cripple, *Deadhand*!"

CHAPTER 49

It was impossible to sleep with the enemy camped outside the walls of Garramide. After tossing in his bed for hours, listening to the blizzard shrieking like the injured men down in the healery, Rix rose and went up to the main watchtower behind the gates. Even wearing a heavy, down-filled coat with a fur-lined hood, it felt petrifyingly cold outside now.

"Lord?" said Nuddell as Rix entered the guardhouse. Nuddell

was warming his hands over the brazier, but must have just come in from the wall – he had an epaulette of snow on each shoulder.

"Hope you haven't been here all night," said Rix, joining him.

"Just an hour. Couldn't sleep."

"Me either. Anything to report?"

"They're still out there – but they're wishing they weren't."

"I'll bet," said Rix. "Even when Tobe and I went hunting in the mountains, I've never known it to be this cold."

"Blizzard's blowing off a thousand miles of ice," said Nuddell. "A man could freeze to death fully dressed out there."

"Let's hope Oosta and her healers are hiding somewhere warm."

"Let's hope they're still alive."

Rix turned away from the brazier, reluctantly. "If anything happens I'll be down at the healery."

Glynnie was already there, changing the dressings on the man with the amputated arm. There were shadows under her eyes and she looked as though she'd had no more sleep than Rix, but she was smiling at the soldier, trying to be cheerful. Despite the pain, he was smiling back. She's done great good here this night, thought Rix.

All the blood and mess had been cleaned away, and so had the amputated limbs and Droag's body. "How are we doing?" Rix said quietly.

"We lost two in the night. Scanzi of a head wound – he never came to, just slipped away – and Pentine with that terrible gash across the belly. I never held any hope for him ... but still ..."

"He was a decent man, a widower with two little kids."

"And now they've got no one."

"They'll have a home here as long as I'm in charge," said Rix.

Dawn was breaking outside, and he was doing the rounds of the wounded, speaking to all those who were awake, when a rosy-cheeked lad came running in, so swathed in coats that he looked like a ball on legs. "Lord, er, Rixium?"

"Yes, lad? You're Thom, aren't you? How's your hand?"

"Can't even see where the splinter was, Lord Deadhand." Thom gazed at Glynnie, worshipfully, then turned back to Rix. "Sergeant Nuddell bids you come at once."

Glynnie swung around, staring at Thom.

"Bad news?" said Rix. "They're not attacking again?"

"Didn't say."

"What are you doing up so early, lad?" said Rix as he accompanied Thom back to the watchtower. Rix wiped his eyes. Even in the sheltered yard the wind was so bitter that his eyes were watering and the tears freezing on his cheeks.

"Cel-celebrating your great victory," said the boy, skipping along.

"We haven't won yet."

"But we're going to."

Nuddell met them at the top of the steps. "You'll want to see this," he said, heading across to the outer wall. Rix followed, impatiently, and looked over.

"Can I see?" said Thom. "Can I see?"

Rix picked the boy up and perched him on his right shoulder.

Thom hooted and waved his fists. "They're running, the cowardly dogs!"

The attacking force was halfway across the plateau, heading for the escarpment and the road down. More than twenty mounds lay in the snow where their camp had been, and many more below the parts of the wall Rix could see from here.

"Whatever they are, Thom, they're not cowards," said Rix. "But they suffered a bitter defeat at the wall yesterday, and last night was a killing cold that would have drained them to the dregs. Few men would be in any condition to fight today, and if they stayed, tonight will be even colder. Off you go."

He walked the length of the wall, speaking to each of the guards and making sure they were up to the job, then headed down to spread the good news, though by the time he was inside the whole fortress knew it.

"They lost a hundred and sixty-six dead, plus many wounded," said Rix to the assembled people. "Such a defeat that they could hardly have attacked again even without the blizzard. They won't be back until the weather improves. Today will be a holiday—"

He paused until the cheering died down. "But after that, we can't rest until we've strengthened Garramide to hold out twice that number."

One after another, the people of Garramide came up to shake
Rix's hand and thank him personally. Protest all he might that it
was a team effort, no one would listen. He had saved them and they
would never forget it.

"That was mightily well done, Rixium," said Swelt, last of all.
"I've written half a dozen dispatches and I'll send them out by carrier hawk within the hour, to the six corners of Hightspall."

"In this weather?" said Rix.

"Carrier hawks fly in any weather, and this is news that can't
wait. Our first true victory over the enemy."

"Well, all right, though it seems a trifle boastful, since the
weather—"

"It's a famous victory. It proves the enemy can be beaten, and it'll
bring hope to our oppressed people wherever they are. And encourage other leaders to step forward, all over the land."

"It might also encourage Lyf to send a full army against us," said
Rix.

CHAPTER 50

Tali scrambled back to the ladder and up six rungs to the seventh level, which was empty. Where was everyone?

"Holm?" she yelled, her voice going shrill. "Where are you? The
top of the spike is on fire."

"I'm here!" Holm called from below. "Come down."

She looked down. "Is Rezire there?"

"No, he went up."

"I've got to warn him."

"You already did."

"Not about the fire."

"Make it quick!"

Tali stood there. "I took too long. I might have stopped
them."

"All twenty-four gauntlings? When all the world's magery is failing? You take too much on yourself."

"I was distracted, and by the time I'd gathered enough magery to attack, it was too late. I've got to warn everyone."

"Then get a move on! I'll tell the people down below."

Tali scrambled up the ladder to the eighth level and screamed, "Rezire! Fire! Fire!"

He did not answer. She looked up the series of ladders, through level after level, hole after hole until she could no longer separate them. It was another eight hundred feet to the top. Tali was a lot stronger than she had been a week ago, but she could not climb all that way.

However the shape of the chambers focused sound upwards, and if she shouted loudly enough it would be heard many levels up. If the librarians and curators on each level repeated the warning, it would pass from the bottom of the tower to the top in a minute or two.

"Fire!" she screamed. "The top of the tower is on fire. Get out *now*!"

A gowned curator, a little, bald gnome of a man, looked down from the ninth level. "Did you call?"

"Fire, you bloody moron. The top level is on fire. Get out now."

He pursed his lips. "There's no excuse for rudeness. Good manners cost nothing, girlie."

"If you don't get out, you're going to burn to death. Warn the people above."

He looked up. "I don't see any fire."

"Hurry, please."

He began to replace books on the shelves as though he had hours. What was the matter with these people? They seemed to live in another world.

Was there time enough to get everyone out? Surely fire would not burn down nearly as quickly as it would go up. Each level would have to catch alight, all the way down, and desperate people could scramble down faster than that.

"Tali?" yelled Holm. "Come down."

She hesitated on the ladder. Had she done enough? No; she had to make up for her failure with the gauntlings. She was climbing up to the ninth level, slowly and wearily, when a hot red dot blossomed an impossible distance above her – fire seen through a succession of ladder holes.

Then a slightly larger dot.

"Tali!" Holm said urgently.

"Yes?" Her voice had a tremor.

"There's nothing more you can do."

She looked up, looked down. With all that magery at her disposal, she must be able to do something. But what? She did not know any spell that would answer in this situation.

"Tali, get down *now*!"

She held on with her left hand, extended her right up towards the distant red dot, and drew power. Her head throbbed.

The ladder shook. Holm was scrambling up it. He came around the other side, level with her.

"What the hell do you think you're doing?"

"Trying to hold back the fire."

"Do you *know* how to stop fire with magery?"

"No, but—"

"It's one of the most difficult of all spells. I've heard of master magians who have spent decades trying to master it – and still failed."

"If I'd stopped the gauntlings—"

Holm let out an inarticulate cry, then held up his right fist in front of her face. "See this?" he said furiously.

The white scars across his knuckles stood out lividly. "Yes."

"If you don't go down *right now*, I'm going to knock you out and carry you down over my shoulder. Of course, I'm an old man, so I'll probably fall off the ladder and break my neck, but—"

"All right," she said quietly. "I'll go. After you."

"You first. I don't trust you."

She looked up. *Whoomph!* A slightly larger dot of red appeared. Another floor ablaze.

"Go!" cried Holm, and she could hear the fear in his voice.

She scrambled down the rungs. He swung around to her side and followed, shaking the ladder in his haste.

"Faster, Tali."

Her knees were already wobbly. "I can't go any faster. I'll fall."

"Better you fall than the fire catches you."

She tried to hurry but her foot slipped. Tali swung by her hands for a few seconds, her heart missing several beats. The holes were directly above one another – she could plunge all the way down, a hundred and eighty feet. She felt for the rungs, settled. Sweat was running down her face.

"Come *on*!" said Holm.

The red dot was much larger now. *Whoomph!* Then again, only seconds later.

She reached the bottom of the ladder and scrambled onto the next one down. "How many levels to go?" she gasped.

"Six."

"I don't think we're going to make it. And what if the fire weakens the spike above us? The floors could fall down on our heads."

"It'll be a quicker way to go than burning to death."

They made it down to the sixth level. Tali looked across the room and saw a curator polishing an orb on a stand.

"Get out!" she screamed. "Tirnan Twil is on fire."

The man did not look up. "Fire or no fire, our work must be done."

"But . . ." She looked up desperately. "Holm, tell them."

"I have told them, but this is the only life they've ever known. We've done all we can."

"I was wrong about the fire," said Tali, who could feel the heat radiation on the top of her head now. "It's coming faster than we can climb down."

"You talk too much," panted Holm.

"And I'm holding you up," she said. "Sorry."

He grunted.

She shot down the next ladder and onto the one after that. She tried to guess how far up the fire was. Surely only ten or twelve levels. Down she hurtled, her sweat-drenched palms slipping on the rungs. Not far to go now.

She reached the bottom, looked up, and choked. There was no sign of Holm.

"Holm, where are you?"

No answer. "Holm?"

She cursed and headed up again, her heart crashing violently. What had happened to him? Had he fallen backwards off the ladder, out of sight?

He wasn't on the second level, the third or fourth or fifth. Pain spread through her chest. He had vanished. She forced herself up towards the sixth, where she had last seen him. Her legs were so wobbly that they would barely support her.

Whoomph!

There was smoke on this level now, stinging her eyes and blinding her with tears. But he wasn't here either. She scrabbled up to the seventh, the portrait gallery.

"Holm?" she said, turning around. There he was, hardly visible through the swirling smoke. "What are you doing?" she screamed.

"I remembered something."

Whoomph! Whoomph!

A pressure wave sent an incandescent blast of heat down at them. That's why it's burning down so fast, she thought. That's why none of the librarians have made it down the ladders. And if it catches us—

Holm sprang down, stuffing something into his coat.

"What's that?" said Tali.

"There isn't time to talk about it."

"You're a fine one to lecture me," cried Tali, fear choking her. "Go down!"

He rattled down the ladder and she followed. When they reached the bottom, the fire was only three levels above. A blistering wind was driven down past them, and on it she could smell burning hair and other unpleasant things. There was no smoke down here, but it was a struggle to breathe nonetheless; the air did not seem to be giving her what she needed.

She looked around frantically. "Which way did we come in?" she said, panting.

"That way." He indicated a closed door. He was breathing heavily too. "But it's not the way we're going out."

"Why not?"

"Do you have to argue every bloody point? Do what I say for once."

He limped to the great door on the other side. It was locked. *Whoomph!*

"Open it," said Holm, and stepped aside.

"How?"

"Use your damned magery. As much raw power as you've got. No subtlety is required."

She extended her hand, drew from the pearl and, with a stone-rending boom, the door tore off its hinges and was blasted outwards. It went tumbling across the ravine, to crash into the yellow cliff a hundred yards away.

"Perhaps a *hint* of subtlety," smiled Holm.

A cold wind rushed in and up the ladder. The fires above glowed red, then blue.

Suddenly there was flame all around, consuming the air, making it impossible to breathe. Holm caught Tali's hand, dragging her outside. It was raining heavily and the air was thick with smoke. The arch stretched before them, across to a ledge. They ran, but were only halfway across when, with a *Whoomph! Whoomph! Whoomph!* fire burst out the door, straight at them.

Tali felt the tips of her hair shrivelling, the fur on the collar of her coat singeing. There came a blast of heat on her exposed skin, then she was pounding away, hauling Holm behind her.

She skidded off the end of the arch, holding her hands out to prevent herself from crashing into the cut-away cliff, then ducked below the level of the arch. Flames roared overhead for a minute or two, bouncing off the cliff in all directions. She was sweltering in her heavy clothes. She sucked at the hot air but still felt suffocated.

Then it was gone into nothing. It might never have been there, save that the yellow cliff was steaming and the moss in the cracks had been charred away. Tali stood up unsteadily and looked back.

Orange flames were visible through the windows of Tirnan Twil, all the way up. Some of the thick panes had burst and flames were licking out, along with yellow, black and brown smoke. The golden stone around the broken windows was already smirched by tarry smoke stains.

Smoke whirled about the spike; rain hissed off the hot stone. The whole structure seemed to shiver slightly, then settle, and for a long moment Tali thought it was going to collapse into the abyss, but it held.

"I almost wish it had fallen," she said quietly. "Apart from the smoke stains, it looks unharmed."

"Just as it ever was," said Holm.

"And even the smoke stains will wash away in time."

"I know what you mean. It doesn't seem right that all those people, and everything they looked after so carefully for so long, should have been destroyed . . ."

"Yet the vainglorious shell remains, untouched. Why didn't they run?" said Tali. Her insides were aching, burning.

"I think some, like Rezire, had invested so much of their lives in Tirnan Twil that they couldn't bear to leave, even in its death agony. Like a captain going down with his ship, perhaps."

"What about the others?"

"It had stood for two millennia, unchanged, untouched. Perhaps the idea of it being destroyed was so preposterous that they could not take it in. Life in Tirnan Twil was slow, contemplative, deliberate."

"I tried to warn them."

"You did everything you could. And at the end, the fire came very fast. Much faster than I expected. By the time they realised how bad it was, it would have been on them."

"It must be a terrible thing, being burned to death." She shuddered violently.

"I think most would have suffocated," he said gently.

"Why do you say that?"

"Remember how hard it was to breathe at the bottom? The burnt air sinks. I doubt they suffered much."

"But still . . ."

"Not the way I would choose to go."

He put an arm around her shoulders. She looked back at Tirnan Twil, one last time.

"As they said, a monument to eternity."

CHAPTER 51

"Was blowing the door off a *great destruction*?" said Tali.

The smoke was thickening, whirling and tumbling in the updrafts created by the ravine. She could hardly see Tirnan Twil now.

"Did it kill anyone, or destroy something vast or vital?"

"No."

"Then the answer is no." He looked down the ravine, then up. "Can you hear them?"

"The people inside?" she whispered, shivering.

"No, the gauntlings."

It was hard to tell over the roar and crackle of the fire, the wind whistling along the gorge, and the pattering rain.

Kaark! Kaark!

"They'll come after us, won't they?"

"Once the smoke clears, they'll come down to check. With the gusting winds around here, it'd be too dangerous right now." He glanced at the sky. "Not much daylight left, which is good. Though it means . . ." He gave her a sympathetic smile.

"What now?" she groaned.

"We'll have to walk the cliff path out – the really dangerous one – in darkness."

"What do you mean the *really dangerous* one? How could it be worse than the one we came in on?"

"It's worse." He was smirking.

Tali could not smile. The destruction of Tirnan Twil had burned all humour out of her.

"However I do know a secret way out," said Holm. "If we can get out of sight we can lose them in the night."

"Luck isn't something we've had much of, lately."

"We're alive, free, and in improving health. I count that as good luck."

"Just as a matter of interest," she said as they trudged along, "where are we going?"

"I thought you'd decided that when I was injured and out of it."

"I was heading in the direction of a place called Garramide. Though I don't know where it is."

"It's a few days east of here, in the middle of the Nandeloch Mountains."

"Good. I've had enough of travel," said Tali. "About the portrait?"

"What portrait?"

"The one you stuffed in your pocket up on the seventh level. I assume it's Lyf's self-portrait. Why did you take it?"

"I suppose, like you, I saw something in it."

"Do you think it's the key?"

"Probably not, but self-portraits are always revealing. If it's cleaned up it could tell us something useful about him."

That night a wicked blizzard blew in and the few days turned into five, the first two of which they spent in a cave, waiting for the weather to improve.

"Go carefully," said Holm, on the fifth afternoon. "These are suspicious times, and isolated fortresses are more likely to shoot strangers than welcome them."

They had spent most of the day labouring up the escarpment through dense forest and heavy snow. They were now standing under the eaves of the forest, studying Fortress Garramide from a quarter of a mile away.

"Better make sure we can't be mistaken for the enemy, then," said Tali.

"Take your hat off. There's never been a Cythonian with golden hair in the history of the world."

From beneath her broad hat brim, Tali looked nervously at the sky. It was heavily overcast and light snow was drifting before a keen southerly.

"I suppose I could manage it – when we're outside the gates."

They headed out of the forest across deep snow, though the surface was hard and it was easy walking, save where a too-hasty step broke through the crust.

"Looks like they've been under attack," said Holm.

"And won."

There were guards all along the walls and carpenters were repairing the main gates. Several large mounds in the snow suggested a lot of enemy dead, but the fortress stood proud and undefeated, and a hundred chimneys were smoking.

They headed across to the road, where the snow had been beaten down by people coming and going, then slowly along it. Tali went first, nervously. The men on the wall to either side of the gate had their bows trained on her all the way.

"No further," said Holm. "You're almost within bowshot. Take off your hat. The scarf too. Let them be in no doubt that you're a Hightspaller, and no threat."

Tali took off her hat, unwound her scarf, then braced herself for the sickening panic of agoraphobia, but it did not rise. Perhaps the sky was too gloomy. The wind ruffled her hair. It was icy on her exposed neck and the driven snowflakes settled there, but did not melt.

"State your name and business," called a tall guard.

"We've been hunted halfway across Hightspall, and seek refuge." Her voice sounded shrill, fearful. "My companion is called Holm and—"

"What is your name?" the guard said curtly.

"I am the Lady Thalalie vi Torgrist."

Silence. The man had disappeared from the wall. None of the other guards spoke. Neither did they lower their weapons.

"He's gone to speak to his captain," Holm said quietly. "We may have a long wait."

Tali drew her coat around her more tightly. Cold was seeping up through the soles of her boots. She stamped her feet but it did not help.

Five minutes passed. Ten. Fifteen. "Why is it taking so long?" said Tali.

Holm did not answer.

"What if they turn us away? We've got no food left."

A huge man appeared on the wall, clad in furs and wearing a hat drawn down over his face against the driving snow. He studied them for a few seconds before turning away.

Tali swallowed. "That doesn't seem like a good sign."

"Depends how you look at it," said Holm.

Shortly a small gate opened beside the main fortress gates. A guard gestured to them.

Tali put on her scarf and hat as she hurried across. The guard held up a square, callused hand, studied their faces as though memorising them, then waved them through.

A tall, weathered man stood waiting in the yard, wearing the insignia of a sergeant. He was quite bald and did not have many teeth. "Sergeant Nuddell," he said courteously. "Your escort to Lord Deadhand."

"Does he always interview refugees personally?" said Holm.

"I don't talk about his business."

They followed Nuddell along paved paths, freshly cleared of snow. Several leafless trees occupied a left-hand corner of the yard. Ahead was a massive castle built from yellow stone. Towers on the corners each had a green, copper-clad dome.

"Garramide looks all very neat and orderly," said Tali.

"The late, great dame ran a tight house," said Nuddell. "Her heir, Lord Deadhand, does things the same way."

He led them inside, along a broad entrance hall and up several levels to a door guarded by a compact, hungry looking fellow, scarred across the throat as if someone had tried to cut it. He nodded to Nuddell, opened the door, stood aside to let them pass and pulled the door closed.

Tali went in, anxiety gnawing at her stomach and acid burning a track up the centre of her chest. She passed across an anteroom, her feet making no sound on an ancient patterned rug, then around through a doorway into a large, panelled room lit only by embers in a large fireplace.

The big man still wore a greatcoat. He had his back to her and was standing in the shadow beside the window, looking out. But there was a presence about him, a familiarity, that swelled and grew until, at the moment he turned, she knew him.

"Rix!" It came out as a shriek of joy.

He stretched out a grey right hand, studied it ruefully for a moment and drew it back. "Around here, they call me Deadhand."

She sprang forwards, thinking to embrace him, for they had been great friends. Then, remembering the manner of their parting, she froze.

Rix frowned. "Am I so very changed? So very ferocious?"

She had to put things right. "I did you wrong, not telling you about Lord and Lady Ricinus's treason. I'm sorry. I was trying to protect you."

"It was my right to know," said Rix coolly.

She could not tell what he was thinking. "I wasn't trying to protect you, as though you were a child," she went on. "But if you'd known, you would have been in an impossible situation—"

"A duty to protect my sovereign in a time of war," said Rix, "utterly in conflict with my duty to honour my parents and safeguard my house. Even so, you should have told me."

"I'm sorry," said Tali, "I've been worrying—"

"Then worry no more. The high treason was revealed, the traitors condemned, the house crushed. Everything I had and everything I was has been swept away. The slate has not just been erased, it's been smashed and thrown out. Come here." He held out his arms.

Tali embraced him, or tried to, though in her heavy coat her arms did not meet around him. He could have enfolded her twice in his arms.

Rix looked over her head towards Holm, then disengaged.

"I'm sorry," he said. "Rixium of Garramide, though I go by Rix. Or Deadhand, whichever you prefer. I won't shake hands, if you don't mind – it rather puts people off."

"I'm Holm," said Holm. "I hear you did away with that hyena, Leatherhead. That must have been a sight to see."

"He might easily have done away with me."

He ushered them to chairs by the fire and called for food and drink, then gave a brief account of the fight with Leatherhead and his time here, though to Tali's mind it raised many questions and provided few answers.

But if he wanted to draw a veil over the time since the fall of Caulderon, that was his right. She'd had a number of experiences in the past weeks that she never wanted to think about again.

Though, as it happened, Rix did not ask her about her time with the chancellor, how she had escaped, or how she had found him.

Shortly a serving maid came in, bearing a heavy tray.

"Glynnie!" Tali cried.

Glynnie set down the tray and turned to her, smiling, though rather formally. Tali, who had been intending to embrace the girl, shook hands instead.

"You look different," said Tali.

She seemed taller, and the slender girl's shape was taking on a woman's curves.

"I get enough to eat here," said Glynnie. "Will that be all, ma'am, *Lord*?"

She shot a glance at Rix, whose jaw tightened. Tali looked from one to the other. There was a tension between them that had not been there back in Caulderon. Rix nodded. Glynnie went out.

"Benn's dead," said Rix. "At least, I lost him when we escaped from Caulderon. I don't see how he can be alive."

"I'm sorry," said Tali. "He was a nice boy."

"Sit down. Eat. And if you have any news, I need to hear it."

"Wherever we go," said Holm, "people are desperate for news of the war. Though there's never any good news."

"There is here," said Rix. "We've beaten off a besieging force of almost five hundred. Inflicted a heavy defeat, in fact. Though the blizzard helped."

"A win is a win," said Tali. "Well done, Rix. Though it doesn't surprise me. You should be a general."

"For the moment, I've got my hands full protecting Garramide. What news do you have?"

"The chancellor never stops scheming," said Tali. "But his schemes don't come to anything. We can't rely on him."

"How big is his army?"

"Not big enough." She frowned. "It was less than five thousand when I escaped, though it'd be bigger by now."

"That's not even enough to hold the south-west," said Rix. "If Lyf attacks it, now he's taken Bleddimire—"

"Bleddimire's fallen?" cried Holm. "When?"

"Weeks ago."

"Then it's over. He holds the best of Hightspall already and we're left with the dregs."

"Be damned!" cried Rix, leaping to his feet and towering over them. "We're *never* giving in. Next time we'll have a bigger victory. And a bigger one after that, until we drive the mongrels back down the rat holes they came from."

He paced around the room, breathing heavily, then sat down with a thump. He looked up, met Tali's eye and said with a rueful smile, "Or, more likely, until me and all my rebels are dead."

"Count me among them," Tali said impulsively. "The rebels, I mean."

"Count *us*!" said Holm. "How dare you leave me out of it?"

Rix's eyes shone. He wiped them hastily. "Thank you," he said, embracing Tali and Holm in turn. "That means everything to me."

"There is one other piece of news," said Tali. "Two pieces, actually. And perhaps you'll find them hopeful."

"Go on."

"From time to time I've been able to spy or eavesdrop on Lyf, via my gift."

"Yes, yes?" said Rix.

"Lyf's victory over Caulderon always seemed uncanny to me. Taking such a great and well-defended city within hours seemed too quick, too complete."

"And to me, too."

"That's because it *was* uncanny."

"How do you know?"

"I overheard him talking to his ghost ancestor, Errek. After Lyf added Deroe's ebony pearls to his own, he drew on vast amounts of magery to attack our armies, and defeat them."

"Why would I find that hopeful?" said Rix.

"Because he took too much. Lyf thought magery was limitless but it isn't. It's failing rapidly – his and the chief magian's. It's failing everywhere, even mine. So next time he fights a battle, he'll have to do it without magery."

"That is good news. I can't fight magery, but I can fight men."

They finished their dinner and a servant appeared to usher them to their quarters. Tali was glad to go. All she wanted was a bath and a bed. She followed the servant to the room prepared for her. It was small and spare, with a low ceiling and bare walls, but she liked small rooms and simple surroundings. It reminded her of the little stone chamber she had shared with her mother in Cython.

It did not remind her of the bad things about Cython, but rather the good ones, and the moment she lay down and blew out the candle, Tali fell asleep.

CHAPTER 52

Why did I withhold the news that Tobry was here? Rix wondered after they were gone. Certainly not to injure Tali. Could it have been to injure Tobry, though? He hadn't stopped talking about Tali since he'd arrived, fretting about her bondage to the chancellor, the dire risk of him finding out that she bore the master pearl and the certainty that Lyf was hunting her.

For Rix, the joy of Tobry's appearance had faded the night he came, when they had discussed Maloch, Herovianism and Rix's mural of the opalised Axil Grandys. Another issue he did not want to talk about.

Since the enemy were unlikely to return until the bad weather broke, he had time on his hands. He found himself constantly drawn to the mural, and more so to the man it portrayed.

Grandys had been hard and ruthless, though that was a necessary characteristic of those who forged nations and won wars, and Rix could not blame the man for what he had done. Grandys had a driving purpose and a self-confidence that Rix himself yearned for.

Tobry mocked Rix mercilessly for this ambition, for his admiration of Grandys and almost everything else that gave Rix's life meaning. Tobry had always poked fun at Rix, but in the past it had been gentle, part of the banter of their relationship. Now Tobry's criticism had a hard edge, and Rix could tolerate less and less of it.

He avoided Tobry most of the time, making excuses where he could.

And Tobry had withdrawn.

One by one I drive my friends away, Rix thought, and soon I'll have none. I've got to do better. I'll make it up to him as soon as he comes in from the hunt.

Tobry had been well liked in Palace Ricinus and almost everywhere in Caulderon, yet, oddly, few people in Garramide had taken to him. Perhaps that was why he had gone off by himself, hunting.

A knock at the outside door. Tobry's knock! Rix's heart jumped. He was back earlier than expected.

"I'm glad you're here," he said, rising and hurrying forwards with his arms outstretched.

Tobry checked. A wary look came and went on his wind-burned face, then he smiled and said lightly, "You're just hoping I had a successful hunt."

"Indeed I am. And did you?"

"You'll be eating your favourite food for a week."

"Not wild boar?"

"The same. Or at least, wild sow – and suckling piglets."

Rix's smile faded. The females could be more dangerous than the males. "Sounds like a dangerous hunt."

"For a minute or two I thought it might go either way. But I prevailed."

"Tell all."

Tobry told the tale of his hunt at length, and for that half hour it was like olden times, when they had been carefree youths and Rix had the world at his feet.

Tobry finished his tale, yawning. "I'm for bed, and a lie-in in the morning – if the enemy allow it. Have you heard anything of them?"

"No, have you?"

"Not a skerrick. I didn't see another soul the whole time. Hardly surprising, considering the weather."

"I suppose not. Good night." Then, in a flash of compassion, Rix picked up the untouched tray on his table. "Could you leave this at the little room on the southern corner, on your way?"

"Of course," said Tobry. "Who is it?"

"Just a visitor," Rix said vaguely. "Sleep well."

Tali was woken from a deep sleep by a quiet tap-tap at the door. It was the first night she had slept in a bed since fleeing Rutherin, and for a few drowsy seconds she thought she was back in that damp cell. But her room and her bed smelled different. It was cold, but it wasn't damp, and the sheets smelled of lavender. She was in an entirely different fortress, hundreds of miles across Hightspall.

Assuming it was Holm, coming to talk to her about something, Tali slipped out of bed. She was padding across the freezing flagstones when the door opened and a man was silhouetted in the dim light.

"Holm?" she said softly. No, it wasn't Holm. The shape wasn't right, though it was familiar. But it couldn't be *him*—

"Tobry?" she gasped. She clutched at her breast; she could hardly breathe. "Tobry, is that you?"

He dropped the tray, smashing the plates and glasses, and scattering cutlery and food everywhere. "Tali?"

Tobry leapt halfway across the room and took her in his arms, and the great nightmare was over.

After a couple of minutes she disengaged herself and lit the candle. The light grew. She held it up so she could see him.

"You're dazzling me," he said, moving it aside. "I can't see your lovely face."

"Never mind my face. I want to see yours." She studied him, moving the candle from side to side. "You look tired. And older."

"I feel older. I've had a hard time of it; at least, until I reached here."

"Why didn't Rix say anything?" said Tali.

"He didn't mention me to you?"

"Not a whisper."

"Nor me to you," said Tobry. "I suppose he wanted it to be a surprise."

Tears blurred her vision. "The best surprise of my life."

"And mine. I was so worried about you."

"I was sure you were dead."

"I should have been . . . but I don't want to talk about it now."

"Sit beside me." She patted the bed. "You don't have to talk at all if you don't want to. Just having you here is all I need."

He sat beside her and took her hand. "You're freezing. Hop back into bed and I'll sit on the end."

"Beside me, I said."

"I've been out hunting and I haven't bathed or washed off the blood and muck."

"Damn you, do as you're told."

He chuckled and sat beside her. "I want to hear all your adventures. Everything that happened since . . ."

"Since you were thrown off the tower," said Tali.

"But not now. Tomorrow. Or the next day. No, one question can't wait."

"Rannilt?" Tali guessed.

"Yes, little Rannilt. She's not . . . ?" He trailed off, swallowing.

"She was very well the last time I saw her. In the dungeons of Fortress Rutherin."

"As long as she's healthy, and you're here, that's all I need." He sniffed and rose hastily.

"Don't go."

"I stink. I have to bathe, then go to my basement bed. The black hole, I call it." He smiled wryly. "I'll see you in the morning."

"Early?"

"Yes, early as you like."

He kissed her on the brow, and left. Tali picked up the broken plates and glasses, the scattered food and cutlery, piled everything on the tray and put it to one side.

She went back to bed, but there was no possibility of sleep now. She wanted to lie awake all night, just thinking about Tobry and the lines of his face and the warmth of his touch, wallowing in him and his miraculous return. She could tell by the look of him, and from the fresh scars on his hands and arms, that he had endured much since their parting.

But she wasn't going to spoil this magical night by thinking about the bad things. There had been far too much of that. For one night she was going to concentrate on the good things. On Tobry.

She wanted to spend the night in his arms and never let him go. She wanted to lie with him—

Tali had never been with a man. Nor, until now, had she ever wanted to. Her romantic soul rebelled at the thought of the casual liaisons that were not uncommon among the Pale.

In Cython the men and women were forced to live apart and the men only allowed home for a few nights a month, to breed more Pale slaves. From an early age she had seen how passionately her mother and father had clung together in those brief visits home, and Tali thought it the only kind of love worth having. And now she could have it for herself, why should she wait?

Life in Hightspall could be violent, brutal and all too short. Doubly so with the war reaching its climax and Garramide bound to be besieged again before long. All the more reason to take what life offered, now.

Assuming Tobry wanted the same thing, of course.

He wasn't like any other man she'd met. Tali was never sure what Tobry was thinking, or what he wanted. At least, she had not been sure until she'd made that disastrous blunder in the palace. The moment she had told the lie, Tali had known what a disastrous folly it was, but it had been too late to take it back. She had saved Rix's life at the expense of Tobry's, or so she had believed.

She leapt out of bed, planning to run down to his room and offer herself to him. But what if he did not want her? How would she bear it? She crept back to bed and pulled the covers around her, teetering one way then the other for hour upon hour.

She had to take the chance. Tali rose, brushed her hair and her teeth, and put on a simple red gown Glynnie had left out for her in lieu of her own worn and filthy garments.

He had mentioned *my basement* and *the black hole*, so she followed the stairs all the way down, praying that she would encounter no servants on the way. In her own eyes she was doing the right thing, the only thing, but she did not want to be judged by anyone else's standards.

Her bare feet were freezing by the time she reached what she assumed to be the basement level. The steps continued down to a low, damp passage, where she encountered a series of padlocked doors. Cellars and storerooms.

She went up the steps, along and back to the darkest corner of the basement. Tali swallowed, told herself to be brave, that Tobry loved her as much as she did him, and lifted the latch.

A candle burned on a small table next to his bed. Tobry was asleep, though he did not seem to be sleeping well. His fists were clenched, his jaw tight and one foot kept kicking against the covers.

She stood there for a long time, gazing at him, immersing herself in the sight of him, then lifted his covers. She was about to slip beneath them when he woke with a terrible cry.

Tali sprang backwards, her heart thundering, then put on a tentative smile. She'd startled him. It would be all right.

He jerked up in bed, saying harshly, "What do you think you're doing?"

Pain sheared through her. Had she got it disastrously wrong? No, she could not have misread his feelings. She had to say it.

"You – you love me, don't you?"

He choked. "With all my heart."

"And I love you. I've come down to – to offer myself to you."

He stared at her as though he did not understand what she was saying. "You – what?"

Her cheeks were burning. How could it be this hard? "To lie with you. In your bed." She came forwards.

He recoiled away from her, his back crashing into the wall, his hands thrust out as if to push her off. "No, *no*!" He was trembling all over.

Sick shame washed through her. She had got it utterly wrong. But before she fled to bury her shame, she had to understand. "Why don't you want me, Tobry?"

"I – *want* – you. You can't know how much I – *want* – you."

"Then why won't you have me?"

Tobry's teeth were chattering. He turned away, jerked open a drawer in the table and took out a series of potion jars. His hands were shaking so wildly that it was a struggle to unstopper the jars. He decanted varying amounts of the potions into a battered enamelled mug. After stirring it with a forefinger, he swallowed the contents in a gulp then set the mug back on the table with a crash that broke pearly flakes of enamel off the sides.

"Can't you tell?" he said, quietly now. His voice was empty, dead.

"Tell what?"

"Your blood didn't heal me."

She looked at him dumbly. She had no idea what he was talking about.

"From being a shifter. There wasn't enough of your healing blood. And it takes more than one dose, apparently."

A black ball of horror swelled inside her. "What are you saying, Tobry?" But she knew, she knew.

"I'm a shifter. A cursed caitsthe, and far gone."

"Give me your knife." She wrenched up her sleeve. "You can take as much blood as you need . . ."

He pushed her away. "Healing blood only works if it's given within days of being turned. Even then, it takes three or four doses. It's over a month since I was turned and I'm way past the point where I can ever be cured. There's no hope for me."

Tali tried to block it out. She refused to accept it. "But . . . why didn't Rix tell me?"

"He doesn't know. No one does." Tobry smiled grimly. "Though the servants and soldiers of Garramide know there's something wrong with me. Something foul. You'd think I'd be high in their esteem, after all I did to help save the fortress, but evidently not. Why do you think I hide out here, in the black hole?"

He looked down, avoiding her gaze. "Please, go. I can't bear to see it in your eyes as well."

CHAPTER 53

Tali wrenched the covers back and climbed into Tobry's bed. "You'll *never* see it in my eyes."

He held her at arm's length. "Anyone who mates with a shifter, male or female, risks becoming one. And if there should be issue—"

"You mean *children?*" she said coolly.

"The *issue* of a shifter is also a shifter. They're condemned before they're even born. This can never be, Tali."

His rejection was like a physical blow, for Tali was strong and proud, and it was a kind of blow she had never had to take before. It hurt more, and deeper, than when Red-whiskers had punched her in the mouth. It was an end to everything between them.

She lay down, her face tilted away so he would not see the tears leaking out from beneath her tightly closed eyelids. He lay still on the other side of the bed, rigid as a post. His heartbeat was a peculiar double thump. A shifter's heartbeat?

All this time she had denied his existence, refused to allow the possibility that, through some miracle, he could have survived. The hope would have been too painful.

Tobry had survived, and there was no joy in it. It would have been better if he had died in the fall from the tower. Not to ease her own loss, but because she knew the terrible fate of a shifter – incurable, violent, foaming-at-the-mouth insanity – and would not wish it on anyone.

But here he was, and she had to deal with it as best she could. It did not make her love him any the less – all it meant was that their love must be narrower, constricted, and all too brief.

"It can never be," she said, moving over and putting her arms around him. "But I'm not getting out of your bed until I hear the full story. From the beginning."

He let out a great sigh. She laid her head against his chest and felt his frantic heartbeat slow.

"All right," he said. "You deserve that much."

She tightened her grip, closed her eyes and let her tears run down onto him.

"I should have died in the fall," said Tobry, "but the ground had collapsed after the tidal wave and the pond of water and mud I landed in saved me – just."

He told her all he had told Rix about that time, and how Salyk had rescued Tobry and helped to heal his injuries, then continued.

"Had I not been half caitsthe I would have died. Your healing blood had started to turn me back, but the physical need of a shifter is almost impossible to deny. Without more doses of healing blood I couldn't fight it, and I soon began to realise that my doom had come upon me. And poor Salyk, hers too."

"Why poor Salyk?"

Tali wasn't sure what to think about a Cythonian soldier girl who had disobeyed her king and saved the portrait, then rescued Tobry. On the one hand, Salyk was a traitor to her king and her country, and Tali had to despise her for that.

On the other, without her compassion for a man who was her king's enemy, and a shifter to boot, Tobry would have drowned in the corpse-filled sump into which he had fallen. He had been badly injured, had lacked the strength to drag himself out and the water had been rising.

"She was greatly troubled. Salyk longed to serve her country and do her duty, but she was soft-hearted, quite unfit for the brutality of war. And her disobedience to her king was tearing her apart."

"Why did she save the portrait?" said Tali. She had never liked Rix's portrait of his father. It had given her the shivers.

"Because it was a masterpiece. Ah, Salyk!" he sighed. "I'm afraid I used her—"

"You *used* her!" cried Tali, her eyes springing open in shock.

He managed a smile. "Not in that way. I took advantage of her soft heart and cajoled her to help me escape. The enemy were hunting everywhere for me, you, Rix and a host of others on Lyf's list. If they'd found me I would have been killed at once."

"How did you get away?"

"The hunted joined the hunters."

"What does that mean?"

"The enemy use hundreds of shifters, but they have a healthy fear of them too. There's a flaw in their design – *our* design, I should say. Once the madness comes upon a shifter, he – or she – is as dangerous to the enemy as to our side."

"How long does it take before the madness comes?"

"It can be years, as in the case of my maternal grandfather. Or only weeks."

"Do you . . . do you know how long you've got?"

"There are signs," said Tobry hoarsely. "Unmistakeable signs."

Tali's bad feeling was getting worse. She felt sure he knew how long he had left, and that it was not long at all, but she wasn't game to ask. Not knowing was definitely better than knowing.

"Salyk took me out of Caulderon as a chained shifter," said Tobry, "one among a group of the beasts being escorted from one part of the hunt to another. It – it wasn't a good time for me. When I was among them I could feel the shifter side becoming stronger, fighting for the upper hand, and it was ever harder to control it. Most shifters are pack animals, you see, and the pack reinforces the individual."

"It must have been horrible," said Tali, taking his hand.

"So horrible that I can't bear to think about it," said Tobry. "Save for one moment I'll tell you about, only so you know what it was like. I owe you that much."

"You owe me nothing," said Tali.

"As you'll see, I owe you everything. There were times, when my shifter side was at its worst, that I was tempted to feed on the dead. And if I had—" He was wracked by shudders. "No man could come back from such bestiality."

Tali was silent. The image was too much to bear.

"I'm not sure how long I spent with the pack," Tobry went on. "It might have been a fortnight. We were heading west. The enemy was using us to track down the chancellor. And you. I had to find you first."

"But you didn't."

"We lost all trace of the chancellor's party in the mountains. Apparently his chief magian lured us in the wrong direction. My quest had failed and I had to break away before the shifter madness took me. You know why I dread it."

Tobry's family had tried to save his shifter grandfather, instead of putting him down as they should have. They had thought they had saved him, and all the while he was stalking the family manors at night, killing the young and the helpless.

When Tobry was a boy of thirteen, his father had gone to put the shifter down, and failed. To save his father, Tobry had been forced to kill his grandfather, and it had destroyed House Lagger. Soon the rest of the family was dead and Tobry had never got over it.

"I was already suffering the first symptoms," said Tobry. "I knew them well; I'd observed them at first hand. Yet again I imposed upon Salyk to help me. By this time she was growing ever more troubled by her own treason – fits of hysteria, nightmares, silences . . . and I was so deep in my own troubles I could not help her. Could not repay a tenth of the debt I owed her."

"What happened?" said Tali. "You talk as though she's dead."

"She was so desperate for absolution that she confessed her treason, knowing what her people would do to her. I could not save her. I saw this gentle, troubled girl executed at Lyf's direct order, torn to pieces by a pack of jackal shifters." He let out a cry of agony. "It was the most terrible thing I've ever seen. I can't get the image out of my mind."

"I fled east across Hightspall, blaming myself. And in truth, I was partly to blame, because I'd taken advantage of her gentle nature. I was so full of self-loathing that I joined a wild shifter pack. I tried to take command of them and turn them away from their vicious path, but I failed. Not cut out to lead the pack," he said wryly.

"You can't imagine the filth I endured, the unbearable bestiality, before they drove me off. I wasn't foul enough for them. I was on the run again, hunted by my own shifter kind, and only my sword and my magery saved me. It's stronger now – perhaps that's the shifter in me.

"But the shifter side was growing ever stronger, and finally I had to prevail on a hedge witch to make me this cocktail of potions." Tobry waved at the potion jars on the bedside table. "It delays the inevitable shift to madness, though it can't prevent it. The side effects are . . . unpleasant, and I have to take ever higher doses.

"When I finally reached the east, I heard stories about Deadhand. I didn't know he was Rix, but he sounded like a man who might take me in and make use of my talents. That's it," he concluded. "You've heard it all. Now tell me that you don't recoil in horror from the beast I've become."

Tali could not speak for a minute or two. "I'm horrified by all you've been through," she said at last. "But I still have my arms around you and I'm not letting go. Once again, I'm offering you my healing blood. If three doses aren't enough, I'll give you five. If not five, then ten. If not ten—"

"You would let me suck you dry like a gigantic leech?"

"I'm not calling you that."

"If there were any hope for me, I'd be tempted. But after the first few days, the shifter change cannot be reversed."

"What about healing magery?"

"No, never!" he cried, pulling her arms from around him and retreating to the other side of the bed.

"Why not?"

"Just no."

"Well," she said, "if that's what you are, I can accept it. I don't care that you're a shifter. I want you anyway."

He shook his head, then urged her off the bed, so gently that it broke her heart.

"You can't have me, Tali. I'd be a danger to you and everyone around you."

"I don't care! I'm not giving you up."

"Then I'll have to put it in terms you can't possibly misunderstand."

"What's that?"

"Were I to look on your loveliness through a shifter's eyes," he said bitterly, "all I would see is *meat*."

Outside the door, Blathy removed her ear from the keyhole, smiled venomously, then ran to spread Tobry's secret through the fortress.

CHAPTER 54

In one of several co-existing shafts of the Abysm, a man hung spreadeagled, trapped in aeons-long crystal dreaming. He was dreaming about the burning of Tirnan Twil and the destruction of the Five Herovians' priceless heritage.

In one of those dreams, he saw the blurred face of a young woman who – he believed – had possessed the magery to save Tirnan Twil, yet at the vital moment had held back. It felt like a personal attack on him and had to be avenged. But it could never be.

He gave way to helpless, choking rage.

CHAPTER 55

Wil's plan had failed utterly.

After weeks of labour he had succeeded in erasing the story Lyf had written on the iron book called *The Consolation of Vengeance*. He had melted the book down, using trickles of heat from a perilous source near the Engine. He had even recast the heavy covers of the book, and the thirty individual cast iron leaves that made it up, and succeeded in binding them together so the pages would turn.

Now he hurled it down in disgust, for it was a lumpen travesty of the beautiful original. Wil knew true beauty when he saw it, but he was utterly incapable of creating it. And his calligraphy was worse. Though he had been practising it on the walls of the Hellish Conduit for weeks, his best attempts were hideous scrawls. He was useless at everything.

Everything save strangling Pale slaves up in Cython.

He was very good at that, very quick, when the need became unbearable and the only way to ease his own pain was to crush the throat of someone smaller than himself. Wil's fingers, hard as the iron he had spent so much time working, closed around their slender necks and squeezed the life out of them. Though none of them was *the one* he wanted to squeeze. He should have done it when he was with *the one*, out in the Seethings. It was all her fault.

But that was not what he was here for.

He was here for the book – and the story it told. He had to

rewrite the book. The story mattered more than anything. He would keep searching until he found a way.

In the meantime, Wil had something else to worry about. The Engine had developed a tiny, intermittent wobble, hardly noticeable, but it bothered him. He had tried to fix it by altering the flow of water through the myriad conduits that flowed through the Engine, but that had made it worse. It had also sent clouds of alkoyl vapour billowing up the fan cracks in the rock above, towards the Abysm.

Wil froze, staring at the cracks, his heart crashing back and forth. What if this changed the story yet again?

But then a tendril of alkoyl drifted towards him, and ah, the chymical bliss.

All his troubles went away.

CHAPTER 56

"Bitch," said Blathy, every second time she passed Tali in the halls. Every other time she said, "Slut!"

Tali had not been to Tobry's room again, nor had he come anywhere near hers, yet vile rumour had spread faster than the fire that had incinerated Tirnan Twil. By the time she entered the breakfast hall the following morning, everyone in Garramide save the lord himself knew that she slept with a filthy shifter. And she wasn't taking the abuse any longer.

Tali spun around, thrusting her right arm out the way she'd done when she had killed Banj, directly up at Blathy's throat. "What did you say?" she hissed.

"'Slut!' I said. What are you going to do about it?"

"I've got magery enough to tear your head from your shoulders," Tali said recklessly.

"I know you have." Blathy opened her blouse to bare her throat, and right down to her cleavage. "Go on, then."

With her hair cascading down her back, her head tilted back and the arrogant smile that dared Tali to do it, Blathy had a barbaric grandeur that was mesmerising. She was prepared to wager her life on her assessment of Tali's character, and take the consequences if her guess was wrong, and that made her a terrifying opponent.

One Tali could not beat. Even had the magery been at her fingertips, she could not kill Blathy in cold blood. Her threat had been empty and now her bluff had been called. She lowered her arm.

Blathy grinned savagely and turned away without a word. None were needed to reinforce her victory.

"It's not true!" Tali cried, in a voice that rang from one end of the hall to the other. "But if it was, I'd be proud to have so brave and decent a man as Tobry Lagger as my mate."

After that, the atmosphere wasn't merely foul. It was poisonous.

"My chambers. *Now!*" said Rix, his face matching the gale raging outside.

Tali put down the potato she was peeling in the galley, washed her hands, then, avoiding all other eyes, headed upstairs.

"Did you see the lord's face?" said a swarthy maid with an unfortunate figure. "He's gunna give the slag what for. Put her out the door, I shouldn't wonder. And serve the scrawny cow right."

Tali was tempted to march back down the steps and punch the maid through the stone wall into the privies behind. She froze in mid-step, rotated on one foot to stare her down, before coming to her senses and turning away.

"She can't get a real man," the maid sneered. "She'll be doing it in the pigsty next."

As Tali whirled, a pair of steely fingers caught her elbow.

"It's not about you," Holm said in her ear. "Don't make it worse." He drew her upwards.

"I've been perfectly nice to them. Why do they have to be so horrible?"

He pretended to consider the question. "Apart from the fact that you're beautiful, clever and famous?"

"I'm not famous."

"Notorious, then. Apart from the fact that you're on speaking terms with the chancellor, the lord of the manor, and Lyf himself, and you've had more adventures in a couple of months than they'll have in ten lifetimes?"

"I wouldn't call them adventures. More like nightmares."

"They seem like adventures to maids who live lives of endless drudgery, and the best man they can hope for is a one-legged veteran with hair growing out of his ears. Of course they want to bring you down to their level."

"Are you escorting me to Rix's chambers, or making sure I don't run away?" said Tali.

"You omitted the third possibility."

"What's that?"

"That I too have been summoned, like a naughty schoolboy."

"You never do anything wrong."

"I suspect the chancellor would have a different view on the matter."

She managed a smile. "Oh yes."

They reached Rix's door. The hungry-looking guard allowed them in. "Lord Rixium will see you in a minute."

They took seats by the fire.

A couple of minutes later, Tobry appeared. He did not appear to have slept in days. "Sorry," he muttered, avoiding their eyes.

"You've got nothing to apologise for," Tali said, more furiously than she had intended.

"Haven't I?"

Rix kept them waiting for half an hour, then the lock clicked and he appeared behind them. For such a big man, he moved quietly.

"Well, Tali?" he said.

She could not think of anything to say. Rix had taken her in, and she had let him down.

"When you arrived," said Rix, "my household was finally running smoothly. Morale was good and the handful of troublemakers had been contained. We'd had a notable victory, and we were united as we prepared ourselves for the greater battle to come – the battle of our lives . . .

"Now people are shouting abuse at each other in the halls and informing on their neighbours in the galleys and workshops, and apparently it's down to you. Why?"

"It's not due to Tali," said Tobry. "I take—"

"I'll get to you in a minute," Rix snarled. "And you'd better have a good explanation – though I can't imagine what justification you can muster for such a betrayal."

Tobry slumped back in his chair, his face in shadow.

"It may have escaped you, Tali," Rix went on, biting each word off, "but we're fighting a desperate battle. And you know, because I often talked about it in Palace Ricinus, that morale is vital to our survival. It wasn't easy getting to Garramide, nor wresting it back. And the time after that, when the only thing people knew about me was the rotting carcass of House Ricinus about my neck, was dire.

"It took everything I had, and a bloody fight for our survival, to win them over. Now morale is in tatters again. Why, Tali?"

"People are spreading filthy lies about me," Tali said defensively. "The whole fortress knew about me and Tobry before I left his room. Someone must have been spying on us. How else could they have known?"

"How could *I* have known, for that matter?" Rix said in a dangerous voice. "But wait, I *didn't* know. I was deliberately kept in the dark."

"I didn't know myself . . ." Tali said feebly.

"*Someone must have been spying on us,*" he quoted in a whiny voice. "What do you expect when you go creeping down the stairs to Tobry's room in the middle of the night? How could you think that someone wouldn't try to find out what you were up to? There's precious little privacy in a place like this, so why should you have any?"

"Don't you believe in love?" she said stupidly.

"Bah!" he said. He turned to Tobry, regarding him for a minute or two in silence. "Why couldn't you confide in me, Tobe?"

"I was going to tell you the moment I got here . . ." said Tobry.
"But?"

"I arrived in the middle of a battle, and when we fought together it was like the good old days before the war. When we sat down by the fire that night, old friends together, I couldn't bear to ruin it."

"Why would it have ruined it?"

"Not even you can be that dense."

"Spell it out for me," Rix grated.

"I thought I had, that first night."

"Say it again."

"Having lost everything in your previous life, you've taken up your Herovian heritage. The Herovians held strong beliefs about cripples, the mentally handicapped and people with 'degenerate' lifestyles, and I know exactly how they feel about shifters."

"Enlighten me."

"In the pantheon of the damned," said Tobry, "nothing is lower or more degenerate than a shifter. Any true Herovian would have no choice but to condemn me."

"And I'm condemned as a *true Herovian*, am I? Just like that."

"Not that I don't warrant it," Tobry said bitterly. "I knew it would come out, and I'd be doomed when it did." His voice dropped, almost to inaudibility. "But just for a few days, I wanted it to be like olden times."

Rix's face grew even colder. "I would have *no choice but to condemn you,* as though our longstanding friendship meant nothing? Do you truly think so little of me, that I would discard you for some petty ideology?"

"I don't call Maloch petty. Nor the *Immortal Text*, nor the mural you painted up in the observatory."

"I noticed the change within days of you coming here," said Rix. "The day after the battle, the whole fortress was as one at dinner time. Two days after that they began to whisper in corners. I assumed it had to do with the enemy. It never occurred to me that they were talking about you."

"Why the hell not?" said Tobry.

"You used to have friends everywhere – among the highest and among the lowest. Everyone liked you—"

"Save the chancellor," said Tobry. "And Lady Ricinus."

"Their hatred counts in your favour. After your heroic deeds on the fortress wall I assumed you'd be accepted at once."

Tobry made as if to speak, but choked it back.

"I was so busy," Rix continued, "that it was almost a week before

I realised people were wary of you. But I rationalised it. Country folk, from one of the oldest and most traditional houses in the land, were bound to take their time to accept a newcomer."

"They could not have said what bothered them about me," said Tobry, "but I knew – *the psychic stink of the shifter*. If I lived here for a thousand years they still would not accept me."

"Why didn't you tell me?"

"We've been through that."

"For the sake of Garramide then? You could have told me, then ridden away. I would have given you half my treasury, such as it is, to help you set up—"

"Or a bribe to keep me from coming back," said Tobry. "A sop to your conscience?"

"Stop it!" screamed Tali. "Both of you. Tobry, how can you say such things about Rix? You know he loves you like a brother. And Rix, can't you see what Tobry has been going through?"

"I might have, had he bothered to tell me," said Rix. "I can't read minds."

"If I might interject," said Holm, "you must have called me here for a reason."

Rix stared at Holm as if he were a stranger. "I suppose I must, though I'm damned if I know what it is."

"Perhaps I can enlighten you. The foregoing discussion, fascinating though it has been, hasn't got to the real point of the problem."

"And that is?" said Tali.

"Until this got out, the people of Garramide didn't know why they felt so badly about Rix's oldest friend. Now they do, and they're angry."

"Angry doesn't cover it," said Rix.

"They're asking why you've allowed a foul shifter to live among them in secret. Why you would so betray them. Their beloved great dame, who was as proud a Herovian as ever lived, would not have allowed a shifter within five miles of the gates."

"Go on," Rix said icily.

"Some of them are wondering if you're a true son of Lord and Lady Ricinus, whose disembowelled corpses still dangle from the traitor's gate of Palace Ricinus. Does the dark blood of House Ricinus run in your veins? Have you come here to betray them too?"

"That's the stupidest thing I've ever heard," said Tali.

"It's what a good few of the people downstairs are thinking, and some are saying."

"Whatever you're working up to," Rix said between his teeth, "spit it out."

"To put it another way," said Holm, "your enemies are starting to contemplate the unthinkable – *mutiny*."

CHAPTER 57

Mutiny was unthinkable in so traditional a house, yet if Tobry stayed here much longer, it could come to pass. And with a great battle looming, Rix could not allow any kind of unrest to divert his people from their preparations, or undermine their morale.

"What am I to do, Glynnie?" he said. They were walking a track that ran along the top of the escarpment, where he could be sure he wasn't overheard.

"Is mutiny certain? I haven't heard anything."

"It's certain that my enemies are whispering about it."

"Who?"

"I don't have any proof."

"But you know who's behind it."

"No, but I can guess."

"Is it imminent?"

"Not according to Swelt. Once the folk of Garramide give their loyalty, they're not easily swayed. Though they're angry and afraid of Tobry, it would take a lot for them to rebel. But if they're pushed too far, they just might."

"Be honest with them," said Glynnie. "Call them together and explain why you took Tobry in. He's a good man – tell them why he's different to other shifters."

"Is he, though – *is* he any different, on the inside?"

"He's fighting it with every ounce of his will. Even I can see that."

"But will it make any difference? I've never heard of anyone breaking the shifter curse, once it takes hold of them."

Glynnie did not answer.

"Tobe and I have been through a lot together," Rix went on. "I love him like a brother. But these people are my people now and I have a duty to them, too. How can I allow a shifter – one who could go mad any minute – to live among them?"

"What if you locked him in at night?"

"Shifters don't only have their mad fits at night. Besides, Tobry's a magian, a good one; I'm not sure any lock could hold him. Must I chain him to a dungeon wall? My oldest friend?"

"You could send him away. He'd understand."

"He's already offered to go," said Rix. "But casting him out would feel like I'd betrayed him ... and as you know, I'm a trifle sensitive about such matters."

They paced across to a mossy outcrop in silence, looped around it and headed back.

"Besides," Rix added, "if he leaves, it's putting the problem on someone else, because—"

"A shifter has to feed," said Glynnie. "Then you only have one option."

"What's that?"

She lowered her voice. "Identify the ringleaders and get rid of them."

"How can I do that? They haven't done anything yet."

"They're encouraging mutiny. Isn't that enough?"

"Do you remember how the chancellor hung all the department heads of Palace Ricinus from the front gates, guilty and innocent alike?"

"Of course I remember," said Glynnie. "He forced us to witness their deaths. I felt sure Benn ... and I were going to be next."

"That day I swore that I would treat everyone fairly and justly. I can't arrest people and cast them out on hearsay."

"Well, if Swelt is right, you've got a few days to uncover the plotters. No matter how careful they are, some of the people they try to recruit will inform on them. And then you can arrest them."

"I hope so . . ." said Rix.

"The longer you leave it, the worse it's going to get. If you're going to be the lord of Garramide you have to take the hard decisions."

"Swelt said the same thing."

Rix stopped by an aged pine whose needles were like stiletto blades, and put his back to the trunk. Glynnie stood waiting several yards away, her hair streaming out in the breeze. She looked at peace, and the bruises were gone.

"How are things downstairs?" said Rix. "Between you and everyone else, I mean?"

"I fixed it."

"How?"

"What happens downstairs stays downstairs."

She headed towards the fortress gates. Rix watched her go. Had she fought the other servants, charmed them, or simply undermined their resentment by doing her best for everyone? He suspected that her work in the healery, where she had saved many lives, was at the heart of it. Not even Blathy took her on now.

Rix spent the day helping with repairs to the gates and the wall, trying not to analyse every sidelong glance among the workers, every low-voiced exchange. Logic said that most of the people were still behind him, that only a few troublemakers were plotting mutiny, but without proof, everyone was a suspect.

And perhaps, he thought as he hefted a block of stone no one else could have lifted, he was using physical labour to avoid facing up to the hard truth – that a mutiny reflected as badly on the leader as it did on the mutineers.

That night, without making any conscious decision, he took the steep stairs to the observatory. It would be bitter up there but he did not take a coat. He felt numb, and maybe the cold would rouse him.

At the top he partly closed the shutter of his lantern and passed the narrow band of light across the mural, left to right – and his skin crawled. It was a crude work, done with vigorous brushstrokes and hardly any touching up, yet the cheeks and eyes of Axil Grandys were so like precious black opal that Rix shivered. How had he had managed such realism from such a casual technique?

It raised the troubling question Tobry had hinted at the first night – had something guided his hand? Maloch?

From childhood, Rix had suffered from a deep-seated fear of anything uncanny. His first divinatory painting, done at the age of nine – a youth cutting down a rabid old shifter – had terrified him. Several months later, Tobry had been forced to kill his mad, shifter grandfather. When Rix heard about it he had blamed himself. He had burned the painting and had never found the courage to tell Tobry about it.

He scanned the Grandys mural again. Where had it come from – memory, divination, or the sword's enchantment? The thought that any aspect of the art he loved could have come from outside him, that he was no more than a conduit for an ancient sword that was using him for its own fell purpose, was too much to contemplate. Yet if it were true—

No! It *could not* be true.

Had Grandys ever suffered from such crippling self-doubt? It was hard to imagine it, but successful men learned to hide their frailties, or overcome them. If Rix could not overcome this one, he would fall, and Garramide with him.

How could he become the leader Garramide needed? How regain the confidence of his people? And even if he did, how could Hightspall be saved now? Or was it already too late?

He passed the band of light across Grandys' face again. It was probably the movement of the light that created the illusion; yes, it had to be. Yet Rix could have sworn the stone lips moved.

And he felt sure he heard a whisper inside his head.

Follow me.

Tali lay on her bed, staring at the ceiling in the dark. She wanted to be with Tobry so desperately that she was tempted to damn the lot of them and creep down to the black hole, which some of the servants now called *the kennel*.

But even if she could defy Rix, Tobry would not. He was deeply ashamed of concealing his true nature from his friend and would turn her away at the door. Tali could take the servants' abuse, their knowing looks and their calling her *slut* and *bitch*, but his rejection had crushed her, and the thought of it happening again was unendurable.

Anyway, after Rix's impassioned pleas last night, she could not undermine him further. She would not be the spark that lit the fire of mutiny.

She closed her eyes and wiped the tears away. Why wouldn't Tobry let her help him with healing magery? Did he know it was impossible – or was there another reason?

His own magery was stronger since becoming a shifter, he had said, but more perilous. And now he was practising it day and night. In the past, he had often joked about what a dilettante he was – a man with many natural gifts who had made no effort to master any of them. He was certainly making the effort now, but was he practising his magery because he hoped to save himself with it? Or in despair that he never would, and would soon be dead?

It reminded her of her own dilemma. She had hesitated too long at Tirnan Twil, possibly because of a subconscious worry that one day she would need her magery for healing. *You can be a destroyer or a healer, but not both.* Her eyes roved across the barely perceptible ceiling, creating images where there were none.

Lyf would soon resume the attack, with far greater force than before. He would throw everything at Garramide and surely must prevail. No matter how bravely Rix fought, he did not have the numbers to hold the walls against a proper army.

This battle could not be won by arms. It had to be fought another way – with magery. She lit a candle, then got out the little self-portrait Holm had taken from Tirnan Twil and lay back on her bed, trying to get into the mind of her enemy. She knew Lyf's story, knew all that had been done to him, but Tali needed more; she needed to understand the process by which the gentle, decent young king had transformed himself into so embittered and vengeful a man.

The miniature could not tell her. The heavy film of grime and smoke stains obscured all but the outlines. If only there were a way to clean it—

Tali sprang up and hurried up to Rix's chambers. He answered the door himself. He was barefoot, his black hair was tousled as if he'd been running his fingers through it and he had a sheaf of papers in his left hand.

"What?" he said curtly.

She thrust the miniature at him. He blinked at it, then took it. "Lyf?"

"A self-portrait, done just after he was crowned."

"You'd better come in."

He tossed his papers onto a pile of papers and ledgers on the table and gestured her to a chair by the fire. "Wine?"

"No, thanks."

"That's right, you don't drink."

"It's too strong. It goes to my head."

"It doesn't go far enough to mine." Rix set a lantern down on a side table, turned the wick up and sat down on the other side of the fire. He studied the portrait for a minute or two. "He wasn't without talent."

"Can you clean it?"

"If I had the time. Is there some reason why I should?"

She told him about her various *seeings* and spyings on Lyf and Errek, the decline of magery, and Lyf's frantic search for the missing key to king-magery, the greatest power of all.

"And he needs it for his *greatest task*," she added.

"A task that's more urgent than winning the war?" said Rix. "I can't imagine what."

"Neither can I. But he's really desperate."

"And you think this image might be the lost key?"

"I don't know – but Lyf did say that the master pearl could lead him to the key, and I felt drawn to the portrait the moment I saw it."

Rix glanced at the huge pile of work on his table and his jaw tightened. "I'll clean it up when I get some time. I don't know when that'll be."

He stood up, and Tali was rising to go when someone slapped a heavy hand on his door, three times.

"Swelt!" Rix muttered. "What the hell does he want?"

He opened the door and Swelt lumbered in, red-faced and panting, followed by Tobry and Holm.

"Carrier hawk just came in," said Swelt.

"News of the war?" said Rix.

"Bad news. From the west."

Rix stood up, offering the castellan his chair by the fire.

Swelt shook his head. "No, thank you – too much to do."

"Well?" said Rix, curbing his impatience.

"It appears the chancellor took heart from the news of your victory, and led his army north to battle."

"Where?" Rix's voice went hoarse.

"Halfway between Rutherin and Bleddimire."

"I assume it didn't go well."

"His officers lost their nerve, and the troops broke and ran at the first charge . . ."

"I can hardly bear to hear the rest. The chancellor's army was wiped out?"

Swelt shook his head. "Through sheer good luck, most of his troops survived."

"Good luck has been a scarce commodity in this war," said Tobry.

"They were racing across a narrow bridge," Swelt went on, "closely pursued. An enemy bombast fell short and destroyed the first span of the bridge. They got across but the enemy couldn't follow."

"I dare say the chancellor counts it as a victory," Tali said sourly.

"No one else does," said Swelt. "I'm told his hold on the southwest is weakening." He went out.

"So nothing's changed," said Tali. "As far as resistance goes, we're it."

"I'm really worried about Lyf's next attack," said Rix. "What if he brings a thousand men?"

"No one could beat off such an attack," said Tobry.

"Save Axil Grandys himself," said Rix, to his own surprise.

"You painted a mural of him," said Holm. "Can I see it?"

"It's not a secret," said Rix. He took a lantern. "Half the servants have been up there. They think highly of Grandys here."

He went ahead up the steep tower stairs, lighting their way with the lantern.

"Careful of the broken steps. The masons are too busy reinforcing the walls."

"What do the servants make of the mural?" said Holm.

"They prefer to see the Five Heroes on horseback, brandishing their swords. Or standing over their fallen enemies, crushing them into the muck."

"And you haven't depicted Axil Grandys that way?"

"You'll see in a minute."

He stepped into the observatory and held the lantern high, illuminating the wall where he'd painted the mural.

Tali let out a little cry, then stepped back, her hand over her mouth.

"What's the matter?" said Rix.

"It's the opal man."

"So what? You saw him in the Abysm. You told us about it, remember?"

"He didn't look like *that*," said Tali.

"I recall you saying he was all twisted and contorted."

"But his face was different."

"I don't follow you."

"In the Abysm, the opalised man was screaming in agony."

"He is screaming."

"Not in agony, Rix. He's screaming in rage."

"What does it matter, after all this time?"

Tali went forwards again, studying the face. "It reminds me of something I've seen before."

"You're an infuriating woman. You must have driven hundreds of men into a rage."

Rix's joke fell flat. "I've seen that expression somewhere –' She broke off, clutching at her heart. "Tirnan Twil."

Rix and Tobry stared at her. "What about it?" said Rix.

"That's where I saw his face – in my mind's eye."

"What were you doing at Tirnan Twil?"

She related the story of the destruction of Tirnan Twil, briefly, baldly.

Rix ground his teeth. Even Tobry looked shocked.

"Why are you only telling me this now?" said Rix in a frighteningly soft voice.

"The night we came, you weren't interested in my story—"

"Nor did you volunteer it."

"I was planning to tell you both, until I discovered Tobry was an incurable shifter. After that, everything's been such a disaster that I didn't get time to tell you."

"I assume that's where you found Lyf's self-portrait," said Rix.

"Um, yes."

"You didn't tell me then, either."

"I would have done, if you hadn't been so busy. But it doesn't change anything, does it?"

"Oh, Tali," said Tobry. "How could you be such a fool?"

"It changes *everything*!" said Rix.

"How?" she whispered. "I don't understand."

"Not only am I harbouring a shifter in my house, and not only are you, according to rumour, debasing the whole fortress by sleeping with him—"

"I'm not!" cried Tali. "He wouldn't have me."

"I'm glad one of you showed some sense." Rix scowled at Tali. "Tirnan Twil was built by the Five Herovians. It contained many of their most precious books and relics, vital objects that can never be replaced."

"And it survived, never seriously threatened, for two thousand years—" said Tobry.

"Yet now you tell me," Rix continued, speaking over Tobry, "that within *hours* of your arrival it was aflame from top to bottom."

"It was attacked by renegade gauntlings, hunting me because—"

"And everything there, and everyone except you and Holm, perished," Rix went on, talking over her. "Can't you see what the Herovians in this house, and every other Herovian house throughout Hightspall, will think when they hear of it?"

"They'll blame you, Tali," said Tobry, looking as though he had aged twenty more years. "You and Holm, but mostly you, because you're the Pale slave who escaped from Cython, and it doesn't take much for Hightspallers to think of the Pale as traitors."

"We're not! We're not!" Tali sank to the icy flagstones.

"They'll say you made a pact with Lyf himself, long ago. And say you've been working for him, spying for him and committing acts of sabotage for him all this time. They'll remember that House Ricinus, the wealthiest and most powerful house in all Hightspall, fell within days of your arrival. And Caulderon only days after that."

"Now you've come to this ancient Herovian house," said Rix. "The moment my people hear about Tirnan Twil they'll draw the inescapable conclusion. That you're here to destroy Garramide as well."

CHAPTER 58

"I won't do you any more damage, Rix," said Tobry early the following morning. "I'll be gone within the hour."

Rix shook his head. "No, you won't. Swelt had a carrier hawk come in at dawn and I need your counsel more than ever, *now*. I need every fighting man I've got, too."

"What's happened?"

"There's an enemy army marching our way. A small army, but—"

"How small?"

"Fifteen hundred men."

Tobry whistled. "Are you a praying man these days?"

"I've worn all the skin off my knees this morning."

"How far away are they?"

"Five or six days. Depends on the weather."

"And if they do a forced march, like last time?"

"The only point to a forced march is to take your enemy by surprise. It doesn't apply here. They know we're expecting them."

"Let's say four days, to be safe."

"Four days or forty, it's not going to make any difference, Tobe. Even a thousand trained soldiers would be too many for us. Fifteen hundred just makes it quicker."

"What's happened to your fighting spirit? The other day—"

"After the battle on the wall, there were times when I truly felt we could take on Lyf. That we could even save Hightspall ..."

"So did I. But ..."

"But the relentless bad news – your doom as a shifter, the talk of mutiny, the destruction of Tirnan Twil – it's shaken my confidence, Tobe."

"You're making Garramide stronger every day. And every day, a few more people turn up at the gates, wanting to fight on your side."

"Not enough to make a difference. It'll take a miracle for us to survive this time."

"You knew that when you decided to take Lyf on. We all did."

"But when I left Caulderon I didn't have anything to lose. Now the lives of hundreds of people depend on me; people I've fought beside; people who'd give everything for me. I'm scared, Tobe. What if I'm not up to the job?"

"You won't let people down. You always do your best."

"If Lyf takes Garramide, he'll put everyone to the sword."

Tobry did not reply.

"I – I need a sign, Tobe. A symbol to rally behind."

"Is that why you painted the Grandys mural? And why you keep going up there to commune with it?"

"He's the most famous name in Hightspall. He was such a brilliant leader – and my ancestor."

"He wasn't a nice fellow, though."

"I know, but he won every battle he fought. Even when his forces were desperately outnumbered, he could turn the tide through sheer, ferocious determination. That's what it's going to take for us to win this battle, Tobe. Nothing else will do."

"Well," Tobry said reluctantly, "if he's the kind of symbol you need, then by all means use him. But be careful."

"I will ... but I'm worried."

"What about?"

"Maloch, for starters."

"What about it?"

"Remember how you warned me about it, the night you came?"

Tobry nodded.

"I think you're right," said Rix. "I sometimes feel it's developing a life of its own."

"What kind of a life?" Tobry seemed to be holding his breath.

"I don't know, but when I draw it I feel strong. Ruthless. Driven."

"Go on."

"Like a drunk who can't stop thinking about his next bottle, the sword is constantly on my mind."

"Perhaps that's the enchantment. Put it away and only use it when you have to fight."

"I need it, Tobe. I've never needed to believe in myself more."

"You looked like a born leader when we fought on the wall."

"I was using Maloch. Perhaps that's why I'm called to the sword, and to Grandys. Because he had the strength I lack. Can the mural divine *my* future, do you think?"

"One or two of your divinations have been right in the past. Though," Tobry mused, "I think it just reflects your own desperate need."

After he had gone down to the black hole, Rix soon found himself standing face to face with the twisted figure again. Tali was right. The expression on Grandys' face was rage, and it made him seem all the stronger.

Help me, Rix thought. Show me how I can win the coming battle.

The problem was twofold: a few weeks' training wasn't enough to make his force of yeomen and farm labourers into professional soldiers, and he simply did not have enough of them to defend the walls against fifteen hundred enemy. Days ago he had sent envoys to all the manors within twenty miles, but few had offered help. Perhaps they'd heard that he harboured a shifter here.

It brought him back to the rumoured mutiny. Further enquiries had told him that there were half a dozen ringleaders and another twenty or thirty sympathisers. But for a mutiny to succeed, they'd need far more sympathisers than that – at least a third of the population of the fortress. It was some way off, then, as Swelt had said. How could he prevent it, *and* strengthen his hand for the coming battle?

Rix was studying the painting, thinking about the opalised Grandys trapped in the Abysm, when an outlandish idea struck him. It would take a miracle to survive the coming battle. A miracle – *or some supernatural aid* – the one way to raise morale in the fortress from the depths to the heights in a moment. The one way to dismay his enemies, even Lyf.

Especially Lyf.

By invoking the memory of the one man everyone in the northeast revered. The one foe Lyf feared more than all the others put together.

Rix took another look at the mural. Was it the right thing to do, or would he be challenging fate? The figure wasn't just a lump of opal – it was a mighty symbol. And if Lyf's victories were largely due to his use of the supernatural force of magery, why not use another supernatural force against him?

Could it be done in time? An hour's study in the library told him that it could. He would need helpers, half a dozen at least. And it would take a day and a half. Plenty of time to go and return before the enemy arrived. If he could bring this symbol back, it could stop any mutiny in its tracks. The plotters wouldn't dare continue then. Yes, he thought, it's the answer to all my problems.

But he wasn't going to tell Tobry in advance. He had a feeling Tobry would disapprove.

Rix would send a select band of men out in the morning, to a rendezvous halfway to the destination. An hour later he would simply say that he was going hunting. No one would query that – in winter, fresh meat was always welcome.

Rix did not know this country and took many wrong turnings before finally locating the rendezvous, hours later than he had planned. By that time the sky had gone the colour of brass, and both men and horses were nervous. Rix did not blame them. A mountain ridge was not the place to be when a storm struck.

"We'll take cover down under that ledge 'til it passes," he said, pointing with Maloch. "Ride!"

His band of ne'er-do-wells roared, raised their fists in the air and pounded down the slope at speeds likely to break their necks, or their horses'. Rix followed more steadily, going over his plan. A forgotten detail niggled at him, but he could not dredge it up.

"The hunt was a cover story," he said once they were under the ledge and the rain was streaming down all around. "I've got a bold and audacious plan that, if we pull it off, will make all our names."

"Bugger our names," said Yudi, a big, foul-mouthed fellow with a pink face and yellow, curling hair. "Can't eat a name, can I?"

"Once you have the name," said Rix, "it's not hard to trade on it for gold, if that's the most important thing in your life."

"It's the second most important thing," Yudi said, nudging his neighbour and sniggering.

"A name will help with that, too," Rix said coldly. "Shut up and listen. A few miles across yonder ridge there's a great sinkhole, sacred to the enemy before Hightspall was founded. Some people say it's one of the co-existing branches of the Abysm—"

"What the hell's an abysm?" said Yudi. "Sounds like a—"

Rix cut him off. "It's the conduit down which the Cythonians' souls pass from life to death. At least, that's what *they* believe." He paused for a full minute. "But it's also the place where their wrythen king, Lyf, hurled Axil Grandys after he killed him – *and turned him to stone.*"

He had their attention now. Every child in Hightspall knew about the Five Heroes' mysterious disappearance, though no one knew what had happened to them until Lyf had admitted it to Rix and Tali almost six weeks ago.

"Co-existing?" said Legz, a slender, black-haired fellow with a hungry eye. "What are you talking about?"

"There's only one Abysm, but it exists in a number of places at the same time."

"That doesn't make any sense."

"Nor to me," said Rix. "But it's so."

"What good's a bloody bit o' stone anyway?" said Yudi disgustedly.

"Actually, Lyf turned Grandys to precious black opal," said Rix. "But the body, not being Cythonian, couldn't pass through the Abysm. It's still floating there, deep down."

Someone whistled, and a small, black-haired fellow said, "All that opal must be worth a chancellor's ransom. And we're going to get it out, right? Then break it to bits and share out the opal?"

"Certainly not! We're going to take it back to Garramide, in one piece."

"What's the use of some crappy old statue?" said Yudi.

"It's not a statue," Rix said. "I just told you, it's Grandys' petrified body. *And it could win the war.*"

They stared at him. No one spoke.

"How?" said a grizzled old fellow with a dingy, stringy beard and ears that stuck out like butterfly wings.

"I'm going to mount his body on top of the main tower at Garramide, behind the gates. Anyone who comes within a mile will see Grandys perched there, watching over the fortress."

"How's that gonna help?"

"The enemy are very superstitious. They wouldn't dare attack while looking their destroyer in the face, even if Lyf himself led them."

"Why not?" said Yudi.

"Because Grandys betrayed Lyf in the first place, then hacked his feet off with this very sword – Maloch."

Rix raised it with a flourish, and felt a surge of strength and certainty burn through him.

"Lyf's terrified of this sword, because it contains one of Grandys' greatest spells." Rix didn't know that, but the deception was justifiable. "I've fought Lyf with Maloch, twice, and I know how it terrifies him. Ready?"

"Yes!" they roared.

"Then let's go and get Grandys."

As he led them back up the ridge, Rix heard Yudi muttering to the man next to him.

"Black opal is priceless, ain't it?"

"A man-size piece would be worth buckets of gold," said the other man. "Maybe barrels."

"And there's no saying Grandys has got to be complete. Bits could have cracked off him at any time, with all those dead souls whizzin' past. Don't reckon old Grandys would miss a finger now. Just snap one off, slip it in your pocket and when we get back home, we're made."

"Reckon I'll snap off something a bit bigger than a finger," said the second man, and they laughed like blocked drains.

CHAPTER 59

Tali could not sleep for thinking about Tobry's fate, and the approaching army that looked likely to end them all, plus the last resistance in Hightspall.

Eventually she gave up and went up to the observatory to study the mural. It looked different now. The body and limbs were less twisted, the florid face showed less pain and more rage, far more menace. Rix must have changed it.

But how could he have? He'd gone out hunting during the day and had not yet returned. She raced down the broken steps.

"Holm?" said Tali, shaking him awake. "I'm worried."

"About something else, you mean? Something *new*?"

"Do you know any way that Rix's portrait of Grandys could change itself?"

"No." He rose at once. "But if it's due to magery, Tobry might."

They found Tobry up under one of the empty domes, where he practised magery in private. He was lathered in sweat.

"I didn't notice any magery in the mural ..." Tali said when she had explained. "But I wasn't looking for it either."

"Let's take a look," said Tobry. "If I'm right in what I'm thinking, every moment matters."

They followed him down, then up the broken steps to the observatory.

"It *is* different," Tobry said after studying the mural for a minute or two. "And if Rix isn't here to change it, who did?"

He waved his elbrot back and forth over the mural, concentrating on the places where the changes had occurred. Tali saw no discernible difference to the elbrot's aura, and neither could her own senses detect any magery.

"Nothing," said Tobry.

"But it's definitely changed," said Tali. "Do you think one of the servants could have done it?"

Tobry snorted. "The brushstrokes are consistent. And masterful."

"Could it be affected by a form of magery we know nothing about?"

"*Anything* could be affected by a form of magery we know nothing about," he said wryly. "But I don't think so. I think it's got something to do with the painting itself, and Rix's gift for producing paintings that are divinations."

"I don't understand."

"Neither do I," said Holm.

"I don't think Rix has gone hunting," Tobry said slowly. "I'm afraid he's gone off to do something so wild that it's actually changing his divination – creating a new future, if you like."

"Where could he have gone?" said Tali.

"No idea."

"Swelt will know," said Holm. "Come on."

"Rix went alone," said Swelt, when they ran him to ground in the buttery where, though it was after 2 a.m., he was taking inventory of the kitchen stores on a grey oval slate. "And no one has left the fortress since."

"Damn," said Tobry.

"But half a dozen fellows, mostly hotheads, left an hour before he did."

"Were they going hunting too?"

"That's what they told the stable boys, but I'm not so sure. Come up."

In his little empire, Swelt consulted a scribbled note in a ledger. "They took a lot of rope, a large block and tackle, canvas and other gear."

"Did they say why they wanted it?"

"No, and no one asked. But clearly, they mean to lift up something heavy."

"Something heavy?" A wave of nausea roiled through Tali's belly.

"But they could be anywhere," said Tobry.

"Not anywhere." Swelt turned to a side table, riffled through a pile of papers and pulled out a small map. "When I came in, this map had been left out. Only Rix and myself have keys to this room."

"Does it give any clues?" said Holm, examining it.

"Yes, it does," said Swelt. He tapped a pudgy finger on a circular feature on the southern side of the map. "Some people say this sinkhole is co-existent with the Cythonian Abysm, so it's obvious what he's up to."

"Unfortunately," said Tali.

"I assume you'll be riding after him."

"At once."

"Rix is a good man," said Swelt. "And he could become a fine leader, assuming he learns when to trust his judgement . . ."

"And when not to," said Tobry.

"Quite so."

They went out. "So Rix means to raise Grandys' petrified body and bring it back," said Tobry.

"Why?" said Tali as they headed for the stables.

"I understand why – I understand that very well."

"I don't!"

"Even without people plotting mutiny, Lyf's approaching army is too big to fight. Rix has always been prone to self-doubt, and he's worried sick. If the enemy take Garramide they'll put everyone to the sword, because that's how rebels are dealt with in wartime. It's going to take a miracle to save us, so is it any wonder he's looking to set up his brilliant ancestor as a symbol?"

"How can that help?"

"In these parts, Grandys is considered the greatest warrior of all time. If Rix held Grandys' long-lost body it would draw fighters from everywhere and make Garramide the centre of resistance. No one would dare talk about mutiny then."

"And," said Holm, "it would terrify Lyf. It's a brilliant plan—"

"Except for one thing," said Tobry.

"What's that?" said Tali.

"I'm worried that it's not Rix's plan."

"How do you mean?"

"He thinks the enchantment on Maloch led him to Garramide, and possibly put the idea into his head to paint the mural of

Grandys – the sword's original owner. Rix is worried that the sword has a mind and purpose of its own, and I think he's right. What if it's also leading him to the Abysm?"

"To throw him in?" said Tali.

"No – to get back to its master. Or perhaps both."

"Come on, come on!" she cried.

They took horses from the stables and set off, riding carefully in the dark, around the edge of the escarpment then up into the most westerly of the mountains at its back. It was slow riding in deep snow. They had not climbed far before Tobry took a winding path up a steep valley, then a track that curved around behind the mountain for several hours, then down steeply.

"What did Swelt mean by *co-existent*?" said Holm. "Tali, when you saw Grandys' petrified body it was in the Abysm, wasn't it?"

"Yes."

"Where was that?"

"Next to Lyf's caverns under Precipitous Crag."

"But this sinkhole has to be a hundred miles from Precipitous Crag. How can the Abysm be here as well?"

"I was drawn through a peculiar crack from Lyf's main cavern," said Tali. "But now you ask, I have no idea where the Abysm was. It could have been next door, or on the other side of the world. I've never been in any place like it."

"I've heard that it co-exists in several places across the realm," said Tobry.

Dawn broke, cold and clear. He consulted the map, headed across into the neighbouring valley and took another path, now heading west. They were still riding down and the snow was scanty here. They followed the path for some hours more, crested a hill and Tobry stopped.

"There it is!"

The sinkhole lay in shadow, surrounded by tall trees, but even so it seemed unusually black, as if a pool of night had collected there and could not escape.

"Why is it black?" said Tali. "When I saw the Abysm before, it was pure white."

Holm and Tobry exchanged glances but no one spoke. On the far side of the sinkhole, something flashed, as if a powerful lantern was being used to probe its depths.

"Hurry. He mustn't get Grandys' body up."

There must have been rain recently, for the snow was gone and every brook running. They galloped across the ridge, angled down the wooded flank and across the valley floor.

"We've got to go faster," said Tobry. "Tali, you're the lightest. Ride ahead."

She urged her mount to give everything it had and the horse lengthened its stride. It flashed between the trees, leapt a rivulet in the valley bottom, slowed momentarily in the soft soil on the far side then accelerated again.

For any non-Cythonian, merely approaching the Abysm was a shocking sacrilege. Stealing Grandys' body from it must be an offence so monstrous that it would shake Cython to its foundations.

Her horse careered up the long slope. Mist wisped from the sinkhole and a halo of green grass surrounded it, out for thirty or forty feet. It looked unnatural at this time of year, when the grass everywhere else was brown and sere. A triangular frame made of freshly cut timbers had been constructed near the downhill edge of the sinkhole, and a wooden beam extended from it over the edge. A thick rope ran across the arm, through a block and tackle at its end and down over the edge into the Abysm. Judging by the tension of the rope, it held something heavy.

Rix's bravos turned away from their work, laughing. Making some offensive joke about me, no doubt, Tali thought. Her horse skidded to a halt, tearing up chunks of moist turf. She tried to scramble off, caught a foot in the stirrup and fell on her head. The men roared.

She got up, wiping her face. "Rix, stop!"

He jerked a thumb at his grinning men. They moved down the slope, reluctantly.

Rix's tanned face was unnaturally pale. "It's the only way to save Garramide."

"Where did you get the idea?"

"It came to me yesterday morning."

"What if it came from Maloch?"

"How do you mean?"

"The sword's enchantment has been working on you since the first time you used it. Tobry thinks it put the idea in your head to come here, and so do I."

"Why would it do that?"

Rix's dead hand stirred. The top of Tali's head throbbed, above the master pearl. He forced his hand down. Maloch rattled in its scabbard, then jerked sideways so wildly that he was heaved towards the edge of the Abysm. He braced himself against the force. The scabbard gave another jerk, tearing one of its leather straps.

"Come away from the edge, Rix. It wants to get back to its master."

Rix tried to move away, but the sword was straining so hard towards the edge that his feet began to slip on the damp grass. Tali took him around the waist and heaved but could not resist the force – it was dragging them both to the brink. Tobry and Holm galloped up.

"Give us a hand, would you?" Rix said in a croaky voice.

The scabbard jerked again. Holm took hold of it and held it until it stilled. Tobry cut a length of rope, took ten turns around the scabbard and tied it down. The three of them held Rix and tried to heave him away, but could not budge him. Tobry tied another rope around Rix's chest, mounted his horse and looped the other end around the saddle horn. He spurred his horse. It strained forwards as though trying to drag a boulder and, with Tali and Holm also heaving, they got Rix away from the edge.

"Further," said Tobry. "Out to the outer rim of the green grass."

The sword was still rattling, though the resistance seemed lesser now, and after a couple of minutes they had Rix out of the halo onto the winter-withered grass. Maloch went still in its scabbard. The rope was so tight around Rix's chest that he was gasping. Tobry untied it; Rix fell to the ground.

"The first time I saw Grandys' body in the Abysm," said Tali, "I had a feeling that something was terribly wrong."

"I'm sorry," said Rix. "It seemed like the answer to all our problems."

"It was a brilliant idea," said Tobry. "And if that's all there was to it, I dare say it would have worked. But Maloch had other ideas."

Rix turned to look back at the black sinkhole. Tendrils of steam, as they rose from it, showed the colours of the rainbow.

Maloch rattled violently and lifted itself a foot out of the scabbard. Rix closed his left hand around the hilt and savagely jammed it back in.

Tali walked up to the edge of the Abysm and a pungent whiff of alkoyl made her head spin. She held her breath, looked down at the writhing shadows and opaline gleams in the uncanny blackness, and felt such fear as she had never known.

As though the world itself stood on the edge of annihilation.

CHAPTER 60

Deep in the blackened shaft of the once-white Abysm, the petrified man who had been Axil Grandys, and was now a solid lump of opal the size and shape of a man, roused from aeons-long crystal dreaming.

What had woken him? His opaline eyes were stinging, his nose burning from a pungent vapour gushing up the shaft. A vapour that made his nose bleed and glorious visions form behind his eyes.

He shook them off. He was not a man to seek refuge in chymical visions. All he craved was reality. But as the reality of what had been done to him and the other four Herovians struck him, he felt such a rage that it shook the shaft.

In the blackness far below, Lirriam and Yulia were also rousing, though they could not move either. Had Grandys' tongue and throat not been solid opal he would have screamed with fury and frustration.

Another memory wisped up from his crystal dreaming. A *recent* memory: the destruction of his heritage at Tirnan Twil. Every book, every paper, every artefact and personal item had been burned in a furious, hour-long conflagration.

How could this have happened? Memory showed him a pale, blurred face – a woman who might have saved Tirnan Twil but had not. Rage, *rage*!

But then – ah, sweet joy! His right hand, his focus, guide and protector. Maloch was nearby! The sword had protected him so well, all his life, that one day Grandys had forgotten the peril he was in and laid it aside while he went for a swim. That day, that very hour, his enemy struck.

Before Grandys had left Thanneron on the First Fleet, in search of the Promised Realm, potent magery had been imbued within the sword to guide and protect him. Now he called to it.

After an agonising delay it recognised him.

Get – me – out! said Grandys.

Maloch's magery continued the de-petrifaction, though painfully slowly, and from the inside out. But the sword-bearer was riding away and the job was not near done. Could Grandys hold him back and draw enough magery to complete the process? Even escape the Abysm?

He tried to call the sword using his own, weaker magery. It would have worked had he been able to utter a single word, but he had not yet regained the ability to speak aloud. He reached towards Maloch, tried to draw the power he needed from it by thought alone, and almost succeeded.

Almost.

Then Maloch was carried out of range and its magery faded. Was he to be trapped here until true death took him? Now that he had been de-petrified internally, he could truly die. Grandys sucked in the alkoyl-laden air, praying it would be enough to restore flesh from stone. It had to.

After a lifetime of gleeful bad deeds, Grandys feared death as no other man could.

CHAPTER 61

Lyf tossed on his modest sleeping pallet in the kings' temple, continually dozing and waking with a jerk after each few minutes of oblivion. Every day his servants cleansed the temple, and every night the stench came back, worse than before, but he would sleep nowhere else. By tradition the king slept in his temple whenever he was in the city, and tradition was one of the things that sustained him. That, and vengeance.

He woke in terror from his recurrent nightmare – the Five Heroes' original attack on him in this temple – to find his shin stumps throbbing mercilessly. The sword, the terrible sword. He could have no rest until it was unmade.

Thought of it hurled him back to the terrible time of his murder, when the whole world of Cythe was toppled.

"No," he cried, "No! Never again!"

His spectral ancestors gathered around him, soothing him.

"Grandys is stone, as ever was," said white-eyed Rovena the Wise. "You need never fear him again. Rise above it, Lyf, and continue with your plans. Crush the upstart at Garramide, then meet with the chancellor's envoys on your terms."

With their support, Lyf rose above his fear. "I will," he said. "But until peace is agreed, if it is, I'll prosecute the war with unmitigated fury. And the first target will be Garramide. *I want that sword.*"

CHAPTER 62

R ix knew there was no hope of saving Garramide now.
He gave no explanation to his ne'er-do-wells, and said not a word on the long ride home. Tali, Tobry and Holm were talking among themselves and shooting him increasingly anxious looks, but he ignored them. He almost wished Maloch had dragged him into the Abysm.

No, never again would he contemplate that way of escape. Even if Garramide was doomed, he was going to fight all the way.

He ran through all the preparations that had been made to defend the fortress. The bombast-battered walls had been repaired, the weakest points strengthened and raised, and the broken gate repaired and reinforced. The storerooms and armouries were full, the cisterns topped up, and his troops were as well trained as they could be in the time. What else could he do?

On reaching Garramide late that night, he dismissed his men and spoke briefly with Swelt, who had no further news of the advancing army. The fortress was calm, so he went to his chambers, put a bottle in one pocket of his coat and a goblet in another, and headed up to the observatory.

Taking a pot of white paint, he blocked out the mural with fierce strokes, then laid a second thick, opaque layer across the brushstrokes of the first, and a third coat diagonally across the others, until no trace of Grandys remained.

That done, he uncorked the bottle, filled the goblet and went to toss it back in a gulp. No, time is rapidly running out. Treat each moment, and each small pleasure, as though it's your last.

Rix turned the lantern down, pulled his coat around him, closed his eyes and took a sip, allowing the wine to flow back across his tongue. Ah, that was good. He had another sip, which was better.

A worry intruded – why the sword wanted to get back to Grandys. Rix put it aside for later but another followed it – the possible mutiny. It could wait until the morning, when he would identify the ringleaders and deal with them. Even the lord of Garramide was entitled to a few moments of peace.

He emptied his mind. The next hour was about the wine. Just savouring the wine, sip by careful sip. Minutes passed between sips; it took half an hour to empty the small goblet. He poured another without opening his eyes, drank it too.

Rix set the goblet down. The urge to swill the whole bottle had passed. He leaned back in the chair and might have dozed for a while. He did not know or care. He roused, yawned, stretched and opened his eyes. And his hair stood up.

The image was reappearing on the wall through three thick layers of white. As he watched it ghosting through, Rix was alarmed to realise that the image had changed. Grandys was still contorted, but definitely not in agony. He was in a crouch, half twisted around so he was looking straight out of the wall, and his right hand was extended as if reaching out for his sword.

Suddenly, Rix was very glad that he had not raised Grandys' petrified body from the Abysm.

"They're back, Deadhand," said Nuddell. He had run all the way from the front watchtower to Rix's chambers and was breathing hard. "The enemy are back in force. Must've come in the night."

Rix grabbed his coat, sword and field glasses, and eased on the steel gauntlet.

"What are they doing?" he said, pretending a casualness he did not feel. The lord of Garramide had to set an example of calm control at all times. Was this it? Would they all be dead by tonight?

"Same as last time. Just sitting there, out of range, setting up camp."

They went down. Swelt met them at the foot of the stairs. He was wearing his sword again.

"You've heard?" said Rix.

"I have. And I've ordered the household to prepare for the worst."

"I'll be on the main watchtower," said Rix. "How many?" he said to Nuddell as they headed that way.

"More than before. Close to a thousand."

"Do you reckon that's all that's coming?"

"I'm just a sergeant, Deadhand. Kicking heads and backsides is more in my line."

"Nonetheless, I'm asking."

"No. I reckon there're more coming."

"So Swelt's information was good. How long can we hold them out?"

"Half a day; maybe a full day if we're lucky . . ."

"How's morale?"

"I've known it to be better."

"What would you say the problem is?"

"Reckon you know that better than I do."

Rix stopped in the middle of the yard. "Answer the damn question, Sergeant."

Nuddell swallowed, avoided Rix's eyes, then said quietly, "It's the shifter."

"Kindly elaborate."

Nuddell cleared his throat. "Personally, I don't mind the fellow. Lagger put up a mighty fight on the wall last time – I wouldn't be here if he hadn't. And he ain't like other shifters. Almost human, he is. Must've been a rare gentleman before he caught the curse."

"He was," said Rix. "I mean, he is."

"But your other men, they haven't seen the world like I have, Lord. Traditional. Closed minds. To name the thing is to condemn it. You let him in, they're saying. You protect him, and what if he starts creeping down the halls at night, at his gory work?"

They reached the watchtower and began to climb the steps. "So that's what they say. What will they *do*?"

"Lord?"

"Will they desert? Refuse to fight? *Mutiny?*"

Nuddell looked everywhere except at Rix. He strained, but no words came out.

"You took the sergeant's badge, Nuddell. You have to do the sergeant's job."

"It's harder than I thought."

Rix waited.

"A handful could be thinking about deserting. I'll give you their names. But refuse to fight an attacking enemy – no, they won't go that far."

"What about mutiny?"

They reached the top of the watchtower. Three guards were on duty, all watching the enemy camp. They turned around, snapping to attention. Rix studied the enemy camp for a minute or two, doing his own estimate of their numbers – the same as Nuddell's count – and their gear, then led him across to the far side where they would not be overheard. The sergeant was sweating now but Rix had to know.

Nuddell glanced at the guards, then lowered his voice. "If anyone was plotting mutiny, reckon they'd slit my throat quick smart if they thought I was informing on them."

"I dare say they will. And my corpse will be lying right beside yours. Give me their names."

Nuddell closed his eyes, then began to tick names off on his fingers. "Bailley. The twin brothers Hox. Rancid—"

"Is there really a man on the rolls called Rancid?" said Rix.

"By nature and by name. Oily fellow, always sucking up, but as soon as your back's turned he's bitching about you. I'll point him out. Knives are his specialty. He likes to slit weasands with them."

"I wonder if he mentions that when he writes home to his mother?" said Rix.

"Doubt if he's got one. Reckon he oozed out from under the jakes."

"Anyone else?"

"Tumblow and Tiddler."

"I know Tiddler," said Rix. "He's the giant."

"Yeah. Blacksmith. Watch out for his hammer. Those six are the worst. Put 'em away and I doubt if you'll have any trouble with the others."

"How long do I have?"

"Until after the battle – assuming we win. And if we don't . . . well, we don't have to worry, do we?"

"Why not before the battle?"

"Mutineers are scum, everyone knows that. But there's no one in this fortress so foul, dishonourable and treacherous that they'd start a mutiny with the enemy at the gates."

"Thank you, Nuddell. I appreciate it."

"Then there's the servants." Nuddell was warming to his task. "I don't know all of them, but there's Blathy, of course, and Porfry—"

"What about Astatin, the witch-woman?"

"Mad as a maggot," said Nuddell, "but desperately loyal. She won't betray you. And that's all I know."

Rix nodded and looked through his field glasses. "Looks like the enemy have brought up a bigger bombast-hurler this time. That could cause us some grief." He turned away. "Keep me informed."

"You going already, Lord Deadhand?"

"Orders to write, messages to send, allies to call upon, scouts and spies to send out. It never stops, Sergeant."

CHAPTER 63

"No one knows who tried to kill Tobry," said Holm, late that night. "It could have been anyone. And they'll try again."

Tali, Rix, Tobry and Holm were in Holm's small room. It had formerly been the sitting room of one of the great dame's ladies and none of the decorations had been changed. The curtains and pillows were festooned with ribbons, the chair covers embroidered in intricate detail, while every surface was covered in crocheted doilies and little china animals. But at least it had a fire.

Tali's stomach cramped. She went to the small window but found no solace there. Outside, the snowy dark was lit by red or white bombast blasts. The enemy had not yet attacked, but their bombasts and grenadoes had already smashed the gates in and were steadily eroding the basalt wall behind it. It was unlikely to last another day.

She turned back to the sombre group. "Can I see it?"

Holm removed a doily draped over an upturned glass resting on a saucer. Inside the glass, a small yellow scorpion struck at the inside wall with its stinger.

Tali shivered. "And it's deadly, you say?"

"It's got enough venom to kill ten people," said Holm. "Slowly and agonisingly."

"How do you know it was a murder attempt?"

"They don't live round here. Too cold. Only place I've seen them is Bleddimire, and that's four hundred miles away."

"It was hidden under the seat of the jakes I use, down near the black hole," said Tobry.

"It could have been intended for anyone," said Tali, trying desperately to deny what was all too obvious. "Why do you think it was for you?"

"No one else has used that jakes since I came to Garramide,"

Tobry said quietly. "They'd sooner die than do their business where a filthy shifter does his. I'm going up to practise my magery."

"You're always practising."

"But I'm not getting any better."

"Why not?"

"Because magery gets weaker every day." He went out.

Tali sat in silence for a few minutes, staring into the fire, then said, "Holm?", in what she imagined to be a cajoling tone.

"No, Tali."

"You don't even know what I'm going to say."

"I've got a fair idea. I can read it in those innocent blue eyes of yours."

"What, then?"

"If there is a way to heal Tobry, no one knows it."

"I have to try."

"He won't allow it."

"Stupid man!"

"He's trying to protect you."

"Did I ask him to?" she flashed. "I don't need looking after."

"I recall a helpless night or two on the iceberg," Holm said mildly.

She ignored that. "I'm entitled to look after my friend, aren't I?"

"Tobry said no to healing, very clearly, because it would endanger you."

"If I could find a way to save him, it might also be the solution to the shifter problems, all the way across Hightspall," she said cunningly.

"Self-justification now?" said Holm.

"Will you help me?"

"No."

"Why not?"

"*I* don't have to justify myself."

"Please, Holm. I'll never ask you for anything else, ever again."

"Of course you will. You'll ask me every time you want something."

"I don't *want* it. Tobry *needs* it."

"No!"

"Why not?"

"Do you realise how exceedingly annoying you are?" he said, looking fondly at her. "First you destroy my lovely boat—"

"*I* didn't destroy it."

"And now you expect me to reveal my darkest and most desperate secret."

From the look on his face, he wasn't joking. "Forget about it. I don't want—"

"No, I've carried it too long. I'm going to tell you why I won't help you with such a healing."

He unlocked his bag, his jaw set.

"I don't want to know," said Tali.

"Then you shouldn't have kept pushing and pushing."

He opened the bag and, from a small, sealed box drew out a scalpel, tongs and other medical tools. They were covered with dry, flaking blood. He held them out on his open palms.

"See these?"

"You were a *healer*?" said Tali.

"A *brilliant* young healer – in fact, a surgeon, taught by the great Stophele himself. He said I was the best of all his students." There was a dark tone to his voice that she had not heard before. "I was wealthy, important, and had everything I wanted. Yet I was proud – so very proud and arrogant that I couldn't bear to take advice from anyone. I also had a demon riding my shoulder and he wouldn't let up, and the only way I could get rid of him was by drinking. Manic drinking."

"Oh," said Tali. Something bad was coming and she did not want to hear it.

"You can imagine what happened."

She shook her head. "Something terrible?"

"One morning I was doing a minor operation on my wife, against all advice. A healer should never treat his loved ones save in an emergency, and this was not."

"What procedure?" she said quietly.

"Just cutting out a cyst. It wasn't a danger to her, but it was exceedingly painful and needed to be removed. And I was so arrogant that I could not trust any other surgeon, not even with so commonplace a procedure." Holm met her eyes, and his were so bleak that she had to look down.

"I was also drunk."

Tali's face must have shown her shock, for he slowly shook his head.

"I wasn't drinking that morning – I wasn't *that* far gone. But, though I denied it to myself and everyone else, I was still drunk from the previous night. And when I drank, I loved to take risks and succeed in spite of them.

"In my drunken stupidity the blade slipped, and an artery was cut, and my hands were trembling so badly I couldn't stitch it. My beautiful wife bled to death in front of me, begging me to save our unborn son. She couldn't understand how so brilliant a surgeon could not do this simple thing, but it was beyond me. I lost them both."

"Oh, Holm," said Tali, reaching out to him.

"Don't try to comfort me. I don't deserve it."

"Everyone deserves a second chance."

"My wife and son didn't get one."

"Neither did my mother," said Tali. "I blame myself, too. If I'd only done something—"

"You were a child in terrible danger beyond your capacity to deal with, yet you did your very best," Holm said harshly. "I was an adult, in full control and working well within my capacities. No one forced me to do what I did. It was my decision to drink, my decision to operate, my decision to do so with reckless disregard for my wife and my unborn child. That night I swore neither to drink nor practise healing again, and I cannot break that vow."

"Not even after, what, thirty years?"

"Thirty-six years; yet there are nights when I still can't sleep for thinking about it. Times when I have to take a sleeping draught to save my sanity."

His eyes went to a little potion bottle on the table, then he stood up wearily. "I'm going to take a turn along the wall before bed and see what the enemy are up to. Good night." He went out.

Tali sat by the fire for a good while, imagining the horror of that fatal day, then his haunted vigil on the wall. She was turning to go when her eye fell upon the bottle containing his sleeping draught.

No! she thought. That would be a monstrous abuse of trust.

Almost as monstrous as what she was contemplating using it for. Holm was right; since Tobry had refused any further attempts to heal him, who was she to interfere?

But she was going to. He would be practising magery up at the dome for another hour, with any luck. She picked up the potion bottle. An eyedropper inside had a mark scored on it, halfway down. Simple enough.

She headed down to the black hole. Knowing that he took his cocktail of potions every night before bed, she dropped the measured amount of sleeping potion in the bottom of his mug, then the same again, to be sure. For her plan to have any chance of succeeding, Tobry must be deeply asleep. The draught did not cover the bottom, so it seemed improbable that he would notice. She went up, replaced the bottle on Holm's table and returned to her room.

And paced, three steps and three, across and back, for hour after hour. What she had done *was* an abuse of her friendship with Holm and Tobry, but it was as nothing compared to what she planned to do next. It had to be done, but she wasn't sure she had the courage for it. She would have to hurt Tobry, do violence to him, *assault* him.

How would she feel if he did to her what she was planning to do to him? Such feelings of outrage rose that she had to block them out. Tali covered her scalding face, for shame – she could not do it to him. It was too wicked to be borne. Tobry would have to die the way other shifters did: either insane, or put to death . . .

The next thing she knew, she was outside his door with the knife in her hand. She set her candle down, lifted the latch and eased the door open. He was asleep. She could tell by the way he was breathing.

She checked behind her, though she already knew there was no one in sight. Tali had learned her lesson last time. She crept in, holding her candle high, and watched him for a minute or two. When he did not react to the light, she put it down on the bedside table.

He was quite still. She drew the covers down to his waist and was briefly surprised that most of the scars he'd had when she'd first met him were gone. Of course they were. Shifting one's flesh from caitsthe to man, or man to caitsthe, healed wounds and did away with all but the largest and deepest scars.

Tali sniffed the cup. She caught a faint whiff of his cocktail of potions, and the sleeping draught beneath that, almost imperceptible. He'd taken it, then. She banged the cup down, as a test. He did not move. He was deeply asleep.

The next part was hard. Having been robbed of so much blood by the chancellor's healers, the sight of her own blood aroused strong emotions in her. She could not bear to spill it, or waste a drop. But she had to. For Tobry.

Tali had sharpened a small knife for the purpose. She held it to her wrist, breathing hard, afraid to cut in case she cut too deep and could not heal it. But that was stupid; of course she could heal it.

She opened her vein with the point of the knife and caught the pumping blood in the cup. Her mistake last time lay in not giving him enough, only a few spoonfuls. This time she would use the whole cup.

When it was full she sealed the vein with healing magery, then had to put the cup down smartly, before she dropped it. Her head was spinning; she was hot and cold, sweaty, faint. She sat on the bed, supporting herself with her arms, until the faintness passed.

Tali took up the knife again. She had to do it now. This was the part she had been dreading, the very worst. This time she would be using the blade, not the point.

Tobry's chest was relatively smooth, which surprised her. She'd expected a coating of downy caitsthe fur, but perhaps his cocktail of potions prevented the fur growth. She reached out to touch his chest, to stroke it, then came to her senses. Do it now!

The blade opened a smooth cut from one side of his chest to the other with almost no resistance. A terrible, appalling cut. Blood followed the blade; far more than she had expected. Tali started to panic. Quickly now. She poured the whole cup of her blood onto his chest, along the deep, spreading cut, then began to rub it in.

She was so concerned to get the shameful business over as

quickly as possible that she did not notice the sudden rigidity of Tobry's muscles or the hooking of his fingers. He made a moaning noise deep in his throat. His eyes fluttered under his lids, as though in panic or terror. She sensed that he was trying to wake, but could not overcome the effects of the sleeping draught. Just as well; she still had most of her blood to rub into him.

His eyes shot open, and they were the golden colour of a caitsthe's eyes. But he hadn't shifted yet. The blood was still running out of him, mingling with her blood which now covered most of his chest. Then, in an instant, down was forming all over him, his fingertips curving and extending into claws, his teeth elongating into fangs.

She had to work faster. Tali ran her fingers along the gash, but now he was shifting too fast for her. He jackknifed up in the bed, blood spattering her clothes and her arms. A backhanded blow drove her three feet across the room, stumbling backwards, her arms windmilling as she struggled to stay on her feet.

He leapt up, now caitsthe-tall, towering over her. Then he went for her, snapping and snarling, and the shifter madness was terrifying. He was many times as strong as her. Too late she understood what he had been trying to tell her before; why he had kept her at bay.

When Tobry was in this state, she *was* just meat to him.

She scrambled away, trying to get to the door, but the shifter leapt past her and put his back to it. His claws extended; he growled low in his throat. Where was the knife? It must have fallen down; she could not see it anywhere.

She had no means of defence. He was going to tear her apart and feed on her, and there was nothing she could do to stop him. She ducked sideways, knowing it was hopeless. He came after her. He opened his maw to its fullest extent—

The door was thrust open violently, pushing Tobry forwards, then Holm leapt into the room, carrying a wooden mallet. As Tobry whirled, Holm struck him hard on the right temple. Tobry fell backwards and lay there, his claws scoring the flagstone floor. He was dazed, but not knocked out.

Tali stood there, gasping. It had happened so fast that she hadn't taken it all in.

"Out of my way!" cried Holm.

He shoved Tali aside and ran to the potion bottles. He poured a dose from each into Tobry's open mouth, one after another, then held his nose until he swallowed. Tobry's eyes closed; he began to revert to his human form, though far more slowly than he had shifted to a caitsthe.

Holm turned to Tali, livid with fury. "You imbecile, you've got his blood all over you. Do you want to be turned as well – to suffer his fate?"

"No," she whispered. Not at any price.

Holm dragged her down the hall into the bathhouse. "Strip! Be quick! Into the tub."

She tore off her clothes, numbly, unable to think, then dragged herself over the side into the square wooden tub. Holm collected her bloody clothes, avoiding the stained areas, and tossed them onto the embers in the fire box under the great coppers used for heating water. He filled two buckets from the nearest copper and thumped them down beside the tub. "I'll pour. You scrub."

She took up a rough sea sponge and some hard yellow soap, and Holm poured the warm contents of the first bucket over her head. Tali scrubbed until all the blood on her front was gone.

"Again!" He poured the other bucket.

He fetched more water and she scrubbed herself again and again, until she stung all over and felt sure she had no skin left. He collected the sponges, tossed them onto the embers as well and washed his hands, three times.

Tali stood there, naked, trembling. He inspected her clinically, nodded, then took off his coat and wrapped it around her.

"How did you know?" she whispered.

"A good healer always knows how much is in his potion bottles."

"I'm sorry."

"Not sorry enough! Now get out of my sight!"

"Please, let me explain."

"Save your breath. You're going to need it when you confess to Rix in the morning."

"Do I have to . . . ?"

"He's the master of this fortress. Of course he has to know. No . . . more . . . secrets!"

She stumbled to her cold bed and lay there, replaying the terrible scene. Confessing her folly to Rix in the morning was going to be bad enough.

But how could she ever look Tobry in the eye again?

CHAPTER 64

Neither Holm nor Tali had seen the majestic figure with the tangled mane of hair, hiding in the shadows beyond the black hole. Nor did they see her in the dark on the far side of the bathhouse, but she saw everything. Blathy waited until they were gone, then slipped upstairs, barefooted and silent. She roused Porfry and her other co-conspirators, and told them of the latest depravity.

"This cannot be borne for another day," she said, hissing between her strong white teeth. "We have to do it now, this very night."

"But the enemy are outside."

"I don't care!" snarled Blathy. "It's got to be done."

"All right, but not yet," said Porfry. "Sometimes the lord isn't in bed 'til three."

"The lord's throat is reserved for my knife," said Blathy savagely. "He killed my man. We'll do it as the clock strikes five. They'll all be sleeping soundly by then. You lot can carve the slut and the old man, then bleed Swelt like the fat old pig he is. He won't give you any trouble. Do the maidservant Glynnie after that, then Nuddell, and the other twenty we have on our list as cleaving to them and their foul, foreign ways."

She inspected the mutineers, one by one. They nodded their agreement to the plan.

"When all is done," said Blathy, "we'll take the lord's treasury and slip out the secret way, into the forest and be gone. And the enemy can burn Garramide to the ground for all I care."

Blathy licked the blade of her knife, spat blood onto her palm, then slid out the door and headed upstairs to await the fifth hour. She was bleeding, bleeding for vengeance.

CHAPTER 65

Neither could Rix sleep that night. The reappearance of the mural had so unnerved him that he had returned to the observatory to scrape off all the white paint. He then chiselled away the painted stone until all trace of the mural was gone.

What would the morrow bring? The bloody end of Garramide, most likely. He looked over the edge. His guards were on duty in the sentry boxes on the towers, and further out the enemy's campfires were blazing. All was still. What were they waiting for? More reinforcements?

He directed his lantern beam to illuminate the wall, drank some wine, dozed in his heavy coat, woke and had another glass, dozed again. The hours passed. It must have been 4 a.m. by now, the darkest time before the dawn, not that there was any difference in the winter night here, with the sky so overcast and the snow falling.

He was watching the wall, dreading that his mural would reappear from the freshly exposed stone, when Tali came stumbling up in her nightgown. Her eyes were raw, her pale skin looked as though it had been scrubbed with a brick and her blonde hair was all a'tangle.

She stared at the bare wall, looked around wildly, then located him in the darkness ten feet away. "Rix?"

"What?" he snapped. Why could he never be left alone?

"I've been a fool."

"You've been a fool, Tobry's been a fool, I've been a fool. Whatever it is, I don't want to hear about it."

"I'm a bigger one," she wailed. She sank to the snow-covered flagstones, put her head in her hands and wept.

Rix stared at her, unnerved. Tali had suffered more and endured more than anyone he could name, yet of all the women he had known, she was the only one he had never seen cry.

"What is it?" he said, falling to his knees beside her.

He held her while she gasped out the dreadful story, covering the front of his coat with tears, and mucus from her running nose.

When she finished, he let out a strangled bark of laughter.

She thrust him away furiously, sure that he was mocking her, and stood up. Rix landed on his back, suppressing the urge to roar like a madman.

"We're a trio, no doubt about it," he said. "Here I am, desperately hacking my mural off the wall, terrified it'll reappear out of nothing and call me to serve a dead man. While, downstairs, you're carving up the man you love like a beast for slaughter."

"It's not funny," she said, still sniffling.

"Our stupidity is hilarious. How could you imagine it would succeed? Any threat to a shifter always makes them shift to the more deadly form."

"It started to work back in Caulderon."

He shook his head in disbelief. "Back then, Tobry had only been a shifter *for an hour*; the curse wouldn't have taken properly. And he was fully conscious, the rational man in control. And," Rix said pointedly, "you weren't hacking a bloody great gash in him with your knife."

"Had to try," she said, almost inaudibly.

"No, you didn't. Tobry refused you more than once. He explained why it couldn't work, and so did Holm."

"How do you know?"

"I make a point of talking to the people in my house. Why won't you ever listen, Tali? Tobry's shifted too many times; he's run with the beasts and been one of them. His nature is fixed and can't be changed, so promise me you won't try again."

"I promise."

"No, look me in the eye when you say that."

"I won't try to heal Tobry with my blood again."

"Do you think I'm stupid, Tali?"

"I don't know what you're talking about."

"Say it properly, without leaving yourself an out — like healing magery."

She swallowed, looked down. He caught her jaw in his big hand and tilted her face up. "Look me in the eye."

She did so. "All right. I won't try to heal Tobry again — with blood or magery."

"Or anything else."

"Or anything else," she repeated.

"I still don't trust you, but let that be the end of it."

"You're not angry with me?"

"I'm furious. You could have been killed or turned into a shifter, trying to do something that never had any hope of success."

"It's over," she said bleakly. "He would have killed me, Rix. Tobry would have killed me — perhaps *eaten* me!" She shuddered.

"It's not him. It's the shifter madness."

"I know, but it's still over between us. My love wasn't as strong as I thought it was."

She shivered. "I'd better go down. I'm freezing."

He took off his coat and put it around her like a cape. It reached all the way to her feet. "Wait a minute. I've got something for you."

"What?" she said dully. Tali sat in one of the chairs, pulled her feet up and wrapped the bottom of the coat around them.

Rix unwrapped a little flat parcel and handed her the miniature of Lyf. "I cleaned it up." He brought the lantern close.

"Thank you."

She studied the miniature. The young Lyf could be seen clearly now, dressed in kingly robes that were a little too big for him, and wearing a simple circlet of filigree silver around his brow. His face wasn't rendered perfectly, but it made him seem younger, more vulnerable and human.

"Does it tell you what you want to know?"

"Not immediately."

"Some of the paint had flaked off," said Rix. "I had to touch it up here and there. Had the devil of a job matching the colours — especially on the silver circlet—"

Tali jumped up and ran on tiptoes to the top of the stair, her head cocked. She had acute senses: her hearing and sense of smell were better than anyone he had ever known. Survival attributes, for a little slave in Cython.

"What is it?" said Rix.

"I heard a cry."

"Someone hurt?"

"Possibly. It was wild, savage. I ... I think it sounded like Blathy."

"Then it's on." Rix ran across and put himself between her and the stairs. "Are you armed?"

"No."

He pulled a knife out of a sheath and handed it to her.

"Do you think it's mutiny?" said Tali.

Rix slid on his steel gauntlet, drew Maloch and headed down. She followed.

"I'd say so. My informant didn't think it would come while the enemy were outside, and neither did I. But if you were seen trying to heal Tobry, you've probably precipitated it."

She stifled a moan. "I'm really sorry. I'm such a fool."

"If so," said Rix, taking pity on her, "you've done everyone a favour. If we were in our beds, they might have cut all our throats as we slept."

She gave him a tremulous smile. "What are you going to do?"

"They'll try to kill you, me, Tobry, Holm and Swelt first. Then everyone else known to be loyal to me. I'll have to play it as it comes. Run and warn the others. Be careful."

"Don't worry," said Tali. "In Cython, I was the best of all the slaves at not being seen."

"To survive this, you're going to need all the skill you have."

Far below, the clock in the hall outside his room bonged five times, its deep note echoing up the stairwell. If I were bent on mutiny and murder, Rix thought, this is the hour I'd do it, while the overworked household lies in an exhausted sleep. More than two hours of winter dark remained to do the bloody business, gather their plunder and get away.

As he reached the bottom of the stairs on the second level, Glynnie screamed. Pain stabbed through his heart. He'd taken her for granted for so long, and had been so busy fretting about Tali and Tobry, that he hadn't given a thought to the young woman who had served him so loyally and quietly.

The girl who had been picked on since the moment they arrived in Garramide, because no one dared to have a go at him. The mutineers could be cutting her throat right now.

Rix raced down the stairs on tiptoes. At the bottom he took off like a thunderbolt, hurtled the corridors to his chambers, then froze. The guard who had been stationed outside his doorway lay dead on the floor, blood spreading from a ragged wound in his side. The blow must have come without warning, from someone he had counted a colleague, if not a friend.

Rix sprang over him and through the door. He moved into his chambers, Maloch extended. His steel gauntlet was clenched into a fist that could have broken the granite jaw of the legendary Hero, Syrten. Two minutes had passed since Glynnie's scream, and two minutes was a long time in a bloody mutiny.

The inner door stood open, a foot away from the wall. Rix pushed it closed. If anyone was behind it he would keep pushing until he crushed them, but he felt no resistance.

A furious rage was growing in him. He had made mistakes, plenty of them, but he had also done everything he could for the hundreds of people who called Garramide home. To have them threatened and murdered, while the enemy were camped outside the gates, was the most monstrous betrayal he could imagine.

His salon was dark. Someone could have been hiding there but his senses suggested otherwise. The same went for the other business rooms of his chambers. That left only his bedchamber, the second-largest room and the one most suited for ambush because of its myriad of hiding places.

He stopped at the door, his night-sensitised eyes sweeping the room. The lamp beside his bed had burned down to a flicker. There was no one on the bed, or behind it that he could tell. What about underneath?

No, Blathy would not hide under the bed, and as he had that thought he knew she was here. She had sworn revenge after he'd killed Leatherhead, and Blathy was not the one to deviate from her purpose. She was a big, vengeful woman, not far short of his own height, and she was here to let every drop of blood out of him.

Yet his chivalrous instincts, and his upbringing, meant that he could not kill a woman. He would have to disarm her, put her to trial and let the judges take care of her. Unless she killed him first.

He moved in, sweeping Maloch from side to side as he searched along the tops of the wardrobes and in the spaces between the furniture. If he saw her, he would strike her down with the flat of the blade, then overpower and bind her.

Blathy was too cunning for him, too quick and too quiet. She must have been lying flat on top of the eight-foot-high wardrobe, out of sight. Her weight landed on his shoulders and a knee drove into the back of his neck, dropping him to the floor beside the bed and paralysing him.

Maloch went skidding and under the bed. She tore off his steel gauntlet and tossed it aside. Rix twisted his head around and caught a glimpse of her – wild-eyed, savage, blood seeping through a bandage on her left shoulder. So he wasn't her first victim.

Blathy knelt on his back, her knees pressing excruciatingly into his kidneys. Her left hand burrowed into his hair, jerked his head back, and her knife rasped as she drew it from its sheath.

"You killed my Arkyz," said Blathy. Her husky voice was trembling with emotion. "You cut off my man's beautiful head and threw it in the offal heap, and I'm going to do the same to you. I'm going to rub your dead face in it."

He could smell her pungent sweat, read the blood lust in her face. She was a strong, coarse woman, and the reek of her would be the last thing he experienced in this life. He was still paralysed and could do nothing to save himself. He could not even speak. All he could do was watch the knife as she brought it slowly and lovingly towards his throat.

CHAPTER 66

Smack! It came out of nowhere, the unpleasant, pulpy sound of metal pounding into flesh and breaking bone. Blathy went over backwards, the tip of the knife raking across Rix's left cheek as she fell.

His paralysis had eased enough for him to roll over, though not enough to get up. Behind him, Blathy was on hands and knees, blood streaming from her broken nose, holding the steel gauntlet that had done the damage. But who had thrown it? She tossed it aside and crawled towards Rix's exposed throat.

Glynnie came out from under the bed, on her knees, swinging Maloch in both hands. She swiped at Blathy, the blade passing so low over Rix's head that he felt the wind. He tried to bury himself in the carpet.

Blathy lurched to her feet, her proud nose dripping blood, and blood running down her arm from the bandaged shoulder wound. Glynnie sprang to her feet and struck upwards, aiming a ferocious blow at the older woman's neck. Blathy leaned backwards to avoid it, then laughed mockingly.

She was almost a foot taller, twice Glynnie's weight, and with the long knife in her hand she had the same reach as Glynnie swinging Maloch two-handed. And Rix could tell she had fought many a battle with that knife. She was fast, skilled and driven by malice.

He groaned and tried to get to his feet. Blathy kicked him in the back of the head, knocking him flat and renewing the paralysis. Clearly, she knew all there was to know about dirty fighting.

Blathy slashed at Glynnie, who avoided the blow with a dexterity Rix would not have thought possible. Blathy struck again; again Glynnie wove aside. They danced their way around the room, past the end of the bed and down the other side.

"No," cried Rix. "She'll pin you in the corner."

Blathy drove Glynnie backwards with a furious set of blows, only ending when Glynnie, with a wild slash, almost took her opponent's knife hand off at the elbow. Blathy drew back. Glynnie leapt up onto the vast bed, rolled across it and landed on her feet beside Rix. She ran around the end and now Blathy was pinned against the wall, though only for a minute. She drove Glynnie backwards again.

They fought up and back, up and back again. Blathy was tiring now, her movements slower. It was always the legs that went first, and she was much older.

The big woman tensed, and Rix could read her plan. Blathy was going to attack in a furious onslaught that would drive her small opponent backwards against the bed, and then she would cut her open.

Glynnie went backwards until her back came up against the side of the bed. Blathy rushed her. Glynnie ducked a savage slash to the throat, raised her sword at the perfect moment and Blathy drove herself onto it, all the way to the heart.

Blathy's eyes were wet. She reached out, as if to her dead lover, and smiled a sweet smile. "Arkyz," she whispered. "At last."

It was over.

Glynnie left Maloch in her opponent's chest, stepped around the body and came across to Rix, wobbly in the knees. Sweat was running down her cheeks, her face was scarlet and blood dripped from her elbow from a gash on her upper arm. He got to his knees, tried to pull himself up on the bed, but failed.

Glynnie's breast was heaving. She looked him up and down.

"Help me up," said Rix, his voice hoarse and crackly.

She put a small hand on each shoulder, holding him down.

"What is it?" A sudden terror struck him; had she joined the mutineers? No, the thought was preposterous.

"Anything you want to say while you're on your knees?"

He swallowed. "Only how desperately ashamed I am. I've treated you badly."

"Abom—" She stumbled over the word. "Abominably."

"Yes. Abominably. I'm deeply sorry. Can you ever forgive me?"

"I have to think about it. Can you get up?"

"I don't think so. My neck—"

She went around behind him. Her damp fingers probed the back of his neck, down the vertebrae. The little hairs stirred there. She shoved hard with her thumbs, he heard a small crack and the numbness faded. He lumbered to his feet, looking down at Blathy. "You were right."

"What about?" said Glynnie.

"The day we came, you said Blathy was one of those women who would only ever have one man. Now death has reunited them."

Distantly, he could hear the sounds of fighting now. "Glynnie, it's mutiny."

"I know."

She jerked the sword from Blathy's chest and handed it to him, then the steel gauntlet, which was covered in Blathy's blood.

His hand shook as he drew it on. "Stay here."

Rix ran out and down, towards the yelling and the sound of blade on blade, which seemed to be coming from the dining hall. Glynnie followed, carrying Blathy's knife. He burst in. The hall was lit only by a couple of lanterns and it took a while to make things out.

Holm had been backed up against the wall. He had a sword in his hand and was fighting two men at once, the brothers Hox. Rix could tell them from behind by their stubby legs and long, rectangular torsos. They weren't skilled swordsmen, though they were tough and tenacious. They ought to be able to take down one old man.

Yet they were the ones flailing away, their wild blows striking sparks out of the wall, while Holm was moving back and forth like a fencing instructor. He was light on his feet for an old coot, using no more energy than he had to and defending effortlessly, though he had passed up several opportunities to kill his opponents. Surely he wasn't a pacifist?

But he hadn't seen the whippet-thin fellow with the strangler's fingers sidling along the wall in the shadows. The long, greasy hair told Rix that he was the aptly named Rancid.

"Holm! Beware on your right."

The brothers Hox turned in identical movements and rushed Rix as though glad of an excuse to get away. Had they ever seen him fight, they would not have been so eager to take him on.

"Rix?" Glynnie choked. "Please be careful."

He did not propose to give any sword-fighting lessons, nor take any prisoners. Mutineers threatened the whole fortress. They were worse than murderers.

He slashed the left-hand brother, Rasti Hox, across the throat, then danced sideways so the dying man would not fall on him. The other brother, Narli Hox, howled like a beast and threw himself at Rix, who killed him with a blow through the chest.

As he turned to scan the hall, Rancid sprang at Holm, six feet into the air, a manoeuvre Rix had never seen before. He had a dagger in each hand and was stabbing downwards, intending to drive them through the top of Holm's head.

But Holm wasn't where he should have been. He ducked low under the flying man, spun on his feet and put his blade in through both of Rancid's kidneys.

"I thought you were never going to move," said Rix. "What took you so long?"

"Used to be a surgeon," said Holm. "It's decades since I practised, but I still prefer patching wounds to making them."

"You don't fight like a healer."

"I had a good instructor."

"You fight as though you *were* an instructor."

"I've done a bit in my time."

"Anything you haven't done in your time?"

"Not much."

"Rix, Holm?" Tali shouting. "We need help."

They ran downstairs and into the main hall, swords at the ready. Glynnie followed, still carrying Blathy's long knife. Tali and half a dozen of the kitchen women were barricaded behind a wall of tumbled tables and chairs. Four mutineers, three men and a woman, were flinging kitchen knives at them. Five bodies were scattered about.

Rix picked up a fallen chair and hurled it at the mutineers, cracking a short, nuggetty man over his shaven head and bringing him to his knees. The others whirled, and their hopeful looks turned to blank despair when they recognised Rix.

"Blathy is dead," said Rix. "Also the brothers Hox. And Rancid. The mutiny is over. Surrender or die."

"Going to die either way," said a giant of a man with biceps the size of Rix's thighs – the blacksmith, Tiddler. "Might as well take you with me, you shifter-loving swine."

He lumbered forwards, swinging a monstrous double-headed war hammer, a terrible weapon in the hands of a strong man. A direct hit would smash Rix to pulp. He dared not take the risk that he might slip on the bloody floor, or stumble over a piece of broken furniture and allow Tiddler to get in a lucky blow.

The war hammer had a major weakness, however. It was so heavy that a blow could not be changed in mid-swing, and it took a long time between swings. Rix watched his opponent, followed his first blow until it had gone past, then killed him the way he had cut down Leatherhead.

The body went one way, the head another, and it took the fight out of the remaining mutineers. They knew they were going to die traitors' deaths but they surrendered anyway. It was over.

"I'm so sick of killing," said Rix, the sleepless nights suddenly catching up with him. "How much longer is it going to go on?"

No one answered. Too damn long, he thought. Until one side or the other is no more.

Glynnie put an arm around his waist. He looked down at her gratefully. "Did I thank you for saving my life?"

"Not adequately, but you will."

"What's the toll down here?" said Rix.

"At least three of the servants were murdered in their bunks," said Holm, "and another four, maybe five, died in the fighting. And I don't think poor old Swelt is going to make it."

"What happened to Swelt?" cried Rix.

"He took up a sword. Said he wasn't going to stand back and see innocent people die. He knew how to use it, too. He fought bravely and gashed Blathy on the shoulder . . ."

"I saw the wound. That must have been the cry Tali heard."

"But he was a fat, tired old man," said Holm.

"Where is he?"

"In the rear corridor where he fell," said Holm. "We couldn't move him."

Rix turned and ran across the bloody hall, out the rear door, then stopped, looking left and right.

Down to the right in the shadowed corridor he made out a still, arching mound. He raced down and went to his knees beside the old man. Swelt's eyes were closed, his flesh sagging.

"Swelt?" whispered Rix. "Don't die. Please."

A small breath sighed out of the old man. He wasn't dead.

"Healer! Light!" Rix yelled. "Quick!"

"No . . . use," said Swelt.

"Where are you hurt?" Rix couldn't see any blood, any wound.

"Stabbed in the back. Noth— nothing anyone can do."

Tali came running with a lantern. Glynnie followed.

"You can't die," said Rix, choking. "How can I ever do without you?"

Swelt smiled, and for a moment he was again the handsome young man he had been so very long ago. "Nicest thing – anyone's ever – said . . ."

"They say you fought like a hero."

"Fought – for my house. What anyone – would do." Swelt's right hand rose. "Come – must pass – secret."

"It's all right," said Rix. "Don't trouble yourself."

The pudgy hand caught Rix's shirt and pulled him down. Swelt's slitted eyes were fixed on Rix's face. "No one knows – you must."

"Knows what?"

"Passed down – great dame – me – now you."

"What is it?" said Rix.

"Grandys – sterile. Daughter – not his. Adopted."

"Why is that important?" said Rix.

Swelt's fingers slipped free. His hand hit the floor with a small thud. He was dead.

Rix took the old man's hand and knelt beside him, remembering all Swelt had done for him and for his beloved Garramide. Had he not marshalled the support of its people behind Rix, he would not have been here now.

"Why did he waste his last breath telling me that?" he said, rising wearily.

"Maybe he wanted you to know that Grandys wasn't your ancestor," Glynnie said quietly.

"No, for such a secret to have been passed down for two thousand years," said Tali, "it must be important – and not just to you."

Rix could not focus. "Poor old Swelt. No more loyal man has ever been. And to think I judged him, when we first met, on his appearance."

"He's at peace now," said Glynnie.

"And will be buried with the highest honour," said Rix, "next to the great dame herself."

"He killed that swine Porfry," said Tali. "And died a contented man, knowing he'd always done his duty." She looked around. "Where's Tobry?"

"I haven't seen him. I thought he'd be with you."

She blanched, then bolted for the door. Rix plodded after her, down the steps to the basement level and along to the black hole. She burst through Tobry's door and stopped, staring at the blood-covered bed and floor, the bed clothes in disarray and the knocked-over table.

"No!" she whispered. "No, no, no!"

"They were all against him," said Glynnie, from the door. "They must have killed him first, in his sleep."

"But where is he?" said Rix. "Where's the ... the body?"

"Maybe they took it out and burned it," said Glynnie.

Tali looked as though she was going to faint. "And I gave him the sleeping potion. Everything that's happened to Tobry since I met him is my fault."

"They'd hardly burn bodies in the middle of a mutiny," said Rix.

"He was a shifter," Glynnie pointed out.

Holm pushed past. "You're taking on more than your due, Tali. And you've got a short memory. The blood is yours and his, from when you tried to heal him."

She looked up at him. "But where's the body?"

Holm sauntered across, flipped the hanging bedclothes up onto the bed and said, "Right here."

Tali looked down. "Why would they dump his body under the bed?"

"They didn't," said Holm. "I did."

"Why the hell would you do that?" said Rix.

"He was sleeping so soundly after Tali's failed healing that I knew he'd be helpless if there was a mutiny. I shoved him under the bed and pulled the bedclothes down so he couldn't be seen. It must have fooled the mutineers, too. Guess they thought someone else had killed him first."

"You mean he's not dead?" Tali scrambled under the bed and took Tobry in her arms. He let out a great snore, but did not wake.

"No," said Holm, "but he's going to murder you when he wakes up."

Rix chuckled. "Serves her right. I think we'll leave them to each other. Come on."

He walked up with Glynnie. "Rix?" she said.

"Yes?"

"If we survive the war, will you come with me to Caulderon and find out what happened to Benn?"

"Yes, I will," said Rix. After this night, he could refuse her nothing. "No matter what."

CHAPTER 67

Dawn finally came, one of the longest nights of Rix's life. He did the rounds with Glynnie and Holm, inspecting the grim tale of the mutiny.

In addition to Swelt, seven servants were dead, three of them murdered while they were asleep. They included a fourteen-year-old serving girl who could not have threatened any of them. Ten mutineers had been killed and another eight captured, five of them by Nuddell's men when the guard mutineers had attacked the barracks.

"This is all my fault," said Rix.

"You didn't mutiny," said Glynnie. "You didn't murder innocent people in their beds."

"But I knew Blathy was trouble; you told me the day we came

here. You told me to get rid of her and I didn't. A good leader would have paid her off and had her escorted from the plateau."

"Yes, but—"

"Let him get it out, Glynnie," said Holm. "Rix is in charge. He needs to say it." He looked at Rix. "If Blathy had been a man, you would have acted instantly, wouldn't you?"

"I was brought up to respect women and treat them fairly."

"So you dithered. You allowed her to stay where she had no right, and now innocent people are dead."

"Yes," said Rix.

"What's done is done," said Holm, "and the only way to make up for it is to be the leader Garramide requires."

"And first of all, there has to be a trial," said Rix wearily.

"Why?" said Glynnie. "Everyone knows they mutinied."

"To show that, in Fortress Garramide if nowhere else, we hold to the rule of law. If *I* put them to death there will be those here, and outside, who'll call it unlawful killing. A trial sets the rules for everyone."

He called the servants together, and those guards who could be spared from the walls, and appointed a jury of three, avoiding both his own allies and the friends and relatives of the murdered servants.

The trial did not take long. The names were read before the assembly, the evidence sworn, the prisoners given a chance to speak in their defence. Five did; the others did not. Some could not even justify their actions to themselves.

"Guilty," said the jury of three.

"Take them out," said Rix to his sergeant.

"Yes, Lord," said Nuddell, sweating profusely, and clearly regretting that he had taken the sergeant's badge. "The sword or the rope?"

"The sword is reserved for those with a shred of honour left. Mutineers get the rope."

The prisoners were taken away and dealt with. The servants and guards returned to their duties. Rix lowered his head to the bench and closed his eyes. No sleep last night, and there would be none today, for the enemy could attack at any time.

"Rix?" said Glynnie.

He sat up. She had changed her clothes, washed the blood off her hands and was standing before him holding a tray. Steam rose from the spout of a teapot and issued from beneath the covers on several plates.

"You saved my life, Glynnie. You don't have to wait on me."

"Would you have me lie idle when there's work to be done and twenty-five less people to do it?" she said coolly. "Besides, you also saved my life."

"I saved *your* life?"

"She knew I was hiding under the bed. She was whispering to me, telling me how she was going to unseam me from top to bottom and spill my guts on your sheets. If you hadn't come in when you did, she would have. She hated me nearly as much as she hated you."

"Why did she hate *you*?" said Rix, bemused.

"She thought I was your woman! She wanted to rob you of everything you'd taken from her."

"But you're not my woman." Rix's head was aching.

"She dropped you beside the bed so I'd have to watch her cutting your throat. It didn't occur to her that I'd fight just as hard for *my man*."

Glynnie gave him a fierce, searching glare. He was trying to think through what she meant – whether she was serious, making a joke or simply being sarcastic – when a cacophony of signal horns sounded outside.

"They're attacking!" Glynnie threw herself into his arms, clinging tightly for a couple of seconds. Just as suddenly, she wrenched free. "We'll need hot water. Bandages. Food and drink."

"Not immediately we won't," said Rix. "Eat first," but she was gone.

He could still feel the impression of her arms around him. He poured a cup of tea and ate some bread and grilled meat. He was trying to clear away all the doings of the night, to concentrate on the coming battle, when Tobry joined him.

"I heard horns," said Tobry. "But . . ."

"They didn't sound like war horns to me, either. Grab some food and come on."

Tobry took tea, glanced at the food, shook his head and winced. "Not sure I can stomach it right now. My head feels peculiar. Never felt quite like it before."

Rix rose and they headed for the wall. "Bad dreams?" he said innocently.

"You might say that." Tobry rubbed his head. "Ahh!"

"Something the matter?"

"Great lump on my head. Feels as though I've been whacked with a mallet."

"Maybe I did it," grinned Rix. "I've wanted to often enough."

"Very funny. And I woke up on the floor under my bed."

They passed out through the doors. In the yard, the wind was howling.

"*Under* your bed? Have you been drinking?"

"With scrape marks across my back, as if someone shoved me underneath."

"Maybe Tali did it, to hide you during the mutiny."

"I'm not in the mood for jokes, Rix."

"It's not something I'd joke about."

"There was a mutiny?" Tobry swung Rix around by the shoulder, eyes wide. "Tell me?"

Rix jerked his head towards the back of the tower, out of sight of the enemy.

Tobry took in the eight bodies dangling there. "I slept through it all? What happened? Is Tali all right? Is—?"

"Tali's all right. But it was a close thing. We might all have been murdered in our beds. As it is, we lost Swelt and seven others."

"That's bad. Strange fellow, Swelt," said Tobry. "Couldn't work him out. But he treated me decently enough . . . considering."

As they were climbing the tower behind the gates, the horns sounded again. They reached the top to see that the enemy were pulling back.

"I don't believe it," said Rix. "They must be trying to lure us out."

"Odd sort of a ploy. Lure us out to what?"

"I don't know." Rix scanned the plateau with his field glasses, in case they had brought a second force up the mountain.

"You're looking in the wrong place," said Tobry. "Down below."

Rix had not noticed the little party because they were already at the gates. Two brightly clad envoys, one in the chancellor's colours, the other in Cythonian garb. Each envoy was led by a standard bearer who bore an identical truce flag, a blue diamond on a white background, and each had an escort of four armed men.

"A joint embassy," said Tobry. "Now I've seen everything."

"Let them through," Rix called to the gate guards. "Have them escorted to the old hall and call for refreshments."

"Why the old hall?" said Tobry, as they headed down. "Why not the main hall?"

"We fought the mutineers there a few hours ago and there could still be a body lying around — or a head. That's hardly going to impress our visitors."

He reached the door and shouted for a housemaid. A girl came running.

"Lord?" she said. Her fingers were blue with cold.

"We've got important visitors. Is the hall presentable?"

"We've taken out the bodies but half the tables are overturned. And the blood's still there."

"Get it cleaned up. You've got half an hour; if it's not finished by then, throw some rugs over the bloodstains."

"Yes, Lord." She ran.

Tali twisted her fingers until the joints ached. How was she to confess to Tobry?

She had to tell him. He would never forgive her if he heard it from anyone else. But what would he say? What would he do? He would be furious, and rightly so. How could she look him in the eyes again? She wanted to run away and hide.

No, Tobry was a good man. He loved her and she loved him; he had to be told. Tali was rehearsing what to say when she remembered the look on his face as he had shifted. There had been nothing good left; nothing kind, loving, or even human. Just the predator, hunting meat. She shivered.

It still had to be done. She slipped up to him when he came in from outside. There was snow in his hair and his eyes were dark as bruises; he looked as though he had not slept for days.

"Tobry?" said Tali, "can we talk?"

"Later," he said wearily. "Ah, I ache all over." He put a hand inside his shirt, rubbed his chest and winced. "Feels like I've been whipped."

Tali stared at him, stricken. She opened her mouth but no words came out.

"I'm sorry," he said, shamefaced. "You've been up all night, fighting mutineers, while I slept through the whole bloody business, and all I can think about is myself." He held out his arms. "Come here."

She wanted to fly into his arms; how she wanted it. But Tali shook her head. She could not bring herself to cross the two yards that separated them. How could she trust Tobry when the monster inside him might burst out at any time?

"What's the matter?" he said. "Please don't be angry with me."

"I'm not angry," she said hoarsely. Her throat hurt.

He frowned and took a step towards her. Tali let out an involuntary cry and scrambled backwards out of his reach. Her heart was battering against her ribs, a bird trying to escape a cage. Her fingers tingled; her mouth was dry as lime. She fought an urge to bolt.

"Have I done something to offend you?" said Tobry. "If I have—"

He focused on his outstretched fingers, which had flakes of dried blood clinging to them. "How the hell did that get there? Did someone attack me in the mutiny?" He stared at her frozen face. "Is there something I'm not being told?"

Tali wanted to vomit. Why hadn't she owned up? She took another step backwards, trembling uncontrollably.

His eyes narrowed. "You're *afraid*? Of *me*? Why would you—"

All colour drained from his face. He wrenched his shirt open and looked down. His front was covered in dried, flaking blood and there was a raised seam across his chest where the long gash had not properly healed before the potion drove him back from shifter to man.

"Sorry," she whispered. "I'm really, really sorry. It was a stupid thing to do . . ."

"*You* did this to me?" said Tobry, in a low, deadly voice. "You tried to heal me with your blood? After I expressly told you not to?"

She could not meet his eyes. Sick with shame, she said, "I had to help you. I thought ... if only I ..."

"You never listen, do you?" Tobry said coldly.

"It might have worked," she said lamely.

"It could *never* have worked. You've been told that by many people – people who know."

"I love you. I had to do something."

"But that's not all," said Tobry, thinking aloud. "It doesn't explain why you're backing away from me; or the terror in your eyes. Why don't you trust me, Tali?"

"I – I do," she lied. "But if ... if Holm hadn't come along ... you – I mean, the caitsthe, it – it attacked me."

His blanched face flushed an ugly purple. "Are you an imbecile?" he bellowed.

"I'm sorry—"

"I could have *killed* you," said Tobry. "Or worse. You could have been turned to a shifter, doomed like me. Did you—?"

"Holm scrubbed me down," she said hastily. "Head to toe."

"And then came the mutiny," Tobry said relentlessly. "Rix begged us to be careful, but you ignored him as well, because you always know best. You came creeping down to my room and the mutineers saw you. *You* precipitated the mutiny. How could you be such a fool?"

"I'm so sorry. Please forgive me." She reached out to him, so desperate now that it overcame her fear of the shifter.

"No," he said softly.

"But – *what did you say?*"

"I don't forgive you." He folded his arms across his chest. "Go away. It's ended."

"I don't understand," said Tali.

"I can't love you. There's nothing between us any more, and there *never* will be. Get out of my sight."

A howl of anguish burst out of her. Tali choked it off and stumbled away, her teeth chattering; she was freezing and sweating at the same time. One minute of folly had shattered her hopes, her dreams, her life.

She knew he would never relent.

"Lord Ricinus," said the Cythonian envoy, a small, white-haired woman of uncertain age, "there is to be a peace conference between King Lyf and the Chancellor of Hightspall at Glimmering-by-the-Water in seven days. You are called to attend." She sat down.

The chancellor's envoy, a pock-marked veteran with a square head and a turned left eye, said, "Lord Ricinus, there is to be a peace conference between the Chancellor of Hightspall and King Lyf at Glimmering-by-the-Water in seven days. You are called to attend." He sat.

Clearly, the precise form of words had been agreed between Lyf and the chancellor in advance. It was the way of such events, Rix knew. There was so little trust that neither side would concede the advantage of a single word to the other.

"Why me?" said Rix.

Neither envoy spoke for some time, though the king's envoy wore a ferocious scowl. Clearly, the question had not been expected and was not included in the protocols.

The chancellor's envoy said quietly, "You defeated and drove off an enemy attack – our first victory of the war and a great boost to morale. You've shown the enemy can be beaten. Naturally, the chancellor requires your presence by his side."

"So he can take credit where none is due."

"You are required to attend, along with the key members of your household, including the Lady Thalalie vi Torgrist."

Rix didn't like the sound of that. "I'm going nowhere while there's an enemy battalion outside my gates."

"The battalion has been ordered to withdraw."

"How far?" said Rix. "And for how long?"

"Until all participants have returned to their original positions. It's detailed on your safe conduct."

"What—?"

The Cythonian envoy rose abruptly. "Here is your safe conduct from King Lyf." She put an engraved platina disc on the table.

The chancellor's envoy, using the same words except that he said "the chancellor" instead of "King Lyf", set an electrum plate beside the platina disc.

Rix bowed, spoke the usual courtesies and took the safe conducts. Then he said, "Why?"

"I beg your pardon?" said the Cythonian envoy.

"Lyf has the upper hand. Why would he make peace when he could soon have it all?"

"Our Lord King is not a vengeful man," said the Cythonian envoy. Tali snorted. The envoy gave her a cold stare. "The lesson has been taught. It's time to end the bloodshed, and the war."

The envoys bowed, withdrew and immediately set off for their next destination.

"Well?" said Rix when the gate had been closed and they returned to his chambers. "What do I do?"

"This reeks of a set-up," said Tobry.

"What if I ignore the summons?"

"By convention," said Tobry, whose knowledge of history and customs was masterly, "ignoring a royal summons, or a summons from the chancellor, is considered a mortal insult. You and your household would be hunted down by both sides."

"So what? I'm already at the top of their death lists," said Rix ruefully.

"Your household isn't. Ignore the summons and you condemn them too."

"So I don't have any choice."

"That's the way these things are usually designed." Tobry rubbed his jaw. "There's another reason why the chancellor wants you there, of course. Possibly a more important reason."

"What's that?"

"You bear Maloch, Grandys' sword. The only weapon that's ever injured Lyf – and you've hurt him with it, twice. Lyf's afraid of it, and having you there, wearing it, makes it a potent symbol for the chancellor."

"What if it's a trap? If I leave, will I ever return?"

"And if the chancellor plans to take Tali's pearl," said Tobry, "how can we defend her in his camp?"

"But you can't come," cried Tali. "The chancellor ordered your death back in Caulderon, and nearly succeeded. He won't fail twice."

"Try and stop me," said Tobry.

CHAPTER 68

"Chancellor!" cried Tali.

She had been dreading this meeting all the week-long trip to Glimmering-by-the-Water, yet still his appearance came as a shock. Was he planning to take her back and start it all over again?

"The Lady Thalalie," he said sourly. "You're looking well."

"I feel well, now you're not sucking my blood. I suppose that's why you had me brought here."

She studied him in the bright sunlight. He did not look a well man, nor a confident one. The failures of the past weeks must have ground him down. Tali felt a shiver of fear. Lyf would see it in an instant; why would he agree to peace when his opponents were so weak?

They were standing on the southernmost tip of the Nusidand Peninsula, which ran south for miles into Lake Fumerous. The peninsula was only a hundred yards across here, with low limestone cliffs all around, falling into deep water.

The roofless temple of Glimmering-by-the-Water, seven lines of columns by nine, stood fifty yards away on the western side of the peninsula. Tali did not know the name of the god the place was dedicated to – presumably one of the Lesser or the Forgotten Gods.

The conference was due to start in an hour, and would be held within the temple, at tables set up on the limestone-paved floor. Entry was controlled by a line of paired guards, one guard of each pair being the chancellor's man, the other, Lyf's.

"I no longer need your healing blood," the chancellor said indifferently.

"Why not?"

"It only works on shifters in the first few days. Those of my people who could be healed were healed long ago, and the ones who could not had to be put down."

"But you still want my master pearl."

He smiled. "I do. Indeed, it's my main hope now, though . . ."

"What?"

"At the rate magery is failing, I'm not sure it'll be much use to me." He looked up at her. "It's time for desperate measures, Tali. But I must go to my pre-conference meet. Good day to you." He walked off, hunch-backed, leaving Tali alone and more troubled than ever.

She looked around but there was no one in sight save the distant guards. Rix, along with Hightspall's other invited leaders, had been called to the chancellor's meeting, which was to be held several hundred yards from the temple. Rix had taken Tobry and Glynnie with him, and Tali had not seen Holm all day. Where could he be?

Tobry had been cold and unforgiving ever since her disastrous attempt to heal him, and Tali had no idea how she felt about him now. He hadn't said *I don't love you*. He had said *I can't love you*. But what did that mean? Could it mean he still loved her, but had rejected his own feelings because their love could never be?

What were *her* own feelings? She had, with great difficulty, come to terms with his first rejection – the night she had come to his bed and he had revealed himself to be a shifter. But his attack in caitsthe form was another matter. Though she understood why it had happened, she could not get past the fact that he would have torn her to pieces.

Were I to look on your loveliness through a shifter's eyes, all I would see is meat.

It had created a barrier that could never be broken. If she were near him when his inevitable descent into shifter madness began, it could happen again. How could her love – *any* love – survive that?

It was too painful to think about. She wandered the other way, down the slope to an oval depression where the cropped grass was starred with little white daisies that flowered here even in winter because the lake was warmed by subterranean fires. Outcrops of white stone around its uphill side mimicked an amphitheatre, though it was only twenty yards across. To the south, across the lake she could see the surviving towers of Caulderon, three miles away.

She was sitting in the sun, her broad hat pulled well down to ward off her agoraphobia, when a child shrieked, "Tali, Tali."

"Rannilt?" said Tali, jumping up.

Rannilt came racing down, tripped, got up, rubbing a grazed knee, ran and threw herself into Tali's arms with such force that she was knocked off her feet.

"I'm sorry!" wept Rannilt, and it burst out of her. "I'm sorry, I'm sorry. It's all my fault Lizue nearly killed ya. You were cross with me for takin' your blood and I wanted to hurt you back, and she was really nice – and how was I supposed to know she was just pre- tendin', and she was there to kill ya?"

"It's all right," said Tali, hugging the skinny child. "It's all right, Rannilt. It wasn't your fault."

"It was, it was!" howled Rannilt.

"She was too clever for us. I thought she seemed nice, too."

"You did?" said Rannilt, looking up at Tali, then wiping her nose on her sleeve.

"Really nice," said Tali, exaggerating more than a little. "But wicked old Lyf sent her, you know. And he'd put some enchantment on her so she seemed nicer than she was, and prettier too, I dare say. She fooled everyone—"

"Except the poor old Sullen Man," said Rannilt. "He didn't trust her a bit, and we were all horrible to him—"

"He hardly ever looked at us. He just kept staring at her the whole time."

"I used to stick my tongue out at him. And now he's dead, stabbed right through the heart and out his back, poor man. There was a hole in him you could have put a cucumber in."

"I don't think we need to dwell on the gory details," said Tali. "Poor man, he risked his life to save me. He was a spy for the chan- cellor, did you know?"

"Of course," said Rannilt. "I could tell the minute I saw him."

"You didn't tell me," Tali exclaimed.

"I was cross with you. I was sure you were fed up with me." She looked hopefully at Tali.

"Never for a second," Tali lied. "I was really sick, Rannilt. The chancellor had robbed me of so much blood I didn't know what I was doing half the time."

"I was sick, too, wasn't I?"

"Very sick. Back in Caulderon, I was terrified you were going to die."

"But your blood healed me. After you gave it to me the first time, wicked old Lyf couldn't reach me any more, and—" Rannilt recoiled, staring up the slope.

Oh no, thought Tali. She rose to her feet, still holding Rannilt's hand, and turned around.

"Eee!" hissed Rannilt, twisting free and trying to hide behind Tali.

It was the very man. Alone, with no guards in sight.

"Many lies have been told about Lord Rixium," said the chancellor to the assembled provincial leaders of Hightspall.

"And you told most of them," Tobry said sourly.

"Don't try my patience, *shifter*, or it'll be the last thing you do."

Tobry yawned. "Rix's whole household is under a sacred safe conduct. Are you saying, publicly, that it means nothing to you?"

"Bah!" said the chancellor.

He was perched on an outcrop of limestone which formed a broad platform six feet above their level. The fifteen provincial leaders and their counsellors were seated on camp chairs on the grassy slope between him and the water, which was a few yards behind them. The stone was white, the grass thick and green, the chancellor pinch-faced and haggard.

Rix was shocked at how old and beaten he looked. The chancellor appeared to have aged ten years since Rix had last seen him. He looked like a man who had lost hope.

"I won't deny that the war is going badly—" said the chancellor.

"How could you?" said Rundi of Notherin, a stocky, purple-faced bruiser who had murdered his ageing lord and seized his vast holdings at the beginning of the war. "You've failed at everything you've done since it began."

"When I called muster, Rundi, you refused to provide a single man to defend your country."

"I have no country. Hightspall is finished and it's every lord for himself."

"But you're not a lord," said the chancellor with a flash of his old menace. "You're just a vicious little thug out for all he can grab, and the moment Lyf turns in your direction you'll be whining and begging the neighbours you brutalised to save your dirty hide. But you'll wait in vain."

The chancellor spat over the edge of the outcrop, onto Rundi's boots.

Rundi scowled and clenched his scarred fists, but said no more. Rix knew the man by reputation – a coward who did his work in the dark, from behind.

"I've not done well," the chancellor went on. "I admit it. Lyf killed all my officers and I don't know how to lead an army in war. Even so, I love my country and would give anything to save it. Can any one of you say the same? Did any one of you give me the support I needed to fight for Hightspall?"

None of the leaders spoke.

"You're gutless, the lot of you," the chancellor said in disgust. "Lyf is going to pick you off, one by one, and good riddance!"

"If things are so bad," said an old, dried-up lord, Carr of Caldees, "what the hell are we doing here? What sort of peace can you hope to negotiate?"

"I'm glad you asked," said the chancellor. "Only one man here has had the courage to stand up to the enemy, and he's a man who, only six weeks ago, had nothing. Rixium of Garramide, come to my side."

"Here we go," Tobry said quietly. "This is why you're here."

As Rix climbed onto the outcrop, the chancellor turned to face him and held out his hand. Hunched as he was, he was a full foot shorter than Rix, and only half his weight, but when Rix looked into the chancellor's eyes he saw dark fires burning there. He wasn't beaten yet, and he had a plan.

It turned Rix's stomach to shake hands with the man who had destroyed House Ricinus and ruined his own good name, but he also loved his country and any alliance was better than none. He drew off the steel gauntlet and extended his dead right hand. The chancellor blanched as he took the hand he had ordered cut off, and quickly withdrew his own, but he was smiling when he turned to the other lords.

"In a few short weeks, Rixium escaped Caulderon, took back his stolen fortress of Garramide and won a mighty victory against the uncounted hordes of the enemy – the first victory of the war."

"It wasn't *that* great," Rix muttered. "And they weren't uncounted hordes, not even five hundred—"

"Do you want to win the war or not?" said the chancellor out of the corner of his mouth.

"Of course, but—"

"If I say it was a great victory, *it was*."

The chancellor raised his voice. "Rixium has shown us that the enemy can be beaten." He stepped to one side to leave Rix at the centre of the platform, then added quietly, "Draw your sword and raise it high."

Rix did so. "Rixium also bears a prodigious weapon," the chancellor went on. "Maloch, the enchanted sword of his towering ancestor, Axil Grandys. And Lyf fears Maloch more than anything in the world. All rise, and acclaim Rixium's victory."

They rose and gave him a perfunctory cheer.

"Louder!" said the chancellor. "I want Lyf to hear it, down at the temple."

This time it was a full-throated roar.

"Excellent," said the chancellor quietly. "It'll help my negotiating position."

"I don't understand why Lyf needs to negotiate," said Rix.

"He's overplayed his hand, driven his people too hard and too far, and they've no stomach for any more bloody destruction. That's why *he's* here." The chancellor looked up at Rix. "Time to go. Say something encouraging."

Rix met the eyes of the provincial leaders, one by one. "I'll tell you something else to give you heart," he said. "Lyf's great victories against Caulderon and Bleddimire weren't won by force of arms alone. They were mainly won by magery – prodigious magery – coming from the stolen ebony pearls."

"How can you possibly know that?" sneered Rundi.

"I have a spy."

"Why should that news give us heart?" said Carr of Caldees, thoughtfully.

"Because Lyf was so desperate to win quickly that he used too much magery," said Rix. "He's almost drained the pearls dry, and now, as everyone knows, magery is failing everywhere. Without Lyf's magery his soldiers are just men, no bigger, no stronger and no better than us. And we're going to fight them! We're going to beat them and take Hightspall back. *Aren't we?*"

"Yes!" they roared, as one this time, and beat their swords on their shields until the din was thunderous.

The chancellor gave Rix an ambiguous stare, then nodded stiffly and turned to the lords. "It's time for the peace conference. I'll do all the talking."

Rix waited until they had gone, then fell in beside Tobry and Glynnie. "Well, I never expected that."

"I did," said Tobry.

"Why didn't you warn me?"

"I thought you'd do better if I didn't. And you did." They walked together for a few paces, then Tobry said suddenly, "If this goes badly, you should challenge him."

Rix froze. "Lyf?"

"No, the chancellor."

"Don't be ridiculous."

"He's just built you up. The provincial leaders see you as one of them, and a fighter, not a schemer. Plus you've got Maloch – never discount it."

"I think so too," said Glynnie. "I've always thought you should be leading Hightspall, Rix."

"I know," snapped Rix. "You and Benn began that nonsense before we escaped from Caulderon. Don't mention it again. I'm not up to it."

He strode ahead to catch up to the others.

CHAPTER 69

Tali swallowed. Had the peace conference been a ploy to bring her here? Did Lyf plan to break the truce and attack her for her pearl? If *he* got it, no way would he agree to peace. Lyf wouldn't need to – the outcome of the war would be certain.

She had to be strong, and ready to fight him if necessary. She stiffened her back, reminding herself that he held the lives of her people in his hands. How would he decide the Pale's fate? Easily, or painfully? She could still see traces of the noble young man from the self-portrait in his ravaged face. But only traces.

Lyf wore long boots over his stumps but he was supporting himself on crutches; his soles did not touch the ground. He carried a rectangular case made from polished stone on a chain around his neck. Heatstone – her head was already starting to throb. Did it hold his ebony pearls? It looked big enough to hold the master pearl as well.

"Ugh!" she said, rubbing her head.

"What did you do with my iron book?" said Lyf.

"One of your people took it."

"One of *my* people?" he exclaimed.

"Mad Wil. Wil the Sump. He carried it down under the palace."

Lyf wrinkled his brow, but did not speak for a long time. Then he dismissed the thought and moved slowly towards Tali.

"I'm tempted," he said. "The master pearl could solve everything."

Because it could lead you to the key, she thought, and give you command of king-magery.

"That's why the chancellor has exactly the same number of guards as you do," she said pointedly.

"And yet," he said, as though she had not spoken, "sometimes I wonder if I've taken the wrong path. Whether it's all been worth it. I'm not sure I know my people any more. My fault – I couldn't let them go, but to save them I had to take them apart and remake them. Did I remake them in the wrong image?"

Tali cracked. "You're just like the bloody chancellor."

He stiffened. He had not expected that. His eyes roved over her, and Rannilt hiding behind her.

"I'm nothing like the chancellor, Lady of the Pale."

"Yes, you are," said Rannilt. "He was always moanin' and wringin' his horrid, twisted fingers. And askin' Tali for advice and confidin' his troubles to her, and the same time he was holdin' her in prison and punishin' her."

"Was he now?" said Lyf. "But I'm not confiding my troubles, child, because I don't have any. Everything is going very well for me."

"Except for the stink in your temple," the child retorted. "You can't get rid of that, can you?"

Lyf almost fell off his crutches. "Who told you that?" he hissed, his breath smoking. "Who's the spy in my camp?"

"You think you're such a big smartypants," said Rannilt, peeping out from behind Tali. "But you don't know nothin'."

"I can force you to tell me," Lyf said menacingly.

"That would break the truce," said Tali, "and prove that your word meant nothing."

"Your treacherous Five Heroes started it," snarled Lyf. "They broke their word and betrayed me in the first place."

"That was two thousand years ago. People change."

"Some people don't."

"Anyway," said Tali, "they were Herovian. They're not my kind."

"You're all Hightspallers. You're all from the same stock."

"Axil Grandys saw us as inferior stock."

Lyf shot forwards, and Tali's head gave such a piercing throb that she fell to her knees on the grass.

"What's the matter?" said Lyf, staring at her.

"Heatstone. It always hurts." And knew she had blundered badly.

"Does it now?" said Lyf. He drifted up in the air for several feet, looking down at her. A gong sounded in the temple. "It's time. Now we shall see." He turned and drifted up the slope.

"He's too strong," said Rannilt. "What are we gonna do, Tali?"

"I don't know, child," Tali said, shivering.

Storm clouds had formed over the lake to the north and light-ning was flickering there, reflecting on the water. Was it always this stormy in Hightspall? she wondered. There seemed to be one every week. Or had Lyf created the storm for some fell purpose?

"Why are you shiverin' when it's so warm?" said Rannilt, put-ting her arms around Tali.

"I don't know."

"You shouldn't have told Lyf that heatstone hurts you. I'm wor-ryin', now."

So am I. Tali moved slowly up the slope, drawn to the drama taking place inside the temple. The columns were vast, dwarfing the dozen or so people gathered at the table in the centre.

A pair of guards stepped into their path. One was a Cythonian man with spiral face tattoos, the other a tall redhead, one of the chancellor's female guards. Tali had seen her on her first visit to the chancellor's red and black palace, a long time ago now. Was her name Verla? The guards studied their faces and checked a list.

"You may pass to the red rope," said the Cythonian, "but no fur-ther."

A great circle of red rope encompassed the conference table, the leaders of both parties, and their personal guards and counsellors, who stood well back. Tali and Rannilt went in slowly until their toes touched the circle, whereupon another guard held up a hand.

Lyf was at one end of the table, the chancellor at the other. Various provincial leaders of Hightspall occupied the right-hand side, including Rix. Lyf's generals sat in the chairs on the left, and after them were three old women dressed in white.

"Are they the Matriarchs of Cython?" Rannilt asked in an awed whisper.

No Pale slave had ever set eyes on the legendary matriarchs, who had assumed leadership when the underground realm of Cython was established. "I suppose they must be. Shh!"

Tobry looked as uneasy as Tali had ever seen him. The dark clouds moved steadily down on a warm breeze. The light faded to an ominous olive gloom. In the distance, thunder rumbled.

After ten minutes, Lyf and the chancellor stood up together and went to the centre of the table, one on either side. An attendant held up a document on heavy paper or parchment. Lyf read it, then the chancellor. Lyf checked it three times, with a variety of implements, and Tali saw the shimmer of magery on the parchment.

"Why's he doin' that?" whispered Rannilt.

"In olden times, the Five Heroes used magery and forced King Lyf to sign a charter giving up the best half of Cythe to Hightspall. Axil Grandys then used the lying charter to prove that the Cythians were wicked cheats, and to justify going to war with them. Lyf has hated our magery ever since."

"He's got magery too!"

"But in the olden days the kings of Cythe only used their magery for healing. That's why Lyf wasn't suspicious of the Herovians' magery. He thought it was the same."

"He uses bad magery now."

Tali sighed. "I suppose he'd say he had to fight bad with bad."

"They're goin' to sign. Does that mean the war will be over?"

"I hope so."

The storm was coming closer, tracking down the peninsula towards Glimmering-by-the-Water. It was less than half a mile away now, and moving rapidly. The air seemed to tingle.

"What's that funny smell?" said Rannilt.

Tali had noticed it too. It was like alkoyl though more acrid, stinging the nose and eyes.

The chancellor signed the charter with a flourish. The attendant held it up so everyone could see his signature, then extended the charter to Lyf. His fingers had just closed over its edge when he went still. He looked over his shoulder, uneasily. Then over the other shoulder.

"What's the matter?" said Tali. "What's he worried about?"

"He's comin'," Rannilt said in a bloodcurdling whisper. "He's comin', Tali."

"Who's coming?"

"*He* is."

The chancellor was whispering in his chief magian's ear. *Time for desperate measures*, he had said. Was this part of a last-ditch plan to even the odds against Lyf?

"Is he on our side?" said Tali

"He's Lyf's enemy," said Rannilt.

Lyf raised his right hand. Tali didn't see anything, but suddenly the tension drained away and he was the one who was smiling.

"What just happened?" said Tali. "I don't understand what's going on."

"Lyf's enemy can't get through. Lyf's blocked him."

Tali didn't ask how the child knew. Rannilt's gift was quite unfathomable. "He must be an ally of the chancellor's, then. I knew he had something up his sleeve."

"Should I let him through?" said Rannilt.

"You can do that?"

"I think so."

There wasn't time to weigh the pros and cons, and without knowing the chancellor's plan Tali had no way of doing so. "Yes, let him through, whoever he is."

Rannilt opened her closed right fist and a stream of tiny golden bubbles streaked out towards the centre of the approaching storm cloud.

Instantly it went dark, then lightning struck the top of the temple, dazzling Tali. The thunder was a simultaneous, deafening blast. The storm exploded around them, four more bolts reflecting off the wind-polished columns, the soldiers' helmets, swords and shields, and a great silver urn in the centre of the table. Then it stopped.

But the dazzling reflections off the urn did not. They grew brighter, extending in gorgeous shimmers and sprays of red and crimson, black and purple and violet. The urn split apart and the pieces rolled off the edges of the table. The brilliant moving colours remained, and grew. They began to take on the form of a man, a huge man, bigger than Rix, with a great bloated head and a vast prow of a nose, armoured in opal. A man whose very skin was armour made from black opal, reflecting the light in every direction.

He's not the chancellor's ally, Tali realised. We shouldn't have let him through. We've done a really stupid thing.

The black opal was beautiful. Beautiful and terrifying. It enclosed the man Tali had seen in the Abysm, turned to stone.

Now the stone had been made flesh.

Grandys.

CHAPTER 70

The chancellor was a cunning and devious man, Rix knew. A man well known for sudden reversals of policy. It wasn't surprising, therefore, that the man who had previously crushed and condemned Rix now treated him as his most important ally. What was he really up to?

Immersed in these worries, he did not take in the gathering storm or notice the acrid smell of ozone. He wasn't paying attention when the chancellor signed the paper, nor when Lyf suddenly checked over his shoulder. Rix was only roused by the lightning bolt striking the top of the temple and the slowly growing shimmer that he should have recognised instantly.

He had first envisioned it months ago, with his hand on Maloch's hilt. He had painted it on the wall of the observatory in Garramide. He had ridden all the way to the sinkhole in that lunatic attempt to recover what he had believed to be Grandys' petrified body. So why did it take so long for him to recognise the man himself? Perhaps he did not want to believe that a petrified man could come back from the dead.

Rix had always been afraid of magery, and now the fear rose in him until it was paralysing. How could a man turned to stone come back to life? Surely the act of petrifaction would destroy every organ in his body. He was rising from his chair, trying to understand, when Grandys caught the movement.

"Who the blazes are you?"

"I'm Rixium Ricinus."

"Ah," said Grandys, rubbing his huge, opal-armoured nose. "You crushed the enemy at the siege of Garramide. Come, I need a bold captain."

As if from a great distance Rix heard Glynnie cry out and he remembered, with a shiver, the night he had been studying the mural upstairs at Garramide. He had been agonising about his own leadership failures and wishing he'd had Grandys' brilliance as a warrior and a leader. The figure on the wall had seemed to speak to him, *Follow me*, and at the time Rix had wanted to. But not for anything would he follow this coarse, brutal man.

"No thanks," said Rix.

"It's an order, not a request."

The man's arrogance was breathtaking and, despite Grandys' size and presence and overwhelming power, Rix wasn't taking it.

"Be damned!" he said recklessly. "I'm no one's man but my own."

Grandys swelled until his crusted skin creaked. Then his opaline eye fixed on the sheath on Rix's hip. And the wire-handled sword.

"Maloch is mine!" he roared. "Give it to me."

Grandys was on the other side of the great conference table but he simply barged through it, knocking everyone aside. His armoured skin shattered the timbers and sent splinters flying in all directions.

Maloch shook wildly, rising halfway out of its sheath as it had at the Abysm. Rix took a firm hold of the hilt, turned towards Grandys, then hesitated. How could he attack his own ancestor, the first of the Five Heroes and the founder of Hightspall? He put up the blade, not knowing what to do, then remembered Swelt's dying words. Grandys was sterile. He'd had no descendants. It also meant that Rix wasn't Herovian. It came as a profound relief. Rix whirled and attacked.

"Maloch!" said Grandys. "Obey my command! Strike him down."

The sword twisted so violently in Rix's hand that he could not hold it, then struck at his face. He ducked and tried to turn the blade away. It struck again, opening a long gash across his forehead.

Blood flooded into Rix's eyes, half blinding him. The sword twisted from his hand, arched upwards and, with a roar of triumph, Grandys caught it.

An arm went around Rix's shoulder, steadying him.

"How did he get free?" said Rix.

"Perhaps he got enough help from Maloch after all." It was Tobry.

"But how the devil did he know to come here?"

"All Hightspall knows about the peace conference. Wipe your eyes." Tobry pressed a rag into Rix's hand. "Grab another sword. I'll keep him at bay betimes."

Rix's head was throbbing. He cleaned the blood out of his eyes and tied the rag around his forehead, across the gash. When he could see again, Tobry was advancing on Grandys, sword in hand. Tobry was a fine swordsman, no doubt of it, but Grandys had been a master. With Maloch and its protective magery, he could kill Tobry with a single blow.

"Tobe, wait."

Wrenching a sword out of a guard's hand, Rix leapt after Tobry. They fought side by side for a minute or two, and even kept Grandys at bay, but he was grinning broadly. He was toying with them. He had been a great magian as well as an invincible warrior, and with Maloch in hand his magery was greatly enhanced.

With a single blow from Maloch, Grandys hacked both their blades in two. He focused on Tobry, his eyes narrowing to points as if trying to peer inside him, then his cruel mouth turned down.

"A bag of gold for anyone who cuts out the obscenity's black livers," he bellowed. "Take the shifter down."

"Tobry, look out!" Tali screamed as a dozen of the chancellor's guards, evidently mesmerised by Grandys' reappearance, stormed towards Tobry.

"Fly, Tobe," Rix hissed. "We've got to live to fight again."

Tobry ran ten steps to the edge of the temple, dived out over the low cliff into the water, and disappeared. As he did, Rix saw Holm's grey head appear over a rock outcrop, then duck down again. Grandys studied Rix for a moment. "I'll deal with you in a minute." He turned away.

Lyf was standing on his crutches, staring at his enemy. A malevolent smile crossed Grandys' opaline face.

"You destroyed Tirnan Twil," he said quietly. "And my Herovian heritage."

"I had nothing to do with it," said Lyf. "The gauntlings went renegade."

"You created them. For my blood-price, I'll accept your king-magery."

Lyf laughed hollowly. "It was lost when you walled me up in the catacombs. When I died, it had nowhere to go."

"It went *somewhere*," said Grandys, "and you know where."

Lyf paled, then extended his right hand towards Grandys, attacking with ferocious flashes of magery. To Rix, it seemed that Lyf was drawing on all the power of the pearls, attempting to overpower his enemy by sheer force. Rix held his breath. He did not want Lyf to win, yet how could Grandys be any better?

The attack failed, for the force never reached its target. Maloch's protective magery diverted the flashes towards the rear of the temple, shattering several columns and causing the corner to collapse in a great tumble of blocks and cylinders of limestone.

Grandys folded his arms, smiling contemptuously, then leapt twenty feet across the temple and struck, wounding Lyf in the shoulder, then the chest. Lyf screamed as the accursed blade parted his flesh. Maloch struck again, shattering the little heatstone case and scattering ebony pearls across the marble flagstones. Grandys swooped on the bouncing pearls, caught two and held them up, roaring in triumph.

Lyf let out a shriek of dismay, called the other two pearls to his hand, then dropped his crutches and fled across the sky, trailing blood. His guards and generals, and the three matriarchs, stared after him, unable to comprehend how the reversal could have come about so easily. Neither could Rix. This changed everything.

The wizened, hunchbacked chancellor approached, extending his hand to Grandys. If they joined forces, could they turn the war Hightspall's way?

"That was well done, Lord Grandys," said the chancellor, gesturing to his own party. "If you would come this way, we have much to talk about."

Grandys looked the chancellor up, looked him down, then spat on his black boots. "I have only one policy, and it is war. War until the enemy have been eliminated from the world."

Turning his back on the apoplectic chancellor, Grandys checked the temple, evidently decided that all threats had been eliminated, then focused on Rix again.

"Since Maloch allowed you to use it, you must be my kinsman." He touched Rix on the chin with the sword. "Follow me."

This time Rix felt a *compulsion* to do so, but he fought it, just as he had fought the compulsion Lyf had put on him as a child, through the heatstone in Rix's salon in Palace Ricinus.

"Nope," he said, as insolently as he could manage.

Grandys pointed Maloch at Rix's heart. "With the magery of this sword, I *command* you to follow."

The spell struck Rix like a physical blow, so hard that he almost went over backwards and his knees turned to water. It was all he could do to stay upright, and he could feel the command beating at him, undermining his free will and trying to take control of him.

Few men could have fought such a spell, but Rix had spent the second ten years of his life fighting Lyf's compulsion, and the struggle had developed an inner strength in him, a resolution that no one not forged in such fires could have had. He drew on every ounce of that strength now, directed it against the command, and broke it.

"Ugh!" grunted Grandys, as if he had taken a painful blow to the midriff. His opaline cheeks flashed red and black. He pointed Maloch again and, groaning with the effort, repeated, "I *command* you to follow."

Again Rix tried to fight the spell, but this time it was stronger. Too strong, for he had given his all the previous time and had nothing left.

"Rix?" Glynnie shouted. "He's ensorcelled you. You've got to fight him."

He wanted to, but Rix could not. It was over. He lurched across on rubbery knees and stood behind Grandys.

"I always win," said Grandys.

He leered at Tali, who was standing on the red circle holding Rannilt's hand and looking as dazed as everyone else. "I have great need of a woman," said Grandys. "You will come to my bed tonight."

Rix felt his outrage rising like a thunderhead, but he could do nothing about it. Tali wouldn't be able to resist his magery either. No one could.

Her jaw knotted. The sinews stood out in her neck and she let out a great groan, then cried, "I will not."

Grandys looked at her in astonishment, as though such a rejection had never happened before. "Who *are* you?"

"I am Pale," she said proudly.

He frowned, and Rix gained the impression that Grandys was trying to remember where he had seen her before. Tali was trembling all over.

Then Grandys' lip curled. "You're an unworthy slave. The command is revoked. Follow me, Ricinus. We're riding to war."

He mounted the largest horse there, ordered Rix to take another, then rode away, leaving a shattered silence behind him.

As Rix followed numbly, he could see the terror in Glynnie's eyes. It was mirrored in his own, for he was starting to realise what a brute Grandys really was. Rix kept fighting the command spell, but it did not relinquish its hold for an instant.

PART THREE

BLOOD OATH

CHAPTER 71

Rix looked sideways at the man who was now his master, and shuddered.

No one would have called Axil Grandys handsome. He was a huge, fleshy man with a red, bloated face, lips as swollen as a burst blood plum, and fists the size of grapefruits. He was boastful, swaggering, supremely confident in everything he said and did. And, Rix had read in one of the books Swelt had given him, that Grandys' appetites were prodigious. All of them.

A mile up the road from Glimmering he dragged Rix's horse, and Rix, sixty yards to a rock platform that looked out over the lake. To the south-west, twenty-odd miles distant, the trio of volcanoes called the Vomits fumed and flowed. South-east only a handful of miles away, a scatter of lights were all that remained of the city of Caulderon, which Lyf's armies and his Hightspaller slaves continued to tear down.

In every other direction, there were no lights.

Grandys took Rix by the throat, heaved him off his horse and forced him to his knees on the brink of the platform. It was several hundred feet down to the water.

"Swear to me, and me alone!" bellowed Grandys, putting Maloch to Rix's throat. "Swear or die."

The sword was quivering, Rix's no longer. Grandys was its master and, no matter what loyalty it had offered to Rix before, no matter what protection it had cast over him, it would quench its blood thirst on him without a second's thought.

He was so sickened at being forced to follow this brute that part of him wanted to take Grandys' second alternative. A part of Rix had craved death ever since the chancellor had forced him to choose between loyalty to his country and betraying his parents. Death meant an end to pain, an end to torment.

Another part longed to be relieved of the burden of responsibility he felt so unsuited to, and simply follow a great leader. Grandys' command spell found the conflict between the two and twisted the knife. Rix, in his turn, twisted to avoid it. What if he hurled himself at Grandys and dragged him over the edge?

The fall would certainly kill Rix, but would it kill a man who had been stone and was now a stone-armoured man? Rix wasn't sure it would.

"Swear a binding oath to serve me, unto death," said Grandys.

Reluctantly, but under his sorcerous thrall, Rix swore.

"What do you know about Lyf's king-magery?" said Grandys that afternoon. They were still riding north up Nusidand Peninsula, which extended into Lake Fumerous for seven miles.

"I know little about any kind of magery," said Rix thoughtlessly, "and want to know less."

Grandys' backhander lifted Rix out of the saddle and the impact with the ground drove the breath out of him.

"I've got to have it," said Grandys. "Tell me all you know."

Rix spat out blood. He'd bitten his tongue. "You rotten mongrel. I'm going to kill you for that!"

"You want to," grinned Grandys. "But you never will. I control you, body and soul. Now speak!"

"The dying king has to go through the death rituals so the king-magery can be released and pass to his successor. But no Cythian knew what had happened to Lyf, or how he died, so he couldn't be given the rituals, and the king-magery wasn't passed on."

"I know all that," snapped Grandys. "What happened to it?"

"No one knows. It left Lyf when he died—"

"That's why we walled him up to starve to death," Grandys grated. "To get the king-magery when death released it. We had everything ready to catch it, but it vanished. Tell me about the ebony pearls. Where did they come from?"

"I don't know," said Rix.

Grandys stalked away, tore up an orange flower that had been foolish enough to emerge in winter, and shredded it in his hairy, sweating fists.

"I've got two ebony pearls," he said, "and Lyf has two. Plus another, weaker kind of magery, some bastard leftover from the lost king-magery, I assume. But I've got Maloch. We'd be evenly matched, save that he commands vast armies, and all I have is you." He raised a fist to the sky. "But I will have my army, and his black pearls too. Then I'll hunt down king-magery and have it all."

"Why do you want it ... Lord Grandys?" said Rix, feigning politeness. He wanted to spit in Grandys' face.

"It's a higher order of magery, and the key to the land. With king-magery I can create the Promised Realm we came all this way to find. But first I must have allies."

He dug the spurs into his mount's bloody flanks and spurred off. Rix followed, hating his master more each time Grandys opened his mouth. What did he mean by *create the Promised Realm*? Tobry had told Rix dark tales about Grandys' conquest of ancient Cythe, and could not bear to think about what he intended now.

They galloped until Grandys' horse fell dead under him. He dragged Rix off his mount, swung into the saddle and ordered him to run behind like a dog. Rix did so, for the command spell would not allow him to do otherwise, but every step of the way he imagined how good it would be to knock the brute off his horse, batter him senseless and choke him to death.

Hours later, at a town in the north, Grandys swaggered into the stables and came out leading six magnificent horses. He did not say how he had obtained them, but there was no outcry or pursuit. They mounted the strongest beasts and galloped into the mountains for hour upon hour, leading the others. Grandys had no map, nor needed one. He knew where he was going, but did not say.

On a windswept peak with a bare, flat top he slowed his headlong pace and began to pick his way between grey rocks. There was little snow; it had all been scoured away by the wind.

"Ah!" he said, spurring up a gentle rise in the moonlight.

An oval chasm yawned before him, a black abyss, but Grandys kept riding full tilt towards it, spurring his horse on even though it was tossing its head, right to the brink. The horse reared up on its back legs, whinnying in terror. Grandys stood up in the saddle, waving Maloch above his head and bellowing with laughter.

The horse dropped to four legs. The wind, which was whistling across the rocks, died away. Rix looked down into the hole, which was pure black even though the rocks it passed through were grey. It was the Abysm, though not the branch of it he had been to near Garramide.

Grandys extended Maloch down into the Abysm. Yellow flickered and shimmered around the blade.

Rix swallowed. He knew what was about to come, and prayed it would fail.

"My friends," Grandys said, speaking downwards in a penetrating voice, "two thousand years ago, as a persecuted people, we took ship from Thanneron to sail to the far side of the world in search of our Promised Realm. We won a glorious realm for others, but we did not find the special place our *Immortal Text* had promised us. Now our time has come. Even as I stand on the brink of this Abysm, so too we stand within an arm's reach of the home we've yearned for so long."

Was that a tear running down Grandys' coarse, bloated cheek? Rix could not credit it.

"Come forth!" Grandys cried. Fire blasted from Maloch's tip, down the Abysm.

In the depths, Rix saw reflections in four places. The reflections twinkled and shimmered and grew until they became four stone figures, no, four people now, slowly rising.

Four Herovians, later renamed Four Heroes.

They reached the top, suspended there by Grandys' magery. They did not look like heroes – not as the history books, the legends and tales of Hightspall had made them out to be.

"Syrten," said Grandys, extending Maloch out with the blade horizontal.

Syrten took hold of the keen blade and was pulled onto the land. He was as massive as a golem and looked like one. His skin had the texture of sandstone and his thighs were so monstrous that they made a grating sound as he moved, like one millstone grinding on another. His mouth hung open, his arms dangled limply, and his skin was not armoured with smooth opal, as Grandys' was. Syrten's skin was encrusted in clots, lumps and nodules of the precious mineral.

"G.r.a.n.d.y.s," Syrten replied, articulating each letter. His rumbling voice reverberated across the Abysm.

"Lirriam," said Grandys.

No greater contrast could be imagined. Lirriam was neither tall like Grandys nor massive like Syrten. She was average height for a woman, but so lushly built that she appeared to be bursting out of her gown, and the only part of her still black opal was her glorious, shimmering hair.

Lirriam did not take hold of the blade. She sprang up on it, the wind plastering her gown to her body and her opaline hair streaming out like a fan.

"What took you so long, Grandys?" Catching sight of Rix, she leapt down, her heavy bosom quivering, and favoured him with a long, tingling look.

Grandys growled in his throat.

Lirriam laughed. "Still as easily provoked as ever. Have two thousand years of crystal reflection taught you nothing?"

Grandys turned back to the Abysm, his jaw clenched. "Rufuss!"

Rufuss was enormously tall and thin – as tall as Arkyz Leatherhead had been, Rix thought, before he'd been deprived of his head – but spare to the point of stringiness. Rufuss's mouth had a sour downturn, as though nothing gave him pleasure save denial. His eyes were opal, and his teeth and fingers, but otherwise he looked like a normal man. At least, any normal man who was utterly insane.

Rufuss waved the sword aside. He stalked across the air above the Abysm, his elongated limbs moving jerkily, and took his place on the other side of Grandys.

"Welcome, Rufuss," said Grandys. "This is a good day."

"Is it?" said Rufuss, biting each word off. "It'll be the first, then."

"Yulia," said Grandys.

She was the most normal of them: tallish, slim, a long austere face, eyes that looked as though they had seen too much and wanted to see no more. Her golden skin was real skin; only her fingernails and toenails were opal. She touched Grandys' blade with a fingertip and a path formed beneath her feet. She walked it to the edge and stood beside Lirriam.

"What is it, Yulia?" said Grandys. "You should be rejoicing in our freedom, yet you seem troubled."

"Two thousand years I've been raking over our deeds," said Yulia. "We did wrong, Grandys. Grave wrong."

A spasm of annoyance crossed his face, but when he spoke it was clear he was deliberately misinterpreting her words. "Yes; we fell into the wrythen's trap. But now we can put it right, Yulia. The Promised Realm!"

"You cannot know how I yearn for it, Axil," she whispered. "Though I fear the price will be too high."

"The price will be high for our enemies," said Grandys. "Mount up and ride – we have an army to form."

CHAPTER 72

"How could he come back from petrifaction?" said Lyf. "It defies the very laws of nature."

Grandys' return from the dead, wielding the accursed sword, had almost unmanned him. And he'd lost two ebony pearls, a crippling blow now that magery was failing and weakening more every day.

Lyf wavered through the air, flying low across Lake Fumerous and trailing blood into the water, then across the city to his temple. He had to drag himself inside, for he had left his crutches behind at Glimmering, but he recoiled at the door. The stench in the temple was unbearable.

He dragged himself up through the heavy air to the top of the leaning tower that had formerly belonged to Rixium Ricinus, and clung to the wall, looking out over Caulderon and all he had won. Had all been in vain? Would it be lost just as quickly?

Grandys had crippled him before with that foul sword, and now he was doing it again. Lyf lay on the cold stone, closed his eyes and set to work to heal the wounds in his chest and shoulder.

They would not heal.

The kings of old Cythe had been masters of healing. It had been one of their three primary duties, and Lyf had been one of the most gifted. Even as a bodiless wrythen he had retained an ability to heal, and since he'd had a body back, imperfect though it was, he had healed hundreds of his wounded and ailing subjects.

Now he could not heal himself at all; not the tiniest bruise or graze. Was it because the injuries had been done with Maloch? He did not think so; he had healed other injuries made with that blade. All injuries save for his amputated feet; but they were a special case.

Lyf took to the air again. It was harder than before. With only two pearls, the powerful magery required to move his body through the air was almost beyond him. In his healery he passed down the lines of injured soldiers, laying his hands on one man, then another.

Nothing.

He could not heal anyone. His healing magery, as essential to him as breathing, was gone. Had Maloch done this to him, or was it Grandys' foul magery? The brute had lusted after king-magery from the moment he stepped ashore from the First Fleet. King-magery was why he had killed Lyf in the first place.

Again Lyf asked himself how Grandys could have come back to life. Then he had an even more chilling thought. What if he brought back the other four Herovians?

He had to act quickly. Lyf returned to his reeking temple, for it contained an ancient portal passage that could carry him instantly to his caverns under Precipitous Crag. Without telling anyone where he was going, he retreated to the flaskoid-shaped cavern, desperate for the security of his aeons-old wrythen home.

And answers.

Once there, he drifted up to the crack – a very different kind of portal – that allowed admittance to the Abysm. He was planning to hurl the other four Heroes down to the bottom and shatter them to a million bits. No one could come back from that.

But he could not gain entrance. The Abysm had been sealed against him. He was locked out of the most sacred place in the land, the place only *he* had the right to enter in life. This was monstrous.

Was it his punishment for perverting the healing magery; for corrupting what had been so pure and beautiful? Or for hurling his opalised enemies into so holy a place? He had to think so; had to blame himself.

Lyf sank to the floor. Had he been set up from the beginning? Had his enemies allowed him to turn them to opal so they could come back and undo all his achievements? Was it all a gigantic conspiracy, another planned betrayal by the despicable Herovians?

Despair overwhelmed him. After all he had done, to be brought down by an enemy he had thought he'd crushed. He had failed his people, given them a hope that could never be fulfilled.

But worse, far worse was the loss of his healing gift, the very foundation of king-magery. Even if he succeeded in his plan to restore the line of Cythian kings, without king-magery he would not be able to heal the troubled land. His disaster-prone land could not thrive, nor his people survive. They would become *degradoes* again, sliding towards annihilation.

He had to save them. But first he must take advice from his ancestor gallery.

And this time he would listen.

CHAPTER 73

"It'll be all right." Rannilt was stroking Tali's burning brow. "You'll get better, I promise. Ooh, that rotten old Grandys. But you showed him, Tali. You showed him good."

Tali lay on the wet flagstones in the temple, wishing the falling rain could quench the fire in her head, though she did not think anything ever would. Why had she interfered? Why had she urged Rannilt to use her unfathomable gift to let Grandys through? She'd thought she was helping to keep Lyf in check. Had she created a disaster?

At least she had broken Grandys' command spell, and that would be worth a song or two when she got home, if she ever did. But why had she attracted his attention in the first place? Why hadn't she hidden, as Rannilt had been urging her to do?

The shattered matriarchs and Lyf's entourage had sailed south to Caulderon, a few miles away across the lake. The provincial leaders were riding north up the long peninsula, then fanning out in all directions, some to shore up their own positions, others to work out how they could capitalise on what had happened at Glimmering. Only Rix's small party remained, leaderless now.

And the chancellor's two hundred.

She had not known him to lose control before, but an hour after Grandys' departure the chancellor was still stalking back and forth, incandescent with rage. Not just because he had been so utterly upstaged. Not just because Grandys had stolen two priceless ebony pearls from under his nose. Not even because Axil Grandys was a despised Herovian and a loose cannon whom no one could predict.

Worse, unimaginably so, Grandys had spat on the chancellor, repudiated him then ignored him, and that could never be endured.

"Clear out!" he raged to his servants and guards. "Get out of my sight."

"Not goin' nowhere," said Rannilt. "Tali needs me."

"Not you! Attendant!" he bawled. A young woman came running, a pretty brunette.

"Get my chief magian!"

She fled.

"What are we gonna do, Tali?" Rannilt said quietly. "Are we gonna escape again?"

"I don't see how we can, child."

"Why not?"

"The chancellor's guards are watching us, see? And if we ran, on this narrow peninsula there's only one way to go, so they'd soon catch us."

"We could try," said Rannilt stubbornly. "We've escaped before, lots of times."

"Where could we go? We're in Lyf's territory here, and everywhere north for many miles. His armies are still hunting me, and anyone who sees us will know that we're Pale."

"Chancellor's a bad man," said Rannilt. "I don't wanna go with him."

Tali looked across at the chancellor, who was pacing across the temple and back. "Me either, but Rix and Tobry are gone. At least, while we're with him, the safe conduct holds."

"He wants your blood."

"Not any more. He has no shifters left to heal."

"The pearl then. He still wants it."

"I know, but I can't do anything about that right now."

Shortly the tubby little chief magian puffed up. "Lord Chancellor?"

"Form an umbrella of magery over Tali, *immediately*. Pull it down so tight that not a glimmer of aura can get in or out. She can't be found or located, *or you lose your head*."

The chief magian jumped. "Immediately, Lord Chancellor. But ... may I ask why?"

"You may not!" The chancellor relented, pulled the chief magian close. "Tali bears the master pearl."

The chief magian's round head shot around. "How do you know?"

"Because Lizue attacked her in Rutherin to get it."

"Then Lyf knows ..."

"And he won't rest until it's his. Need I say that if he gets Tali's pearl, it's all over for Hightspall. And," the chancellor continued with a nasty grin, "you know how the enemy hate magery and magians. You'll be number one on their disembowelling list."

"I'll get the umbrella started right away."

The chief magian fetched a silver elbrot, a larger and far more ornate one than the wooden elbrot Tali had seen Tobry use. He walked around her, chanting and moving it in snail-trail patterns.

The bones of her skull creaked and a soothing numbness spread through her. Tali could not see the umbrella aura, but she could feel it closing around her and Rannilt. She let out a little sigh. Not safe from Lyf, but safer.

"Is that *it*?" said the chancellor.

The chief magian's nostrils pinched in, as if his art had been insulted. "'Tis but the first stage of five. Each succeeding stage of the spell is more difficult and painful than the one before, and requires study and practice. Once the fifth stage is in place, in a few days' time, you may send Tali wherever you wish, confident that Lyf's magery will never find her."

"What about Grandys' magery?"

The chief magian paled. "You need Tali hidden from him as well?"

"More than the other, and more urgently. If Grandys realises she's got the master pearl, he'll be back here in an instant. He'll certainly wonder, once he has time from other pressing duties, how an *unworthy slave* was able to break his command. And he's a far more vengeful man than I am. Get it done."

The chancellor gave orders for camp to be struck, then stood looking down at Tali. "Every one of my troops is watching you, so don't try another escape. Right now, you're my best hope of survival – and I'm yours."

"Until you gouge the master pearl out of my head."

"Did I say I was going to take it?"

She snorted.

"Are you ready to travel?" he added.

"Where are you taking me? Not back to Rutherin, I hope. I had an experience in your care that wasn't much to my liking."

"Speaking of Rutherin, where's your treacherous friend Holm, formerly known as Kroni?"

"No idea," Tali lied. "Haven't seen him all day."

He walked away, calling his retinue together.

"I saw a grey-haired old man lurkin' down by the water," said Rannilt. "Was that him?"

"Yes."

"Why is he hidin'?"

"He helped me escape from Rutherin, so it wouldn't be a good idea for the chancellor to set eyes on him. Especially in his present mood. Shh!"

The chancellor's retinue, half of them guards, had assembled in the middle of the temple.

"Rixium Ricinus is condemned as a traitor and is to be killed on sight," the chancellor announced. "The reward for his head is half a pound of gold." He waved a small leather bag above his head to reinforce the message. "The shifter called Tobry Lagger, and the so-called clock attendant, Holm, alias Kroni, who betrayed me by helping Tali to escape my prison, are also condemned. One eleventh of a pound of gold for each of them – dead or alive. Get moving!"

After days of cold, arduous travel under the fifth stage of the sorcerous shield that blurred everything around Tali, the shield was lowered a fraction. The thirty-foot wall loomed before her, the battered gate, the copper-clad domes.

"Why have you brought me to Garramide?" said Tali.

"For much the same reasons that Rix came here," said the chancellor. "It's inaccessible but not remote, readily defended with a sufficiently powerful force, and well resourced save for the treasury, which I can supply. And, you may recall, I have a great love of beautiful things. Rutherin was a cultural desert. Garramide contains treasures you have never seen, collected by the great dame herself. I want to see them."

One of them turned out to be a seeing stone with which he sent messages to his army in Rutherin, to other allies across the land, and to those he would have as allies.

On the way he had swallowed his bile and sent three envoys to Grandys. The chancellor stalked the halls, waiting wild-eyed for Grandys' reply.

CHAPTER 74

"Swire," said Grandys, reining in at the top of the hill and looking down at the town nestled in a loop of the river. Swire was small, two thousand inhabitants at the most, though it looked prosperous. The castle, on a flat hill beside it, guarded the way in by both road and river. "In two hours both the town and the castle will be ours."

"How, when you only have one soldier?" said Rix.

Lirriam gave a throaty laugh. "Shall I show the boy how we take what we want?"

Grandys scowled, then said, "The ride of glory. Go ahead and announce us, Ricinus. Make them sit up and take notice."

Rix nodded stiffly. He had no idea how to announce the return of the Five Heroes, but one did not say no to Grandys. To him, all things were possible and he did not tolerate failure.

As Rix rode down the winding track, Lirriam's laughter followed him.

"The boy," he fumed. "After all I've done, she calls me *the boy*."

But then, since he was obeying their every command, perhaps to them he was a child.

He reached the town. The gates stood open, it being daytime and the truce still in force. Rix rode in. It must have been market day for the streets were crowded. He looked back and saw a dust cloud a mile up the road – the Heroes coming at full gallop. He had only two minutes.

How was he to announce the ride of glory? Well, he made an imposing figure on the great horse, and Swire was a simple country town, so perhaps the simplest way was best. He clamped onto his shield with his dead hand, raised it above his head and struck it hard with his sword, again and again, until every eye in the square was on him. A hushed silence fell.

"Axil Grandys has been reborn!" said Rix. "The Five Heroes return. Hightspall is saved."

Everyone stared at him as though he was mad. No one spoke for a few seconds, then everyone at once.

Rix stood up in his stirrups, pointed towards the racing dust cloud and said, "They come."

And come they did, pounding towards the gate, their swords held high.

"Make way!" Rix shouted, afraid that they would ride down anyone in their way. "Make way for Axil Grandys. Make way for the Five Heroes."

The crowd parted, barely in time. Grandys flashed through the gate, a majestic sight with his great sword and opal-armoured skin glistening, and then the others. No one could have doubted what they were seeing: the Five Heroes had truly returned. They skidded to a stop, their horses' shoes striking sparks from the cobbles, then walked with majestic slowness to the centre of the square. What was Grandys going to do? What would he say?

The Five Heroes formed their horses into a circle, facing out. Grandys flicked his fingers at Rix, as if to say, *Get out of our way, boy*. Rix moved into the background, awed by the display, yet fuming at their contemptuous treatment.

Grandys stared down everyone who met his eyes, but did not speak.

"Hightspall is saved," cried a brown-haired, pigtailed girl at the front of the crowd. She was no older than ten. "Hail Axil Grandys."

"Hail Axil Grandys," the crowd echoed. "Hail the Five Heroes, hail, hail!"

The Heroes formed a procession, Grandys leading. They rode slowly down the main street to the far gate, turned and rode back, still silent.

I'll say one thing for the swine, Rix thought. He knows how to make an entrance.

At the square again, Grandys rose in his stirrups and searched the crowd, looking for one particular face.

"You, girl," he said. "You who first hailed me. Come forward."

The little girl did so, stumbling on the rough stones. She made him a rude curtsy. "Y-yes, Lord Grandys?"

"Who's the lord of yonder Castle Swire?"

"It's Lord Bondy, Lord Grandys."

"Is Bondy a good man, child? Does he treat his people well?"

The girl gulped, looked around her, then said, "Not very well."

"Is that so," said Grandys. "Then I'll have to chastise him, won't I?"

"Yes, you will, Lord Grandys."

"Come up here, child. Show me the way."

Someone cried out, her mother perhaps, then fell silent. The girl walked slowly towards the enormous horse and its imperious rider.

"Don't be afraid," said Grandys. "I would never hurt a child."

He heaved her up and seated her in front of him. "Hold on to the saddle horn."

She did so, biting her lip.

"You are my first, my chosen people," he said to the assembled townsfolk of Swire. "Follow me to the castle."

He turned to the town gates, never doubting that they would

follow, walking his horse so the people could keep up with him. The other Heroes fell in beside him, buxom Lirriam and golem-like Syrten on the left, cadaverous Rufuss and slender, grave Yulia to the right.

Rix's heart was pounding and a sick dread washed back and forth through his belly. One part of him could admire Grandys, his confidence and his swagger. Another part knew him for an arrogant brute who served no one's purposes but his own.

More worryingly, Rix saw echoes of Grandys' character in his own mother, and even himself. Was this his true inheritance? No, he thought, he's not my ancestor. *I won't have it.*

The Five Heroes rode through the gates of Castle Swire, followed by Rix and the entire population of Swire. All were agog to see how Grandys planned to chastise their lord. Rix was not. Sickness was churning in his gut.

Grandys dismounted, leaving the girl on the horse. He strode up the steps of the castle, pounded on the great iron-reinforced door with the butt of his sword and took several steps to the left.

"Lord Bondy, come forth."

Shortly the door opened and a short, plump man came out onto the terrace.

"What the devil do you mean, hammering on my door like that?" he said furiously. He turned and saw the enormous figure standing there, armoured in black opal. Then the other four Heroes, and the townsfolk still flooding through the gates. Bondy blanched and made a dart for the door. Grandys blocked his path.

"Are you Bondy?"

"Yes," whispered the plump man.

"The child on my horse said you don't treat your people well."

Bondy looked from Grandys to the girl in the saddle, and back again. He frowned. "I'm a good overlord. Are you playing some kind of joke, sir?"

"I never joke, Bondy. I could have your head for that."

Bondy relaxed.

Grandys added, "In fact, I will."

"Lord?" said Bondy.

Maloch flashed out, faster than Rix's eye could follow, then returned to its sheath. Rix blinked. What had just happened?

Bondy's eyes rolled up, then Grandys reached out and lifted the man's neatly severed head from his neck. He strode down the steps and handed the dripping extremity to the girl.

"You won't have any more trouble with him, child."

Grandys raised his voice. "Castle Swire is mine. Turn its inhabitants into the street. Bid the servants here, either to swear to me – or die like their master."

The girl dropped Bondy's gory head and screamed.

Irritably, Grandys gestured to her mother to take her away, then reached out to the townsfolk.

"I am raising an army, and I'm going to take back our land. Who will join me?"

He said it with such self-confidence that no one could doubt him. Rix felt it too, despite himself: the pride that he had played a small part in an event of momentous importance, and the feeling – no, the unshakeable belief – that if he followed Grandys, together they *would* cast out the enemy and take Hightspall back.

It was clear that everyone else felt the same. Within an hour Grandys had signed up six hundred men. Messengers were sent to all the surrounding towns, villages and manors, bidding their youths to hasten to Swire, to Axil Grandys' service.

In four days, he was training an army of thousands and planning his first attack, a demonstration of his power that no one could deny.

"Get your troops ready, Captain Rixium," he said to Rix that morning. "Tonight we march on Castle Rebroff."

"But ... that's the enemy's most powerful fortress outside Caulderon," said Rix.

"And led by Lyf's greatest and most experienced general, Rochlis. That's why I've chosen it."

"How are you going to attack it with a few thousand untrained troops?" said Rix.

"I'm not merely going to attack Rebroff. I'm going to take it. We'll feast like carrion crows in Castle Rebroff's Great Hall, this time tomorrow night."

It was impossible to doubt him. Was Grandys the leader Hightspall needed to hold back the Cythonian hordes, even defeat them? Despite his hatred of the man, Rix was beginning to think so.

He was also thinking that he could learn much about the art of leadership from Grandys – assuming he survived long enough.

CHAPTER 75

"The – the envoys have returned, Chancellor," stammered his aide, from the door.

Tali and the chancellor were in the great dame's chambers, which he had appropriated, by a blazing fire.

"Then send them in. What did Grandys say?"

"Th-there's a m-message," said the aide. His arms hung low, his feet dragged.

"What is it, damn you?"

The aide opened a brown sack and dumped the contents on the chancellor's gleaming table. "This."

The severed heads of the chancellor's three envoys rolled halfway across and stopped, their clouded eyes staring at him.

Tali recoiled. The chancellor let out a strangled gasp.

"What's Grandys saying?" said Tali, turning so she would not have to look at the heads, which had been severed a good few days ago and were past their best.

"I should have thought that was obvious."

"Not to me."

"It means that he, unlike every other foe I've ever dealt with, is utterly unpredictable. How can I fight such a man? I've no idea what he'll do next."

"I don't know." And Rix was in the hands of this monster, unable to help himself.

The chancellor's sardonic eye turned to her, as if he had read her thought. "How could Rixium have gone off with the man? How could he be so weak-willed?" He spat into the fire.

In the shadows behind him, Tali saw Glynnie stiffen. The chancellor had taken her on because she was the perfect maidservant, but if he could have seen the look in her eyes now he might have thought otherwise. Was she grieving for Rix, Tali wondered, or burning for him?

He cleared his throat, pointedly. Rix's betrayal was a theme the chancellor kept returning to, like a dog to a bone he'd gnawed all the meat off but could not let go.

"Grandys ensorcelled him," said Tali, wishing the chancellor would have the severed heads removed. "You know that."

"But for Grandys to do it so easily, surely Rix must have wanted it, subconsciously?"

"What if the enchantment on Maloch wasn't protecting Rix for himself," said Tali, "but because of the connection to Grandys?"

The chancellor started, and so did Glynnie, though she recovered quickly and stepped further back into the shadows.

"How do you mean?" said the chancellor.

"Did Maloch deliberately lead Rix to Precipitous Crag so he could attack the wrythen, terrorise Lyf with the reappearance of the sword that had cut his feet off, and weaken him from fear? Did Maloch direct Rix to Garramide so he'd paint the mural of the opalised man from images Maloch had previously shown him? A mural that would call Rix to recover Grandys' petrified body from the Abysm."

"Are you suggesting all this was foreordained?" said the chancellor.

"Not foreordained. But I do think there's a malign purpose at work, and it comes from the enchantment on the sword."

"Which makes this just the latest step in a two-thousand-year-old battle."

"Lady Ricinus gave Maloch to Rix and told him to wear it, but he disliked the sword on sight," said Tali. "Perhaps he sensed the magery in it. And the moment he strapped it on, he must have come under its influence. What if his great-aunt didn't sent it to Rix as an innocent gift, but in the hope that it would influence him to bring Grandys back?"

In the shadows, Glynnie drew in a long, hissing breath. The chancellor's dark brows knitted.

"If you're right, the sword was never protecting Rix for himself, but only for what he could do for its master."

"How are you going to save him?" Glynnie's face was twisted in anguish.

"Save Rixium?" barked the chancellor. "I've already condemned the swine twice. I hope Grandys puts him down like the Herovian dog he is."

"No, you don't," said Tali.

"Why the hell not?"

"Because Rix may be the only one who can save us from Grandys."

"Right now I'm more concerned about saving us from Lyf. Now get out!"

Tali went.

Given the way the peace conference had ended, Lyf must feel more embittered than ever, and more convinced that Hightspall had planned the breach of the safe conduct to bring Grandys there. What would Lyf do? He must be watching the news of his old enemy's progress with alarm, perhaps terror.

Was he planning a great new campaign? Or thinking that, before the worst happened, he had better secure his people's ultimate refuge, Cython? Either way, Lyf must also be giving thought to the Pale, and whether he could allow them to remain at the heart of his empire.

Their doom, she felt sure, was coming ever closer. She had to find out what Lyf was up to, and there was only one way to do that. Despite the risk, she would have to spy on him again.

CHAPTER 76

"It's impossible," Rix said quietly, when the sun rose to reveal the mighty fortress that was Castle Rebroff. "It's got every form of defence known. And what do we have?"

A thousand young, foolish men, most of whom had never picked up a sword until a few days ago. Only a thousand, because Grandys had left most of his recruits behind. None of his men had ever fought in a proper battle, and their opponent was the brilliant Cythonian general, Rochlis, who had won dozens of battles and lost none.

Grandys had marched his force the thirteen miles from Swire to Rebroff in darkness, arriving at their destination an hour before dawn. The castle was half a mile away, over the hill and down. They had to advance across a meadow that provided no cover, then pass a thirty-foot-wide moat before they could attack the walls or the gate. The attack would not happen until the mid-afternoon, for he wanted his men rested and fed. It was his only concession to the rules of warfare.

Once the camp was quiet, Rix went across to Grandys, who was perched on a boulder, his eyes glittering like black opals in the starlight. They were on the flank of a stony hill; knee-high tussocks of a coarse, sharp-bladed grass were scattered all around.

"How are we going to attack?" said Rix. "The wall or the gate? Or both at once?"

"The gate," Grandys said impatiently, as though that were obvious. "Only divide your forces when you can delegate them to another leader as good as you are."

"How can we breach the gate? It looks mighty strong, and we don't have a ram."

"I'll think of something when we come to it."

Had any other man said that, Rix would have known they were insane. And maybe Grandys was. Who knew what might have gone wrong inside him in all those ages he had spent petrified? Yet he exuded such arrogant self-confidence that Rix half believed him.

"What about the moat?" said Rix.

"You don't have to worry about that."

"Why not?"

"I'm beginning to have doubts about you, Ricinus. You obsess about every tiny detail."

"My instructors taught me that a good leader has to know every detail of his command. And control every aspect of the battle plan."

Grandys sneered. "Any of them ever won a battle? Or even fought one?"

"Well, no," Rix admitted. "Until this war started, there hadn't been one for a thousand years."

"No wars? None at all?"

"No."

Grandys looked incredulous. "Why didn't somebody start one?"

"Start a war just so the men could get battle practice?" cried Rix.

"Of course. Heroism in battle is man's highest ideal."

Rix took a while to come to terms with that. Whenever he thought Grandys could sink no lower he revealed an even baser iniquity. "Did you start wars to get battle practice?"

"At least a dozen."

"A lot of men must have been killed. Good men, maimed and brutalised, dying in agony."

Grandys yawned. "But the ones who survived were all the better for the practice."

He lay back on the snowy grass, wearing only his shirt and kilt, and did not seem to be troubled by the cold. Was that a side effect of being turned to stone?

"You can't know every detail of your command," said Grandys, harking back to what they had been talking about several minutes ago, "That's your officers' job, not yours. Nor can you control every aspect of the battle plan. There are too many imponderables, too many loose cannons, too many fingers of fate."

"What do you see as the commander's job?" asked Rix, fascinated despite his reservations, or because of them.

"To have a vision no one else has ever had before," said Grandys, holding up a thick finger. He raised a second finger. "To lead by example, so forcefully that your men will follow you anywhere." He studied his ring finger for a minute or so, then raised it as well. "To be a master of improvisation. No matter what the situation, to turn whatever is to hand to your advantage."

"What if you can't?"

"There's always a way."

"I don't see it," said Rix.

"Suppose you were to attack me now, while I'm unarmed. I left Maloch in my tent."

Grandys reached out lazily, plucked a blade from one of the

coarse yellow tussocks of razor grass and drew its edge across his unarmoured palm. A line of blood welled out. "With this I could sever your jugular before you realised I held a weapon."

He tore a long spine off one of the low thorn bushes scattered around the boulders. Milky sap oozed from the base of the spine. Grandys held it up.

"You wouldn't even see this in my hand, yet in under a second I could have it through your heart, your kidney, or any other vulnerable place that presented itself." He reversed the spine. "If I were to dab the white sap into your eye, it would burn it out of your head.

"Weapons lie in the most innocent of objects," Grandys went on, reflectively. "Any good general can design a battle plan. And once the plan is recognised, any good opponent can make a new plan to defeat the first. But how can they defeat an enemy who has no plan, who's so trained to improvise that he can turn any object, and any situation, to his advantage? They can't, and it drives them mad with frustration."

Grandys chuckled, lay back and closed his eyes.

"Besides," he said a few minutes later, "I thrive on being the underdog, on taking on foes with far greater armies in impregnable positions – *and destroying them.*"

"But even so, to attack such a mighty fortress with only a thousand raw recruits – why didn't you bring the rest?"

"If I had, I wouldn't be the underdog, would I?"

A minute later he was snoring as though he had not a worry in his opal-armoured head.

Rix eyed the razor grass, then Grandys' exposed throat. The armour had gaps there, where the muscles flexed. It was tempting, but the command spell still held him and he did not think he could ever break it. Was he bound to Grandys unto death?

Grandys roused at 1 p.m. "Get the men up. We march at one-thirty."

"You're attacking in full daylight?" said Rix. "We'll have no element of surprise."

"We don't need it," said Grandys, impatiently. "Besides, if we don't go now we won't be feasting in the Great Hall by dinner time."

He had to be insane, and there was nothing Rix could do.

He made sure the men were in their ranks, and all had their water bottles, rations, weapons, shields and helmets. You could never tell what unblooded men would leave behind, or forget to do. Grandys might not care about the little details, but Rix tried to think of everything.

Grandys raised his voice so all could hear him. "I lead the march, and the attack. We'll head down the track until we're just outside arrow-shot from the walls. On my signal, we charge the gates. Keep watch on me. I'll give new orders when we're close. March!"

They began to march out.

"That's the entirety of the plan?" said Rix. "But they'll see us. They'll be ready with archers and shriek-arrows, bombasts and grenadoes and fire-flitters, and all their other chymical weaponry we can't fight—"

"Weren't you listening?" said Grandys. He thumped Rix playfully on the shoulder and turned away.

This was going to go wrong. Disastrously wrong, and Rix would be stuck in the middle while a thousand poor, stupid kids were slaughtered. And he, leading the attack with Grandys, would be one of the first to die.

Marching in their ranks, they passed down the slope to the meadow and across until they were almost within range of the walls. Grandys raised his right arm. Everyone stopped.

Castle Rebroff looked even more formidable from here. It had towering granite walls, not cored with rubble but solid stone all the way through. The gates were made from many crisscrossing layers of hardwood, each layer reinforced with iron on both sides. The water in the moat was at least ten feet deep and the steep banks were bare, greasy clay that would be a nightmare to climb. How many of the men could swim? Few people in Hightspall could. And there were hundreds of guards on the walls, able to fire on the unprotected army from shelter, while Rochlis was said to have another thousand battle hardened troops inside.

"I am Axil Grandys," Grandys bellowed at the gates. "The Five

Herovians have come back from the dead. With might and magery I will take Castle Rebroff by nightfall. Surrender now or die, for I take no prisoners."

Several of the guards on the wall laughed, though the mirth soon died into an uneasy silence. Every Cythonian had been taught about Grandys and his impossibly daring deeds in the early days of the Two Hundred and Fifty Years War. Now the man himself had come back from the dead. Back from stone.

An archer fired an arrow, which soared out towards Grandys. He watched it fall, unmoved, until it smashed against his opalised chest.

"You cannot win," he said.

A guard let out a fearful cry. He was hastily dragged out of sight.

"No?" said Grandys. "Excellent. I hate surrenders. Charge!" He spurred his horse forward.

Rix had no choice but to go with him. The golem-like Syrten was on his left, on foot; the cadaverous Rufuss riding a long way to the right. Rix could not see Lirriam or Yulia, though he had no doubt they were there, if only to prove Grandys' initial words.

Arrows began to fall. Rix held his shield up but it only covered part of his body and his horse not at all. Behind him, men were screaming in agony, falling, dying. He did not look back.

A bombast came spinning through the air towards them. It was the size of a large beer barrel and packed with enough alchymical material to blow down a three-foot-thick wall – or kill several hundred soldiers if it landed among them. No Hightspaller had yet mastered the basis of its shattering power. The rare bombasts that did not go off on impact were liable to explode when anyone tried to open them.

Grandys spurred across until the bombast was flying directly for him. Yet again, Rix wondered if the Herovian was insane. If it exploded, not even he could survive it.

Grandys reached up with both hands as if to catch the bombast like a football. The impact drove him backwards out of the saddle and slammed him into the ground. Rix froze. The soldiers let out a great cry of dismay. Was Grandys dead? Had he broken his neck? Was the bombast about to explode?

He rolled over, bounced to his feet, then punched his right fist through the end of the bombast. Tearing out a thick fuse like a red chuck-lash, he raised the bombast high. Evidently he had rendered it harmless.

Grandys signalled to Syrten, who went lumbering across to intercept a second bombast in one arm, and then a third with the other. Dozens of arrows were fired at him, and many hit, but none could penetrate the thick opal encrustations that had been created by Lyf's own magery.

A fourth bombast, aimed higher, soared way over their heads and landed in the middle of the army, going off with a shattering blast and scattering men, and pieces of men, across a hundred yards of the meadow. Rix could not help himself. He looked back and the carnage was so terrible that he threw up on his saddle horn.

"On!" roared Grandys, waving Maloch above his head. "No setback can stop us. On!"

He sprang into the saddle and spurred on, holding the bombast under his left arm and Maloch with his right. Whether through sheer luck or the protective magery of Maloch, no arrow fell on him or his horse.

He calls the death of a hundred man a *setback*? Rix thought. He's a monster; and I'm following him, so what does that make me? But the command spell would not let him go.

He hurtled in Grandys' wake. No magery protected Rix now, and until a few days ago he had been Lyf's number one enemy, so every soldier on the wall would want the credit for killing him. His shield could not protect him from a side-on shot, and he expected to die with an arrow through the head or belly at any moment.

His horse, struck by three arrows at once, stumbled and went down. Rix barely heaved his feet from the stirrups before it hit the ground and rolled. Had he been trapped in the saddle it would have broken his pelvis, if not his backbone.

He got up, aching all over, and ran. Grandys was a hundred yards ahead, approaching the moat, beyond which was the great gate. But he wasn't stopping. He was spurring his horse on as though intending to jump the moat.

It wasn't possible. No horse could jump that distance.

And neither could Grandys. His horse was falling towards the water when Grandys scrambled up onto the saddle, his broad feet spread, and leapt forwards. His weight pushed the unfortunate horse down and it hit the grey water with a colossal splash. When it cleared Rix saw Grandys, who had landed halfway up the greasy clay slope, dig in his heels and drive himself upwards. Arrows were raining down around him, and breaking on his chest armour, but none hit any unarmoured place.

Away to the left, Syrten was lumbering towards the moat, converging on the gate with a bombast under each arm. Dozens of arrows shattered on his encrusted skin. As many more were stuck into the bombasts, quivering with each of Syrten's thumping footfalls. Fifty yards to the right, Rufuss was across the moat and climbing the wall like an armoured stick insect. He reached the top unharmed and began dealing death to the defenders with cold deliberation.

An arrow sliced across Rix's right arm and blood flooded out, but if he stopped to attend it the archers would pierce him with a hundred more. He leapt over the edge of the moat, skidding on his boot soles down the slippery clay towards the water, then dropped his shield. He was a strong swimmer and could go a reasonable distance bearing the weight of his sword, but carrying a shield was out of the question.

Now Syrten was running straight down the bank of the moat. Could he swim? Would he even float? Rix could not imagine it. Syrten ran into the water and disappeared in spray, as if he were intending to pound across the bottom and up the other side.

Rix sheathed his sword and dived deep, arms out in front of him. The water was deeper than he had thought, around fifteen feet. At least, at that depth, the force of the arrows would be spent.

He swam slowly, conserving his strength. He had to burst out of the water and scramble up the greasy slope in seconds or they would shoot him dead. The water was murky and he could not see a thing. He swam ten yards to his left, so the archers could not predict his exit point, and shot out.

Syrten was immediately ahead, driving upwards, his great weight forcing his square boots deep into the slippery slope and giving him purchase. Rix scrambled up behind him, crouched low to avoid the arrows, then in a moment of inspiration, thrust his fingers through Syrten's opaline belt.

Syrten did not appear to notice. Could he feel anything through that heavily encrusted skin? The driving thighs towed Rix up, and at the top he rolled away and ran to the shelter of the wall. Lirriam was walking calmly towards the wall, fifty yards to Rix's left. A dozen archers were shooting at her but she must have been protecting herself with magery, for the arrows were shattering in mid-air before they reached her.

"Get the bridge down, Ricinus," yelled Grandys, who was so close to the gate that the archers struggled to bear on him. "Syrten, here."

Syrten ran across, gave Grandys the two bombasts, then lurched, more golem-like than ever, across to the raised moat bridge. Lirriam was on its far side. The bridge stood vertically against the wall, held there by its lifting chains. They ran from the upper end of the bridge, fifty feet above him, across the wall and down to a treadmill-driven winch on the other side. There was no way to lower the bridge from outside.

"It can't be done," Rix said, cursing.

Without the bridge, the troops could not cross the moat, and when they stopped on the other side they would be cut down in minutes. The archers on the walls could then pick Rix and Grandys off at their leisure, and drop a bombast on Syrten's head if he could not be killed any other way.

"Get it down!" bellowed Grandys.

Rix ran across to the gates. Grandys was packing the bombasts against them.

"We can't release it," Rix panted. "The chains are out of reach."

Grandys clouted Rix out of the way, took the red fuses from a pocket, poked one end deep into a bombast and ran towards the vertical bridge, carrying it.

Where was Syrten? Rix could not see him until the timbers of the bridge began to creak and groan, when he caught an opaline flash from the gap between the bridge and the wall. Syrten had forced his way into the gap and was pushing with his massive legs, his back against the stone wall, trying to force the gate down.

The chains clanked and tightened; from the top of the wall Rix heard someone shout a warning. Syrten let out a wrenching groan. It sounded as though the strain was tearing him apart. One of his armoured feet burst through the boards of the bridge, then the other.

"That's not the way," said Grandys. "Out!"

He ran back to the gate, set down the bombast, struck sparks off his armoured chest with Maloch and ignited the three red fuses. Picking up one of the bombasts, he took careful aim and hurled it high above the wall. For a few seconds Rix thought it was going to fall back on them, but it plunged down, grazed the other side of the wall and struck something inside. A monumental explosion shook stones down around them and cleared the guards off the wall for fifty yards.

It must have destroyed the winch, for suddenly the chains were running. The bridge fell outwards with Syrten, a foolish expression on his swart face, still embedded through the planking to the knees. The bridge slammed down on the other side of the moat, driving him into the planking until he was stopped by his groin. He bellowed in agony.

"Down!" roared Grandys.

Rix threw himself behind a projection of the wall and wrapped his arms around his head as the remaining two bombasts exploded, sending earth, rocks, splinters and multi-coloured fire in all directions.

"Charge!" said Grandys.

His troops charged across the bridge, swerving around Syrten, who was trying to heave himself out of the planking.

"You!" said Grandys to Rix. "Time to earn your keep. With me."

They charged the breach together. Most of the gate was gone, just a few splintered timbers still hanging from the left-hand side, and there were no live guards to be seen. Grandys and Rix scrambled through, leaping over rubble and stone, logs and bodies. Then they were faced with a dozen of the enemy – more. They were coming from everywhere.

A guard came at Rix from the left. He cut him down with a wild sweep to the neck and kept swinging to take down the fellow next to him. On his right, Grandys was wreaking havoc with Maloch. Rix had never seen such sword work, or such bloody death at close quarters. Lirriam was directly behind, killing gleefully, protected by magery that deflected both arrows and sword blows.

They cut and hacked their way for several dozen yards until they were surrounded by enemy. Rix's sword arm was already tiring. The butchery was horrific but if he stopped for a second he would die.

"On!" said Grandys, his eyes wild with exhilaration. "Ah, this is living!"

As if to prove the point, he hacked an enemy soldier down, then another.

The enemy counterattacked, forming an impenetrable wall ahead of them. Suddenly Grandys, struck by many weapons at once, faltered. His blows were failing to make impact; the enemy were closing in around, a dozen of them attacking him at once. Not even he could survive that.

Then Syrten was behind them, pushing between them, driving forwards on his own, bursting through the enemy's shield wall and trampling them underfoot. Yulia came after, stone-faced, striking her opponents down with precise thrusts of a small black rapier. Rix followed Syrten, and between the four of them the enemy gave.

Grandys' army came surging through the gap, and though few of them were a match for Rochlis's experienced men, the Cythonians were so demoralised by the swift destruction of their unbreachable gate, by the appearance of the Five Heroes who had brought Cythe down in the first place, and their forbidden magery, that they turned and ran.

"To me," bellowed a heavyset, broad-faced fellow in the uniform of a Cythonian general. "Drive them out the gates and into the ditch."

"That's Rochlis," said Grandys. "I want him alive."

He hurtled through the ranks of the enemy, knocking them down to right and left, and up the slope to where General Rochlis stood. Rochlis fought as bravely as any man, but he was outmatched, and Rix's heart went out to the fellow. He'd seen enough bloodshed today, and caused enough, to last him a lifetime.

A blow from Syrten's armoured fist brought Rochlis down.

Grandys heaved the general above his head and shook him like a dog with a rat.

"It's over! Castle Rebroff is mine."

He dropped the general on his face and turned to Rix. "I always get what I want, Rixium. Remember that and you'll come to no harm."

And you don't give a damn about Hightspall, Rix thought. You're the most dangerous man in the world and someone has to stop you.

If any man can.

CHAPTER 77

Tali rounded a corner of the fortress wall and stopped dead. Tobry and Holm were strolling along the wall, chatting as though they weren't condemned traitors with a reward for their severed heads. She ran down to them, throwing her arms out to embrace Tobry, then froze.

"Tobry, Holm? What are you doing here? The chancellor will kill you."

She had taken to walking along the top of the escarpment wall, because walking helped her to think. And she had much to think about; not least, what Lyf was up to. There had been no news of him since he fled Glimmering, which allowed her worries free rein. Three times she had tried to spy on him, and three times she had failed. Was he blocking her?

Tobry sidestepped her, took her right hand in his and released it at once. He had not forgiven her for using her healing blood on him. She, in turn, had felt her love die when he had attacked her as a caitsthe. Tobry would always be a friend but there could be no more.

"Not when he hears my plan," said Tobry, answering her previous question.

"What plan? What's going on?"

Tobry and Holm exchanged glances.

"Can't talk about it yet," said Tobry.

"Why did you come back? What if there's another mutiny?"

"Don't be silly," said Holm. "All the plotters are dead."

"Besides," said Tobry, "the chancellor has two hundred guards and servants, and if there's anyone who knows how to control a fortress, he does. If there was one whisper of a plot his spies would tell him about it, and the plotters' bodies would be dangling from the battle tower within the hour."

Tali felt foolish for having asked. "Well, there's still a price on your head – both your heads."

"I *really* think you should tell her," Holm murmured. "Tali has a right to know."

"If it involves you," said Tali, hands on her hips, "I damn well do."

"I can't," said Tobry.

"Is it dangerous?"

Again that exchange of glances.

"There are certain risks," said Tobry.

"*Certain risks!* You sound like one of the chancellor's war advisors. This is me you're talking to. The woman who—" She couldn't say it; it wasn't true any more.

"Loved you?" Holm said helpfully.

"Who asked you to interfere?" she snapped. "Go away."

Holm spread his hands as if to say, *I did my best*. He gave Tobry another of those enigmatic looks and continued along the wall.

"What kind of risks?" said Tali.

"I can't talk about it yet. Sorry."

"Not as sorry as you're going to be."

"Why?" he said wryly. "Are you going to cut me open again?"

"I wouldn't waste my healing blood on you! Now clear out. I've got important things to think about. *Things that matter.*"

"Don't be like that," said Tobry. "I've had a hard time of it on the run."

"And I haven't?" said Tali, not disposed to forgive him that easily. "The chancellor could decide to hack the pearl out any day now. Lyf is also after me, and back at Glimmering I revealed myself to Grandys—"

His tanned face went white. "You did what?"

She related the incident. Tobry gripped her by the shoulders. "This is bad, bad. I wish you hadn't done that."

"And then there's Rix."

"What's happened to him? I assumed he'd be here."

"But ... how could you not know?"

"Know *what*?"

"Grandys used a command spell at Glimmering and ordered Rix follow him. Surely you knew that?"

No – Tobry had dived off the cliff to escape, *before* Grandys took Rix. And Holm hadn't been there either – he had been keeping out of sight of the chancellor.

"Holm heard that the chancellor had put a price on our heads," said Tobry, "but we haven't heard any other news. What's going on?"

"Grandys has brought back the other four Heroes, and he's like a ravening wolf. He killed the lord of Swire, formed an army of villagers then took Castle Rebroff in a couple of hours and put everyone to the sword. He's called—"

"He captured Castle Rebroff with *an army of villagers*?" said Tobry. "But ... it's supposed to be impregnable." He stared over the wall, shivering. "This is bad."

"Grandys has put out a call for every Herovian in the land to rise in rebellion and flock to his banner," said Tali. "And according to the chancellor's spies, thousands have come out of hiding already, bearing their ancient house arms."

"Martial training is part of Herovian culture, for both girls and boys, from the time they can walk. They're formidable fighters."

"The chancellor sent envoys to Grandys. He sent their severed heads back in a bag. What does he want, Tobry?"

"What the Herovians ever wanted. Their Promised Realm, all to themselves."

"They're greatly outnumbered by Hightspallers, and Cythonians," said Tali.

"Maybe Grandys believes a Herovian uprising can destroy both enemies," said Tobry. "And take the prize for himself."

"You're shivering. Here, take my coat."

"It would hardly fit. I'm all right. I've suffered worse. Let's walk."

She went to slip her arm through his, then remembered that they didn't do that any more. They turned the corner and headed down the high wall that ran along the escarpment.

"Grandys built this place for his daughter," said Tali. "He must have known it well, and maybe it's important to him, too. Do you think he'll come here?"

"Yes. Sooner or later."

"If Lyf's best general couldn't defend Castle Rebroff, how can we defend Garramide?"

"Maybe we can't."

She looked down the escarpment, at the snow on the leaves of the forest trees. From this angle she could see nothing but forest and mountains. There was not a sign that humanity existed.

Tali wished they'd all go away and take their stupid fights with them. Damn the Herovians, and damn the Five Heroes. They had cheated and lied to start the first war, and two thousand years later innocent people were still dying. It had to be stopped.

"I've been thinking about Grandys and Maloch," she said. "I'm starting to think this business was set in motion a long time ago."

"What do you mean?"

"I don't think Maloch was ever Rix's. Nor do I think it was ever protecting him."

"I've heard it said that the sword contained an enchantment to protect Grandys, *and his direct descendants*."

"But he had no descendants. He was sterile."

"What are you getting at?"

"The enchantment was designed to protect one man, Grandys himself."

"And from the moment Rix took up Maloch," said Tobry, "it was leading him: to the Crag, to the wrythen, to Garramide, to the Abysm."

"So what happens if he wins?"

"Hightspall is finished."

"And what happens if Lyf wins?"

"Hightspall is finished. Which is why I'm going ahead with my plan."

"Why?"

"Because I'm going to die, Tali, and it won't be long. The shifter madness is creeping nearer; I can see it from the corner of my eye. I'm not going through what my grandfather suffered, and I'm not inflicting it on anyone else either."

Before Tali could reply, a trio of guards advanced towards them along the wall from the left, and another pair appeared on the right.

"Then why did you come back?" said Tali.

CHAPTER 78

"Ahh! That was glorious," said Grandys after Castle Rebroff had been secured. "I love the smell of blood on the battlefield. It makes me feel so alive."

Rix's mood broke. He had fought beside the man like a barbarian of old, glorying in his own ability to face seasoned warriors, yet survive. He had felt the euphoria of fighting against impossible odds, of being part of a team that had pulled off an astonishing victory.

Now vomit rose up the back of his throat as he walked past the heaps of butchered men. Men like himself. Good, decent men, most of them, he felt sure. They were the enemy, but had they deserved to die this way?

Grandys was obsessed by winning, by proving himself the best, over and again, and war was just a game, one where his strength and magery gave him an unfair advantage. He did not care how many men died, on the enemy's side or his own. The more bloodshed, the better he liked it, and his own men were just ciphers. All that mattered was that he prevail where no one else could have.

No, there had to be more to it. Grandys was here for a reason. What he really wanted was the Promised Realm – though how did he plan to set it up? There was only one way to find out; by spying on him.

Rix fought the spell and felt it slip a little, though it still bound him. Would it allow him to spy on Grandys? Or would it lure him in, only to betray him?

"Hoy, you!" Grandys said to a tall young fellow from the town of Swire, a lad who could not have been more than sixteen. "I've got a job for you. Come in here."

Grandys put an arm around the young man's shoulders and led him into the Great Hall. Rix followed, curious to know what he was up to. He looked around the hall and lost his breath for a few seconds.

Though the enemy had only held Rebroff for a month, the hall had been beautifully decorated in the Cythonian manner, with paintings large and small, wall carvings, vases and sculpture, and simple but exquisitely carved tables and chairs. Their art was vital to them and Rix wanted to see more of it.

He turned, gazing in wonder at a wall sculpture in a niche, a leaning, weathered tree carved from stone. It was astonishing.

Crash! Crash!

Rix turned as Grandys thrust Maloch through a lovely painted vase. Two others like it lay shattered on the floor.

"What are you doing?" Rix cried.

"Disgusting, decadent rubbish," said Grandys, smashing another vase, and another. He tore a tapestry off the wall, a woodland scene in scarlet, blue and gold that must have taken a team of weavers months. He threw it over a table and hacked it to pieces.

"Get a gang in here, lad," said Grandys, "and destroy the lot. Take nothing; leave nothing; hide nothing. Understood?"

"Yes, Lord Grandys," the boy whispered.

"You know what happens to people who disobey me, don't you?"

"Yes, Lord."

"Of course you do," said Grandys, smiling menacingly. "Run! The Great Hall must be cleared before the feast, and that's only two hours away."

The boy ran. Rix went up to Grandys.

"Lord," he said, though the title was bitter in his mouth, "these are priceless works of art."

A thin smile stretched Grandys' bloated lips. "You think so? You know about art?"

"Yes, I do. And I—"

The blow came out of nowhere, driving so hard into Rix's belly that the air was expelled from his lungs. He hit the floor and lay there, gasping. In all his life he had never taken such a blow. It felt as though a stone pile-driver had been driven into him.

Grandys picked up Rix's sword, which had gone skidding from his scabbard, then methodically smashed every pot, vase and sculpture in the Great Hall, before tossing it back at Rix's face. He stopped it with his dead hand, only inches away.

The spell slipped a little more. Damn you, Grandys. I'm not serving you a minute longer. Again Rix tried to break the command, but it had been created with magery and would not release him.

"There's only one sort of art worth having," said Grandys. "Herovian art is simple, hand-made, abjuring all polish and ornamentation. Once the enemy are vanquished, which will not take me long, all art in Hightspall save our own will be destroyed."

He looked down at Rix's furious, impotent face and laughed.

"I'm going to put you in charge of its destruction – assuming I allow you to live that long."

All the art in the Great Hall had been smashed, hacked, burned or defiled by the time the feast was ready. The last tragic threads and shards were being barrowed out and dumped in a corner of the castle yard as Grandys' victorious troops marched in.

At least, the elite among them, those of Herovian descent. The common soldiers were holding their own feast out in the yard, by a bonfire fuelled by the furniture from Castle Rebroff. Grandys would allow nothing to remain that had been made by the enemy – save the drink in the cellars.

Nor their cooks, serving gear or eating utensils. The victors would feast the Herovian way, on beasts roasted over an open fire and vegetables cooked in the coals. The only implement permitted was a cutting knife. All eating was done with the fingers.

And all drinking, of which there was a great deal, was from two-handled tankards brought with them. They held half a gallon each and passed continually along the tables, and woe to any man who handed on the tankard untasted.

"You!" bellowed Grandys at a thin, unhealthy looking fellow who had only pretended to sip, then passed the tankard on. Grandys' eyes were everywhere and nothing escaped him. "You didn't drink."

"Lord," the man protested. "I sipped, I really did. But I got a bad liver – the pain, it's chronic—"

Grandys stalked across and dragged the fellow up by the front. "Damn your liver. Are you Herovian or not?"

"Yes, Lord. You can ask anyone."

"A Herovian soldier drinks with his comrades. To do otherwise is an insult to every man who fell today. Hold him down."

The unfortunate man was pinned down while a funnel was fetched. A flagon of red wine was poured down his throat and he was dragged into a corner, where he twitched for a while, then slumped, unconscious or dead. It didn't matter to Grandys either way. Not even his own people were immune from his brutality.

All day Rix had been trying to make allowances. The Cythonians had done equally terrible things, he knew. Worse things, perhaps, and if they won, or if the war dragged on for years or even centuries, as the first war had done, it would ruin Hightspall. Perhaps it was for the best if Grandys, swine though he was, had a swift and total victory. The destruction would surely be less in the long run.

But when he ordered the best looking of the enemy dead brought in and their bodies hacked and despoiled in the middle of the Great Hall, and when the helpless prisoners were tormented for the amusement of the Five Heroes, Rix could endure no more.

"Enough!" he cried. "What are you, Grandys? A man or an animal?"

Grandys turned, his bloated face red from drink. His mouth set in a snarl. "Are you speaking to me?"

"You know I am," said Rix, shaking inwardly but determined not to back down. "Leave them alone. If you must fight, pick on someone your own size."

"Since you're my only living descendant," said Grandys, "and you fought beside me with courage and skill, I'll assume you can't hold your drink. Sit down, have another mug and keep your mouth shut."

It was a way of saving face for both of them, and Rix wasn't having it.

"As it happens," he said through his teeth, "I can hold my drink. Better than you can, I'm thinking. Leave the prisoners be."

"Why?" said Grandys coldly. "Are you a friend of the enemy? *Or are you in their pay?*"

The room went still. The accusations were insults no man could tolerate.

Rix had no choice now. He had to fight Grandys, bare-handed. And though he had never lost such a fight, he knew he was going to lose this one. There was not a man in the Great Hall who would back him against the First of the Five Heroes. Whatever they thought of Grandys, deep down, he was their master and they would support him all the way.

Rix drew his sword and put it on the table in full view, so everyone could see he was unarmed. His eyes met Grandys', challenging him to do the same, though there was no reason to assume he would. Grandys might draw Maloch and hack Rix to pieces. He might do anything.

But not this time.

Grandys laid down his own sword and stepped forwards. He had taken off his boots at the beginning of the feast, but even in bare feet he was inches taller than Rix, and broader. He had drunk an enormous amount of wine, at least a gallon, enough to put a normal man on his back.

But Grandys was no normal man. The only symptoms Rix noticed were a slowness to his speech and a slight unsteadiness on his feet. There was still stone in him, and perhaps it stiffened him in other ways, too. The battle had exhausted Rix, yet Grandys had seemed as strong and energetic at the end as he had been at the beginning. Rix had to win the bout quickly, or Grandys would wear him down and batter him to death.

He glories in being unpredictable, Rix thought, so I must do the same. What's the most unpredictable way to start the bout? Don't think about it, or his magery might read it. Just do it.

Grandys stepped forwards, raising his fists. Rix did too, alternately watching Grandys' fists, then his eyes. The eyes often gave a feint away. Grandys was doing the same. Rix gave a little, stifled jab with his right, and at the same time glanced down at Grandys' groin, then away.

Grandys threw his right leg forward and bent the knee, instinctively trying to protect his groin, and Rix jammed his boot heel down on Grandys' bare toes with all his weight, shattering the opal armour and grinding it into flesh and bone. Grandys reared back, his teeth bared, and Rix brought his left hand up from floor level in an uppercut that would have knocked any normal man onto his back, unconscious.

Grandys rocked backwards, his eyes glazed, and for several seconds Rix thought he was going to topple. But he remained on his feet and Rix made his fatal mistake. He acted honourably to a man who lacked all honour.

He should have gone on the attack, battering Grandys about the head until he fell senseless. Foolishly, Rix allowed him a few seconds to recover.

He was watching Grandys' fists when he should have been checking his feet. Grandys' right foot struck Rix in the groin so hard that tears burst from his eyes. Before he could see again, Grandys punched him in the mouth, the nose, the throat, then so hard over the heart that it missed a number of beats and for several seconds he wasn't sure it was going to start again. Rix swayed like a drunken man, took another blow to the chin, landed flat on his back and could not get up.

He lay there, expecting to die. Every man in the Great Hall was on his feet, and it was clear that half of them wanted to see Grandys finish Rix. Lirriam was licking her plump lips. Rufuss's eyes pierced Rix like black beams.

Grandys might have killed Rix, had the whim taken him. Perhaps he didn't know what he was going to do until he did it. But after a minute or two he let out a roar of laughter and hauled Rix to his feet.

"Well done, Ricinus," he said clapping him on the back and nearly driving Rix's backbone through his lower intestine. "Stamp on my toes – I'll make an innovator of you yet. If I don't kill you first."

He picked up Maloch and raised it. Again the room held its breath.

"What are you doing?" said Rix, thinking that he was going to die after all.

"Promoting you to my first lieutenant, of course."

He tapped Rix on the right shoulder with the blade, then added quietly, "Clearly my command spell has been slipping. You won't find this one so easy to fight. Back to your bench now, lad, and we'll toast your promotion with another flagon."

No sooner than Rix had regained his seat than Grandys walked up to the first prisoner, General Rochlis, put Maloch's tip against his chest and, ever so slowly, pushed it in. He watched Rochlis die, then strolled around the hall, putting the remaining prisoners to death with no more concern than if he had been dicing carrots. After each man he put down, Grandys turned to study the expression on Rix's face.

Rix tried to remain impassive, but inside he was screaming in outrage. Grandys was a brilliant, ruthless leader, but he was thoroughly evil and would not rest until he had brought Rix down to his own level.

CHAPTER 79

Tali edged through the door into the chancellor's quarters and slipped behind the floor-to-ceiling drapes. She had to know what he was going to do to Tobry and Holm.

"You're condemned men," said the chancellor, when they were brought before his table, in rattling chains. "Is there anything you'd like to say before I order your execution for treason?"

"I've got a plan to deal with Grandys," said Tobry.

"I've never liked you, Lagger—" began the chancellor.

"So *that* explains why you ordered me thrown from the top of Rix's tower," Tobry said drily. "All this time I've been trying to work it out."

Tobry, don't! You've no idea what a vengeful man he is. But Tali had to admire his composure in the face of death. Her knees would barely hold her up.

"How *did* you survive?" said the chancellor. "Never mind. The fact that you did, and even managed to escape so thorough a hunt as Lyf had set for you, suggests that there's more to you than I'd imagined."

"And now your *tediously conventional* plans have failed so dismally, you're prepared to clutch at the most desperate straws to get yourself out of trouble."

"Speaking as one condemned man to *two* others," said Holm, "the noose is tightening every minute. If you hope to slip it, you'd better get on with it."

"You're overly bold for a humble clock attendant," said the chancellor.

"And you've become unwontedly timid since you fled Caulderon, Chancellor. Tell him the plan, Tobry."

"I'm going to join Grandys' army, in the guise of a Herovian, then shift to a caitsthe after he's gone to bed and claw his heart out."

"No!" cried Tali, forgetting herself.

A guard hauled her out from behind the drape.

"What the hell are you doing here?" growled the chancellor.

"Whatever you're planning to do to them, I've a right to know," she said defiantly.

"You've a right to know nothing. You're an interfering little know-it-all."

Tali reached out to Tobry. "Tobry, you can't disguise yourself from Grandys. At Glimmering, he picked that you were a shifter in seconds. He'll put you straight to death."

"Not if I disguise myself with magery," said Tobry.

"He's got two ebony pearls, remember? And even if you could

fool him, you can't fool Maloch. It knows you. Chancellor," said Tali. "Don't let him do it. It's suicide."

"You're appealing to me now?" said the chancellor. "What a fruity irony."

"I can heal Tobry," said Rannilt's shrill little voice from the other side of the room. "Let me try."

"Guard!" bellowed the chancellor. "How did that brat get in?"

"I don't know, Chancellor," said the guard, "but she didn't come through the door."

"How am I supposed to discuss secret strategies when half the fortress is lurking behind the drapes?"

"I don't know, Chancellor."

"Put the little twerp out. Don't damage her."

The guard gave the chancellor a reproachful look and picked Rannilt up by the scruff of the neck and the seat of her pants.

"I can heal Tobry, I can heal Tobry!" she wailed, kicking her thin legs and arms.

"Rannilt, you can't," said Tali. "You lost your gift after Lyf stole power from you in the caverns. Your blood doesn't heal any more."

The guard took her out, her cries dwindling down the hall.

"Well?" said Tobry, after a considerable silence.

"Well what?" said the chancellor.

"Will you allow me out, to try and kill Grandys?"

"No."

"Why not?"

"To win the aftermath I'm going to need a mighty army, but my forces are being eaten away by desertion to Grandys. I can't strike at him until I've rebuilt my army, or defeating him will merely give victory to Lyf.

"I've got a better plan," the chancellor said, leaning back in his chair. "Let Grandys turn the war our way first. Then you can kill him, *shifter*."

CHAPTER 80

Rix tightened his defiance of the command spell until it hurt, then crawled along the dusty ceiling beam until he was above Grandys' bedchamber. If he failed, or the spell betrayed him, he would die.

A few minutes ago, an unobtrusive little man had given the password to the guards outside Grandys' room, and slipped inside. Rix had seen the man before and felt sure he was a spy.

What was Grandys really up to? There was an implacable purpose behind his bloody ruthlessness, and it had to do with the Herovian goal of reaching their Promised Realm. But how were they to get to it? And what did that mean for Hightspall?

The ceiling plaster was old and cracked. Not cracked enough for Rix to see into the bedchamber, though he might be able to hear. He lowered his ear to the surface, but heard not a sound.

Everything was so thickly coated with dust here that even his gentle movements had stirred it up. The dust was tickling the back of his nose. He suppressed a sneeze and kept very still, knowing that his weight on the beam could be enough to crack the plaster, and that would give him away at once.

"There's *another* ebony pearl?" said Grandys.

"Yes, Lord Grandys," said the spy. "My sources tell me that there are five, and it is the fifth."

"A fifth! And the way magery is failing, I'm soon going to need it."

So Grandys' magery was also failing. That was the best news Rix had heard since Glimmering. The command spell must be weakening too, and if he fought it hard enough he might be able to break it again. But this time he would be more careful; he would not reveal that he had done so.

"Where do they come from?" said Grandys.

"Some magians say that ebony pearls just happened," said the spy, "that they're a freak of nature. Others believe that Lyf manipulated the lost king-magery so the pearls would form in suitable hosts—"

"Suitable hosts?"

"Pale slaves—"

"How can such priceless artefacts form in a people so unworthy?" Grandys cried.

"I cannot say, my Lord."

"Which Pale slaves?"

"Certain young females. Unusual Pale, you can be sure, though we only have the name of one."

"How did you learn this name?"

"It was mentioned at the trial of Lord and Lady Ricinus, Lord."

Grandys clenched a fist. "Lady Ricinus was the mother of my troublesome lieutenant. A noble Herovian, and she was hanged and drawn on her palace gates by this miserable chancellor. He must be put down. And the name of this Pale?"

"Iusia vi Torgrist, Lord. Lady Ricinus killed her and took her pearl ten years ago."

"Vi Torgrist, vi Torgrist? Where have I heard that name recently?"

"It's an ancient house," said the spy.

"*I know*!" snapped Grandys. "The founding family came on the Second Fleet."

"But the house is long extinct in Hightspall. It only survives in the Pale."

"Tell me about the fifth pearl."

"It has not yet been harvested from its host."

"Why not?"

"Ebony pearls take many years to grow and mature. They can only be harvested from the host after she comes of age."

"So the development of the pearl is linked to the development and maturity of the host," said Grandys. "Go on."

"My sources say the fifth pearl is the strongest of all. It's been called the master pearl."

"The *master* pearl. To the nub: who is the host?"

"A Pale who escaped from Cython. As far as I can discover, the only people who know her name are Lyf and the chancellor. They're both after it, of course."

"But the host has eluded them. The pearl must have given her exceptional gifts."

"Quite so, Lord," said the spy. "Will that be all?"

"For the moment."

Rix heard the door open and close. Then it opened again.

"You heard all that?" Grandys said quietly.

"Yes," said Lirriam. "Can you name the Pale?"

Grandys did not answer.

"Only two have escaped from Cython," Lirriam went on, slowly, as though assembling lines of evidence, "and one was a child who could not host a mature pearl. Therefore it has to be the other, Tali vi Torgrist. She gave evidence about the murder of her mother at the trial of Lady Ricinus. *Which means that pearls must be familial.*"

"I'm remembering something," said Grandys.

"About the Pale?"

"No, from my crystal dreaming, before Maloch woke me in the Abysm. I was dreaming about Tirnan Twil."

"What about it?" Lirriam said sharply.

"When the gauntlings burned Tirnan Twil, I dreamed that a Pale woman was there."

"So what?"

"If Tali is the only adult Pale to have escaped, it must have been her. And if she has the fifth pearl, surely she had the magery to defend Tirnan Twil. But she did not act. Why not?"

"Perhaps she doesn't know how to use her power."

"It was her!" cried Grandys.

"You're beginning to sound obsessed," Lirriam said with a hint of a sneer.

"The small blonde Pale who refused me at Glimmering-by-the-Water. Before that she cried out. She was distraught at something I'd done. What, *what?*"

"You *are* obsessed with her," said Lirriam. "Don't let yet another woman impair your judgement."

"No, this is monstrous!" said Grandys. "It was when I tried to kill the shifter, the mongrel who dived over the cliff and escaped. She cried out in fear for a filthy shifter."

"Are you saying that Tali held back her magery for *him*?"

"Yes! Tirnan Twil was destroyed because she's a despicable shifter lover, and when I find her, I'll have her for it."

"And the pearl," said Lirriam. "Don't forget what's important here."

Rix's next two spying missions revealed nothing. Was Grandys onto him, and allowing him to compromise himself ever more deeply? If Grandys was, his wrath would be terrible. But Rix could not stop now. He went back for a fourth evening, and this time found a tiny hole that allowed him to see a small part of the bedchamber.

"What do you mean, Tali can't be found?" said Grandys, stalking back and forth, Maloch in one hand, wine jug in the other. "We know she left Glimmering with the chancellor's party."

He hacked a chunk out of the windowsill in his fury. His magery had failed to locate her and he'd reluctantly enlisted the assistance of Lirriam and Rufuss, whose command of sorcery, while not as powerful as his own, had certain advantages in subtlety. He had not wanted to; he did not trust either of them, and especially not Rufuss, whose opalisation had further damaged an already unstable mind.

"She's been hidden with powerful magery," said Lirriam. "Under such concealment, she could have gone anywhere and we wouldn't know."

"The chancellor knows she bears the pearl," said Grandys. "Do you think for one minute that he'll let her out of his sight? I'll bet he has her at Garramide."

"If he does, whoever hid her has done it with rare skill."

"It'll be the chief magian," said Rufuss. "What's his name?"

No one knew.

"It wouldn't be hard to take Garramide," said Lirriam.

"We're not going near it," said Grandys in a tone that brooked no argument.

"Why not?" said Rufuss.

"I built it for a purpose—"

"Your *adopted* daughter has been dead 1950 years," she sneered.

"But my purpose has not yet come to completion," Grandys said coldly. "If we attack Garramide, the chancellor might destroy the place rather than surrender. He's a spiteful little man."

"I was wondering when you would remember our noble purpose," said Yulia. Rix started and nearly fell. He had not realised she was there. "I thought you'd lost sight of it completely, in your ceaseless attempts to prove yourself by slaughtering everyone who stands in your way."

"I haven't lost sight of it," Grandys growled.

"I hope not. This land is ours by right – a right laid down in the *Immortal Text*."

"Why do you think I'm fighting for it?"

"For the joy of killing," she said coldly.

"Why are recruits flocking to us by the thousand?" said Grandys. "Why do the enemy cower in terror when they hear we're coming? Why is Lyf hiding in Caulderon? Because of my name, Yulia!" He hacked into the windowsill again. "My name and reputation. Once they're established, I'll continue with our noble purpose."

"They *are* established," said Yulia. "Two thousand years ago, we came here to create the Promised Realm, and we failed. Why was that?"

Rix sat up. What did she mean by *create* the Promised Realm.

"Because the wrythen petrified us," Grandys said sullenly.

"That's not the real reason, and you know it. We failed because you acted like the brute and sadist you are."

"Lyf had to die. There was no other way to get the king-magery. And without it, we could not create the Promised Realm."

"You didn't have to hack his feet off. You didn't have to inflict all the pain and suffering on him you could. You didn't have to carry out all those massacres, or destroy every precious item of Cythe's great civilisation."

"They had to go. What does it matter?"

"It matters," said Yulia, and Rix could tell she was speaking between her clenched teeth, "because your viciousness brought out something in Lyf he never knew he had. That's how the departing king-magery created his undying wrythen. That's where he found the strength to hunt us down and turn us to opal. That gave him the burning urge to vengeance that's brought him, and his people, all the way down the aeons to today, and his boot across the throat of our land. It matters because your failure lost us the Promised Realm."

"It's not lost," said Grandys, defensively. "Just delayed."

"Then delay no longer. You swore a binding oath to do this. Do it now."

"To tear Hightspall down and reshape the island into the Promised Realm, I have to have king-magery. Nothing else will do."

Tear Hightspall down? Reshape the island? Did Grandys mean to destroy everything in Hightspall and create the Promised Realm from scratch? This was worse than Rix had imagined. Worse than he *could* have imagined. And it raised an even more troubling problem, though he could not bring it to mind.

"Then get it," said Yulia.

"I will – just as soon as I get Lyf's two pearls, and the master pearl."

"Take the master pearl first," said Lirriam.

"It won't be easy to lure the craven dog of a chancellor from his kennel," said Grandys.

"It will if we move to all-out war."

"Go on."

"Were we to wage war with the same ferocity that we used to take Rebroff," said Lirriam, "we could control Lakeland, Fennery and Gordion within a week. The chancellor couldn't hide in Garramide then – he'd be too afraid we'd sweep all the way south and take Caulderon back."

"Especially if I drop hints to his spies that I'm planning to," said Grandys. "He'll have to come out of his lair then, and he'll want Tali close by, in case he needs to take the pearl for himself. As soon as he moves, I'll take an elite raiding party, capture his chief magian and force him to reveal Tali."

"What if he won't?"

"I'll squeeze him until his eyeballs pop. There aren't many men I can't break, Lirriam."

"I can break them all," said Lirriam, smoothing her hands over the curve of her belly.

He scowled and rubbed his bloodshot eyes. "Ahh, I do need war."

"With all this feasting and lazing around," said Lirriam provocatively, "you look a wreck."

"But my armies are far smaller than Lyf's," said Grandys, testing her. "And he holds very strong positions."

"Just the way we like it." The blood lust in his eyes was reflected in her own.

"Call the men together. We march tonight – to exterminate the enemy in the north and destroy all his works. Then, once we have the remaining pearls, we recover the lost king-magery and create our Promised Realm at last."

A cold wave passed through Rix's head and down into his middle. Grandys did not understand what king-magery was, or how it worked. He assumed it was just another form of magery, an incredibly powerful tool that could be used for any purpose. But it wasn't.

Rix knew, because Tali and Holm had told him, that king-magery was fundamentally a healing force that could not safely be used in any other way. If it were twisted to destructive purposes, such as tearing the land down and rebuilding it, the consequences for Hightspall could be dire.

Rix had no choice now. He had to break the command spell, take Grandys on, and kill him. It was the only way Hightspall could be saved.

CHAPTER 81

"Grandys has taken Lakeland and Fennery," said the chancellor, agitatedly. "Now he's marching on Gordion. What's he going to do next?"

He'll come for me, Tali thought. He wants revenge for Tirnan Twil, he wants my pearl, and he's not a patient man.

His violent onslaught on the north after a week of peace had taken everyone by surprise, including Lyf. Grandys, with his unbeatable sword, his combination of old and new magery, his brilliantly unpredictable leadership and utter ruthlessness, had one astounding victory after another. The survivors of Lyf's routed armies were retreating towards Cauldfron as fast as they could go, and the chancellor was starting to panic.

Tali was too. No one understood Grandys, and no one knew what he would do next. She had a mental flash of the envoys' heads rolling across the table. He might turn up here tonight and there was no reasoning with him, no fighting him either. He would simply have his way.

"If the passes are clear of snow, it's only a day's march over the mountains from Gordion to Cauldfron," said Holm, answering the chancellor's question. "He could do another of those overnight forced marches and be at the gates of the city at daybreak tomorrow. If he chose to, he could attack Cauldfron before we heard he was on his way."

"He won't find it easy to win," said the chancellor, sounding like a man trying to convince himself. "Capturing a great city isn't like taking a fortress defended by a thousand soldiers, or beating an army out on the open plain. Lyf's got fifty thousand troops in Cauldfron and they're well dug in. Not even Grandys could take it with a ragtag army of ten thousand."

"He could take *part* of it, though," said Tobry. "With the lake walls destroyed by the tidal wave it's a difficult city to defend."

"And most of the people still live there," said Holm. "If he took the southern shanty towns, say, then called on the people to rise in rebellion, he could make things awkward for Lyf."

It's coming, Tali thought. The end of the Pale is coming and I'm trapped here where I can't do anything about it. I've got to spy on Lyf again, tonight.

The chancellor gnawed a reddened knuckle. "And I'm stuck in Garramide. Whatever possessed me to come here?"

"How were you to know Grandys would move so fast, and have such brilliant victories?" said Tali.

"Any student of history might have predicted—" began Tobry.

"Thank you, shifter!" the chancellor snapped. "You're here on tolerance and mine is limited."

"But he's right," said Holm. "Grandys is doing exactly what he did before, when . . ."

"When he was alive?" said Tali.

"I don't know that he ever died, exactly . . ."

"My tutors in Cython taught me that—"

"What would your tutors know?" said the chancellor. "The Pale went to Cython as children."

"*Went* isn't the word I'd use," Tali said coldly. "They were given to the enemy as child hostages. *And never ransomed*. Hightspall abandoned its noble children, then blackened their name to cover its own shame."

"Grandys started the first war with a brilliant, ruthless stroke," the chancellor said, ignoring her outburst. "His armies were vastly outnumbered by the enemy, yet he had victory upon victory. No one could predict what he would do next because he didn't know himself."

"Then how come the war went on for two hundred and fifty years?" said Tali.

"Didn't your tutors explain that?" the chancellor said nastily. "A decade after the war began, Lyf and the other four Heroes all disappeared within a few months, and the war turned bad. They were like demi-gods by then, and their disappearance was a shattering blow to morale."

"No one ever discovered what had happened to the Five Heroes," said Tobry, "but everyone knew the enemy had done it."

"To lose Grandys was bad enough," said the chancellor. "But to lose the other four Heroes when they were all on high alert, was devastating. It meant that no one was safe."

"Hightspall had no one fit for command," said Tobry. "The Five Heroes had been too dominant for too long, and they had wanted all the glory for themselves. The younger officers tried to emulate Grandys' tactics, failed, and were ruinously defeated. In a few months the Cythians had taken back most of the territory they'd lost in a decade of war – and it took another two hundred and forty years to beat them."

"Enough talk." The chancellor rose abruptly. "I can't be stuck here, so far away. If an opportunity comes, it'll be over before I hear about it."

"Are we going somewhere?" said Tali.

"I sent messages to my army in Rutherin, weeks ago. And to my other allies, to come east. We're riding west to join them in the morning."

"I don't want you to spy on him again," said Tobry, late that night.

They were up under the dome where he was accustomed to practise magery. Though it was exceedingly cold, it was a large open space where there was no chance of anyone eavesdropping on them.

"And I don't want you going off to kill Grandys, so we're even."

"If you're finished arguing," said Holm, "can you get on with it? We've got an early start in the morning and I need my sleep."

Tali sat on the blanket she'd brought up, studied the self-portrait of Lyf for a minute to fix him in mind, then closed her eyes and focused her magery on his temple. She hadn't needed such help last time.

"It's a lot harder to *see* than before," she said after several fruitless minutes. "Is the temple protected, I wonder, or is it my weakening gift?"

Neither Holm nor Tobry replied. She tried again and, with no warning, broke through.

"*If you'd kept the catalyz on—*" Errek was saying.

"*Don't speak the name!*" hissed Lyf. After a long pause he went on. "*Besides, my father the king cautioned me not to wear it unless I was about to use it. It's our most precious secret.*"

"*Do you think I don't know that?*" growled Errek. "*I created king-magery in the first place – and the key.*"

"*I know you did,*" Lyf said hastily. "*But—*"

"*Some secrets are best hidden in plain view.*"

"*What's that?*" cried Lyf.

Tali withdrew hastily. Her heart was pounding as if she had just climbed a high ladder.

"Did you see anything?" said Tobry.

"He mentioned something called a *catalyz*. Wearing it."

"What were their words, exactly?" said Holm.

She repeated them. "Is a catalyz a magical talisman? In olden times, Grandys stripped the temple looking for a talisman. At least, that's what Wiven said before Lyf had him put to death."

"It's an alchymical term," said Tobry. "A catalyz isn't magical in any way. It's just something that needs to be present before something else can occur."

"Like the detonator in a grenado?" said Holm.

"No, the detonator explodes and makes the grenado go off. A catalyz doesn't *make* anything happen – it simply *allows* it to happen, when conditions are right."

"Is the catalyz the key to king-magery?" said Tali.

"Possibly."

"So that's why Grandys could never find a talisman," said Tali. "There wasn't one, because the catalyz isn't the least bit magical."

"If Errek First-King created king-magery to heal the land, why did he also make the catalyz? What's it really for?"

"I think I can answer that," said Holm. "From my study of history."

"You must have studied it more deeply than I have," said Tobry.

"I've certainly studied it a lot longer. In old Cythe, magery was forbidden to anyone save the king, and bound around with all kinds of punishments if anyone else tried to learn even the tiniest spell. But why?"

"To preserve the mystique of the king," Tobry said cynically.

"Perhaps. But here's a thought – what if any adept who learned the procedures – the spells, if you like – could use king-magery? It would put the whole realm in peril, and most of all, the king. Perhaps that's why Errek created the *catalyz*."

"Why?" said Tali.

"To be a secret key, known only to the current king or ruling queen, without which king-magery could not be used. And the secret would only be passed on as the old king passed on king-magery to his heir."

"It fits the evidence," said Tobry.

"If we can find the key, the catalyz," said Tali, "we might command king-magery. It's the greatest magery of all; it could win us the war."

"Nothing is that simple," said Tobry. "Even the kings of old Cythe had a long and difficult struggle to learn king-magery, I've heard, and some never did."

"All right," said Tali. "But if Grandys gets it—"

"That," said Holm, "is a truly terrifying prospect."

"It would certainly make him invincible," said Tobry.

"That's not what I meant. Errek designed king-magery to heal the land, and every king had to swear publicly that he'd made that choice. If Grandys tries to twist king-magery to destructive purposes, instead of healing the land, it could destroy it."

"How does that work?" Tobry said curiously.

"I don't know. But this land can be deadly when things get out of balance. Lake Fumerous was created when the fourth Vomit blew itself to pieces in ancient times. If it happened again, would any human life survive in Hightspall?"

"I doubt it," said Tobry.

"But surely Grandys would understand the risk," said Tali. "He'd know not to go too far."

"A man like him?" said Holm. "He never listens; he would never believe that such a rule would apply to him. What megalomaniac would?"

Tali looked down at Lyf's self-portrait, which was still resting in her lap. "This circlet looks a bit out of place, wouldn't you say?"

"Why so?" said Tobry.

"Lyf's wearing elaborate kingly robes, yet his crown is a simple silver circlet."

"The kings of Cythe never wore crowns," said Holm. "Perhaps it's something he had as a boy and put on to give himself confidence."

"Then why paint himself wearing it as a newly crowned king?" said Tali.

"To remind himself to stay humble? Lyf never wanted to be king. It fell to him when his older brother died suddenly."

"What if the circlet is the catalyz," Tali said slowly. "Holm, was there a circlet among all the artefacts in Tirnan Twil?"

"I wouldn't know. There are whole floors of artefacts and we didn't go up there."

"It doesn't take a very hot fire to melt silver," said Tobry, "and from what you said about that fire, it was a conflagration. If the circlet was there, it would have been fused into a useless lump."

"Wait a minute," said Holm.

"What?" said Tali.

"Silver was never used by the kings of Cythe – not for ceremonial purposes, anyway."

"Why not?"

"It was considered an ignoble metal."

"What did they use?"

"Gold, mostly," said Tobry. "Sometimes platina which, as I recall, Lyf had a lot of in his caverns."

"Gold or platina, it would still have melted in a fire like that," said Holm.

"Gold, maybe, though it's harder to melt than silver," said Tobry. "But not platina – it takes an exceedingly hot fire to even soften it. Any ordinary fire, fuelled by wood and paper, wouldn't affect it."

"So if the circlet is platina, and it was at Tirnan Twil," said Tali, "it could still be there. And sooner or later, Lyf is going to reach the same conclusion."

"Can't say I'd want to go back and see what fire did to all those people," said Holm.

CHAPTER 82

"They're comin', Tali," moaned Rannilt, shaking her. "They're comin' for you. You gotta get out."

The chancellor's entourage had camped in a steep valley four days' ride west of Garramide. Tali could not see Rannilt's face; their tent was dark as the inside of a rock. The child's warnings weren't always reliable but Tali did not ask questions. She began heaving on her boots; they had all slept in their clothes. Down the other end she could hear Glynnie, who shared the tent with them, doing the same.

Belt, knife, journey-cake, fur-lined coat, and Tali was ready. "Which way, Rannilt?"

"Don't know." She let out a sob. "Stupid buttons! Can't do 'em up in the dark."

"Let me," said Glynnie. Clothing rustled. "There you are. Got your knife, water bottle, food and kindling?"

There was a faint rustling as Glynnie checked her pockets. In this weather, going outside without food and a pocketful of dry kindling could mean the difference between death and survival.

Tali eased open the tent flap. Snow was driven into her eyes. She shielded them with her hand and looked around, but it was as dark outside as in. The wind howling through the tent ropes was a hedge witch crying out their doom.

"We'd better hold hands."

Tali took Rannilt's left hand and Glynnie her right. "Should we run and warn the others?"

"No time," Rannilt said hoarsely.

"What are you seeing?"

"They're comin' over the ridges."

"Who?"

"Don't know. Lots. They're after you, Tali. They really hate you."

That doesn't narrow the list down much, Tali thought.

Further up the slope, a guard bellowed over the howling wind, "Chancellor! We're attacked—" His voice ended in a scream.

Tali's hair stood up and a jolt of sick fear rippled through her belly. How could she run when she didn't know which way to run to?

The camp was set at the upper end of a windswept, U-shaped valley. There were steep ridges on either side and a cliff at the upper end.

Red flared up and out like a three-lobed leaf, some kind of mage-light at the top of the camp, and Tali saw a horde of shadows creeping upon the tents from either side of the valley. She crawled away for ten or fifteen yards, then pulled Rannilt and Glynnie close.

"There's too many of them. We'll never get out."

"If we can get away from the camp," said Glynnie, "they won't know where to look."

"If they've come all this way for me they won't give up easily. Keep low."

"Why don't we head for the entrance to the valley—?"

"That's what they'll expect us to do. It's the only way to get out."

"Up," said Rannilt in a cracked voice.

"If they know we're up there, they'll easily trap us."

"Up!" Rannilt repeated. "No, wait. I can hear somethin'."

"Get down!" Glynnie shoved them both into the snow.

Now Tali heard it too, a thundering roar that was shaking the hillside through the snow. What could it be? It did not sound right for a man on horseback.

She looked up as it came. *He* came. The Third Hero, Syrten. Massive, his monstrous hams pounding down the snow and driving that boulder-like body along relentlessly, the sandpaper thighs rasping together like grinding wheels. The opaline encrustations on his skin winked red and green and blue as they reflected the magelight.

"It's Grandys," said Glynnie. "He's come for you, Tali."

One of the chancellor's horses whinnied, another let out a scream of fear, then in a mass the horses broke through the side of their sapling corral and stampeded down the valley.

Syrten was driving down the slope directly towards them and it was too late to move. All they could do was lie still, half buried in snow, and pray that he missed them.

"Golem," whispered Rannilt. "Golem gunna get us."

"He's just a man." Tali gripped Rannilt's hand and squeezed. The child was gasping as if she was about to scream, and if she gave way to it they were lost.

Syrten thumped closer. Judging by the way his footsteps shook the ground, he must weigh half a ton. If he ran over them he would crush their skulls or snap their bones. Then Grandys would finish the job.

Tali pulled herself into the tightest line she could manage. If Syrten caught them, she would have to use magery. Destructive magery, whatever the cost, though she did not think it would avail her against him. And it would instantly reveal her to Grandys.

The bursts of light from up the hill were more frequent now, and stronger, highlighting struggling groups of figures in many places. Battle was being done with magery up there and every blast sent needle pains through the top of her skull.

Syrten was hurtling down and it seemed impossible that he could miss them. Tali put her hands over the top of her head, scrunched herself further into the snow, and prayed.

A blast inside a tent, a hundred yards up the valley, lit the night sky – orange flame, human outlines wheeling through the air, a bellow of pain. Syrten propped, skidding sideways down the slope towards them and sending up a great deluge of snow. Was he going to skid right over them?

The golem feet broke through the snow, found purchase on rock beneath, then he shot away at right angles, directly for Tali's tent.

"Come on," she whispered. "We'll go up in his tracks."

Taking advantage of a momentary darkness, they scurried up the pounded snow to the ridge crest, which was tipped with slabs of slate like the plates running down the back of a land leviathan of olden times. The wind was howling up here, lifting the fallen snow and whirling it around in clouds.

"At least they won't be able to track us," said Tali, though she did not think anyone could have heard. "Glynnie, which way?"

No answer. "Glynnie?" said Tali. "Rannilt?"

"Right here," said Rannilt after a pause. "But Glynnie ain't."

"What happened to her?"

"Don't know."

"She didn't . . . get trampled?"

"Don't think so. I thought she was comin' behind. Couldn't see nothin', but."

"We'll have to go back for her."

"Better wait," said Rannilt. "They're searchin' below."

"How many do you think there are?" said Tali. "I thought about a hundred."

"Wasn't countin'."

"So it's not his army, just a raiding party that can move quickly. Grandys, Syrten, and a bunch of experienced fighters."

"Do you think Rix—?"

"Grandys would hardly take Rix on a raid against his friends."

Another flash revealed a line of men moving across the snow below them. "They're cuttin' us off," said Rannilt. "We can't go back."

They scrambled up the ridge, which rose ever steeper, groping their way through a darkness illuminated by flashes from the head of the valley.

"This isn't right," said Tali, clinging to a slab to catch her breath. "People are dying and I'm running away."

"Dyin' to protect ya," said Rannilt. "Chief magian's umbrella spell will stop them trackin' ya, but it won't hide ya if you're seen."

"I know, but my friends are down there. Tobry, Holm, Glynnie . . ." The catalogue of her friends was a short one.

"If they had to escape," said Rannilt, "you'd be fightin' so they could. Up there." She was indicating the dark mass of the cliff where the ridge ran up into it.

"What's up there?"

"Bit of a cave. Go in the back, and don't look out. They can't even get a glimpse of ya."

They huddled in a broad, shallow space no bigger than the bed of a wagon, Tali facing away from the entrance.

"You'll tell me if anything happens."

"Don't think they're doin' much killin'," said Rannilt a while later. "They're roundin' people up. Settin' up magery lights and searchin' for ya."

Tali desperately wanted to look around, to see for herself. "Can you tell who they've caught?"

"Too far away."

The minutes passed.

"They're still searchin'," said Rannilt. "They're brightenin' up the mage-lights. Draggin' someone out into the centre. Oh, don't look—"

"Can you tell who?" Tali held her breath.

"A short, round little bloke."

"Not the chief magian?"

Rannilt didn't answer. She was breathing heavily. The blizzard squall passed and suddenly the night was ablaze with stars. Rannilt cried out, and at the same moment Tali felt a piercing pain pass through her from top to bottom. Suddenly she felt naked, exposed, vulnerable.

"They've killed him," Tali said dully.

"Chopped his poor old head right off. How did you know?"

"The shield broke. They'll be able to use magery to find me now."

Who else were they going to kill? Grandys had already condemned Tobry, and if they had Glynnie, as Tali assumed, she would probably die as well. Grandys might put the whole camp to death. He had the reputation for it.

A tremendous flare of emerald green fire lit the night, bursting up and out in all directions and carrying what looked like dozens of people – or bodies – with it. Pain jagged through Tali's skull.

"What was that?"

"Powerful magery," said Rannilt. "Chief magian's."

"But he's dead."

"Must've left a booby trap behind. Killed dozens of them." She paused. "They're goin'."

The raiders raced up the slope, over the ridge, and disappeared.

"Gone to their horses, I expect," said Rannilt sagely.

"Do you think it's a trick?" said Tali once they were gone. "Are they lurking nearby in case I go back?"

"Don't know."

Tali waited another ten minutes, then said, "I'm not game to go back, just in case. Come on."

"Where are we goin'?"

"Down the ridge to the mouth of the valley. The horses stampeded that way, but I don't think they'd go too far."

"Are we leavin' the wicked old chancellor?" said Rannilt. "Goody."

"In a way. We're going to Tirnan Twil."

CHAPTER 83

"I just heard about the chancellor," said Tobry as he entered the healer's tent at dawn. He was grey-faced and covered in snow. "How is he?"

"Rage doesn't begin to describe his mood," said Holm exhaustedly. It had been an eternal night and the day didn't promise any better. "Grandys cut down his guards, stabbed the chancellor in the left arm with Maloch and left without saying a word."

"Why?"

"A warning. *I could have killed you but this time I chose not to. But wherever you go, and no matter how many guards and magians you surround yourself with, you're at my mercy.*"

"Bastard!"

"Did you find Tali, Rannilt or Glynnie?"

"Yes and no."

"They're not—?"

"No," Tobry said quietly. He took Holm by the arm and led him outside where they wouldn't be overheard. "Tali and Rannilt are gone."

"What do you mean, *gone?*"

"I lost their tracks in the falling snow, so I went down to help round up the horses. There was one missing, the one Tali and Rannilt had been riding. And I found this, tied into my horse's mane."

He handed Holm a little twisted strip of paper, unsigned. It said, *You know where we've gone.*

"Tirnan Twil?" said Holm.

"Where else?"

"It's about eight hours' ride from here. They'd be halfway there by now. Is there any point—?"

"We'd never catch them," said Tobry. "Besides, we can't go after them without alerting the chancellor – and Tali's search is something we definitely don't want him to know about."

"What about Glynnie?"

Tobry let out his breath in a rush. "I'm pretty sure Grandys has her."

"Why would he take Glynnie?"

"To get at Rix," Tobry replied. "Maybe he won't do what Grandys wants. It's no secret that Rix and Glynnie are close."

"No chance of a rescue, I suppose?"

Tobry shook his head. "What a rotten, lousy night." He turned back to the tent. "How's his arm?

"Not good. When Grandys uses Maloch, it's cursed, and with the chief magian dead, nothing can be done about the curse. It's as though the arm is poisoned."

They went into the tent, where the chancellor lay on a stretcher. Several healers were gathered around, applying one balm after another to the livid gash on his upper arm, but his twisted fingers had already gone black to the second joints and even as they watched the blackness inched up.

"Enough, dammit," he said roughly. "You're making it worse. Bandage it up and get out."

"Bandaging such a wound can do no good," said the first healer through pursed lips.

"Do you think I don't know that? You'll have to come back and cut the arm off. Get out!"

He looked up at Holm and Tobry. "What the hell do you want?"

"Tali and Rannilt have run off," said Holm.

The chancellor cursed. "Take a squad and find her."

"No tracks. The snow fills them in in minutes."

"Wonderful! Have you got any other good news?"

"Grandys has taken Glynnie, presumably to get at Rix."

The chancellor tried to shrug and gasped with the pain. "Nothing – I can do."

"Why did he attack you?" said Tobry.

"He holds me in contempt." The chancellor smiled through his pain. "It's how I like to be held."

"Why?"

"Contempt is a mind-addling emotion that obscures reason. The more contempt he feels for me, the more he'll underestimate me – to his cost."

"Then you have a plan," said Tobry.

"I've always got a plan. Most of the time I have too many. Grandys is more dangerous than a wounded caitsthe." The chancellor shot Tobry a sardonic glance. "Yet he commands fanatical loyalty."

"But surely, after this—" said Holm.

"Don't think it for a minute," said the chancellor. "The common people, who have been suffering under the nobility for centuries—"

"And under the chancellors too," said Tobry.

"You've no idea what a pleasure it's going to be to see your blood spilled, shifter."

"Death is like an old friend. I'm looking forward to opening the door to her."

The chancellor scowled. "As I was saying, the common folk will be delighted to hear that Grandys strikes down and humiliates the mighty. They'll forgive him anything."

"What are you going to do?"

"He's gone south, back to Gordion, I assume. We're riding west with all possible speed, to meet my army near Nyrdly."

CHAPTER 84

"Are we there yet?" said Rannilt, snuggling up against Tali. The child's capacity for sleep was almost infinite.

"Nearly," said Tali for the tenth time. The horses had been unsaddled when they stampeded, and after nine hours of riding bare-back her hips and backside ached abominably. "We'll have to leave the horse in a minute. It's a steep climb from here."

She wasn't looking forward to the cliff track, though this path into Tirnan Twil – the way Tali and Holm had departed last time – was shorter than their eternal first approach, and much of the way passed through a series of tunnels.

Tali wasn't looking forward to Tirnan Twil, either, and wished she had not brought Rannilt with her, though there had been no alternative. A tower full of corpses was no sight for a child. A part of Tali hoped that the great tower, that spike impaling the dome of the sky, had collapsed into the ravine and buried the bodies decently under ten thousand tons of rubble.

Near the bottom of the first cliff path she found a safe place to leave the horse – as safe as anywhere could be in a land at war – woke Rannilt and dismounted wearily.

"Why are you walkin' like that," said Rannilt, who had spent most of the ride on Tali's lap.

"It feels like all the skin has been chafed off my bottom."

It was snowing gently, though there was no wind and it wasn't as cold as the past few days had been.

"Come on, then," said Tali. "The sooner we begin, the sooner we'll get there. Are you afraid of heights?"

"No."

"Well, I am, so I may need to hold your hand later on."

When they finally emerged from the last tunnel onto the high cliff path, however, the snow was falling so thickly that they could only see a few yards ahead, and the precipice on their right was invisible. It helped.

"Go slowly and tread carefully, child. If you slip here, you can fall a thousand feet."

"Better take my hand," said Rannilt. "Walk next to the cliff and you'll be all right."

"You're a great improvement on Holm," said Tali when they were halfway up. "He made jokes at my expense all the way."

"Probably tryin' to distract ya from falling over," Rannilt said wisely.

Finally they reached the top and turned onto the broader cliff path along the ravine. A cold wind blew down it, driving the snow into their eyes and plastering it on their cheeks. Tali's belly ached — they had eaten the last of her food hours ago.

They turned the corner, the snow thinned and there it was, still standing, a slender, towering spike mounted over the ravine at the intersection of five colossal stone arches.

"Have you ever seen anything like it?" said Tali.

"It's ugly," said Rannilt. "I hate it."

Tali thought it astoundingly beautiful, but did not say so. A beautiful coffin, marred only by yellow and brown smoke-staining around the small windows.

As they trudged down to the central of the five arches, the knot grew in her stomach. What would it be like inside? She prayed that the bodies had burned to ash and there would be nothing recognisable of the people she had met here.

"We'll have to be really careful crossing the arch," said Tali. "It could be icy."

Rannilt took her hand again and they crept across. The wind was stronger here and kept tugging at them as if it wanted to hurl them off. Tali's foreboding grew. They reached the entrance, which was open – she had blasted the door off as she and Holm escaped.

"You'd better wait outside," said Tali.

Rannilt, even enveloped in her thick coat and fur-lined trousers, was shivering. "Why?"

"It's not going to be very nice inside."

"Seen hundreds of dead bodies. Not waitin' here. Too cold."

Rannilt had seen far more than any child her age ever should, but Tali conceded that she was right. It was miserably exposed here on the centre of the arches. "I suppose so."

They went in. The lowest level was heaped hip-high with ash and debris that had fallen down through the ladder hole from the upper floors. In places, the ash had been scoured into ripples and little dunes by wind, and the walls were covered in soot. Thankfully there were no bodies, no bones, and the tapestry of Axil Grandys that had so alarmed her last time had burned away, leaving only a heap of carbonised threads.

"What are you lookin' for?" said Rannilt.

Tali had known Rannilt would ask, and for hours she had been debating what to tell the child. The key was a deadly secret and Rannilt did not need to know about it, but she had to tell her something.

"A silvery circlet that's worn around the forehead." She drew a fore-finger across the top of Rannilt's forehead and around to complete a circle.

"What's it for?"

"I can't tell you that, but it is important."

"Has it got magery in it?"

"Not a skerrick."

"Oh!" said Rannilt.

"You sound disappointed."

"If it did have magery, I could have found it for ya."

"Could you really?"

"Of course."

Tali couldn't always tell whether Rannilt was stating a fact or being fanciful, as with her absurd contention that she could heal Tobry. She filed her statement away for later.

"If it's here, my pearl should tell me," said Tali.

"Then you don't need me at all."

"Of course I need you. Coming up?"

"Think I'll wait here," Rannilt said sniffily.

Tali climbed the steel ladder, which ran up thirty feet to the circular hole through into the next level. The ladder was unaffected by the fire, though each rung bore a little pile of ash or flakes of charred paper.

There was ash on this floor, too, a peaked ring of it around the ladder, tapering away on all sides to a fine powder. Other little heaps marked the spaces where things had burned away – in one embayment, two square piles were all that remained of Syrten's oddly shaped baby shoes. In another, an elongated pile must be the ash from Lirriam's wooden flute, carved for her by her grandfather an impossible age ago in the ancestral homeland, Thanneron.

But neither was what Tali was looking for, and thus far there had not been a peep from her pearl. Surely, if the circlet was here, the master pearl ought to have woken.

Had it done anything unusual the last time she was here? The pearl had troubled her, she recalled, and the premonitions had led her to discover the attacking gauntlings.

She went up several more levels. Nothing. Nothing.

She climbed into the seventh, the portrait gallery, looked around and let out a shriek.

"Tali?" called Rannilt, from below.

"It's all right." Tali pressed her hand to her thundering heart. "I was just startled." She could hear Rannilt coming up the rungs. "Stay there. You don't need to see this."

"Comin' up."

The walls were coated with greasy soot, the kind that comes from burning meat. The portraits had all burned away save one that had been painted on an iron plate. No trace of the image remained apart from a few darker patches. But that was not what had startled her.

It was the bodies.

Twenty-one of them, evenly spaced around the embayed walls. All seated with their backs to the wall, their legs crossed and their hands resting on their knees. All looking upwards, as if to infinity. All charred, though none of them had burned away. Perhaps the smoke and the heavy air had put the fire out. Enough remained for her to identify several of them – the neat, compact form of the curator, Rezire; the three pilgrims, their yellow robes burned away; and the gawky figure of the young archivist who had opened the window for Tali.

"Why are they sittin' like that?" said Rannilt, eyes wide.

"Maybe they didn't want to leave their home."

"But it was on fire!"

"Or maybe they got this far and could go no further ... Come on."

She climbed several more ladders and saw more bodies, but the master pearl remained silent, and Tali knew in her heart that it was not going to tell her anything.

"It's not here. We've come all this way for nothing. Let's go down."

"If it's not here," said Rannilt, "where can it be?"

"I don't know, child," Tali said heavily. "But I need to find out fast, before our enemies do. Let's go."

Despite the risk, she would have to spy on Lyf again, and she'd better do it as soon as possible. But not here.

In the middle of the arch Rannilt looked back. "It's horrible. You should bring it down."

"Even if I could, it would be a *great destruction*. Tirnan Twil should stand, as a monument to failed ambition." Tali frowned. "This is the second time I've been here looking for the key, and the second time I've found nothing ..." She paused. "What does that remind me of?"

Rannilt shrugged.

They went out and retraced their steps: across the arch, along the cliff paths, now terrifying because the snow had stopped and Tali could see all the way down to the rocks at the bottom of the ravine, then through the tunnels and down, finally, to the place where they had tethered the horse. It was just on darkness when they got there.

It had pawed away the snow in a circle to get at the withered grass and moss beneath. They gathered wood, drank from an ice-covered stream and Tali lit a fire.

"What's for dinner?" said Rannilt.

"Nothing."

Tali contemplated the prospect of a cold night with an empty belly and the same for breakfast. Her stomach growled.

"Nothin'?" Rannilt repeated.

"We left the camp last night with nothing save what we had in our pockets, remember?"

"But we didn't eat my food. We ate yours."

"You mean you've got some left?"

Rannilt turned out her pockets. A cube of journey-cake the size of a man's fist, a thick, spicy sausage six inches long, a handful of nuts and a purple carrot. Having spent most of her life in a half-starved state, because the other slave children had picked on her and stolen her dinner, Rannilt pilfered food wherever she found it and squirrelled it away for later.

"What a treasure you are," cried Tali, embracing her.

The word reminded her about Tirnan Twil being a monument to failed ambition – but not Grandys. "The objects there weren't *his* treasures," Tali said aloud. "Rezire said, they were *things that would be seen as treasures by those who worshipped him.*"

"Don't know what you're talkin' about," Rannilt said sleepily.

"Grandys would never have put his own treasures on display at Tirnan Twil. We've been looking in the wrong place. He was still hoping to uncover the secret of king-magery, so he would have hidden everything carefully."

"The servants of Garramide were always talkin' about ancient treasures," said Rannilt.

"That must be what Swelt was hinting at when he died," cried Tali.

"About Grandys' daughter?"

"Yes, but she wasn't his real daughter. It explains everything."

Rannilt yawned.

"Garramide is one of the greatest fortresses in Hightspall," Tali went on. "It must have cost a fortune, but blood was everything to the Herovians. Grandys woudn't have gone to all that expense to protect an *adopted* daughter."

"Why not?"

"She wasn't of his blood – so she wouldn't be that important to him. What if she was part of his cover, to conceal that Garramide was built to protect his real treasures – including everything he'd taken from Lyf's temple? *And it's all still there?*"

"Are we goin' back to Garramide?" said Rannilt.

"We'd better – before Grandys hears that Lyf is searching for the key."

Once the child was asleep, Tali prepared herself, then probed out with exquisite care towards Lyf's temple. She thought he had detected her before, and if he had, he was bound to be on alert, but she had to know what he was doing.

The connection was easy this time. Too easy? She waited until her heart had steadied, then peered into the temple.

Lyf was standing on his crutches, looking towards the rear of his temple, where all one hundred and six of his ghostly ancestors were arrayed in a semicircle, facing him.

"We've been over this a dozen times," said Errek First-King. "The balance is tipping rapidly, and if it goes much further, the Engine will shake the land to pieces."

"I fear to go near it," said Lyf. "I still remember the agony when those specks of alkoyl landed on me in my caverns – and that was spent *alkoyl. In its native form—" He shuddered.*

"Lucky none landed on the little heatstone," Errek said wryly. "But you must go on. You've got to heal the land while it's still possible. It's your first and most important duty."

"How can I? The key hasn't been found."

"Then find it, before Grandys does."

"I don't know where else to look."

"If you can't, it's the end," said Errek.

"If it is, I'm going to make sure of him first," Lyf said grimly. "I'm striking with everything I have."

"He'll be expecting that."

"*I dare say, but my forces outnumber his five to one. And we have weapons we haven't used yet. Weapons he's never seen before. We'll crush him.*"

"*What if you don't? Have you considered that?*"

"*I've considered everything. If the worst happens, we still have Cython.*"

"*Which has eighty-five thousand Pale. Eighty-five thousand too many, if it's our final bolthole. What are you going to do about them?*"

Lyf did not speak for a long time. Then he said in a flat voice, "*The Pale cannot stay. Nor can we allow them to leave, knowing all the secrets of Cython.*"

"*Then the Pale must die,*" *said Errek.*

As Tali wrenched free, her binding oath tightened until it was choking her. This was the moment she had been dreading. She had to return to slavery and save the Pale. And she had no idea how it could be done.

There was no possibility of going to Garramide now. There wasn't time. She would have to pray that Grandys did not realise Lyf was searching for the key. If he discovered it was the circlet, he would know exactly where to find it.

Her ride west to join her allies at Nyrdly felt like the ride of the damned.

CHAPTER 85

"Tali, can we talk about this mad plan of yours?" said Tobry, moving his horse alongside hers.

It was the day after she had rejoined the chancellor's company at Nyrdly. Tali and Tobry were riding across the plain of Reffering, the site of an ancient battle a few miles from the chancellor's camp.

"Not now," she said. "I'm trying to think."

"I don't want you going back to Cython."

"Neither do I, but I swore a blood oath."

"Nobody could hold you to it. Not for this."

"The point of a blood oath, as you well know, is to hold *oneself* to the purpose."

"Even so——"

"My friend Mia was executed in Cython for using magery – magery she was only using because of something stupid *I'd* done. I swore to make up for what had been done to her, and my mother, by saving the Pale. I can't break that oath."

"It doesn't mean you have to go back. We should be looking for the circlet."

"There isn't time. Lyf's planning to put the Pale to death. I heard him say so."

"If you do this, you'll either end up dead, or enslaved again."

"Do you think I don't know that?" she shouted. "Do you imagine I don't think about it constantly? Go away. You're only making things worse."

Tobry whirled his horse and rode off. Tali immediately regretted her outburst, but she felt relieved, too. He radiated anxiety and she could not deal with it as well.

If they caught her, and they probably would, they would make an example of her to rival the greatest horrors of the war.

When she returned, the chancellor was alone in his quarters, a large space created by stretching tent canvas over four walls of the ruined fortress at Nyrdly. He spent all his time there these days. The old chancellor would have punished her for riding off after Grandys' attack, but when she had returned with Rannilt all he'd said was, "You're back! About bloody time."

His poisoned arm had been amputated but it had not cured what ailed him. He was in great pain and increasingly withdrawn. If it came to war, how could he hope to lead his troops?

"My army still hasn't arrived and now I'm worried," he said as she entered.

"The weather's been bad."

"Not that bad. And few of my former allies have answered my call. There's anarchy and rebellion in the south-west, around Rutherin. Lyf holds Bleddimire, and the centre and the south, while Grandys will soon have everything north of Lake Fumerous."

"That still leaves the Nandelochs."

"For how long? My army, *if it gets here*, comprises only nine thousand men, and I'm struggling to recruit more because they're all flocking to Grandys."

"Nine thousand makes a fine army," Tali said more stoutly than she felt.

"The Cythonians have crushed bigger ones, and they've got ten times that many, most dug in, in cities where it would take many times their number to get them out. I can't beat them, Tali. I have to face that."

"So you're saying Hightspall is lost."

"The Hightspall we knew, yes."

"What about Grandys?"

"He's recruited an army of ten thousand in a few weeks and led them to a succession of brilliant victories. Their morale is so high that in a month he could double that number. But he's not going to do anything for us."

All the more reason for Tali to go her own way — to Cython.

"This plan is lunacy," said Tobry that night. "The matriarchs have had months to put new defences in place."

Tali, Tobry and Holm were in a large tent on the far side of the encampment from the chancellor's quarters. In his increasingly reclusive state there was little chance of him catching them, but Tali was keeping as far away as possible. If he heard about her plan he would have her locked away. Though he had threatened to send her to Cython months ago, Tali now knew that he could not have been serious. Not for a second would he risk the loss of her master pearl.

"I know," said Tali. "But if I can't save the Pale, who can? Will you come with me — just until I get inside? I . . . I know it's a lot to ask, but I need magery to get in — your kind of magery."

"If you're determined to go, I'll go with you, all the way. What have I, a doomed shifter, got to lose?" There was no bitterness in Tobry's voice now. He had come to terms with his fate.

"I'm coming too," said Holm.

"No, you're not," said Tali. "I couldn't possibly ask it."

"You're not asking. I'm offering."

"You'll probably be killed."

"I'm an old man, and I've got much to atone for. It's my choice."

Tali wiped tears out of her eyes. "Thank you."

"How many enemy are there in Cython?"

"Um, before the war, there were about three hundred thousand. But a hundred thousand troops came out, men and women."

"And most have been joined by their families," said Tobry. "It's said that more than a quarter of a million Cythonians came out, all up."

"So there might be thirty thousand left in Cython," said Tali, "and a third of them trained guards and soldiers."

"Ten thousand isn't many to guard eighty-five thousand Pale," said Holm. "No wonder Lyf wants to get rid of them."

"The Pale are unarmed," cried Tali. "Untrained! They've got no leaders and they've been bred to be docile and apathetic. I don't see the threat."

"But you must see the problem. How the hell are you going to get them to rebel?"

"I don't know?"

"And if they have to fight—"

"I'm hoping not to fight – just to make a break for the closest exit."

"If you don't mind me saying so," said Holm, "that's not a very good plan."

"I know!" cried Tali, "but it's the best I can come up with."

"Putting the escape plan aside for the moment," said Tobry, "how are we to get into Cython? The defences are supposed to be unbreachable."

"Holm's already thought of that."

Holm went out, shortly returning with a little old man whose back was as curved as a bow. When she'd first met the fellow, Tali had assumed that he never washed, but he was not so much grimy as encrusted with dark grit. His cracked hands and arms, his gnarled and twisted feet, and even the top of his head, were embedded with particles of rock ground into him over a lifetime of labour.

"This is Aditty," said Tali. His head was no higher than her chest. "He's been fifty years a miner."

Aditty did not shake hands, only nodded so stiffly that she heard his neck bones grind together. His breath crackled in his lungs.

"Where have you mined?" said Holm. "I've done a bit of delving myself."

"Wherever there wuz work," said Aditty. His voice was small, dry and breathless, as if his lungs were as encrusted as the rest of him. "Gold, coal, oil shale, copper, platina, you name it. Don't pay much, mining. You got to keep going, going ..." He trailed off, shuffling his battered bare feet.

"Ever worked in the abandoned mines of old Cythe?" said Tobry.

"'Course. Great miners, they wuz. Took the best ore, though."

"If we were looking to get into an underground place," said Tali, "a heavily guarded place, where would we start?"

"Like Cython, you mean?" said Aditty.

"Why Cython, in particular?" said Tali, exchanging troubled glances with Tobry and Holm. Could the secret have got out already?

"You didn't say *mine*, you said *place*. There's only one underground place I know of."

"Suppose we did want to get in, *secretly*," said Tobry, leaning close to the old fellow, "how would we approach it?"

"Air and water," said Aditty.

"Can you elaborate?"

"Elab – elab—?" He went into a fit of coughing that turned his face scarlet and made his eyes water.

"It means *explain*," said Holm. "Tell us what you mean by air and water."

Aditty wiped his eyes. "They got to have fresh air underground, and clean water. Got to get rid of the breathed air and the dirty water, or they die. Big problem, especially air."

"Go on," said Tali.

"Can be all kinds of bad air underground. There's fire-damp: you can't smell it, can't see it, but one spark and," he clapped his hands together, "*bang*! And there's stink-damp, like what they burn in the street lights of Caulderon. Not so common, but it's deadly poison, and it also goes off, *bang*."

He paused for a moment, staring at his feet. "Then there's heavy air, collects in low places. Put a group of people in a hole and they'll breathe out enough heavy air to suffocate 'emselves." He looked up, and Tali saw a keen interest in his tired eyes. "If you build a city underground, you got to have good air, lots of it. Where do you get it?"

"An air shaft," said Tobry.

"An air shaft does for a small mine. But for a city, what runs underground for miles, you need lots of air shafts, one for each area."

"Why can't you have a fan in one entrance," said Tobry, "and blow it through the city and out the other side?"

"Never seen a fan strong enough. Like I said," said Aditty, "the heavy air builds up quick. You got to get rid of it straight away. Need lots of air shafts."

"The problem is finding them," said Holm. "They'll be carefully concealed—"

"And guarded," said Aditty.

"— and the Seethings above Cython is Lyf's territory. If we try to search it we're bound to be seen. We've got to go straight to the spot."

"What about water?" said Tali. "It's not so easy to hide where water goes underground."

"Water ain't such a problem," said Aditty. "Mines often got too much water, though you can't always drink it. Can be salty. And in a lead or arsenic or cinnabar mine, it'll kill you quick. But then," he mused, "just mining lead or arsenic ore, or cinnabar, can kill you quick. Or coal, for that matter. Dangerous business, mining."

"Can you read mine maps?" said Holm.

"Wouldn't be in such health if I couldn't." Aditty coughed up grit into a grubby rag, inspected it and put it in his pocket.

Tali unrolled another map on the folding table. "This is Cython as it is now. At least, it's the main level of Cython, where the Pale live and work. And the enemy live."

"Reliable?" said Aditty.

"It was made for the chancellor before Caulderon fell, from details tortured out of enemy prisoners. I've checked it."

"How did you get it?" said Tobry.

"Snaffled it from his chart room. He had a plan to attack Cython at one stage."

They gathered around the table and Tali pointed out the main features of Cython – the enemy's living quarters, the Pale's Empound where the women lived, the farms, eeleries, toadstool grottoes, heat-stone mine, the men's quarters and the main Floatillery, an underground canal that ran all the way to Merchantery Exit.

Tali produced a second map. It had been drawn in blue ink on fine leather, but was now cracked and worn, and the ink was badly faded.

"I found this in the same place. It's a two-thousand-year-old Cythian mine plan. It shows the workings of the labyrinth of mines underneath the Seethings, as they were at the time of the First Fleet. I'm not sure what all the symbols mean."

Aditty bent so low over the map that his nose touched the surface. He moved his head around for several minutes, his breath crackling. He checked the Cythonian map, then returned to the mine plan. He stepped away, coughed more grit up into his rag and nodded to himself.

"Well?" said Tobry, impatiently.

"Here," said Aditty, stabbing a dust-impregnated thumb at the left side of the mine plan.

Tali could only see meaningless lines and symbols. "What is it?"

"A forgotten air shaft from ancient times."

"How do you know it's forgotten?"

"I've prospected all through the Seethings. Seen no sign of it. I reckon it runs through to Cython, about here." Aditty gestured to the other map.

"That's at the water supply pondages," said Tali. "Why would an air shaft run there?"

"Mines in that area make water, don't they? When the old mine was abandoned, it would have flooded in a few years."

"The enemy went underground five hundred years after the first war started," said Tobry. "If the old maps were lost, they wouldn't have known the flooded air shaft was there. Good place for the water pondages, though."

"How deep would the water be?" said Tali.

"How far underground is Cython?" said Holm.

"The climb up the sunstone shaft is a thousand steps – three hundred feet or more."

"The bottom of the air shaft could be flooded twenty feet deep," said Aditty. "Or sixty." He nodded and went out.

"If we go down the shaft to the water," said Tobry, "we might be able to dive and come up in the flooded area."

"Twenty feet we *might* manage," said Holm. "I can't dive sixty." He shuddered.

"There's magery for that kind of thing," Tobry said vaguely.

"What kind of thing?" said Holm.

"Breathing underwater. I'll start working on it."

"I can't swim," said Tali, another of her personal nightmares closing in around her.

CHAPTER 86

"No, like this." Tobry supported Tali in the water with one hand and demonstrated the breaststroke with the other, for the tenth time.

"I can't do it!" she wailed. The water was miserably cold and terrifyingly alien. "I'm not meant to swim. Get me out!"

He pulled her three yards to the edge of the river pool and helped her onto the bank. Holm, who was waiting beside a fire, wrapped a blanket around her. Tali sat down in the chair and lifted her blue feet onto a wrapped stone he'd heated in the fire. He handed her a large mug of sweet, steaming tea. She curled her hands around it.

"Then we'll have to go to Cython without you," grinned Holm. "Though I don't see how *we're* going to convince the Pale to rebel."

"You two couldn't masquerade as Pale in pitch darkness," she muttered.

Tali had looked forward to this. Not for the swimming lessons, which she had known would be an ordeal, but because she'd be with

Tobry. Now that they were just friends again, and working together on her plan, the tension between them was gone and it was a pleasure to be with him. It reminded her of old times.

But the water was so cold that it took her breath away, and Tobry had turned out to be a stern teacher who expected her to be able to swim after one lesson. The first time he let her go she began to flounder, panic set in and she sank. It had set the pattern for the day.

She could only last five minutes in the cold water, and each time she got out and warmed up it was harder to go back in. She eyed Tobry resentfully. His chest was bare and he hadn't bothered to stand by the fire.

"One more go," he said, rubbing his hands together.

"You're a horrible man. I don't know what I ever saw in you."

"I never understood it either," he said, smirking.

"You're enjoying my suffering, you beast."

"Get in!"

She stood up. Holm took the blanket away, and the breeze struck through her wet shirt and knickers. "No more!" she gasped, staring at the hostile water.

"In, or I'll throw you in."

"One day I'm going to murder you, Lagger. One day!"

He rolled his eyes. Tali stepped in and all the carefully nurtured warmth was gone in an instant. She pushed her arms out, attempting a stroke, but her legs sank and she plunged to the bottom, thrashing and choking.

Tobry hauled her up by the hair and extended her horizontally along the surface. "Well done. You almost did a *stroke* that time."

She thumped him and sank.

It was forty miles from Nyrdly to the forgotten air shaft that led into Cython, by the winding route they had to take to avoid detection, and it had taken them two nights to get there. Two exceedingly tense nights.

On Tali's right, the mighty volcano called the Brown Vomit was erupting, casting an ominous red glare over the landscape. Fine ash was sifting down, getting into their eyes, noses and ears, and the ground quivered constantly.

Tobry had barely spoken the whole time. The magery to allow them to breathe underwater was proving a far bigger challenge than he had anticipated, and he was still struggling with it as they rode between the boiling pools of the Seethings, and across the boulder-strewn badlands between the Vomits and Lake Fumerous.

It wasn't the only thing bothering him – or her. The eruption flares glistened on his sweaty face, and every so often he would twist around in the saddle and thrust out a hand, as if to ward something off, though there was nothing to be seen in the empty landscape. Was it a sign that shifter madness was closing in? An attack was often preceded by hallucinations and, she knew, could be brought on by stress.

If he had a bout of madness on the way down the shaft, when they were reliant on his magery, none of them would survive. But Tali could not do it without *him*. Without his underwater breathing spell she could not hope to get inside.

And then there was the circlet to worry about. How long before Lyf decided to look for it in Garramide? Or Grandys went there? Leaderless, Garramide would fall in a day, and there was nothing she could do about that either. She could not spare Tobry or Holm, and could not trust anyone else with the secret.

"I've just thought of another problem," said Holm. "A big one."

Tali groaned. "I don't want to know. What?"

"If the worst happens, and we end up in a battle, what are you going to do?"

"We'll have to fight."

"Even if we can arm the Pale, they've no training with weapons."

"Heatstone!" said Tali.

"What about it?"

"We chuck it at the enemy. When heatstone breaks, it's like a grenado going off."

"And wasn't there something about it knocking the enemy unconscious, but not the Pale?"

"That was sunstone, but I'm hoping heatstone will have the same effect, since it's stronger. Anyway, apart from Tobry's magery, heatstone is the one advantage we have over them."

"Why can't they chuck it back at us?"

"They're very superstitious about it; won't touch the stuff."

"Perhaps they sense its connection with king-magery," Holm said thoughtfully. "That's a good idea, but if you do end up in a battle, how are you going to direct it? It won't be anything like directing a normal battle from the top of a hill where you can see everything."

"Um . . ." said Tali.

"Cython is a maze of tunnels," said Tobry. "And you're . . ."

"Short?"

"I would have said *petite*. If there's a row of enemy troops in front of you, you won't be able to tell if there's twenty of them, or a thousand."

"And you won't have a clue what's going on in any of the other tunnels," said Holm.

"What's your solution?" said Tali.

"I don't have one."

"Then we'd better not get into a battle," she said quietly.

As she rode, she checked on Lyf again, but her gift was weak today. And all she saw were disconnected images of the temple walls . . .

"What can you see?" said Holm quietly.

She roused slowly. "How did you know I was looking?"

"A particular blankness in your eyes."

"Thanks!" She looked again. "Lyf's pacing. Looks worried. Now he seems to be arguing with his ghost ancestors. No, I've lost him."

Several hours before dawn they reached the rocky little hill which, according to Aditty, should contain the forgotten air shaft. The hill was only a few hundred yards across and rose from the flatlands like a door knob before flattening on top, eighty feet above the plain. They walked the horses up and made camp among scrubby trees and grey-leaved bushes.

"We can't move until after dark tonight," said Tali. "I want to get into the Empound around midnight, when the slaves are in their beds and there aren't many guards around."

"First, let's see if the air shaft is here," said Holm. "After all this time it could have collapsed."

Tobry wiped his dripping face and twisted around, staring

behind him and swallowing audibly. "Get on with it. I've got to complete the water-breathing spell and I need peace and quiet."

"What if you can't complete it?" said Tali. Part of her hoped he would fail. Hoped there was no way in and she wouldn't have to go through with it.

"What if you can't find the shaft?" he snapped. "What if it's blocked, or there's no way into the pondages, or—"

"I think we'd better leave him to it," Holm said pointedly. The stress was getting to everyone.

"Do you know what you've got to do?" Tali said to Holm as they began to circumnavigate the hill, working in along a spiral.

"I ought to, the number of times you've asked me."

Something was bothering him, too. "Sorry. I'm not used to leading a team."

"I identify and disarm any enemy traps," said Holm. "When we get inside and you're inciting the Pale to rebellion, I help Tobry break open the armouries and heatstone stores. Sounds simple enough."

She stared at him in the red glare from the erupting volcano. "*Simple?*"

"I was attempting a joke."

"A *joke?*"

He chuckled. "You know – to relieve the tension and lighten the mood."

"Well, don't!"

Nothing could lighten Tali's mood save being a thousand miles from here. If the maps were wrong, or this route was known to the enemy, or the traps they would encounter could not be disarmed, they would die.

"Seems to me you've got a lot to learn about leadership," said Holm.

"What's the matter with you? You haven't been your normal self since we left . . ."

"And only now do you think to ask? A good leader has to be sensitive to—"

"If there's something the matter, *just tell me*," she hissed. "Don't drop hints so I'll dig it out of you. I've got enough worries as it is."

"Well, here's another one. When I was a kid, my big brother

used to hold a pillow over my face until I thought I was going to suffocate. Ever since then, I've been afraid of being buried alive. Going down this shaft isn't the deepest desire of my heart."

"I wish you'd told me."

"It would have been one more thing for you to worry about," he said pointedly.

"Speaking of which, have you been keeping an eye on Tobry?"

"I have," said Holm.

"Would you say he's more twitchy than usual?"

He ran his fingers through his thin hair.

"Holm?"

"Judging by the heavy doses of potion he's been taking the past few days, I'd say he thinks he's not far off shifting – involuntarily."

"Fantastic!" said Tali. "I'm terrified of drowning, you're afraid of being buried alive and we're going down a bottomless well with a madman whom we can't do without."

"And that's the easy part."

They continued on their inward spiral, probing ahead with sticks so they didn't accidentally walk into the shaft. Some minutes later, Tali's stick broke through a layer of rotting vegetation. They cleared it away. Holm unshuttered his lantern and shone it down.

An oval shaft, six feet by five, cut through hard volcanic rock. The light did not reveal how deep it was. Tali dropped a stone. It took four or five seconds before she heard the splash.

"Few hundred feet down to the water," grunted Holm. "I hope our ropes are long enough."

"You packed them. You ought to know."

He chuckled. "Just testing you. Of course they're long enough, and a bit more."

She got out the chancellor's map of Cython, studied it carefully, then folded it and packed it in its envelope of waterproof waxed cloth. She could need the map in Cython, since some parts of the city had been forbidden to her.

It was getting light as they headed back to the camp, but when they were ten yards away Holm thrust out a hand. They stopped in the gloom under a copse of trees.

Tobry had lain his potion bottles out on a flat rock and was measuring the doses into a cup. He held it up in a shaking hand then swallowed it in a gulp. He wiped his face, checked behind him then, furtively, began to measure a second dose. After draining the cup, wiping out the residue with a forefinger and licking it off, he stood up, shuddering.

"A double dose," Holm said in Tali's ear. "It's worse than I thought."

They continued to the camp. "We found the shaft," said Holm with exaggerated good cheer. "How's it going?"

"I've done the spell," said Tobry, wiping his face again.

He was sweating more than ever. This was not going to go well.

CHAPTER 87

"Before we go, it might be an idea to check on Lyf again," said Holm that night. They were waiting by the shaft, and all was ready.

She used her failing magery to peer through the hazy distance to Lyf's temple. It took three attempts before she saw anything, but this time she could only see, not hear.

"He's stalking across to a table," said Tali. "There's a small sheet of iron on it—"

"Iron?" said Holm.

"Like a loose leaf from the iron book he made, but it's blank. He's writing on it. No, etching it with a scriber. He used to use alkoyl for that, back in his caverns."

"What's he writing?"

"I can't read it. But it's only a few words. Lyf's put the scriber down. Now he's using his hands, as if working magery. The iron page is rising in the air – no, it's crashed down on the table. I'd say he's trying to send it somewhere."

"I think I can guess what it is, and where he's sending it," said Holm.

"Where?"

"We know he's planning to put the Pale down, so I'd reckon this is the death order. And a highly symbolic one, since he's written it on a page of the iron book."

"*The Consolation of Vengeance*," whispered Tali. "And the book was unfinished. The ending hadn't been written."

"It has now," said Holm. "What's he doing?"

"I – I can't see," said Tali. Her heart was hammering in her ears, yet so little blood was going to her head that she felt faint. She forced herself to focus. "He's calling someone in. A servant. No, a courier."

"What's he saying?"

"The only word I could lip-read was *matriarchs*. Now the courier's put the iron page into a bag. He's running out."

"How far is it from Caulderon to Cython?" said Holm. "Quick!"

"Um . . . the nearest entrance is nine or ten miles, on horseback."

"Once he gets out the gates of Caulderon, a courier could ride that in an hour, even through the rough country of the Seethings."

"Add another hour to get out of the city," said Tali, "and to reach the matriarchs way across Cython, but in two hours they'll have the order."

"Will they act on it straight away?" said Holm. "Or wait until morning?"

"I don't know. I can't think."

"It must take an hour or two to get ready, surely? Four hours, say, before the Pale start to die. Can we do it in time?"

Tali ran through her mental map. "If we can get in, and we're not discovered, and everything goes well, we can reach the Pale in an hour and a half. But to get them out, first I've got to convince them to rebel."

"Surely they'll want to escape," said Tobry, speaking for the first time.

"They're not like me. In Cython, any slaves who cause trouble, or show initiative, are sent to the heatstone mines to die. For a thousand years the fate of the brave and the bold has been an unpleasant death, and every Pale knows that the only way to survive is to be docile and obedient. Getting them to rebel won't be easy."

"But when you tell them about the death order—" said Holm.

"What if they refuse to listen?"

"We'd better get moving," said Tobry. He took hold of the ropes and went over the edge.

Because of the underground heat, even a cold winter was mild in the Seethings, and once they were fifty feet down the air shaft Tali was sweating as profusely as Tobry. He was twitchy, looking behind him all the time now. Holm seemed unnaturally calm but it was all an act. She knew he was terrified.

He was a far better actor than she was.

Though Holm had spliced loops into the rope every two feet, climbing down it was tricky and dangerous. Once they passed below the level of the hill, the hard volcanic rock gave way to layers of welded ash, some crumbling. The wall of the shaft was covered in slimy growths and the air had a dead reek.

"Smells like something fell in here long ago and is quietly rotting at the bottom," said Tali, who had her feet in one loop and was hanging onto another.

"I imagine many animals have fallen in and drowned since the air shaft was last used," said Holm. "And perhaps one or two unwary people."

And soon, *us*?

They settled into the black water. A shudder rose up Tali's back.

"At least it's warm," said Tobry, holding up his elbrot to provide an eerie emerald light. "Hope you've remembered your swimming lessons, Tali."

He forced a smile but Tali could not reciprocate. *I – can't – do – it.*

Holm counted the loops. "We're a hundred and eighty feet below the level of the Seethings. That means the water could be a hundred feet deep . . ."

"That's a hell of a dive," said Tobry, gnawing on a thumb. "I'm not sure the spell is up to it."

"Then fix the damn thing," snapped Holm, his voice cracking.

Tobry made a few adjustments, using his elbrot. "All right." He tapped Tali on the head with it, then Holm and lastly himself.

Nothing happened for a few seconds, then Tali's lungs spasmed and she began to choke. "Can't breathe," she gasped.

"Get–under–water," said Tobry.

Holm, his eyes protruding, slid beneath the surface. Tobry
dropped off the rope. Tali didn't move. She was too afraid of the
black water. She clung to the loop, wanting to scream but lacking
the breath to do so. It was getting worse. Her head was spinning,
her fingers slipping—

Someone clamped onto her left ankle and yanked. She hit the
water with a stinging splash and sank, thrashing wildly. There came
a cold pain in her chest, a sharp ache that spread through her along
a thousand little branches, and she could breathe again. She could
breathe – *underwater*!

Her terror faded as a light appeared below her, Tobry's elbrot,
now glowing orange. He pulled her down to his level. Holm was
a few feet below them, his eyes bulging more than before and his
jaw clenched. He jerked a finger at the side of the shaft, where a
rock layer had crumbled away. The rock above and below looked
none too secure either.

Don't show me anything else, she thought. If that's how we're
going to die, I don't want to know.

Down they went. Down, down. She could not tell how deep; the
shaft felt as though it was running all the way to the centre of the
world. Down, down, down. The water grew warmer, and murkier.
She lost sight of Tobry and Holm. Tali thrashed a couple of times,
overcome by a momentary panic, then calmed herself by an effort
of will. They had to be close by; there was nowhere else they could
be. She settled on crumbling, silt-covered stone and they appeared
on either side.

Tobry forced more orange light from his elbrot but it did not
help. They had stirred up the silt and the water was cloudy, visibility only a foot. He began to feel along the rock, looking for a way
through. Tali and Holm did the same. It did not take them long.
Crumbling rock covered the bottom of the shaft to an unknown
depth. There was no way through.

Tali perched on the pile, head in hands. What now? Even with
the loops in the rope, it would be a struggle to climb all the way
back up. Tobry was creeping around the oval wall of the shaft. Every
so often she caught a glimpse of him through the increasingly
murky water.

He caught her arm from behind. He was pointing to the wall. She pulled herself across. A smaller air shaft led off horizontally, its entrance only partly blocked. Tali was helping to heave the rubble aside when another pain passed through her chest and for a second she felt breathless, stifled. Was Tobry's spell wearing off too soon?

She caught his arm, urgently pointing to her chest. He nodded. He'd felt it too. *What do I do?* she mimed.

He raised his hands, palms up. He didn't know either.

She gestured to the elbrot. *Re-do the spell.*

I can't.

Had the overdose of potion affected his ability to work magery? His chest heaved and he whipped around, staring behind him again. His eyes were wild, his mouth gaping. Was the shifter madness coming?

Holm hurled the last rock aside. Tobry wriggled into the horizontal shaft, his broad shoulders touching the sides, and held the elbrot out to light the way. The water was clearer here; she could see for yards. She followed, expecting the shaft to turn upwards, but it kept going, and going.

And going.

The breathless feeling was growing by the minute, draining the energy from her. She could not last much longer. Neither could Holm, who still wore that stricken look. *Tobry, help! Do something.*

She could not reach him. He was too far ahead and going faster than she could.

Then his light disappeared.

Behind her, Holm let out a frenzied cry that was throttled by the water. Tali reached back, caught his hand and gave it a jerk. Her head struck rock. She groped all around, discovered that the shaft took an upwards bend, and kicked upwards. The orange light of the elbrot was dwindling above them as Tobry raced for the surface. Tali struggled after him, lungs heaving, breath gone. She had nothing left.

She ran out of steam twenty feet from the surface. Her muscles stopped working, as though her last air had been diverted to her brain. For what? She wasn't capable of thought, much less of some magery that could save them . . .

CHAPTER 88

Holm was drifting up past her, unmoving, when Tobry came spearing down. He caught her hand with his, and the back of Holm's belt with the other hand, and with mighty kicks drove them to the surface.

Tali turned onto her back and floated there, staring up at the dark roof and gasping as she dragged the unfamiliar air into her lungs. It hurt. It hurt dreadfully. She was drifting in a circle when she realised that her fear of the water was gone. She rolled over, pushed her arms forward and out, the way Tobry had tried so hard to teach her – and it worked. She was breathing and swimming at the same time!

The elbrot's light reflected off distant stone walls, and along to a heavy iron grating that ran from stone ceiling to stone floor. They had emerged in the pondages, and they were locked.

Tobry swam across to the edge. Holm was already there. Tali followed and hung onto the low side wall, getting her breath. After a minute Holm climbed out and went, wobbly-kneed, to the grating. It was made of thick iron, rusty on the outside but solid underneath. The central part opened to let people in, though there was a massive lock on the other side.

He did not look at it. Holm was down on hands and knees, studying the floor where the grating passed into it. He began to pick at the edge with his knife, prising the caked dust away, then stood up wearily.

"There's a second gate down there, spring operated, I'd say. Looks like it's got a shearing blade on top. Even if I could pick the lock without springing the gate and cutting myself in two, I don't think we can get through without setting off one of their clangours . . ."

Tali, who knew Holm by now, waited for him to go on. Tobry stared at Holm, a muscle jumping in his left cheek. It was warm

and humid here, and rivers of sweat were pouring down his stub-
bled cheeks.

"Whatever you're planning, you'd better make it snappy."
Tobry's voice had a hint of caitsthe roar in it. "Don't think I've got
long left."

"But you took two doses," said Tali.

"Saw that, did you? It wasn't enough. Could be touch and go, if
you aren't quick."

Tobry got out his potion bottles and mixed a third dose. He
poured the thick grey liquid into an empty potion bottle and held
it out to Tali.

"What's that for?" she said, not taking it.

"An emergency. You'll need to force it down my throat . . ."

"I don't think I could force it down a shifter's throat."

"You'll see the signs. You'll have a minute . . . *if* you're lucky."

"That'll make it a triple dose," said Tali. "It could kill you."

"If I shift involuntarily, I could kill you both."

With deep misgivings, she took the little, thick-walled bottle
and tucked it away in her small pack. Holm was feeling in his own
pack. He brought out a small package, carefully wrapped, and
opened it to reveal a glass phial, tightly stoppered.

"Not you, too?" said Tali. "Bloody shifters, they're everywhere."
She had seen a phial like it before but could not remember where.

Holm smiled at the feeble joke. "Lizue dropped this one in your
cell in Rutherin. I've been carrying it ever since."

He twisted the stopper out and white fumes wisped up. Holding
the phial out carefully, he ran a line of liquid onto the bars in a large
rectangle. The bars fizzed and dripped, and after several minutes he
heaved and the section came away.

Holm put it down carefully. "We're in."

"But there's still a long, long way to go," said Tobry.

Tali did not need reminding. Nor what was at the end of it.
"How long did all that take?"

"About twenty minutes," said Holm, who always seemed to
know the time.

"Lyf's courier will be out the city gates by now."

"And racing towards the Seethings."

As they moved out into a carved and painted tunnel, she caught the faint, familiar scent of Cython: the quiet odour of the rock, an occasional whiff of sulphur from the hot springs that broke through the walls here and there, and the distant tang of the fish tanks and eeleries.

Her eyes stung, but she dashed the tears away. How could she possibly be feeling homesick for Cython? But she was. Her first eighteen years, and the lives of her ancestors for the past thousand years, had been lived here, and she had felt more at home in Cython than she ever had in Hightspall.

She took a few steps forward, a few steps back, listening to the rock and tasting the air with her nose. She could sense Tobry's churning emotions but she put him out of mind. All depended on her now. Her knowledge and her instincts about Cython.

Tali knew vaguely where she was; as a child she had wandered down to the pondages several times. After being put to full-time slavery at the age of ten, however, she'd had no right to be in this area and would have been chuck-lashed if she had ever come here.

A faint boot scrape told her someone was coming; one of the enemy. The Pale slaves were mostly small, slender people and they went barefoot, making no sound on the stone floors.

"Enemy!" she whispered, drawing Tobry and Holm back to the dark pondages. "Put out the light. No fighting unless I give the signal."

Tobry extinguished his elbrot and they crouched in the dark, hands on their blades. It would be a bad sign if they had to fight so soon after getting in. Any ruckus risked the enemy being alerted, and if that happened, they would have to try and get out the way they had come, impossible though that seemed. If the enemy knew they were in Cython there would be no hope of completing their mission.

The bluish light of a glowstone lantern cast streaks down the passage. It must be a pair of guards, patrolling the halls as they did every day and night. But there were many halls to monitor, so why had they come this way at this particular moment? Had the break-in set off a clangour somewhere else?

Their footfalls were regular; there was nothing to suggest that it was anything but a routine patrol. The light was bright now, and Tali edged back. They would pass by any second.

They reached the entrance to the pondages. A man and a woman, both big and strong. Then they stopped.

"What's that smell?" said the woman, who was closest to the entrance. She held up her lantern. It revealed a broad, mannish face, black hair cut short, and tattoos like a pair of crossed ribbons across her forehead.

Tobry was still sweating rivers but Tali did not think the female had scented him. Now she noticed the smell too – a faint, acrid odour drifting from the grating, coming from the corrosive fluid Holm had used to eat through the metal.

"Alkoyl?" said the male guard.

"No," said the woman, sniffing. "It smells like the new kind of vitriol." She took a chuck-lash from her belt, a red and black one almost as thick as Tali's little finger, and raised it over her shoulder.

The man drew a curved sword and followed.

Tali had been lashed with little chuck-lashes several times, which exploded against the skin with excruciating, blistering pain. But the big ones could take an arm off, or a lower leg, and if they hit in the face, throat or belly, they usually killed.

She made the agreed sign to Tobry and Holm, slashing her fingers across her throat. Silence the guards – as quickly as possible.

They already had a plan for this. Tali and Tobry would attack, while Holm stood by to cut down anyone who got away or went for the clangours, the system of alarms that ran along the ceiling of every tunnel in Cython. If the clangours were sounded, the alarm would be carried, and repeated, by a series of bell-pipes throughout Cython. Every Cythonian, anywhere in the underground city, would hear the sound within minutes.

The woman passed by. One step. Two steps. She raised her glow-stone lantern, extended it ahead of her towards the pondages, and the light fell directly on the rectangular section that Holm's phial of acid had eaten through the grating.

She spun around and raced for the clangours, shouting, "Intruders, intruders!"

CHAPTER 89

"Tali's taken the bait," Lyf exulted, rising up into the air for a second or two. Then sense prevailed. He must not waste what remained of his magery. "She's on her way to Cython. Now to close the trap."

"How do you know this?" said General Hillish.

"A while back, I discovered that she'd been using the master pearl to spy on me. I've been trying to put a trace on her ever since, and it's finally worked." Lyf circled his hands and Tali's voice came forth from the air before him.

"Lyf's put the scriber down. Now he's using his hands, as if working magery. The iron page is rising in the air — no, it's crashed down on the table. I'd say he's trying to send it somewhere."

"I think I can guess what it is, and where he's sending it," said a man's voice, broad and slow.

"Where?" said Tali.

"We know he's planning to put the Pale down, so I'd reckon this is the death order. And a highly symbolic one, since he's written it on a page of the iron book."

"The Consolation of Vengeance," whispered Tali. *"And the book was unfinished. The ending hadn't been written."*

"It has now," said the man. *"What's he doing?"*

"I — I can't see," said Tali. She did not speak for a minute. *"He's calling someone in. A servant. No, a courier."*

"What's he saying?"

"The only word I could lip-read was matriarchs. *Now the courier's put the iron page into a bag. He's running out."*

"How far is it from Caulderon to Cython? Quick!"

"Um . . . the nearest entrance is nine or ten miles, on horseback."

"That's all I got before the trace broke," said Lyf. "But it's enough."

"Where is she?" said Hillish.

"Somewhere in the Seethings, I'd say. Close to Cython."

"Do you know how she plans to get in?"

"No."

"Can you get the trace back?"

"Not unless she spies on me again. But I don't need to."

"Why not, Lord King?"

"She'll have to use magery to sneak through any of the entrances, unseen, and I've had spy devices fitted to all of them, linked to the clangours. The moment she sets one off, she'll be taken."

"She's clever," said Hillish grudgingly. "Better warn the matri-archs she's coming. Should I call another courier?"

"No," said Lyf. "I'm riding to Cython at once. I want to be there when she's taken."

CHAPTER 90

Grandys reached over and scratched Rix under the chin, like a grandmother with a baby. "You hate me, and you can't do a thing about it. I love that."

"It's the only way you can command loyalty," Rix forced out.

Grandys snorted. "My men love me. I give them power for the first time in their lives."

"Power to die for your own aggrandisement."

"Any of us can die. But unlike Hightspall's gutless generals, when my men look up they see me at the front, risking my life as I lead them to victory."

"With power and magery none of your opponents can match," Rix sneered, "and an enchanted sword protecting you all the way. You're not taking much of a risk."

"Maloch only protects to a degree," said Grandys. "An arrow in the eye, the throat or the heart can kill me as easily as any man." He sauntered out, grinning.

Oh, for an arrow in your eye! The moment Grandys was gone, Rix lay on his mattress, closed his eyes and started attacking the command spell afresh.

A fortnight had passed since Rix's vow to kill Grandys, a time of frustration and failure as the army had gone back and forth, attacking enemy fortresses and Hightspaller manors indiscriminately. Rix had to find a way; it had to be now.

For years he had fought the compulsion Lyf had put on him via the heatstone, and the battle had strengthened his will immeasurably. Could that be why Grandys' command spell had slipped before, when they had fought at the feast after the capture of Rebroff? Because Rix had recoiled so violently from Grandys' atrocities?

The spell always felt tightest when Rix was fighting beside Grandys, overcome by the euphoria of following a charismatic leader. But once the battle had been won, and Grandys was despoiling the bodies and tormenting the prisoners, or revelling in the destruction of priceless artwork and libraries, Rix's fury rose to the surface and the command spell weakened. It had not yet slipped enough for him to kill his master, though.

He debated his plan again, wishing Tobry were here, for he saw the flaws in a plan far more clearly than Rix. Nor was Tobry troubled by the self-doubt that sometimes crippled Rix. What if he succeeded in killing Grandys, but it made things worse? Would it be better to wait and see if Grandys could defeat Lyf first?

But the more Rix saw of Grandys, the more he knew what a monster the man was, far worse than Lyf who, for all his flaws, wanted to heal the land, not tear it apart. If Grandys defeated Lyf he would be too strong; there would be no check on him. Besides, Grandys no longer trusted Rix and might cut him down at any time.

He could not beat Grandys in a fair fight. The man was too tough, skilled and ruthless, and he would use every dirty trick he knew. Neither Grandys' ego nor his reputation could allow him to lose.

How Rix wanted to crush and humiliate the brute; to inflict the same misery of defeat on him that he had done to so many others.

It was unworthy, he knew. Well, he thought wryly, I never claimed to be a saint.

If he attacked Grandys, would the other officers intervene? No, they wouldn't dare. Intervening would be saying that Grandys could not take care of himself. But if Rix should win by foul means, since fair ones offered no hope, Grandys' men would probably tear him to pieces.

He was going to do it anyway. There was a faint hope that, if he did kill Grandys, he might wrest command of his army the way he had taken over Leatherhead's raiders, then take on Lyf. Rix had no hope of beating Lyf's vast forces with an army of ten thousand, but for the sake of his country he was prepared to try. A man who wasn't prepared to die for his country was no man at all.

His plan was simple. He would avoid fighting side by side with Grandys, since that strengthened the command spell, yet stay as close as possible when he was committing his atrocities, in the hope that this would crack the spell completely.

But this time Rix must restrain his horror and his disgust. If he gave any hint of his true feelings, Grandys would tighten the spell anew.

You've got to kill him tonight. You can't risk it any longer.

It was a strange feeling to be cold-bloodedly planning the death, no, murder – or would it be easier if he thought of it as an execution? – of the Hero Rix had admired all his life, the legendary founder of Hightspall.

He would call Grandys out. Then Rix planned to publicly repudiate the oath he had sworn after they left Glimmering. What kind of a man am I, he thought, that I'm prepared to commit murder, yet can't do it while I'm sworn to the brute? Then, unless Rix was killed first, he would drive a dagger through Grandys' weakest point – his eye.

Only one obstacle remained, the command spell. It had to be cracking if Rix could actually plan his master's murder, but it was far from broken. He prayed that the afternoon's attack would shatter it – Grandys' planned onslaught, using just a hundred of his men, on a castle that had already offered to surrender.

The attack was so unnecessary. Half the men of Bastion Cowly, a small fortress in Lakeland, had marched off to join the chancellor's army this morning. Several hours later its remaining inhabitants, desperate to avoid the fate that so many other fortresses in the north had suffered, had run up white flags the moment Grandys' small force had appeared.

"How dare they?" Grandys fumed. "No Herovian would ever surrender. But to surrender without a fight, when the attacking force is far smaller than their own, is utter cowardice."

Rix had been restraining himself for days now, but could hold back no longer. "What the hell does it matter? You wanted Cowly, and now you can take it with no bloodshed and none of your men lost."

"I don't want the damn castle, and I couldn't care less about the lives saved," snapped Grandys. "I want the fight, miserable though it will be with such an easy target. What's the matter with these people?"

"They're just trying to live their normal lives."

"Well, I'm not having it."

Rix let out his breath in a rush. "We're going home?"

"The *surrender*," said Grandys, as though Rix was an idiot. "I'm not accepting it. Prepare to attack."

"You can't attack a castle that's offered to surrender," said Rix.

Grandys swung around in the saddle, his meaty face choleric. "How dare you tell me what I can and can't do?"

"It's a dishonourable act."

"In war there are no dishonourable acts. If it helps you win, it's the right thing to do. If it doesn't help, it was wrong." Grandys raised his sword, roaring, "Attack! Show the craven curs no shred of mercy."

He turned to Rix. "You're fighting by my side, Ricinus. If you're not drenched in the enemy's blood by the time we break through, I'll cut your guts out and make you eat them."

Rix tried to stare Grandys down, but could not defeat that ferocious glare and was the first to look away. Fear thrilled through him. Did Grandys know what he was planning? Was he setting his own trap? Curse you, he thought, to the depths of the Abysm. Whether it's a trap, or not, I've got to go through with it.

Grandys raised Maloch and spurred his horse. Rix kicked his

own mount into a gallop and they raced across the meadow towards the gates. He prayed that Grandys' horse would step in a rabbit hole and fall, and that he would break his thick and partly armoured neck, but it would never happen. The Herovian's life was charmed.

What if he rode up beside Grandys and skewered him when he wasn't looking? No, that would be like stabbing him in the back. Rix was prepared to kill Grandys, even murder him if he had to, but it must be face to face.

After withdrawing his oath.

CHAPTER 91

Tali had only seconds to stop the Cythonian guard. She swung at her but the guard must have sensed the movement and turned at the same time. Tali's blade struck the dangling chuck-lash and it went off in a series of violent red bursts, *crack-crack-crack*. The sword blade shattered six inches from the hilt, spraying shards of metal everywhere and wrenching Tali's wrist so violently that she felt something tear.

A shard caught the guard in the right cheek. She reached up dazedly to pull it out, then stared at her hand in disbelief. All the fingers were gone, amputated in a second by the exploding chuck-lash. But she was well trained and determined to do her duty. She swung her lantern at Tali's face.

She could not get out of the way in time and the base of the lantern caught her on the side of the head. The lantern went flying, hit the floor and rolled away though, being glowstone, it continued to shine. The guard went for her own sword, left-handed. Tali leapt forwards, thrusting at her middle with the shattered remnant of her blade, and the guard fell.

In the dim light, Tali could not tell where her thrust had gone. Was the guard dying, injured, or shamming? She lay on the floor, unmoving.

To Tali's left, Tobry was struggling. He was normally cool under pressure, but his blade kept slipping in his sweat-drenched hand and his strokes were hasty, mis-timed. His tanned face had gone grey and he looked as though he were about to throw up.

His potion caused nausea and severe gut pain. Had the double dose, on top of the strain of working that powerful magery, been too much for him? And where was Holm? Why hadn't he come to Tobry's aid? Had he been killed already? Tali raised her broken blade to hurl it at his opponent's throat, then lowered it. That would leave her weaponless.

Metal scraped on stone behind her. The female guard was still lying on the floor but she had raised her sword to the horizontal, and now she swung it awkwardly at Tali's ankles.

Tali sprang high. The sword shaved leather off the heel of her left boot, slipped from the guard's hand and went skidding across the floor. The male guard looked around, thinking he was under attack, and Tobry thrust his blade home.

Tali went for the female guard but the woman's head thudded backwards into the stone floor. She was bleeding to death from her belly wound. Holm raced out of the passage, sword in hand.

"Where have you been?" whispered Tali.

"Guarding the clangours and watching the hall. We'd better get moving. When they don't return, they'll be missed. How long have we got?"

"Depends on their rounds. Two hours at most." She turned, her voice rising. "Tobry?"

He was standing listlessly, the bloody sword dangling, and his eyes were glazed. He was going paler by the second.

"Are you hurt?" said Tali. She could see no mark on him.

"Just – overdose."

"Maybe you'd better wait here."

He grimaced. "I'll cope. Which way?"

Tali struggled to remember; too much had happened too quickly. "Er . . . left. What time is it?"

"Must be after eleven," said Holm.

"Then the slaves will be in their beds. We'll head to the men's quarters first."

Tali knew quite a few Pale men by sight but had no friends among them. And the men were beaten down by exhausting labour in the mines and foundries. Why would they listen to her?

She put that problem aside and focused on the immediate one – getting there. The men's quarters, which were past the heatstone mine, were about a mile away. She wasn't looking forward to going that way – a whole mine full of heatstone was bound to cause her excruciating pain.

She took the guard's sword in place of her own and they set off along the carved and painted tunnels. This time their luck held and they encountered no one on the way. It was just as well; Tobry was staggering and Tali's wrenched wrist was so painful she could barely raise the sword.

As they approached the barred entrance to the heatstone mine, the wall art became ever more dark and threatening. It was always so in places where the Pale lived and worked. The art in the rest of Cython depicted gentle scenes from nature, seldom showing humans, but here the walls were sculpted into wild scenes of jungle, storm and moor, and there were eyes in the darkness. Hunters. Predators.

It was a warning to the Pale. Try to escape and this is what you will face.

Tali crept past the mine entrance, keeping to the outside wall of the tunnel and as far away as possible from any heatstone. The pain was like being stabbed through the skull but she could not stop.

"Heatstone?" said Holm.

"Help me past."

He put an arm around her waist and heaved her along. Tobry lurched in their wake, twitching, sweating and still looking as though he was going to throw up. Once they had gone a couple of hundred yards past the mine, her headache began to ease.

"What a miserable crew we are," she said.

"Speak for yourself," said Holm, who had perked up since leaving the pondages.

"The men's quarters are around the next corner and down a hundred yards. Tobry, I'll need you to work a concealing magery to get me past the guard post."

"What's wrong with your magery?" Tobry said limply.

"It's weakening. I'm saving it for an emergency."

They struggled on. "Knock the guards down," said Tali. "Stun them ... or whatever ... then deal with them while I rouse the men."

Her biggest challenge. The only time she had addressed a multitude had been at Lady and Lord Ricinus's trial. Her tutors had not given her instruction in rhetoric, which was forbidden in Cython and would have earned her a chuck-lashing. How was she to convince all those worn-out men that rebellion and probable death in Hightspall was preferable to their miserable existence in Cython?

They crept around the corner.

"I can see the guard post," said Holm, "but there aren't any guards."

"What if we're too late?" whispered Tali.

"Get going!" said Tobry. "Courier must be – through – Seethings by now." He slumped against the wall, holding his belly. His lips were an ugly grey, his eyes dilated.

She bit her lip. There was nothing she could do for him. And he was right. Lyf's courier would have reached the entrance to Cython by now. In half an hour he could be handing the death order to the matriarchs. All depended on how urgent it was, and how long they took to act on it. What if the enemy already had a plan and were just waiting for the order? There might not be much time at all.

The men's Empound, which consisted of banks of tiny, individual cells arranged around a large assembly area, was as neat and well scrubbed as everywhere else in Cython.

But the place felt empty.

Tali eased open a cell door and peeped in. She saw an empty stone bunk, a neatly folded ragweed blanket, a full water jug and a peg in the wall where the slave would hang his loincloth at bedtime. Every slave's home looked like that. Few had any other possessions.

She checked several other cells, randomly. They were all the same – like the women's cells, only smaller. She tasted water from one of the jugs, and it was fresh. What could have happened to the men? The cells did not look abandoned – just empty.

She went back to Tobry and Holm. "They're not here. What do I do now?"

"Where could they have gone?" said Holm.

When she thought about it, the answer was obvious. "Mating nights."

"Which are?"

"The three nights a month when the mated men are allowed to visit their women folk, and the younger men and boys go home to their families. They'll be in the women's Empound."

"Then your call to rebellion will have to be absolutely brilliant," said Holm.

"Why so?"

"If you were seeing your partner for the first time in a month, would you go out to listen to some rabblerouser who was probably going to get you both killed?"

CHAPTER 92

"Wan' me to take – guard down?" Tobry was worse, slurring his words. He was constantly checking behind himself now, his eyes wide and fearful.

It was midnight, and the entrance to the women's Empound was guarded. Tali pulled him back out of sight.

"We can't risk magery here." Can't risk you using it either, in your condition, she thought. You'd get it wrong and give us away.

"Why not?"

"The enemy's quarters are just up there." Tali pointed back to a broad tunnel leading off this one, "and the entrance is heavily guarded. If they hear anything suspicious they'll be out in force."

"How are you planning to get into the Empound?" said Holm.

"As a slave," said Tali. The condition she most feared, but there was no other way.

They went back and hid in an empty storeroom a hundred yards away. Tali tried to prepare herself mentally, but it was hard to focus when Tobry was throwing up blood in a corner.

He wiped his mouth and staggered across. "What if you're seen?" He sounded a little better.

"Slaves are allowed to leave the Empound at night to relieve themselves. The squatteries are around the corner."

"Why don't they have them inside the Empound?" said Holm. "That'd make more sense."

"Cythonians are fanatical about cleanliness. Even with all the lime they use, the squatteries stink. They're all well away from the living areas, with special air wafters and pipework to get rid of the smell."

"But if they recognise you—"

"Why would they? Lots of Pale are blonde, and most are small. I'm a common type."

"Never *common*," said Tobry. "I'd better come with you."

"You're tanned and weathered! Any fool would know you're not one of us. Why do you think we're called the Pale?"

"That's not the real reason, is it?" said Tobry bitterly. "You're afraid I'll crack up."

Tali couldn't deal with his troubles as well. The challenge facing her once she got into the Empound – *if* she did – was too over-whelming. "You said it. I didn't."

His look told her he knew exactly what she meant.

"You know what you've got to do," said Tali. "Go down past the subsistery – the Pale's dining hall – the entrance looks like the mouth of a grinning eel. Then head around and to the right. Break into the weapons stores and the tool stores—"

"What if we can't?" said Holm.

"If your lock-breaking skills don't work, Tobry will have to use magery. Find anything that can be used as weapons – enough for thousands. Especially heatstone – there's a storeroom full of it, here." She showed him on the map. "Once you've done that, come back, deal with the Empound guard and keep watch. If you run into any of the enemy, and you probably will, you know what to do."

"Why not deal with the guard now?" said Holm.

"The guards change in an hour, and it's going to take me longer than that to get thousands of Pale up and talk them into rebelling." Assuming she could. "Off you go; I've got to get undressed."

They went out. Tali took a length of green rag from her pack, stripped and put her clothes, boots and knife in. She rumpled up her hair and fastened the loincloth around her hips.

And she was a slave again. A half-naked, helpless slave that any Cythonian could strike down. She could feel the slave's mind-set rousing, the hope draining out of her. Tali fought it. No matter how she was dressed, she was the Lady Thalalie vi Torgrist, here to save her people.

After taking a deep breath, she adjusted her loincloth, readjusted it, then went out, practising the slave's listless walk, the downcast eyes and dangling arms. Around the corner, up the gentle slope towards the guard post.

It was hard to breathe; a knot tightened in her belly. You look like a common slave, she reminded herself, like all the others here. Why would any guard take notice of you?

She watched him from the corner of an eye as she passed. He looked up, then down again. Slaves went in, slaves went out. As long as there was no ruckus in the Empound, he wasn't concerned. In a couple of hours there would be a huge ruckus, but by then Tobry and Holm would have dealt with the new guard. If Tobry was still on his feet.

And if he hadn't had an attack of shifter madness. She should have given Holm the emergency potion, which was in the bottom of her pack in the storeroom. Too late now. She couldn't go back.

Tali followed the tunnel in. It curved around to the right and the wall art here was ferocious and threatening, full of toothed beasts in savage landscapes under lowering skies.

Her greatest challenge was yet to come, and it was the one she - was least well equipped for. What if the Pale wouldn't rebel? Why would they listen to her, an escaped slave who had stupidly come back to slavery? What if they laughed at her or mocked her? The thought of standing up before such a vast sea of hostile faces almost made her wet herself.

Tali plodded to a stop, feeling the panic rising. The courier could have reached the matriarchs by now; he could be handing them the death order. Would they debate it, wait until the morning, or act at once? Eighty-five thousand lives depended on the answer.

The women's Empound had the same layout as the men's quarters, curving slices like honeycomb each containing thousands of little cells arranged around a circular assembly area a couple of hundred yards across. The arching ceiling was held up by thick, octagonal columns arranged in arcs, carved from the native rock. The only difference was that the cells and the assembly area were larger here. On mating nights the Empound had to accommodate many more Pale.

She crossed the assembly area, went to the first cell, shoved the door open and said, "Get up. The enemy are coming to kill you."

"What?" a man's voice said thickly.

"Kill us?" cried a woman.

Tali did not reply. She ran down several doors and said the same thing, then scrambled up to the next level of the honeycomb of cells, then along and up again, repeating her message but offering no explanation. She crossed to the next section of the honeycomb, then to the section after that.

She could not go to every cell, or even every row; that would have taken hours. Tali was trusting to the slaves' natural curiosity and ever-present fear to get them outside and rouse their neighbours.

Their lives being mind-numbingly tedious, the smallest bit of news or gossip fascinated them, as did any kind of violence against their fellow slaves. Her well-chosen words offered both and soon thousands of Pale were outside, all whispering at once.

In fifteen minutes, she judged that everyone who was coming out had done so. There were people everywhere along the walkways to the cells and in the assembly area, tens of thousands of them. Such an assembly was forbidden, so she had to sway them quickly. The strong slaves preyed on the weak and anyone who could gain favour by denouncing her was likely to do so, unless she convinced them that their own lives were in peril.

Tali stood at the edge of one of the walkways, halfway up a bank of cells where the maximum number of people could see her. She held up a hand and the talking ceased. She had to be quick, and she had to put it simply, clearly, persuasively.

"You know me," she said. "I am Tali vi Torgrist, the first Pale ever to escape from Cython. I killed Overseer Banj with mighty magery. I know the way out. I've come back to free you, because—"

"Why would we listen to *you*?" sneered a familiar voice, off to her right. It was a tall, beautiful slave with a fall of shining black hair and skin like rubbed amber. Radl.

Tali's heart stopped, then restarted, beating twice as fast. Radl had been her enemy since childhood, and since her man had been executed in the heatstone mine last year she burned with barely suppressed fury. But she was a natural leader who kept the Pale in her group in line better than their masters could, and she had saved many a life by doing so.

"There's a death order out for the Pale."

"Explain!"

"Up above, the war's turning against Lyf," said Tali. "He has to make sure Cython is safe, in case he has to retreat here. He's just issued a death order on the Pale."

"I don't believe you," said Radl.

"It's true," Tali said desperately. "His courier will be here by now, handing the death order to the matriarchs."

"How could you know that?"

"There isn't time for this," said Tali. "Please, Radl, we've got to get them out."

"Answer the question."

"I've been spying on Lyf with magery. For weeks. I was afraid this would happen."

"I think you're lying," said Radl, smiling thinly.

"Why would I come back to slavery? If they catch me, I'm going to suffer the most agonising death they can create."

"Yes, you are." Radl licked her lips. "But the slave who betrays you will be well rewarded."

"Are you prepared to bet your neck on that?"

Radl frowned.

"If I'm telling the truth, you'll lose your head to the Living Blade, like everyone else," said Tali. She reached out to Radl. "I've seen the death order. And I saw the courier leaving Caulderon, *two hours ago*. He'll be here by now."

"How's the war going?" Radl said abruptly.

The Pale had only one source of news – what their masters told them. Most of the time that was nothing, though of course they knew there was a war on. Keeping one eye on the gathering, Tali sketched the situation in Hightspall in as few words as possible.

When she finished, Radl just stared at her, and Tali began to sweat. Even if the courier wasn't here yet, more than an hour had passed since she and Tobry had killed the guards at the pondages. The moment their bodies were discovered, the hunt would be on and all Cython would be roused. Then the rebellion would be crushed before it begun.

"All right," said Radl. "I believe you. But they won't listen."

Some of the slaves were already heading back to their cells, their minds closed.

"Why not?"

"Because I've spent all my hours since Mia's death blackening your name."

"Why would you do that?" Tali said hoarsely.

Radl shrugged. "She was my friend and you caused her death. And I've never liked you. I was working on a similar plan, and your escape ruined mine."

Tali shivered. She felt sure Radl was going to betray her.

"But I love my people and I want them to escape," Radl said unexpectedly. "What's your plan?"

"I've got two allies here. They're breaking into the armouries right now. We arm our people, as many as we can, and run for the nearest exit."

"All the exits are guarded and booby trapped."

"But the enemy are expecting an attack from outside, not inside. Holm knows how to disable traps, and Tobry can blast down the guards with magery."

"It's not much of a plan," said Radl. "The enemy have thousands of trained fighters; we have none."

"I was hoping not to fight. Have you got a better plan?"

"Not yet."

"Wait; there's one other thing." Tali explained how small pieces of heatstone could be used like grenadoes. "We can attack the enemy with heatstone if we have to, and since they're superstitious about the stuff, I don't think they'll use it against us."

"I like it," said Radl.

"Also, when I dropped that huge piece of sunstone in the shaft the day I escaped, it knocked all the Cythonians unconscious—"

"So *that's* how you got away. The enemy cleaned the whole shaft up themselves; they wouldn't allow us near."

"They didn't want you to know how I escaped."

"But there's no sunstone near here," said Radl.

"I'm hoping that heatstone, being stronger, will also knock them out."

"I wouldn't bet on it." Radl thought for a moment. "All right, I'll help you . . . if you can beat me in a fight."

CHAPTER 93

"A *fight?*" said Tali.
"Right here, right now."

There wasn't time to debate the matter. The enemy could be on their way, and the moment they entered the Empound every slave would denounce Tali.

"All right," she said.

Without warning, or any hint of what she had in mind, Radl struck Tali across the face so hard that it knocked her sideways. She staggered a couple of steps, her head ringing. The low buzz of talk throughout the assembly area stopped. Radl had everyone's attention. The slaves loved a fight, loved to see someone else's blood, and loved a winner, too.

Tali hurled herself at the taller woman. Radl struck at her again but this time Tali was ready. And she had learned a lot about fighting since her escape from Cython. She caught Radl's arm, yanked

her forwards and brought her knee up into Radl's belly, driving the
wind out of her. Radl stumbled backwards, fell, and Tali went after
her, realising too late that it was a trick. Radl thrust two long feet
into Tali's belly, snapped her legs straight and catapulted her ten
feet backwards, knocking down half a dozen staring Pale.

She rose, hurting all over. She'd landed on the wrist she had
wrenched earlier and it was throbbing mercilessly again. Was Radl
genuine, or was she planning to kill her? It wasn't uncommon for
slaves to be killed in fights.

Tali moved forwards, reviewing the lessons Nurse Bet had taught
her and all the dirty fighting she'd learned since. Though how could
she fight with only one hand?

Think, think. And then she had it.

"Throw the match," said Tali quietly as they circled each other,
"and I won't kill you the way I killed Banj."

"You can't. Your power comes and goes."

Tali extended her right hand, the fingers pointing at Radl's
throat. "Want to bet your life on it? I've been schooled by some
mighty magians in Hightspall." It was almost true. "I've learned a
lot from them."

After a long hesitation, Radl said, "All right." Then added, nastily, "I was going to let you win anyway. It's the only way you could
ever beat me."

She struck at Tali, missed. Tali struck back and also missed. Radl
aimed a tremendous blow at Tali's face. She ducked, took hold of
Radl's arm with both hands and, ignoring the excruciating pain in
her wrist, threw the taller woman over her shoulder. Radl hit the
floor hard. Tali sprang onto her chest with both feet, raised her arms
to signal victory, then stepped aside briskly, just in case.

"Cheat," muttered Radl, but she got up, came to Tali's side and
raised her arm. From the corner of her mouth she added, "In return
for my support, I want your man."

Tali ground her teeth. "I don't have a man."

"Well, if you ever get one, old or young, handsome young giant
or toothless dwarf, I'm having him."

"Whatever you say," said Tali. It hardly mattered, since they
were bound to die anyway.

Radl pushed Tali aside, faced the staring Pale, then spoke, just loudly enough to be heard by all.

"Only two hours ago, Lyf issued a death order – *on all the Pale.*" Radl paused. "If we don't rise up against the enemy right now, they're going to put every one of us to death."

"When?" said a small, white-blonde woman at the front.

"Maybe tomorrow, Nizzy," said Radl. "*Or maybe tonight!* They could come for us at any time."

"We can't stop them with our bare hands," said Nizzy.

"Tali killed her overseer with magery and she's got allies here who can arm us. Are you going to join us – or lie down and wait to die?"

They stared at her, unmoving. This had always been Tali's greatest fear. Like mice trapped by a cat, the Pale were too cowed. After a thousand years of slavery, their natural instinct was to close their eyes to what was happening. Not even Radl could convince them to rebel.

"What are you going to do?" Tali muttered.

"Pick the best natural leaders."

"And then?"

"You'll see. You, Lenz," said Radl, pointing to a stocky, brown-haired man. "Come here."

He obeyed. If there was one thing the Pale knew, it was obedience.

"And you, Nizzy. And you, Balun."

The small, white-blonde woman came down, then a middle-aged man followed, limping. He had big fists and a slightly twisted left foot.

Radl walked back and forth, picking out another dozen people and calling them forwards by name. When they stood before her, she walked up to Lenz, drew back her fist and punched him in the mouth, knocking him down.

She stood over him. "Round up your people. You're going to war."

He got up sullenly, but headed up to the cells.

Radl laid Nizzy low with a vicious blow to the belly, and was turning on Balun when he put his hands in the air. "I get the message."

Radl dropped him anyway, though with less ferocity. "Bring

down your men, and your fighting women. Don't take no for an answer."

Nizzy went cheerfully enough, Balun with a ferocious grin, and the other twelve leaders scattered to fetch their own people. Radl sent three of her own loyal followers to guard the exit, to prevent any slave from sneaking out and betraying them, then turned to Tali, rubbing her bruised knuckles. For a second Tali thought the tall woman was going to thump her as well. Radl laughed, showing strong white teeth.

"See how it's done?"

"Was that necessary?" said Tali.

"It's the only argument they understand. You should try it."

"I'll leave it to you. You're so much better at it."

"Yes, I am," said Radl. "I've been planning this day for a very long time."

"Really?"

"I love my people," said Radl. "And I *burn* to see them delivered from slavery."

"But for as long as I've known you, you've treated them badly."

"They're so cowed, nothing else would work."

Radl proceeded along the rows of cells, beating and bullying selected male and female Pale, and ordering them to do the same. After fifteen minutes, a little over three thousand slaves stood in the assembly area, in groups of a hundred, each behind their captain. Radl went from group to group, giving them soft-voiced instructions emphasised with a punch here, a slap there. Tali could not hear what she was saying, but judging by Radl's hand movements she was telling them how to fight.

She came back. "There, I've done your job for you."

"But there's only three thousand. What about the rest?"

"You know what they're like," said Radl. "Heads in the sand."

"We have to save them all."

"This is all you're going to get."

"What about the children, the nursing mothers, the old folk?"

"They can't fight armed guards. If we win, we'll come back for them."

Tali swallowed, stared at the taller woman. Clearly, Radl had decided to take over, but Tali didn't see how this new plan could succeed. "But . . . we're not supposed to be attacking the enemy – just making a run for the exits."

"That can't work," said Radl.

"Why not?"

"Thousands of Pale can't run for the exits in secret – the enemy would know about it in seconds. They'd signal the exit guards to lock the exits, then they'd attack from behind and butcher us. There's only one thing to do."

"What's that?"

"Attack the enemy, *right now*, and defeat them. Then lead out everyone who wants to go."

"That's not my plan," said Tali.

Radl knocked Tali onto her back with a blow to the belly she did not see coming, then put her foot on Tali's chest, holding her down. "I've changed the plan."

The blow had winded Tali. "Have you – ever – led an army – to battle?"

"Have you?" Radl retorted. "I've been planning a rebellion ever since they killed my man. This is the only way that has a hope of working."

Radl thought for a moment, then removed her foot and offered Tali a hand. She took it and Radl lifted her to her feet. Tali studied the taller woman from under her lashes. She would never understand Radl, but if this was the only way to save the Pale, she would find a way to work with her.

"What's the matter with your wrist?" Radl said suddenly.

"A bad wrench."

Radl took it in both hands; her lips moved in a healing, and the pain eased.

"Thanks," said Tali.

"I did it for them, not you. Once we've armed everyone," said Radl, "we'll attack the enemy in their quarters. Nearly everyone will be there at this time of night. If your magian can blast down the gates and kill their guards, we can take them by surprise. We'll try to bring the entrance roof down with heatstone and trap them in their quarters. Then we can get *everyone* out."

"It's a better plan," Tali said grudgingly.

Radl grinned. "Of course it is."

"But the matriarchs could be issuing the death order by now."

"Then we've got nothing to lose, have we? Lead the way."

"Three thousand Pale aren't enough to attack ten thousand armed enemy. Not nearly enough."

"They will be if we can catch them in their beds. Come on."

CHAPTER 94

The guard post was open, the guard lying dead inside. The Pale streamed out behind Tali, men and women both, barefooted and silent.

She led them along to the subsistery. Outside its grinning-eel-shaped entrance was an open assembly area, the roof of which was held up with a dozen slender, carved columns. It was about fifty yards by forty, barely large enough to accommodate the three thousand Pale who had followed.

Holm and Tobry were waiting in the service corridor beside the assembly area, with Tali's pack.

"It worked, then?" said Holm.

"Not exactly. Radl's taken over." Tali explained the new plan.

"It's better than the previous plan," said Holm. "I can't say I ever liked it."

"Neither did I," said Tali. She slipped her pack on; there wasn't time to get dressed. She felt hideously self-conscious wearing only a loincloth in front of her friends, but arming the Pale was more important than her own modesty. "Any news?"

"Had to kill a few guards," said Tobry. "No sight of a courier, though."

"Doesn't mean anything," said Tali. "He could have come a number of ways."

Tobry was looking better since he'd thrown up, though it aroused the old fear – if he'd thrown up the potion before he'd absorbed all of it, how long before the shifter madness rose again?

It was another pointless worry. She would keep an eye on him and be ready to use the emergency dose if he started to shift ... assuming she could. Tobry was a strong man and, in shifter form, twice as strong again. With an effort she buried that worry as well.

"Take this with you," said Holm, handing her a little brass implement on a lanyard; a stubby cylinder with lenses at either end, like an inch-long telescope. "It'll help with that problem we talked about earlier."

"What problem?"

"Getting an overview of an underground battle. Tobry and I put it together while we waited."

"But what is it?"

"A mage glass," said Tobry. "Focus it on any part of your map and it'll show you what's happening there."

"More or less," said Holm.

"Can I talk to our captains with it? Give them orders?"

"Of course not."

Then it probably wasn't going to be much use, but she hung it around her neck.

"Have you got the map?" said Holm.

"In my pack." She looked around. "Let's get the Pale armed."

Tobry and Holm had cracked the locks on the armoury and the nearby storerooms and laid out crates of swords, knives, chisels, hammers and many other kinds of tools. They had also broken into the heatstone store and opened boxes containing small cut pieces of heatstone, which were used for a myriad of heating purposes. As the last of the Pale collected their weapons, Tali's head began to throb.

She was explaining how to hurl pieces of heatstone so they would break and go off like grenadoes when the clangours sounded from a dozen places at once, and a terrified cry echoed down the corridor.

"They're coming!"

There was instant panic, Pale running in all directions, crashing into one another, jamming in the exits and trampling any who fell. Radl's plan had failed before it began. The element of surprise had been lost, the guards at the exits were alerted, and now the little Pale army faced a greatly superior enemy.

"What do we do?" said Tali. They could not collapse the tunnel into the enemy quarters now – they could not get to it.

"Only two choices," said Holm. "Attack or run. And I don't like either."

"We've nowhere to run to – if we can't beat them, we'll never get out. We've got to fight. Form up your ranks," she yelled. "Weapons at the ready."

No one took any notice. "This is hopeless," said Tali, arming herself with more pieces of heatstone. "I don't know why I came here."

"At least they'll die on their feet, not their knees." Holm looked over her shoulder. "Here they come."

A band of Cythonians were forcing their way in through the main entrance, at least fifty, though Tali wasn't tall enough to see how many ranks there were behind the leaders. They were armed with short swords, the best weapon for fighting in confined spaces, and the officers among them wore leather armour.

Radl sprang up on a table. "They're only a handful," she bellowed. "We can take them."

She leapt down with a chunk of heatstone in each hand, hurled them across the assembly area at the advancing enemy, and before the missiles landed she was racing forwards, armoured only by her loincloth and her amber skin.

Tali flung her heatstone at the same time. It burst at the feet of the leading rank of the enemy, the blast killing several and knocking others down, shrivelling their hair and setting their clothes alight. The Pale let out a ragged cheer.

"Come on!" screamed Radl.

Pain speared through Tali's skull, as it always did when heatstone or sunstone was broken nearby though, to her dismay, none of the enemy had been knocked unconscious. Maybe that only happened with sunstone.

She staggered after Radl, and so did a horde of Pale. The enemy, disconcerted by the unprecedented defiance of their slaves, beat out the flames and retreated, leaving their dead and injured. The Pale swarmed over the bodies, arming themselves with swords, knives and chuck-lashes, which they hurled after the retreating Cythonians.

"Don't waste the chuck-lashes," Tali yelled, donning a leather chest plate and helmet from a small Cythonian woman, and taking an odd-shaped crossbow and a bag of quarrels. "Hold onto them until the enemy are close."

The enemy surged again, and were again driven back, though this time more than half of the fallen were Pale. Tali wound the crossbow, aimed and fired. One less Cythonian to fight. But then they came again, in armour in a flying wedge.

"Use the heatstones!" Tali screamed. "Throw them all at the same time."

It was no use. The Pale weren't trained to fight as a team. The enemy drove deep into the milling slaves, and the slaughter was terrible.

The Pale dropped their heatstones, broke and ran backwards into the broad tunnel that ran from the assembly area towards the toadstool grottoes. The enemy came after them, killing more and more.

Holm caught Tali's arm and shouted in her ear, though she could not make out what he was saying over the clamour.

"What?" she yelled, dropping the crossbow, which was an encumbrance at close quarters, and duelling a tall Cythonian left-handed.

Holm jerked her backwards just in time. "This isn't working! They know how to fight down here and the Pale don't. They aren't using heatstone effectively – they're letting the enemy get too close. Weight, strength and armour are everything in hand-to-hand battles, and the Pale don't have it."

"I know. But I don't know what to do."

"See if you can bring the roof down in front of the enemy."

"How's that going to help?"

"It'll give the Pale a chance to regroup, and you the time to beat some useful tactics into them."

"Have you got any heatstone?"

"Yes, here." He thrust several chunks into her hands.

Tali's head shrieked but she had to ignore it. "Radl! Bring them back. Back!"

The bloodiest fighting was just ahead, and Tali recognised Radl's tall, splendid figure, fighting a desperate rear-guard action that was doomed to failure.

Tali hurled a piece of heatstone past her, taking down the two people Radl was fighting and opening up a gap between her and the next squad of the enemy. She checked the roof rock. She wasn't sure how well heatstone would work against solid rock, so a spot where the roof was fissured was her best hope.

Several dozen armoured Cythonians were lumbering towards her, brandishing swords and flinging chuck-lashes that exploded to her left and right. She waited until they were only twenty feet away, then hurled another piece of heatstone up at the fissured tunnel roof, ten feet above them.

The burst brought down yards of rock and three of the enemy disappeared beneath the fall. The ones behind retreated, their clothes smoking, watching her warily. She hurled another chunk of heatstone and more roof caved in, rubble bouncing on rubble until billowing dust blocked all sight of the enemy.

Tali shoved the littlest piece of heatstone into her pouch and made her way back through the Pale to Holm. "Boost me up, quick."

He lifted her onto his shoulders.

"Retreat," Tali screamed. She had to scream or she would never have been heard. "This way." She pointed down the tunnel, away from the enemy.

"Where to?" yelled the man with the big fists and the twisted foot. What was his name? Balun.

"To the exit," someone shouted, and a band of Pale stampeded, carrying Holm and Tali along with them.

"We can't reach the Merchantery Exit from here," yelled another Pale. "We can't get to any exit."

CHAPTER 95

Bastion Cowly had taken the message. The gate guards were swinging the wooden gates shut and the guards were scrambling up onto the wall, but too late. Before they could slide the heavy bars across the inside of the gates, Grandys and Syrten struck them together and forced them open.

Then it was on, Grandys attacking the hapless defenders with unusual savagery, even for him. Rix was sickened by the bloodshed. He could not stay close to the man, could not take part in it. He allowed a gap to open up between himself and the two Heroes, trying to knock his opponents out rather than kill them. Rufuss stalked past, killing like a blank-faced automaton. The doomed defenders counterattacked bravely; the battle broke up with dozens of little melees, and Rix lost sight of Grandys.

Rix fought half-heartedly, never wanting to raise a sword again, and when a big guard came at him, swinging a club, he was too slow to avoid it. It struck him on the side of the head and he went down.

He lay there, seeing double, so dazed that he lost track of what was happening. Grandys' army surged past, chasing the defenders and hacking them down. Rix crawled several yards, bumped into a heap of bodies and stalled. He could hear shouting, the clash of swords, the screams of men, women and children, but they seemed to be coming from further and further away . . .

"There he is, the craven bastard," said Grandys. An iron-shod boot thumped Rix in the ribs. "Get up!"

He groaned and gave a feeble heave. It felt as though his head was tearing open, but he could not come to his knees.

"Pick the cur up!"

Two soldiers lifted Rix to his feet, then had to hold him upright. He forced his eyes open. It was dark and a fire blazed not far away. He must have been unconscious for hours. He was drenched in dried blood, though only the flaking blood on his face and in his hair was his own.

"Well?" said Grandys. He was drunk, as he was at every feast. It only made him meaner.

"Hit with a club," said Rix. "Didn't see him."

"It didn't look like you wanted to fight today," said Grandys. "Drag him up to the feast, lads. We'll show him how we treat cowards around here."

The castle was small, and it was only a hundred yards to the bonfire they had made from the furniture. A bonfire so huge that it shouted *Grandys is here* to anyone within five miles. Butchered beasts were roasting on spits. Light rain was falling and an icy wind curled around the castle yard.

In the background Rix saw a row of bound prisoners. His gut tightened. He knew what was in store for them after the feast and, judging by the despairing looks they were giving one another, so did they.

Benches were drawn up before the fire and the troops were eating and drinking, wrapped in coats and blankets. The soldiers dumped Rix on a bench by himself and he slumped there, freezing on one side and roasting on the other. Platters of greasy, half-raw meat were carried around, along with jugs of beer and flagons of a purple wine so strong that it stripped the enamel off teeth. Rix knew he would have to drink, so he forced down several mouthfuls of stringy horse-meat. At least the grease would put a lining on his stomach.

It seemed to help. By the time he swallowed the last of it, he felt a little steadier, and even took his turn at jug and flagon without disgracing himself by throwing up. But all the while, the knot in his gut was growing. Grandys kept looking his way, then eyeing the prisoners and grinning. He always carried out his threats.

Rix could not watch any more prisoners put down, especially not these innocent folk, none of whom were soldiers. He had to strike now, before Grandys began. At least he might save a few lives in exchange for his own.

Grandys wiped his greasy hands on his month's growth of beard, then took up Maloch, leering at Rix as if defying him to intervene. The feast went silent. Everyone was looking from Grandys to Rix, waiting for him to challenge, and be killed.

He forced himself to his feet. His head spun, but settled. He propped himself on the point of his sword for a moment, then stood upright. Had the command spell broken? If it had not, he would die for nothing.

"No more killing of innocent prisoners," he croaked.

Grandys beckoned to the guards. A man and a woman were hauled up. Grandys put them to death with no more feeling than if they were bags of wheat.

The drunken soldiers roared, "More, more!"

"That's enough!" cried Rix.

The pain in his gut was so bad that Maloch might already have been embedded there. He looked around at the soldiers, then back to Grandys, and met his eye. Be strong, Rix thought. This is your hour, and it could save the world – or if you fail, doom it.

"Before all these witnesses," he said in a voice that echoed back from the bastion walls, "I repudiate my oath. You're a mongrel, Grandys, and I can serve you no longer."

"Your oath stands," snarled Grandys, "until the moment you die."

"An oath given under duress of sorcery is meaningless."

"Then why are you repudiating it?"

"Because I'm a man of my word."

"An oath is an oath. No conditions can be placed on it."

"Then prove your mastery over me in combat," said Rix. "*If you dare.*"

It was a challenge Grandys could not refuse, even had he wanted to. Which of course he did not. His triumphant leer suggested that he had been expecting it. I'm predictable, thought Rix, and he isn't. But give me the tiniest chance and I'll drive my concealed dagger into his eye so hard it'll come out the back of his head. Let's see him come back from that.

"Bring the third prisoner," said Grandys, grinning so broadly that it was almost tearing his bloated face in two.

Another prisoner was dragged out, a slender young woman with a cloud of wavy hair that flamed in the firelight. The lump in Rix's belly became a spiked ball rolling back and forth, tearing through him. No!

The guard yanked her head up by the hair.

Her name burst out of Rix, "*Glynnie!*" Only now did he truly realise how much she meant to him. He lurched around, staring at Grandys. "How did you know about her?"

"She cried out your name when I commanded you at Glimmering. I see everything, Rixium. And when I happened on her in the raid on the chancellor's camp last week, I knew she'd come in handy."

"Sorry, Rix." Glynnie bowed her head.

"Enough of the cooing and the cow eyes," said Grandys. "Your little maidservant is the prize – for the winner."

"What?" Rix croaked.

"You win, you get her," Grandys said carelessly. "I win, I get her."

Rix dragged out his sword. For Glynnie's sake he must not fail. With his right hand he had been a brilliant swordsman; the match of most men in the land. And Grandys was drunk, which must slow him a little.

Rix wasn't as dexterous with the left but after all the practice he was very good. Now he fought as though possessed, using every ounce of his skill and creative flair. He could not afford to be predictable, or allow his strokes to repeat themselves. The moment Grandys identified a pattern he would strike, and that would be the end of him – and Glynnie.

Rix could not afford a long battle, either. The longer he fought, the more likely his injury would bring him down. He attacked with a hail of blows, testing one weakness then another, and as he fought, and Grandys defended, Rix saw a reluctant admiration creeping into the Herovian's eyes.

"You're testing me," said Grandys in amazement. "You're actually testing *me*. Who taught you?"

Rix did not reply. He could not spare the energy. He drove Grandys back with another fusillade of blows, then rocked him with three blows in succession from his dead hand – a punch in the mouth, another to the right eye and a third to the bearded chin. The last would have knocked out most men, and it rocked Grandys back on his feet, but he did not go down.

He spat out two broken, opal front teeth. His eye was swelling badly; Rix could see red through the cracked armour around it. He looked down at his dead hand, which had been badly lacerated from Grandys' opal armour, exposing the bone on two knuckles. Had it not been dead, he would have been in agony.

As he leapt forwards to strike a killing blow, his foot came down on a greasy platter someone had dropped on the cobblestones, and he slipped and nearly fell. Instantly Grandys was on him and Rix only kept Maloch out of his heart by the most desperate of efforts.

He was losing strength, losing heart. He could not win. Then he caught the look in Glynnie's eyes and remembered how utter her faith in him had been, when he had promised to go with her after the war and find out what had happened to Benn. He could not let her down.

When fighting Grandys, the only defence was attack. Rix began another brilliant onslaught and knew it was his last, for his strength was failing and his vision beginning to blur. Twice he got his sword to Grandys' chest, and once to his throat, drawing blood there, but could not penetrate the man's defences. It was time for the last throw.

He slipped his dead hand into a sheath he'd stitched into an inner pocket. He'd previously practised clamping onto the dagger with his dead hand, then throwing the weapon using his arm rather than his hand. It was a desperate ploy and if he missed, as he probably would, Grandys would tear his throat out.

But the knife wasn't there.

Grandys guffawed, exposing the huge gap where Rix had knocked out his front teeth, and fished the knife out of his own pocket. "Looking for something?"

Rix attacked desperately but the best of his strength was gone. He knew he was beaten; Glynnie was lost.

"Had you watched ever since I renewed the command spell, *boy*," sneered Grandys, "the moment you started practising knife throwing with your dead hand, I knew what you were up to. I was going to bait my trap with the Pale slave but your maidservant is even better. And now she gets to watch you die – proof that I'm the better man for her."

"Rix, behind you," cried Glynnie.

Too late. The sword was struck from his hand and he was caught from behind in a wrestler's grip he could not break.

"Bring him here," said Grandys, dropping Maloch on a bench.

His right eye was turning purple through the cracked opal armour; it was so swollen that he could only see out through a slit. He tore a flagon from a soldier's hand and drained it, spilling wine down his front like purple blood then, staggering drunkenly, headed down the slope to a water cistern on the left side of the open gates of Bastion Cowly. Grandys never shut the gates of his fortresses, for he had no fear of any man.

"You know what to do," said Grandys, jerking a thumb at the cistern.

Lengths of broken timber were scattered all around, from the breaking of the gates. They would have made useful weapons if Rix had been able to reach one, but he was securely held.

The wrestler lifted Rix upright. Grandys gave him a blow in the mouth that loosened his front teeth, another to the chest that almost stopped his heart and a third to the groin that made him shriek. A second man seized his feet and they heaved him over the low side of the cistern. He crashed through a thin sheet of ice into the freezing water.

"Gather – gather round, one and all," Grandys said, now slurring his words. He was drunker than Rix had ever seen him, but still strong, still dangerous. "Ounce of gold to the man who can guess ... who can guess how many seconds Ricinus ... survive. Bring the maid. Might make her more friendly."

CHAPTER 96

The rebellion was going to end in a massacre. Tali had to come up with a new plan, fast.

"Holm?" she yelled. "Radl?"

They did not answer, and she had no idea where to look for them.

"Balun?"

He was gone too.

She had to know how the battle was going and where the fighting was. Tali got out the mage glass, held it over the map, put her eye to the lens and twisted the ring to focus it. The map went out of focus and an image grew in its place, as though she were looking down from the ceiling at the empty assembly area outside the sub-sistery. The floor was littered with dead and dying but the battle had moved on.

She moved the mage glass back and forth. The view was slightly blurred now and she could not make it any clearer, but in a broad grey tunnel several hundred yards away she made out a band of about forty Cythonians, fighting a couple of hundred Pale. And the Cythonians had the advantage.

They were forcing the Pale backwards, using their superior height and weight. The Pale could not use their far greater numbers because the passage was only wide enough for a dozen people to fight side by side. Even if they had outnumbered the enemy ten to one it would not have availed them.

She checked a nearby passage, then another. The story was the same everywhere – the Pale were either in fighting retreat, or bloody rout. Nowhere could she see them winning.

Where was Radl? Given the reckless way she fought, she was probably dead by now. Where were Tobry and Holm? She could not pick them out anywhere. What if they were dead as well, and she were all alone, leading a battle that was already lost?

Another band of Pale ran her way. Many had bloody wounds, and most had lost their weapons. "Don't give up!" Tali yelled. "We've got heatstone and the enemy are afraid of it. We can still win."

They took no notice.

"Holm, Holm?" she yelled.

"Here!" He forced his way through the Pale, who were milling about aimlessly. Holm was thickly coated in dust, even his eye-lashes.

"I brought the roof down," she said, "but they'll come at us from another direction. Our only hope is to go down."

"Where to?"

"The next level – the chymical level."

"What's it like?" said Holm.

"No idea; no Pale has ever been allowed in. But it'll give us other options. And other weapons too."

"How do we get down?"

"This way." She pointed down past the entrance to the toadstool

grottoes, where she had laboured for many years with Mia. It felt
like a lifetime ago. "Not far. They started cutting a drift down
before I escaped. I imagine it was finished a long time ago, but it'll
be blocked off."

"What do you want from me?" said Holm.

"Bring a dozen helpers – people with initiative, if you can find
any – and heatstone, as much as they can carry. If you see Radl, tell
her to come here."

He nodded and ran off.

Shortly Radl appeared with a dozen Pale behind her. Tali's heart
skipped a beat. "Are they . . . all that's left?"

Radl's full lip curled. "Do you truly think so little of your
people? They've fought bravely, and we've won a skirmish or two."

"It's not enough and we both know it."

"What do you want?"

"Teach them how to use heatstone properly. They're letting the
enemy get too close. They've got to use it from a distance, and if
they can hurl it in a volley, all the better. But not at the enemy –
if it hits them it won't go off. It needs to land at their feet."

"I'll get onto it," said Radl. "What's your new plan?" She wasn't
so arrogant now that her own plan had failed so badly.

"Holm is going to break a way down to the chymical level. He
needs sl—" Tali had almost said *slaves*. "He needs people with initiative, and heatstone, plenty of it. Can you—?"

"Damn right," said Radl, raising a bloody sword. She wore an
enemy's belt over her loincloth, with a dozen red chuck-lashes dangling from it. She gestured to her followers. "Come on!"

"Then round everyone up and bring them here," Tali yelled after
her.

She picked up a small crate of heatstone pieces in her good hand,
using her gift to try and block the pain that speared through her
head. She was heading past the toadstool grottoes when she caught
a whiff of its heavy, cloying smell, a mixture of earthy, fishy, fetid
and foul odours. Dozens of kinds of edible toadstools were cultured
there, plus some of the dangerous ones.

In an instant she was back in the grottoes, reliving her years of
slavery with Mia. Poor, hapless Mia. She had been a good friend,

better than Tali had deserved, and her own recklessness had led to Mia's death.

She balanced the box on her knee, wiped her eyes with her free hand and hurried on. Past the breeze-room where she had hidden the day of Mia's death, and where she had first met Rannilt. Tali could hear the water-driven box fans ticking, pumping fresh air down to the lower levels. She continued along to the sloping drive, twenty feet wide and nine feet high, that ran down to the chymical level.

The floor of the drive was scored with paired wheel grooves where hundreds of laden wagons had been hauled up the slope by teams of Pale women. Tali assumed the wagons had been laden with chymical weapons for the war. As she had expected, the drive was now closed off a third of the way down by a wall of stone. There was an iron door in the left-hand side but it was locked.

Holm was already at the wall with two other Pale, a thin man with his arm in a sling made from a yellow loincloth, and a white-haired young woman. Under his direction they were attaching clusters of heatstone pieces to the wall with eel glue. Tali could smell it from here. Holm was fitting together a small clockwork device.

Radl ran by, carrying a large crate on her shoulder. Tali stumbled after, her breasts bouncing painfully with each movement. Her feet hurt, too. It was months since she had gone barefoot and her soles had lost their former toughness. She stumbled, fell forwards and dropped her crate with a crash.

Radl spun around. So did Holm. They were staring at the crate. How much force did it take to set off a piece of heatstone? Some burst easily when thrown, others not at all. And if one piece went off, would it detonate all the others? Was that what Holm was relying on here?

The crate did not go off. Radl shook her head pityingly and ran back the way she had come.

"Try not to do that again," said Holm. He tightened three nuts, then wound his mechanism with a brass key, *clack, clack*. "Not sure my old heart can take it."

"Sorry. Where's Tobry? I haven't seen him since we armed the Pale."

"No idea."

Tali could hear distant shouting and the sound of sword on sword, but it was impossible to tell which direction the racket was coming from. She had a bad feeling, though.

She checked with the mage glass. Fighting was now going in so many places that she could not keep the whole battle in her head. The Pale were advancing in a couple of small tunnels, but retreating everywhere else.

"What do you know about the chymical level?" said Holm.

"Only rumours. It's secret, because it's where they make a lot of their weapons – chuck-lashes, shriek-arrows, bombasts, grenadoes, and so on. I've heard they have great retorts there, and furnaces, kilns, distilling apparatuses . . ."

"Anything useful to us?" Holm fitted his apparatus in the middle of the central heatstone cluster.

"I don't know. The only time we heard anything about the chymical level was after accidents. Last year an explosion at one of the acidulators sent a green mist gushing up into our level. Burned out the lungs of dozens of Pale; some of the enemy too."

"Sounds unpleasant."

"People are always dying in horrible accidents here. There was one at the elixerater just before I escaped. A woman had her thigh eaten through from spilled alkoyl . . . I saw it. Her leg just . . . fell off." She shuddered. "Why do you ask?"

"If this bang smashes something nasty on the chymical level, it could make it awkward." Holm stood up, his knees cracking, and rubbed his back. "Why am I doing this, at my age? I should be tucked safely in my bed."

"Hoy, old man!" It was Radl, at the top of the drive. "Make it quick. They're breaking through."

Holm flicked off a latch. His mechanism made a series of clicking sounds, each louder than the previous one.

"Go!" he said to the two Pale who had been helping him.

They ran up the slope. Tali and Holm followed hastily.

"Around the corner, I think," he said. "You never know . . ."

They turned the corner. Tali could hear fighting coming from both directions. She checked the map with her mage glass, and wished she hadn't.

"I hate this thing," she muttered.

"And I went to so much trouble to make it," he said, mock sorrowfully.

"It shows me how the battle is going, and tells me every bit of bad news, but I can't do anything about any of it. Like here, for instance."

She focused on the main tunnel up near the subsistery. "A hundred enemy are finishing off a small band of Pale. In the next tunnel, I can see hundreds of armed Pale who could come to the rescue – if only they knew help was needed. But they don't and I've no way of telling them."

"Send a messenger."

"He'd be cut down before he got there. I need more people, Holm. I need the ones who stayed behind in the Empound, but I can't get to them either."

"Didn't you say there were eighty-five thousand Pale?" said Holm.

"Counting children and mothers with young children. Maybe thirty thousand could fight, though only a tenth of those followed us."

"And the rest will die anyway." He shook his head. "Poor fools."

Tali shivered. It did not bear thinking about, but she could not stop herself. "If there was a way to get them out ..."

She checked with the mage glass, and swore. "The enemy have blocked the Empound off with an iron gate."

Thousands of slaves had gathered on the Empound side of the gate. They would be able to hear the fighting but they could not get out.

Holm didn't answer. "It's been too long," he said, frowning. "It should have gone off minutes ago."

As he put his head around the corner of the drive, the clusters of heatstone went off in a series of shattering blasts. Holm reeled backwards, his arms outspread, then landed on his back.

Tali ran to him. Blood was pouring from a triangular gash on his forehead and it brought back bad memories of the time he'd been struck down on the south coast. She studied the wound, put her hand on his forehead and tried to heal it.

A series of small thumping bangs shook the tunnel behind her. It sounded as though the Pale were using heatstone more effectively now. The blasts must have temporarily stopped the enemy advance, for a host of Pale surged past. Many had bloody, untended wounds but there was nothing Tali could do for them. Holm had to take precedence.

Another group appeared, sent by Radl, then another. There were more blasts in the other direction and more Pale appeared, wild-eyed and desperate.

"We're the last," said a hairy, bloody-chested man. "Ah! So many dead."

Tali tried to estimate how many Pale had passed. Surely less than two thousand. So few. How could they hope to win now? Or had they already failed?

Holm wasn't responding. She lifted her hand, checked the wound in case she had missed something, and began the healing again.

Radl stopped beside her, covered in sweat and gasping. "Damage won't hold the enemy back for long. Is the way open?"

Tali peered through the whirling dust. "Looks like it's still blocked. You might have to blast it again."

"I'll get onto it." Radl looked down at Holm. "Leave him. He's finished."

Radl checked the tunnel behind her, then took a red chuck-lash from her belt and hurled it up to the left. Someone shrieked.

"I can't leave him," said Tali. "Help me."

"Do you know how many of my people I've had to abandon to die alone?" Radl said furiously.

For a moment, Tali thought Radl was going to stab her. "Holm understands the enemy's devices and traps," she said hastily. "Without him, we can't get out the exit."

"How the hell are we going to get out if we go down to the chymical level?"

"Have you got a better idea?"

"No."

Tali gnawed her lower lip. "Where's Tobry?"

"No idea."

"I've got to find him. We need his magery more than ever now."

Radl heaved Holm over her shoulder and carried him down towards the wall, which was cracked in several places but not broken through. The biggest Pale began attacking it with sledge-hammers.

Tali went the other way. "Anyone seen Tobry?"

No answer.

She heard shouting from up the drive, then the clashing of weapons and the screams of the dying. A band of some twenty Pale, mostly women, ran down. Two thin, leathery men followed, looking as though they had been baked in the heatstone mines, like Tali's poor father.

They were so dazed that she did not think they recognised her. She picked up a fragment of heatstone and held it in her fist, waiting for the pursuing enemy. There they were, half a dozen of them. She hurled the fragment to land at their feet. Two soldiers fell and the rest retreated.

Using the mage glass, she scanned the tunnels for Tobry and saw him at once. He was several hundred yards away, and this time the image was absolutely clear. He was backing along the passage, bleeding from both upper arms and the right shoulder, and shaking badly.

And, she noted with alarm, there was a downy growth on his cheeks, between the four days' growth of beard. Was he *turning*?

"Tali?" he said, his voice the barest croak. "Need my potion, *now*."

If he could not take it in the next few minutes, he would have a full-blown attack of shifter madness. And she had it in her pack.

Tali checked on the map to make sure of the quickest route, then turned and ran, along the main tunnel and around a corner. Three passages opened up before her. She took the left one and was racing along it when she realised that she had never been this way before; this passage had not been here when she was a slave. But the floor was worn, and there was dust on the wall carvings, so it wasn't newly built, either.

She stopped. This wasn't right. Many parts of Cython were forbidden to the Pale, but how had she got into one? As she turned back, a door slid across ahead of her, sealing the passage. She turned again and her nemesis stood there.

"You fell into my trap," said Lyf.

CHAPTER 97

"I lured you to Cython with a lie," said Lyf, smiling. He wore boots and still supported himself on crutches, though he wasn't holding them – they were moving of their own accord.

"W-what?" Tali felt numb; she couldn't think.

"I never planned to put the Pale to death. Do you really think I'm such a monster as to repay Hightspall's genocide with my own?"

She didn't reply. Yes, she thought. I think you are such a monster.

"But now your people have rebelled and attacked their lawful masters," he went on, "what can my people do but cut them down – in self-defence?"

Tali's knees wobbled. She had given him the justification he needed, and this was his revenge for what she had done to him in the murder cellar. She had doomed the people she had come here to save.

"You manipulated me all along," she whispered. "Your revenge must be sweet indeed."

He clunked towards her. "This isn't revenge, it's *war*, and I didn't incite your people to rebel and attack their lawful masters. You did!"

"You're not our lawful masters," she said dully. "You enslaved us."

"Slavery is perfectly legal."

"Not in my country."

"Ah, but you aren't in your country, are you? You're in mine, the Pale too, and my laws apply."

In the distance she could hear the clash of swords, an occasional thump as a piece of heatstone went off, and the distinctive, high-voiced cries of her people. Death cries. "How long have I been your dupe?"

"I discovered that you were spying on me a few weeks ago," said Lyf.

"And you've been feeding me lies ever since."

"Didn't you wonder that, every time you spied on me, I was talking about the same thing?"

"The key to king-magery." What a fool she'd been to think she could outwit Lyf.

"Just so. I needed the master pearl to lead me to the key, but you were too well guarded. So why not put the idea into your head – perhaps you would find the key for me."

"It wasn't at Tirnan Twil."

He came forwards again, shrugged. "No matter. I've had a better idea."

The piece of heatstone in her loincloth pouch was hot against her belly. She felt its square outline through the fabric. Was there a way to use it?

"How did you know?" she said limply.

"I've been aware of your blood oath for some time. It showed me the way to lure you here, and the last time you spied on me I managed to overhear you, briefly."

"So that's what the leaf of the iron book was all about – to lure me here like the fool I am."

"There's no shame in being fooled by *me*." Lyf was only a few feet away. Within striking distance.

What was his weakness? Magery might be weakening everywhere, but here in his realm, so close to the vast heatstone deposit that held his lost king-magery, his gift was bound to be stronger than hers.

She could not harm him with heatstone, either. In the caverns, when she had broken that little heatstone, it had empowered him. What about his legs? Since he still used crutches, she assumed that he had not found a way to restore his amputated feet.

His eyes narrowed; he was about to attack. Tali dived, not at him but for the left-hand crutch, which supported his most damaged leg. She caught hold of it and wrenched. He teetered but it didn't come free – it was bound to him with magery. She landed on her back, kicked upwards with both legs at the other crutch and sent it flying.

As Lyf crashed to the floor, he reached out and called the crutch to him; he was already rising as it came skidding across the stone. Tali couldn't fight him, he was too strong. She turned and bolted down the dimly lit tunnel.

Shortly she reached an intersection. She had planned to go left and circle around to get back to the Pale, but the left passage was blocked. She went right, loping along, trying to get ahead. The next passage to the left was also blocked, and so was the way directly ahead.

He seemed to be driving her to the right, but why? What was down that way? The whole world was silent now, save for the audible thumping of her heart. She stopped, checked the passage each way, then located herself with the map. She wasn't far from the heatstone mine, though this passage approached it from an unfamiliar direction. Was he driving her that way, deliberately exposing her to the heatstone that would hurt her and strengthen him?

The mage glass revealed fighting all around the toadstool grottoes and the drive down to the chymical level. The Pale still had not broken through and now they appeared to be trapped; the enemy were advancing along the main tunnel from either direction. She put map and glass in her pack and stumbled on.

Tali didn't know this passage, which was cut through grey stone with a bluish tint. Her head began to throb, the bones of her skull to creak – she must be approaching the heatstone mine.

There was no sign of Lyf so she checked the map again – and wished she had not. The blurry image in the centre of the lens was Tobry, shifted to a caitsthe and rampaging up a tunnel, his great mouth stretched wide in an insane howl. He had gone berserker and was flinging bloody bodies to right and left, but the scene was out of focus all around him and she could not tell if the bodies were Pale or the enemy. She frantically tried to focus the mage glass, but lost him, and in the chaos she could not find him again.

"Tobry!" she screamed. It was one of her darkest moments; the berserker madness meant that his end could not be far away. And Holm could not help him, even if he were able to get close, because Tali still had the emergency potion in her pack.

She plodded on down the blue tunnel, the emanations from the unseen heatstone mine hurting more with every step. She had to keep ahead of Lyf, though she felt sure he was driving her, herding her.

I can heal him . . . It was Lyf, speaking into her mind.

He was either trying to tempt her, or rattle her so she gave herself away, and she wasn't having it. She could play that game too. *It's the* catalyz *you're looking for, isn't it?*

Lyf did not reply, and she sensed that he was thinking fast. If she knew its name, did she also know its purpose – the deadly secret that only one person in the world was allowed to know?

And I know what *it is,* said Tali. *The platina circlet.*

She sensed rage – or was it fear? She could not tell. She tried to check on Tobry but using the mage glass hurt her now and she could not get it to focus. All she could see was a surge of bodies – one mass dark, the other pale – and a blurred mass of running people flecked with red.

She had to keep ahead of Lyf long enough to find a way to beat him. But the longer she took, the stronger the heatstone would make him, and the more of her people would be killed. They needed her desperately but there was no way to get back to them.

Tali rounded a corner. The passage opened out and was joined by another, a broad down-sloping ramp that she had never seen before, curving down to her left. She was hesitating at the intersection when she saw someone moving up, stumbling and lurching wildly from side to side as though drunk. But not mildly drunk – intoxicated to the point that he could barely stand up.

"War!" Wil wailed, blood and mucus dribbling from his alkoyl-eaten nose. "War in beautiful Cython. *Not the right ending,"* he screamed, waving a fuming platina flask in the air.

Who's there? said Lyf sharply.

It's Mad Wil, said Tali. *Your man. And he's carrying a flask of alkoyl. I seem to remember that alkoyl hurts you, Lyf.*

Ah, but Wil does what I tell him to, and he wants to glide his fingers around your pretty white throat and choke the life out of you. He wants that, desperately, Tali. Should I let him?

CHAPTER 98

Grandys' troops gathered around, swilling from their flagons and calling out bets on how many seconds Rix could survive in the icy cistern. Few wagers were over a hundred seconds. His cretinous thugs can't count any higher, Rix thought sourly.

The cold was seeping into his muscles by the time he saw Glynnie's white, desperate face appear at the far side. She was held by the same two fellows who had thrown Rix in. Were they going to cast her in as well?

He floundered through sharp pieces of ice like broken glass, reached the side and tried to pull himself out, but the inner wall of the cistern was covered in slime and he could not get a grip. He pushed upwards and caught the rim. Grandys, swaying drunkenly, put his hand in the middle of Rix's forehead and shoved him back in.

Rix trod water, the cold leaching his strength. A hand reached out to him. He made a grab for it. It was slim and pale, a woman's cold hand. He looked up. Lirriam! She met his eyes, smiled, then shook him free and thrust him under. Everyone roared with drunken laughter.

Rix knew he was beaten. He had failed Glynnie, and failed Hightspall too. But he fought the despair. He was never giving in.

The cold was making his bones ache, slowing his movements and undermining his will to keep going. How long could he last? Another few minutes in the icy water would finish him, though he suspected he would be hauled out before the end and subjected to a worse fate. Drowning was too good for a traitor, would-be deserter, oath-breaker and attempted murderer.

He was splashing feebly when he realised that the atmosphere around the cistern had changed. The troops closest to the gates were lurching around, calling out drunken warnings.

Rix caught the rim and, after several attempts, managed to pull himself up until he could see over. A flight of arrows came whistling through the open gates and two soldiers slumped over the side of the cistern. One had a red-and-yellow feathered arrow right through his neck, the other was dead with three similar arrows in a tight group in the middle of his back. Several more men were hit and fell the other way.

His teeth chattered. What was going on? He was so cold that it was hard to think. The arrows bore the colours of Bastion Cowly. Someone must have got away during the attack and called back the men who had marched out that morning. Or perhaps they had seen the bonfire and knew what it meant. Grandys' drunken debauches after taking a castle were legendary.

A second flight of arrows tore into Grandys' troops, cutting down another seven, then a third flight. Grandys staggered around, an arrow deep in his right shoulder where the opal armour had cracked.

He reached back and after several attempts snapped off the shaft. "Attack, attack!" he bellowed.

But at the sight of their leader's blood, and a quarter of their friends fallen to an enemy shooting from the darkness, a drunken panic set in and his troops fell over themselves to get away. Lirriam and the other three Heroes had disappeared.

The cold was unbearable now. Rix tried to pull himself out but his arms lacked the strength to heave his weight up the slime-covered side of the cistern.

Grandys fumbled for his sword but his sheath was empty. "Maloch?" he said thickly, looking around. "Maloch?"

He'd dropped the sword on a bench up near the bonfire, earlier, but perhaps was too drunk to remember. He caught sight of Rix, clinging to the edge, grinned and clenched an opal-crusted fist. As he was lurching towards Rix with murder in his eye, little Glynnie appeared to his left, swinging a six-foot baulk of timber.

"Try me, you stinking mongrel!"

Grandys turned and reached out, swaying, but too late. The baulk of timber, swung with all her strength, slammed into his face, breaking the opal armour off his nose and driving him backwards. He staggered around, then crashed against the side of the cistern next to Rix, blood pouring from his smashed nose.

"Rix is mine," Glynnie said with deadly menace, and whacked Grandys again, splitting his left ear. "Touch him again and you die."

Grandys' eyes almost popped with astonishment and fury. He bellowed and tried to heave himself upright to go for her, and he was such a strong brawler that he could end her life with a single blow. Rix swung his right arm around Grandys' throat and pulled it tight, trying to choke the life out of him, but did not have the strength.

Glynnie reversed the length of timber and jammed the broken end into Grandys' belly. Brittle opal cracked and a grunt was forced out of him, though he did not seem badly harmed. She struck him between the legs. He let out a strangled roar, prised Rix's arm from around his throat and swayed on his feet. Glynnie thumped Grandys over the back of the head, driving him to his knees.

"After them," a man bellowed from outside the gateway. "Cut the gutless dogs down. Avenge our dead and restore the honour of Bastion Cowly."

"Get out of sight!" hissed Rix, terrified that Glynnie would be shot by mistake.

CHAPTER 99

"All Wil's fault, Lord King," said Wil as he reached the top, slobbering and gasping. He wiped his nose on his arm, which was crusted with dried blood and muck to the elbow. "Wil changed the ending. Wil got to atone."

Tali looked over her shoulder. Lyf was only twenty yards away. "How could *you* change the story, worm?" Lyf said coldly.

"Tried to fix Engine but everything went wrong."

"Your mind is addled; you couldn't get anywhere near the Engine. Where did you get alkoyl from? Have you been stealing from the stores again?"

"Wil not steal!" cried Wil, staggering towards Lyf and reaching out with his bony arms. "Collected it from Engine's weepings."

"Liar! Get out of my sight – no, first bring me the iron book you stole from Palace Ricinus."

"Book gone, Lord King," whispered Wil.

The feet of Lyf's crutches squealed against the stone floor as he twisted around. "What happened to it?" he thundered.

"Melted book down, Lord King. Reforged the pages. Tried to write it again, but it didn't work!" Wil howled. "Couldn't make the writing go right."

Tali looked from Wil to Lyf, whose face was drained of colour. He shot into the air so rapidly that his long boots slipped down, exposing his weakness, the stumps of his legs. "Go!" he thundered.

Wil cried out, tilted the flask up to his nose cavity and tilted it. Alkoyl fumed out, flesh sizzled, he gasped and cringed away down the ramp, weeping piteously.

Now! Tali thought. She slipped the small piece of heatstone out of her pouch and hurled it at Lyf's stumps. It struck the left-hand stump with a loud crack, then clattered to the floor. Lyf let out a cry of agony and doubled over, clutching his shinbones.

Tali dared not try to get past him; her only choice was to flee down the curving ramp. She did not know where it went, but at least it led away from the heatstone deposit. She bolted down and, after a vertical descent of some fifty feet, entered a vast, open chamber several hundred yards long and wide, carved from the native rock, white marble.

Tali looked back. Lyf wasn't in sight though she could hear his crutches on the ramp. Where could she hide?

The chamber's rocky ceiling, more than thirty feet above her, was supported by pillars of carved stone, six feet square at their bases, arranged in intersecting arcs which resembled alchymical symbols. She ran down and took cover behind the nearest pillar. Wil had disappeared.

To her left, stacked against the side wall of the great chamber near the base of the ramp, was a hip-high cube of heatstone bricks. She wasn't going anywhere near it. The chamber was softly lit by a number of glowstone plates mounted on the ceiling, but there were deep shadows too, plenty of places for her to hide – and for Wil to have hidden.

Where was he? Though he was addled, and seemed pitiful, Tali knew how dangerous he was. She had seen him choke Tinyhead, a big man, to death with those long, callused fingers. She could not see Wil, for the chamber was crowded with large, complicated pieces of equipment the like of which she had never seen before. He could be lurking anywhere.

Ahead were a variety of furnaces, some tall, narrow and made of grey iron, others squat constructions built from small, lime-green firebricks. Flues mounted beneath the ceiling carried the fumes away. She was on the forbidden alchymical level, and this curving ramp must be the way the Cythonians went up and down. Did the walled-off drive emerge somewhere on the other side? If it did not, she would be trapped here.

Tali scurried behind one of the firebrick furnaces and peered back towards the ramp. She could hear Lyf coming, the click of his crutches slow and deliberate. Keeping behind the furnaces, she scurried across towards the centre of the chymical level, to a cluster of distilling apparatuses.

The equipment in the room, she now realised, was arranged in clusters according to purpose – furnaces behind her, stills, alembics and retorts here, and to her right was an array of enormous flasks, their contents seething and bubbling on beds of heatstone bricks. One flask held a yellow fluid, thick as porridge. Another was watery and purple, with scintillas of silver rising and falling as it boiled.

Other clusters contained kinds of equipment she could not identify, although she had heard the names mentioned in her slave days – abluters, sublimaters, crystallisers, elixerators, calciners . . .

Something clacked behind her and she spun around, thinking that Wil was creeping up on her. *Clack-clack*. All she could see were a dozen kinds of stills, any of which would suffice to hide the little man.

Three towering stills made of glass reminded her of Lyf's great glass still that she had seen in his caverns. She crept between them, knife in hand. Nothing to her left; nothing to her right. *Clack-clack.* The tallest glass still, twenty feet high, hissed steam from a top vent, *ssss*. Tali stifled a screech.

Steady, steady – you're jumping at shadows. But Wil was lurking somewhere in these shadows, and he had cause to hate her.

She edged around a pot-bellied still made from sections of riveted copper. Pipes arose from its top, looping and twisting before passing through a water bath and then into glass flasks. Ahead, a small platina still was set in an open space well apart from everything else. Thick stone walls curved around it, though she could not tell whether they were intended to protect the platina still, or the equipment nearby.

Away to her right, some tall pieces of glassy equipment were illuminated by yellow lights so bright that they dazzled her. Tali didn't know what they were and wasn't planning to go that way. In here, the light was her enemy.

Then she saw Wil – the wretched creature was down the back of the chamber, creeping up an iron ladder towards a rack of silvery demijohns. He had a furtive air. What was he up to? She looked back but Lyf still wasn't in sight. Why was he taking so long? Waiting for reinforcements?

Tali crept after Wil. The nearest half of the rear wall, a hundred yards long, was covered in shelves and racks of chymicals stored in glass bottles, jars and demijohns. There were huge flasks full of deadly quick-silver, the liquid metal that was heavier than lead, jars of powders that were coloured viridian, lurid orange, bright yellow, blue, and many that were white or black. Jars full of waxy-looking metals, stored under oil. Flasks that fumed and jugs that smoked. The air had a peculiar metallic tang.

The second half of the rear wall was stacked with crates that bore the rictus symbol of death-lashes. Other stacks were marked with the symbols for grenadoes and pyrotechnic flares. She also recognised barrel-shaped bombasts, and there were stacks of crates that could have had any kind of horror inside.

A faint whistling sound alerted her. Lyf was drifting down the ramp, flying five feet above the floor, his dark eyes darting this way and that. Tali armed herself with a death-lash and took cover behind a stack of barrels. Where was Wil? He had disappeared again. She scurried across the chymical level, darting from one piece of equipment to another, looking for a way out.

Her legs ached, and so did her back; it must be three in the morning, at least. She had been going full bore for many hours, without food or drink.

On the far side she spied another ramp leading up, a straight one this time. It had to be the walled-off drive Holm had tried to break through. She scuttled that way, took cover behind one of the square pillars and looked up the drive. Hammers were pounding on the wall and she could see a number of cracks in it, but the Pale did not look like breaking through.

And even if they did, all they would find down here was Lyf. Tali hastily scanned the tunnel above with her mage glass. The image was clear this time, and perfectly in focus, though she wished it was not.

The tunnel was empty – she saw no sign of friend or foe. But a stream of blood, several feet wide, was creeping along the floor towards her viewpoint. Tali gasped and clutched at her chest, for she had seen that image before somewhere. Where?

It had been in Madam Dibly's wagon, on the way across the mountains to Rutherin. Tali's mental image of that moment was so clear that she could still remember how sluggishly the blood had flowed, still smell the faint tang of iron. She could smell it now. Tali sniffed, took her eye from the mage glass and looked around, puzzled.

And then it came, first a series of finger-width trickles seeping through cracks at the base of the wall and flowing down the centre of the drive. But as she watched, the skin on the back of her neck crawling, the trickles strengthened and merged, and slowly widened until flowing blood covered the floor of the drive from wall to wall.

Pale blood, she had no doubt. Gallons and gallons. The slaughter had begun.

She had to take Lyf on right now, or her people were going to be exterminated. She looked around frantically. The alchymical level was a dangerous place; what could she use to attack him? Her pil-fered death-lash would not suffice.

Again the bright lights caught her eye. Fifty yards away, green mist was rising from three exotic apparatuses, each a honeycomb of yellow glass with green fluids bubbling through a network of inter-nal conduits. Ten-foot-wide squares of glowing sunstone, suspended above each apparatus, lit it with a brilliant yellow light. Bricks of heatstone were stacked around the bulbous bases, heating the acid-green fluid to a furious boil.

She felt sure that these devices were acidulators, because the green mist looked like the blistering fumes that had burst up through the floor last year. What if she lured Lyf towards the near-est acidulator, then hurled a piece of heatstone and smashed it to bits? It would be a deadly ploy, as liable to kill herself as him, but she could not last much longer. It was time for desperate measures.

She plodded towards the acidulators, keeping out in the open this time so Lyf would see her, and watching him from the corner of an eye. He changed course and raced through the air in her direc-tion.

She hurled her death-lash at him, missed, and scrambled in under the base of the first acidulator, to the stacked bricks of heat-stone. Pain sheared through her head, as bad as she had ever felt, and the heat radiating down onto her was blistering. The acids in the acidulator boiled and seethed, right above her head. If the flask burst, or Lyf broke it, her death would be agony beyond description.

She jerked out a heatstone brick, rolled over and scrabbled out the other side of the acidulator as Lyf came hurtling across. He hov-ered, fifteen feet away. Tali held the brick up.

"Stop, or I'll use it."

"Smash the acidulator and it'll do you far more damage than me."

She knew it, too; most of it was above her. But trying to kill Lyf wasn't the answer. His death wouldn't stop his people from killing the slaves – it would only make their vengeance more furious.

Wait! Could she turn her earlier, bitter moment back on him? Could she make him think that *his* failure to stop her had put his people at risk? If she could, it would give the Pale a chance.

"Give up," he said. "There's no way out, and I can summon my people in an instant."

"Then why haven't you?"

He did not reply.

"I can knock some of your people unconscious," said Tali. "Maybe even all of them." It was a bluff – she had no idea how far the effects would extend, if it worked at all. There was also a possibility that the burst would strengthen him.

He eyed the brick of heatstone in her hand. "How?"

"The same way as I did in the shaft when I escaped from Cython – when I dropped my sunstone down the shaft and it imploded. It knocked all the Cythonians nearby unconscious – those it didn't kill outright – yet it had no effect on the Pale."

"The ones who were knocked unconscious woke within half an hour, unharmed."

"Half an hour is a long time to be unconscious in the middle of a battle," Tali said pointedly. "It only takes a slave ten seconds to cut a throat."

He blanched. "Anyway, heatstone doesn't have the same effect."

"But *sunstone* does," said Tali.

She hurled her heatstone brick up at the centre of the huge sunstone above the acidulator and ran for her very life, towards a cube-shaped iron furnace ten yards away.

The heatstone burst against the lower side of the sunstone, *crump*, imploding with a hot flash of light and causing a sharp pain behind her ears. She looked back. The sunstone seemed to be undamaged. No, cracks were radiating out from the centre. Get to shelter, quick!

She dived over the left side of the furnace and threw herself into shelter behind it. From the corner of an eye she saw Lyf streaking away, covering his face. Tali covered hers with her arms, put her head between her knees and—

The sunstone implosion occurred in absolute silence but with a light so bright that she could see it even with her arms over her eyes. The pain was so bad that she screamed. Heat washed over her – a torrid incandescence that would have turned her to char in an instant had she been in its direct path; just as the unfortunate guards in the sunstone shaft had been carbonised that day.

Then it was gone, still in silence. Now a hissing whistle began behind her and rose up the register until it was so banshee-shrill that her teeth began to ache. A dreadful fear struck her as she realised what was happening. Most of that burst of radiant heat had passed directly down onto the acidulator, superheating the acids inside to steam, and when the glass could take no more pressure—

She leapt up and ran. Nothing mattered now save getting as far away as possible, and keeping as much heavy apparatus between her and the acidulator as she could.

She had just passed behind the platina still when the acidulator went off with a shattering blast that hurled glass and fuming green fluids halfway across the chymical level. Green fumes boiled out and up – the same deadly, blistering fumes that had killed dozens of Pale after the accident last year. Tali covered her face with her hands and prepared to die.

CHAPTER 100

Glynnie bent to pick something up, then scuttled around behind the cistern, into the shadows. Grandys reeled up the yard into the darkness as several dozen troops stormed through the gates. Rix assumed they were the men who had marched off to join the chancellor's army. He lowered himself into the water until they passed, then scrabbled helplessly at the edge.

"Here," whispered Glynnie, who had crept around the side of the cistern and was sliding one end of her bloodstained length of timber in.

With his failing strength, Rix dragged himself onto it and clung there, panting. It was all he could do.

"Give me your hand," said Glynnie.

He reached up. She caught his left hand, and with Glynnie pulling and Rix heaving, he reached the rim and toppled off onto the cobblestones.

"So cold." He wrapped his arms around himself, shuddering violently.

"Wait here," said Glynnie, looking around. "Won't be long." She darted up towards the fire.

"What – you doing?" said Rix. "If he comes back –'

Neither Grandys nor the other Heroes were anywhere to be seen, though Rix could hear fighting not far away. His teeth chattered.

"Glynnie?" he said hoarsely.

Never before had he felt so afraid. Even in Grandys' drunken state he was a ferocious enemy. He could well rally his troops and defeat the attackers, and the moment he did he would be back, intent on bloody vengeance against the woman who had struck him down.

Rix crawled across to the dead men, found the heaviest sword and used it to push himself to his feet. A cold wind gusted in through the gates, striking through his wet clothes to the bone, for it was well below freezing now. Without dry gear he would soon collapse. Rix began to strip the biggest of the dead men, though it was slow work one-handed; his good fingers were as numb as the dead ones.

Glynnie came running back, carrying a chunk of roast rump the size of a pumpkin and dragging a sack. She wrenched the coat and pants off the man who had the arrow through his neck, and threw them into the sack.

"Horses, quick!" said Glynnie. "Where are the stables?"

"Don't know," said Rix.

"Hold this." Glynnie thrust the roast into his hands. She must have taken it from a spit because it was still gloriously hot. She looked around. "Down there. Come on."

He held it against his chest. The warmth helped. He staggered after her, his boots squelching with every step. The horses had been unsaddled and fed, and were in their stalls.

Glynnie chose a bay mare with dark brown ears, Lirriam's mount. Rix looked around for the biggest. Grandys was constantly riding his horses to death and his latest mount, down the far end, was a wild-eyed black stallion some eighteen hands high.

Rix stuffed the piece of beef in one of Grandys' saddlebags, calmed the horse with his hands, then heaved the saddle on and tightened the straps. It was all he could do to mount the beast via the side of the stall. Glynnie was waiting near the doors. She took a blanket from the sack, cut a hole through the middle and threw it to him. He put his head through the hole and gathered the blanket around him.

"How are you doing?" she said anxiously.

"Better."

"How long can you ride without getting warmed up?" She studied him in the light slanting in through the doorway. "You saved me when we were in the lake, remember? I know how bad it gets."

"Death from hypothermia is a risk I'll have to take. If Grandys catches us—"

"I know. How long?"

He got out the hot slab of beef and held it against his chest, under the blanket.

"Can probably manage an hour."

"Which way?" said Glynnie. "I don't know this country."

"North," said Rix.

"Which way is that?"

"Keep the moon on your right. The deeper we go into Lakeland, the more little lakes there are, and the harder it'll be to trace us."

They rode quietly away, and only when they were out of sight over the hill did they spur their horses to a trot, the fastest pace that was safe over rough ground in darkness. It was a clear night lit by a half moon, but windy and miserably cold, and the quicker they went the more it penetrated Rix's damp blanket. Finally, when they were five or six miles away, some time after midnight and in broken country with hundreds of little lakes and pools, he signed to her to stop.

"Can't go – any further."

She went ahead, riding around the edge of a lake until she found a protected spot against a north-facing cliff, where it would be safe to light a fire. They dismounted and Glynnie kindled a little blaze, then held a blanket up to break the breeze while Rix stripped, dried himself and put on the dry clothes taken from the dead man. He donned two coats, wrapped the blanket around himself and sat by the fire.

"You smell like roast beef," said Glynnie, kneeling before him with a little pot of a Herovian ointment she must have stolen from Bastion Cowly.

"Feel like frozen beef."

She dug her fingers into the ointment and began to smooth it across his battered face. He winced.

"You're going to look a mess in the morning," said Glynnie.

"Least – there'll be – a morning."

"Don't talk. It wastes warmth."

Glynnie laid a spare blanket on the ground between the fire and the cliff, sat down and began to cut pieces off the slab of beef. It was still steaming in the middle. Rix slumped opposite her.

"Eat!" she said, handing him a piece.

"Don't think I can swallow."

"Try. It'll warm you."

He swallowed a small piece, then another.

"Thank you," he said hoarsely.

"We did it together."

He didn't have the strength to argue. "I was so afraid for you. I was sure—"

"But you never gave in. Will he come after us?" said Glynnie. "If he survives the fight?"

"He'll survive. And come after us."

"Now?" Her voice was a little higher than usual.

Rix shook his head. "Too drunk. His debauches always end with him collapsing, unconscious. He'll sleep for ten hours, then wake with a bad head and more bile than a wounded caitsthe. He'll rant and swear bloody revenge, and run anyone through who looks at him sideways, but he won't come after us until he's stone sober and has finished brooding about his humiliation."

"And then . . ."

Rix felt sick at the thought of what Grandys would do to Glynnie. "He may not come for a week. But when he does, he'll hunt us with the same viciousness as he storms a castle. Nothing and no one will stand in his way. He always wins."

She trembled. "Not always. We beat him last night."

"*You* did. And we were lucky."

"It still counts as a win." She got up and made tea, stirred in honey from the honeycomb and handed him the mug. "Well, if we're going to die, let's make our deaths worthwhile."

He wrapped his bruised fingers around the hot mug. "Er – what do you have in mind?"

"Would you say that Grandys' reputation is the key to his success?"

"It's a big part," said Rix, unsure where she was going.

"Then the best way to undermine him would be to make people laugh at him."

Rix shivered. "I don't think that's ever happened."

"If it got out that he'd been beaten up by a woman, a no-account little maidservant, it'd do him more damage than a defeat on the battlefield."

"How would it get out?"

"We're riding west to join the chancellor's army. It should be at Nyrdly by now. We'll announce Grandys' defeat at every town and village on the way. In a couple of days, the way news spreads in Hightspall, the whole country will know about it."

"What if they don't believe us?"

"They'll believe us," said Glynnie. "You're riding Grandys' horse. And . . ."

"And?" said Rix.

"And I've got this." She reached into her pocket, but did not pull her hand out at once. She was grinning, teasing him, making him wait.

"You've got what?" cried Rix.

She drew out her hand and held it palm up. Precious opal shone in the firelight – a single piece of armour in the shape of Axil Grandys' huge nose.

Rix roared with laughter, though briefly. His battered mouth hurt too much. "Where did you get that?"

"It cracked off when I whacked him one. Thought it might come in handy."

He threw his arms around her. "Grandys' famous nose. No one can argue with that. Glynnie, you're brilliant."

"It's taken you long enough to realise it," she muttered, then smiled. "What are you going to do when we get to Nyrdly?"

"Ask the chancellor for a captain's commission, then fight for Hightspall."

"What makes you think he'll give you one?" she said mischievously. "He used to hate you."

"I *hope* he will," said Rix, suddenly uncertain. "He was happy to make use of my reputation at Glimmering. And I've learned a lot since then. A lot about leadership. A lot about right and wrong. A lot about war."

"And a lot about Grandys," said Glynnie. "You know more about how he fights, and thinks, than anyone on our side. Of course the chancellor will make you an officer. You should be our commander-in-chief."

"So you've been saying since before we left Caulderon," said Rix. "A captain's rank will do me nicely, if he'll allow it. It's an unforgiving business, leading an army." He studied her face in the firelight. "Glynnie . . . ?"

"Yes?"

He swallowed. "Something occurred to me when I was in the cistern, just before you helped me out."

"What's that?"

"How much has changed since Glimmering. We've been friends for a good while now, but . . ." He faded out, not sure how to put it.

"But you were the lord of a great fortress, and I was just a humble maidservant," she said helpfully.

"Not *just* a maidservant. But yes – that was always between us."

"You're still the lord of a fortress. I'm still a maidservant." But her eyes twinkled as she said it.

"Not here. Not now. Not if we never get back."

"I'm not sure what you're saying, Rix."

"I've plumbed the depths. You've done tremendous things. The balance has tipped. You're the strong one now."

"We're both strong," said Glynnie.

"And that's a good thing."

Neither spoke for a while. Rix stared into the fire. He could feel her gaze on him.

"Rix?" said Glynnie tentatively. "Can I ask you something?"

"Anything. Anything at all."

"Can I ride with you?"

"For the rest of your life," said Rix.

CHAPTER 101

Green acid fumes were whirling all around, condensing on the coils of the still, fizzing on the zinc plates of some arcane apparatus beyond, stinging her cheeks, burning her ears and nose. Tali closed her eyes and held her breath, though that would only gain her one more minute of life.

She fumbled a shirt out of her pack, wiped her face and spat out bloody saliva. All her exposed skin was stinging now.

Thump! She was caught around the waist, heaved effortlessly into the air and carried away, just ahead of the rolling green cloud. The implosion must have strengthened Lyf for he was carrying her weight without effort.

It had given her a painful, temporary power as well, just as it had that time in the sunstone shaft, but not enough to take him on. Lyf shot through roiling fumes towards the side wall, wrenched open a heavy glass door and dropped her onto the floor. He slammed the door and shoved a rubbery seal against it at the base.

They were in a small, square emergency chamber, empty save for a water barrel and a bank of seven levers on the right-hand side. Lyf thrust the levers forward, one by one, and Tali heard sets of water-driven box fans start up outside. He turned and studied her enigmatically.

"You would suffer so agonising a death to save your people?"

"I swore an unbreakable oath," said Tali. "Why did you save my life?"

"I saved the master pearl. Your life was incidental."

"Are you going to cut it out now?"

"After I've checked on my people. If the sunstone knocked them unconscious—"

"If you want to save them, you'd better hurry," she said exhaustedly.

Her eyes were burning again. She felt her way across to the water barrel and ducked her head. When she cleaned her eyes, Lyf was gone.

Tali checked the door. It was locked. She reached out with her gift, to see if she could unlock it, but it did not budge.

She dressed hastily, knowing Lyf could come back at any moment, then hurled her loincloth, the symbol of her enslavement, into the darkest corner. Even if she only had minutes to live she wasn't wearing it any longer.

Since she could not get out, she began to check the tunnels with the mage glass, one by one. Lyf was flitting back and forth, rousing his people. The bursting sunstone had knocked most of the enemy unconscious, but there was still fighting here and there. She had saved the Pale from immediate destruction, but for how long?

Tobry should have stood out among both the Pale and the grey-skinned enemy, but she saw no sign of him, or Holm. She closed her eyes, remembering Tobry as she had last seen him through the mage glass, rampaging up and down the tunnels, gone berserker in his madness. Tears leaked from her eyes. How had such a wonderful man been reduced to this.

Could he be healed with magery? Both Holm and Tobry had said no, but no one really knew. If it was possible at all, the best chance must be here in Cython, close to the greatest source of healing power of all – the heatstone mine. But to attempt it she would have to make the irrevocable choice between healing and destruction, and if she chose healing she could never use destructive magery to help the Pale.

Alkoyl ate through the lock, silently. The door opened, closed again, then Wil's callused fingers closed around Tali's throat from behind.

"All Wil's fault," he slurred. "Should have betrayed you to Matriarch Ady when she asked."

Tali fought her instinctive urge to struggle – he was too strong.

His fingers opened and closed, opened and closed, squeezing her throat so hard that her windpipe was flattening. He was playing with her life, drawing out the delicious moments before he took it. Tali waited until he was directly behind her then slammed her head backwards into his ruined nose, caving it in.

Wil screamed. She slammed her head back again and again, until his hands relaxed. He was lurching around, blinded by tears of agony. His face and hands were red from the acid fumes he had walked through to get to her and blood was flooding from his nose. She shouldered him aside, stumbled for the door, and out.

Most of the green mist had cleared, though the air still stung her nose and made her eyes water. She pounded across to the walled-off drive. Blood was still dribbling from the cracks, low down, and she could hear a few desultory hammer blows on it, but it was clear the Pale weren't going to break through without assistance.

Tali ran down to the back of the chamber, to the racks and crates she had seen earlier. Her lungs were burning now, her eyes watering so badly that she could barely see. She stuffed half a dozen grenadoes into her pack, strapped on a belt of death-lashes and plodded back to the wall.

"Stand back!" she yelled through the biggest crack.

The hammering stopped. Tali hurled the first of her grenadoes at the centre of the wall, where it was cracked from Holm's earlier blast. *Boom!* The centre of the wall crazed. She hurled the second grenado at the base, a third of the wall fell away and she saw the desperate Pale on the other side. They kicked and smashed the broken stone out of the way and burst through, slipping and skidding on the bloody drive.

What a pitiful remnant they were. Tali peered through, trying to count the ones up the drive. They numbered twelve hundred at most, less than half of those who had followed her out of the Empound only hours ago. Many were injured and all looked exhausted. The rebellion could not last much longer.

Radl was at their head, wounded in many places and trembling with weariness, but the light had not gone out in her eyes. And, to Tali's joy, Holm was beside her.

"This way," said Tali. "There are grenadoes and all kinds of other weapons down the back, in those crates." She pointed. "Hurry! There's a ramp on the other side – they may come that way."

"Did you do that?" said Radl.

"What?"

"Knock down three thousand of the enemy."

"I broke a great sunstone," said Tali. "Nearly killed me."

"You saved us. Without that reprieve, they would have slaughtered us all."

To Tali's astonishment, Radl, her enemy since childhood, threw her arms around her. After a few seconds she broke away and clambered onto the top of a steel retort.

"Arm yourselves and get ready to fight," she yelled. "The enemy will soon be back; we've got to be ready."

The Pale did not move. They seemed to be in shock, which was not surprising after all they had seen and done, and in the brief hiatus from fighting many had reverted to their apathetic former selves. They had to be roused again, quickly, otherwise the last resistance would be crushed and Lyf would *lawfully* order the rest of the Pale put to death.

Tali scrambled up beside Radl. "Do you have loved ones back in the Empound?" she said to the Pale.

They stared at her, sullen, afraid.

"Answer me!"

Nothing.

Radl growled, deep in her throat. Springing lightly down, she stalked to the nearest group of Pale and seized a woman by the throat. After shaking her like a cat with a rat, Radl threw her down, then slammed her fist into the jaw of the next man, rocking him backwards.

"Well?" she said.

"Yes. My family are back in the Empound."

"Well?" Radl demanded, looking down on the gathered Pale.

"Yes," shouted the Pale.

"You know what will happen to your families if our rebellion fails."

They stood there in slack-jawed silence. Clearly, they did not want to think about it.

"We know," said the woman Radl had shaken by the throat. "Lyf has issued the death warrant. The enemy will slaughter them all."

"Every Pale in Cython will die," said Radl. "All your wives and husbands, all your children."

"Your families can't help themselves; the Empound has been sealed off," said Tali. "If *you* don't save them, they die. Down the back there are crates of death-lashes, bombasts, grenadoes and fire-flitters—"

Radl thrust her aside. "Arm yourselves and get ready to fight. Hurry – if we can get up the ramp quickly enough, we can take them by surprise."

Hundreds of Pale stormed down to the back to the weapons shelves. Others gathered heatstones from around the retorts and stills, or wrenched iron bars and other implements off the alchymical equipment, taking anything that could be used as a weapon. Tali returned to Holm, who was leaning against the wall, holding his head.

"Have you seen Tobry?"

"No," said Holm.

"I have. He'd turned shifter and was going berserker."

"Then I dare say they've cut him down by now," Holm said quietly. He put a bloody arm around her shoulders.

Tali glanced across to the ramp and her heart missed a beat. Lyf was halfway down it, a host of troops at his back. She pulled free. "They're coming!"

"Attack!" bellowed Lyf.

Three hundred enemy charged down the ramp. Though they were greatly outnumbered by the Pale, the Cythonians wore chest armour and carried oval shields, and their first charge drove thirty yards across the chymical level before the Pale stopped them, fighting desperately with chuck-lashes and grenadoes, swords and knives, and drove them back to the foot of the ramp.

"Attack from a distance with your grenadoes," Radl shouted. "Don't let them get close."

Enemy reinforcements appeared around the curve of the ramp, another couple of hundred. The company at the bottom assembled in ranks and charged again, and this time the Pale could not drive them all the way back. Their only advantage was in numbers and it was rapidly being neutralised. They were no match for the enemy in size, weaponry, armour or training, and if the Cythonians gained a foothold in the chymical level, the battle and the rebellion were lost.

As Tali ran, she fumbled a couple of grenadoes out of her pack. Her breath was rasping in her throat and her legs were giving out. Thirty yards from the foot of the ramp she propped and hurled the first missile.

"Like this!" she yelled.

It went off at the feet of the enemy, taking down half a dozen of them. She hurled the second grenado but it slipped in her sweaty hand and fell short, exploding and blasting white stone everywhere, and leaving a foot-wide hole in the floor.

The fighting was furious now, the bodies of Cythonians and Pale piled in heaps all around the base of the ramp and scattered across the floor for a hundred feet. There was so much blood that the fighters were slipping in it.

It was Tali's first close experience of a major battle, and it was horrible. People lay maimed and dying everywhere, screaming in agony, begging for help or to be put down, gasping farewell to loved ones or bitterly regretting that they had joined the failing rebellion. A few were cursing Tali's name and all her ancestors.

"Attack!" said Lyf, who was hovering twenty feet up, not far from the cube of heatstone blocks.

The enemy re-formed their ranks and charged, driving through the front ranks of the Pale. Tali scrabbled frantically for another grenado, but the fighting was hand-to-hand now and she could not use it without endangering her own people. She hurled it up at Lyf instead. It burst on the wall next to him, showering him in chips of white stone. He zoomed away, bleeding from half a dozen small cuts, and she lost sight of him.

The Pale were being driven back when a vast animal howl rang down the ramp. Suddenly the enemy were screaming and shouting and scrambling out of the way as a seven-foot caitsthe stormed through them, its claws tearing through leather armour into flesh and flinging bodies to left and right.

"Stand firm," said a burly sergeant. He put himself in the path of the beast and thrust out a javelin.

The caitsthe smashed the shaft to pieces with a contemptuous backhander. Its next blow lifted the sergeant off his feet and drove him into the wall, breaking his neck. As it came raging down the ramp, the rest of the Cythonians scattered. It reached the floor, slipped in blood, then turned towards the nearest group of Pale, who stood there, mesmerised.

The beast – Tali could not think of it as Tobry, for there was no more humanity in its eyes than when he had attacked her after her disastrous attempt to heal him – would tear them apart.

"Emergency potion!" hissed Holm.

Tali felt in her pack for the little bottle. Where had she put it? Her fingers closed on a bundle deep down and she heaved it out, praying that the bottle hadn't been broken in all the fighting.

"Hurry!" said Holm, running out and putting himself between the caitsthe and the Pale.

Her injured wrist throbbed. It was a struggle to get the bottle out, and then she could not open it. Holm ducked around the caitsthe and caught it from behind but it whirled and hurled him ten feet across the floor.

The caitsthe bounded after the Pale. Tali leapt between it and them. "Tobry, stop!"

It gave no hint of recognition. Tali could not open the tightly sealed bottle so she flung it into the caitsthe's gaping mouth. Broken glass could do no lasting harm to a shifter that could heal any injury in minutes.

It crunched up the bottle, the thick grey contents oozing out and mixing with its blood. It grabbed Tali and drew her towards the great maw that could tear her arm off in a single snap. She screamed and tried to pull free but it was many times as strong as she was.

"Stop it!" roared Holm, thumping the caitsthe over the back of the head with a heatstone brick.

It turned slowly, extending its claws, then fell to its knees. The potion was working. Its claws were retreating back into its fingers, the cat jaw slowly changing to a man's.

Tobry's eyes looked out of the caitsthe's yellow eyes. They met hers and recognised her. Tali saw a deep shame in his eyes, and a flush passed up his downy cheeks.

"Thanks," he said in a thick, growling voice, and fell on his face.

"But for what?" she said quietly.

Holm dragged Tobry away from the arena of battle, which now resumed.

There was a colossal boom behind her. She looked around as the great glass still toppled. It looked as though someone had thrown a grenado at it. Behind it, one of those large flasks of quicksilver had been broken by a projectile and the silvery metal was creeping across the floor. And quicksilver was poisonous to breathe.

"More grenadoes!" she yelled. "Drive them back."

"It's not working," said Holm. "Their reinforcements are still coming down." He surveyed the battle. "And I can see them at the drive now. We've got nowhere to go, and they can attack us from both sides. It'll all be over in ten minutes ... Unless ..."

"What?" said Tali.

"The time has come for you to make the final choice about your magery."

A brick descended into the pit of her stomach. *You can be a destroyer or a healer, but not both.*

CHAPTER 102

Had Tali acted more quickly to attack the gauntlings at Tirnan Twil, its people and its treasures might have survived. Now she faced the choice again. Her life was going around in circles.

Tobry was on his feet, though he was grey and exhausted. His skin had gone baggy and he looked shrunken, for the caitsthe state burned energy at a staggering rate. His eyes were still yellow and he was covered in down – this time he hadn't turned all the way back.

The only hope for him, and that a tiny one, was healing magery, which would definitely be a *great healing*, if it could be done at all. But the chance of success was tiny, and the risk enormous. Could she justify it?

She looked around at the dying Pale and knew that she could not. If she used her gift on a healing, she would not just be condemning these Pale here, but the others as well – all eighty-five thousand of them.

"I'm sorry, Tobry," she said. "I can't choose healing."

"I never wanted you to," said Tobry. "Saving your people is the only thing to do."

That did not make it any easier.

"All right." Tali looked across at the base of the ramp, where the fighting was again furious. "Holm, what do you want me to do?"

"Can you even the odds a little?"

She studied the lines of pillars arcing across the chymical level. "There are two ways to even the odds – by reducing their numbers, or increasing ours."

"Yes," said Holm.

"And I'm thinking that those pillars aren't far from the entrance to the Empound . . ."

"How can you be sure?" said Tobry.

"Remember that green mist I mentioned earlier? It burst through into the wax-nut grottoes last year, and they're around to the left from the Empound. And that acidulator is where the mist came from." She indicated its shattered ruins.

"Might be an idea to check your map first."

"I don't have it." She had dropped it when Wil attacked. There wasn't time to go looking for it.

"If I can bring down *those* pillars," Tali continued, indicating two beyond the apparatus, "it might crack open the entrance to the Empound and free all the Pale. With luck . . ."

"Better hurry," said Tobry, glancing across the bloody battlefield.

"Is your magery strong enough to bring down those columns?" said Holm. "They're massive."

"No, it isn't. I was thinking about heatstone."

Holm shook his head. "It works all right on cracked rock, but doesn't do much to the solid stuff."

"What if we stacked half a dozen bombasts around one of the pillars and set them off?"

"Too powerful," said Holm. "It'd probably kill everyone here."

"I don't know what else to do," said Tali.

"Better think, fast."

"I need time," she snapped. "Create a diversion!"

"I'm not sure . . ."

"Find a way to distract them from me – *and make it big*!"

Holm ran across to the nearest melee, then led dozens of Pale to the rear of the chymical level. Shortly a signal rocket soared across the ceiling, struck the wall near the ramp and exploded with a shower of pyrotechnic sparks and clouds of red smoke.

Another followed it, but dipped low and shattered one of the great glass alembics to pieces. It must have been a rocket flare for it burned with a dazzling blue-white light. A brown, fizzing liquid began to creep from the alembic, across the floor.

In the far corner, a bombast went off with a shattering roar, hurling pieces of rock and metal for fifty yards. A furnace toppled, scattering glowing coals everywhere and adding its white smoke to the thickening air. A swarm of shriek-arrows screamed across towards the ramp, followed by the brilliant red sparks of a dozen fire-flitters.

Now *that's* a distraction, Tali thought. How could she help the Pale, though?

It occurred to Tali that, when she'd whacked Lyf's wrythen with the iron book in his caverns, months ago, those few droplets of diluted alkoyl had hurt him badly. Could she attack Lyf with alkoyl? Wil had carried a flask of the stuff, though he had probably taken it with him, wherever he had gone. *If* he had gone. No, she dared not let Lyf get close enough to toss alkoyl at him. But it reminded her of something else . . .

Lucky none landed on the little heatstone, Errek had once said. Why not? What was alkoyl, anyway? She knew that it was obtained from somewhere way down the Hellish Conduit, but where did it come from? Could it truly come from the Engine's *weepings*, as Wil had said?

It fostered an alarming chain of thought. Cythonians believed that the Engine was a destructive force, forever trying to tear the land apart with great eruptions, earthquakes and other catastrophes. The king-magery that Errek had invented ten thousand years ago was a healing force and, as long as the two were in balance, all was well.

The balance between healing and destruction had been maintained for eight thousand years, until Grandys had killed Lyf in an attempt to seize king-magery for himself. Instead, king-magery had been lost and the land had not been healed in the two thousand years since.

Now the balance was rapidly tipping towards destruction, the eruptions and quakes were increasing, and Errek had said it was almost at the point where it could not be stopped. Where a cataclysm could destroy the land itself.

Alkoyl, alkoyl? It wept from the destructive Engine, while king-magery was somehow locked up in heatstone. Could alkoyl be the *antithesis* to heatstone, just as king-magery was the healing force that balanced the chaos of the Engine? And if so, what would happen if alkoyl and heatstone were combined? Was that what Errek had been talking about?

Alkoyl was stored on this level, she knew. It had been mentioned during her escape from Cython, when the young woman's leg had been eaten right through—

"She were up on the third elixerater," the foreman had said, *"toppin' up the alkoyl level, but someone had taken the dribbler out. The whole flask poured in. Blew the elixerator to pieces, and a whole flask of precious alkoyl lost—"*

The *someone* who had done it surely had to be Wil, who knew where the alkoyl stocks were held; she had seen him sniffing it even before her escape from Cython. Was that what he had been up to when she'd glimpsed him earlier? Had he been looking for alkoyl on the store's racks?

Tali had no idea what combining alkoyl and heatstone would do, but she had no other options. The enemy were still coming down the ramp and if she didn't do something fast, the rebellion would end here.

Another rocket shot across the ceiling, then two more, each exploding in brilliant blue-white flares. A second bombast went off, followed by a long line of white fire that snaked a quarter of the way across the chymical level. Someone must have laid out a barrier of the red powder called *thermitto*, which burned so hot that it could cut straight through solid stone. Cythonian miners used it to cut and shape rock.

There was fighting everywhere now, furnaces and stills being toppled, retorts exploding in showers of glass, battles raging back and forth through the wreckage, though how they could see to fight Tali did not know. The smoke was thickening; in some places the visibility was only a few yards, and before long the fumes must bring everyone down.

She heard coughing behind her. Tali whirled. Lyf was hovering only ten yards away. She jumped.

"It's time," he said.

She bolted into the smoke, turned right around the smashed acidulator then left past a badly burned cluster of bodies. Lyf was not far behind, appearing and disappearing through the smoke. She ducked down, ran the other way and scuttled through the wreckage towards the shelves Wil had been climbing, taking advantage of every bit of cover she could. Lyf zoomed overhead; she froze under the overhang of what she assumed to be an elixerator until he disappeared in the smoke.

As she reached the rear of the chymical level she saw Wil again. He must have been lurking here all this time.

"Got to write ending," he howled. "Engine going to end *everything*."

He was staggering across the floor, dragging a platina demijohn behind him. He passed through the smoking crevice in the end wall and headed downwards.

Good riddance! She darted along the wall until she reached the shelves that held the alkoyl stores. The platina flasks were high up; she could see six of them. The walls and the shelves were badly corroded, the stone and metal partly eaten away. It was deadly stuff, and she shivered at the thought of what she was planning to do with it.

Tali dared not climb the shelves the way Wil had earlier – since Lyf was flying up near the ceiling, he was bound to spot her. What if she used magery to levitate a flask down? That would be perilous too; if she dropped it and alkoyl spilled on her, even a single drop, it would eat right through her.

Would levitating a flask of alkoyl constitute a great destruction?

She did not think so — but what she was planning to do with it might. She focused her magery on the central flask. *Rise*. It rose too quickly, and so did the one on its right. They were empty.

The third one was considerably heavier — so heavy that it wobbled as she levitated it and Tali felt a moment of panic that it was going to fall. It couldn't break, being platina, but if the cap came off . . .

She managed to steady it and brought it down to the floor. Tali eyed the flask. A wisp of vapour was oozing out around the cap and she did not want to go anywhere near it, but everyone else here was putting their lives at risk and she could do no less.

"Charge!" an officer yelled in the guttural Cythonian accent. "Cut them down!"

The chymical level echoed to the sounds of hundreds of booted feet. She looked around but could see nothing through the smoke and wreckage save glows and flashes all over the place. Then she heard the distinctive thump of the seven fan levers being thrown, and the great box fans began to tick.

"Driving us into a corner!" yelled Holm. "If there's anything you can do, do it *now*!"

She picked up the flask by its handle and headed across to where the spare heatstone blocks were stacked in that hip-high cube against the wall, not far from the bottom of the ramp where the battle had begun. If alkoyl set the heatstone off, it could knock most of the enemy down, perhaps block the ramp, and give the Pale the advantage. The cube wasn't in the perfect place for that — it was a bit far away from the ramp — but she had to work with what she had.

The air thinned a little and she saw that there was still fighting at the ramp. She could go no further. She ducked beneath the overhang of a toppled furnace, took a deep breath, wrapped her hands in a piece of rag torn from the bottom of her shirt and twisted the cap off the flask.

The rag began to smoke; her fingers and palms were blistering. She wiped them on the floor. It began to smoke as well. She scrubbed her fingers against the stone. All right. She had to do it now.

She began to levitate the flask across the alchymical level. Did such magery constitute a great destruction? Not yet. Twenty yards to go. Ten.

"Don't do it!" Lyf roared, and she saw him streaking towards the flask. "Everyone, get to shelter!"

Tali felt a twinge of alarm, but she had no choice; nothing else could help the Pale now. She tightened the grip of her magery on the flask. Five yards; three; one. The flask was above the cube of heatstone blocks when Lyf caught hold of it and tried to heave it away. She held it with all the strength of her magery; she had been saving it for this moment. But her strength wasn't equal to his. He was dragging the flask out of her grasp.

She forced on the base and tried to tip the flask upside-down. He jerked it out of her grip. She thrust hard and the flask tipped sideways.

Tali was too far away to see what happened, but she envisaged it clearly in her mind's eye. A single thick drop of alkoyl, glowing a faintly luminous green, quivered on the lip of the flask, then fell.

Lyf turned in mid-air and fled, still holding the flask. A stream of alkoyl poured from it, unheeded, onto the floor, which began to fizz and fume.

"Up the ramp!" he said in a magnified voice that echoed back and forth across the ruined chymical level.

The disciplined Cythonian troops disengaged from the fighting and obeyed instantly. Tali scrambled behind a column and covered her face with her hands.

Nothing happened. A minute passed. She could hear her heart thumping, but nothing else save the Cythonians pounding up the ramp and the soft-footed Pale pattering the other way.

She was about to peer around the side of the column when she remembered what had happened to Holm. Tali tightened her fists and counted down another minute. As she said *fifty-four*, something went *zipppp* from the direction of the cube of heatstone. There came a monumental flash of green light, which darkened to blue then violet.

She went blind for a few seconds. Her whole body began shuddering violently and she could not stop it. Her head was so heavy that she could not hold it up. Then the whole world seemed to implode, and a green flash, the echo of the first, speared through her head. She felt pain such as she had never felt before, as if something inside her head was collapsing into a mote and dragging everything surrounding it, including the bones of her skull, into the centre, to annihilation.

The pain vanished and she could see and hear again. Behind her, rock was shrieking and crashing and grinding as it was torn apart, but, oddly, there weren't any pieces falling around her. There was no dust, either, though she could feel the air rushing past towards the cube of heatstone, faster and faster. She wasn't game to move, or even open her eyes, but Tali dared a quick check with her gift.

And gasped. The cube of heatstone was gone, and so was the floor beneath it and the wall immediately behind it – it had been annihilated. The wall rock was shattering to small pieces, which were drawn down so fast that they made streaks, into the incandescent spot where the cube had been, then vanishing. The dust and smoke were hurtling into it too, and every object on the floor nearby, including the many dead and dying.

A great bite had been taken out of the enemy ranks – all those who had passed within thirty yards of the cube as they raced for the ramp had vanished. But that wasn't all. Not nearly.

The incandescence faded, revealing a large hole in the floor. The hole in the wall behind it, and in the rocky ceiling above, were widening – the ceiling hole was already twenty yards across and growing rapidly as the unsupported rock crumbled and fell into oblivion. Thirty yards, fifty, eighty, a hundred and fifty, three hundred – was it going to suck all Cython down there?

Then it stopped.

Tali opened her eyes. She was trembling all over and her fingers and palms were still stinging. She rubbed them on the floor; several layers of blistered skin sloughed off. She rose slowly and looked around the other side of the pillar.

Lyf was nowhere to be seen. There was no dust in the air. No smoke. Nothing save a blue-green, shimmering rainbow arching above the hole in the floor, now slowly fading.

The annihilation hole formed a perfect oval five or six yards across, though behind it the wall rock had been eaten away for three or four times that distance, and it had led to the collapse of an enormous area above. Near the left-hand corner of the rear wall, the crevice down which Wil had passed was blackened and smoking.

Lyf came hurtling across from the far side. She expected him to turn on her, and if he had she could not have defended herself, but he raced past and up the curving ramp. At the top he scanned the collapsed area and his face hardened. He looked down at Tali.

"You've made your choice. *Destruction*. It can never be unmade."

CHAPTER 103

Axil Grandys thrust aside the naked brunette he had been groping for the past hour, put the spy-scope to his eye and touched the wire-bound hilt of Maloch with his free hand. The *trace* slid into view, showing Rix and Glynnie together. Sooner or later they would lead him to Tali and, when he took the three of them, his revenge would be such a horror that people would still be talking about it in a thousand years.

The humiliation of Rix's escape must be avenged, though Grandys had been planning to let him get away, anyway. The trace on Rix was intended to show Grandys where Tali had been hidden, and soon it would.

"Rufuss!" he bellowed.

The cadaverous man appeared at once, as if he had been lurking outside. He probably had. He was quite insane. But he could be relied on in certain matters.

"Grandys?" said Rufuss.

Grandys tossed him the spy-scope. "Follow Rixium, but don't alert him. Eventually, he will lead you to Tali. When you can do so without being discovered, bring her to me unharmed."

"What about the other two?"

"They can wait. Just Tali."

"What will you do to her?" said Rufuss, licking his lips.

Grandys wasn't going to mention the master pearl. He didn't trust anyone with that knowledge, and certainly not Rufuss. "I'm going to have my revenge."

"Shall I bring her back here?"

Grandys suppressed his impatience. "Of course not – we won't be here. We're marching to war, overnight."

"War with whom?"

"With *everyone*, of course."

"But we'll be outnumbered many times."

"That's how I like it. It will make my victory all the greater. Bring her to me at the battle plain of Reffering."

CHAPTER 104

What had she done? Tali did not know. She looked across to the ramp. There was no fighting, no noise save for the rhythm of marching soldiers and the groans of the injured. The Pale stood in a circular mass in the wreckage-clotted centre of the chymical level, pressed close together as if for comfort. The enemy were racing up the ramp towards the part of Cython that had collapsed.

She used the pillar to pull herself to her feet and was edging towards the annihilation hole when she heard that sound again, *zipppp*, and felt a breeze on the back of her neck. Something that had been suspended in the hole had hurtled down like a piston, drawing air after it.

The rock around the hole looked solid. She crept to the edge and peered in, gingerly. All was black. Something glowed orange, deep down, then it went black again and the breeze died away.

"You all right?" said Holm.

His face was soot-stained, his grey hair had gone a smoky yellow-brown, and his eyes were red and watering.

"Don't know," said Tali, trembling. "I feel a trifle ... fragile. Hot and cold at the same time."

He peered up through the enormous hole in the wall and ceiling. It was dark up there and she could not tell what part of Cython had collapsed.

"What did you do?" said Holm.

"One drop of alkoyl landed on the heatstone stack. Just one drop."

He frowned at her. She explained what she had done, and how Errek's words had inspired her to do it.

"I think you're right," said Holm. "Alkoyl and heatstone must be the antithesis of each other, just as king-magery and the Engine are opposites. One creates, the other destroys, and both are necessary. But if that balance tilts—"

The ground shook.

"Have I helped, or made things worse?" she said quietly.

"Another minute and they would have overwhelmed us."

She looked up to the dark collapse zone. "I've got a bad feeling, Holm."

"About where the collapse took place?"

"It can't have been far from the Empound. What if ... what if it was right underneath?"

Holm looked grave. "We'd better go up."

Something rumbled in the depths. The floor shook violently and more rock fell, though this time it was just an ordinary rock fall – whatever had happened at the heatstone cube, the point of annihilation, had completed itself.

Tali felt the last of her gift drain away. She swayed and almost fell. "Something's wrong," she croaked. "Something's very wrong."

Lyf reappeared at the curve of the ramp, moving slowly and wearily, as though his magery could barely support him. What had he seen up there?

"What have you done now?" he cried. "Something has just changed, deep down. The balance is tipping towards the point of no return."

"Wil went down ..." Tali was so exhausted that she could barely speak.

"When?" Lyf shook her. Holm pushed him away.

"Half an hour ago," said Tali.

"Where did he go?"

Tali pointed to the fuming crevice.

"He went down the *Hellish Conduit?*"

"Where does it lead?"

"Way down. To the Engine at the heart of the world, eventually. But surely Wil can't do any damage down there," Lyf said, as if to himself. "He wouldn't know . . ."

"He said, *Got to write ending. Engine going to end* everything," said Tali. "And he was dragging a great platina demijohn. I . . . I think it held alkoyl."

"He wouldn't!" whispered Lyf. "He can't get to the Engine, surely. And he wouldn't know how to do any harm . . . Or would he?" He looked up. "*Errek?*"

The wispy old ghost-king appeared in the air before him.

"Did you hear?" said Lyf.

"Of course I heard," said Errek. "I'm your creation."

"Sometimes I forget."

"Wil reforged the iron book," said Errek. "He could not have done that in Cython without the matriarchs being informed. Where else would he find the heat for so mighty a forging? Only near the Engine."

"Is that why magery has been failing?" said Tali. "Because Wil's been rewriting the iron book?"

"The way the balance has been tilting," said Errek, "he must have been interfering with the Engine. You've got to stop him, Lyf. *Right now!*"

Lyf looked up at the collapsed area. "But . . . my people need me. I can't turn my back on them now, when they need me most."

"When you swore your kingly oath all those years ago, when you chose the way of healing magery, you also swore that the king's noble purpose would always come first."

"What noble purpose?" said Tali.

"Healing the land and maintaining the balance?" said Holm, low-voiced.

"Since you became king again," said Errek, "you've neglected that responsibility. Now you have no choice. Go!"

"How can I heal the land?" said Lyf. "Without the catalyz, I can't use king-magery."

"Kill Wil, then brake the Engine. Use your bare hands, if you must."

"That won't heal the land. It can't."

"But it can delay the catastrophe."

"First, I'll take the master pearl," snarled Lyf. "Tali created this mess."

"Grandys created it," said Errek. "With Maloch, two thousand years ago. Leave her – she's bound up with the fate of the world, somehow. Go!"

Lyf wobbled towards the smoking entrance to the Hellish Conduit and disappeared as Wil had done. Errek vanished. Tali's legs gave beneath her and she slid to the floor. She had nothing left.

"We'd better go up and see what the damage is," said Holm. "Hoy, Tobry?"

He came across, wearily.

"Give us a hand with her," said Holm. "She's all in."

Tobry looked pale, shrunken and further aged. It was not a good sign.

He picked Tali up and began to carry her up the ramp, but she found no comfort in his arms. All she could think about was his terrible end that could not be far away.

Every jolt sent hot pain spearing through Tali's head. She closed her eyes; it hurt too much with them open. Around her, hundreds of Pale were panting as they scrambled up.

"What's happened?" someone asked.

"I don't know," said another. "Where have the enemy gone?"

There was no reply. Tali could hear the Pale's bare feet slapping the stone all around. They ran in a mass for a minute or two, then stopped.

"To their armouries," Radl was shouting. "Arm yourselves and hold the passages against the enemy. Pale in the Empound, come forth and take up arms."

A great cheering rent the air. Tali forced her eyes open. The area was lit with lanterns and glowstones now, though it took a while to recognise what she was seeing.

The collapse had torn open the edge of the Empound and freed the trapped Pale who were streaming forth in their thousands. She could see the huge assembly area and some of the honeycomb cells, though there did not seem to be much damage there.

But there was massive damage in the other direction, where the Cythonian living quarters had been. The entrance tunnel was gone and hundreds of yards of the floor inside had vanished, drawn down into the annihilation hole. Much of the ceiling was gone as well, and the rest had fallen, destroying thousands of the small stone apartments in which the enemy dwelt.

"Most would have been unoccupied, their people long gone to Hightspall," said Tobry, who must have sensed Tali's horror. He put her down on her feet, but held her. "There might not have been too many killed."

Tali blocked his voice out. She had made her choice, destruction over healing, and this was the result. She could not shy away from it. The victims, enemy though they were, were owed that much. And there would be many of them. Very many.

A great wailing arose from the passage to the right; she saw the enemy troops clustered there. The soldiers who had come so close to victory down below now faced a disaster they could not comprehend.

They made their slow way around the broken edges of the collapsed area and into their living quarters, crying out for the survivors, but they did not find many.

As the first of the injured Cythonians were brought out, the rescuers were confronted by ten thousand armed Pale. Many wore armour, and their numbers and new-found determination made them a formidable force. For the first time the enemy realised how the situation had been overturned; how drastically they were outnumbered.

"You can fight, or you can leave Cython," said Radl quietly. "If you leave we will not hinder you, and you may take what weapons and possessions you will. But if you fight, know that we will fight you to the death."

The Cythonians consulted among themselves, but they had taken thousands of casualties in the hours-long battle and all were exhausted. Now, as they looked upon the destruction of the homes they had lived in for the past fifteen hundred years, Tali saw the heart go out of them.

"Our matriarchs are dead, crushed in their apartments, and Lyf has abandoned us for a higher duty," said a tall Cythonian with zigzag face tattoos. "We cannot make this choice."

"You must," said Radl, "or we will deal with you the way you planned to deal with us."

After another long consultation, the tall Cythonian said, "We will go." They began to gather their injured, and their meagre possessions, and then they went.

"Happy now?" said Radl to Tali.

Radl was covered in blood and had suffered many small injuries, though none marred her beauty nor hindered her determination to lead her people.

"No, I'm not," said Tali.

It was a victory she had never dreamed of achieving, from an attack that had not been planned, but she could take no joy from it. Thousands of lives had been lost on each side, and not just soldiers. Old men and women had been killed, girls and boys and infants. She put her head in her hands and wept.

"It's not finished yet," said Holm. "You've got to go on."

"No, I've done enough damage."

"There's still a war up above, and we're losing badly."

"What can I do about it?"

"The chancellor needs soldiers, blooded in battle. The Pale can provide them."

"I'm not leading anyone else to their death. I've too many on my conscience already."

"You've got to ask them."

"Why me? Why can't you do it?"

"If we don't defeat Lyf, he'll try to take Cython back, and the blood bath will make today look like a tea party."

He was right – she had to go on. Tobry boosted Tali up onto a heap of rubble where she could see the Pale and they could see her. Holm banged on a shield until people looked her way.

"You have won your freedom," she shouted. "But your people in

Hightspall are in the thrall of the enemy and cry out for your aid. Today I'm marching north to Nyrdly, to the aid of our country. Will you march with me?"

No one moved. No one spoke. They just stared at her with hostile eyes.

"Why won't they answer?" she said to Radl.

"You're not wearing your loincloth."

"I don't understand."

"You're *dressed*. You're not one of us." Radl scrambled up onto the pile of rubble. "The battle has been won but the war continues. We have to fight Lyf, and defeat him, or he will come at the head of an army to take Cython back. Will you march under *my* leadership?"

Thousands of Pale raised their hands, though not nearly as many as Tali had hoped.

"Is that all?" she said.

"Hightspall sent our ancestors here as child hostages," said a gaunt man with bloodshot, staring eyes. "Hightspall refused to ransom us, then made us out to be traitors and enemy collaborators. Why should we fight for a land that despises us, when we can have Cython for ourselves?"

"He'll come back," said Tali.

"And if he does, we'll fight for our country. But we're not fighting for yours."

Tali climbed down, more exhausted than she had ever felt. "I want to go home."

"You and I still remember our noble heritage," said Radl. "We still think of ourselves as Hightspallers, and all our lives we've yearned to go home, but most of the Pale forgot their ancestors and lost their heritage long ago. Cython *is* their home, the only one they've ever known."

"And even with all the destruction in this area," said Holm, "the rest of Cython is warm, productive and safe. Why would they leave it for the bitter cold of Hightspall, and an uncertain war in a land that has long despised them?"

CHAPTER 105

"Did you kill Wil?" said Errek First-King late that afternoon.

"He eluded me," Lyf replied, wincing as a healer finished binding his cruelly burned hands. "He crept down into cracks where I could not follow."

"But you did brake the Engine?"

Lyf looked down at his bound hands. "Thank you," he said to the healer. "You may go." Once she had gone, and the door was sealed, he resumed. "As best I could, though it won't last. I stopped the balance tilting all the way to disaster, but it can only be restored with king-magery. And—"

"Lacking the catalyz . . ." said Errek.

"Where can it be? Unless it's found, the balance can't be restored, nor the land saved."

"I would guess," said Errek, "that it still lies in one of Grandys' hoards, hidden before the time of his death, its true value never recognised."

"But Tali knows our secret now, and so do her friends."

"And a secret known to so many people cannot be kept. Sooner or later, Grandys will hear of it."

"He'll know where to go for the catalyz, and once he gets it, we're lost."

"Unless . . ." said Errek. He whispered in Lyf's ear.

"I'll call the ancestors into the temple," said Lyf. Clumsily, with his bandaged hands, he inserted his nose plugs and led the way.

Within, the stench was now so foul that not even his hardiest workmen could enter. It was sickening even through the nose plugs. Did it presage the doom of his people, and the land as well?

"This sacred temple has been defiled beyond redemption," he said to his ancestors, "but is that due to my crimes when it was the murder cellar, or to Grandys' two thousand years ago?"

The ancestors did not speak. They were gazing at him in alarm.

"It should be torn down," he continued, though the symbolism of such an act made him shudder. "But that would be like tearing down my own realm, my people, my land."

"With Cython fallen, our final refuge lost," said Errek, "our people are more troubled than ever."

The eruptions at the Vomits had picked up in the past day and the land was quaking all the time now. Though Lyf had not told his people the true reason for it, every Cythonian knew that something was badly wrong, deep down.

"It will take a great victory to turn their morale around," said Bloody Herrie.

"That's what I'm planning." Lyf opened the door and called to his attendant. "Order my armies to get ready. We're marching north to Reffering in the morning."

Lyf came back inside and closed the door.

"Are you intending to fight the chancellor?" said Errek.

"Not unless I'm forced to it. Our real enemy is Grandys, and if two sides are there, preparing to do battle, you can be sure he'll turn up."

"And then?"

"Grandys doesn't know what the key is, but he knows where he hid everything he stole from my temple. I'm going to deal with him and get the key," said Lyf.

CHAPTER 106

"You look dreadful," said Rix from the entrance to the chancellor's quarters. He could see the man himself, at the rear, bent over a stack of papers.

The chancellor's head lifted and he gave a sardonic smile. "If I looked as bad as you do, I'd know I was about to die. Come in and get it over with, whatever it is you want."

Rix limped in on Glynnie's arm. Three days had passed since the fight with Grandys but his face was still swollen and covered in yellowing bruises, his split lip was scabbed and blue, and he ached all over. But at least he was getting better. Whatever ailed the chancellor appeared terminal and it had affected the whole army. The officers Rix had met on his way through the camp all looked defeated. They were going through the motions, waiting for the inevitable end.

Nonetheless, he felt that familiar gnawing in his belly. The chancellor had publicly condemned him and there was no saying he felt the way he had at Glimmering, when he had held Rix up to the world as a hero. If the chancellor was on the way out, he might feel that it was time to settle old scores, permanently.

They stared at one another for a long time. Finally the chancellor said, "Well?"

"You may take it that I'm no longer under the thrall of Grandys' command spell," said Rix.

"So I've heard."

"What have you heard?"

"The tale spread across Hightspall like a forest fire." The chancellor's eyes slid sideways onto Glynnie. "May I see it?" He held out his hand.

After a brief hesitation, she reached into her bag, brought out the black opal armour broken off Grandys' nose and dropped it in the chancellor's small, wrinkled hand. He looked down at it, then laughed until tears flooded from his eyes.

"How tall are you, Glynnie?"

"Five foot two," she said, frowning.

"And Grandys is six foot eight." He looked up at Rix. "It's true then? She knocked the bastard down?"

"Glynnie got in five blows with a six-foot baulk of timber," Rix said proudly. "Flattened his ugly nose against his bloated face, knocked him to his knees and had him howling and spitting blood."

"Ah, thank you, thank you," said the chancellor. "You've done me more good in a minute than all my healers and all their blasted potions have in a week." He handed the piece of opal back and wiped his face. "You'll want to keep that to show your grandchildren."

"It wasn't just me," said Glynnie. "Rix fought Grandys to a standstill. He knocked out two front teeth, gave him a black eye and, but for a greasy plate underfoot, would have won. And Rix stole his horse. Don't forget that."

The chancellor's lip twitched. "Did he now? Ah, that's the icing. Well, Ricinus, you find me brought to a new low. My arm gone—" He flapped his stump. "Half my army lost or deserted. Hope fading by the minute and, according to my spies, Lyf is already marching north to attack us. I'm in such desperate straits that I'm even prepared to enlist vagabonds, traitors and condemned shifters, so why should I baulk at a Herovian, dead-handed horse thief?"

"I don't believe I am Herovian," said Rix. "And I can't say I go for their ideals."

"Whatever! Is that what you came for – to hear that all is forgiven?"

"No," said Rix. "*I* haven't forgiven anything. I want a commission in your army – a captain's rank."

"*A captain's rank?*"

"At Glimmering you sang my praises," Rix said defensively. "You told the world how greatly my victory had improved morale."

"Glimmering, yes," said the chancellor, as though that had been a lifetime away. "But a captain's rank ... I'll have to think about that."

Rix swallowed. It did not appear as though the chancellor had forgiven anything either.

"But, surely—?" said Glynnie.

"I said I'd think about it," the chancellor said mildly. "In a day or two we'll ride to Reffering. You can be sure Grandys won't be far away, but which side will he fight on? Sit down. Eat, drink. We're all going to die and I've broken out the best bottles I have. Let's raise a glass to the end of the world."

CHAPTER 107

"I should have realised I had no talent for leadership," said Tali as she, Tobry and Holm headed across country to the hill where they had left the horses. "Let Radl lead the Pale to war. She seems born to it."

"Leadership is a thankless job," said Holm. "You're well shot of it."

Since the land seemed empty and there was no longer any need for secrecy, they rode through the day and well into the night. The ground shook a number of times on the journey, though not in the way Tali remembered from the time, months back, when the Vomits had been building up to an eruption. Those quakes had been short, sharp jolts, quickly over. The ones she felt now were deep, rolling shudders that began gently, built up to a climax over a minute or two and slowly died away, as though the whole of Hightspall was being shaken.

"I'm worried about the circlet," said Tali. "We should go—"

"Shh!" said Holm. "Lyf might still have a trace on you."

"I've got to do something."

"Wherever you go, someone will see you. You'll lead Lyf – or Grandys – to it. We'll go back to the camp and ask the chancellor's advice."

"I wonder what he's planning," said Tali. "Do you think he's strong enough for war?

"No," said Holm. "What do you reckon, Tobry?"

Tobry grunted. He had barely said a word since leaving Cython, and Tali knew what ailed him. His physical decline was accelerating, his ability to hold back the shifter madness weaker every day, and he had retreated to a place where no one could reach him. That was the saddest part of all.

They arrived to find that the camp at Nyrdly had grown

enormously. Tents now extended out from the ruins for half a mile, and even at this hour the lantern lights were like nets of small, bright jewels draped across the gently undulating landscape.

They were challenged three times on the way in, and each checkpoint had the same message. "You are to report to the chancellor with the utmost dispatch."

"You've got a nerve, Tali," he said when they were finally brought before him, in his quarters in the haunted ruins.

The draped canvas had been replaced with a proper tent the size of a small house, otherwise everything was as it had been when they had left. Everything except the chancellor himself. He was more hunchbacked and twisted than ever, and seemed to have shrunk.

"What do you mean?" said Tali. "Risking the master pearl in Cython? Or coming back?"

"Both." Before Tali could respond he said, "Have you eaten? Drunk? Washed?"

"No," said Tali. "We haven't stopped all the way."

It was as if the chancellor was putting off hearing their news. He called for food and wine, bowls of water and towels. They washed their faces and hands. Platters of hot meat and bread were set before them, a jug of wine and a goblet of cordial for Tali.

"I've heard rumours from the south," he said, smiling and pouring the wine liberally.

"They must have flown here," said Tali.

"They say that Cython has fallen to rebellion and its masters have abandoned it."

"They speak truly."

"A famous, unprecedented victory." The chancellor went to rub his hands together, remembered he only had one, and dropped his hand, frowning.

"It changes the landscape," said Tali.

"Rumour also says that a great army is marching north from Cython to join us. An army of small, pale folk."

"An army, though not a great one," said Tali.

The chancellor's smile faded. "I heard figures of fifteen, even twenty thousand."

"The figures are right – but only a quarter are fighters. The rest are mothers and children."

"Five thousand? You've only brought me *five thousand men*?"

"I haven't brought you anyone. Radl is leading them, not me."

"Only five thousand?" he repeated. "What's the matter with them?"

"The Pale fought bravely for their own realm," said Tali, "and thousands of them died for it."

"What do you mean, *their own realm*? Hightspall is their realm and it's their duty—"

"Give over, you bloody old fool," snapped Holm. "Hightspall abandoned them a thousand years ago. Hightspall refused to ransom them, then blackened the Pale's name to cover up its own betrayal. Do you think the Pale don't know this? It's burned into their very bones."

"Are you saying most of them *stayed*?" the chancellor said savagely. "In the foul, stinking dungeon where they've been enslaved?"

"Cython is beautiful," said Tali. "It's spacious, airy, productive, clean – and warm. Above all, it's safe. At least, it's a lot safer than Hightspall can ever be."

The chancellor sank his head in his hands. "Five thousand. Five – miserable – thousand!"

"Until a day ago, you weren't expecting any aid from that quarter."

"Got my damn hopes up when I heard the news."

"It gives you fourteen or fifteen thousand, a mighty force. More than Grandys has."

"It doesn't give me anything like it," said the chancellor. "My army lost two thousand on the way here, in a disastrous battle in the mountains. Another three thousand have deserted to Grandys since they crossed. I've only got five thousand men left." He paused. "Five thousand and one, if one counts Rixium Ricinus, and I suppose I must."

"Rix is here?" cried Tali and Tobry at the same time.

"Where have you been? His escape has been the talk of Hightspall for days."

*

"Grandys is planning to hunt you down like a dog, Tali," Rix said later that night. "He wants you desperately. He'll never give in."

Rix, Tali, Tobry, Holm, Rannilt and Glynnie had camped at the back of the ruins, in a small space where four broken walls rose above them to various heights. It was very cold, but Holm and Tobry had cut down a dead tree and made a roaring fire, and Rix and Glynnie had threaded chunks of meat and small whole onions onto skewers. With the heat reflected back from the pale walls it was pleasant enough, though the ground was quaking and shuddering again.

"I know," said Tali, who was under a blanket with Rannilt snuggled up against her. Grandys was a problem she had no idea how to deal with.

Glynnie and Rix had made a rude couch from half a dozen slabs of fallen stone, which they had cushioned with dry bracken and covered in blankets and coats. They were sitting so close together that they touched from her shoulder to her ankle. Tali smiled to see it.

Holm had formed a chair by lashing tent canvas across an arrangement of bound branches. He had made it while talking, not even looking at what he was doing, and she marvelled at his ability to create what he wanted from whatever was to hand.

Tobry was the only one on his feet. Holm had offered to make him a chair but Tobry had refused, curtly. He kept pacing around the walls, feeling his beard and the hair on his arms as if afraid it might, any moment, change to fur.

After his berserker horror in Cython, Tali also feared it. Tobry's prodigious water-breathing magery, and then the treble dose of potion, had left him with no reserves. He had lost so much weight that he looked gaunt. She also knew, though he had tried to conceal it from her, that his attacks were getting worse and the after effects of the ever-higher doses of potion more terrible.

It was eating him away on the inside. How much longer could he keep the madness at bay?

Rix rose and came across to Tali. He looked almost serene, and that bothered her.

"I wanted to say how sorry I am, while I still can," said Rix.

"What are you talking about?"

"I repudiated my oath to Grandys. And even though he forced the oath from me with magery, he won't let go."

"What a load of rubbish!"

"*An oath is an oath*, Grandys says. Once given, it holds, no matter the circumstances. And *forever*, no matter the circumstances. To Grandys I'm the worst traitor of all, an oath-breaker and deserter who's helped to publicly humiliate him. When he finds me, he's going to kill me. I know it in my bones, and I've got to make amends before I die."

"There's nothing to make amends for," said Tali. "I treated you badly too. We're even."

"Told you," said Glynnie to Rix. She patted the bench beside her. He sat down gingerly and she pulled the blankets around them both.

Rannilt wriggled but did not wake. Holm leaned back in his chair, staring up at the stars. Glynnie laid her head on Rix's broad chest. Tali's eyes followed Tobry as he stalked around the walls, never stopping. Why wouldn't he let anyone in?

There has to be a way, she said to herself.

Later that night, when everyone else had gone to their blankets, she cornered Holm by the fire.

"What would happen if I used my magery on Tobry anyway?"

He spun around in his chair, appalled. "Try to heal him when you've already chosen the path of *destructive* magery?" he whispered.

"Yes," she said, already backing away from the idea.

"Your path is set, Tali. Set to destruction. You may still be able to heal small injuries in the old way, by laying on your hands, but healing with magery is forever closed to you."

"What if I tried anyway?" she persisted.

"You wouldn't heal – you would destroy."

"Destroy what?"

"Maybe Tobry. Maybe yourself. Maybe both of you. But if you were able to fight those destructive forces, or Tobry did, they would burst out somewhere else. Kill an innocent child, perhaps."

"I didn't think of that," she said, remembering the trusting way Rannilt had snuggled up to her.

"I assumed you understood the consequences of your choice. We've talked about it often enough."

"I did, but . . ."

"But you feel the rule shouldn't apply to you? That if you search hard enough for a loophole, you'll be able to get out of your choice?"

"I suppose so."

"That's exactly what I was like, Tali."

"When you . . . ?"

"Yes," said Holm. "When my reckless arrogance killed my wife and unborn son."

CHAPTER 108

"Tali! Holm!" yelled Rix, galloping up. "Come on. It's Tobry."

"What's happened?"

"Shifter madness. Worse than I've ever seen it."

He wheeled his horse and galloped to the rear. Tali followed as fast as she dared. Though she had done a lot of riding lately, she was never sure that her seat was secure at full gallop.

She could hear the howling from two hundred yards away. Tobry had partly shifted, he was more caitsthe than man, and it was taking six soldiers to hold him. He was making incoherent howling noises, punctuated by shrieks and savage growls. Slimy foam hung in festoons from his gaping mouth, where the teeth of a caitsthe gruesomely distended his man-shaped lower jaw. He snarled, slashed with claw-tipped fingers, lunged and tried to tear the throat out of one of the men holding him, with his teeth.

Rix leapt off his horse while it was still running.

"Should I knock him out, Lord?" said another soldier, who held a makeshift club.

"Stand aside," said Holm. He dismounted, drew a little brown sachet from his pocket, walked up to Tobry and, as the shifter tried to tear his face off, tossed the sachet into his open mouth.

It must have passed straight down his throat for Tobry gave no sign that he had noticed. He kept lunging and shrieking for another minute or two, then folded up, deeply unconscious.

"Chain him," said Rix. "Double manacles – wrists and ankles. Bind his mouth and blindfold him so he can't see to bite anyone, then put him in one of the wagons. Four men on guard at all times. I'll take the first watch."

He came across to Tali's stirrup. "I'm sorry you had to see that. It – it signals the end is close."

"How close?" said Tali.

"Days."

"Will he shift back at all?"

"Probably not."

Tali watched as they put the manacles on Tobry and fixed them to the bed of the wagon. It was the saddest moment of her life. The kind and gentle man she had once loved with all her heart was now reduced to a chained, mindless beast.

CHAPTER 109

Fortress Togl was small, squat and cramped, a rambling structure of yellow sandstone lumped on top of a flat-topped hill that overlooked the battle plain of Reffering. The chancellor's sadly reduced army from Rutherin was camped on the eastern slopes of the hill. In the distance to the south, Tali could see the dust of what she assumed to be Radl's Pale army and, miles behind it, a far greater dust cloud approaching from Caulderon.

Tobry had been chained in a vacant outbuilding a quarter of a mile down the hill, on the opposite side to Reffering, though his howls and shrieks could still be heard from the fortress.

"The final madness has come on quickly," said Rix that after-noon. He was as pale as chalk beneath his tan. "They say the more you try to hold it off, the faster it comes at the end. Ah, Tobry, no

man ever had a better friend. He laid down his life to save my unde-
serving life, and I'm not ashamed to cry for him."

"How – long?" Tali whispered.

"Not long," said Holm.

"He has brief moments," said Rix. "Lucid moments, I mean.
Sometimes only a minute."

"What does he say?" said Tali. "Does he remember us – *me* – at all?"

"He remembers. And – and then he begs to be put down."

Put down. Such a dreadful phrase. Put to death. Got rid of.
Destroyed as useless, dangerous.

"It – it must be done soon," said Rix. "It's no kindness to pro-
long his torment because we can't bear to do it . . . or because we
hope for a miracle that's never going to come."

"There hasn't been a miracle in Hightspall in a thousand years,"
said Holm, harshly. "This land has been cursed ever since our *noble*
ancestors abandoned their children to slavery."

"Tali," said Rix, reaching out to her. "You and I, we're his dearest friends. And . . . I can't bear for the chancellor's butchers to do
it, the way they'd slaughter a beast for the kitchen."

"No, never that," said Tali.

"We can't wait until the war begins, in case the worst happens
and we . . . we're not around. It's the one thing left we can do for our
friend."

Tali could not move. Could not speak.

"You and I," said Rix. "We've got to put Tobry down. In the
morning."

CHAPTER 110

At dawn of the following day, the four armies – Hightspallers,
Herovians, Cythonians and Pale – took up their positions on
the battle plain. The chancellor called his generals, plus Rix,
Glynnie, Tali and Holm, into the big war tent.

"The Herovians and Cythonians are determined to annihilate each other," Rix said quietly to Holm and Tali. "And neither side takes prisoners. The winner takes all, the loser is extinguished."

"What about us?" said Tali.

"They're the sandwich, we're the meat," said Holm. "But at least Radl's Pale have agreed to support us."

"I'm not sure they'll be much use," said Rix. "They're more a rabble than an army."

"Any alliance is better than being alone."

"Shh!" said an adjutant, primly. "The chancellor is about to address his generals."

The ground shook, more violently than any of the previous quakes over the past days, overturning the map table. There was a brief moment of laughter and levity while everything was put back in place and the water jugs refilled.

The chancellor stood up, a little, hunchbacked man, rubbing the stump of his left arm and wincing. He poured another glass of water, sipped it, and picked up his map pointer.

The ground shook again, not so violently this time. The chancellor took another sip, then the glass slipped from his hand. He choked and doubled over, coughing blood.

"Chancellor?" someone cried.

"What's going on?" said a voice at the back. "Has he been poisoned?"

Suddenly everyone was talking at once. With an effort of will he stood upright again. He dabbed at his mouth with a handkerchief, then looked around, smiling enigmatically.

"Order!" he said in a rasping voice. "Order."

The assembly fell silent.

"I'm dying," said the chancellor. "I've known it for days. The moment Grandys hacked into my arm with that accursed blade, he doomed me. I'd hoped to lead you into battle, to die better than I've lived, but my time has run out."

"Then who's going to lead us?" cried his pink-mouthed adjutant.

"Who indeed?" said the chancellor, eyeing his officers malevolently. "Should it be General Libbens, who led you to a crushing defeat north of Rutherin? General Grasbee, who demonstrated his incompetence with an even worse defeat in the mountains on the way here? Or Colonel Krabb, who's such an uninspiring leader that a third of his troops deserted to Axil Grandys in only two days? Well?"

None of his officers spoke. None met his eye.

"If not them," said the chancellor, "name your own man."

Silence.

"You can't," the chancellor said quietly. "There's not an officer among you could lead a dog to its dinner bowl, and I'll have none of you."

"But Chancellor," said his adjutant, "what are we to do? We must have a commander."

"We must. But to survive, we need an officer who's been forged in white-hot fires and emerged the stronger."

"Who, Lord Chancellor?"

"My chosen commander must be a hero who's demonstrated courage and leadership in battle. A man of principle who's prepared to lay down his life to protect the country he loves. A creative thinker who isn't trapped in the strategies of the last war."

The officers were staring at each other. Who was he talking about?

"A man who has fought beside Axil Grandys; who understands how Grandys fights and knows how to combat him."

"Is he talking about Syrten?" whispered the officer in front of Rix. "Has Syrten deserted to our side?"

"Or Rufuss?" said the man next to him. "Please, let it not be Rufuss."

The chancellor stared them to silence. "My commander will be the only man who has fought both Lyf and Grandys. The only man to have hurt both Lyf and Grandys, and survived."

"He means you, Rix," said Glynnie, giving him a little shove.

"No!" whispered Rix, shaking his head dazedly. "He hates my guts."

"Rixium of Garramide," said the chancellor. "Come forward."

Rix lurched to his feet. His belly was throbbing, his chest so tight that he could hardly draw breath. This had to be a cruel joke at his expense.

There was a moment of uproar, quelled by a savage down-slash of the chancellor's hand. "Silence!"

"He's a dishonoured man," said Libbens, forcing the words between his angled teeth.

"Not so!" said the chancellor. "Through black-hearted malice, I forced Rixium to make the impossible choice between his country and his house; I threatened to kill his closest friend if he did not make the choice I required. No man should be put to such a choice. *I* dishonoured him, yet by his actions since that day, he's proven that his own honour stands intact. Come forward, Rixium."

Rix wove between the officers and stepped up onto the dais. His knees were shaking. The chancellor extended his hand. Rix took it.

"Why?" he said quietly, struggling to overcome his distrust of the man who had so betrayed him. But then, Rix recalled, the chancellor was also famous for sudden reversals of policy.

The chancellor swayed on his feet. His lips were turning blue. "Imminent death makes old enmities irrelevant. I too love my country, Rixium, and I want the best man to lead it."

"I'm not up to it, Chancellor. I've never led an army, I'm not good enough—"

"I never said you were. But the need is now, and you're the best we have."

"But—"

"Can any of this pathetic rabble lead Hightspall?"

Rix surveyed the officers, many of whom he knew by dismal reputation. "No."

"Would you refuse your country when it needs you most?"

"Of course not."

"Then raise your hand and take the oath, Commander."

Rix hesitated.

"It'll make things awkward if I die without appointing a commander," said the chancellor wryly.

Rix raised his hand and swore to serve his country until his dying breath. This was an oath he could swear with all his heart.

The chancellor shook his hand. "Good luck, Commander," he whispered, then his small hand relaxed in Rix's and he fell backwards, dead.

What the hell do I do now? Rix thought. Our combined army is outnumbered by both Grandys' army and Lyf's. Am I doomed to fight a battle that must surely end in Hightspall's annihilation?

CHAPTER 111

L yf looked up from his spyglass. "The chancellor is dead."

"Then the war has returned to its two-thousand-year-old starting point," said Errek. "Grandys versus you."

"He'll make no alliances and give no quarter. And neither can I. The fight for our world has begun."

CHAPTER 112

"C an Wil do it?" said Wil, swaying, for he was alkoyled to the eyeballs. "Can Wil undo Lyf's work, and destroy the enemy too? Yes, yes he can. Wil can do *anything*."

Three days had passed since Lyf had come after him, and only now was Wil game to creep out of his hiding place.

The great story of Cythe and Cython could not end this way. Something had to be done but the iron book was not ready. He had forged it for a third time, and thought the quality of the pages would do, but it would take months to etch the story into them. It could not be done in time because the story was racing off on its own, outside anyone's control.

That could not be allowed.

Wil was going to make the Engine take charge.

Sobbing with terror, he lurched down the Hellish Conduit, going further than he had ever been before. He was carrying a platina bucket full of the purest form of alkoyl, a substance so rare and valuable that he could have bought half of Hightspall with it.

Wil went further than anyone had ever been. Right to the terror of the Engine he went, until his skin blistered like a roast chicken from the heat and the infernal radiance. But he felt no pain, only ecstasy.

He climbed up on top, his feet charring, and poured alkoyl in the one place where it should never go. Right into the works of the Engine at the heart of the world.

CHAPTER 113

The dreadful hour had come. Before Rix led his army out to an impossible battle, he had to do his tragic duty to a friend.

Tali and Rix slipped out of the chaos of the war tent and went up the hill, then down the other side to the outbuilding where Tobry was chained. Rix dismissed the guards, who were glad to go — even to bloody war.

Tali took hold of the left-hand set of chains, and Rix the right, and they led the hopelessly mad shifter that had once been Tobry Lagger out for a last look at the land he had loved.

They took him further down the hill, heading away from the battle plain to a chuckling, pebbly-bottomed stream. Despite the season there was a scattering of wildflowers across the meadow by the water and, in the distance, a view of snowy mountains. By the big trees and the sweet water, they stopped and chained Tobry to the trunk of the largest tree.

"He was a dreadful cynic," said Rix. "He mocked every convention, and everything I ever believed in. But it was just an expression of his pain at losing the house and the family that had been everything to him. I know that now."

"He took me to the Honouring Ball," said Tali, "and though I couldn't dance a step, in his arms I was the queen of the ball."

They bowed to their ruined friend. Momentarily, the shifter's eyes – Tobry's eyes – shone with love and regret. For a few seconds he was a noble man again, not a rabid beast.

Tali's own eyes burned, but she could not weep, and the moment passed. He was a beast again, snarling and slavering. And she was just meat that he could not reach.

She opened Tobry's shirt down the front, baring his chest and belly. Rix prepared the brazier and laid the packet of powdered lead beside it. Burning the twin livers on a fire fuelled with powdered lead was the one sure way to kill a caitsthe.

"Now?" said Rix.

"Now," said Tali.

He embraced her. She clung desperately to him, as old friends do. In her right hand she held the disembowelling knife. Her eyes drifted to the brazier. Burning Tobry's livers would rob her of her life's greatest joy and worst pain in the same moment.

Rix shook his head in grief, then raised his sword and prepared to strike. Only now did he realise the truth of the mural he had painted in the vault below Palace Ricinus, eleven weeks and a full lifetime ago.

GLOSSARY

Abysm: The conduit down which Cythonian souls are believed to pass after death. It exists in several places at once in Hightspall.

Acidulator: A perilous piece of alchymical equipment in which powerful acids are boiled.

Aditty: A little old miner.

Alkoyl: A deadly alchymical fluid used for a myriad of purposes by the Cythonians. It will dissolve anything, even stone and flesh. Said to be wept by the Engine.

Ancestor Gallery: Spirit versions of the 106 most important kings and ruling queens of old Cythe, recreated by Lyf as advisors, though they're more prone to lecture and hector him.

Arkyz Leatherhead: A gigantic, murderous bandit whose gang of thugs has been terrorising the Nandeloch Mountains for a decade. After the war begins, he seizes Garramide.

Astatin: A witch-woman in Garramide.

Banj: Tali's overseer when she was a slave in Cython. She killed him during her escape, with an uncontrollable blast of magery.

Bedderlees: A local lord who agrees to help Rix in the raid on Jadgery.

Benn: Glynnie's little brother, aged ten.

Blathy: Leatherhead's mistress, a bold and dominating woman who is willing to risk all on a bluff. Blathy is also vengeful and malicious.

Bledd: The capital of Bleddimire.

Bleddimire: The wealthy north-western peninsula of Hightspall.

Bloody Herrie: An angry shade, one of Lyf's ancestor gallery.

Bombast: A barrel-shaped explosive weapon hurled by a catapult.

Bondy, Lord: The lord of Castle Swire.

Caitsthe: The most powerful and savage of all shifters, a cat or cat-man, seven feet tall, which can heal wounds quickly by partial shifting. The one sure way to kill a caitsthe is by burning its twin livers on a fire fuelled with powdered lead.

Carr of Caldees: A provincial leader at the peace conference.

Castle Rebroff: The strongest fortress north of Lake Fumerous, held by Lyf's greatest general, Rochlis.

Caulderon: The capital city of Hightspall, on the south-eastern shore of Lake Fumerous. Caulderon was built on the site of the Cythian city of Lucidand, which the Hightspallers largely tore down.

Caverns, the: The uncanny chambers deep below Precipitous Crag where Lyf's wrythen dwelt and plotted for almost two thousand years after his death.

Cellar/Murder Cellar: A skull-shaped chamber deep beneath Palace Ricinus where Tali's ancestors were killed for their ebony pearls. In ancient times it had been the Cythian kings' private temple but it was defiled by Grandys' treachery there, and his assault and abduction of King Lyf.

Chancellor, the: The leader of Hightspall, a small, twisted, cunning man. After ordering Tobry hurled off the tower to his death, and Rix's right hand severed, the chancellor fled Caulderon when it fell to the enemy, with a small band of retainers. He took Tali and Rannilt with them, for their healing blood.

Chuck-lash: A chymical device like a thick bootlace. When thrown at someone, it explodes against the skin leaving a burned wound like a whip lash. Heavier versions, such as death-lashes, can blast a limb off, or kill outright.

Chymical or Alchymical Art: An art practised with considerable mastery by the Cythonians, lately used to create many new kinds of weapons of war.

Chymical Level: The secret level below the main level of Cython, where the enemy practise alchymical arts and build weapons of war.

Clangours: A sound-based alarm system in Cython, in which bell tones are carried throughout the underground city by a series of pipes.

Command: A powerful compulsion spell.

Crebb: A black-bearded thug who attacks Tali and Holm on the south coast.

Cythe: The name of the Cythians' island realm in ancient times.

Cythian: Pertaining to Cythe, the name of the land and the kingdom in ancient times.

Cython: The underground city of the Cythonians. After losing the Two Hundred and Fifty Years War, some of the surviving Cythians went into the mines of Cythe fifteen hundred years ago and built a great city there. Cython lies under part of the Seethings, a thermal wasteland.

Cythonian: Pertaining to Cython; also, the people of Cython.

Deadhand: Rixium Ricinus.

Degradoes: The Cythians who survived the Two Hundred and Fifty Years War were herded into filthy camps, and became known as *degradoes*. Several hundred years later Hightspall burned the camps and the *degradoes* were killed, save for a group of innocent children who disappeared underground, led by three matriarchs, who founded Cython following the instructions set down by Lyf in the Books of the Solaces.

Deroe: A magian possessed by Lyf's wrythen over a hundred years ago and used by him to cut out the first ebony pearl. Deroe subsequently rebelled and stole the next three pearls. He was killed by Lyf in *Vengeance*.

Dibly, Madam: An aged healer, tasked with drawing Tali's healing blood.

Droag: A lazy guard at Garramide.

Elbrot: A focus used by magians, an elbrot is often in the form of a swirling pattern cut from wood or cast in metal.

Empound: The Pale's living quarters in Cython.

Engine, the: At the lower end of the Hellish Conduit, in the deep heart of the land, Cythonians believe that a great subterranean Engine powers the workings of the land itself, causing volcanic eruptions, earthquakes and other phenomena. The Engine has to be kept in balance by the king's healing magery, but since king-magery was lost on Lyf's death two thousand years ago, the land has not been healed and the Engine is increasingly out of balance.

Errek First-King: The first known king of Cythe; the legendary inventor of king-magery. Lyf has recreated a spirit version of Errek, to advise him.

Facinore: A vicious shifter-beast created by Lyf, and subsequently cannibalised to give him a body again, so he would be able to leave his caverns and take charge of the war.

First Fleet: The original fleet that came from ancestral Thanneron to Cythe, two thousand years ago, bearing the Hightspallers (and some Herovians, including those later known as the Five Heroes). Three more fleets came, though the Third or Herovian Fleet was wrecked by a storm and only one person out of seven thousand survived, a girl said to be Grandys' daughter, but actually adopted by him.

Five Heroes, the: The Five Herovians – Grandys, Syrten, Rufuss, Lirriam and Yulia (later called the Five Heroes) began the war that led to Cythe falling to the Hightspallers, and are credited with founding Hightspall. They all disappeared mysteriously, however. In fact they were hunted down by Lyf's wrythen, turned to opal, agonisingly, and hurled into the Abysm.

Floatillery, the: An underground canal running from Cython to the Merchantery Exit, where heatstones and other things were traded with Hightspall.

Fortress Rutherin: A grim old fortress on the cliff-top above Rutherin, where the chancellor takes refuge after fleeing from Caulderon.

Garramide: A vast, strong fortress on a high plateau in the Nandeloch Mountains, built by Grandys for his daughter nearly two thousand years ago. Rix's great-aunt left it to him on her death.

Gauntlings: Humanoid, winged shifters created by Lyf for spying and for carrying his human spies. Gauntlings are prone to insubordination, vengeful malice and madness.

Gift, the: Magery.

Gift, Healing: The ability to heal by the laying on of hands. It's related to magery, though many people consider it separate from magery. This kind of healing is unrelated to the kind of healing that the kings of Cythe could do, which *was* a form of magery.

Glimmering-by-the-Water: An ancient temple site on the southern tip of the Nusidand Peninsula in Lake Fumerous; site of the peace conference.

Glowstone: A kind of rock, mined in Cython, which emits a feeble bluish glow. Used for lighting in Cython, and elsewhere.

Glynnie: A young maidservant from Palace Ricinus, aged seventeen. Glynnie begged Rix to allow her and her little brother, Benn, to stay after House Ricinus fell and the chancellor cast out all the house's servants.

Grandys, Axil: A great warrior and leader; a brutal and treacherous man who was the first of the Five Heroes and the legendary founder of Hightspall. He betrayed the young King Lyf in his own temple, hacked his feet off then walled him up in the catacombs to die, in an attempt to seize Lyf's powerful king-magery when he died. Grandys failed and the king-magery was lost, but at the point of death Lyf managed to form himself into a wrythen which existed for two thousand years.

Grenado: A hand-thrown exploding weapon.

Grizel: Ugly name the chancellor gives to Tali while she is disguised by his chief magian's magery.

Healing blood: Tali's blood, and perhaps the blood of some other Pale slaves, has the virtue of healing. It can even heal some people who have been turned to shifters, if given soon enough. This virtue may be due to exposure to emanations from heatstone.

Heatstone: A kind of rock, mined in Cython, which can be used for a myriad of heating purposes. Rebellious male slaves in Cython are condemned to work in the heatstone mine, which soon bakes them to death. Breaking a heatstone can be fatal because of the vast power released. The heatstone deposit is surrounded by a halo of sunstone, and that by a halo of glowstone.

Hellish Conduit: A winding, exotic passage that leads down from Cython towards the subterranean Engine.

Herovians, the: A persecuted minority who came to Hightspall on the first fleets, seeking their Promised Realm, two thousand years ago. Due to their fanaticism and brutal excess they fell from power and many now conceal their true heritage.

Hightspall: The nation founded by the people who came on the First Fleet, after taking Cythe from the Cythians.

Hillish: One of Lyf's generals.

Holm: An oldish man, very clever with his hands, who helps Tali. He uses the alias Kroni.

Hox: Twin brothers in Garramide; mutineers.

Hramm: One of Lyf's generals.

Ice, the: Ice sheets spreading up from the southern pole, and down from the north, are steadily cutting Hightspall off from the rest of the world. The ice is thought due to the Engine at the heart of the land getting out of balance. Many Hightspallers also believe that the land is rising up against them because of the evil way they took it from the Cythians two thousand years ago.

Immortal Text, the: The sacred book of the Herovians. It sets out the guiding beliefs of their faith, tells them where to seek the Promised Realm, and how to take it. Other people believe the *Immortal Text* to be a pernicious, racist tract which should be destroyed.

Iron Book, the: A book, *The Consolation of Vengeance*, written by Lyf for his people; the final book thus far of the Solaces. He etched the words of the book onto sheet iron pages, using alkoyl. The book's appearance in Cython was a call to war, though the iron book was not yet complete when Tali stole it from Lyf. It was subsequently stolen by Mad Wil, a blind Cythonian seer and killer who is obsessed by completing the story in the book.

Iusia (vi Torgrist): Tali's mother, murdered in front of Tali by Lord and Lady Ricinus for her ebony pearl, at the beginning of *Vengeance*. They on-sold the pearl to Deroe.

Jadgery: A town in the lower Nandelochs; the enemy have a garrison there.

King-Magery: Magery used by the king or ruling queen of Cythe to heal the land or the people. No one else in Cythe was permitted to use magery. King-magery was only passed on to the new king on the death of the old king. But because Lyf died alone and his body was never found, the death rituals could not be enacted, his king-magery was never passed on, and it was lost. King-magery is different from, and far more powerful than, other forms of magery.

Kroni: An old clock attendant in Fortress Rutherin. Also known as Holm.

Lady Ricinus: Rix's late mother, a cold, manipulative woman, obsessed with raising the social position of House Ricinus at any cost. She was executed at the end of *Vengeance* for high treason, and the murder of Tali's mother and grandmother for their ebony pearls.

Lirriam: One of the Five Heroes, a cold, buxom temptress.

Lizue: A beautiful prisoner in Fortress Rutherin.

Lord Ricinus: Rix's father, and lord of House Ricinus, formerly one of the wealthiest and most powerful Houses in Hightspall. A foul drunkard, sick with guilt at the crimes his wife forced him to commit. Executed at the end of *Vengeance* for high treason and murder.

Lucidand: The capital city of Cythe, in ancient times.

Lyf, King Lyf: The eighteen-year-old king of Cythe at the time the first war began. He was betrayed in his own temple by Grandys and the other Heroes, maimed and walled up to die in the catacombs. But after death Lyf's soul could not pass on, and he used the last of his king-magery to become a wrythen, so as to protect his people and take revenge on the enemy. Later Lyf wrote the Solaces, a series of books which showed his people how to live underground. As a wrythen, he spent the next two thousand years harrying Hightspall, and trying to get his king-magery, and a body, back. He eventually did, partly by using ebony pearls. Then he ordered war against Hightspall.

Magery: Wizardry, sorcery. Magery was brought by the Hightspallers from Thanneron, but has been failing ever since. This is believed to be due to the land they conquered rising up against them. Magery has a different origin to king-magery.

Magian: A wizard or sorcerer.

Maloch: An old sword, made from titane, given to Rix by his mother. It bears an enchantment of protection against magery. Rix is somewhat unnerved by this, though the sword has saved his life more than once. Maloch is a Herovian sword and originally belonged to Axil Grandys.

Matriarchs: When the king-magery was lost, Cythe could no longer have a king, and after the Cythonians took refuge in

Cython they were ruled by a trio of matriarchs, who were themselves advised by the Solaces.

Mia: Tali's best friend, executed in Cython for using magery. Tali blames herself and swore a blood oath to make up for failing Mia. This subsequently became a blood oath to save her people, the Pale.

Mimoy, Mimula: Tali's great-great-great-grandmother, an irascible, foul-mouthed old woman.

Moley Gryle: Lyf's personal attendant.

Nandelochs, Nandeloch Mountains: A high and rugged range of mountains in north-east Hightspall. A Herovian stronghold.

Noys: Rix's captain at Garramide.

Nuddell: One of Leatherhead's gang, later Rix's loyal sergeant.

Nurse Bet: An old Pale healer in Cython. She taught Tali self-defence, among other things.

Nusee: Tali's grandmother, murdered for an ebony pearl.

Oosta: The chief healer at Garramide.

Pale, the: A thousand years ago, a host of noble Hightspaller children were given to the enemy as hostages, but, oddly, never ransomed. Their enslaved descendants are known as the Pale because, having lived underground in Cython all their lives, their skin has never been exposed to the sun.

Pearl, Ebony: Black, marble-sized objects that have grown inside the heads of certain Pale women in Cython, due to radiance from the heatstone deposit. Ebony pearls can enhance a gift for magery many times over, and are beyond price. Only five can exist at any one time. Four of Tali's ancestors were killed for their ebony pearls and Tali bears the fifth, the master pearl, though few people know this deadly secret.

Porfry: The Keeper of the Records at Garramide; a fanatical Herovian.

Poulter: A four-legged fowl, supposedly created by Lyf to help feed his people after they took refuge in Cython.

Promised Realm: The legendary land the Herovians came to Cythe in search of, but have not yet found (or created).

Radl: A tall, beautiful Pale in Cython. Tali's enemy since childhood.

Rancid: An oily, vicious guard in Garramide; a mutineer.

Rannilt: A much-bullied slave girl, about ten years old, who escaped from Cython with Tali. Rannilt has an enigmatic gift for magery, manifested by displays of golden radiance. In an attack in Lyf's caverns he appeared to steal much of her gift and she lay near death for some time afterwards.

Rezire: The curator at Tirnan Twil.

Ricinus: A fabulously wealthy house in Hightspall, toppled by the chancellor after the discovery that the basis of its wealth was the depraved trade in ebony pearls. The name comes from the deadly poison ricin, obtained from the castor oil plant.

Riddum: One of Leatherhead's gang, later one of Rix's raiders.

Rixium (Rix): Formerly heir to the vast estates of House Ricinus, he was stripped of this inheritance by the chancellor due to the high treason of Rix's parents. Rix is a brilliant swordsman, and also a masterful artist, though some of his paintings have been disturbingly divinatory. Rix has recently discovered that he's Herovian, descended from Axil Grandys himself; he is ambivalent about this. Also known as Deadhand.

Rochlis: Lyf's greatest general. A man with a conscience.

Rufuss: One of the Five Heroes, a tall, gaunt man whose only pleasure is denial.

Rundi of Notherin: A provincial leader, a murderous coward.

Rutherin: An old fishing port on the south-west coast of Hightspall, now in decline because the sea level has fallen and the coast is well offshore of its former position.

Salyk: A compassionate female Cythonian soldier who found Rix's brilliant portrait of his father, and saved it, disobeying Lyf's order to burn it. She later rescued Tobry but was put to death by her own people for aiding the enemy.

Seethings, the: A thermal wasteland of boiling pools, chymical lakes and deadly sinkholes.

Shell racer: Small, light sailboats which can also be rowed by four rowers. Very fast and manoeuvrable, but fragile.

Shifters: Vicious, bastard creatures created by Lyf with the blasphemous art of *germine*, in order to harry the Hightspallers. Shifters come in a number of kinds, such as hyena and jackal shifters, caitsthes and gauntlings. All are prone to insanity. Exposure to their bite or blood can cause others to become shifters.

Shillilar: A foreseeing. It was Wil's foreseeing that identified Tali as *the one* who would change the story Lyf had written in his iron book, *The Consolation of Vengeance*, and thus change the world.

Solaces: A series of books written by Lyf, detailing various aspects of living underground, which he sorcerously transmitted to the matriarchs of Cython. They are held in the Chamber of the Solaces. There, Wil was the first to glimpse the iron book. He had a *shillilar* or foreseeing about *the one* (Tali) but the book burned his eyes out, and he never told the matriarchs the truth about her.

Spectible: A device that can see the aura associated with an enchanted object, or with the use of magery.

Squattery: A communal toilet in Cython.

Stink-damp: Rotten egg gas that seeps up from underground. It's used for lighting in Cauldron though it's both poisonous and explosive.

Subsistery: The Pale's dining hall in Cython.

Suden: The large island south of Hightspall, now covered by the creeping ice sheets.

Sulien: Tali's great-great-grandmother, murdered for an ebony pearl.

Sullen Man, the: A cold-eyed prisoner in Fortress Rutherin.

Sunstone: A kind of rock, mined in Cython. After exposure to sunlight, sunstone emits a bright light for days or weeks. It's used to provide "sunlight' in the underground green farms in Cython. Breaking a sunstone releases all its stored power at once, which is deadly to those directly exposed, and Cythonians (but not Pale) nearby but not directly exposed will be knocked unconscious.

Swelt: The castellan of Garramide, a gross-looking man, but loyal.

Swire: A town in Fennery, scene of the Five Heroes' ride of glory and initial recruitment drive.

Syrten: One of the Five Heroes, a massive, golem-like man.

Tali, AKA the one: The familiar name of Thalalie vi Torgrist, a Pale slave. She was the first person in a thousand years to escape from Cython. Tali's mother and three other female ancestors were murdered for magical ebony pearls grown inside their heads, and Tali is being hunted because she bears the fifth pearl, the master pearl, which Lyf needs to complete his plan.

Thanneron: The ancestral homeland of the Hightspallers, on the far side of the world. They came from Thanneron in four fleets, two thousand years ago. All contact with Thanneron was lost after the Fourth Fleet, and it is believed to have disappeared under the ice long ago.

Thermitto: An alchymical powder which burns so hot that it can melt rock; used for mining in Cython by the technique known as *splittery*.

Thom: A wood boy in Garramide.

Tiddler: A giant of a man in Garramide. A hammer-wielding mutineer.

Tirnan Twil: A remote tower, a kind of museum to the Five Heroes and their heritage.

Titane: A light, immensely strong metal. The secret of how to forge it has been lost.

Tobry Lagger: Rix's brave, clever but disreputable friend, Tobry lost everything when House Lagger fell when he was about thirteen. Tobry had a mortal fear of shifters, and of becoming one himself, because his maternal grandfather became one and stalked the house, and Tobry was forced to kill him to save his father. At the end of *Vengeance*, Tobry became a caitsthe because it was the only way to save his friends. He survived, but the chancellor subsequently ordered him hurled from the top of Rix's tower to his death. Rix calls him Tobe.

Tordy: One of Leatherhead's thugs, whom Rix casts out of Garramide.

Two Hundred and Fifty Years War, the: The war that Grandys began a couple of years after the arrival of the First Fleet. It ended 250 years later (1,750 years ago) with the utter defeat of Cythe.

Vi Torgrist: Tali's family name. Vi Torgrist is an ancient house which first came to Hightspall on the Second Fleet, but is now extinct except in the Pale.

Vomits, the: A trio of immense active volcanoes, the Red, Brown and Black Vomits, south-west of Caulderon. Cythonian legend holds that a fourth Vomit blew itself to bits in ancient times, creating the vast crater now filled by Lake Fumerous.

Wil, Mad Wil, Wil the Sump: A lowly, blind Cythonian who has *shillilars*, and is addicted to sniffing alkoyl. Wil is obsessed by the story set down in the iron book; but the story has gone wrong and he wants to set it right by rewriting the prophetic book.

Wiven: An old historian-mage Tali sees while using her gift to spy on Lyf.

Wrythen: The semi-solid shape Lyf's spirit takes on after he dies.

Yestin: A local lord who helps Rix in the raid on Jadgery.

Yudi: One of Rix's ne'er-do-wells, a crude fellow.

Yulia: One of the Five Heroes, she is the conscience of the group.

Zenda: Tali's great-grandmother, murdered for an ebony pearl.

The End of Book Two

The story continues in book three of
The Tainted Realm Trilogy:
Justice

extras

orbit

meet the author

Mike Benveniste

IAN IRVINE, a marine scientist who has developed some of Australia's national guidelines for protection of the marine environment, has also written twenty-seven novels. These include the internationally bestselling Three Worlds fantasy sequence (The View from the Mirror, The Well of Echoes and Song of the Tears), which has sold over a million copies, a trilogy of thrillers set in a world undergoing catastrophic climate change, Human Rites, and twelve books for younger readers, the latest being the humorous fantasy quartet Grim and Grimmer.

Email Ian: ianirvine@ozemail.com.au
Ian's website: www.ian-irvine.com
Ian's Facebook page: http://www.facebook.com/ianirvine.author

introducing

If you enjoyed
REBELLION,
look out for

ICE FORGED

by Gail Z. Martin

Condemned as a murderer for killing the man who dishonored his sister, Blaine "Mick" McFadden has spent the past six years in Velant, a penal colony in the frigid northern wastelands. Harsh military discipline and the oppressive magic keep a fragile peace as colonists struggle against a hostile environment. But the supply ships from Dondareth have stopped coming, boding ill for the kingdom that banished the colonists.

Now, as the world's magic runs wild, McFadden and the people of Velant must fight to survive and decide their fate...

"This has to end." Blaine McFadden looked at his sister Mari huddled in the bed, covers drawn up to her chin. She was sobbing hard enough that it nearly robbed her of breath and was leaning against Aunt Judith, who murmured consolations. Just sixteen, Mari looked small and lost. A vivid bruise marked one cheek. She struggled to hold her nightgown together where it had been ripped down the front.

"You're upsetting her more." Judith cast a reproving glance his way.

"I'm upsetting her? Father's the one to blame for this. That drunken son of a bitch…" Blaine's right hand opened and closed, itching for the pommel of his sword.

"Blaine…" Judith's voice warned him off.

"After what he did… you stand up for him?"

Judith McFadden Ainsworth raised her head to meet his gaze. She was a thin, handsome woman in her middle years; and when she dressed for court, it was still possible to see a glimpse of the beauty she had been in her youth. Tonight, she looked worn. "Of course not."

"I'm sick of his rages. Sick of being beaten when he's on one of his binges…"

Judith's lips quirked. "You've been too tall for him to beat for years now."

At twenty years old and a few inches over six feet tall, Blaine stood a hand's breadth taller than Lord McFadden. While he had his mother's dark chestnut hair, his blue eyes were a match in color and determination to his father's. Blaine had always been secretly pleased that while he resembled his father enough to avoid questions of paternity, in build and features he took after his mother's side of the family. Where his father was short and round, Blaine was tall and rangy. Ian McFadden's features had the smashed look of a brawler; Blaine's were more regular, and if not quite handsome, better than passable. He was honest enough to know that though he might not be the first man in a room to catch a lady's eye, he was pleasant enough in face and manner to attract the attention of at least one female by the end of the evening. The work he did around the manor and its lands had filled out his chest and arms. He was no longer the small, thin boy his father caned for the slightest infraction.

"He killed our mother when she got between him and me. He took his temper out on my hide until I was tall enough to fight back. He started beating Carr when I got too big to thrash. I had to put his horse down after he'd beaten it and broken its legs. Now this...it has to stop!"

"Blaine, please." Judith turned, and Blaine could see tears in her eyes. "Anything you do will only make it worse. I know my brother's tempers better than anyone." Absently, she stroked Mari's hair.

"By the gods...did he..." But the shamed look on Judith's face as she turned away answered Blaine's question.

"I'll kill that son of a bitch," Blaine muttered, turning away and sprinting down the hall.

"Blaine, don't. Blaine—"

He took the stairs at a run. Above the fireplace in the parlor hung two broadswords, weapons that had once belonged to his grandfather. Blaine snatched down the lowest broadsword. Its grip felt heavy and familiar in his hand.

"Master Blaine..." Edward followed him into the room. The elderly man was alarmed as his gaze fell from Blaine's face to the weapon in his hand. Edward had been Glenreith's seneschal for longer than Blaine had been alive. Edward: the expert manager, the budget master, and the family's secret-keeper.

"Where is he?"

"Who, m'lord?"

Blaine caught Edward by the arm and Edward shrank back from his gaze. "My whore-spawned father, that's who. Where is he?"

"Master Blaine, I beg you..."

"Where is he?"

"He headed for the gardens. He had his pipe with him."

Blaine headed for the manor's front entrance at a dead run. Judith was halfway down the stairs. "Blaine, think about this. Blaine—"

He flung open the door so hard that it crashed against the wall. Blaine ran down the manor's sweeping stone steps. A full moon lit the sloping lawn well enough for Blaine to make out the figure of a man in the distance, strolling down the carriage lane. The smell of his father's pipe smoke wafted back to him, as hated as the odor of camphor that always clung to Lord McFadden's clothing.

The older man turned at the sound of Blaine's running footsteps. "You bastard! You bloody bastard!" Blaine shouted.

Lord Ian McFadden's eyes narrowed as he saw the sword in Blaine's hand. Dropping his pipe, the man grabbed a rake that leaned against the stone fence edging the carriageway. He held its thick oak handle across his body like a staff. Lord McFadden might be well into his fifth decade, but in his youth he had been an officer in the king's army, where he had earned King Merrill's notice and his gratitude. "Go back inside, boy. Don't make me hurt you."

Blaine did not slow down or lower his sword. "Why? Why Mari? There's no shortage of court whores. Why Mari?"

Lord McFadden's face reddened. "Because I can. Now drop that sword if you know what's good for you."

Blaine's blood thundered in his ears. In the distance, he could hear Judith screaming his name.

"I guess this cur needs to be taught a lesson." Lord McFadden swung at Blaine with enough force to have shattered his skull if Blaine had not ducked the heavy rake. McFadden gave a roar and swung again, but Blaine lurched forward, taking the blow on his shoulder to get inside McFadden's guard. The broadsword sank hilt-deep into the man's chest, slicing through his waistcoat.

Lord McFadden's body shuddered, and he dropped the rake. He met Blaine's gaze, his eyes wide with surprise. "Didn't think you had it in you," he gasped.

Behind him, Blaine could hear footsteps pounding on the cobblestones; he heard panicked shouts and Judith's scream. Nothing mattered to him, nothing at all except for the ashen face of his father. Blood soaked Lord McFadden's clothing, and gobbets of it splashed Blaine's hand and shirt. He gasped for breath, his mouth working like a hooked fish out of water. Blaine let him slide from the sword, watched numbly as his father fell backward onto the carriageway in a spreading pool of blood.

"Master Blaine, what have you done?" Selden, the ground-skeeper, was the first to reach the scene. He gazed in horror at Lord McFadden, who lay twitching on the ground, breathing in labored, slow gasps.

Blaine's grip tightened on the sword in his hand. "Something someone should have done years ago."

A crowd of servants was gathering; Blaine could hear their whispers and the sound of their steps on the cobblestones. "Blaine! Blaine!" He barely recognized Judith's voice. Raw from screaming, choked with tears, his aunt must have gathered her skirts like a milkmaid to run from the house this quickly. "Let me through!"

Heaving for breath, Judith pushed past Selden and grabbed Blaine's left arm to steady herself. "Oh, by the gods, Blaine, what will become of us now?"

Lord McFadden wheezed painfully and went still.

Shock replaced numbness as the rage drained from Blaine's body. *It's actually over. He's finally dead.*

"Blaine, can you hear me?" Judith was shaking his left arm. Her tone had regained control, alarmed but no longer panicked.

"He swung first," Blaine replied distantly. "I don't think he realized, until the end, that I actually meant to do it."

"When the king hears—"

Blaine snapped back to himself and turned toward Judith. "Say nothing about Mari to anyone," he growled in a voice low enough that only she could hear. "I'll pay the consequences. But it's for naught if she's shamed. I've thrown my life away for nothing if she's dishonored." He dropped the bloody sword, gripping Judith by the forearm. "Swear to it."

Judith's eyes were wide, but Blaine could see she was calm. "I swear."

Selden and several of the other servants moved around them, giving Blaine a wary glance as they bent to carry Lord McFadden's body back to the manor.

"The king will find out. He'll take your title...Oh, Blaine, you'll hang for this."

Blaine swallowed hard. A knot of fear tightened in his stomach as he stared at the blood on his hand and the darkening stain on the cobblestones. *Better to die avenged than crouch like a beaten dog.* He met Judith's eyes and a wave of cold resignation washed over him.

"He won't hurt Mari or Carr again. Ever. Carr will inherit when he's old enough. Odds are the king will name you guardian until then. Nothing will change—"

"Except that you'll hang for murder," Judith said miserably.

"Yes," Blaine replied, folding his aunt against his chest as she sobbed. "Except for that."

"You have been charged with murder. Murder of a lord, and murder of your own father." King Merrill's voice thundered through the judgment hall. "How do you plead?" A muted buzz of whispered conversation hummed from the packed audience in the galleries. Blaine McFadden knelt where the guards had forced him down, shackled at the wrists and ankles, his long brown hair hanging loose around his face. Unshaven and filthy from more than a week in the king's dungeon, he lifted his head to look at the king defiantly.

"Guilty as charged, Your Majesty. He was a murdering son of a bitch—"

"Silence!"

The guard at Blaine's right shoulder cuffed him hard. Blaine straightened, and lifted his head once more. *I'm not sorry and I'll be damned if I'll apologize, even to the king. Let's get this over with.* He avoided the curious stares of the courtiers and nobles in the gallery, those for whom death and punishment were nothing more than gossip and entertainment.

Only two faces caught his eye. Judith sat stiffly, her face unreadable although her eyes glinted angrily. Beside her sat Carensa, daughter of the Earl of Rhystorp. He and Carensa had been betrothed to wed later that spring. Carensa was dressed in mourning clothes; her face was ashen and her eyes were red-rimmed. Blaine could not meet her gaze. Of all that his actions cost him—title, lands, fortune, and life—losing Carensa was the only loss that mattered.

The king turned his attention back to Blaine. "The penalty for common murder is hanging. For killing a noble—not to mention your own father—the penalty is beheading."

A gasp went up from the crowd. Carensa swayed in her seat as if she might faint, and Judith reached out to steady her.

"Lord Ian McFadden was a loyal member of my Council. I valued his presence beside me whether we rode to war or in the hunt." The king's voice dropped, and Blaine doubted that few aside from the guards could hear his next words. "Yet I was not blind to his faults.

"For that reason," the king said, raising his voice once more, "I will show mercy."

It seemed as if the entire crowd held its breath. Blaine steeled himself, willing his expression to show nothing of his fear.

"Blaine McFadden, I strip from you the title of Lord of Glenreith, and give that title in trust to your brother, Carr, when he reaches his majority. Your lands and your holdings are likewise no longer your own. For your crime, I sentence you to transportation to the penal colony on Velant, where you will live out the rest of your days. So be it."

The king rose and swept from the room in a blur of crimson and ermine, followed by a brace of guards. A stunned silence hung over the crowd, broken only by Carensa's sobbing. As the guards wrestled Blaine to his feet, he dared to look back. Judith's face was drawn and her eyes held a hopelessness that made Blaine wince. Carensa's face was buried in her hands, and although Judith placed an arm around her, Carensa would not be comforted.

The soldiers shoved him hard enough that he stumbled, and the gallery crowd awoke from its momentary silence. Jeers and catcalls followed him until the huge mahogany doors of the judgment chamber slammed shut.

Blaine sat on the floor of his cell, head back and eyes closed. Not too far away, he heard the squeal of a rat. His cell had a small barred window too high for him to peer out, barely enough to allow for a dim shaft of light to enter. The floor was covered with filthy straw. The far corner of the room had a small drain for him to relieve himself. Like the rest of the dungeon, it stank. Near the iron-bound door was a bucket of brackish water and an empty tin tray that had held a heel of stale bread and chunk of spoiled cheese.

For lesser crimes, noble-born prisoners were accorded the dignity of confinement in one of the rooms in the tower, away from the filth of the dungeon and its common criminals. Blaine guessed that his crime had caused scandal enough that Merrill felt the need to make an example, after the leniency of Blaine's sentencing.

I'd much prefer death to banishment. If the executioner's blade is sharp, it would be over in a moment. I've heard tales of Velant. A frozen wasteland at the top of the world. Guards that are the dregs of His Majesty's service, sent to Velant because no one else will have them. Forced labor in the mines, or the chance to drown on board one of the fishing boats. How long will it take to die there? Will I freeze in my sleep or starve, or will one of my fellow inmates do me a real mercy and slip a shiv between my ribs?

The clatter of the key in the heavy iron lock made Blaine open his eyes, though he did not stir from where he sat. *Are the guards come early to take me to the ship? I didn't think we sailed until tomorrow.* Another, darker possibility occurred to him. *Perhaps Merrill's "mercy" was for show. If the guards were to take me to the wharves by night, who would ever know if I didn't make it onto the ship? Merrill would be blameless, and no one would be the wiser.* Blaine let out a long breath. *Let it come. I did what I had to do.*

The door squealed on its hinges to frame a guard whose broad shoulders barely fit between the doorposts. To Blaine's astonishment, the guard did not move to come into the room. "I can only give you a few minutes. Even for another coin, I don't dare do more. Say what you must and leave."

The guard stood back, and a hooded figure in a gray cloak rushed into the room. Edward, Glenreith's seneschal, entered behind the figure, but stayed just inside the doorway, shaking his head to prevent Blaine from saying anything. The hooded visitor slipped across the small cell to kneel beside Blaine. The hood fell back, revealing Carensa's face.

"How did you get in?" Blaine whispered. "You shouldn't have come. Bad enough that I've shamed you—"

Carensa grasped him by the shoulders and kissed him hard on the lips. He could taste the salt of her tears. She let go, moving away just far enough that he got a good look at her face. Her eyes were red and puffy, with dark circles. Though barely twenty summers old, she looked careworn and haggard. She was a shadow of the vibrant, glowing girl who had led all the young men at court on a merry chase before accepting Blaine's proposal, as everyone knew she had intended all along.

"Oh, Blaine," she whispered. "Your father deserved what he got. I don't know what he did to push you this far." Her voice caught.

"Carensa," Blaine said softly, savoring the sound of her name, knowing it was the last time they would be together. "It'll be worse for you if someone finds you here."

Carensa straightened her shoulders and swallowed back her tears. "I bribed the guards. But I had to come."

Blaine shifted, trying to minimize the noise as his heavy wrist shackles clinked with the movement. He took her hand in both of his. "Forget me. I release you. No one ever comes back from Velant. Give me the comfort of knowing that you'll find someone else who'll take good care of you."

"And will you forget me?" She lifted her chin, and her blue eyes sparked in challenge.

Blaine looked down. "No. But I'm a dead man. If the voyage doesn't kill me, the winter will. Say a prayer to the gods for me and light a candle for my soul. Please, Carensa, just because I'm going to die doesn't mean that you can't live."

Carensa's long red hair veiled her face as she looked down, trying to collect herself. "I can't promise that, Blaine. Please, don't make me. Not now. Maybe not ever." She looked up again. "I'll be there at the wharf when your ship leaves. You may not see me, but I'll be there."

Blaine reached up to stroke her cheek. "Save your reputation. Renounce me. I won't mind."

Carensa's eyes took on a determined glint. "As if no one knew we were betrothed? As if the whole court didn't guess that we were lovers? No, the only thing I'm sorry about is that we didn't make a handfasting before the guards took you. I don't regret a single thing, Blaine McFadden. I love you and I always will."

Blaine squeezed his eyes shut, willing himself to maintain control. He pulled her gently to him for another kiss, long and lingering, in lieu of everything he could not find the words to say.

The footsteps of the guard in the doorway made Carensa draw back and pull up her hood. She gave his hand one last squeeze and then walked to the door. She looked back, just for a moment, but neither one of them spoke. She followed the guard out the door.

Edward paused, and sadly shook his head. "Gods be with you, Master Blaine. I'll pray that your ship sails safely."

"Pray it sinks, Edward. If you ever cared at all for me, pray it sinks."

Edward nodded. "As you wish, Master Blaine." He turned and followed Carensa, leaving the guard to pull the door shut behind them.

"Get on your feet. Time to go."

The guard's voice woke Blaine from uneasy sleep. He staggered to his feet, hobbled by the ankle chains, and managed to make it to the door without falling. Outside, it was barely dawn. Several hundred men and a few dozen women, all shackled at the wrists and ankles, stood nervously as the guards rounded up the group for the walk to the wharves where the transport ship waited.

Early as it was, jeers greeted them as they stumbled down the narrow lanes. Blaine was glad to be in the center of the group. More than once, women in the upper floors of the hard-used buildings that crowded the twisting streets laughed as they poured out their chamber pots on the prisoners below. Young boys pelted them from the alleyways with rotting produce. Once in a while, the boys' aim went astray, hitting a guard, who gave chase for a block or two, shouting curses.

Blaine knew that the distance from the castle to the wharves was less than a mile, but the walk seemed to take forever. He kept his head down, intent on trying to walk without stumbling as the manacles bit into his ankles and the short chain hobbled his stride. They walked five abreast with guards every few rows, shoulder to shoulder.

"There it is—your new home for the next forty days," one of the guards announced as they reached the end of the street at the waterfront. A large carrack sat in the harbor with sails furled. In groups of ten, the prisoners queued up to be loaded into flat-bottomed rowboats and taken out to the waiting ship.

"Rather a dead man in Donderath's ocean than a slave on Velant's ice!" One of the prisoners in the front wrested free from the guard who was attempting to load him onto the boat. He twisted, needing only a few inches to gain his freedom, falling from the dock into the water where his heavy chains dragged him under.

"It's all the same to me whether you drown or get aboard the boat," shouted the captain of the guards, breaking the silence as the prisoners stared into the water where the man had disappeared. "If you're of a mind to do it, there'll be more food for the rest."

"Bloody bastard!" A big man threw his weight against the nearest guard, shoving him out of the way, and hurtled toward the captain. "Let's see how well you swim!" He bent over and butted the captain in the gut, and the momentum took them both over the side. The captain flailed, trying to keep his head above water while the prisoner's manacled hands closed around his neck, forcing him under. Two soldiers aboard the rowboat beat with their oars at the spot where the burly man had gone down. Four soldiers, cursing under their breath, jumped in after the captain.

After considerable splashing, the captain was hauled onto the deck, sputtering water and coughing. Two of the other soldiers had a grip on the big man by the shoulders, keeping his head above the water. One of the soldiers held a knife under the man's chin. The captain dragged himself to his feet and stood on the dock for a moment, looking down at them.

"What do we do with him, sir?"

The captain's expression hardened. "Give him gills, lad, to help him on his way."

The soldier's knife made a swift slash, cutting the big man's throat from ear to ear. Blood tinged the water crimson as the soldiers let go of the man's body, and it sank beneath the waves. When the soldiers had been dragged onto the deck, the captain glared at the prisoners.

"Any further disturbances and I'll see to it that you're all put on half rations for the duration." His smile was unpleasant. "And I assure you, full rations are little enough." He turned to his second in command. "Load the boats, and be quick about it."

The group fell silent as the guards prodded them into boats. From the other wharf, Blaine could hear women's voices and the muffled sobbing of children. He looked to the edge of the wharf crowded with women. Most had the look of scullery maids, with tattered dresses, and shawls pulled tight around their shoulders. A few wore the garish colors and low-cut gowns of seaport whores. They shouted a babble of names, calling to the men who crawled into the boats.

One figure stood apart from the others, near the end of the wharf. A gray cloak fluttered in the wind, and as Blaine watched, the hood fell back, freeing long red hair to tangle on the cold breeze. Carensa did not shout to him. She did not move at all, but he felt her gaze, as if she could pick him out of the crowded mass of prisoners. Not a word, not a gesture, just a mute witness to his banishment. Blaine never took his eyes off her as he stumbled into the boat, earning a cuff on the ear for his clumsiness from the guard. He twisted as far as he dared in his seat to keep her in sight as the boat rowed toward the transport ship.

When they reached the side of the *Cutlass*, rope ladders hung from its deck.

"Climb," ordered the soldier behind Blaine, giving him a poke in the ribs for good measure. A few of the prisoners lost their footing, screaming as they fell into the black water of the bay. The guards glanced at each other and shrugged. Blaine began to climb, and only the knowledge that Carensa would be witness to his suicide kept him from letting himself fall backward into the waves.